Copyright © 2017 by Ben Thomas

All rights reserved. This book or any portion thereof may not be reproduced or used in any manner whatsoever without the express written permission of the publisher, except for the use of brief quotations in a book review.

Printed in the United States of America
10 9 8 7 6 5 4 3 2 1

First Edition, Second Printing, 2017

ISBN 0-692-92263-6

This book is a work of fiction. Although it makes reference to many historical events, cultures, languages, and individuals, none of these depictions are meant to serve as factual representations of those cultures, or of their descendants, living or dead.

Cover by Nada Orlic

TheStrangeContinent.com

The Cradle and the Sword

A NOVEL

Ben Thomas

Acknowledgments

Credit for this book must go first to Laszlo Xalieri, my friend, fellow writer, and peer in obsession with the oldest of old cultures, who told me in the spring of 2016 that someone needed to write this book, and that someone needed to be me. I owe equal thanks to my editor Yolande McLean, who somehow always understands just what I mean to say, and shows me how to say it, even when I keep getting in the way. This book wouldn't be nearly so unusual without a lot of late-night bull sessions with my friend Devin O'Neill, who's never afraid to ask if things could be bigger, wilder, weirder. Daniel Kenis, writer and ancient-history geek *par excellence*, read the first drafts of what later became this book's early chapters, and opened my eyes to the true scale of what it could be, sparking its transformation from a few small slices of ancient life into a full-blown historical epic. More than a year later, my historical compatriot Bettina Joy de Guzman read the almost-final draft of each chapter, and helped bring every scene into sharp focus with her uncanny gift for inhabiting a character's skin. And last—but certainly the polar opposite of least—I have to thank my mom, Cindy Thomas, who recognized I was a writer before I even knew how to read, and put pen and paper in my hands for the very first time.

Contents

Acknowledgements 5

Map 11

Prelude 13

Chapter 1: 286 BC 17

Chapter 2: 395 BC 63

Chapter 3: 530 BC 107

Chapter 4: 631 BC 165

Chapter 5: 920 BC 211

Chapter 6: 1216 BC 265

Chapter 7: 1334 BC 321

Chapter 8: 1531 BC 397

Chapter 9: 1882 BC 445

Chapter 10: 1991 BC 489

Chapter 11: 2149 BC 539

Chapter 12: 2287 BC 601

Chapter 13: 2490 BC 669

Chapter 14: 3057 BC 731

Chapter 15: 5765 BC 781

Believe me,
We stand amidst sacraments
And mysteries of awe.
Mankind is the secret
Which I am about to explore,
And before I can discover him
I must cross over weltering seas indeed,
And oceans and mists
Of many thousand years.

— Arthur Machen

Prelude

The Land Between the Rivers swallows empires and centuries whole. Flat-bottomed boats have plied these marshes since the world's first morning, as they will until the twilight of its final day.

Here, in the sun-baked shadows of the tall palms, among the reed-hidden islands of the Swift and Slow Rivers, the winds and waters devour cities beyond number; and, as the vault of the stars turns above, they churn new empires from the wet clay. Those empires, in their turn, are baked brittle and weathered to dust, and still others rise amid the ruins of ziggurats and mud-brick palaces that stand like naked sentinels on the plains.

The wind whistles through the cracks in these old stones; singing, perhaps, of those faraway days when—so it is said—Heaven talked with Earth, and men and women took their first steps on the banks of these rivers in the mists of the world's dawn, guided by the Gods of the deep waters to lay the bricks of the first city, whose name was Eridu.

Now Eridu lies long in ruins, a windswept ghost-city of the marshes. Setting off from those ruins, poling and gliding up the great Slow River, one might glimpse other cities along the shore: Kish, whose god-kings conquered and ruled this plain in the half-remembered morning of mankind's childhood. Urim, whose primordial stepped pyramids tower atop the ruins of temples far more ancient still. And on the bank of the Swift River, a day's march east, the once-mighty citadel of Lagash, where scholars kept their lamps alight through the long night of the world's first dark age.

At the heart of these plains sprawls the immortal Babili, once the crown of the world; a citadel of jewelled blue gateways and terraced temples whose towers pierced the sky. A paradise of fountained gardens and golden palaces, of markets where travelers bargained in a hundred tongues for treasures and beasts from exotic lands; a shrine of wild, debauched worship, where sacred courtesans took lovers from all quarters of the Earth, and showed them the way to the Gods.

But even now that Babili wears the yoke of a foreign conqueror, and her manor-houses have crumbled to heaps of moss-tufted rubble—now that makeshift aqueducts of cracked clay cough muddy water into the ruins of her plazas, where sheep and cattle graze on weeds amid the fallen pillars, and rats scurry among the broken flagstones of her boulevards, and the old, true names of Gods and stars are long forgotten among the babble of new tongues that fills her streets—

Perhaps, despite all this, she is still the same city she has always been.

2,303 YEARS AGO
286 BC

On the banks of the Two Rivers,
Only weeds now grow.
The cities are razed to ruin.
The land's fate cannot be changed.
Who can overturn it?

— The Lament for Shumér

"In those days, in those faraway days; in those years, in those long-ago years..." So began many old poems in the Land Between the Rivers.

Someday, thought Zaidu, *a poet might sing the same of this very night.*

He trudged alone through narrow streets between mud-daubed walls, along alleys framed with rotting timber, his sandaled feet crunching softly on the overgrown weeds and hard-packed dirt. *But Dipti would laugh at me for saying such a thing*, he mused, ducking through the low doorway of his favorite tavern, tucking his wood stylus-box into his tunic's rough-spun sash.

Once his eyes adjusted to the tavern's lamp-lit interior, he caught sight of his friend sitting at a corner table, polishing off the dregs of foamy sweet-beer from a clay mug, waving for the barmaid to bring him another.

"Dipti!" he cried, wrapping his fellow scribe in a rough hug, kissing one cheek and the other. "Where've you been lately?" His eyes widened in mock concern. "Have you forgotten where we live?"

"Yes, Zaidu, that's exactly what's happened," Dipti replied drily, squeezing back into the corner behind the table. "Truth is, I've just been so damned busy at Master—*gah!*" He'd knocked his stylus-box to the floor, scattering pens and writing-reeds across the sawdust.

"Ah, so *that's* why they call you Dipti Steady-Hands," said Zaidu, bending to help his friend gather his styluses and return them to the box.

"Steady enough to snap your neck," Dipti sighed, holding out the box for Zaidu to return a handful of pens.

Grinning, Zaidu muttered his favorite Elline curse. "*Metrókoítes.*"

"Did you just—" Dipti's jaw dropped in a parody of outrage. "Did you just say I... fornicate with my mother, in Elline common-tongue?"

"You? Never," Zaidu replied. "I was talking of our friend here." He gestured at the cramped corner next to the table they'd secured, where a drunkard in a rough wool tunic slouched, snoring raucously, his meaty head on his chest.

Dipti wrinkled his nose as he squeezed back onto his stool in the corner. "At least he kept this table clear for us."

"He's keeping the beer away, too," Zaidu said, waving to get the barmaid's attention. The girl ignored him, rushing from table to table, smiling distractedly at the neighborhood bricklayers, carpenters, sandal-makers, rat-killers, and barbers, setting mugs of fresh, foaming sweet-beer before them, sloshing foam onto the stained wood.

"You know," Dipti said, "Master Izdubar has us speaking Elline common-tongue in his work chambers now. He says we must become—*ahem*—'fluent in our rulers' tongue.'" He enunciated each word, imitating the master's archaic accent.

"Gods, what an ugly language it is," Zaidu sighed. "Why can't they call a house *beytheyn*, as we do? *Oikos* sounds like a pig. *Oik oik*."

"And their word for 'fish': *ikhthýs*." Dipti gagged theatrically.

"Gibberish! Sounds like you've got something caught in your throat."

Dipti shot Zaidu a warning glare. "I keep telling you, tone it down with the anti-Elline talk. They speak common-tongue in the throne room now. One of these days a soldier's going to overhear..." He glanced around the tavern nervously but saw no soldiers.

"Gibberish," Zaidu repeated. "Just how you'd expect illiterate war-grunts to talk. Call themselves kings of our city, and name it *Babylon*. What kind of word is that? This is Babili. It's always been Babili."

"Master Izdubar says their Elláda is—" Dipti imitated the master's pompous voice again: "—filled with mighty cities and holy temples of marble, nearly as impressive as our own."

Zaidu snorted. "So *they* say. Pour a few beers into any man and he'll spin you tales of his homeland."

"And, oh, the tales these Ellines spin." Dipti peered into his empty mug, and frowned. "They claim to have perfected the arts of astrology and poetry. Even mathematics. And painting, too. I once heard an Elline artist brag of painting grapes that looked so real, birds flew down to peck them."

"As if that were the purpose of art. To paint realistic fruit." Zaidu rolled his eyes. He waved at the barmaid again, more energetically this time, but she was busy with a table of raucous dockworkers, and didn't see him. He shook his head and turned back to Dipti.

"Master Izdubar's mind must be warping with old age," he continued, sighing. "I mean, think about what he's telling you. How could that be? We've been developing tables for multiplication and the movements of the stars for hundreds of years."

"And poetry," Dipti replied. "How could that possibly—?"

"Our poetry's been refined over millennia, Dipti. All the way back to ancient Shumér, before the Flood."

"I know. I sat in those history classes, too, remember?"

"How could I forget?" Zaidu rolled his eyes. "Master Shamas loved that whip-rod, didn't he? Remember how he yelled? 'Your father will thank me for this!'"

"That horrid reedy voice of his. 'This is what your father pays me for!' *Whack! Whack!*"

Zaidu groaned. "If we forgot one line of a poem, we'd be sleeping on our stomachs that night."

"Don't remind me." Dipti shivered.

"But really," Zaidu went on, "how could the Ellines write anything like the great Shuméru epics? *Uruba kienedibe mir insi*—'A tempest has filled the dancing of the city.' *Kurgulgul ude a ba'esi*—'Devastatrix of the lands, you are lent wings by the storm.' Can an Elline poet write like that?"

Dipti snorted. "You really love those old Shuméru poems, don't you?"

"Of course I do," Zaidu said. "No one writes like that anymore. I don't think anyone ever will."

"Because no one's spoken Shuméru for a thousand years! What are you going to do, recite that to the barmaid? '*Kurgulgul*.' She'll think you've lost your mind."

As if on cue, the barmaid chose that moment to appear at their table at last, carrying two clay mugs. As she set them on the table, Zaidu looked up into her eyes and said, "*Saibbaza aba itenten, kiag.*"

She looked at him as if he'd gone mad. Then she laughed. "What does that mean?"

Zaidu made a show of pouting. Dipti covered his mouth, shaking with suppressed laughter.

The Cradle and the Sword

"Don't laugh," Zaidu said. "It's Shuméru. It means, 'Who can temper your raging heart, my love?'"

She raised her eyebrows and grinned. "You speak Shuméru?"

"Of course! It's the most beautiful language that ever was."

"I thought only priests spoke it—folk in temples," she said.

"That *is* where they speak it," said Dipti. "Except my friend here thinks it should be spoken in taverns, too."

"I hear it's almost impossible to learn," she said.

"The grammar is complicated, it's true," said Zaidu. "But it's so worth it, for the beautiful things you'll read. *A single glance from you shakes the hearts of mountains. Like a wild bull whose horns pierce the heavens—*" He stopped, his gaze falling to the beer in his mug.

For a long silent moment, he was certain he'd made an utter fool of himself.

But then, in a soft voice, she spoke. "No, keep going," she said. "Please."

He looked up and watched a smile spread across her lips. Something in her eyes made his heart hum and made him want to tell her every line of poetry he knew.

"*In Dilmun's garden did he lay her down,*" he recited, trying to keep the tremble out of his voice. "*Upon that untouched land where never a furrow had been plowed.*"

She laughed softly, covering her mouth.

He felt as if he might melt right through the floor.

"I could teach you," he said. "If you like."

"First I'd have to learn to read," she said, "and I've heard that's hard enough."

"It takes a few years," Dipti broke in. "And oh so many whippings."

"How awful!" she said. "I'm too old to put up with being whipped, really, but my father—"

"Arwia!" The proprietor, a balding, middle-aged man behind the bar, tore her attention away. "What in the Seven Stars do you think you're doing, besides wasting our customers' time? I swear before all the Gods, you're the laziest daughter I ever had!" He howled, tearing at his beard theatrically.

She smiled at Zaidu and rolled her eyes, then dashed off to refill other patrons' mugs.

"I didn't know her name was Arwia," said Zaidu, smiling as if surfacing from a dream.

"How could you not know that?" said Dipti. "We come here every week, and you never asked her?"

"Did you?"

"Of course I did!" Dipti barked a laugh. "The first night we came here, what, three years ago now."

Zaidu shrugged. "After a certain point, I got too embarrassed to ask."

Dipti raised his eyebrows. "Frankly, I'm amazed the word 'embarrassed' even exists in your vocabulary, Zaidu. Come on, finish your drink and let's go home."

"I want to stay," said Zaidu. "I want to talk to Arwia."

"Then stay if you want," said Dipti. "But I'm exhausted, and I have to be at Master Izdubar's chambers at sunup tomorrow."

"You," Zaidu replied, "are the enemy of fun."

"Come on," Dipti heaved himself up. "Let's go home."

Dipti pulled Zaidu up from the table and over to the bar where he dropped a few copper obols on the beer-stained wood of the countertop. Zaidu tried to catch Arwia's eye as they made their way to the door, but she was busy flirting with a table of tan men in clay-stained leather aprons—bricklayers, Zaidu guessed. One looked up and caught Zaidu's eye. His expression darkened and he started to get up from the table. Dipti pulled him out the door before anything dangerous could unfold.

"This whole city is full of madmen," Dipti said as they stumbled out into the moonlit street that was little more than an alley, a narrow dirt trail winding between mud-plastered shacks.

"There's an old joke, you know, that they tell about this city," Zaidu said, orienting himself in the direction of home.

"What joke is that?" Dipti asked, only half interested.

"It's not a very funny joke," Zaidu said. "But here it is."

"Well, if it's not funny," Dipti asked, "then why are you telling it?"

Zaidu waved his hand. "Just listen."

"You're drunk, Zaidu." Dipti turned away and started walking for home.

"Maybe so," Zaidu slurred. "But I want to tell this story. So we live in 'Godgate,' right?"

"'Gate of the Gods,' more properly," Dipti replied. "I mean, *Bab-Ili* in the old Akkadu tongue—"

"I know more old Akkadu than you do, you ass." Zaidu waved a hand dismissively. "Do you want to hear this story or not?"

"I thought it was a joke," Dipti said.

"Story, joke, whatever," Zaidu answered. He began to trudge homeward, and Dipti followed. "Anyway, this was a few hundred years ago, back when Ashûru kings ruled Babili. One of those kings uprooted a lot of Yehudu people, brought them east from Yerushalem and made them live here."

"That would be Emperor Nabû-kudurri-ushûr." Dipti pronounced it carefully, imitating Master Izdubar's stodgy accent again.

"That's a mouthful," said Zaidu. "Gods, those Ashûru throne-names."

"I knew a priest once who took the name Adad-apla-iddína," said Dipti.

"Wonder if he made the priestesses call him that in bed," Zaidu mused, running his hand along the wall. "Anyhow, the Yehudu people were force-marched here to Babili. And when they arrived, they were appalled to hear such a riot of foreign tongues in the streets. You know how it is in this city. You ask someone for directions, you never know if they'll speak proper Aramaya or one of those thick northern dialects, or Parsa, or Yehud, or—"

"Elline common-tongue." Dipti nodded. "Yes, it's a mess. We all know."

"Well, like I said," Zaidu went on, "they heard this cacophony and couldn't make any sense of it." He paused and turned to Dipti, raising a finger, a wry grin crossing his lips. "So instead of Babili, they called this city *Babel*, which means 'confused.'"

Dipti stood in silence for a moment, waiting expectantly. "That's it?" he asked at last.

"I guess it's not very funny." Zaidu shrugged.

"Not even a joke, really," Dipti said. "More of a pun, I suppose."

"Well," said Zaidu. "Here our city still stands, just as confused as it ever was."

"You're the one who's confused," Dipti replied. "Home is down this alley, not that one."

Zaidu and Dipti stumbled homeward through the tightly winding alleys, between densely packed and stacked houses of mud-brick, all their wood shutters locked tight. They climbed over the bricks of crumbling ancient walls, amid cracked and defaced mosaics and reliefs: lions, bulls, dragons whose eyes had been gouged from the stone.

They crept past the smooth-plastered walls of new houses raised on the ruins of crumbling ones, some already bearing painted graffiti in the letters of Aramaya—"*Hanina, why won't you love me?*"—or of the Elline alphabet—"*I'll race my horse against any in Babili, and I'll win*"—or of the ancient and universal signs of stars and faces. Still others bore drawings of sleek horses and broad-winged eagles; wide eyes and grotesque phalluses, and the more abstract swirls and zigzags that marked safe houses or generous bakeries in the cipher of some tribe or other.

In the shadowy alleys under wooden arches, beneath bridges of apartments and shops, Zaidu caught sight of thieves, dashing down side-streets so narrow they had to turn sideways to fit through them.

They saw a dim flicker of firelight around the next corner, and rounded it to come face to face with a pair of Elline soldiers in polished iron helmets, their red tunics trimmed in white, oil lamps upraised as they scanned the street with narrowed eyes. These pale-skinned foreigners clutched long iron-tipped spears, and swords hung at their sides. After a long moment of silent scrutiny by lamplight, Zaidu and Dipti nodded, and the Ellines nodded, and they moved on.

On the next street they passed a pack of furtive men standing in a huddle, tapping knives and wood cudgels against their palms. The men fell abruptly silent, waited for Zaidu and Dipti to pass, then began muttering again once they were out of range.

Zaidu glanced back at the huddle of men, and tripped in a pothole amid the weeds, barely managing to stay upright.

"This city used to be so beautiful," he murmured, regaining his balance.

Dipti raised an eyebrow. "Getting nostalgic now, are we? As far as I can remember, Babili's always been a reeking ruin."

"In our lifetimes, yes." Zaidu nodded, falling back into a wavering walk in the direction of home. "But before these Ellines came, it was the heart of the greatest empire on earth. Home of the Hanging Gardens. The glimmering blue gates."

Dipti snorted, matching his friend's pace. "You mean the gates where soldiers go to piss?"

Zaidu ignored him. "The observatories where brilliant priests studied the movements of the stars."

"We still have those," Dipti pointed out. "You work in one of them."

"Libraries," Zaidu went on, strolling and gesturing like a temple lecturer. "Theaters. Museums. Banquet halls. Markets filled with exotic spices and fabrics, and strange beasts from faraway lands. Festivals where crowds of ten-thousands gathered to celebrate the glory of the Gods."

"Yes, I suppose it must've been a lovely city before the Parsa came, and the Ellines after them." Dipti sighed. "We were born too late to see it."

"Not just lovely." Zaidu shook his head. "Magnificent. A wonder of the world. An earthly paradise without equal."

"I don't know if I'd go *that* far—"

"And look at it now. Potholes in the streets. Trash piled in the doorways. Husks of dead trees in the gardens. Temples and palaces crumbling to rubble. Cattle grazing in the avenues. All because a pack of scheming, backstabbing, illiterate Ellines are squatting in the royal palace."

"Shh!" Dipti hissed as they rounded another corner.

"Ellines ruling Babili," Zaidu went on. "Ellines ruling Misr on the Nile. They even tried to conquer Hindush in the east, word has it, until some king drove them out. They *infest* this wide world of ours."

Dipti winced. "One of these days you're going to say that where the wrong person can hear you."

"I honestly don't care anymore." Zaidu shrugged. "This has happened before, and it'll happen again—if we manage to survive this age of savagery." He shook his head. "Sometimes I feel like old king Gudea, fighting to preserve Shumér through the First Dark Age, when the Guti barbarians swept over the land two thousand years ago."

"Here we go again." Dipti sighed.

"Or the kings of Babili, fighting their way up out of the Second Dark Age a thousand years after that, amid the wars with Ash'shúr and the Khatti, and the Kalshu and Elamu, and only the Gods know how many other squabbling kingdoms. In every dark time, there's always been a lamp in the night."

Dipti grunted a laugh. "And you're that lamp? That's what you're saying?"

Zaidu fell silent for a moment, plodding slowly around the potholes.

"Somebody's got to be," he muttered. He drew a deep breath, then sighed. "Sometimes I truly hate this city."

"No," Dipti said. "You adore it. That much is clear. You love it with your whole heart."

"I love what it used to be," Zaidu said. "What it once was."

"How do you know what it used to be?" Dipti asked. "You weren't there. Now look, here's our door."

Dipti knocked softly, and a sleepy-eyed scribe opened the worn wood door, then shuffled back to his mat, lay down, and promptly fell asleep. Zaidu and Dipti made their way across the dark apartment, past floormats where a few other scribes lay snoring. They found their own mats, unstrapped their sandals, lay down on the soft wool, and closed their eyes in the dark.

And Zaidu slipped into dreams of a Babili that was no more, and perhaps never would be again—a city of wondrous temples, grand palaces, and wide avenues where royal processions paraded solid-gold statues of the Gods amid the jubilation of tens of thousands. It was here, in *this* Babili, that he felt most truly at home.

HE WOKE TO dim predawn light, and the sound of arguing.

"I don't know what happened to your stylus-box, Gibil," Dipti was saying.

"I'm telling you, it isn't here," said Gibil, pulling off his wool headband and running his hands through his black hair. "I've looked everywhere."

All the other scribes had already left, either because they'd had their own pre-dawn appointments, or because they'd gotten tired of listening to the bickering.

"How many places could it be, Gibil?" Zaidu said, sitting up and rubbing his eyes. "We all sleep in the same room. Did you look in the clothing chest?"

"Yes I looked in the Gods-damned clothing chest."

"All right, all right," said Zaidu, rubbing his aching head. "Calm down. It's too early for this."

"It's too late for this, is what it is," said Gibil. "I'm supposed to be at the courthouse by sunup, and now I'm going to be late. It takes half an hour to walk over there."

"That reminds me," said Dipti. "I've got to get to work, too."

"And what do I do?" cried Gibil. "Show up late, with no stylus?"

"Good Gods, just use one of mine, Gibil," said Zaidu, taking his own stylus-box from the small wood chest next to his bed. He lifted a thin reed stylus from the box and handed it to Gibil, who took it with a quiet "Thank you."

"If I find your box, I'll let you know," said Dipti. He glanced out the window. "Now look what time it is. Didn't even have time for breakfast." He clutched his stylus-box to his chest, running out the door, calling, "See you tonight" to Zaidu as he closed it behind him.

"I'd better go, too," said Gibil. "Really, thanks for the stylus. I mean it."

"Don't mention it," said Zaidu, as Gibil hurried out the door.

Zaidu rubbed his eyes and his head, but none of that made the ache go away. He shuffled through the back of the house into the complex's courtyard, pumped some water from the well, and drank it straight from the bucket in big draughts. His stomach protested, but it made him feel a little better. He muttered a quick prayer to Nabû, the God of scribes and writing, just for good measure. Then he hurried back inside, grabbed his stylus-box, strapped on his sandals, and hustled out the door.

Rushing through the narrow streets, Zaidu dodged around the early-morning crowds of cloth-sellers and trinket-hawkers, the wood poles over their shoulders dangling with carved amulets for warding off demons, or tiny votive statues for the temple. He ducked down a side street and took a shortcut he knew, passing into the cleaner brick walls and broader avenues of the temple district as he headed for the astrological observatory.

The mud-brick edifice would stand out in any city, but the planners of Babili had surrounded it with a flat open courtyard of flowerbeds and tree planters, just to make sure all passers-by gave proper attention to its magnificence—its tall columns painted blue and gold, capped by friezes carved with the symbols of the Gods: stars, the sun, the moon, and other heavenly bodies. On any other day, Zaidu might have paused to admire it in the golden morning light.

This morning, though, he tore across that courtyard at a speed just short of a dead run, drawing disapproving gazes from the priests and eunuchs who shuffled pensively in their colorful linen robes. He ran up the steps into the observatory's lower foyer, then up the winding brick staircase that led to Master Tattannu's private chambers. By the time he reached the chamber's door—fine dark wood, polished to a gleam, on which hung a wood plaque neatly painted with the the master's name in Aramaya letters—he was gasping and panting like a dog.

He took a moment to compose himself, then knocked.

"Come!" called a voice from inside.

Zaidu opened the door and stepped into the master's chamber. As he shut the door carefully behind him, he glanced at a table of work that'd evidently been piling up since last night, to judge by the burned-out oil lamps and candles. The table held tall piles of papyrus scrolls, and stacks of thick wax scratch-pads and clay tablets, many of them etched with dense patterns of tiny wedge-shaped symbols.

Master Tattannu hunched over the table, shuffling his notes, his long gray hair and beard hanging over his burgundy linen robe. He glanced up as Zaidu entered, raising his thick eyebrows.

"You're late," the master said.

"You're quite right, master," said Zaidu. "I was, eh, unavoidably detained, preparing my materials."

"You lost your stylus-box."

"I had to calm another scribe who'd lost his, and lend him a stylus."

The master shook his head. "It's not proper for all you young scribes to live together. You should have your own house. A wife and children. That's how we did things when I was young."

"Quite right, master, as always. I'm sorry."

The master waved a hand absentmindedly. "Never mind that now. I need you to transcribe my notes onto tablets, and have them baked."

"Certainly. What exactly will I be transcribing, if I may ask?"

Master Tattannu looked up, and a smile crossed his wrinkled face. "Let me show you."

The master laid out a series of tablets and scrolls across the table, along with an assortment of six-sided prisms of baked clay, their faces engraved with tables of cramped symbols so tiny they were scarcely legible, recording the positions of stars and planets on each day of the year. The sheer breadth of languages represented on this desk astonished even Zaidu, lettered as he was. Some older prisms were inscribed in classical Akkadu, while the parchments and papyri bore the squat rounded letters of modern Aramaya, or of Yehudu, which Zaidu hadn't even known the master could read.

Other tablets were inscribed with the sharp triangular glyphs of Elamu, and—Zaidu could scarce believe his eyes—even pale, spiderweb-cracked lumps of clay, stamped with the crisscrossed needle-hashes and pictoglyphs of archaic Shuméru. *Those tablets must be two thousand years old, at the very least*, Zaidu thought. It took a master's credentials to even be allowed to handle texts of that age, let alone remove them from the archive building.

Master Tattannu caught Zaidu's eye, smiled, and said, "Yes, those are tablets from old Shumér."

"I must admit, master," said Zaidu, "now you've sparked my curiosity."

"Then let us begin," said the master.

MASTER TATTANNU BEGAN by explaining that he'd perfected a method of pinpointing the position of Marutúk—the purple wandering star which bore the name of the father-God—in the night sky on any day of the year, without having to refer to the dense tables of recorded positions covering the clay prisms on his desk. The master was well aware that other astrologers had conceived of this approach before him. Its basic outlines, at least, had been known in Babili for nearly a hundred years. But over a few weeks of feverish work, Master Tattannu believed, he had carried the technique to a new height of simplicity and precision.

The method involved a long list of complicated fractions, and a trapezoid divided in half, and a lot of calculations about time and speed, most of which Zaidu didn't really understand. He'd never had much of a head for numbers, and last night's sweet-beer wasn't helping.

"So this shape represents Marutúk's speed as he traverses the heavens," Zaidu said, pointing at a trapezoid the master had drawn, wider at the top than at the bottom.

"No, not his speed," said Master Tattannu. "The *pace of change* in his speed."

Zaidu wrinkled his brow. "I'm sorry, master, but what's the difference?"

"As Marutúk moves across the heavens," said Master Tattannu, tracing a line across the trapezoid with his finger. "His speed changes, yes—but so does the *rate* at which his speed changes over time." He tapped the curved line with his finger to emphasize his point. "Ha! You see?"

"I'm afraid I don't," said Zaidu, his head feeling cloudy and sore. Why did the master have to choose this morning, of all mornings, for a lesson in advanced mathematics? "Please forgive my stupidity, master," he said. "Perhaps it's best if I simply copy it as you've drawn it—"

"No no! You must understand what you're transcribing. This is very important." He lifted out a soft clay tablet marked with a large circle. "Now, this shape, you see, represents the sky, the dome of the heavens. Yes?"

"I see, master."

"Now, on the first night, Marutúk moves one-sixty-fourth part across this half of the heavens." Master Tattannu took the reed stylus from Zaidu and made a mark in the clay, just slightly to the right of the circle's left edge. "You see?"

"I think so, master."

"Excellent. Now, on the second night, he moves one-sixty-*sixth* part." The master made a second mark, a bit farther to the right of the first mark. "His speed is decreasing as he nears the center of the heavenly dome. Only the Gods, in their wisdom, know why."

"Yes, master. He slows as he nears the center."

"Precisely. Now on the third, fourth, and fifth nights, Marutúk travels one-seventieth part. Then one-eightieth part. Then ninety-sixth part." The master made a series of marks at decreasing distances toward the center of the circle. "His speed is decreasing, yes. But here is the crucial insight: the *pace* at which he slows—is *increasing*!"

Zaidu nodded, still not quite sure this was making sense.

"By the time Marutúk reaches the center of the heavens," Master Tattannu said, "He is moving at one-one-hundred-twelfth part per night. So slow, he's barely moving at all. Were his speed to keep decreasing at this rate, he would almost cease to move altogether in another—"

"—ten days," whispered Zaidu, then said, "I'm sorry for interrupting, master."

Master Tattannu smiled. "Nine, in fact," he said. "You're a quick study, Zaidu."

"Thank you, master," said Zaidu. "But I'm afraid I fail to see why this is so important."

"Ah!" said Master Tattannu, and bent over the tablet again. "Well, you see, Marutúk, in his wisdom, does not stop. He pauses and rests when he reaches the center of the heavens. Then, after a few days tarrying there, he reverses course. As he descends the dome of the sky—" the master tapped the marks he'd made, from the center outward, farther and farther apart, "his speed begins to quicken, at *precisely the same pace* as it slowed."

Zaidu stared at the diagram for a few moments, repeating the master's words under his breath: *pace of quickening. Pace of slowing. Both paces are the same.*

"Is this really true?" he asked at last.

"So I have calculated," said the master. "Until at last Marutúk reaches the far edge of the heavens, and immediately begins to climb back toward the center, along the very same path as before, at exactly the same rate of quickening. Gods be praised for creating such an ordered universe."

"Gods be praised," echoed Zaidu out of habit, concentrating on the marks in the clay.

"And when we weave together the threads of the pace—you see, the *pace*—at which Marutúk's speed changes each night," said the master, "We assemble a figure: this trapezoid." He tapped the asymmetrical shape again.

Zaidu was nodding slowly. "Which means if you know how much Marutúk moves on any given night..."

"Yes, go on," said the master, smiling gently.

"Immortal Gods! If you knew the pace of change for every star, you wouldn't need the check the tables on those clay prisms, or anything—"

"Precisely," said Master Tattannu.

"To calculate where a star would be on any night, all you'd need to know is its position one night and the night after." Zaidu clapped his hand to his forehead. "By Énlil's breath!" He winced. "Sorry, master."

Tattannu smiled gently. "Quite a gift from Énki, the Father of Cleverness, don't you think?"

Zaidu shook his head. "The other astrologers will lavish you with prizes—"

"—or they might drag me outside the walls and stone me. The minds of priests are known to have a... rather slow pace of change." Master Tattannu laughed softly at his little joke. "In any case, I think it's important to make a record of this method. Someone might find it useful."

Zaidu rubbed his chin. "What about other objects, master?"

"Other—objects?" Tattannu raised a bushy eyebrow.

"What if—" Zaidu struggled to fit his thought into words. "Well, you say the speeds of all stars in the heavens have their ordained rates of change."

The master nodded. "I believe it is so."

"Well, what about objects here on Earth?" Zaidu asked. "What if you could, you know, throw a stone, or launch an arrow, and calculate exactly where it would be—"

The old master laughed softly. "It would be nice, wouldn't it, if our earthly world were as predictable and orderly as the stars?"

"Yes," said Zaidu. "I suppose it would be."

"I think we'd best stick to the heavens," said the master, handing the stylus back to Zaidu.

"Of course, master," said Zaidu. "I'll get started on the tablets now. And—thank you. Thank you very much for the lesson."

Master Tattannu smiled. "I'm glad you enjoyed it. And now, I believe it's time for this old man to take a nap."

Zaidu worked on the transcription for the next few hours, carefully copying diagrams and fractions and tiny clusters of triangle-shaped symbols from wax pads and papyrus scrolls to clay tablets, which—since the master was paying extra—would be baked to rock-hardness, so they'd last for centuries. Zaidu tried to focus on the formulas and their meanings, but after a while he got lost in the copying, as he always did, seeing nothing but lines of symbols, knowing nothing but the flow of the work, like water along a riverbank.

When he looked up at the window it was nearly sunset, and Master Tattannu was still sleeping. Zaidu decided to let him sleep. In the last of the sunlight he finished copying a few pages of notes, then arranged everything neatly on the table, packed up his stylus-box, and headed downstairs into the courtyard. Most of the priests and eunuchs were gone by this time of the evening, which was a relief.

ZAIDU WALKED HOME, thinking of stars and Gods and the heavens, and nearly bumped into a trinket-seller returning from the market, who cursed him loudly in some crass southern dialect.

Once he'd deposited his stylus-box in the chest next to his sleeping-mat, he walked the few blocks to the tavern, where he found Dipti already a few beers deep.

"That kind of day, was it?" Zaidu asked as he waved down Arwia to bring him a mug.

"You wouldn't believe it," said Dipti.

"Try me." Zaidu settled in at the table.

"The Gods-damned scribal school double-booked me!" Dipti cried. "Can you believe that? I had Master Izdubar and

Master Shamas yelling at me at the same time—both their transcriptions were absolute top priority, of course—and I worked all day and still didn't finish either of them. Both of those bastards are too cheap to give me a candle or—Gods forbid—light a damned lamp, so when the sun went down they finally let me go home."

Zaidu groaned. "And you're going back there tomorrow?"

"Do I have a choice?" Dipti sighed, long and tired.

"Maybe you should talk to the scribal school," Zaidu offered.

"And say what?" Dipti threw up his hands. "I'm lucky to have the work, in this economy."

Zaidu nodded and sipped his beer. "Well," he said, after a moment, "you won't believe what happened to me today."

Dipti groaned. "Don't tell me they double-booked you, too."

"No, thank the Gods." Zaidu said. "But Master Tattannu told me something very interesting."

"Oh, well, I'm glad one of us learned something interesting today." Dipti rubbed his brow.

Arwia arrived at the table with Zaidu's mug of beer, which she set on the stained wood with a smile. "Got any Shuméru for me today, scribe?" she asked, smiling.

"Maybe later," said Zaidu. "Come back and we'll see."

She bit her lip and winked, and he smiled back. She hurried off to other tables before her father could shout at her.

"Master Tattannu told me," Zaidu began. "Well, I don't know how much I should reveal, but he explained there's a way to calculate the position of any star in the heavens, without using the tables."

"Fascinating," said Dipti dryly.

"And it got me thinking—"

"You think there's any money in that?" asked Dipti.

"In what? In these calculations?" Zaidu shook his head. "I don't know. I hadn't really thought about it. There could be."

"Maybe you could, you know, sneak some of them out with you."

Zaidu slapped the table, splashing beer foam. "Come on, man! I'm trying to explain something important here, and you're talking about stealing from clients. What's wrong with you?"

"Oh, sorry," said Dipti, taking a slow sip of his beer. "I didn't have as *interesting* a day as you. Please, by all means, continue."

"Well," said Zaidu, "I was just thinking—I mean, Master Tattannu said this probably wouldn't work, but I was thinking, what if everything that moves in both the heavens and the earth really does follow the same laws?"

Dipti rubbed at his temples. "What laws? What are you talking about, Zaidu? Gods help me, this is worse than your Shuméru rant last night."

Zaidu waved a hand dismissively. "Fine. You know what? Forget it. It's probably not important anyway." He raised his clay mug and took a long series of swallows.

"I'll tell you what's important," said Dipti. "The way Arwia looked at you a minute ago. Did you see that? She winked at you. Actually winked at you."

"Yeah, I guess I did see that." Zaidu grinned.

Dipti spread his hands. "You're not going to get more of an invitation than that. You need to give her the answer she's hoping for."

Zaidu glanced over at the counter. "Her father's standing right there, Dipti."

"After closing time, then." Dipti flicked his eyes toward the door. "Meet her outside."

Zaidu sighed. "I'll think about it."

"You'll do it," said Dipti. "I swear by all the Gods, if I catch you coming home alone tonight, I'll beat you worse than Master Shamas ever did."

Zaidu laughed. A long, tired, shaking laugh.

"If not for you, do it for me," said Dipti. He downed the rest of his beer, and waved down Arwia for another.

They sat and drank and cracked jokes and traded complaints for a while, waiting for Arwia to finish her work for the night. Dipti got very drunk and tried to pick a fight with a chariot-builder. Zaidu stopped him before anything could happen.

And when the night was over they stumbled out into the street, and Arwia was there waiting for them. Zaidu talked to her and made her laugh while Dipti slipped away, and Zaidu told Arwia some more poetry in Shuméru, and she loved every line of it.

She wrapped her arms gently around his neck and kissed him slow and lazily, and he kissed her back, long and soft, then harder, and he thought about the big house they'd move into in a nicer part of town, and the home they'd make together there. Gods and mathematics were the very furthest things from his mind.

▼▼▼
▼▼▼

"Hey! Boy. Yes, you." The voice echoed from a nearby alley.

Zaidu turned, his mind still swirling with the smell of Arwia's breath. The taste of her tongue.

A bearded man in a tattered tunic emerged from the shadows, his face lit by the flickering flame of the small torch in his hand.

Zaidu raised his hands. "I haven't got any coin!" he gasped. "I swear. Spent the last of it at the tavern."

"I'm not here to rob you, boy," the man snarled, twisting the scar that ran along his upper lip. "Those swine in the palace do enough of that already."

"I'm sorry?" Zaidu's brow furrowed.

"We're not deaf," the man replied. "We've heard you, every night outside the tavern. And you're right. Those Elline sons-of-whores are raping this city. You're not the only one who thinks so."

"I'm, eh, glad to hear it," Zaidu stammered. "But I've really got to be going now."

"Oh, that's right," the man sneered. "Hurry home to your soft bed, while savages sleep in the palace, lining their pockets with stolen gold. Keep spilling words and cowering from action. 'The wolf circles around it and the lion picks it up.' Are you a wolf or a lion?"

Zaidu whirled on him. "What do you expect me to do? There's no room for lions anymore."

The man smiled crookedly. "Ah, now that's where we disagree, son."

"What are you talking about?" Zaidu shook his head.

"Follow me," said the man, and turned away down the alley.

Zaidu followed the torchlight through the narrow gaps between buildings, around tight corners and switchbacks, deeper into the entrails of this tumbledown neighborhood. He caught torch-lit glimpses of rats swarming around trash-piles; rag-clad men sleeping in doorways; wild dogs looking up from their sleep, growling softly, eyes shining in the blackness.

The man knocked at a door, which swung aside to reveal a suspicious-looking woman, her head wrapped in rags.

"It's me," the man whispered. "And I've brought a guest."

The woman looked Zaidu up and down in a glance, then nodded curtly and stepped aside to let them in.

Two more men and a younger woman sat on battered cushions in the cramped interior, amid the guttering flame of a cheap fat-burning lamp.

"This is Zaidu," said the man who'd brought him here.

The others nodded in greeting, announcing their names: Mushezibti, Palusum, Sheshkala, Tilhar; though he immediately forgot whose name was whose. He was still a bit wobbly from the beer, though he felt he was concealing it well. He lowered himself onto a cushion, feeling slightly claustrophobic—though perhaps that was because they were all eyeing him with open suspicion.

"I'm Kutik," said the man who'd brought him here, extinguishing his torch. "Welcome to the family."

"Family?" Zaidu asked. "I'm still not sure I understand." He was fairly sure, though, that he did.

"'When liars enter by the city gate,'" Kutik said, "'fingers point at them from the front, and from behind.' We all know who the liars in our city are."

"'And a fettered dog stands ready to bite,'" Zaidu quoted in response. "Are you a scribe?"

Kutik shook his head. "Never learned the trick of it. But I listen. I listen to everything and everyone. That's how I heard your complaints. And you're right—we're all fettered dogs these days. All except those filthy Ellines, and the nobles who dance at the ends of their puppet-strings."

"We'll have them dancing at the ends of ropes soon enough," muttered a potbellied man in a long, loose toga, who Zaidu thought was probably the one called Palusum.

The woman who'd answered the door—Sheshkala, was it?—set a small tray of barley-cakes near the fire and offered one to Zaidu. He accepted it, though he had no appetite.

"Listen, I—" Zaidu raised his hands. "I'm just a scribe. I transcribe documents. I hate these Elline savages as much as you do, and I wish they were gone. I support your cause. Truly, I do. But I'm not your man."

They all watched him for a long, acutely uncomfortable moment.

"We haven't even told you what we're planning yet," Kutik said at last.

Zaidu looked around, meeting each man's eyes in turn. They looked disappointed with him, which somehow felt much worse than if they'd been angry.

"Oh, all right," he said at last. "Tell me what you plan to do."

Kutik smiled tightly. "Show him, Tilhar."

The gaunt, sour-faced man rose from his cushion and ducked behind the cloth curtain in the back doorway. He emerged cradling a clay barrel, stoppered tightly and bound with leather straps and set it with utmost delicacy on the cushion he'd just vacated. The woman Sheshkala reached out and lifted the lamp away, setting it as far away from the barrel as possible.

"War-fire," Tilhar said, his voice like wind through a reed.

Zaidu's eyes widened. "The liquid flame?" he whispered.

"The same." Kutik smiled, nodding.

"How did you acquire it?" Zaidu asked.

Kutik snorted. "Does it matter? All that matters now is how we use it."

Zaidu stared at the small clay vessel, half-expecting it to explode in flame any moment, consuming them all. "How do you plan to use it?"

"We have word," Kutik said, "that the despot Seleukos plans to celebrate his birthday on the seventh day of the month of Simanu."

"That's five days from now," Zaidu murmured.

"Word is," Kutik continued, "the Elline tyrant will celebrate by sailing his royal barque down the Slow River, packed with his barbaric family, concubines, musicians—even a few traitorous nobles, if we're lucky."

Zaidu's breath caught in his throat. "And with one spark—"

Tilhar grinned. "The whole boat goes up in flame."

"Liquid, resinous, inextinguishable flame," Kutik added approvingly.

"But how will you hurl the vessel?" Zaidu asked. "You have a catapult hidden away in that back room, too?"

Kutik laughed softly. "If only." He sighed. "No, I'm afraid one of us will have to board the boat, light the fuse, and smash the clay at the opportune moment."

"Someone who loves Babili more than his own life," Palusum huffed from his cushion in the corner.

Zaidu met the pudgy man's eyes. No mistaking the meaning in that look—the look that all the others were now giving him, too.

"Surely you can't mean me," he said softly.

"Look at us." Kutik gestured around at the others. "Peasants. Wool-spinners. Butchers. None of us would get within a league of the royal barque. Now a well-respected scribe, on the other hand—one with connections at the temple..."

"I'm a transcriber!" Zaidu burst out. "I just copy texts! I've never even been to the palace. And no one at the temple gives a damn what I think."

But Kutik was shaking his head. "That's not what I hear."

Zaidu's brow furrowed. "What do you hear?"

"That a young scribe named Zaidu dreams of applying the mathematics of Heaven to the movement of objects on Earth." Kutik grinned. "Just the sort of topic to intrigue and entertain an upstart Elline tyrant—even one as illiterate and barbaric as ours."

"How did—" Zaidu stammered. "How can you possibly know about that? I only told—"

"—a certain master of astronomy," Kutik finished, "who is most sympathetic to our cause, and has already been invited to join the tyrant on his little river outing."

Zaidu's eyes widened. He shook his head, as if that might cause these new facts to fall into some sort of rational array. This was too much to process all at once. "All the same," he said, barely hearing his own words, "I'm not your man. I love Babili. Love it with my whole heart. But—"

"Think about it." Kutik raised a hand, smiling gently. "That's all I ask. Take the next two days and think it over. Search your heart. Find clarity."

None of this seemed clear at all. The mathematics, the tavern, Arwia, the vessel of war-fire—it all whirled madly in his mind, like a dream. He barely remembered how he bid the plotters goodnight, or how he found his way home.

ZAIDU WAS DREAMING. He knew he must be dreaming because he walked not in Babili, but in an older city: a place of columns tiled in mosaics of red, black and white; of temples and stepped pyramids of mud-brick, where men and women in shaggy fleece garments carried reed baskets along dirt paths beneath the palms, and—so it was said—fish-scaled sages had come forth from the depths of the Two Rivers, to teach the crafts and sciences of civilization to the first men and women.

He could use some of that wisdom now, he thought. But everyone knew that after the great Flood, the sages had stopped coming forth from the Rivers, and the Gods had stopped speaking freely with mankind, as they had before. Zaidu wasn't sure how much of the old stories he believed. But judging by the state of Babili today, it seemed abundantly clear that the people of the Land Between the Rivers had been abandoned to fend for themselves.

Even as he thought this, Zaidu suddenly found that another man had appeared at his side. The man had long, shaggy black hair, and thick eyebrows that joined in the middle. Zaidu would've recognized his garb anywhere: the high-waisted kilt of thick-curled fleece worn by Shuméru men in the most ancient mosaics, and a bare chest tattooed with zigzagged patterns of red and black. Perhaps, Zaidu thought, his wish for heavenly wisdom from before the Flood had summoned this man—whoever he was—from the Sea of Dreams.

"That's quite a costume," Zaidu commented, by way of introduction.

"Costume?" The Shuméru man glanced down at himself and shrugged. "I could say the same of you," he replied. "What land do you come from?"

Zaidu was really beginning to enjoy this. "From Babili," he said. "And you—I can see you've come all the way from ancient Shumér, before the Flood."

"The Flood—?" The kilted man looked astonished. He raised a hand to stop Zaidu, gazing into his eyes with fear. "Are you saying this flood really happens?" he demanded.

Sadness filled Zaidu. *I am warning this man of his own doom*, he thought. *A doom he cannot escape.* "Yes," he said at last. "The Flood washed away all the cities of Shumér. Only a few people survived. They became the founders of the new dynasties."

The man's eyes widened. "What can we do?" he asked.

"Is this some kind of a test?" Zaidu's raised an eyebrow, suspicious.

"Yes," said the kilted man, nodding eagerly. "A test. How did people survive the Flood?"

Zaidu knew the tale by heart, as did all children of Babili. "I only know the story of one survivor," he told the Shuméru man. "The stories say he built some kind of strange vessel that carried him over the waves."

"A strange vessel," the man muttered. After a moment, he shook his head. "Perhaps that will prove to be the answer," he said.

Zaidu hadn't the slightest idea what that meant. A new question rose to his lips, unbidden. "What about my questions?" he asked. "The wisdom I asked for?"

The shaggy-kilted man only shook his head. "What wisdom? What are you talking about?"

With the strange logic of dreams, Zaidu chose to ask about a problem that had scarcely crossed his thoughts lately: "What of the movement of objects on earth? Do they obey the same laws as bodies in the heavens?" Surely, he thought, men from before the Flood must have understood such matters perfectly, guided as they were by the Gods themselves.

But the Shuméru man only gazed back at him, his face a mask of confusion. "I know nothing of the heavens," he said at last. "But so far as I have seen, all things obey the same law: the faster one rises, the faster one falls."

And in this dream, that answer somehow made perfect sense. Zaidu's heart swelled with joy. "Thank you," he told the man.

Then the mud-brick city was fading, and Zaidu was plummeting up from the Sea of Dreams into blinding daylight. Someone was calling his name.

"Hey, stop napping!" It was Arwia's voice.

The waking world flooded back. He was lying on the grass, and the sun was in his eyes. Arwia sat next to him, a baked clay tablet in her hands. They lay beneath the shade of a great juniper tree, in the last surviving garden of the royal park of Babili.

"Isn't it the student who's supposed to fall asleep?" Arwia teased. "Not the teacher?"

"Right." Zaidu blinked, raising himself upright. "Where were we?" he asked her, the dream already fading from memory.

"I was showing you the signs I remember from last time," she said. "Ah! I recognize this one!" She pointed to an intricate Shuméru glyph among the hundreds stamped into the clay. "It means 'man.'"

"You're close." Zaidu smiled. "But it's also got the sign for *gál*, 'big,' there on the left side. See? So it means *lugál*, 'big man' or 'king.'"

She wrinkled her nose, sighing in exasperation as she looked up from the clay tablet they held. "How do you keep all this straight?"

He snorted a laugh. "Don't forget, I had to beg Master Tattannu for permission to take this tablet out of the archives. It's not everyone who gets to read writing this ancient."

She fell back on the grass theatrically, throwing a hand over her eyes, as he carefully tucked the tablet back into his shoulder-bag. "I can see why it's not a popular pastime. One tiny mistake reading one little character," she said, "and the message changes from 'Please send barley' to 'Let's make war on Misr.' It's amazing this hasn't thrown the world into chaos by now."

He lay down beside her, wrapping his arm around her waist to pull her close. "Well, modern Aramaya is much simpler. We write it on parchment with an *aleph-bet* script. Just forty-four letters. Much less chance of confusion. But it'll never be as beautiful as Shuméru."

"It's beautiful when you speak it," she said, planting kisses against his cheek. "Tell me some more."

"*Something which has never occurred since time immemorial*," he recited solemnly. "*A young woman did not fart in her husband's embrace.*"

She rolled away from him, making an annoyed sound. He climbed on top of her, straddling her, pulling her hands away from her face as she struggled and squealed with laughter.

"I didn't like that one." She pouted.

He kissed her. "I'm sorry." And again. "I promise I'll tell you more." And again. "Soon."

She made a happy, humming sound, and they rolled on the grass together. Even now, pressed tightly against her, smelling her breath and tasting her skin, the city's melancholy pulled at him, like a thread of a garment slowly coming unwoven.

"What's in your mind, Zaidu?" she asked after a while. "You're not all here."

He drew a deep breath and sighed slowly, searching for some way to translate the feeling into words.

"Do you ever think about what this city used to be like?" he asked her at last. "I mean, before the Ellines came, or the Parsa kings before them. Back when Babili ruled herself."

She stroked his cheek. "My mother used to sing me tales of the old Empire, when I was a little girl. The gardens of a thousand flowers. The shining golden gates. I saw them in my dreams, sometimes."

"What about now?" he asked.

"What about what, now?" she replied, kissing his cheek.

"Do you ever see those places in your dreams anymore?"

She laughed softly. "Not for a long time. I can't even remember the last dream I had. After a long night at the tavern, I'm just glad to be in my own bed."

"The other night," he said, "I dreamed of walking down the Processional Way in the new year's festival. The king and nobles in jewels and furs. The solid-gold statues of the Gods. The crowds of dancers and musicians from all across the Empire. When I woke up, I felt cheated."

"Was I there, in your dream?" She nuzzled against his neck.

"No," he said. "I don't think so."

"Well then," she slipped on top of him. "You should be glad you woke up."

"Sometimes I think I'd trade my life," he said, "just to resurrect this city."

"Except it doesn't work that way," she murmured in his ear. "This city is what it is, and we've all got to live in it. But if you want to give your life away, I'll be glad to accept it."

He met her gaze, unsure if she meant what she seemed to be saying. She bit her lip, smiling shyly.

"Arwia, I—"

"Arwia, what?" she mocked.

"Yes," he answered. "I—I think I'm supposed to ask that question, but yes. I'm yours."

She kissed him again, harder than before.

"Then it's settled," she said. "I'll take care of you, you'll take care of me, and everyone else can take care of themselves."

"And the city—"

"Not another word about the city," she said, placing a finger on his lips. "I'm here. Now. What are you going to do with me?"

He rolled over on top of her, and gave her an answer.

HE WAS STROLLING back to the archives to return the clay tablet he'd shared with Arwia when he felt a presence behind him.

Trying not to appear too obvious, he turned and glanced back. Three Elline soldiers, armored and crimson-cloaked, unshaven and leering, about half a block behind him. He could almost smell them from where he was.

He turned a tight corner next to a bakery, hurrying down the narrow alley between two apartment blocks, as cats hissed and leaped out of his way. But somehow the soldiers were there at the end of the alley, waiting for him—how had they gotten there so quickly?—blocking his way, hairy hands resting casually on the worn pommels of their swords.

"*Poú pas se mia tétoia viasýni?*" one of them sneered. Zaidu's command of common-tongue Elline was nowhere near as practiced as Dipti's, but he still caught the meaning: "Where are you off to in such a hurry?"

"Sorry!" He raised his hands defensively, frantically trying to remember the rudiments of common-tongue grammar. "My Elline, not so good."

The three soldiers exchanged glances, sharing a laugh. "Oh no! My Elline, not so good!" one of them mocked him in a high-pitched voice.

"Now isn't that strange?" the leader remarked. "A scribe who can't be bothered to learn the common language of his empire. Why, it's almost as if he doesn't recognize what a blessing it is to live under our benevolence."

One word leaped out at Zaidu amid all the others.

"How—how you know I am a scribe?" he asked.

The leader grinned. "Oh, we've been watching you, we have. Isn't that right, boys?" The others grunted in agreement.

Zaidu's stomach plummeted, leaving a cold emptiness in its place.

"You lead quite the interesting life," the leader continued, picking his teeth with a splinter of wood. "Temple scribe by day, lover in the afternoon—and plotter against the throne by night."

Zaidu backed away. "Please, I don't know—I don't understand."

"Oh, I think you understand just fine," said the soldier, his grin widening. Zaidu smelled stale beer on the man's breath. "That sweet little thing of yours, though—she may not understand why you've up and disappeared. Perhaps I'll have to give her a bit of comfort myself—"

"Don't you touch her!" Zaidu howled in Aramaya, provoking laughs and gibberish from the soldiers.

Then everything seemed to happen at once. Zaidu swung his shoulder-bag like a sling, connecting hard with the side of the leader's head, cracking the tablet inside with a crunch like old bone. He winced, imagining the scolding he'd get from Master Tattannu.

Meanwhile the other two soldiers stepped out around the leader, grabbing the strap of the bag, tugging Zaidu away, tripping him so he stumbled backward and landed hard on the stones—

And suddenly the alley was full of fighters: Kutik and the others from the night-meeting; even fat Palusum, cracking a walking-stick over a soldier's head. The scarfed woman lashed out with a dagger, spilling the third soldier's blood as he fell screaming.

Kutik grabbed Zaidu by the collar and pulled him up. Then they were all running, rounding angled corners between tight-pressed buildings, leaping over trash-heaps, climbing fences and dashing through courtyards as old women leaped away in surprise, spilling laundry and buckets of water.

They reached a small low-set door. Kutik yanked it open and they piled inside and down the stairs, into a shadowy room that turned pitch-black when someone slammed the door behind them.

Kutik lit a lamp, filling the room with a dim orange glow. It was another cramped chamber: bare walls, a low table, a few cushions.

Zaidu took it all in, panting, trying to slow his breath. Suddenly he remembered his shoulder-bag, and the tablet he'd sneaked away from the archives after his morning session with Master Tattannu. He opened the bag, wincing: the tablet lay in dozens of pieces, shattered beyond repair.

"I'm sorry," Kutik said.

Zaidu shook his head. "It's not just the punishment I face," he said softly. "This tablet was centuries old. Now it's just another piece of old Babili that's been smashed to rubble."

He sank onto a cushion, letting out a long, slow breath.

"There's no going back now," Kutik said, sinking onto the cushion next to Zaidu as the others busied themselves double-checking the room's supplies. "You realize that, don't you?"

Zaidu looked up sharply and met the man's eyes. "Did you set this up? Tell me the truth, Kutik."

The silence between them stretched tightly, until at last Kutik broke it.

"Those men had been following you for days," he said.

"That's not what I asked."

Kutik nodded. "Our man told them where you'd be this afternoon. That's all—"

"I knew it!" Zaidu leaped up, his face contorted with rage. "All you care about is your stupid plot! I'm not your puppet—I'm a human being! I have—" He trailed off.

"What do you have?" Kutik asked.

"I have my own life," Zaidu finished weakly.

Kutik watched him for a long moment.

"Is that truly what you want?" the other man asked at last. "To marry that girl, settle down, raise your children in a Babili ruled by Ellines? Live out your days as a scribe, all the while forced to learn more common-tongue and forget Shuméru? To watch this city crumble slowly to dust before your eyes?"

Zaidu sank back down to the cushion. "What's the alternative?" he asked quietly. "Cast myself into the Underworld? Leave behind everything I love?"

Kutik leaned in close. "If you do this for Babili," he said, his voice almost a whisper, "whether you succeed or fail, we will make sure she is provided for. A high position at a faraway temple. A quiet farm in the countryside. Anything she desires, as long as it's within our reach. I promise this."

Zaidu looked into Kutik's eyes, then down at his hands.

"But that's not why you'll do this," Kutik said. "You'll do it because you know, in your heart, that it is the only path. I see it in your eyes, clear as a morning sky."

Hot tears welled up in Zaidu's eyes. He fought them back down. "I can't leave her," he said. "I can't."

"Zaidu," Kutik said. "After what you've done today, she will never be safe. You must know this."

"After what *you've* done!" Zaidu cried. "You did this to me!"

"No." Kutik shook his head calmly. "The enemy did it to all of us."

Zaidu stared at him, his face a mask of incredulity.

"I had a wife," Kutik said. "And I once thought like you. Thought that as long as I kept my head down, everything would be all right. But one day, some bastard of an Elline general took a liking to my beautiful Inu. We fought back, of course. I and every man and woman on my block. But of course, the soldiers won in the end." He tapped the scar on his upper lip. "They took her away, and I've been in hiding ever since. Don't even know if she's alive or dead."

A long silence hung in the air. Zaidu had no words to offer.

"And as long as an outsider sits on our throne," Kutik said. "This will never stop. Do you see that? They have stolen all choices from us—all but one: the choice of what to do now. Here. In this moment."

Zaidu shook his head. "There's always another choice."

"Then name it," Kutik said. "Zaidu, if there is any other path from here, then show it to me. I beg you."

Zaidu sat for what seemed hours, searching for any crack in the wall; any glimmer of hope that might light the way to a life with Arwia—a long, peaceful life in some corner of the earth where empires and kings would simply leave them alone. But there was no such corner. The earth was ruled by Ellines now; and if their empire fell, then after them would come others still more barbaric. This was it. This was the end of history. But if Babili was to burn, then her conquerors must burn, too.

"I want her taken care of," Zaidu said at last, letting the tears come. It was a relief to let them rise in his eyes, softening the world with their warmth, running down his cheeks. "Whatever she wants, I want her to have."

"Of course." Kutik smiled softly. "I have already promised this."

"Tomorrow, then," Zaidu said. "The king's birthday."

"Tomorrow," Kutik agreed.

※※※

"I KNOW THIS can't be easy for you," Seleukos Nikator—"the Victor," white-haired Elline king of Babili and the Eastern Provinces—was saying.

Zaidu could barely concentrate. His mind was on the sealed clay vessel of war-fire that was concealed belowdecks, waiting for the right moment.

"The way my soldiers behaved toward you was atrocious," Seleukos was saying in fluent, Elline-accented Aramaya. "Simply barbaric. Inexcusable. I've already had them flogged."

The Cradle and the Sword

The king reclined in a solid-gold throne near the stern of the royal barque, which rocked gently as it sailed down the Slow River. Jewelled dragons crawled about the throne's legs, extending their claws to form the chair's feet. The aged king sat draped in purple Parsa silk embroidered with circular golden flowers, in classic Babili style. Atop his blocky, wispy-haired head sat a gold laurel wreath: a typical fashion for Elline conquerors.

"That wasn't necessary, Your Majesty," Zaidu replied, without really hearing the words.

"Oh, but it was!" exclaimed the king. "It most certainly was. I hear a tablet was damaged in the brawl. An irreplaceable relic of ancient Shumér."

"That was my fault, Majesty," Zaidu said drily. "In the heat of battle, I defended myself by cracking the tablet against your soldier's head."

"Ha!" The king threw back his head and barked a laugh. "If only it were as easy to transmit culture as to transmit force of motion. Am I right?"

"A most erudite observation, sire," commented Master Tattannu, who stood at Zaidu's right. He shot Zaidu a sharply disappointed glance that somehow stung worse than any whipping.

"I must be honest, gentlemen," the old king mused, looking out over the calm water. "This is not the Babili I dreamed of. The city was already half in ruins when General Alexandros liberated it from the Parsa kings, nearly fifty years ago. And I fear we've only made things worse since then."

"'Liberated,'" Zaidu muttered.

The king cocked his head. "What's that you say?"

"Eh—he means to say, Majesty," Master Tattannu put in, "that perhaps it is liberation itself that creates many of our problems. Our people have been ruled by great kings since time immemorial. We require a strong, firm hand to guide us."

"Perhaps it is as you say." The king nodded thoughtfully, stroking his bare chin. "And in that case, I owe you all the more apology for my poor control of my own soldiers."

"Seleukos Nikator owes me nothing," Zaidu said, careful to cloak his bitterness with a humble tone.

"And I am honored," the king concluded, "that you have elected to join me here today, in celebration of my seventy-first birthday." He shook his head. "Seventy-one years. To think that an old war-horse should live so long."

The king stared off over the water for a few uncomfortable moments, while a band of musicians played a hymn to the Goddess Ishtar. Nobles and royals in long silken robes mingled around a long golden table laid with gem-encrusted plates of fruits and candied nuts.

A pair of gray-haired Ellines—probably generals-turned-statesmen, judging by the scars on their arms—flirted with a gaggle of young Babili heiresses by the wine-pitchers. A bald bureaucrat from Misr—an ambassador of the Nile kingdom's latest Elline overlord—stood draped in white linen, his kohl-shadowed eyes narrowing with concentration as he chatted with three chestnut-skinned gentleman in bejewelled vests and red silk trousers: diplomats from the jungle-lords of Hindush, far to the east, unless Zaidu missed his guess. *Not that these nobles' origins and names will count for anything*, he thought, *once they've joined the king at the bottom of this river.*

"So tell me, young scribe," Seleukos said, "of your plan to apply the mathematics of Heaven to the movement of objects here on Earth."

At that moment, Zaidu felt like a ship abandoned by the wind. He felt no great love for this king, or any softening toward the Elline conquerors. But he realized—"clear as a morning sky," as Kutik would say—that killing this old man and his family would accomplish nothing. Elline soldiers would swarm through the city in vengeance, slaughtering plotters and innocents alike. Arwia and Dipti and everyone who'd known him would die by the sword, or worse. And in this king's place would rise some new usurper, even more illiterate and uncultured. The king would suffer only for a few moments, and Babili would suffer for centuries to come.

The king's gaze—sharp as a blade, despite the old man's years—pulled Zaidu back to the moment.

"I have no great plan, Majesty," he said. "Only an idea."

A smile crossed the king's wrinkled face. "Then I would hear this idea of yours, young Zaidu."

"It's quite simple, really," he said. "Master Tattannu has amply demonstrated that the speeds of the Gods change at consistent rates as they traverse the heavens. I proposed that the same might be true of objects here on Earth."

"Perhaps you might—" Master Tattannu met Zaidu's eyes. He nodded toward the boat's hold, where the clay vessel was hidden. "—retrieve that bit of parchment with my calculations, to better demonstrate the principle."

The king waved a hand dismissively. "You know, I never learned to read. Never seemed to find the time. I have the greatest respect for anyone who masters that art."

"All the same, Majesty," said Master Tattannu, "my illustrations might prove helpful."

"Ah yes. Illustrations." The king nodded. "Yes, why not? Anything to liven up this dreary party."

Zaidu's walk to the door of the hold seemed to last for ages. With every step, possible plans multiplied in his mind: hurl the vessel overboard. Bring it before the king and report the plot. Pretend to drop it, then flee in the ensuing panic. Every one of the schemes seemed fraught with danger, filled with holes. Zaidu wished he could undo all this: step back to the night when he'd kissed Arwia, and take a different turn on the walk home—one that steered a wide berth around Kutik's alley.

Somehow, he kept moving—opened the door to the hold, ducked down into the darkness, and retrieved the vessel. It felt heavy in his hands, its surface cool to the touch.

As he lifted it out into daylight, he bumped into someone tall and perfumed.

"I say! What's that you've got there?" a voice cried in Elline.

"Gods save us!" a general howled. "He's got a fire-vessel!"

Suddenly all was panic. Shrieking men and women pushed for the sideboards, leaped overboard into the river, or clambered away from him.

Down near the stern, the king was pushing himself up from his golden throne, crying, "What is this madness?" as Master Tattannu gestured desperately, trying to get him to return to his seat.

Without really knowing why, Zaidu did the least dangerous thing he could think of: he set the vessel down carefully on the deck, and rolled it away toward the boat's bow. It rolled back and forth in a snakelike pattern as the boat rocked wildly from side to side, abandoned by its rudderman.

"What in the Gods' names are you doing?" Master Tattannu screamed at him, spittle flying from his beard. "Finish it!"

At that moment, Zaidu locked eyes with the king, and all was known.

The king's eyes widened with rage. "Seize them!" he shrieked to his guards, who pushed through the thrashing crowd, grabbing hold of Master Tattannu and forcing their way to Zaidu.

The vessel rolled to the left, then to the right—then the boat bucked, and the vessel reversed course and rolled straight toward Master Tattannu, who caught it with his foot—lifted it to his chest—produced tinder from a fold of his cloak—struck a spark and lit the fuse—and hurled the vessel to the sky.

Zaidu wouldn't have believed the master had so much strength in his body. He watched, as if in a dream, as the lit vessel rose upward toward the heavens, its speed slowing at at an ever-increasing rate. At last it reached its peak, stopped, and plunged back toward Earth, its speed growing ever more quickly.

He had the briefest moment to think: *I was right!*

The vessel exploded against the boat's railing, spilling half its viscid flame into the river, spraying half across the side of the boat. A blaze leaped up from the wood, roaring like thunder, lashing Zaidu's face with tongues of heat.

Everyone was screaming now, leaping overboard, splashing into the river, swimming back toward the banks or foundering wildly amid the waves, howling for help.

Zaidu leaped, too. He hit the water with a splash, felt its coolness envelop him; then burst from the surface amid the smoke and timber, swimming frantically from the collapsing wreckage of the boat, which sank slowly amid roiling smoke and coruscating flame.

He had nowhere to go. No one to return to. No hope of safety. But he swam for the shore anyway, because there was nothing else to be done.

⟨

"For the attempted murder of the king," the priest recited, "by a man of the laboring class, the ancient Law Code of King Ammurapi of Babili prescribes no specific punishment."

Zaidu gazed up at the man who recited the charges against him: young, scarcely older than he was, swathed in a long robe of deep blue trimmed in gold tassel, with an undergarment of white linen, and a breastplate of polished bronze set with neat rows of emeralds and carnelian and agate. The young priest's beard was long and stringy, like that of a goat, and he wore it awkwardly. He tried to speak in a booming voice, but it cracked on the high notes.

"But it is decreed," the priest droned on, "in the ancient Shuméru law code of Én Ur-Nammu of Urim, and in the still more venerable code of Énsi Iri'inimgina of Lagash, that the penalty for this crime shall be death."

Zaidu barely heard the words. In the hours since he'd escaped the boat, he'd felt he scarcely existed in the world. He'd hurried to Arwia's tavern, but she was nowhere to be found. He'd paced the streets like a madman, knowing nowhere he could hide; nowhere they wouldn't expect him and root him out in minutes.

In the end, he strode out onto the Processional Way, amid the potholes and piles of trash, and the weeds sprouting up through cracks in the ancient tiled flagstone. He stepped across the drainage channel clogged with reeking fly-swarmed sewage. Along the moss-grown walls on his left and right marched great bulls and roaring lions and long-necked dragons in relief, once painted proud gold and emerald green against a background that had gleamed bright blue; the glaze now cracked and faded in the sun. He stood among the ruins and waited for them to come.

The Elline soldiers arrived in minutes—alerted, no doubt, by the women who watched from high apartment balconies for anything suspicious—tied his hands behind his back, and marched him straight to a tiny brick shack near the soldiers' barracks, where he spent a long, sleepless night.

Now he stood before the king and a small crowd of nobles in robes of purple and emerald and crimson, who looked down on him from cracked stone benches. The morning sun was in his eyes, but he could see that the king looked most regal of all, in a loose silk gown as blue as the sky, embroidered with intricate golden vines and flowers. Atop his head sat the tiered crown of Babili, its rim adorned with every kind of precious stone. It looked heavy and hot.

"The choice of the manner of death, however," the priest continued, "is left to the intended victim—in this case, the king Seleukos Nikator."

A long silence hung over the square.

"What manner of death," the priest asked at last, "do you decree for this criminal, Supreme Majesty?"

The old king shook his head sadly.

"Was it really necessary to kill an old man?" he asked Zaidu, his voice resonating with surprising strength across the morning air. "What can I do to Babili that has not already been done to her, in this century and in twenty others?"

Zaidu licked his lips. "No," he called up to the king. "It was not necessary. And there is nothing you can do to me, or to Babili, that has not been done already."

The king nodded, as if in approval.

"If I had your master here before me now," said the king, "the man who lit the vessel and would have burned me and my family alive, had my men not carried me to safety—I would have him crucified and burned."

The priest opened his mouth to declare the punishment, but the king raised a hand to cut him off.

"But I am not convinced that was your aim, boy," he said. "You did not light the vessel. Why not?"

Zaidu tried to swallow, but only clenched his dry throat. "I saw there was no point," he said. "In killing you."

"No point." The king nodded again. "In that case, why did you not warn me?"

"Because there was no point," Zaidu said, "in trying to stop it."

The king's face hardened. "And it is for that, young scribe," he said, "you will die." He turned to the priest. "Make it quick," he said. "A blade to the throat."

The priest nodded. "Beheading!" he cried.

"Not beheading, damn you!" cried the king. "This isn't a bloody spectacle. Slit his throat and be done with it."

The priest backed away, glaring at Zaidu as he departed. "As the king commands," he said.

Two soldiers forced Zaidu to his knees on the hard stone. He did not resist.

He lifted his head. There, at the upper edge of the stands, stood Arwia. She was too far away to see clearly, but he could tell she was crying. What was there to say, now? In all the thousands of years of poetry he'd learned, he knew no words that would make sense of this.

He settled for five simple ones: "Be done with it, then."

A hand gripped his hair and jerked his head back. Something cool and sharp pressed against the skin of his neck. Sharp, cold pain lanced beneath his chin. Warm wetness spread downward onto his chest.

As the darkness crept in from the edges of his vision, it was not Arwia he thought of, nor the king, or even Babili. He thought instead of the movements of stars and Gods, and of earthly kingdoms. And he thought: *The faster one rises, the faster one falls. Every act produces its own opposite.*

Then the darkness swept inward, and all was at an end.

109 YEARS EARLIER
395 BC

They came to a great city,
Inhabited by the Mída in ancient times,
Now deserted and lying in ruins.

— The Expedition to the Interior

Y

The afternoon sunlight blinded Leander. In the shadow of the little mud-brick shack stood an old man, shouting and pointing at the far-off hills and the dense woods in the distance, chattering in some thick rural dialect of Aramaya as if he expected Leander to understand.

"Elline?" he tried hopelessly. "Do you speak a word of any Elline dialect, by chance?"

The man kept chattering and gesturing.

"No, of course you don't," Leander muttered. His own army spoke half a dozen different regional Elline dialects. It was a miracle they could coordinate their tactics at all.

He was feeling the weight of his helmet and breastplate today, and the shield on his back. Armor always started to feel heavy like this in the afternoons, when the hot sun beat down on the rocky hills. Especially when they'd been marching all day, which, as usual, they had been.

"Sir," he said in careful Aramaya, "I need you to listen to me."

That set off a fresh explosion of pointing and chattering.

"Can we get the translator over here?" Leander called back to his band of fighters, ten tired mercenaries in mismatched bronze helmets and breastplates. They were canvassing the mostly deserted mud-brick village in pairs, finding no people; just chickens and goats. Bareil, their local translator, was nowhere to be seen.

"Where in hell is Bareil?" Leander shouted. "I've got an old man here who may know where the enemy garrison is. Bareil!"

The translator came running from behind one of the shacks, clutching a bronze helmet under his arm.

"Never take that helmet off, Bareil," said Leander. "The enemy love to surprise us."

"Yes sir," said Bareil in thickly accented Elline, sliding the helmet onto his head. "Sorry, sir."

"I think this old-timer knows where the enemy garrison is," Leander told him.

Bareil nodded, and started up a storm of Aramaya chatter with the old man, who gestured and pointed and recited a whole oration in response to every question Bareil asked.

At the end of this long, dramatic production, Bareil nodded and turned to Leander, saying, "He saw a few horsemen near the woods, day before yesterday. Scouts, he thinks."

"Why does he think that?" Leander asked.

"They were only a few. Seemed to be in a hurry. Then they retreated back around the woods there." Bareil pointed at the distant tree-line, up in the foothills of the mountains.

The old man nodded and chattered in agreement and pointed enthusiastically.

"All right," said Leander. "Now ask him where everyone in this village went."

Bareil asked the old man, who gave another oration and wept and tore his hair. Leander caught the word *keshet*, which meant "archer" in Aramaya.

"*Iy, keshet*," he said, stretching the limits of his Aramaya. "*Keshet okad?*" Where are the archers?

Bareil held up a hand for him to wait a moment. "He says the *satrap*—" Bareil started, then had to pause for a moment longer while the old man added more details. "—the local *satrap* sent some soldiers here about three years ago. Ordered all the men in the village to join King Kurosh's army, as archers. Most of them refused—" Here the old man cried out and tore at his hair some more. "—and when the men refused to join, the soldiers chased them down and carried them off as slaves. Took all the young women, too, and the children, and most of the cattle. They only left a few elders behind. He's the only one left alive."

Leander wasn't sure if he believed that or not. But as all the Gods knew, his men had seen worse things in this part of the world.

"What's his name?" he asked Bareil.

Bariel muttered a quick question to the man, who said "Mardeen."

"All right, Mardeen," Leander said. "Now I need you to show me exactly where those archers went. *Keshet okad*, Mardeen?"

They walked up to the hills near the woods, and the enemy garrison turned out to be long-gone from there—two days gone, at least, to judge by the remains of their camps and cook-fires. By the time the fighters had humped all the way over there, the sun had sunk until it touched the tips of the distant mountains.

"We're not going to make it back before dark," said Bareil quietly, so the others wouldn't overhear.

"You don't have to whisper," said Leander. "They know. Gods know we've walked enough of these patrols."

"I hope we get some sleep tonight, at least."

"Well," said Leander, "at least we know there aren't any surprises lurking for us tonight."

ϒϒ

IT WAS WELL past dark by the time they made their way back to the main Arkadian camp, which was set up on a plateau that had good visibility on the surrounding hills—in the daylight, anyway. Pulling their helmets from their sweat-soaked heads, the men shuffled through long rows of tents and cook-fires, calling out greetings to friends here and there, looking for the red-and-green flags that marked their band's section of camp.

They joined the men already seated around the fire, and tore chunks of roasted mutton from the spit, and accepted skins of wine, which they gulped down greedily. Once they were settled in, cracking jokes and commiserating, Leander walked a few rows of tents down, and found the commanders' private camp. He saluted the two guards outside the tent, who nodded and let him duck inside.

"So, where were the archers?" asked one of the commanders, a middle-aged man called Kratippus, who sat with a few other officers, tearing up a plate of bread and mutton.

"Not in the woods," said Leander. "We canvassed all the villages around here. A few of them saw scouts, but that was days ago. No one knows where they've gone."

"That's bad news," said another commander, a tough-skinned man called Eusebios.

"I have to tell you," said Leander, "my men are getting pretty tired of walking these patrols."

"You'd better not be thinking of leaving," said Eusebios.

"Believe me, we've thought about it. But not tonight."

Kratippus sighed. "The ones we don't lose to arrows, we lose to disease," he said, "and the rest just walk away. Aren't we paying you enough? Is that it?"

"The pay's fine," said Leander. "But we came here to fight, not to argue with old men in villages."

"Then find me some Gods-damned enemies," Kratippus snarled.

"What are we supposed to do?" Leander asked. "Keep knocking on doors like a mob of politicians, until finally some farmer tells us, 'Oh, those archers? They're behind that tree over there'—is that what this campaign is turning into? Because I'll tell you right now, my men are not—"

"Do you want to stand here yelling all night?" Kratippus cut him off. "Or do you want to go get drunk with your men? Because that's what I strongly recommend you do right now."

"What I want," said Leander, "is to finish this war and go back to a civilized country, and kiss my wife. That's what I want to do."

"That's what we all want," said Eusebios.

"You've got me and my men through the end of the week," said Leander. "After that, I can't promise you anything. I'll do my best to hold them together for a few more days."

"You know," said Kratippus, "sometimes I wish I was a despot like this Parsa king Kurosh who hired us. If you threatened to leave, I'd just have your eyes put out."

"Lord Kratippus, King of Kings," said Leander. He bent down, dug a clump of dirt from the earthen floor, and tossed it at the commander, who dodged, but caught it on the shoulder. Eusebios started laughing.

"There's your offering of earth, Great King," said Leander, then fiddled under his tunic and spread his feet apart. "And, just a moment, your offering of water will arrive any instant now—"

"Get out of here, you mercenary piece of shit," said Kratippus, and now Eusebios and the other commanders were laughing, too.

"Same to you, Supreme Majesty," said Leander, bowing dramatically, flipping the fig sign with both hands. "And a very good night to you all."

He ducked out of the tent, their laughter roaring behind him, and found his way back to his men's tents.

Dinner had turned into a drunken singalong, with accompaniment by Eteokles on the lyre and Leotykhides on the panpipes. The wine and song had attracted a company of Kórinthi whores—camp followers, who sat on the men's laps, their hair braided elaborately and done up with gold pins, their long dresses dyed pastel purple and green, all of them clapping happily in time as the men belted out the bouncy chorus of "The Temple Virgin's Robes."

Leander tore a leg from the pig roasting from the spit and took a seat on the log next to Ikarion. The youth's full lips parted into a slight smile as he passed Leander the wineskin he'd been sipping from. He pushed his long blond hair back from his face, revealing deep green eyes.

"How was the village?" Ikarion asked.

"Pointless, as usual." Leander grunted, lowering himself onto the log next to him.

Ikarion ran a hand along Leander's shoulder. "Kill any Parsa?"

"No. I just told you, it was a pointless day," Leander snapped.

Ikarion drew back, a wounded look crossing his face. Such an innocent face, Leander thought. So smooth, soft with just the barest hint of a beard, without a single crease of worry or exhaustion.

Ikarion gazed into the fire. "I only meant—"

"Don't apologize," Leander muttered.

The youth looked up, green eyes meeting his. Leander took another swig from the wineskin, sloshing the tart liquid around in his mouth.

"You're the only person around here who listens to me," he said at last, wiping wine from his beard. "I mean, really listens. That means you see—" He gestured vaguely at the fire. "Well, this. This side of me. I'm not proud of it."

"We're all tired," Ikarion said softly, reaching up to stroke Leander's chest. "We all want to go home."

Leander put his face in his hands, rubbing at his temples, eyes, cheeks. "Ikarion, I—"

The youth gazed up at him, green eyes wide, his brow creased with delicate furrows.

"I want you to promise me something," he said.

Ikarion shook his head. "No," he said. "I know what you're going to say. I don't want to hear it."

Leander reached up and placed his calloused hand against Ikarion's cheek. "If one day I don't come back—"

"No," Ikarion said again, tears rising in his eyes. "Don't say that."

"If I don't come back," Leander persisted, "promise me you'll stay in camp. That you won't volunteer for scouting, or—if it comes to it—a battle."

"You *will* come back." The youth's lip trembled. "You always come back."

"Just promise me," Leander said, squeezing Ikarion's forehead tight against his. He smelled the salt on the youth's skin; the wine on his breath.

"I won't promise that," Ikarion whispered, shaking. "Because it'll never happen."

Leander sighed. The youth's hope twisted an invisible knife in his gut, more painful than despair.

"We're going to make it home," Ikarion said through his tears.

"You must barely remember home," Leander said. "You had—what—ten summers to your name when we shipped out?"

"Eleven," Ikarion reminded him. "I'm seventeen now. I was old enough to volunteer as a kitchen-boy, and plenty old enough to remember the green hills of Arkadia."

"The forests and the fields," Leander muttered.

"Yes," said Ikarion, planting kisses on Leander's forehead. "And the mountain streams and lakes. And we're going to make it back there together, my love."

"I'm not sure how well that'll please my wife." Leander huffed a dry laugh.

"Your wife will understand." Ikarion kissed Leander's rough cheeks and cracked lips. "You're not the first soldier to love a beautiful boy." He smiled, clearly fishing for a compliment. "Is it not so?"

"Beauty is beauty, or so the sages say." Leander took the boy's head in his hands, gazing deep into those green eyes. How lovely they were! Like precious stones.

A smile crossed Ikarion's soft lips. "And I'll grow my beard, and learn a trade, and take a wife of my own in time, but we'll stay the best of friends. And someday, when we're wrinkled and gray, we'll sit on the porch and tell tales of our adventures in the East."

"Is that what this is?" Leander asked drily. "An adventure?"

"This war?" The youth shook his head, smiling. "No, of course not. But you and I, we're on an adventure all our own."

Leander kissed Ikarion, full and hard, felt him sigh, felt his body soften and lean into his. Around the fire, soldiers whooped and whistled. They were singing "Satyr in the Garden" now, throwing in some creatively explicit verses contributed by the Kórinthi whores in their laps:

The boy looked back and asked the faun,
"Say you love me, sir, I beg!"
Said the faun, "I do,"
And he loved him true,
For the boy now walks bow-legg'd!
Ho! There's a satyr in the garden...

"They're singing about us, you know," Leander said, swallowing another mouthful of wine.

Ikarion sent an exploring hand up Leander's leg. "Well then," he said softly. "Let's give them something to sing about."

Leander grabbed the youth, picked him up and swung him around, drawing more cheers and whoops from the men and women around the fire. Then he wrapped an arm around Ikarion's shoulder, and together they made a straight line for their tent. Ikarion had Leander's toga unbelted before they could even crawl inside. He remembered to close the tent flap, just in time.

ʎʎ

AFTERWARD, WHEN THE moon sat high in the starry sky, Leander and Ikarion slipped back into their tunics, washed the sweat from their bodies, and rejoined their companions around the fire. Leander's whole body hummed serenely, like after a hot bath. For the first time in days, he felt something approaching contentment.

The soldiers had grown drunk enough to wobble when they stood and to slur their words, and they moved on to calmer songs. They tried to sing "Make My Bed in Kórinth," which should've been another raunchy one. But they sang it slowly, sadly, dreaming of faraway Elláda and the comforts of home.

Silence fell around the dying fire. After a long moment, a swordsman called Dexios sang out the first few notes of "On Lake Koroneia" in a surprisingly sweet voice, and everyone joined in. After that came the sadder songs: "The Fields of Marathon" and "How Far From the Sea." By then, some of the men were close to tears, thinking of the homes and families they'd likely never see again. The women from Kórinth comforted them and offered them more wine, leading them back to the tents to do what women of Kórinth were famous for.

Leander and Ikarion remained by the fire, passing the wineskin back and forth, staring into the flickering flames, along with a few men stretched out near the fire. After a while, Dexios, the sweet-voiced soldier, lurched up from his seat, sauntered across the circle, and plopped down on the log next to the two companions, belching loudly.

"Six years, Leander." Dexios rubbed at his temples. "Can you believe that?"

Leander glanced at Ikarion, who only smiled and shrugged. With a sigh, he turned to the drunk soldier next to him.

"Seventy-five months in the world's arsehole," he said. "I've been counting every one."

"Far from home as a man can march," Dexios replied.

"Not quite," said Leander. "Some of them marched even farther."

Dexios huffed. "Xenias and his bunch, you mean."

Ikarion spit into the fire. "Deserter pieces of shit," the youth snarled. "As if we don't have it hard enough without them switching sides."

Leander shrugged. "We're on the side that pays the most for the least work."

"We were," Dexios slurred. "Now our employer's dead and we're stuck at the arse end of the world, to pick our own way north to the sea, then west and home, if any of us ever make it that far."

Leander raised his eyebrows. "You thinking of staying around? Selling your sword-arm to some other despot?"

Dexios shrugged. "Why not? It's just one tyrant against another. What difference does it make whose crest is on the banners?"

"Ellines killing Ellines for Parsa gold." Leander sighed.

"Spare me the morality," Dexios spat. "If these Eastern despots want to grind each other to dust, I might as well make some gold off their family squabbles."

Ikarion looked up at that, catching Leander's eye; but the older man looked away. And so the three of them stared into the fire: two old soldiers and one youth, too soft and sweet to belong here.

The last of the flames began to flicker out. Ikarion laid a few more branches on the dying embers, and fresh flames

The Cradle and the Sword

leaped up. He took a sip from the wineskin and passed it to Leander, who took a long, deep drink from it, his throat working as he gulped it down, then burped softly and wiped his mouth.

"You sure that's what you want?" Leander asked Dexios. "Fight for some despot? Die under the hot sun?"

The drunk soldier made no answer, watching the flames for a long time. At last he muttered, "Better than dying old and toothless, shitting my bed."

Leander looked down at the wineskin and remembered he hadn't drunk from it in a while, and passed it to Ikarion, who took another sip.

After a while, Leander said, "I had a wife, you know. Back in Arkadia."

Ikarion stared down at his hands, his body tensing slightly.

Dexios took a sip from the wineskin. "I didn't know that," he said.

"Aella," said Leander. "That's her name. 'Whirlwind.' It suits her. That wild black hair. Some nights I still dream of taking hold of that hair and—"

He stopped there, glancing over at Ikarion; but the youth only smiled tightly, and reached up to stroke Leander's arm.

"It's all right to have dreams," Ikarion said softly.

"Mine was called Korinna," Dexios put in. "She wouldn't promise me anything." He laughed dryly. "Said no woman in her right mind would marry a mercenary. That's probably true, actually." He shook his head. "I do miss those hips, though. Hips like Aphrodíti."

Leander started to say something, stopped, started again and couldn't get himself to say it. Then, quietly, so softly the men could barely hear him, he said, "Aella had a baby inside her when I left."

Ikarion looked at him, eyes wide, but said nothing.

"That means I've got a child old enough to be a schoolboy," Leander went on. "And I've never even seen him. Don't even know his name."

"Or *her* name," Ikarion said, passing the wineskin and putting his hand on Leander's shoulder.

Leander laughed without smiling. "Or her name."

"This war fell apart months ago," Dexios grunted. "We all know it. We're not even trying to liberate cities anymore. Just trying to get out. Get back to the sea. And we can't even do that."

"It's a bloody mess," Leander agreed. "You're right."

Dexios huffed again. "Most of the senior officers have deserted, or are dead now, or—only the Gods know what."

Leander rubbed his brow. "That Parsa king who hired us wasn't so bad, I suppose. Paid on time, anyway. These Ashûru, on the other hand… they're paid in the same Parsa gold we are, but sometimes I wonder who they're really fighting for. The things we've seen them do… impale men on stakes and parade them in public. Chain mothers up and behead their children while they watch, one after another. What compels a man…?" He watched the dancing flames for a long time, as if scrying some message only he could see.

"I hear the Ashûru used to be even worse in the old days," Dexios said. "Before the Parsa swept in and got 'em under control. This whole land was a dog-pit back then, you believe half the stories you hear. They say one of those old Ashûru kings flayed the skin off every last man, woman and child in a city he conquered. Every one of them. Did you know that? Nailed all the skins to a pillar and put it on display in his palace. Proud of the thing."

Ikarion stared into the fire, a sour look on his soft-downed face. "That's just a tall tale," he said at last; but his tone was unsure. "Isn't it?"

"Who knows?" Leander shrugged. "Even the roughest Parsa shock-troops steer a wide berth around the Ashûru tents. We've all seen it. They call them jackals. Evil spirits."

Dexios shook his head slowly and took another long drink from the wineskin. "I've never seen an evil spirit," he said after a time. "Seen my share of evil men, though."

"Sometimes," Leander sighed, after a moment, "I think we've already died and fallen into in the Underworld. Nothing but flames and foul spirits and torture, far as the eye can see."

Dexios spat into the fire. "No, this is worse. What do you do in the Underworld? Push a rock uphill for eternity. Starve next to a tree whose fruit you can't reach. Not so bad. No worse than a hard day's march, you ask me." He took another long drink of the wine, and passed the skin to Ikarion. "This, though. This is just—mud. The whole place is a swamp. Quicksand. The harder we fight, the deeper we sink."

They watched the fire for a while more, thinking their own thoughts.

"I talked to an old farmer the other day," said Leander after a while. "Bareil translated for me. Old man told me there used to be big sweetwater lake south of here, a long time ago. They called the lake *Abzu*. The Abyss. Mankind crawled up out of those waters, he told me. And there was a salt sea, too, called Tiamat. The dragon. Chaos. And he told me the war between the two of them is called… civilization."

He glanced up at Dexios, who only grunted and swallowed another sip of wine.

"Anyway, you're right, nowadays it's just a swamp," Leander said. "A mire that sucks down armies and never lets 'em go."

Dexios still stared into the fire, as if he hoped to discern some sign inscribed on its coals. "There's no end to it, is there?" he asked, quietly, as if for his own ears. "No end. Maybe no beginning, either."

"Then he asked me where we were from, this farmer," Leander went on. "What kind of country. I told him we're from a place called Arkadia, and we have no kings there. And you know what did? He laughed at me." Ikarion took a drink from the wineskin. "'No kings?' he said. 'That's impossible.' That's what he said to me. 'That's impossible.'"

"It's all they know here," said Dexios. "Warlords and despots and fanatics lopping each other's heads off. A guaranteed living for pieces of shit like us."

"And here's the strange thing about it," Leander said. "You talk to them, and you see they're just regular people. Intelligent folk. They have homes and families, and houses and farms. And you'd think they'd have dreams, like we do. Hopes for the future. But they don't. I can't understand it."

"Well, like you said," said Ikarion, "they're smart. They've seen what happens to anyone around here who makes a fortune, or tries to build something." He shrugged. "Someone comes and takes it from you, or just burns it down. They see it every day."

Leander looked up to meet his eyes. Sometimes, those green pools seemed to glisten with a strange wisdom beyond their years.

"And I have to say," said Dexios, "after six years of this..." He sighed. "After everything I've seen over here..." He sighed again and shook his head. "Gods help me, I'm starting to think that way too."

"That's the saddest thing I ever heard," said Ikarion.

"Before these Parsa kings, it was the Mída horse-tribes," Dexios went on. "Some other damned tribe before them. And a thousand years from now, new conquerors will come riding out of the desert with another new God, and—oh, of course they'll be riding in the name of peace this time. Of course. An end to all this barbarism. And then fifty years later, it'll be right back to this again."

"I was wrong," said Ikarion. "*That's* the saddest thing I ever heard. And I don't think it's true. People learn. They change."

"Sure, for a while," said Leander. "Then they change back."

Ikarion looked up into Leander's eyes, his face a mask of sadness. Leander had never seen such despair in the youth's eyes before, and suddenly he felt a wave of guilt wash over him, as though he'd inflicted some irreparable harm, darkening Ikarion's innocent mind by telling these stories. But Ikarion was no naive farmboy. He'd marched through these lands with the rest of them, bathed in the same blood and sweat they all had. Anyway, he could find no words to say to the boy, so he sat in silence.

The three of them finished off the last of the wine together, until Leander turned the wineskin upside down and only a few drops fell to the ground. Then Dexios bid them goodnight and stumbled back to his tent to catch a few hours' sleep.

At last only Leander and Ikarion remained, sitting by themselves under the stars, watching the fire slowly flicker out, and saying nothing.

Leander woke to shouting, and to the feel of dirt and gravel on his face. Apparently he'd lain down and fallen asleep next to the fire. But now the sky was turning from dark blue to pale pink, and all around, men were running and shouting "Throw me my helmet!" and "Spear! Where's my fucking spear?" and in the air were humming and zipping sounds, and thuds and angry screams, and an arrow fell from nowhere and buried itself in the tent. Then two more—*zip-thud*, *zip-thud*—in the dirt near his head.

He was up and running for the tent, finding it empty, heaving his breastplate up and tying it on quick as he could, strapping on his sword and grabbing his helmet and shield, racing across the camp through the tents in the direction the arrows were coming from.

So many of those arrows, dozens of them every moment, raining like hail into the tents and the fire-pits and the legs and shoulders of men who fell to the ground screaming, and others who limped along with two or three of the wood shafts sticking out from them, howling about "Gods shit on the Parsa" and "I'll skin your children" and other things that made no sense that came out of angry men in agony, and nearby on the ground lay three of the Kórinthi women in their pretty pastel dresses, two dead and bleeding out with arrows through their eyes and chests; the third one huddled on the ground next to them, covering herself with some dead man's shield, her hair undone and gold pins fallen everywhere as the arrows clattered onto the shield and she wept and screamed at everything around her.

Leander crept forward in a crouch with his shield held over him, feeling it thump against his back each time an arrow hit it, two hits, then three, then more, and he must've been carrying at least twenty arrows by the time he found Kratippus and a few of the other commanders. A few of his men were here, too, though Ikarion wasn't. Together, they huddled under an overturned arrow-bristled supply wagon.

"This was a stupid place to make camp," Leander said as he climbed under the wagon.

"This was orders," said Kratippus. "Direct from the generals. This place was supposed to have visibility over all the surrounding hills."

"What happened? Did the sentry fall asleep?" Leander asked.

"Sentry was one of the first to die," said Eusebios. "They came up just before dawn, we don't know where from. Just lay up in the hills and started raining arrows on us, the *dog-fucking cowards*!" He howled in the direction the arrows were coming from.

"Must be at least a few hundred of them, judging by the arrows," said Leander.

"Trying to cut us off from the rest," said Kratippus. "Divide and kill."

"Why are they still trying to kill us?" Eusebios demanded. "Our employer surrendered. Then they killed him. What more do they want with us?"

"Loose ends," Kratippus muttered.

"We just need to wait awhile," said Leander. "They can't keep this up for long. I'd say it's more than half over already. When they stop, we gather up whoever's left and run straight for their line. They won't stand a chance."

The Cradle and the Sword

"Unless they've got some other surprise for us," said Eusebios.

"They might," said Leander. "And we'll deal with it when we get there. We don't have a choice."

Kratippus and Eusebios looked at each other. "You're right," said Eusebios. "We don't."

Leander started counting his breaths. In-*one*-then-out. In-*two*-then-out. By the time he'd counted up to one hundred twenty-three, the hail of arrows was thinning. By one hundred thirty, it had stopped completely. The screams and curses were still coming, though, from all over camp.

"Let's go," said Kratippus, and they pushed up and out from under the wagon and ran at a dead sprint across camp toward the source of the attack, shields slung across their backs, praying no more arrows were coming.

"To us!" they shouted; but few answered the call. Dexios crawled out from under a wagon, and one of the Kórinthi whores climbed out of a pit where she'd huddled under a shield, which was studded thickly with arrows. They charged for the edge of camp, these ghosts pierced with wood shafts in arms and shoulders, seeping dark brownish blood from a hundred tiny gashes where arrows had sliced their faces and hands.

They made their way between arrow-studded wreckages of tents, long rows of them, where men and camp-women lay pinned to the ground in lakes of blood, forests of feathered shafts sprouting where they lay. Some were still alive and groaning, others fading in and out of awareness, waking in fits to howl and shout curses. When they ran close by one of those in agony, one of the men would dash over and thrust a sword into the sufferer's chest or neck, stopping the screams; and they'd all mutter a prayer for the dead man, promising before running onward to come back later and laid coins on his eyes; passage for the ferry to the Underworld.

By the time they'd reached the edge of the plateau, they'd gathered a group of five: Leander, thick-shouldered Eusebios, sweet-voiced Dexios, the commander Kratippus, and Ourania, one of the Kórinthi whores. The only survivors of the hundred or so who'd sung and slept and fucked here last night.

And still no sign of Ikarion, Leander couldn't help noticing.

At last they caught sight of the Parsa archers—about two hundred of them, Leander guessed, in brightly colored trousers and vests, protected by a front line of Elline mercenaries with tall iron shields and long spears. The enemy Ellines were already closing ranks around their retreating archers, protecting their flight back into the woods. Too far away to catch up to now, especially for a band of wounded soldiers in heavy armor.

"Gods-damned cowards," Dexios screamed at them. "Cowards!"

"They're probably out of hearing range," said Leander, catching his breath.

"I piss on your mothers!" Dexios shouted anyway. "All of you!"

The last of the archers vanished into the trees.

Kratippus shook his head slowly. "Why can't they just fight like men?"

"They used to, sometimes," Leander said. "Remember Kunaxa? All of them along the left bank, thick as wheat in a field. All those spears."

"That was six years ago," said Ourania.

"Six years ago," said Kratippus, "we had an army worth fighting. Now they just pick us off out here in the wilderness, like ducks by a lake."

"This is no way for men to fight," said Eusebios.

Leander shook his head. "No way for anyone to fight."

Once they felt fairly sure the archers and spearmen weren't coming back, they trudged back to camp. They spent the rest of the day gathering up what they could carry from the tents and supply wagons, and looking for survivors. But these were few. Two men begged to be put out of their suffering and have coins placed on their eyes and prayers said for them, and Eusebios fulfilled those requests.

Leander didn't see anyone crying. They were probably too tired, he thought. He did hear Dexios singing "How Far From the Sea," though, and that made his eyes fill with tears, but he blinked them back.

He found Ikarion not too far from their band's part of camp. The youth had taken an arrow to the back of the head and had probably died instantly. So there was that, at least. After he'd fallen he'd taken a few dozen more arrows, to all parts of his body.

Leander snapped off the shafts and rolled the body over, and gently closed the deep green eyes and placed coins on each of them, and said a prayer for Ikarion's soul in its passage across the river to the Underworld. Now the tears burned in his eyes until they rolled down his cheeks and mixed with the dirt and the blood, and this time, he didn't care. He wept so hard he shook, and the other five stood and watched him, saying nothing.

ALONG WITH THE five of them, six horses had survived. One had taken an arrow in its hip, and could not stand; only lay on its side, whinnying frantically. Eusebios inspected the wound, wiping away the drying blood with a wet cloth, careful not to prod too deeply lest the beast's hoof kick out and crack his ribs.

After a delicate inspection, he looked up and shook his head sadly. "She won't be getting up any time soon," he sighed.

"Kindest thing is to put her out of her misery," said Dexios.

"It's only an arrow in the hip," said Ourania. "We could—"

"We could what?" Kratippus cut her off. "Bind the wound? Bring back a physician from the main army?"

Her lip began to tremble, and Kratippus's expression softened. He extended a hand, as if to comfort her, but she pulled away.

"I'll do it," Leander said. "Quick and painless."

"You don't have to," Dexios said. "I can take care—"

"I'm not infirm," Leander snapped, and the other man drew back.

He knelt next to the horse and stroked her head and nose, tutting softly to keep her calm as he drew his dagger. Ourania turned away, covering her mouth.

"So we're just not going to talk about him, then," Dexios said, leaning in to speak softly in Leander's ear.

"What is there to talk about?" Leander replied. "He's in some garden with the Gods now."

"And you want to join him there," Dexios said.

Leander glared at him. "I want to get out of this shithole and back to Arkadia," he snapped. "Back to my wife and child."

"I know that look in your eye, Leander," Dexios said after a moment.

"I don't have a look," Leander said. "I'm just watching the horizon for enemies."

"Yes, you do," Dexios retorted. "You have a look on you. You'll charge the first enemy you see, hoping for a sharp spearpoint right to the heart."

Leander only glared at him, positioning his blade next to the horse's heart.

"See to the other horses," Kratippus ordered as Leander plunged his blade in. The horse bucked once, twice, then trembled as she fell still, blood pouring down Leander's arm. He rose and wiped the blade on the grass.

Eusebios was scanning the horizon. "They'll be sending mounted archers to pick us off," he muttered. "We need to be long gone by nightfall."

"There's a road, runs by the base of this hill," Leander told them. "Back toward that field where the rest of the army's camped. Saw it with my own eyes yesterday morning. Not much more than a dirt track, but..." He nodded toward a wagon near the horses. Its bed was laden with swords and shields and tent-stakes, but with a lighter load, it'd be much quicker than walking.

"Clear out that weight from the back," Kratippus said. "Let's be quick about it."

As the sun climbed high above the distant western mountains, the survivors loaded a few sacks of dried meat onto the now-empty bed of the wagon, along with a few skins of water and wine that had been lucky enough to escape the arrows. The men strapped axes, swords and shields across their backs. Kratippus and Dexios mounted two of the horses, wiry long-maned bays bred more for scouting than for charges or long marches.

Leander and Eusebios yoked the other four horses to the wagon, in teams of two. Eusebios, the most skilled archer among them, climbed into the back with a longbow, while Ourania settled in beside him. Leander climbed up into the wagon's seat, taking the reins.

They clattered down the hillside, bouncing over hillocks and holes, each lurch of the wagon's spoked wheels juddering their teeth, until Ourania and Eusebios called for Leander to stop, and climbed out of the wagon-bed to descend the hill on foot. At last, though, they reached the road; a dirt track winding around the base of the hill and off across the plain; its surface rough, but packed hard and baked by the sun.

Dexios and Kratippus reigned up their horses on either side of the wagon, as Eusebios and Ourania climbed back into its bed. All eyes converged on Leander, as if waiting for him to announce the start of the race; this mad dash to reach the main army before Parsa horse-archers caught up and picked them off.

Glancing over the wagon now, and ahead at the dirt track, Leander suddenly doubted they had any chance at all. Their pursuers knew where they were, and where they were headed.

Parsa horses were famously swift, and could easily outpace a wagon, even one as lightly loaded as this.

All the same, Leander gave a nod of assent, flicked the reigns hard, and yelled "Hyaa!"

The four horses erupted into a gallop. The wagon lurched forward. Kratippus and Dexios spurred their mounts, spreading out ahead of the bouncing, shuddering cart. Dust swirled, hooves pounded, and the caravan raced across the plain in a thundering cloud of dust.

※

Four horses sprinted north along a packed dirt trail through a sea of tall dead grass. The wagon bounced and shuddered behind them, swaying in a swirl of dust. To the left of the trail, a blinding white sun cast sharp shadows from the mountains in the west.

Leander lashed the reins, scanning the horizon for a rising plume of dust or smoke, but could scry no sign in that emptiness, whose only inhabitants were groves of tall palms baked brown in the heat.

Dexios and Kratippus swept on ahead, tracking back and forth across the trail, like twin heads of a serpent coursing across the plain; a riot of hooves and foam and hot breath racing toward the rim of the world.

Six Parsa horse-archers swept out from a ridge of rocky bluffs amid the foothills, off to the left. Kratippus called out a warning, pointing toward the columns of dust sweeping toward the wagon; and suddenly there they came: men on fast, lithe horses, tearing through the tall grass, notching arrows to the strings of great bows even as they spurred their beasts to the charge.

As the horsemen matched pace with the wagon, Leander caught a closer look at their brightly patterned tunics and trousers; almost comical counterpoints to the ferocity of their pursuit. From their reins and saddled bounced trains of small trophies: knuckle-bones and jaws; ears dried to black figs; fingers weathered to half-naked bone, rattling and spinning, pointing incoherently at ground and sky.

At their head rode a tall, broad-shouldered Parsa on a titan chestnut steed, heavier and more muscled than the others. Gold ringlets jingled in his beard, from his ears and nose, as his beast split the tall grass at a dead gallop, chains of bleached bones rattling and whirling on its reins. Emerald peacock feathers bounced atop his gleaming bronze helmet, and the bow he drew stretched the length of a grown man's arms.

The giant locked eyes with Leander; eyes like night, sharp as a hawk's. He raised a hand and flicked it left, then right. Instantly the horse-archers broke off to both sides of the trail, twisting in their saddles to loose arrows behind them. Even as the shafts flew, the men were drawing others from the quivers on their backs, pulling bowstrings, loosing fresh volleys.

Arrows arced overhead, hissing, thunking into the wood of the rattling cart-bed. Leander whipped the reins, shouting at the charging horses; his cries inarticulate and wordless as the whoops and ululations of the Parsa horsemen.

Behind him, Ourania raised a great wooden shield, stopping one arrow, then another, with splintering cracks. The riders swept left, then right, arrows in twos and threes lancing the air with low-pitched hisses, striking the wagon's sides.

Eusebios worked frantically at his own bow, loosing arrows at the horse-archers as the riders dodged and whirled; but every jolt of the wagon tossed him, shifting his aim. Bolt after bolt flew uselessly into the empty air, descending and disappearing into the dead brown grass.

"Stop wasting arrows!" Leander called back after another of Eusebios's bolts flew long of its mark.

"Slow down," Eusebios snarled. "Stop bouncing so much and I'll hit something!"

Kratippus and Dexios wheeled their horses for a charge, dashing headlong toward two of the galloping archers, spear raised for a throw. The bright-coated Parsa horsemen dodged left, then right, cutting back and forth across the trail before the hurtling wagon. One turned in his saddle and loosed an arrow—behind Dexios, another archer fired.

Leander roared, "Dexios, look out—!"

Dexios turned, just in time to catch an arrow in the neck, then another in the ribs. He leaned over in his saddle, gasping, eyes wide, blood seeping from the wounds. For a long moment he was suspended in midair, the horse running on as he tumbled slowly from its back. Suddenly he was gone, swallowed in a sea of tall brown grass, and all was in motion again. The wagon rattled past in a cloud of dust.

"We can't leave him!" Eusebios cried.

"Jump off, then, if you're that stupid," Leander howled back, lashing the horses faster.

Kratippus roared in fury, spurring his horse around the front of the wagon, charging at the other Parsa archers, who parted and fled, only to whirl about and charge from the rear, loosing another wave of arrows before them.

Eusebios turned and loosed arrows straight back at them. One of the Parsa cried out, clutched at his chest and slipped from his saddle and fell into the tall grass. Eusebios whooped.

"That's one down," Ourania called, catching another two arrows with the broad wooden shield.

The five remaining riders swept out around the front of the wagon, led by the giant archer atop his massive horse, charging alongside the cart. They loosed arrows, notched more, loosed a second wave as they sprinted back and forth across the trail. Arrows zipped past and thunked into the seat and the wheels, their shafts shattering under the rolling wagon. One of the horses took a shaft in the shoulder, bucking and whinnying in a spray of blood. It galloped on, mouth foaming, trying to keep pace with the others. But soon it began to stumble.

Ourania craned over the front of the wagon to inspect the wound. "He won't last long," she declared.

"We need a plan," Eusebios said.

"This is our plan," Leander said. "We're running."

"That's not a plan!" Ourania cried.

Up ahead, Kratippus was shouting at them, pointing at a rise of hills that loomed ahead, off to the left of the trail. The commander kicked his horse, galloping through the tall grass toward a cleft in the piles of great gray boulders.

"There's no road up there," Leander called after him, but the commander didn't seem to hear.

"We've got no choice," Eusebios hollered.

"We'll lose speed," Leander called back.

"They'll catch us anyway!" Ourania shouted, throwing herself against Leander, grabbing at the reins in his hand, yanking them toward the rocks.

The horses wheeled to the left, hard, stumbling as they dragged the wagon off the road, into the high grass and onto rocky soil that bounced the cart high and jerked them from side to side. Sunlight lanced into Leander's eyes and blinded him. They all held on, knuckles white, as horses and cart careened through a storm of sharp, dry grass blades that lashed their hands and faces, explosions of dry seedpods choking the air.

"There's a road here," Kratippus called back to them, galloping out of a wide cleft in the rocks, then wheeling about and vanishing again between the boulders.

Leander held on tight, flying as much as riding the wagon; but at last the ground began to level off, and soon they were rolling through a passage between the rocks at a trot. None of the wheels had broken, mercifully, but the wounded horse was limping badly. The path was flat and rocky; a narrow corridor between rocky cliffs.

"Those Parsa bastards won't come through here," Kratippus said, reining up his horse beside them. "It's too narrow. They'll look for a way to ride up over the bluffs. Try to rain arrows down on us."

As if to prove the commander's point, the Parsa riders reined up a good distance back, hurling taunts and curses at their escaped prey. After a few moments, the brightly clothed archers wheeled their mounts about, and galloped off in search of a better vantage.

But the giant sat his horse at the entrance to the ravine, dark eyes locked on Leander, arrow notched on his bowstring, waiting for a clear shot. At last he slung his bow on his back, leaned forward, gripping his horse's thick neck, and roared like a wild beast. He roared again, and once more, his cries echoing through the canyon, putting a flock of crows to flight; a storm of tiny black wings swirling in the red sunset above. And as the final echoes faded, the hunter yanked the reins, spun his horse about, and departed.

THEY WERE RIDING through the ravine, a narrow rift between rocky cliffs, beneath bluffs overhung with dry grass and dead flowers, when they saw silhouettes creeping like slender phantoms above them casting long shadows in the afternoon sun across the cool shade of the ravine's belly.

"Duck and cover!" Eusebios shouted from the bed of the wagon.

Leander ducked, raising his shield above his head, waiting for the hail of arrows. He glanced back east along the narrow ravine, a chasm of rock barely wide enough to admit the wagon; the only level passage through this range of rough-hewn cliffs.

A swarm of painted warriors strode along the bluffs above carrying axes, and wearing copperscale armor that jingled atop their tunics. Several crouched for a better look at the newcomers.

"Forward!" Kratippus cried, spurring his horse to gallop ahead.

Leander snapped the reins, but the horses stumbled over boulders and potholes, shaking the wagon so hard that Leander was nearly thrown from his seat.

"Stop!" Leander shouted up to Kratippus. The commander wheeled his horse around and glanced back at the wagon. "We'll shatter a wheel if we don't slow down," Leander told him.

More warriors gathered on the bluffs above; first a dozen, then twenty or more. On a closer look, they seemed a sorry lot, scarred and dirt-caked; the colorful patterns of their rough-spun tunics faded by sun and dusted with ashes and soot, worn away at the shoulders and elbows; leather trousers grass-stained and shiny at the knees; copperscale armor rusted green and gapped like rotting teeth. They carried bows; copper chisel-axes; bronze daggers and maces, most looking dull. But their eyes glinted.

Kratippus called up to them in Aramaya, then in Elline: "If you're with the Parsa, know that we will fight to the death!"

Leander drew his sword, as Eusebios notched an arrow to his bow.

Ourania dug two daggers from beneath the canvas, and clutched them tightly, wide-eyed and frantic. "We don't want to fight," she called up to the the warriors, as Kratippus tried to hush her. "We just want to leave this place!"

The fighters continued to clamber down into the ravine, tensing themselves for an attack.

"*Bagash!*" cried a woman's voice in Aramaya—then in Elline: "Wait! Stop!"

The painted warriors froze.

Kratippus raised a hand. "Hold!"

Leander scanned the cliffs and found the source of the voice: a young woman draped in the tattered remains of what had once been a regal cloak, woven in stripes of blue and amber and vermilion. Her reddish hair hung in a long braid slung forward over her shoulder, and her eyes were outlined sharply in black kohl. A chain of copper breastplates, joined with beaded chains, hung down her chest and belly, greenish in spots, intricately worked with beads of turquoise and carnelian.

The woman stared Kratippus dead in the eye. "Who are you?" she asked in thickly accented Elline.

"We're scouts," Kratippus replied. "Or rather, we're all that remains of a scouting party."

"What happened to the rest?" she demanded.

"Dead," Leander told her.

"Most of ours are dead, too," she replied.

"All we want is to get out of this wretched place," Ourania cried.

"That's what we want," the woman said. "Lay down your weapons and we'll both go in peace."

"And why should we believe you, Parsa bitch?" Eusebios growled.

"We are not Parsa!" the woman snapped.

"You were about to attack us without provocation," said Eusebios. "That makes you Parsa as far as I'm concerned."

"Enough!" Kratippus bellowed. He fixed the woman with a sharp gaze. "If you're not Parsa, then who are you?"

The woman raised her head. "We are Kalshu," she said proudly.

Her few surviving companions raised a rough cheer in agreement. Leander glanced at the men next to him, mouthing "Kalshu?" Eusebios and Ourania shrugged.

"I am Miriash," she said. "Princess of the tribe of Karduniash, last daughter of the noble line of King Ulamburiash the Great, Conqueror of Babili."

Her companions barked a rough cheer of affirmation. Eusebios whistled, mock-impressed.

Kratippus scowled at him. "I am Kratippus," he said to the woman atop the cliff, "a very tired old bastard from Arkadia. The last of my noble patience is running out. And in case you haven't heard, a Parsa king rules Babili now."

Miriash spat on the ground. "We have been press-ganged into this Parsa army—the army of King Artakshacha," Miriash replied. "But we have no love for Artakshacha, or for his brother Kurosh who fights against him."

"Well we can agree on that," Eusebios replied. "Artakshacha's men killed plenty on our side."

"We have no love for you Ellines, either," she continued. "Or for any Parsa king you may fight for."

"King Kurosh is dead," Kratippus told her. "Haven't you heard? The war's over. We've been paid. We're going home."

"Or trying to," Ourania muttered.

Miriash shrugged, as if it made no matter. "I would gladly kill all you foreigners, Parsa and Elline alike," she said, "if I had the men. But I have only what you see here. Our horses are all dead. We are tired, as you are. We want to go home, to the mountains. To Kalsh."

"Then come down here," Kratippus called up to her. "Let's strike a bargain."

Miriash glanced to the warriors by her side, who only stared back at her, unsure. After a moment, she clambered down the wall of the ravine, leaping from one boulder to the next with the balance of a leopard, her shadow dancing before her in the red light of the sunset.

"What in the Gods' names is Kalsh?" Ourania muttered to no one in particular as the princess descended.

Eusebios shrugged. "Six years in this hellhole and I've never heard that name."

"Few of us remain today, it is true," Miriash said, leaping from a boulder to land on the trail with a soft crunch, her chain of breastplates jingling. "But once we were the mightiest people between the Two Rivers. As I said, my ancestors sat the throne of Babili itself in days long-gone."

"And yet, strangely, I've never heard of you," Eusebios remarked drily.

Miriash smiled. Rusted and ragged though she was, she stood straight-backed and proud before the commander, looking just as much at ease in her many-colored cloak and breastplates as she would've looked in a crown and furs.

"I've never heard of this—what did you call it? Arkadia—of yours, either," the princess said. "Perhaps someday you'll conquer Babili for yourselves, only to be cast out into the hills like we were. And the world will forget your tribe's name, as it has forgotten mine."

Silence fell as Kratippus pondered this.

"Babili, ruled by Ellines!" Eusebios broke the silence. "Now that'd be a sight to see."

"I could go for some of that fine Parsa wine," Ourania muttered. "I'd park my arse on a golden throne and gulp that sweet nectar till I couldn't see straight."

"Aye, and Khaldaian whores in our laps," Eusebios added.

"Khaldaians now, is it?" Ourania put in, crossing her arms in mock-offense. "Everyone knows a Kórinthi lady will— "

"Shut it!" Kratippus growled. "Both of you!"

They fell silent, shooting each other baleful glances.

"Princess Miriash," Kratippus said. "I don't trust you as far as I can piss."

"Nor I, you," she replied smoothly.

"But we've taken enough losses today. You'll march in front, with our spears at your back. One false move and you'll feel Elline iron through your heart."

Miriash barked a laugh. "I don't think you're in any position to bargain," she declared.

Kratippus chewed his lip for a moment. "Name your terms then," he said at last.

"We march together," Miriash said at once. "If we meet any Parsa, we kill them, if we can. If they are too strong, we run. When we find your army's camp, you give us safe passage, and water and food. Then we go east to Kalsh, and you go—wherever it is you're going."

"Agreed," Kratippus said. He extended his arm, and she clasped it, formally, as if concluding a treaty. "One last thing," he added. "We've a wounded horse. Can you patch her up?"

Miriash stepped close to the horse, running her hand along its thigh, probing ever so gently at the arrow-shaft protruding from the bloody, raw wound as she stroked the horse's nose, muttering kind words in a language Leander did not recognize.

After a moment, the princess shook her head. "It will be some months before she can run," she said. "But you would be wise to let her live."

Kratippus sighed. "What does that mean?"

"We believe it is bad luck to kill a healthy horse," Miriash said. She glanced up at her men along the rim of the ravine, and whistled. "Indash!" she called, then barked out an order in her strange tongue.

A short, hook-nosed man in a green-and-black tunic came scrambling down the rocks, nimble as a monkey. As he descended, Miriash abruptly ripped the arrow from the horse's flank. Leander leaped back, expecting the beast to buck madly; but the princess had done the job so deftly that the horse only kicked a few times, stumbled, and fell still, wounded leg upraised.

Meanwhile, the man in the green tunic—Indash, apparently—drew some herbs from a sackcloth pouch at his side, and began to chew them, spitting out mouthfuls of greenish mush to press into the horse's wound.

"We don't have time for this," Kratippus said. The sunset was already fading to deep red, the vault of the sky dimming into a blue, cloudless dusk.

"Release her from these reins," Miriash said to Leander, in a tone that sounded distinctly like a direct command.

Leander glanced at Kratippus, who nodded. He undid the reins from the wounded horse's harness, drawing the slack up into the seat beside him.

"We'll have to leave this one behind, too," he said, nodding at the horse who now lacked a teammate. Two horses would pull slowly but evenly; two horses plus one would make a disaster.

"No," said Miriash. "I will ride him."

Kratippus nodded. "Let's go, then," he said.

Leander unhooked the other horse from the harness, leaving the two others yoked in tandem before the wagon. "We don't have another saddle," he told Miriash.

The princess laughed, swinging herself up over the newly freed horse's side and onto its back as if she'd been best friends with the beast all her life. "Saddles," she taunted. "Is that what you Ellines teach your young men? I've never used a saddle in my life. Let's be off."

Leander snapped the reigns of the wagon, and the great cart rattled forward, deeper into the ravine. Miriash galloped on ahead of him, side by side with Kratippus. On the bluffs above, the proud, painted, fur-clad warriors of Kalsh marched solemnly, scanning the hills for sign of Parsa riders beneath a deep-red sky fading quickly to the blue of twilight.

THEY RODE BENEATH a dusky sky in the deep shadows of the ravine, until they reached its mouth and Miriash raised her hand for a halt.

"Keep quiet," the princess whispered. "I'll be back shortly."

As Leander reigned up the horses drawing the wagon, Miriash nudged her horse into a trot, riding out of the rocky throat of the ravine and onto the hilly plains, where only isolated elms and junipers offered cover.

Night had nearly fallen. Pale blue limned the world's rim behind the western mountains, and a crescent moon hung high in a dark-bruised sky. A chill breeze whistled among hollows in the rocks, raising the hairs on Leander's arms and neck.

While they waited for the princess to return from scouting, Leander gazed up to find the first shimmering constellations of the evening: the Hunter; the Scorpion; the Great and Small Dogs.

"What do you call that one?" asked one of the Kalshu warriors atop the bluffs, pointing up toward the west, where Leander could just make out three bright stars arranged in a triangle.

"That's the Goat's Horn," Eusebios told him.

"Sometimes we call it the Aegipan," Ourania added. "He was a satyr who fled into the sky, and took the form of a fish-tailed goat."

The man's bushy eyebrows rose. "How strange," he said.

Eusebios shrugged. "No stranger than any other story of Gods and monsters, if you ask me."

"No, not the story," said the Kalshu warrior. "It's strange because—people here have always called those stars the Goat-Fish. Since the most ancient times."

"Really?" Ourania's eyes widened with surprise.

"It is a name for the God Énki," the warrior told them, "who came forth from the sea at the dawn of time to teach crafts and letters to mankind—or so the old songs say. He is known to wear goat's hooves and a fish's tail when the mood takes him. And look: even now, after all these centuries, he still rises from the deep every evening. To check in on us, perhaps."

Leander gazed up at the lopsided triangle of stars, trying to imagine a God with goat's hooves and a fish's tail. The legend seemed to fall short of the reality, as did so many legends in this place.

"Quiet, all of you," Kratippus hissed from horseback at the mouth of the ravine. The Kalshu warrior stepped back from the ledge, though no one had anything else to say. They waited in tense silence for Miriash to return.

At last she came riding back through the ravine's mouth. "Fires," she said. "I saw campfires on the hills, just northwest of here. Dozens of them. Enough for a few hundred men. Maybe a thousand. I don't think they are Parsa."

"You don't think?" Kratippus raised an eyebrow. "What does that mean?"

"Parsa always raise big tents for the noblemen," the princess answered. "Build big cookfires for their feasts. All I saw were small tents and small fires. So, I do not think they are Parsa."

"Could be ours," Eusebios said.

"You sure enough to stake your life on it?" Kratippus snapped back at him.

"Our employer is dead," Eusebios snarled. "That means it's either his brother's army, or our lot. By the size, it's got to be ours."

"Doesn't mean there aren't any Parsa out there," Ourania said.

Everyone looked to Miriash. "The fires aren't far," she said after a moment. "If we move quick and quiet, we may reach the camp before any Parsa riders catch us."

"Think about that," Leander said quietly. It was the first thing he'd said all evening, and all heads turned to hear the rest. "We come galloping out of the dark, into an Elline camp, with Parsa riders galloping and whooping behind us. If I saw that, I'd loose arrows first and ask questions afterward."

"The Parsa riders will not whoop," Miriash said drily. "They will be stealthy at night."

"I say we wait," Ourania said. "Move in the dead of night, while the riders sleep."

"Or give them time to creep up behind us in the dark and slay us all," Eusebios put in.

"We wait until full dark," Kratippus declared. "Then we'll send a rider to the camp; alert them we're coming. The rest of us will follow, quick and quiet as we can." After a moment he turned to look at Miriash, who nodded in agreement.

"Who'll be the messenger?" the princess asked. "I would volunteer, but those men in the camp would not recognize me."

Kratippus looked to Leander, then to Eusebios and Ourania in the back of the wagon.

Eusebios's eyes widened. "Well I'm not doing it," he exclaimed.

"I don't know how to ride," Ourania said.

"I'll do it," Leander said.

Everyone turned to look at him again. He hated the feeling of so many eyes on him, especially when people stared in such silence. The wind whistled softly through the ravine, over the songs of night insects.

"We don't even know they're still out there," Leander said after a moment.

"Of course they are," Eusebios said. "They never give up a pursuit. I don't know how Miriash slipped past them—"

"Because I am quiet," Miriash said. "And I know how to hide."

"—but they won't miss you, Leander," Eusebios said. "Not with you tilting across the meadow. There's plenty of moonlight. They'll see you, and they'll catch you."

Leander drew a deep breath and let it out in a long, tired sigh. "I do not care. Truly."

"You'd better care about reaching that camp," Kratippus told him.

Eusebios gaped at Leander. "You've really got a deathwish, haven't you?"

Kratippus ignored Eusebios's incredulous stare and turned to Ourania. "Let's get these cart-horses out of their harnesses. The more of us who can go on horseback, the more of us who are likely to make it."

"By 'us,' I presume you mean *all* of us," Miriash said, glancing at him sharply, flicking her chin to indicate the warriors watching from the top of the ravine. Kratippus glanced up at them and saw some of them tense and shift their weight subtly, wrapping fingers around sword-hilts and axe-handles.

"Yes, of course, I mean all of us," the commander said. "We've got three horses left, so we'll take six riders. The rest will have to go on foot."

"And then, of course," Eusebios said, fixing Leander with a dark stare, "there's our messenger. The one who's marked himself to die."

Leander met the man's gaze evenly, but said nothing.

⁂

LEANDER'S HORSE RAN. He held on tight, legs gripping its ribs, fingers tight on reins as the beast raced among the rolling moonlit hills, past oaks and elms and junipers whose branches clutched at the starry sky. The air chilled his throat and lungs, making steam of his breath, and of the horse's. Hooves thundered on hard-packed earth; night insects sang. All else was still and silent, as if this place refused to acknowledge his presence or his purpose.

Five riders in shadow swept out behind him; centaurs in silhouette, men and beasts and bows, tightening arrows against the strings amidst the rattle of leather and bone, all motion and muted breath. The giant charged at their head.

There was no trail here, no hard-packed dirt on which to outpace his pursuers; only soil and stone, twig and grass, each hoofbeat the threat of shattered ankles and headlong crashes, and where would he be then? Perhaps he truly did not care, as he'd said; perhaps he only pushed the thoughts from his mind. He spurred his horse onward, and it ran, and they came quick behind, closing the distance.

He could hear their hooves, close, as he crested a rise and saw the campfires on a distant ridge, tiny lamplights softening the dark with a faint orange glow. The camps were farther than the woman had said. Or farther than he'd pictured. An arrow hummed past his left ear, then two more from the right. He huddled low against the horse's back and rode onward.

Down one hillside, up the next, through a valley and across another rise. They were fanning out on both sides of him now, shadows with hooves and bows. The giant rode up close on his right, feathers bobbing atop his helmet, face shrouded in shadow. The absence of a man; a void from which arrows issued, splitting the night with hisses.

Leander guided the horse with his knees, dodging left and right, like he'd done when he was a boy, riding across the green fields of Arkadia in the summer; crashing through berry bushes, splashing through warm streams, hunting a hare, or carrying Aella out into the forest to bed her down somewhere soft on the pine needles. Aella. He cast her face away and kept his eyes on the fires ahead.

An arrow flew from the left; another from the right; two more from the silent pursuers on each side of him. He swung down, gripping the horse tight with his legs, clinging to its side, feeling its heartbeat and breath against its ribs. Two more arrows flew up and over the horse, and down onto the other side. He heard an arrow hiss, and felt a sharp pain in his side, then wet warmth spreading out from his back, down his hip. When he tried to draw a breath, he felt the cold sharp point buried under his shoulder blade.

The fires were closer. Just one more hillside to climb.

⟨

THE MEN AROUND the campfire were tearing off the night's first round of fresh-spitted pig when the rider came thundering out of the night. The soldiers leaped up, raising shields and drawing swords; but they could see the wounded man was one of them: Elline, and badly hurt, slumped over his horse's side, dripping bright red onto the grass.

"It's a lung wound," said one of the soldiers, a fur-clad Thrakian with a missing eye and a deep pitted scar along his cheek, as he reached up to inspect the wounded rider.

"Look!" called another, pointing out beyond the firelight. The men followed his gaze and saw shadows with bows, wheeling and racing away beneath the stars.

The man on the horse groaned and forced himself up. "More are..." he wheezed, and blood ran from the corner of his mouth to drip and pool on the dirt. The soldiers lifted him carefully from his mount, laying him on soft blankets by the fireside. Someone summoned a physician for the arrows in his back.

"Don't try to talk," the soldiers told him.

"More," the wounded man said, "are coming."

"More Parsa?" The Thrakian eyed the hills suspiciously.

"More... Ellines," the wounded man said. "And... Kalshu."

The soldiers looked at one another, questions in their eyes.

"Help," the wounded man said. "Please... Help my friends... Coming..."

He raised an arm, gesturing out across the moonlit hills.

"Right," growled the Thrakian. "Ten men w' torches, now. Let's go."

Fur-cloaked soldiers lit torches from the fire. They marched out beneath the stars, and met two horses galloping across those desolate hills: one bearing a commander called Kratippus and a dark-skinned local with painted face and tattered tunic, the other carrying a similarly painted warrior, and a long-braided woman who called herself a princess. There had been a third horse, they said. But as the torch-bearers fanned out across the hills, calling for a soldier and a whore, no one called back.

In the firelight, Kratippus and the princess strode through rows of tents with their escort of strangely painted, blanketed warriors. Soldiers looked up from their roasting pork and mutton and their wineskins, and stared at the silent line of dirt-caked men with bloody faces and empty eyes, and they gulped and said nothing.

Once they'd reached a quiet area, Kratippus told the princess and her men to stay put and sleep where they could, and set off to find the main command tent, somewhere far toward the center of the camp. Those among the Kalsh-men with a few words of Elline drifted over to the cooking pits, asking about meat and wine.

Leander lay on the blankets, each breath a battle. A physician came and tutted over the arrow in his back. At last the man shook his head sadly.

"You've got a few days, at most," the physician told him. "I can give you some poppy's-milk to help you sleep. Around here they call it 'joyplant,' though I can't say it'll bring you much joy tonight."

Leander nodded, and the physician tipped a vial of white, milky fluid past his lips. It tasted sweet, like flowers, and it helped the pain. Soon he was dreaming of the green fields and forests of Arkadia; the wild mountains where satyrs still hid among the trees, and one might catch a nymph bathing in a lake, if one crept up quietly.

He dreamed of Aella; how they'd lain in the forest when they were young. And he dreamed of Ikarion; how the beautiful youth's eyes had shone when he'd returned to camp on quiet nights; and Ikarion as he might have been, back in Arkadia, building a house by the lake, growing wrinkled and grey with a good wife by his side. He dreamed of how they might've been old friends, and traded war stories beneath the quiet stars.

⟨Y

THE MORNING DAWNED gray and chilly. After a hurried breakfast of cold porridge and rough black bread, the generals announced that the army would be continuing its march northward toward the sea.

As Princess Miriash and her band thanked their hosts and prepared to depart, Kratippus helped the band of Thrakians pack up their tents. They thanked him in throaty accents, casting baleful glances at Leander, who lay gray-faced on a litter, gazing off into some other place.

Then they were on the march, across flat plains covered in tall grass and scrub, men belting out marching songs and the others taking up the rhythm, drums and pan-pipes joining in, and to Leander it almost felt like a festival compared to the days leading up to this one. They saw no enemy scouts, and their own scouts caught no glimpse of any.

The Thrakians had claimed Leander as their own. They carried his litter close by the army commanders; and for the first time since he'd come to this part of the world, Leander saw them up close: Khrisophus and Timasion and the other generals, marching easily in their brightly dyed tunics, their attendants driving wagons that carried their breastplates and weapons and private tents.

By the time the sun reached its peak, they'd arrived at the bank of a great river—the one called the Swift, Leander guessed, down which they'd fought their way southeastward six long years ago, and were now following back northwest, to the sea.

Khrisophus stopped and raised a hand and conferred with the other generals. They called a halt for lunch, which the commanders spread outward across the camp.

They'd stopped near an old wall—very old, by the looks of it. Not that Leander was much of a judge. It was built of mud-brick, taller than a man standing on another man's shoulders, built atop a thick stone foundation packed with shells, running far off toward the horizon in both directions, its flatness interrupted periodically by taller towers with narrow windows. The brick and stone were weathered and cracked, and the gates were long crumbled and rotted away. Leander could see nothing inside the walls except wind-blown mounds of dirt and stone.

Close by, Leander heard an excited voice call out "Pakor! Nirar!" and two of the local translators came running. "What is this place?" asked the man who'd summoned them. Leander didn't recognize him, but his indigo tunic and plaited hair marked him out as a rich man. The son of some merchant prince, most likely, thoroughly enjoying his excursion in the wild East. He held a wax tablet and a stylus, and scratched notes as he consulted with the translators. "Do you know what this place is?" he was asking.

"It is a great deserted city, sir," said one of the translators.

"I can see that, Pakor," said the young man. "What is it called?"

Pakor and Nirar conferred, arguing and pointing and shoving. Finally Pakor, the older, said, "It is the ruin of the city of Mespila."

Nirar raised a hand. "That isn't true—!"

"Whose city was it, Pakor?" the rich young man interrupted.

"It was inhabited by the Mída in ancient times," Pakor said, "before the Parsa came."

"No, that's not true!" Nirar cried. "It is much more ancient. It was once a city of my people, the Ashůru, centuries before the Mída came down from the hills. Its name was Ninua, and it was the mightiest city in all the world, where a great library was built by the World-King—"

"How can you possibly know all this?" Pakor cried.

"It is a true story," Nirar said, "told to my grandfather by his grandfather, and to him by his grandfather—"

"All the way back to the very first man, I suppose," said Pakor, smiling indulgently for the young man's sake. "I'm sorry, sir, but you can't believe—"

"If no one can agree who created this city," the young man cut him off, "or even what it is called, then I feel very sorry for the people who built it."

He walked closer to the walls, scanning them with practiced eyes. "They clearly wanted these walls to stand forever. So similar to the Parsa style, and yet—simpler. Less ornate. The raw form, so to speak. And quite ancient indeed, to judge by their state of decay."

"As I said, sir," Nirar said, "this city is centuries old, far older than the Mída—"

"Artemios!" the young man called out, cutting him off. An army messenger came running. "Go tell Epiktetos I'll need a small guard," the young man said, scratching more marks on his wax tablet. "Five men should do it. I wish to inspect these walls."

"Of course, sir," said Artemios, and hurried off into the camp.

"Now," said the young man, turning back to the translators. "Can we agree on who built this city, or can't we?"

The translators stood in silence for a moment, glancing at each other, each daring the other to go first.

Finally Pakor blurted out, "As I explained, sir, before I was interrupted, it is the city of Mespila, which was built by the Mída in ancient times."

Nirar threw up his hands and made an exasperated sound, and stalked off toward the translators' camp.

"Very well, then," said the young man, nodding. "It is Mespila, and it was once inhabited by the Mída."

Epiktetos came with his five spearmen, and they and the young man walked away down the length of the wall, which the young man scrutinized it at every step, asking Epiktetos to keep track of the distance he walked.

A Thrakian approached Leander and offered him a wineskin, which he took and drank from eagerly, breathing a little easier as the warm sweet liquid washed the dust from his throat.

"Who's the rich lad?" asked the Thrakian.

"Damned if I know," said Leander. "Not a general, I don't think. But they jump to follow his orders; that's for certain. He's asking all kinds of questions about these walls."

"Whose walls?" asked the Thrakian.

"We're not sure," said Leander. "Some people who won a lot of battles, I suppose. And then lost the war."

The Thrakian considered this. "Long time ago," he said.

Leander took another long drink from the wineskin, and sighed deeply. "Right," he said. "A long time ago."

The Thrakian shook his head. "No'un here to fight," he said.

"Well," said Leander, "you're right about that."

The Thrakian grunted his disapproval, took back the wineskin, and went to rejoin his friends.

135 YEARS EARLIER
530 BC

Woman clothed in radiance,
The great rites are yours:
Who can fathom them?

— The Exaltation of Inanna

丫

The whole world seemed to have come to the city of Urim today. Standing outside the sanctuary atop the highest level of the Great Ziggurat, gazing beyond the tiled courtyards and gardens of the temple complex, one could see men and women in their thousands, milling like ants among the palms of the broad avenues, hurrying with reed baskets, barrels and bundles of river-trout around the vast honeycomb of mud shacks stretching far as the horizon.

Off the main streets, flat roofs of every shape and size framed tangled mazes of alleys and private courtyards, tightly packed against their neighbors, from the walls of the temple complex to the towering stone embankments of the broad canal that split the city in two—and across the precincts on the canal's far side, all the way to the distant city walls, and the sprawling barley-fields and olive farms beyond. To the east, great flat-bottomed cargo ships maneuvered into berths in the walled harbor at the city's edge, or crept out through its mighty cedar gates, to rejoin the lazy current of the Slow River.

If, running and leaping across the city's flat-topped roofs, one paused to peer with special alertness at the lower layers of that mud-brick honeycomb, one might see how houses were built atop the crumbling foundations of buildings far older: collapsed walls whose sculpted reliefs now wore many layers of painted graffiti; buckled columns once mosaicked in blue and gold and aquamarine, tumbling from their fittings to mingle with the garbage of the street. Always the older layers remained, interwoven like bones and veins among the new, as if the city's inhabitants could conceive of no architecture whose foundation did not wear the dust of centuries.

And if, jumping from one roof to the next, one chanced to land on the canopied balcony of a certain manor-house, and craned in close against the balcony doors to peer through their tamarisk-wood lattice entwined with carved vines and pomegranates, one might glimpse through the pinholes a pale young lady in a white silk nightgown, lying silent in her shadowy bedchamber, amid the embroidered pillows and sheets of a vast four-poster bed.

But then, suddenly, came the sound of a heavy fist knocking against the chamber door.

From some far-distant place, Ninsunu heard that pounding, loud and insistent, though it seemed to come from another world. Rolling over on the enormous bed, she twisted away from the sound, pulling the linen blankets tight around her shoulders and knocking glass vials of joyplant milk from the wood nightstand. The vials shattered on the tiled limestone floor, splashing their dregs of brown-speckled white across the rugs.

Ninsunu pressed the silk pillows tight against her ears. But the pounding continued.

From a far-off land, she heard her father's voice. "I'm here with a guard, Ninsunu. Open the door or I will command him to break it down. I give you until I count three."

In her faraway dreamland, Ninsunu smiled softly. This was a funny game her father was playing.

"One," he shouted.

She hummed a few bars of "Lovers' Quarrel."

Don't come to the bridge tonight,
For you won't find me there.
I've gone to a distant land,
And you'll never know where...

"Two!" He bellowed. "Last chance, Ninsunu."

Now his voice was getting distracting. She pressed the pillow tightly against her head.

"Three!" he shouted, and Ninsunu heard a crash—a distant booming sound—and there he was, stern and imposing in his sashed blue robes, with coiffed black hair and beard, standing among shattered timbers, behind the thick-muscled slave who'd smashed her chamber door down.

Stepping past the slave into her shadowy bedchamber, her father glared at her through the translucent drapes hanging about the posts of her bed.

"Wake up," he called, his voice sounding far away, though it seemed to be growing closer. "Please." The warm softness of everything was sharpening, and she didn't like that, not one bit.

Her father's burly attendant marched across the room, tripping on overturned chairs and rumpled carpets and scattered satin couch-cushions, to thrust open the latticed balcony doors that afforded a pinhole mosaic of the sky. Long shadows of vines and fruits cast by the lattice gave way to dazzling sunlight and a full view of the boulevard below, where onion-sellers and rat-killers wove among trenches of palms, dodging braying donkeys and rattling carts heaped with grain.

Blinding sun flooded the bedchamber, illuminating pillars mosaicked in blue stone and gold-leaf beneath the mural of palm trees and flowers adorning the room's high ceiling. Real palm trees and flowers wilted, dead and brown, in painted urns in the room's far corners, and in vases on the marbled tabletops, where moldy figs and dates, oranges and pomegranates, green pistachios and flaky pastries lay scattered from their silver plates. Some tumbled onto the patterned rugs between the tables' claw-carved feet.

Ninsunu squinted, raising herself on her elbow to get a better look at the intruders, shielding her eyes with one hand and feeling her head sway gently from side to side. A warm breeze caressed her pale skin, but with it came a reek of rotting vegetables and manure that turned her stomach.

"Ninsunu, how can you live like this?" Her father muttered. He glanced down at the bed and saw an empty glass vial lying next to her on the mattress, still stained brown-speckled white with the dregs of poppy's-milk. Joyplant, everyone had called it for as long as anyone could remember.

"Take that away. Now," he said to the slave, who retrieved the vial and departed.

Her father took a few deep breaths, and calmed down. He walked slowly to the bed, sank onto the cushioned mattress and stroked her hair, like he'd done when she was a little girl.

"Why do you do this, Ninsunu?" he asked softly. "Is your life so miserable?" He waited for an answer, but she only pouted at him, her head still swaying like a snake's, eyes not focusing. "What is it you lack? Name it and I will have it brought for you."

"Sleep," she said, soft and slowly.

He leaned in closer. "What's that?"

"I lack sleep," she murmured. "Let me sleep."

He hit her then—not hard enough to knock her over, but hard enough to sting, even with the joyplant in her veins. She wobbled back and forth for a moment, then began to cry.

"Why did you do that, Daddy?" she asked.

The Cradle and the Sword

"Because," he said, leaning close to her face, "I have sacrificed everything for you—bowed and scraped before withered old men who had no more idea of—" he trailed off, shaking his head. "You could have been high priestess, you realize that?" he snapped suddenly. "I would have spoken to the temple elders and made it so. You could have married any man in the city. A general, even a governor. Seven Stars, Ninsunu! The Gods know I've counted out enough gold over the years. All for—" he glanced around the bedchamber, as if unsure of something. "All for you, of course. All for you."

"But I don't want to marry some wrinkled old man," she said.

"You want nothing!" he cried. "What was this all for, all of this—?" he gestured wildly around the room, "if not to secure a future for you? I would bring you the whole city of Urim on a platter, and you lie here gulping down joyplant milk like a cheap barmaid—"

"That's enough," came her mother's voice from the doorway.

She came and sat next to Ninsunu on the bed, as her father stood up to pace, crossing his silk-draped arms, clenching a hand around his mouth as he gazed down on her, sadness in his eyes.

"Your father shouldn't speak to you that way," said her mother, stroking Ninsunu's tangled hair.

"Father," Ninsunu began. She took a long, deep breath, then finished, "is cruel."

"Your father is afraid for you," her mother replied. "He has seen what happens to those who drink the joyplant as you do. Their lives are not long or happy."

"No one's life is happy," she whispered.

Her mother sighed. "That isn't true, dear. Your father and I were very happy." Her voice faded. "Once. We were so happy." Her eyes flickered up to her husband, then down at her hands, folded in her lap.

"Once?" Ninsunu asked, searching her mother's eyes.

"Ninsunu." Her mother suddenly took a stern tone, setting her jaw. "You're not going to like this, but, well… your father and I have discussed it, and—"

"It's time for you to choose a path," said her father. "A real path in the world."

"You can do anything you wish, dear," said her mother. "If you don't want to take a husband, don't take one. But become a priestess, then, if you like, or a scribe. Several schools take on female scribes, you know."

"I don't want any of those things," Ninsunu murmured.

Her mother nodded, eyes wet with tears. "We know, sweetlove. But this can't go on."

"Can't you see how this hurts your mother?" said her father. "Look what you're doing to her."

"If you will agree to stop taking this drink," her mother said, "you'll have the very best physicians to cure you of the pain. But we can no longer…" She trailed off, gazing down at her hands again.

"What your mother means, is…" Her father spoke up, trying to fill the silence. "You'll either stop the joyplant now, today, or you'll leave this house. We love you, truly. But…" He shook his head, as if he'd run out of words.

What her parents were telling her seemed almost important enough to cut through the warm softness of Ninsunu's dreamland and make its meaning felt. But try as she might, she could not feel it.

"Out of this house," she muttered. "Where will I go?"

Her mother's lip was trembling. "That would be up to you, dear. But please, we beg you, do not force us down that path. Choose to stay here with us."

"I choose," sighed Ninsunu, then forgot what she was going to say. "I choose to sleep," she said at last, and closed her eyes and fell back into the warm soft place.

NEXT MORNING, IT was the headache that woke her first. Then the stomping of feet and the opening and slamming closed of the chests around her bed brought her out of half-wakefulness and made her sit up and see what was happening. Three of her father's slaves were clattering around the room, opening her heavy wood clothing chests and packing her dresses and jewelry into smaller travel boxes.

"What are you doing?" she cried.

Fragments of last night came back to her. *You'll either stop the joyplant now, today, or you'll leave this house.* What had she said in response? Was it tomorrow already?

"Mother!" she screamed, racing out the door and down the stairs. "Father!" But they were nowhere to be found—not in the dining room, or in the central courtyard with its pools and fountains, or in the study with its stacks of scrolls and clay tablets, or in their bedroom, or even out in the foyer.

She ran back up the stairs to her chamber. "Where are Mother and Father?" she demanded of a servant.

"They have departed," he responded. "I have orders that you are to be gone from the house by the time they return."

"What?" she screamed at him.

His face remained impassive. "I'm sorry. That is all I know. If you'll excuse me, I will escort you outside once we have packed up your essentials."

"Escort me—" she half-gasped, half-laughed. But the slave had already returned to his task, carefully collecting the gold mirrors and combs from her dressing table and packing them into a small, daintily painted box.

A few minutes later, she stood out on the street in front of her family's townhouse, watching the household slaves load her boxes and chests onto a donkey-drawn cart; one that bore a palanquin on top, with ornately stitched curtains drawn around it.

"If my lady would kindly embark," said the man who'd kicked down her door the day before.

"Where are you taking me?" she demanded.

"It pains me that I am not at liberty to say. If your ladyship would be so kind as to board the carriage, however, you will soon see."

"I want to talk to Mother," she said, but the slave only shook his head.

"I'm afraid that is not possible. However, your mother and father wish me to assure you that they have personally chosen your destination."

"*What* destination?" she cried.

"My lady, if you would kindly embark."

He bowed low, held out his hand to her, and remained in that pose until finally, with an exasperated gasp, she took his hand and climbed up onto the wagon, and sat down on a small padded chair inside the palanquin. Another slave climbed up and drew the curtains tightly around the palanquin and tied them shut, blocking any view of the outside, shrouding her in dimness, as in her bedchamber. After a pause, she heard him cry "ha!" as he tapped the donkey with his riding-stick, and the wagon jerked and began to roll forward over the cobblestones.

The long, winding, bumpy ride made Ninsunu's headache worse. She felt sick to her stomach, with a tense cramping in her bowels, and all her limbs seemed to ache down to the bones. By the time they reached their destination, she was shivering in spite of the heat.

A servant opened the curtains around the palanquin, and helped Ninsunu down from the wagon, which was parked in front of a small door in a narrow street next to a tall, sheer wall.

"What is this place?" she asked.

The only walls this size she knew were the one surrounding the entire city, and the one surrounding the base of the temple precinct. She looked up and saw, at the top of the wall, the flat courtyard; and atop that, the glimmering blue-and-gold facades of the Great Ziggurat of Urim, its top levels towering so high that they seemed to scrape the clouds.

The door in the wall opened, and a small woman peeked out. She was not much older than Ninsunu, dressed simply and neatly in a clean white dress of rough-spun wool, her black hair pulled back into a tight bun.

"You must be Ninsunu," said the woman.

"Lady Ninsunu, to you," said Ninsunu.

The woman smiled gently. "We're all ladies here, Ninsunu, no matter where we come from. I'm Belessa. Welcome."

"Welcome to *where*?" Ninsunu asked, but Belessa didn't answer.

THE SERVANTS WERE already unloading her chests and Belessa began dragging them inside, helped by two similarly dressed women who appeared from behind the door.

"You might give us a hand," said one.

Ninsunu was about to make a sharp-tongued reply, but instead she said, "I feel sick."

Belessa glanced at her, and she must've looked as bad as she felt, because the woman snapped, "Get her inside."

The other two women threw her arms over their shoulders and supported her through the doorway, down a winding series of candlelit hallways, out across a daylit courtyard where a dozen more women in white dresses sat cross-legged on the floor, writing on wax tablets, and down another hallway with tiny bedchambers opening off both sides, to the lavatory at the end of the hall, just in time for Ninsunu to lean over the hole and retch up everything in her stomach.

When she was finished, the women helped her to a bedchamber that contained two small beds, two desks with chairs, and a narrow window looking out onto the courtyard. They laid her on the bed, placed two pitchers—one full of water, one empty—next to it, and left the room, locking the door behind them.

Ninsunu didn't know how long the next part lasted. Every minute felt like a day of aches and dizziness and stomach pains that made her grope for the pitcher next to the bed. Hours flew by in blurs, shadowy times when she thought she heard voices far away, some speaking in worried tones, others chanting prayers. She smelled incense in the air. Then the voices faded.

She woke once, alone, and the early morning light came through the window. She tried to drink water, vomited it back up, and lay on the bed again. This happened several more times, and each time, she woke to find the dirty pitcher replaced with a clean one, and the one with water had been refilled. So passed—Days? Weeks?—until she no longer knew whether it was day or night, where she was, or what she was doing here. All she knew was sickness and pain, hot and cold sweats.

Another time when she woke it was night, and all was quiet, aside from her own moaning. The sheets were soaked with sweat, and other worse-smelling fluids. She tried calling for help, but no one came, and soon the dreams took her again.

She dreamed of great stone vaults beneath the earth, where endless shelves cradled thousands upon thousands of clay tablets from every era of the world's past, all the way back to before the great Flood.

Shadowy figures moved among these shelves, withdrawing and consulting cracked, ancient tablets; inscribing notes on plaques of wood and clay; ascending and descending stone staircases that led to deeper vaults below. She followed the shadowy forms, calling out to them, asking them to stop and answer her, but they moved in silence without turning or showing their faces.

She was searching for something—what, she could not say. But she yearned for it, ached for it, as she ached for the joyplant. Her search drove her down the stone stairs, into rooms lit by torchlight, where stones inscribed with jagged symbols lay piled at the feet of engravings of forgotten Gods; deities with heads of birds and tails like fish, clasping branches and bowls overflowing with water.

In one chamber she found a wood door in the floor. Heaving it back on its rusty hinges, she uncovered a ladder descending into the shadows. Her feet moved of their own will, placing themselves on each step of the ladder, pulling her down until cool water lapped at her ankles; and deeper, until waves splashed at her chin, and she felt herself slip under.

There in the depths, strange colored lights seemed to dance around her, and a voice hummed in her marrow.

This place has no bottom, it said.

She panicked, thrashing and gulping for air. The lights pressed in around her, coalescing into a blinding halo of white—

Suddenly she was walking in the temple courtyard. It was midday, and the palm trees cast long shadows across the flagstones. Birds sang from their nests atop the walls.

Another woman walked beside her, clad not in an embroidered satin dress or in the pale flax habit of the temple, but in a long skirt and shawl of pleated wool, like the Shuméru women in the ancient mosaics. She wore her hair neatly braided and coiffed, and atop her head sat a strange domed hat of polished bronze.

"There's a lot more down there than you can see," said the woman.

Ninsunu tried to tease meaning from those words, but could find none.

"The halls and chambers extend deeper than anyone guesses," the woman said.

Utterly confused, Ninsunu searched for some question to make sense of this dream. "What's in those halls you speak of?" she asked the woman.

"Monsters, of course," the woman said, smiling. "The ones you most dread, and most yearn to face. The Gods in the Abyss."

At those words, Ninsunu tried to scream; but only a weak groan issued from her mouth. She closed her eyes tightly and screamed and screamed as hard as she could, thrashing her limbs frantically—

GASPING, SHE AWOKE in her moonlit bedchamber, the rough flax of her bedclothes soaked with cold sweat. Gratefully, feeling the world return to focus around her, she pushed herself up and sat panting.

She was hungry and feeling clear-headed. The pains had faded. Easing herself up from the bed, she found her shaky footing, and tried the door. Still locked. She knocked gently.

"If it's all right," she said, "I'd like to have something to eat."

She heard footsteps padding away down the hallway, then two pairs of them returning.

"What are you asking for?" asked a voice she thought she recognized as Belessa's.

"Just a bit of bread, if you have it," she said. "I'm very hungry."

The door unlocked and opened, and in the doorway stood Belessa, with a younger, frightened-looking woman at her side. Belessa looked Ninsunu up and down, nodded, turned to the younger woman and said, "Amata, bring some bread and vegetables, and milk."

Amata hurried off down the hallway, and Belessa continued to scrutinize Ninsunu in a way that, until very recently, would have made her furious. Today she was just glad to have the company.

"How long was I—" she asked. "Like that?"

"It is called the Expulsion," said Belessa. "It normally lasts five days. Yours lasted eight."

Ninsunu sat on the bed, staring at the floor. "Eight days—"

"I believe the worst has passed," said Belessa. "Once you've eaten, you may feel stronger. Then I can begin to show you around."

Ninsunu was about to ask Belessa what this place was, but then Amata came running back in with a tray of rough bread and fresh vegetables and a clay cup of milk, and Belessa was hurrying out of the room, saying, "Eat slowly," without turning around. Amata set on the tray on the table, bowed slightly, and also hurried out into the hallway. This time, though, she didn't lock the door behind her.

Ninsunu tore into the crusty bread. It tasted savory and satisfying on her tongue, though it was baked blandly, with no spices or herbs she could taste. She bit into a cucumber, which tasted more refreshing than anything she'd ever eaten. Then she tried a fresh date, and an apple, washing them down with the fresh cool milk. Her stomach grumbled, and for a moment she thought it was all about to come back up. But she slowed her chewing and her insides settled.

She'd barely eaten enough for a small child, but she felt nourishment flowing outward from her stomach, down her arms and legs and up into her heart. For the first time in days, she didn't have a headache or an urge to void her stomach. She took one last sip of the milk, then stepped out into the hallway and called for Belessa in the politest voice she could summon.

Belessa came striding up the hallway, looked Ninsunu up and down again, and asked, "Ready to take a walk?"

"I think so," said Ninsunu, mostly because she was tired of not knowing where she was.

"Well then," said Belessa, cracking the slightest smile, "follow me."

Belessa led the way back up the hall and out into the sunny courtyard, where the other women were sitting cross-legged, using reed styluses to etch intricate clusters of triangular marks into blocks of clay. Some of them hummed as they worked—a tune Ninsunu had never heard; something wordless and lilting, with a simple rhythm.

A middle-aged woman sat at a desk at the far end of the courtyard, writing carefully on a papyrus scroll. She was the only one not dressed in white, clad instead like a temple priestess in a deep red robe, and a simple gold necklace. Unlike the other women, whose hair was pulled back into simple buns, this woman's hair was braided and arranged carefully, with gold pins.

The woman looked up, caught Ninsunu's eye, smiled, carefully returned her ink-reed to its tray, and rose with leisurely grace to stroll over and greet them.

"Welcome to the Scribal School for Women," she said, taking Ninsunu's hand in hers. "Where, for eight centuries, we have produced the finest archivists and poetesses between the Two Rivers."

"I am the Lady Ninsunu," said Ninsunu.

The woman smiled gently, her lips full and plump; her face broad, yet not quite square; soft, somehow, about the edges. Her skin was smooth, creased by slight wrinkles about the eyes and cheeks. "So I've heard," she said. "Though, as Belessa has probably told you, we are all ladies here, regardless of our birth."

"I see." Ninsunu was still trying to size this woman up. Her manners and poise marked her as belonging to the uppermost echelons of Urim society. "And what might I call you, lady?" she asked.

The woman laughed unselfconsciously, like a child. "You might call me Én-nigaldi-Nannár, Princess of Urim, daughter of Emperor Nabu-na'id of Babili." Ninsunu's eyes widened slightly, despite herself. "Or you might call me Bel-shalti-Nannár, High Priestess of the moon-God Nannár."

Ninsunu's childhood training took hold. By instinct she dropped into an extremely low curtsy. But now both women were laughing gently again, so she felt foolish and drew herself back up.

"Or," said the princess, "if you'd prefer to stay here and study with us, you may simply call me by my name—Shala. Or 'Mother of Scribes,' if you wish—but I prefer Shala." She smiled again, looking into Ninsunu's eyes in a way that made Ninsunu feel naked—no, transparent—as though this royal-born woman could see every thought in her mind, but neither judged nor condemned those thoughts.

For perhaps the first time in her life, Ninsunu realized she was thoroughly outclassed by another woman. It was a thrilling feeling, but not a comfortable one.

"I would be pleased to call you Shala, Your Radiance," she said, "if you would permit me."

Shala made a tutting sound. "Please, none of that bowing-and-scraping 'radiance' nonsense here," she said. "I used to get enough of that at home, thank you very much."

Ninsunu realized that when Shala said *home*, she meant the Royal Palace of Babili, though she held onto enough poise to keep from blurting this out.

"So you'll be staying and studying with us, then?" Belessa asked.

"I—" Ninsunu began, then asked, "Do I have a choice?"

Shala smiled. "Yes, of course. You always have a choice."

"But my parents," Ninsunu said. "They told me—at least I think, they said—"

"Your father made the terms of the arrangement very clear," said Shala. "He will not allow you to return to his house until circumstances change."

"What does that mean?"

Shala shrugged. "We shall see. Circumstances always change, do they not?"

Ninsunu didn't know how to answer that, so she asked, "What, precisely, are my options?"

"If you choose to stay here and study," said Shala, "your room and board will be paid for, for the duration of your education. You will retain your belongings. And when your scribal training is complete, you will regain control of your inheritance as well."

Ninsunu nodded slowly. "Or—?"

"Or you may come work in the archive. The same stipulations would apply. Or you may relinquish your worldly possessions and become a priestess at the temple of Nannár, also under my tutelage."

"Are those the only choices?"

Shala smiled, slipping gracefully back into her chair behind the desk. "Of course not, dear," she said. "You are always free to leave here and pursue any life you choose. Of course, then you'd forfeit all your possessions, as well as your inheritance—not to mention that this would grieve your parents even more deeply."

Ninsunu stood silently for a moment, her mind churning through her options. Over the past few days, she'd come to feel she'd been hurled off a cliff into a deep pool of water and forced to swim.

"But there are other reasons to say here, child," Shala said softly.

Ninsunu raised an eyebrow. "Other reasons?"

Shala glanced up at her. "You may discover serenity in this work." She ran her fingers gently over the scrolls scattered across her desk.

"But isn't it a dull ritual?" Ninsunu asked. "Rising before dawn, repeating the same prayers every morning, noon, and night."

Shala smiled. "All ritual can be difficult at first, it's true," she said. "But over time, it's like wearing familiar clothes. We'd feel naked without them." She raised her eyes, searching for the right words. "And ritual reminds us that events happen in cycles. Some things arise. Others pass away. But through it all, the cycles themselves remain."

Ninsunu furrowed her brow. "I've never had much of a mind for mysticism."

Shala laughed, suddenly and sweetly, like a young girl. "I said just the same, when I first came here," the priestess told her. "I remember well."

"What convinced you to stay?" Ninsunu asked.

Shala glanced up at Belessa and fixed the young priestess with a meaningful glance. Belessa bowed politely and padded out of the room.

"Would you like to hear a secret, Ninsunu?" Shala asked, when the other priestess had gone.

"I—" Ninsunu stammered, surprised by the question.

"It's not a trick question, dear." Shala laughed again. "I'm offering."

"Yes, please," Ninsunu said.

"When I was your age," said Shala, "I loved a boy with all my heart."

I knew it! thought Ninsunu.

"His name was Rimush," the priestess went on. "A stable-boy, every bit as handsome as the ancient king who was his namesake. Rimush and I met in secret almost every night, beneath a pomegranate tree in the royal garden. We knew it was forbidden. But we were in love."

Ninsunu nodded for her to continue.

"One month my blood did not come," Shala went on. "I told no one, not even Rimush. I hoped it was only late. But another week passed, and then another, and when I began to feel ill in the mornings, I knew I could deny the truth no longer."

"What did you do?" Ninsunu gasped.

"I told Rimush. I promised I'd go into town and buy the herbs to end it. But Rimush refused."

Ninsunu's brow furrowed. "What do you mean, he refused?"

Shala shook her head and wiped a tiny tear from her eye. "That stupid, proud stable-boy had heard too many tales of honor, I suppose. He somehow arranged a private moment with my father—while saddling his horse, I think—and told him the truth."

Ninsunu's eyes went wide. "What did your father do?" she whispered, though she suspected she already knew how this story ended.

Shala blinked, wiping at her eyes. After a moment, she said, "He did what a king does. He hanged my dear, proud Rimush like a common thief from a tree outside the city walls. And that night, an old woman came to my bedchamber, with a drink of bitter herbs that brought the matter to an end."

Ninsunu gazed at the priestess wordlessly, watching her wipe her eyes, straighten her robes and recompose herself.

"The next day," Shala said, "I was bundled into a carriage and sent south to Urim. I arrived at the temple here to find a position already prepared for me. And I suppose I just never found it in me to leave."

Ninsunu waited for Shala to continue. But the priestess only gazed into Ninsunu's eyes, as if watching the thousand thoughts that swirled in her mind.

At last Ninsunu asked, "May I think about this offer for a day or so?"

Shala nodded. Any hint of the sad young woman had vanished, replaced with the serene middle-aged priestess who'd greeted Ninsunu this morning. "Of course, dear," she said. "However, while you think it over, I hope you will tour our various projects with Belessa. I think you will find them most interesting—and she is a superb tour guide."

"I'm sure she is," said Ninsunu.

"Well then!" Shala clapped her hands. "I'll see you this evening. Please excuse me—I really am hip-deep in this poem.

It's Énheduanna. Difficult stuff. Heady. But—you really must read her sometime."

Ninsunu had never heard of a poet called Énheduanna, but she said it sounded interesting, and thanked the Mother of Scribes for her time—to which Shala only asked her, again, to please dispense with all that nonsense.

Belessa led her through the scribal school, showing her the rooms where students stacked the clay tablets and scrolls for storage, and the ovens where they baked the tablets to rock-hardness, and the brightly lit room where a few scribes labored carefully, inking line upon line of tiny letters onto papyrus scrolls.

Then they walked out into the broad temple courtyard, between gardens of bright yellow and purple flowers, and tall palm and date trees, to the Great Ziggurat. There, they climbed hundreds of mud-brick steps, more steps than she'd ever climbed in her life. By the time they reached the outer court of the mezzanine sanctuary, both of them were gasping and panting.

Once Ninsunu had caught her breath, she walked to the edge of the terrace and looked out over the great city of Urim. She'd never seen it like this before—the way a bird would see it: tight clusters of mud-brick houses stacked haphazardly atop each other, reaching far to the horizon like a labyrinth, interrupted only by the lush gardens here and there, and by the grand causeway, running straight outward from the temple to the gate in the far wall—the road Urim's army marched in triumph after a great victory, and the king and priests paraded the statues of the Gods along on festival days. Today, though, the causeway was packed with wagons and oxen and hundreds of people, all tiny as ants.

Ninsunu turned back to the temple courtyard, and watched small groups of priestesses walking slowly, silently, meditatively, to and from the inner chambers on mysterious errands.

"They don't seem very happy," said Ninsunu after a while.

Belessa shrugged. "This life is not for everyone. A priestess of our order is married only to Nannár, God of the moon, and of scribes and writing. She must live here in the temple for the rest of her days. The work is easy, we say, but the life itself can be hard."

"And Shala oversees all these women?"

Belessa nodded. "Her private chambers are up there, in the upper sanctuary." She pointed toward the highest level of the Ziggurat, which towered even above the level where they stood now.

"I'm not walking up there," said Ninsunu.

Belessa laughed. "Come on," she said. "Let's go down to the courtyard and have a bite to eat."

By the time they'd descended the steps of the Great Ziggurat, the sun had passed its peak in the sky. They went to the temple storehouse and got dates and bread and milk, then found a broad shady palm tree, where Belessa decided they'd sit and eat their lunch. As they sat on the soft grass, picking the pits out of the dates, Ninsunu said, "I don't think I can do that. Work in the sanctuary."

Belessa shrugged. "It isn't for everyone."

"I'm not so sure about the scribe school, either," she said. "All those long days sitting cross-legged on the floor, copying page after page of those tiny symbols. I think I might go mad."

Belessa chuckled. "I thought the same, when I first came here."

"You didn't want to be a scribe?"

"I wanted to be a courtesan," she said, "in the harem of the King of Babili. A life of leisure and pleasure, reclining on cushions in water-gardens, sipping wine and eating grapes."

"Until one night, the king sends for you."

"Oh, I wouldn't have minded that. Might even have enjoyed it. It's a sacred thing, you know, when the temple prostitutes do it."

"Well, as you said, we can't all work at the temple."

"Though I tried. I surely did. And when my father found out—"

Ninsunu's eyes widened. "Your father caught you—soliciting? At the temple?"

Belessa smiled. "And the next thing I knew, I was packed off to scribal school."

Ninsunu shook her head and laughed. "You are full of surprises, Belessa."

"You have no idea," Belessa said. "But that was a long time ago."

After lunch, Belessa said they'd be walking over to the archive next. This turned out to be housed in a long, wide building, a bit like a one-story temple. Its outside walls were decorated with beautiful blue stones and golden reliefs depicting dragons, lions, and other heraldic beasts of Urim, along with great heroes and kings of the past, most of whom Ninsunu didn't recognize.

As they stepped into the cool, shadowy halls of the archive, and Ninsunu's eyes adjusted to the light, her first thought was that this was some kind of art shop for very wealthy people. Long shelves and display cases ran along the walls, and each shelf held collections of clay tablets, statues, sculptures, clay cones, cylinders, and diverse other shapes. As Ninsunu looked closer, she saw that the items were organized into groups, and that each group was labeled by a clay plaque, neatly printed with an inscription. Each individual item had its own neatly printed plaque, too.

"Shala made most of these plaques herself," said Belessa.

"What do they say?" Ninsunu asked.

"The large plaques tell where each group of artifacts comes from, and their time period," said Belessa. "The small ones explain what each artifact says, who it depicts, and so on."

"Some look quite old," Ninsunu said, peering at a polished white statue of a bald man with a beard and a wool kilt, clasping his hands as if in prayer. His blue stone eyes looked almost alive.

"Some are thousands of years old," Belessa said. "Older, perhaps."

Ninsunu turned to her, raising an eyebrow. "How can anyone know that?"

"Many are inscribed with the names of ancient kings. We can compare those names against our own archival king lists, and lists of year-names, in libraries here in Urim; as well as with similar lists in Babili and other modern cities. Those lists are quite precise, reaching back—"

"Why?" Ninsunu interrupted. "I mean, why dig up all these old things? Do you sell them?"

Belessa looked disappointed. "Of course not. These are our people, Ninsunu." She spread her hands. "These people are *us*."

"I don't see any people," said Ninsunu. "I see a lot of statues and bricks, and—I don't know, clay cones. What are these cones, anyway?"

"Please don't touch that!" Belessa gasped as Ninsunu reached out to pick one up. She drew her hand back, feeling like a small child, scolded for reaching for a piece of cake.

"These artifacts are very old," Belessa said, more kindly. "They can crumble to dust at the slightest touch."

"Perhaps that's for the best," Ninsunu muttered.

Belessa threw her another disappointed look.

"Those cones," said Belessa, "if you really did want to know, were buried in the foundations of ancient temples. Others like them are buried here, we believe, in the ground beneath our own Great Ziggurat, by the king who rebuilt it a few centuries ago, and named it *É-temen-ní-gùru*, 'The House Whose Foundation Creates a Fearful Aura.'"

"Rebuilt it?" Ninsunu's brow furrowed. "I didn't know it was damaged."

"This whole temple precinct," said Belessa, "where we're standing now, is built atop the ruins of an older one—a whole temple complex that fell into ruin centuries ago."

"I had no idea," said Ninsunu. "So we're standing on the ruins of the original temple of Urim."

Belessa shook her head, laughing. "No, it just keeps going back, as far as we can tell. That ancient temple precinct was itself built on the ruins of one even more ancient, built atop ruins even more ancient than that—and so on, down through thousands upon thousands of years, back to the very first temple of Old Urim, which, I suppose, must be buried at the very bottom, beneath all this."

Ninsunu wasn't sure how much of this she believed. "And at each level, you find those cones," she said. "Saying who commissioned the job."

"Something like that."

"That's interesting," said Ninsunu. Belessa smiled, but Ninsunu raised a cautionary hand. "Nowhere near interesting enough to devote my whole life to, Belessa. But you're right. It's a curious idea. Kings digging up the brags of older kings, praying someone will dig up *their* brags one day." She shook her head. "I suppose it's a good hobby for bored old rich men."

Belessa burst out laughing at that, and then they were laughing together, strolling through the tree-lined courtyard in the golden late-afternoon light, back to Shala's scribal school.

𒀭𒀭

Most of the scribes had left the writing-hall, leaving their tablets neatly stacked in the corner of the courtyard. Presumably they'd gone to evening prayers, or to duties elsewhere in the temple district.

Shala herself, however, was still at her desk, though, studying her scrolls and tablets by the fire of an oil lamp. "So," she said, giving a nod to Belessa as she rose to greet Ninsunu, "what do you think of my little enterprises?"

"The temple is beautiful," said Ninsunu. "It's grand and lovely and—"

"I have no time for flattery," said Shala, but she smiled. "Please, tell me your true thoughts. I promise, you will not injure my feelings."

Ninsunu took a deep breath, glancing nervously at Belessa.

"Belessa," said Shala, "would you mind if we spoke alone for a moment?"

"Certainly," said Belessa, and hurried off down the hall to some other errand.

Once Belessa was out of hearing range, Ninsunu said, "The temple looks deathly boring." She swallowed. "To be perfectly honest."

Shala spread her hands. "Please continue."

"And the scribal work—I just can't see myself sitting on the floor like that all day, every day, making tiny marks on papyrus scrolls."

Shala nodded. "I understand. Although it's not so much the marks themselves that are interesting, as what they mean to you, and who they introduce you to."

"Maybe so," said Ninsunu. "But I still don't think it's for me."

"And my archive?" Shala asked.

"The archive, right. Belessa told me you organized most of that yourself."

"Not just organized. Found. Went out myself and explored and dug up from the ruins of old palaces and temples."

"Sounds like sweaty work."

"Lovemaking is sweaty work, too," Shala said with a smile. "But the secrets you bring forth are oh, so worth the sweat. Wouldn't you agree?"

Ninsunu looked down at her feet. "I, eh, I suppose so—"

"My, my," said Shala, laughing gently. "I would have thought you were quite the woman of the world. Our veteran joyplant drinker, passionate seeker of all sensual pleasures."

Ninsunu swallowed, coughed. "Not so passionate as that, Your Radia—er, I mean, Shala."

Shala chuckled and turned back to her work desk where she began rolling up scrolls and stacking up tablets.

"What you said about digging up secrets," Ninsunu ventured. "It makes me think of something Belessa told me today."

Shala turned, still smiling, and nodded for her to continue.

"We were talking about how this temple complex is built on all these layers and layers," Ninsunu went on. "Ancient temples on top of even more ancient ones, all the way back to—well, in the beginning, I suppose."

"It's true," Shala replied.

Ninsunu suddenly felt overcome with the desire to tell Shala of her dream: the misty corridors and vaults beneath the earth; the depths of water and the voice that hummed inside her. She hadn't told anyone about it, and surely Shala would know what to do. But perhaps now wasn't the right time.

"Just think how many ancient corridors must be down there," Ninsunu tried. "Older and older chambers, all the way back to—to who knows when!"

Shala looked at her very strangely. "There are many ancient ruins buried beneath the temple grounds, no question," the priestess said at last. "But there are no hidden chambers or secret passageways. Only heaps of stone, grinding themselves slowly to dust beneath the weight of the buildings above."

Ninsunu's face fell. "But my dream—" she blurted, then stopped.

Shala's brow furrowed. "What dream?"

It was too late to back out now. "I—had a strange dream last night," she said; and then the words came pouring forth. She told Shala of the tablet-filled vaults beneath the earth; the chambers of shadow and the staircases receding into the depths; the strange old Shuméru priestess who'd spoken mysteries. The God whose voice hummed in her bones.

When at last Ninsunu fell silent, Shala gazed into her eyes for a long time.

"It is a very unusual dream," the priestess said at last. "I don't know who this ancient priestess was, but I can certainly tell you who the God was, as well as his meaning."

Ninsunu nodded for her to continue.

"It was none other than Énki," Shala said. "Lord of the Abyss, God of crafts and writing, of cleverness and invention. Énki isn't just any minor God. He's one of the Seven Gods who Decree, which means a visit from him is a rare honor, to be sure. But the depths he spoke of are no secret corridors beneath the temple. They're the abysses of your own mind."

Ninsunu's brow furrowed. "My mind?"

"Of course," Shala replied. "Énki urges you to plunge into the depths of your heart, and seek the monsters within you. All those fears and weaknesses that first drove you to seek comfort in the joyplant. A worthy commission, to be sure. Oh, don't look so despondent, dear! You've been visited by one of the supreme Gods, and given a profound calling. Any woman here would envy you." She chuckled softly, sipping at her wine. "Many will, I'll wager, once word gets out."

That night, Ninsunu dreamed of the vaults again, of walking with shadowy figures among endless shelves filled with ancient clay tablets. Of descending a stone staircase into lightless hallways where mist swirled, smelling like earthy incense. She called out for Énki, and for the priestess, but the only answer was the echo of her own voice.

How long she wandered in that labyrinth, she did not know. When she awoke, the first rays of dawn were creeping over the temple courtyard, casting her room in pale golden light.

She rose, and without pausing to wash, drifted down the corridor, across the cold courtyard where long-plumed *irsaj* birds had begun to flap and peck amid the branches of the palm trees, rousing themselves to sing the first songs of the new day. Something pulled her toward the archive. Its door was barred but unlocked, and Ninsunu managed to lift the heavy wooden bar and squeeze through the doorway, closing the door behind her.

She lit a small lamp and hurried between the shelves of ancient artifacts: statues of long-dead lords; mosaics of forgotten battles; inscriptions testifying to the power of kingdoms now crumbled to dust. At the cavernous room's far end, she descended a stairway and at the foot of the stairs found a heavy wood doorway blocking her way; barred and locked this time. She pushed and pulled at the bolt with all her strength, but it would not budge.

Cursing, she glanced about for any likely hiding spots for a key, but saw only bare walls of mud-brick upon stone foundations; not a crack or crevice that might conceal the solution.

Giving up, she decided to abandon the archive before Belessa or anyone else showed up to make the morning rounds. But reaching the top of the stairs, she stumbled on a wooden box. Digging through it, she found a rusted brass key, and suppressing a squeal of glee, she hurried back down the stairs, fitted the key in the lock, and turned it, feeling the click. The wooden bar lifted easily, and the door swung inward, casting up a storm of moldy dust that made Ninsunu cough and gag.

Footsteps rang on the floor-tiles at the far end of the room. Ninsunu tucked the key in her belt, and closed the door behind her, feeling the heavy wood bolt drop into place. She had no way to replace the lock from the inside, but perhaps no one would check. It wasn't until she'd padded a fair way down the musty corridor that she realized she might've blocked off her only means of exit.

Pushing such thoughts from her mind, she trod deeper, following the downward-sloping corridor. Luckily this was no maze, just a straight hallway that descended, switched back around a corner, and descended again. After three or four corners, Ninsunu had begun to wonder if this corridor sank forever into the earth—and remembered the God's words: *It has no bottom*—but at last she reached a square doorway of half-rotted wood. Taking a deep breath, she plunged through it.

Her lamp's flickering flame cast a soft reddish glow across small white mountains covering the floor. She crept closer, reaching out to brush her fingers against soft linen, damp with moisture. Lifting the corner of the cloth, she felt fresh clay beneath. Red and soft, it left stains on her fingertips.

As she raised her lamp, its warm light illumined dozens of these clay-and-cloth mounds; perhaps hundreds. She padded quietly toward the chamber's far wall, glancing up to see walls adorned with old reliefs depicting kings in gold crowns, carrying gold sceptres, battling long-tongued dragons and enormous lions. The kings' robes were painted indigo and crimson, their hair and eyelids the blackest kohl. All were glazed in faience that had cracked and sloughed away, leaving rough patches of bare stone across the faces of holy warriors and monsters. Shadows played about the flickering flame of her lamp, making the figures seem to dance.

"Centuries old," she muttered, hearing her voice echo thinly from the far wall.

Along the wall ran many wood tables, set with the tools and props of every refined profession: scribes' writing-reeds and clay tablets, robes and mitres for priests and priestesses, swords in ornate scabbards, senatorial togas and even a royal sceptre. She reached out and stroked its golden handle, her fingers brushing off a thick caking of dust. She tried to imagine herself as a queen, but the thought only filled her with fear.

"I don't want to be a queen," she whispered. "I don't want—"

All at once, a panic rose up from her belly, and she yearned for a draught of joyplant. Just a sip to soften the world's edges a bit; to make her forget what a labyrinth the world was. But she had no joyplant, of course; not here or anywhere in the temple complex.

Suddenly she wanted to escape this place; to see the light and speak with Belessa or Shala; to feel the way she'd felt yesterday, when they'd spoken with her.

She turned and rushed back toward the doorway she'd entered through. In her rush, the lamp's flame blew out. Ninsunu panicked. She could not breathe. Certainly she would die in this place. She groped her way blindly through the darkness, finding the wall of the corridor, following it seemingly without end until she reached the first corner; rounding the switchback and ascending, climbing toward the light she could not see, but imagined waiting for her at the top.

But when at last she reached the door she'd unlocked, it would not budge, no matter how she pushed and pulled and threw her weight against it.

"Help!" she screamed. "Someone, help me, please!"

After much pounding and screaming, she heard a heavy hammer-blow against the door's bolt. She stepped back, and a second blow sounded, then a third. She heard the wooden bar slide up against the door, which cracked open, flooding her eyes with light, even here in the dimness of the museum.

"Oh, thank the Gods!" she gasped, throwing her arms around her rescuer.

The man only grunted and pushed her away. His bald head and hairless arms marked him as a priest, and his expression was unamused. He plucked the keys from Ninsunu's belt and handed them to Belessa, who stood behind him, arms crossed.

"What in the Seven Stars were you doing down in the clay-vault?" the priestess demanded. "How did you even get down there?"

Ninsunu glanced from the priest to Belessa, and back again. "I—" she began, but did not know how to continue.

"We're not hiding any joyplant down there," Belessa said drily.

"I know that," Ninsunu exclaimed. "That's not what I—I mean, that's not at all—I would never—"

"Come on," Belessa cut her off. "I'm sure Shala will know how to get an explanation out of you."

▼▼▼
▼▼▼
▼▼

SHALA SAT BACK in her cushioned, claw-armed chair, sipped at her chilled wine, and stared sharply into Ninsunu's eyes. Plates of fresh oranges, grapes, figs, and dates sat ignored amid rays of morning sunlight filtering down through the vine-covered trellises above the high priestess's private terrace garden.

Ninsunu had scarcely touched her goblet. She could hardly even look Shala in the eye.

"I have heard," the high priestess said at last, "that the visions evoked by joyplant can linger for days, sometimes. But so long after the Expulsion..."

"It wasn't a vision!" Ninsunu burst out, drawing an icy glance from Shala. "It was a dream," she said, more respectfully. "Like the one I had before."

Shala sighed and sipped her wine again, delicate fingers rubbing at her brow. "Ninsunu, there are no ancient carvings in the clay-vault. No deep descending corridors. It's just a moldy basement on the other side of an old door."

Ninsunu's eyes widened. A chill rippled across her skin. "But—the paintings! The crowns and sceptres—" Could the high priestess really be telling the truth?

"Belessa!" Shala called.

The younger priestess came trotting across the terrace, looking none too pleased to see Ninsunu sharing the high priestess's breakfast table.

"Let us all take a walk to the archive," Shala said.

Ninsunu followed the two women across the courtyard, her throat dry with dread. The sun was fully risen now, and Shala and Belessa nodded warmly to acolytes and priestesses who padded across the courtyard on their way to midmorning prayers, or kitchen duty, or the washing-tubs. All the women smiled back mildly, their faces betraying no hint of the gossip that must be forming in their minds even now.

The archive's door stood open, though only one acolyte attended the shelves, dusting with a broom of feathers, and adjusting plaques that hung slightly askew. The young woman bowed low as Shala entered, and watched in silence as the three women strode toward the heavy wood door at the bottom of the back staircase.

"Open it," Shala commanded.

Belessa unlocked the door and lit a lamp from a stand just inside, casting a dim glow across the white-shrouded mounds inside. For a moment, Ninsunu could not move. She forced herself to step through the doorway, peering inside. The room was an ordinary basement. No colorful bas-reliefs, no tables laden with crowns and sceptres and swords. Just lumps of clay draped in linen sheets, and moist walls sprouting with efflorescences of mold.

Belessa shot her a look that demanded, *are you satisfied?* Ninsunu nodded numbly as Belessa extinguished the lamp, pulled the heavy door closed, and barred and locked it.

Ninsunu looked from Belessa's cold eyes to meet Shala's gaze. "What can this mean?" she asked, her voice scarcely more than a whisper.

"Belessa," said Shala. "Would you give us a moment to talk?"

The younger priestess barely concealed a roll of her eyes. But she nodded curtly and padded away across the archive, calling out to her acolyte to help her with some task.

Shala waited until Belessa was out of earshot, then placed a gentle arm around Ninsunu and sat down next to her on the stone stairs above the basement.

"Do you remember what I told you about your dream?" the high priestess asked.

Ninsunu nodded. "You said all those corridors Énki bid me to explore are really in my own mind."

"I wonder," Shala said, "if this vision is your way of exploring those depths."

Ninsunu shook her head, her brow furrowing. "I know what I saw," she insisted.

"We know," Shala raised a finger, "that you woke—or believed you woke—from a second dream of exploring corridors beneath the temple. We know that you returned to your senses this morning, having locked yourself in the clay-cellar."

Ninsunu coughed a humorless laugh. "So you're saying— what? That I was sleepwalking?"

"I am saying," Shala said, "that the boundaries between dream and waking, vision and reality—even between past and future—are not always so sharp as we believe them to be." She patted Ninsunu's knee. "Tell me, the last time you drowned your mind in joyplant, what was the reason?"

Ninsunu shrugged. "A thousand reasons. My father and mother drove me mad. I hated my life, day after boring day—"

"Yes, but what was it about that particular day?" Shala persisted.

Ninsunu shook her head, unsure if she even wanted to remember. She cast her mind back to the evening when she'd run out to buy the bottle from her trusted seller; an Elamu gentleman who went only by the name Nialu: "Sleep." What had sent her down the alley where Nialu kept his little shop? A memory tugged at her—a fear—

"Father and Mother confronted me at dinner that evening," she told Shala. "Told me it was time to choose a place in the world, or else choose a worthy husband."

She glanced at Shala, whose eyes were fixed on hers, wide and attentive. The high priestess nodded for her to continue.

"Father began to list so many trades and professions to me. Told me I could be a scribe, or a priestess, or marry a general or a baron—perhaps even a prince if I had the will to pursue one." She paused, shaking her head. "The more paths he spoke of, the more my head spun. I felt the weight of all these great deeds and honors of other men and women like a millstone pressing on my chest."

"You wanted none of them," Shala said softly.

"I didn't know," Ninsunu cried. "I didn't know what I wanted. I didn't want to choose, at least not right then. But Father kept pushing me, pressing me for an answer. I screamed at him to shut up, and then he—" Her voice choked, and she drew a few quick breaths. "He hit me, across the face, right there at the table. Hadn't done that since I was a girl."

Shala nodded gently. "That must've been humiliating."

Ninsunu shook her head. "I wanted to run away, and sleep, or just not think anymore. I leaped up and ran out into the street. Didn't even take my cloak with me. Father chased me, but I heard Mother telling him to let me go. I guess he did. I snuck back in through my window late that night, already half-asleep with joyplant, and two more vials unopened for later." She laughed drily. "Funny, isn't it, how our lives turn on the smallest of things. A crown. A tablet. A little vial of poppy's-milk."

Shala pursed her lips, as if pondering this. "And tell me, what you found in the clay-vault last night."

"I already told you," Ninsunu said. "Carvings of great kings and warriors. Swords and sceptres and—" She gasped, eyes widening.

Shala shrugged, a slight grin playing about her lips. "It seems as if Énki has guided you to one of those chambers he spoke of. The vaults you feared, yet yearned to explore."

"The Abyss," Ninsunu breathed. "But then—was it real, or only—?"

Shala patted Ninsunu's knee again. "We have learned something real about *you*, Ninsunu," she said, heaving herself up from the stairs with a soft grunt. "In some cases, it is wisest to let mysteries remain mysteries, to take what we can from them, and to be grateful for the opportunity."

"Wait. You said 'vaults,'" Ninsunu said, rising to join her.

Shala raised an eyebrow quizzically.

"'Vaults,' not 'vault,'" Ninsunu said. "You're saying there are more."

Shala shrugged again. "You've drunk the milk of the joyplant more than once, haven't you?"

"Well, yes." Ninsunu's eyes fell, a blush filling her cheeks. "Many more times than once."

Shala nodded. "Then I'd say we can expect further dreams. More visions, and deeper chambers."

The high priestess turned and shuffled up the stairs, across the shadowy interior of the archive.

"What do I do?" Ninsunu called after her, hurrying to keep up.

The Cradle and the Sword 141

"Why, whatever you'd like, of course," Shala answered, a playful smile dancing about her lips again. "I told you that on the day I met you."

𒐘𒐘𒐘
𒐘𒐘𒐘
𒐘𒐘𒐘

"You know," said Belessa, "You're not the only girl here who's run a bit wild in your life."

She and Ninsunu worked side by side at the laundry vats, thrusting washing-bats into big wooden barrels, where gray soapy water swirled and bubbled around tangles of linens. Ninsunu felt her strokes slipping wildly around the bottom of the barrel, and was sure one of the other acolytes would snatch her bat out of her hands in disgust. But all the other women kept their eyes on their own barrels, amusing themselves with their own quiet chatter.

"And you're far from being the only lady here," Belessa continued, grunting as the swirled the linens in her barrel, "who wanted to escape a golden cage."

Ninsunu remembered what Belessa had told her a few days ago, about how she'd gotten caught soliciting men outside the temple; how her father had flown into a rage and forced her to join herself to the temple, to join herself in marriage to the Gods, and serve as a priestess.

"I know you think I look unkindly on you," Belessa said, "but that's—to tell the truth, that's not it at all."

"I have to say," Ninsunu replied, "you haven't been very kind to me lately."

A snort of laughter escaped Belessa's lips. "After you broke into the clay-vault, then woke me up, screaming for someone to let you out?" She shook her head. "I've got a long temper,

Ninsunu, but imagine if our roles were reversed, and you'd been given charge of the archive."

Ninsunu stared into Belessa's eyes for a long moment. "I've been seeing things," she said at last, so quietly the priestess had to lean close to hear her.

Belessa's brow furrowed. "What things?" Her expression darkened. "I swear by all the Gods, if you've been sneaking joy-plant in here—"

"I told you, I haven't touched a drop!" Ninsunu snapped. "It's not like that."

Belessa shook her head. "Then what is it like? Please, tell me."

Ninsunu drew a long, deep breath, let it out slowly, and raised her eyes to meet Belessa's. "I've been having dreams," she said. "Of walking in strange corridors beneath the earth, descending deeper, searching for something. I don't know what. In the dreams, I hear this voice. A voice that hums in my bones, telling me to search in deep places. Shala says—" She paused, swallowing, unsure if she should go on. "Shala says it's the voice of Énki himself."

She half-expected Belessa to laugh, or turn away in disgust, but the woman watched her with wide, curious eyes. "That's what drove you to break into the clay-vault."

"I didn't think it was a clay-vault," Ninsunu said. "I woke up just before dawn—or thought I woke up. I felt something pulling me to the archive down those stairs, toward that door. And it wasn't just a clay-vault I found. You have to believe me. I found ancient carvings of kings and monsters. Tables covered with gold sceptres and crowns and swords and priestly clothes. But when we returned with Shala, it was all gone."

Belessa's eyes turned away. For long moments, the woman seemed lost in her own thoughts.

"Perhaps it's both," she said at last.

Ninsunu's brow furrowed. "Both what?"

"Maybe this vault you found, with all these carvings and sceptres and crowns—maybe that's your vault, too." Belessa's eyes sparkled with excitement.

Ninsunu nodded. "All the things in that vault—they're all the reasons I drowned my mind in joyplant. At least, the most recent reasons."

Belessa laughed softly. "Do you know why I started selling my services outside the temple?"

Ninsunu shrugged. "Boredom?"

"My parents threw a party one night," Belessa said. "All the eligible bachelors were there. Army commanders and ship's captains and head scribes. My father pressed me to choose one of them that night. Any one of those assembled, he said; it didn't matter to him. He'd brought in the finest red wine, and beer, and joyplant and spinplant. And for the first time in—well, perhaps ever, he let me drink and smoke all I desired."

"He wanted you pliable," Ninsunu said with disgust. "Accepting."

"He wanted me to flirt shamelessly," said Belessa, "so he could auction me off, like a prize horse. Gods, he was fond of his horses, my father." She shook her head. "Anyway, he got what he wanted, though not in the way he'd hoped. I drank and smoked so much that I lost all interest in the party. I thought, why whore myself out to marry someone old and boring and rich, when I could make my own money whoring on my own terms?" She giggled. "So I snuck out the back and went to the temple to make some silver!"

Ninsunu gaped, her eyes wide with astonishment. The two women collapsed in a fit of laugher. When they'd regained some measure of composure, Belessa said, "See? You and I are not so different after all."

"But you still think I'm mad, for having these visions." Ninsunu sighed.

"I've never once called you mad." Belessa looked genuinely shocked. "Never. I only want you to stop keeping secrets from me. I'd like us to be friends. And the next time you set off on one of your nocturnal adventures, I'd like to join you. Who knows, maybe I'll get to see one of these magic chambers for myself."

For a moment, Ninsunu found herself too stunned to speak. A smile crept across her lips, and she threw her arms around Belessa's neck. The other woman patted her arm gently, and they drew apart wearing bright smiles.

"Next time," said Ninsunu.

"Wake me," Belessa replied. "Even if you think you're dreaming, come and wake me, and we'll descend into the vaults together."

"I don't think it works that way," Ninsunu said.

Belessa shrugged. "Try anyway. Promise me."

Ninsunu smiled. "All right, I promise," she said. "Of course I promise."

⟨

Ninsunu did not see Shala that evening, nor the next day, nor all the next week. She worked with Belessa, sorting artifacts in the archive, washing linen sheets and robes, chopping up mint and coriander and onions in the kitchens. She memorized most of the sunrise prayer to Shamash that was chanted each morning, though it had many verses. She learned her way around the stables, and the dormitories, and the chapels where men and women came to pray for deliverance from illness, poverty, loneliness, and many other afflictions.

And though Ninsunu dreamed of Mother and Father, and her home, and her old friends, and many other times and places, she did not dream of Énki or the vaults.

"I'm starting to think it was just an echo of the joyplant," she told Belessa one day as they swept dead leaves and stray bits of wool from the courtyard flagstones with straw brooms. "I drank two whole vials the night before they brought me here."

"But what about the deeper passages?" Belessa asked. "Didn't Shala say you had more depths to dream of?"

"I wish I knew where those depths were." Ninsunu sighed. "It was so easy the first two times. It just... happened to me, somehow."

"Have you considered..." Belessa trailed off.

"Considered what?" Ninsunu met the other woman's eyes, searching for some hint of an answer there. "I've already tried all the prayers I know and all the chants. None seem to work."

"Sacred bread," Belessa whispered. "Have you thought of trying it?"

Ninsunu's brow furrowed. "You mean the bread the priests offer to the Gods? How's that going to help us?"

Belessa shook her head. "No. There's a special kind of bread, baked from grain on which these strange little black tongues grow."

"Little tongues?" Now Ninsunu was more perplexed than before. "What are you talking about?"

"All I know is," Belessa said, "The temple pays extra for grain with these little black tongues growing on it. They make it into a secret kind of bread, for special rituals, like the Ceremony of the Descent." Belessa glanced around to make sure no one was listening, and lowered her voice to a whisper. "The bread makes you see things, dream strange dreams. It's forbidden food, of course. Food of the Gods. But I know where they keep it."

Ninsunu laughed, incredulous. But her smile fell away when she saw Belessa's solemn expression. "You can't be serious," she said. "Forbidden food? Strange dreams? Can you imagine what Shala would say? The whole reason I'm here in the first place is to stop me from drinking joyplant."

"Yes," Belessa agreed. "But you drank joyplant to make you forget. This would help you remember."

Ninsunu chewed her lip.

"If we try it, it has to be only this one time," she said after a long silence.

"'We?'" Belessa asked, a grin crossing her lips.

"Yes, both of us, on the same night." Ninsunu clenched the handle of her broom, excitement twisting in her belly. "Just enough to make us dream."

"And see if we can walk together in that place." Belessa smiled.

Ninsunu shook her head. "I don't know. You saw how much trouble I got in for breaking into the clay-vault. Why risk it?"

Belessa laughed softly. "It's easier than you think. I know a place in the spice-cellar where they keep a few loaves."

Ninsunu's eyes widened. "You mean you've—?"

"Just sampled a few bites, once or twice." Belessa grinned mischievously. "Like I said, you're not the only girl here who's a bit wild. Shh! Here come the sacrifice-priestesses!"

Securing the sacred bread turned out to be even easier than Ninsunu expected. She and Belessa had kitchen duty that afternoon, which meant both of them spent hours scurrying around the spice-cellar to fetch salt and cumin and black pepper. The cookery-priestesses kept close eyes on Ninsunu, but Belessa neatly palmed a small loaf when no one was looking, and slipped it into her belt.

Ninsunu was almost too excited to eat dinner or remember her sunset prayers. Her heart pounded—not only at the prospect of tasting the strange bread, but at the chance of walking those mysterious corridors beneath the earth; and at the thrill of doing something so wrong. She hadn't felt so clever since she was a little girl. She'd forgotten how delicious it tasted.

That night after sunset, Belessa knocked quietly at Ninsunu's bedroom door. Ninsunu opened it quickly and practically yanked Belessa inside, drawing a surprised squeal from the other woman.

"Did anyone see you?" Ninsunu demanded.

Belessa laughed. "Who do you think I am? Of course no one saw me."

She drew a small round loaf out of a fold in her robe. The bread was flecked with tiny seeds, and strange dark swirls ran through it.

Ninsunu wrinkled her nose. "Are you sure this is safe?"

Belessa laughed, broke the loaf in half, and devoured her portion in a few bites.

Ninsunu took a careful bite of her own half. The bread was dry and slightly bitter, with an undertaste like mold that made her gag faintly. Somehow she choked it down.

"I'd better go," said Belessa.

"Go?" Ninsunu's eyes widened. "I thought we were doing this together."

"We are," Belessa said softly. "In our dreams. But if anyone sees I'm not in my room..." She mimed locking a door and throwing away the key.

Then suddenly, Belessa leaned forward and kissed her, full on the lips. Just a peck, but enough to make Ninsunu squeal with surprise. She grasped Belessa's head and kissed her again, harder. Now both of them were laughing quietly, and Ninsunu wanted to run her hands all over Belessa's body, but Belessa pulled away.

"Before anyone notices," she said, giving Ninsunu's hand a final squeeze, and throwing a smile behind her as she slipped out the door.

Ninsunu lay back on her small, lumpy mattress, tasting the bread on her lips, its earthy scent mingling wonderfully with the taste of Belessa.

"How strange," she whispered to herself. "How strange life is."

A softness spread through her, covering her like a soft blanket, lifting her like a mattress. As she floated, a smile began to cross her lips. She closed her eyes. Just before the dream carried her away, she remembered what she and Belessa had agreed.

"The vaults," she whispered. "We will go to the vaults."

She repeated these words until they transmuted themselves into a song of foreign syllables and lost all meaning. Still she muttered them, these strange words whose meaning she had forgotten.

Then, at last, the dream took her.

⟨Y

Perhaps it was not a dream. Perhaps she really did rise from her bed in the moonlight, to pad softly down the hall where Belessa waited for her, silent as a ghost. Perhaps the two of them really did creep out across the courtyard, amid the ranks of shadows cast by palm trees, beneath the stars.

But if this was not a dream, the archive building seemed to rush toward Ninsunu in a way unknown in waking life, as if this journey unspooled according to some predetermined rhythm of its own.

They hurried among high shelves packed with statues and tablets of every time and provenance, down the staircase at the back, Belessa clicking the lock in the key; Ninsunu lifting the heavy bolt and swinging the door wide.

Together they lit lamps and glided down the descending corridors, switching back and back again as they plunged deeper beneath the earth. They passed through the clay-vault with its white-shrouded mounds and cracked carvings, and saw the tables set with swords and sceptres, crowns and tablets. But they passed on, through that room and down a staircase at its far side, whose stone-hewn steps gave way to blocks of cracked mud-brick, each step casting up centuries of cobwebbed dust.

Down those clay stairs they climbed, to arrive at a door of gnarled, frail wood, its surface painted in whorls of red and black. It bore no lock; only a clay seal, which Ninsunu broke.

Belessa swung the door aside, and together they passed through the archway into a room vaster than the first.

Flames leaped up in braziers, illuminating walls covered with delicately carved reliefs in rusted copper, far more cracked and weathered than those of the room above. Thousands of tiny men and women marched like ants in neat rows striped across the walls. Some rode in chariot-wagons behind horses leaping and trampling their tiny enemies. Men carried baskets, bows, spears and daggers, leading camels, bulls and apes. They raised their hands in greeting, made ritual gestures, genuflected to one another beneath tents. Sharp-bearded kings in togas and horned helmets led armies up hills forested with green-leafed oaks and pines and junipers, where winged and haloed Gods held bowls in upraised hands, spilling streams of glimmering water onto the earth.

The room was set for a banquet. Cushioned couches waited beside hoof-legged marble tables laden with steaming plates of duck roasted in honey and cardamom; whole trout baked in butter and black pepper; racks of lamb stuffed with caramelized onions and rare black truffles; fresh-sliced cucumbers and salted lentils; sweet date rolls, soft white cheese and barley flatbread, flaky almond pastries, green figs, oranges, pomegranates, and clusters of plump purple grapes; chilled flagons of wine and pitchers of foaming beer. Ninsunu and Belessa scanned the room for any hint of the banquet's hosts or guests, but no other attendees made their presence known.

"I know this should make me hungry," Belessa said, "but I can't seem to find my appetite."

Ninsunu nodded in agreement. "This reminds me of my family's house. I used to hate banquets like this."

"Impossible to enjoy yourself among so much ritual and ceremony," Belessa said. "Mother's gossip-partners trying to tease family secrets out of you. Father's gray-haired patrons eyeing you up and down, like so much meat."

"It was on nights like this that I started drinking joyplant," Ninsunu said. She strode around the nearest couch, running a finger along its delicate brass-work. "It was at a banquet just like this, actually. You know, there's no lonelier feeling than sitting in a room full of people who don't understand you."

Belessa hummed in agreement.

"My friend Rubati would bring a vial," Ninsunu went on. "We'd sneak sips under the tablecloth. Before long, I found I didn't mind hearing about who wanted to sleep with whom, who was richer than whom, who was heading out on which campaign. Someone was playing a lyre. It sounded so sweet, and I just... let the song carry me away."

Belessa huffed. "Who ever came up with all this nonsense? Banquets and marriages. Kings and Gods. Such a strange game."

Ninsunu gazed over the ornate furniture; the plates piled high with fruits and meats; the tall lyres in the corners and the carvings on the walls. "It's just... life, I suppose," she said.

"Someone had to come up with it first," Belessa said.

Ninsunu turned to her. "What does it matter now? It's the game everyone plays. Well, everyone except us, I suppose. Lucky ones that we are."

A smile crossed Belessa's face. "Does that mean you'll stay?"

"Stay?" Ninsunu shook her head, confused. She had no wish to stay at this ghostly banquet.

"At the temple, silly," said Belessa, throwing her arms around Ninsunu's shoulders. "Stay with us. No need to play those silly games anymore."

Part of Ninsunu wanted to say yes, but she couldn't seem to form the words. "I—I need to—"

A deep groan echoed through the chamber. Both women whirled, raising lamps to seek its source, but no movement disturbed the dust. The sound rose again: a low, deep rumbling that shook the cobwebs. It seemed to emanate from the far end of the banquet-hall. Ninsunu glanced at Belessa, paralyzed by dream-fear, frozen in terror, yet compelled to seek the source.

She felt herself drawn toward the sound. Even as Belessa reached out to hold her back, she raced across the floor, knocking cushions off couches, scattering platters of fruit; clouds of dust erupting in the firelight.

The thrumming echoed up from a vast round well; a stone shaft large enough to swallow a small house. A staircase coiled around its edges, spiraling downward into shadow. Behind her, Belessa was crying out, pleading with her to stop. Ninsunu placed a slipper on the first stair, her other foot on the second, and began to pad down the steps, around the rim of the well.

Her lamp's flickering glow cast shadows across mosaics of shell and deep blue stone: parades of bald-headed men in shaggy sheepskin kilts, carrying fish and birds and vessels of beer to smiling lords seated in tall chairs; laborers bearing baskets of bricks toward great temples; men in donkey-drawn wagons, spears upraised against enemies trampled beneath their wheels; women in long wool garments, plucking lyres and scattering flower-petals.

All these scenes she passed, and many more besides; all mosaicked in rough, simple style, inlaid with fragments of red and blue limestone, pale alabaster, and gleaming mother-of-pearl. Down and down she climbed, winding serpentine around the neck of that great chasm, past scenes of slain armies pecked at by vultures; rows of marching warriors in leopardskin cloaks and round bronze helmets; hooved men dancing in thickets; men with the bodies of scorpions, or of bulls; great birds with lions' heads. Belessa's voice faded to a faint echo, then to nothing, as the upper reaches of the well closed in, far above Ninsunu's head.

She did not know how long she descended. Hours, perhaps, or days, as she trod on thousands of steps, feeling no hunger or thirst but the yearning to reach the bottom and find what lay there.

Until at last she stepped from stair onto hard-packed dirt, and knew she could descend no further. She raised her lamp and scanned the walls of a cavern whose ceiling soared too high for lamplight to reach, leaving the rooms' upper reaches blanketed in shadow.

Bones littered the floor of the cavern: skulls and ribs and jawbones of men and women, and wolves and gazelle and oryx, and many other beasts besides; the newest of them gleaming white, the oldest yellowed, cracking and crumbling to dust as she trod on them.

The paintings and carvings on these walls seemed older than any on the way down. No long-robed women here, no kilted men on thrones. Here on these rock walls, naked warriors thrust knives into the bellies of black-spotted leopards. Great clawed serpents coiled about shaggy beasts like oryx and bulls, biting into necks and backs, spilling bright red blood while broad-winged white birds with lions' heads soared above.

It all looked so terribly violent and cruel; yet, at the same time, so simple and straightforward. No temples or palaces here. No banquets or kings or fine linens. Just the earth and its beasts, and the men and women who brought forth the will of their hearts into the world.

Though she could not say why, Ninsunu felt hot tears rising in her eyes. She felt as if she could sit down right here with her lamp. She wished she could watch these scenes dance in the firelight forever.

But that is exactly what's happening, a familiar voice hummed in her bones.

She jumped, startled. Though she'd heard nothing, she could feel the God speaking to her; within her. Énki was here.

"I thought you'd forgotten me," she whispered into the lamplit darkness, her eyes darting over the bright reds and blacks and whites of the murals.

Do you like my stories? the God's voice thrummed.

"You—you made all these paintings and carvings?" Ninsunu asked.

Not I, hummed the God. *You made them. All of you.*

Ninsunu thought of the hunters and beasts on the walls of this cave; the kilted priests and wool-clad women on the well-shaft; the warriors and armies in the banquet-hall above; the gold-crowned kings and dragons in the clay-vault. "There are so many," she said, feeling stupid for having nothing more clever to offer.

Indeed there are, the God replied. *I am proud to say so.*

"But I like these best," she told him. "The simple ones. The men and women, and the animals, and the earth. Nothing else."

She felt something like a smile hum through her body. *I loved it too*, the God's voice hummed.

"Then why did you let it change?" she asked.

I did not change anything, the God told her.

She shook her head. "I don't understand. Why couldn't everything stay like this? Why'd we have to have kings and cities, palaces and banquets and wars? Why can't we just live the way these people did?"

But you do, hummed the God's voice. *You do, and always have.*

"No we don't!" she cried. "The world isn't like this anymore."

Your world is this world, hummed the voice. *This is easy to see, when you start the story from the beginning and follow it straight through. There is no yesterday. There is only—*

A great clap like thunder shook the cavern. Suddenly Ninsunu knew the God was gone. She panted in the sudden silence, trying to catch her breath.

Hearing footsteps from the shadows, she raised her lamp. A young girl was creeping out of the darkness. For an instant, Ninsunu thought this might be a sign from the God. A vision of her younger self, sent to remind her where her own story started.

"Are you me?" she asked the girl.

The girl furrowed her brow, perplexed. It had been a silly question; the girl looked nothing like Ninsunu, even when she'd been young. This girl's hair was lighter, decked with colorful feathers, her arms crisscrossed by tattoos of strange geometric design. She was wrapped in a loose garment of woven flax, fringed with tassels of polished shell and bone.

"No, you can't be me," Ninsunu said. "We don't look anything alike. So who are you?"

"I'm Zeru," said the girl. "Who are you?"

What did the God mean, sending this strange young girl to her? Ninsunu laughed, unable to make any sense of this vision. "First paintings, then riddles. Now some girl who's just as confused as I am."

"Which people do you come from?" the girl asked suddenly, jarring Ninsunu.

What a strange question. "I'm from Urim, of course," Ninsunu said. "Where are you from?"

"I'm of the Fishing People," said the girl. "What kind of place is Urim?"

This conversation was making less sense with every word. Everyone knew Urim. How could she describe it?

"It's a city," Ninsunu said. "You know, Urim? The great ancient city of Urim?" Surely the girl must recognize the name. Urim had been a holy city for four thousand years.

The girl furrowed her brow. "I've never heard of it. Do you have a temple there?"

Another unexpected question. Ninsunu couldn't help it; she burst out laughing, unable to find any thread to follow. "Well, yes," she said after a moment. "We have the temple, and underneath that we have the ruins of an older one, and beneath that one older still, all the way down to—to this, I suppose. Wherever this is."

"They say the temple at the Abzu is very old," said the girl. "I wonder if yours is older."

"The Abzu?" That name tugged at a vague memory in Ninsunu. An old piece of poetry; something she'd heard as a child: *All the lands were sea, then Eridu was made on the shores of the Abzu.* That was it—Eridu was said to be the first city on earth, built on the shore of a great freshwater lake called the Abzu, in whose depths the God Énki was said to dwell. Eridu must be no more than ruins now, if it ever existed in the first place.

"The Abzu? But Eridu hasn't existed for—" Ninsunu started to say. But as she spoke the words, everything suddenly snapped into place. "That's who you are!" Ninsunu's eyes went wide. "You're the very first!"

The girl flinched away. "The first what? What are you talking about?"

The God had brought her down here, through vaults of stories reaching further and deeper back in time. He'd told her to find the beginning of the story, and follow it from there. Then he'd disappeared, and now here stood—

"I don't expect you to believe me," Ninsunu said, "but—on some far-distant day, people like me are going to dig up the stories left by people like you."

The girl wrinkled her nose. "How can you dig up a story?"

Ninsunu laughed with the thrill of it. "That's it exactly!" she exclaimed, waving a finger at the girl. "You don't have any way to write your stories yet. There's no writing yet. Ha! Which is why you have to tell them. But someday, someone will stamp them on clay. And we'll be able to dig them up, and find out what this was all about, at the very beginning! You see? That's how we'll find out what all this was meant to be, when it all started!"

That yearning pulled Ninsunu deeper into the cavern, toward a place where the bone-littered floor cracked and yawned, and a chasm plunged away beneath her feet, its fathoms swirling with deep blue water. She plummeted down the chasm and into the sea, surprised to find the water warm. Great river-carp swam slowly, gracefully around her, their long moustaches waving in the current, their eyes alive with unspoken wisdom. Sparkling lights of every color swum above and below and all around her, dancing like millions of shooting stars.

Not yet, the God's voice hummed within her. *You will know this place, but not yet.*

Still further below, darker waters swirled; a vortex of impenetrable shadow that drew her ever downward. She tried to kick and swum upward, but the dark, salty water pulled at her; tendrils of icy cold caressed her legs, her belly, her arms.

The colored lights fell away above her. The titan river-carp whirled and fled upward into the luminous depths. From somewhere deep within the darkness below her, a voice rumbled; or rather, a thousand voices—a swarm, hissing and buzzing, arguing and berating in a babble of tongues.

Ninsunu screamed, but only bubbles burst forth from her mouth. She called for the God, but no answer came. The thousand voices howled, and she screamed harder, and harder still, until at last a thin wail rose from her, and she was plummeting upward out of the salt-choked depths; up through the warm water, up out of the chasm and through the caverns beneath the world.

She reeled through paintings of red and black and white; carvings of obsidian and mother-of-pearl; banquets and mosaics and swords and sceptres and crowns and inscriptions on clay. And out of that darkness, she plunged up into her body and her bed, lurching upright to gasp and shake, sweat-covered, in the first rays of dawn.

〈𒀭𒀭

Belessa ran to Ninsunu at sunrise prayers, giddy with excitement.

"We did it," she whispered. "Didn't we?"

"I—I'm not sure." Ninsunu shook her head, wrapping her arms around her friend. "Tell me what you saw."

"The same things you saw, silly." Belessa laughed. "We went down to that room with all the old carvings and paintings, with the tables set for a banquet."

They gazed into each others' eyes, astonished.

"Were we dreaming?" Ninsunu whispered.

Belessa shrugged. "I'm not sure. I think so. Anyway, you disappeared. We heard a noise, and you ran off."

Ninsunu nodded. "Something pulled at me."

"Where did you go?" Belessa asked.

But the older priestesses were pulling them apart, reminding them to go splash their foreheads with water from the basin at the sanctuary's entrance—a reminder of the waters of the Abzu, from which all craft and creativity had sprung forth at the world's dawn—then to kneel before the altar and recite the morning liturgy to Shamash, God of the warm and nourishing sun.

After prayers, Belessa had to go help in the kitchens, while Ninsunu was assigned to feed the temple's sheep and goats. As she paced around the sheep-pen, scattering grain from a basket, Ninsunu tried to think of how to tell Belessa of her descent into the well; the cavern of paintings and bones, and the strange young girl, and the riddles of the God who'd spoken within her. She couldn't find any words that fit. She could scarcely make sense of it herself. Yet she felt sure the God had spoken the truth: *start the story from the beginning and follow it straight through...*

That evening, she went to see Shala. The high priestess was poring over old clay tablets in her office, a small blue-painted room at the very top of the great ziggurat, high above the temple complex. Ninsunu arrived panting and gasping, the only other sounds the whistling of the wind and the songs of twilight insects, and the scratching of the high priestess's reed against papyrus. As Ninsunu stumbled into the chambers, Shala rose from behind her ornate dragon-footed desk, greeting the young girl with a formal bow and a tight smile, as if she had better things to do.

"I'm sorry to bother you," Ninsunu said.

"Well, you've climbed all this way." Shala smiled and shrugged. "What's on your mind, my dear?"

"It's just—" Ninsunu began, and found, once again, that the right words would not come.

Shala pulled out a chair for her. "Sit," she said. "Take your time."

"I've been talking with Belessa," Ninsunu said, sinking to the chair's cushioned seat.

"I thought you girls would get along," Shala replied.

"Yes, we—" Ninsunu nearly let slip a word about the sacred bread and the dreams, but decided to hold that secret back for now. "We've been spending a lot of time in the archives." That much was true. "And I've been thinking about—well, about stories, I suppose. Stories of where we come from."

"You've had more of those dreams," Shala said. "Haven't you?"

Ninsunu blushed. She yearned to tell Shala everything, but the truth might get her expelled from this place forever. "Yes," she said at last. "I've had more of the dreams."

Shala nodded. "And what depths in yourself has the God led you to explore?"

Ninsunu bit her lip, unsure if she could put her thought into words. "I went back to the beginning," she said after a moment. "Back before anything went wrong. I needed the joy-plant, you see—or thought I needed it—because everything had gotten so tangled up, and I didn't know how to untangle it. But I realized, I don't have to untangle it. I can start from the beginning, and then maybe it won't seem so tangled anymore. Oh, I'm not making any sense, am I?"

"You're making more sense than you know, child," Shala said softly.

Ninsunu stared at her hands in her lap, her face still flushed with embarrassment.

"I want to show you something," Shala said after a moment.

Ninsunu gulped. "What sort of thing?"

Shala looked up and laughed softly. "Just a place I like to walk, when I lose sight of myself. Would you walk with me?"

"It's almost dark," said Ninsunu.

"And I," said Shala, "am Princess and High Priestess of Urim. Come on. It isn't far."

They descended the ziggurat's thousand steps together, their lamps casting soft orange glows into the darkness. They strolled across the temple's tiled courtyard under the moonlight—almost alone in all that space, except for the palms, rustling in the night breeze, and the occasional acolyte who hurried from one building to another, barely sparing them a glance; then past the vast sanctuary building, around its soaring limestone arches and colonnaded walls mosaicked in intricate geometries of blue and yellow stone.

At least they reached the far side of the temple complex, where only a few old buildings stood. Among those small mud-brick shacks, a labyrinth of short crumbled walls of ancient mud-brick lay sunken into the earth.

"What is this place?" asked Ninsunu.

"It is called the Gipáru," Shala replied, raising her lamp to illuminate the winding pits. "It was a beautiful sanctuary once, long ago. Only for women. Men were forbidden to enter, on pain of death."

Ninsunu nodded, impressed. "Won't someone rebuild it, like the ziggurat?"

"Someday, perhaps. But for now, only I may explore these ruins, to retrieve what artifacts I can for my archive."

Shala hiked up her skirts and climbed down into a narrow pit between two walls of crumbled brick.

"Artifacts," said Ninsunu. "You mean like those cones and statues?"

"Maybe," said Shala. "But mostly what I've found here are tablets."

"Like the ones the scribes write at the school."

"Well, something like that," said Shala. "I find poetry, mostly. Particularly the poetry of a priestess named Énheduanna."

"I remember that name. You were translating her poems on the day I—well, the day first met you."

"Indeed I was." Shala smiled softly. "Would you like to hear a bit of one? It's called 'The Exaltation of Inanna.'"

Ninsunu shrugged. "Why not?"

"You don't speak any classical Shuméru, by any chance?"

"I'm afraid I don't." Ninsunu cast her eyes down, faintly ashamed.

"Not to worry," Shala said. "I'll recite a bit in Aramaya."

She sat on the edge of a collapsed wall and recited these lines in a soft, sweet voice:

I have been driven forth from my house,
Forced to flee the nest like a bird.
My life is devoured,
And I walk among the mountain thorns.
My boat has landed in an enemy land.
There will I die, singing my song.

They sat in silence for a while, breathing the cool night air, listening to the chirp of insects and the whistle of the wind through the crumbled bricks.

"Of course, it's much more beautiful in the original Shuméru," said Shala, smiling.

"When did she write that?" Ninsunu asked.

"A long time ago," said Shala. "Long before the Ashůru Empire's reign of terror. Before the First Empire of Babili before them, or the great Shuméru Renaissance centuries before that. Long before all those things, Énheduanna wrote those words. Two thousand years ago, or more."

"All those names and years," said Ninsunu. "My mind can't make any sense of them."

"Nor mine, sometimes." Shala laughed.

"I mean—no offense, but it's all just ancient history, isn't it?"

"And yet," said Shala, "two thousand years back in that ancient history, a woman sat right here—right where we're sitting, right now—and wept for her lost home, and wrote a beautiful poem about it. A poem I love. A poem whose hurt I still feel."

"It's like those cones, isn't it?" said Ninsunu.

"How's that?"

"Those cones, in your archive. The ones the kings buried under their temples, with their names and all that inscribed on them."

"Hmm. Perhaps I should bury my own poetry for some future priestess to find."

"Maybe," said Ninsunu. "Or maybe you've already built your own—what's this place called?—your own Gipáru. That archive of yours. I mean, it seems like a wonderful place, and I hope it stands for a thousand years. I truly do. But, you know, someday—"

Ninsunu glanced over to see if she'd said something out of order, but Shala was already nodding in agreement.

"You know, I'd been wondering about that," Shala said. "How to leave something of myself for excavators like me, long centuries in the future. But I hadn't even thought of what you just said." She smiled. "Perhaps you're right. Perhaps I've already made the work they'll dig up."

"Some priestess can build an archive of your archive someday. 'An Exhibit on the Ancient Archive of Én-nigaldi-Nannár.' Wouldn't that be a sight to see?"

Shala laughed. "Well, all things rise and pass away."

"And through it all," Ninsunu said, "the cycles themselves remain."

"That's right," said Shala, smiling. "Quite a memory you've got there."

They sat in silence a while longer, listening to the insects sing in the night.

"I've got to teach an early-morning class tomorrow," Shala said at last. "I hope I'll see you there."

Ninsunu thought for a moment. "Will you be teaching—Shuméru, you said? The language this priestess wrote in?"

Shala smiled. "If that's what you'd like to learn, then that's what I'll teach you. Of course, we'll have to start off with basic reading and writing, and then classical Shuméru grammar—" Ninsunu's face fell, and Shala chuckled softly. "Or perhaps not. Perhaps we can begin with some of Énheduanna's poems, have you translate them sign by sign, and learn that way. I always say, there's no better way to learn a language than to translate a poet you love."

Ninsunu nodded. "Yes," she said. "I'd like that. I'd like that a lot."

Shala grinned. "Tomorrow morning, then. Bright and early. And in the meantime, I'd better catch what sleep these old bones can."

Ninsunu helped her up out of the ruins of the Gíparu. They made their way back around the base of the Great Ziggurat, the Étemenníguru, built on the bones of so many ziggurats and temples before it. Ninsunu had never given any of that the slightest thought before, but she was thinking about it now. She thought of that sad priestess so long ago, writing poems in this very same place, and suddenly nothing felt distant at all. Everything felt near, and very warm and familiar, all at the same time.

That was what Ninsunu thought about as she walked back to her small room with Shala leaning on her arm under the moonlight, listening to the soft night breeze and the chirping of the insects in the palms.

101 YEARS EARLIER
631 BC

*I read the cunning tablets of Shumér,
And the dark Akkadu language
Which is difficult to rightly use.
I took my pleasure in reading stones
Inscribed before the Flood.*

— The History of Ash'shúr-bani-apli

𐎊

The King of Kings was dying. This in itself was no great surprise, as dying was what old men did. And had the emperor been any ordinary man, his dying might have caused no great disturbance. But he was the Emperor of the World, Lord of the Four Quarters; and rumors of his illness fueled a whispered panic throughout the palace complex. The star called Marutúk was in the House of the Scorpion. Flocks of crows had been sighted flying west. The omens were dark.

Slipping through the gardens of the Royal Palace of Ninua, Nura overheard men muttering on the other side of a topiary. "Twin sons," said one.

The speaker hadn't the slightest idea Nura was there, and she paused for a moment to listen.

"None of us says what we all know is true," he was saying. "With the twins, there's no chance of a clean succession. Whichever son he appoints, the other will challenge."

"Fifty years of peace and profit, and now this," another voice sighed. "We'll have a grand old civil war, like in my grandfather's time."

"Will you back us, then, when the time comes?" asked the first voice.

"What's the offer?" said the other. "I assume we're talking about a council post, at the very—" He paused. "Wait. Do you hear that?"

"Hear what?"

"Someone's there."

By the time they peered through the topiary, she was gone, strolling with calculated casualness next to the fish pond a good distance away. That had been close. The lawful penalty for speaking with one of the emperor's women—even looking at one unveiled—was execution; often for both parties. Such ancient punishments weren't enforced now as often as they were centuries before, under less enlightened monarchs. But one could never be too careful.

Still, she'd managed to catch a glimpse of the would-be conspirators: the older one half-bald, plump but muscular, square-jawed and thick of beard, wearing a loose tunic of deep crimson, belted with a thick leather strap that held two sharp bronze daggers, wrapped in a long indigo cloak fringed in soft fleece; the younger one slender, with a carefully preened goatee and a lush emerald-dyed robe fringed in gold, draped in a finely worked silver necklace studded with rubies. She imprinted these details on her mind and stowed them away for later use.

A litany from her eshêru training, practiced in secret by a small cabal of women in the emperor's harem, ran through her mind:

Even in motion, I am still.
Even in sight, I walk invisibly.
I move as the world moves.
The world moves as I will.

She slipped beneath the towering archway that divided the complex's outer gardens and buildings from the halls of the central palace itself, where thin shafts of evening sunlight lanced down through narrow, high-set windows. Her black robes wafted loosely around her body; black veil covering her face. She headed for a doorway flanked by stone statues of ancient Shuméru gods with the stern, bearded faces and torsos of men, but the tails and fins of fish. Strange old gods, she thought. So utterly unlike the one true God, Ash'shûr.

Two spearmen in full copperscale armor stood guard in front of the statues, on either side of the door.

Her first thought was that she could take both of them down. In an eyeblink, her muscles and mind mapped the sequence of steps: *a fake lunge toward the guard on the left, then a step aside and a tap at just the right point on the other's neck as he made a grab for her...*

The guards nodded curtly, and tipped their spears aside to let her pass.

She moved on, black robes swirling, through that looming doorway, down a narrower series of hallways leading to the palace's maze of inner buildings and gardens—and ultimately, to the central keep where the emperor's bedroom lay. She walked briskly under the glow of flickering torches, past intricate mosaics of polished stone, and brightly glazed bas-reliefs of the emperor plunging his holy spear down the throats of lions and foreigners and rebellious tribal chiefs.

As she turned a corner, she passed two men she barely knew—a high-ranking eunuch of some sort, all coiffed curls and embroidered robes; and a lower-ranking eunuch, plump and bald-headed, wearing only a simple toga. The eunuchs were whispering intently, their faces cast in shadow by the torches. They fell silent, eyeing her carefully as she hurried by.

Even in motion, I am still, she thought. *Even in sight, I walk invisibly.*

As she slipped out of hearing range, she heard the high-ranking eunuch say, "I recognize her steps. She's his latest favorite. We'll have to—"

But she didn't hear the rest, because now she'd turned down a narrower passage, its walls adorned with natural scenes of birds and fishes among the reeds of a river. Behind heavy iron-barred doors, she dimly heard—or thought she heard—the emperor's pet lions roaring in the yard; his elephants trumpeting; his apes hooting and his hawks and falcons screeching, and the exotic birds in his menagerie singing their thousand songs.

At the end of this passage lay a locked door, its archway framed in dim torchlight. Nura knocked twice, then three times, then once, then twice again. The door opened. A slave-girl bowed and smiled as Nura passed through, then closed and bolted the thick door behind her.

She strode down a narrower hallway: one of the palace complex's many hidden corridors, whose entrances and passwords were closely guarded, revealed only to those servants of the emperor who'd been summoned for some special task. On the evening Nura had first been summoned to the emperor's bed, a eunuch had visited her in the harem, leaned in close and whispered the location of the door, along with the sequence of knocks to access this particular passage. But she knew many more existed, whose doors and knocks she would never learn. Legend held that the emperor's father had kidnapped seventy-seven architects to design these secret corridors, then buried them all alive beneath the palace's walls, so none but the emperor and his line would ever know the labyrinth's full extent.

Inward Nura hurried, through honeycombs of small, ornate buildings scented with sandalwood and attar, whose smoke drifted in lazy strands up from braziers in the corners, amid the soft light of oil lamps, so much smoother and steadier than the light of the torches in the outer hallways. Here there were no sculptures of battle—only painted reliefs of flowers and bushes, and carefully tended beds of flowers, and trimmed little trees bearing oranges and lemons, and burbling fountains filled with darting golden fish.

Some harpist in a nearby alcove plucked out the familiar strains of "The Lion and the Dog," each ringing note as languid as the smoke and lamplight. Nura found herself half-humming a few lines:

"Weigh your worth against me," the false king howled,
Atop his high wall, across the rushing river...

No upstart noblemen haunting these gardens, thank Heaven. A few eunuchs shuffling quietly by; high-born women and their retinues reclining on enormous silk cushions, plucking figs and grapes and baked delicacies from gold platters. Almond-skinned ladies of Misr, dragged here from their palaces on the Nile; dark-haired Urartu women from the mountainous plateaus in the north; pale, freckled Adnanu girls from the islands of the Great Western Sea; princesses of Babili, dripping with gold rings and glimmering jewels; warrior-queens of Kush, with braided black hair and skin as brown as earth; narrow-eyed Elamu women from the Zagros Mountains far to the east, their tan faces tattooed with strange cyphers of dots and stripes. Princesses and chieftains' daughters hauled from provinces near and far, like the fine Adnanu wine in their gold goblets and the Babili dates they nibbled—an empire in miniature, existing at the World-Lord's whim and pleasure.

Nura passed quietly among the trellises and trees, attracting little notice, aside from a few stares from jealous women in the baths. She supposed she'd have felt the same in their position. There they sat, naked in the wine-stained water, waiting for a call from the emperor, turning to watch her hurry to his quarters.

After the baths, Nura passed through the nursery, where a gaggle of royal children played on wood horses and dolls, or chased wildly after each other, or after balls and hoops and other toys, in games of their own invention. Nura dodged through the mess, passed down a long flower-lined promenade, to arrive at last at the entryway of the palace's central keep.

The outer foyer stood mostly bare, aside from two small claw-footed chairs near the great inner door, and great wall carvings of the Emperor-as-High-Priest, offering incense and herbs to the God Ash'shûr. Two helmeted guards stood at attention to either side of the inner chamber's door, iron-tipped spears upraised.

Nura approached them and spoke a password. One asked her a question in response, and she responded with the second password. Eyeing her carefully, though she knew he'd seen her before, the guard stood aside, and the two guards together unbolted the heavy wooden door and heaved it open.

The emperor's chambers dwarfed every other room in the palace complex, aside from the throne room itself. The bedroom's ceiling soared above the roofs of the surrounding rooms, admitting rays of pale moonlight through tiny, high-set windows. Sweet-smelling braziers and lamps cast their soft glow across a polished limestone floor covered in embroidered carpets of the finest patterned silk, and in the skins of lions and leopards, and of stranger beasts: horses striped black-and-white; long-necked creatures with brown-mottled skin; great lizards with gnarled dark-green hides—all sent as gifts from vassal-kings in the far-off reaches of the empire, to receive the honor of being trampled by the World-Lord's bedroom slippers.

A vast marble table, long enough for a banquet, had been set with fattened duck baked in honeyed pistachios; rack of lamb roasted in wine and black truffles; plates of white and blue-marbled cheeses; loaves of sesame wheat-bread and flaky pastry; black and green olives; towers of sweet Babili dates, ripe purple figs, grapes, and pomegranates; sweet-rolls spiced with cardamom. And more exotic fruits lay on platters, candied or soaked in honey: green and yellow melons brought from Misr, plump quinces from K'nan, pink Elamu melons with green-striped rinds, and berries of deep blue and bright red sent from the island lords of the Great Sea, far in the west.

This feast sat mostly untouched, as did the great writing-desk with its stacks of scrolls and clay tablets. At the far end of the room—so far it almost looked small—sprawled the emperor's bed, a mountain of tasseled cushions and pillows of golden silk, draped in soft, ornate curtains from the carved cedar posts at its corners.

And on that bed, his head propped up by cushions and pillows, his body shrouded in an embroidered robe of deepest purple silk, lay the most powerful man on earth.

NURA BOWED LOW, into her knees, forehead touching the rugs. But the emperor was already saying, "Stop that, Nura."

"I beg your forgiveness, Lord Emperor," she said, approaching the bed without looking up.

"Nura," he said, "If you don't stop that this instant, I shall hurl this pillow at you."

"Can you score a hit from that angle?" she asked, a smile spreading across her face.

"You dare question my aim?"

"I am too afraid to find out, O Perfect One," she said, pulling off her veil and headscarf and tossing them to the floor. She leapt up onto the bed and plumped down beside him, setting off an avalanche of cushions and pillows, both of them laughing and pulling each other close as she planted tiny kisses about his forehead and neck.

The emperor lay in a voluminous indigo robe, fringed with tassels of gold thread; belted with thick golden ropes; filigreed with an intricate honeycomb of dragons' claws, among which a thousand tiny suns shone against tiles of white. His skin was thin and mottled, yet hard old muscles rolled beneath that wrinkled parchment. His face, like his hands, bore deep creases; chasms between his thick black brows; at the edges of his pursed, hawk-like lips. The vast curls of hair and beard about that face were dyed black to hide the whiteness that crept up from their roots. But his dark eyes—such deep chestnut that they, too, seemed almost black—still gazed at her with a young man's sharpness.

She'd heard tales of those sharp eyes from some of the old generals. Eyes that could stare right into the eyes of a rebellious chieftain, look inside that man and see every detail of his plans, and stay locked on that man's eyes as the emperor commanded, *Let this man's last sight in this world be that of his sons, flayed and crucified before him.* Eyes that could gaze into the eyes of wild lions without wavering, so the lions would flinch for a moment, and in that moment the emperor would plunge his spear straight down the lion's throat.

Nura wasn't sure how many of these stories she believed. But here, looking into those eyes for herself, she understood the feeling that must have inspired them—the sense that the emperor knew everything about you just by looking into your eyes, and through them. Maybe that was why he trusted her.

"You are frightened, my love," said the emperor.

"Not of you," she said.

"Not of me now, no," he said, "but what I'm capable of."

How quickly he saw the heart and struck at it!

She tried changing the subject. "You are capable of more than many assume, Lord Emperor," she said. "How goes your work translating the tablets from before the Flood?"

He stared at her—into her—for a long moment.

"Who says I am incapable of this?" he asked.

She stammered for a moment, then caught and composed herself, scolding herself for letting him catch her off guard like this.

"No one has said it out loud, lord, at least not that I recall. But for the world's mightiest warrior-king to also be such an advanced scholar in ancient texts—" She trailed off.

He sighed, and sat silently for a few breaths. "Shuméru is an impossible language," he said. "Even classical Akkadu is dark and difficult. It seems so similar to modern Aramaya, but that ancient grammar is enough to drive a man mad. I don't know how people kept it all straight."

"I love the old Akkadu poetry you've taught me. '*Enûma elish la nabu shámamu*'—"

"'*La nabu'ú shámamu*,'" he corrected her gently. "'When the sky above was not yet named'—"

"—'*Shaplish ammatum shuma la zakrat*,'" she finished.

"—'Nor did the earth below yet bear a name,'" he echoed. "A thousand years old, that poem is. Did you know that? I ordered it brought here all the way from the archives of Urim. I'm blessed to have it in my library."

"Your library is blessed with many ancient writings. This is why you are the wisest among all rulers."

He looked at her and frowned. "You should know better than to try that kind of flattery on me. I'm an old man, Nura, and I'm tired of that shit."

"You're right, my lord. It was a stupid thing to say."

"Anyway, I'm not wise enough to make much sense of these ancient Shuméru texts." He laughed. "You know I had a monument made a few years ago with an inscription—I had the scribe write, 'I, the World-Lord, read the tablets from before the Flood.' Oh, I can read the symbols all right—some of them, anyway."

He heaved himself out of bed and padded over to his gilded work-desk, his thick-folded purple robes dragging behind him.

He shuffled through some of the oldest clay tablets; the palest and most cracked; the ones as old as stone but as fragile as plaster.

"I'll be damned if I can make sense of these sentences," he said, gesturing with one tablet that looked as though it might crumble to dust at any moment. "It's the grammar of madmen, all backward and upside-down. Ha!" He barked a laugh. "Maybe the Shuméru were all mad. Maybe that's the key. Maybe I should go mad, too! Then I'll understand what they were trying to say. There've been mad kings before, haven't there? What's one more mad king, in the great sweep of history?"

"One thing's certain," said Nura. "You're not mad."

"Oh no?"

"No. I've known mad men. And you, lord, are not numbered among them."

He humphed softly, laid the tablet down with great care, and returned to the bed to lie among the pillows. She stroked his chest and rubbed his shoulders, making him wince and stretch so she could adjust her grip to massage those spots.

Unlike some women in the World-Lord's harem, she made no attempt to reach downward now, or to nibble his ear or kiss his neck. The emperor had sent many women away for trying these things at the wrong moment. That was the gossip in the harem, and some of those women were never seen again.

Instead, Nura simply lay next to him, caressing him attentively but not insistently, rubbing the little muscles that ached. She felt those muscles relax, and before long the rest of him was relaxing too.

He let out a long sigh, that sounded like he'd been holding it in for a very long time.

"Am I not?" he asked.

Her brow furrowed, ever so slightly. "Are you not what, lord?"

"'Not to be numbered among the mad men you've known.'" He used his word-for-word quoting tone, the way he did when he repeated orations, speeches, passages of poetry without hesitation, precisely as they'd been spoken to him; and now with her, for the words she'd spoken.

"Your mind works with the speed of a man of twenty years, the memory of a man of thirty, and the cunning of a man of forty." She looked into his eyes. "And you know, lord, that I know better than to flatter you."

He grinned. "And here I am in a fifty-one-year-old body. Too slow to hunt lions, too sick to slay enemies, and too—" he gestured downward "—soft, to reap the fruits of my cunning."

"Do you not enjoy your time with me, lord?"

He made a soft *tsk* sound. "Don't fish for compliments, Nura. You're better than that."

She bit back a response and continued massaging his shoulders.

"Besides," he said, "I was going to say something else." He sighed. "The memory. 'The memory of a man of thirty.' That's the part that never fades."

He lay silent for a long while after that, staring at nothing, so at last she asked, "This troubles you, lord?"

"One sees a lot, in fifty-one years," he said. "One remembers a lot. Perhaps more than one should."

She gathered her thoughts for a few moments, choosing her words carefully. "If I were some other woman," she said slowly, "I would tell the Lord Emperor that, no doubt, every memory has only made you wiser, stronger, better able to rule." She paused for effect. "But I am not that other woman."

She looked to see how he'd react, but he only looked sharply into her eyes, waiting for the rest.

"I will tell you only, lord, that I, with my twenty-six years, am also troubled by many memories. I suppose the details would only bore your majesty, but... memories come to me at night, sometimes. I wake screaming from my dreams, they tell me."

"Who tells you—the other women?" the emperor asked "Do they treat you well?" The change of topic surprised her, as did his concern for her treatment in the harem.

"When I was first brought here," she told him, rising from the bed and padding over to the banquet-table, "from my village in the Silver Mountains, the women beat and cursed me when my screams woke them." She took a golden pitcher, its sides delicately chased with images of roaring lions, and poured a dark red wine into a gem-encrusted goblet. "But I think it was because I was new here. As we grew to be friends, and they heard my story, they treated me more kindly. Now when it happens, they comfort me, and soothe me back to sleep." She padded back to the bed, and gently placed the goblet in the emperor's hand.

He gulped the wine, his body visibly relaxing with each swallow. "Good," he said, after a few gulps. "I don't want you mistreated."

She sidled up next to him again. They sat in silence for a while more after that, the emperor gulping down the rest of goblet. When he'd drained the last dregs, he handed the cup back to her and said, "I would like you to stay here with me tonight."

Her eyes widened a bit, though she tried to hide it. "As His Sublime Majesty commands," she said.

He shook his head gently. "No. I don't command it," he said. "I ask it. I ask you to do this of your own free will, because it pleases you. You may say no. I will not be angry, and I will summon you again tomorrow evening, just as before."

"Of course it would please me, Exalted One," she said.

He smiled, ever so slightly behind that coiffed black-dyed beard. "In that case," he said, "do not call me 'Majesty' or 'Exalted One' or any of that nonsense. Call me Pul. That is my name."

"As you wish, Maj—" she stopped, laughed. "As you wish, Pul."

He smiled then, a real smile, a happy one. "Good. I ask only for you to share my bed, Nura. Forget about trying to please me, or entertain me, or otherwise convince me of your value. You are here because I *know* your value—a value as rare as that of a prize jewel. Though I suppose prize jewels are no rarity here. Rare as an honest courtier, then."

She looked down, biting her lip. "I have no answer for that."

"Then say nothing," he said.

He clapped his hands. "Come, it's getting late," he said, and called for the slaves to come extinguish the oil lamps, which was done with great speed; and to arrange the pillows on the bed and draw the curtains around it, all of which was done with great expeditiousness and politeness. The slaves bowed and wished the King of Kings the most restful sleep and the sweetest of dreams, until at last they exited the room, still bowing.

When the room was dark and the slaves were gone, Nura and Pul lay together on the soft pillows of the bed, and he stroked her hair, and she stroked his beard. And slowly, without either of them noticing it was happening, they both drifted to sleep.

ᚼᚼᚼ

She woke in the dark some time later, a nameless dread twisting in her belly.

Casting her gaze around the bedchamber, she saw only shadows; vague shapes lit by dim shafts of moonlight through the tiny windows along the upper edges of the walls. No movement but the slight shifting of the bed curtains in the night breeze.

Still, something was wrong. She slipped soundlessly from the bed, watching the emperor to make sure he didn't stir. He snored soundly, arms thrown across gold-stitched pillows, embroidered blankets twisted around his knees. Careless, for the only hours he was allowed to be so.

A tapestry on the far wall stirred. A hunting scene sprawled across the vast fabric: the emperor in his chariot, cold pride on his bearded face, a spear in his hand, poised to thrust down the throat of a charging lion. At the edge of the tapestry, a section of wall had swung aside, revealing a narrow rectangle of shadow: one of the palace's secret passageways; this one unknown to her until this very moment. Someone had opened it from the other side tonight, which meant—

An arm gripped her around the shoulders. A hand clamped over her mouth. She struggled but her captor was too strong. She kicked and he pinned her leg, expertly, efficiently. Without a sound.

Another man stepped into view before her. She recognized him: Ilani, one of the emperor's twin sons. Barely twenty years old, with the sharp eyes and aquiline nose of his father, but none of the emperor's grace of movement. He spared her a glance, then slipped like a wolf, swift and nervous, for the bed where the emperor snored.

She tried to cry out, but only a muffled squeak escaped through her captor's hand. She squeaked again and his other hand moved around to the back of her neck, pressing on a pressure point there. Pain exploded outward, down her arms and across her back, and she cried out.

Ilani looked up and hissed, "Get rid of her!" He'd drawn a gold dagger from his belt, and raised it above the emperor, ready to strike.

Her captor had made a mistake—moving his arm to hurt her had loosed his grip, and she managed to wrench her mouth away from his hand long enough to shout "Pul!"

The emperor sat up, eyes wide. In a flash of an instant, his face showed shock, disbelief, then rage. He pulled his own dagger from beneath the pillows; his other hand shot out and gripped his son by the throat. Muscles bulged beneath the skin of his arm. She'd never have thought him so strong, but he held on, choking the young man.

She stomped on her captor's foot, hard. He snarled and stepped back. Eshêru moved her muscles, shifting her body slightly to the side, using the huge man's weight and force against him, tipping him forward, tripping him, letting him hit the stone floor face-first with a grunt.

The emperor was shouting "Guards!" as Ilani gasped and slashed at his father's arm with the dagger. The effort made him cough, thick and loud. But he held onto Ilani's neck, the veins in his red face bulging. He coughed blood and spat it into the boy's face.

The guards burst in; first the two from just outside the door, then more from farther down the hallway, until the whole bedchamber was swarming with anxious men in copperscale, lighting all the candles and lamps, lifting the heavy attacker from the floor, pinning Ilani's hands behind his back as he sneered and spat curses. At some point, Nura remembered to throw on her robes and veil her face; not that anyone seemed especially concerned about her at the moment.

"What does the Exalted One wish us to do with them?" asked the captain of the guard.

The emperor nodded toward the heavy one who'd attacked Nura. He had a thick, lumpy face, already starting to bruise from his fall to the floor. His eyes stared vacantly. "Throw him in the House of Darkness," the emperor said, referring to the palace's deepest dungeon. "We'll execute him at dawn."

Then the emperor looked into the eyes of his son, who stared back at him coldly, hatefully. Such similarity in those faces, young and old, Nura thought. Yet such a chasm between them. One that would never be crossed.

"Why, Ilani?" the emperor asked. "I am old. You didn't have long to wait."

Ilani only glared back, radiant with hate.

At last the emperor sighed, shaking his head. "Place my son in the House of Darkness as well. At dawn—" He hesitated, glancing around the room: tapestries torn from the wall, disordered bedclothes, gold daggers on the floor. "At dawn," he continued, "he will bear the punishment for high treason."

"Behold the Lord of Nations!" Ilani roared. "Behold my father, who loves his people, his sons, most of all!"

The guards dragged him away out the bedchamber door, down the hallway and out of hearing range. Meanwhile an *ásu*-physician was summoned to tend to the dagger wounds on the emperor's arm. The birdlike little man tutted and pressed a poultice of herbs to the shallow cuts, then wrapped the arm in a bandage.

As the physician worked, an *ashípu*-healer entered and joined him at the emperor's bedside, clad in the pleated linen robe of a priest, carrying a white dove in a golden basin. At the instant he reached the bedside, the plump little man broke the bird's neck, then drew a small bronze dagger from his sash and sliced its belly open, prodding at its gleaming red innards with delicate fingers, waving his hands about the emperor's wound and muttering incantations with closed eyes.

"The omens are favorable," the healer said matter-of-factly, after a moment. "At sunrise, make an offering of pure water and unleavened bread to Gula, the spirit of health, and wash the royal person thrice in the House of Ablution. Once you have done this, evil spirits will not trouble this arm."

The emperor glanced up at the *ashípu*-healer. "It's only a few cuts," he said tiredly. "I'm covered with scars already, can't you see? A few more won't hurt."

The healer gasped. "Highest Holiness," he stammered. "This is the remedy prescribed in the ancient lore of Eridu itself. My augury foretells the course of your sickness, and—"

"Next time I'm girding up for a great battle, I'll be sure to call for one of your auguries," the emperor snarled, drawing stares from all assembled. "I do not need them tonight, healer. Thank you for your concern. You may go."

For an instant, the plump, linen-robed man looked as if he might burst with indignation. At last he turned on his heel and declared, "A wound without a healer is like hunger without food," to no one in particular. He stomped out of the bedchamber, his eviscerated dove sloshing in its gold basin with every step.

The physician, who was still binding the emperor's arm, took the opportunity to comment, "This palace is crawling with odd creatures, is it not, my Lord Emperor?"

The man's words awoke a memory in Nura: the two men she'd overheard in the garden this evening. She moved close to the emperor, bending her veiled face to his ear as the *ásu*-physician tended to his arm.

"Pul," she whispered.

"Not now, Nura," he said, waving her away.

She remained where she was. "I heard two men talking in the garden today," she said. "On the way here."

The physician froze.

"Return in a moment," the emperor said to him. He bowed and retreated.

"Tell me *precisely* what you saw and heard," the emperor said to Nura.

"Two men," she said. "The older one plump and half-bald, bearded, wearing a crimson tunic and an indigo cloak. The younger one slender, wearing a robe the color of emerald, and a necklace with rubies. He had a goatee. The younger one said, 'We'll have a grand old civil war, like in my grandfather's time.' The older one replied, 'Will you back us, then, when the time comes?' Then the younger one asked for a council post. I remember it clear as water."

The emperor looked at her sharply, mute with rage. "Nusku and Harshu," he hissed. "Guards!"

Two guards appeared instantly at the emperor's side. "Find the Grand Duke Nusku and the Baron Harshu," the emperor told them. "Arrest them, and place them in the House of Darkness. They too will be executed at dawn."

The guards hesitated, glancing at Nura. "Sire," one of them said quietly, "are you absolutely sure—"

"You dare ask me—!" The emperor snarled, then bit back a cough that shook his body. Everyone watched silently for a long few moments, while the emperor wrestled with the coughing fit and conquered it. "Of course I'm sure," he said, more quietly. "Do it immediately, before word gets out."

The guards saluted and hurried off to find the conspirators.

Nura faded into the background as the emperor summoned the physician back to his side. *Even in sight, I walk invisibly.*

When the bandaging was finished, the physician also insisted on checking the emperor's breathing. The man's eyes grew wide as he pressed his ear to the emperor's chest and listened. He was about to voice a warning when the emperor's expression darkened, and he waved the physician away. The little man advised the emperor to get plenty of rest, bowed discreetly, and hurried out the door.

After the guards had checked and double-checked every corner and shadow of the bedchamber, they finally bowed and disappeared, swinging the heavy wood door closed behind them. Nura and the emperor returned to the bed.

❦

"They'll be standing double watches until morning," she said, having no words for the moment, but feeling she should break the silence somehow.

"No one else is coming tonight," the emperor said.

"I would not think so," she agreed, fetching him a fresh goblet of wine from the table across the room.

"I only have one other living son, you know," the emperor said. "And Lishir is far away. I made him king in Babili."

"I've never met Lishir," she said, handing him the goblet. "But if you appointed him Lord of Babili, he must be wiser than his twin."

The emperor shook his head and sipped the dark wine. "Perhaps he has the potential to become wise," he said. "I sent him there when he was fifteen. Put him under the tutelage of the palace eunuchs. He's made sure Babili pays its taxes on time. The people don't seem to riot. What more can I say? I hardly know the boy."

She walked around the room slowly, blowing out the candles and lamps, listening to him talk quietly as he stared up at the gold-trimmed hunting mural on the ceiling.

"My firstborn son was becoming wise," he said.

Nura paused and looked at him, startled. She'd never heard of a son before the twins.

"He would've been about the same age as you," said the emperor, "perhaps the same age, in fact."

She chose her next words with great care. "I would've liked to have met him," she said.

The emperor sighed. "His name was Apli. He was a good hunter. A better swordsman. I made him commander of a regiment when he was only nineteen. Brought him with me to put down a rebellion in Elam."

The emperor fell silent. Nura came and lay on the bed next to him.

"I shouldn't have done that," the emperor said. "Put him in command. Great fighters aren't always great tacticians. Especially young ones."

"You were proud of him," said Nura. She felt strange talking about Apli like this; a ghost her own age, whose much older father lay here beside her.

"Proud enough to send him to his death," said the king.

"You didn't know," said Nura.

"They cut him up in pieces," the emperor said, his voice trembling. "Put the pieces in a clay pot and delivered them to me, in my war-tent outside their city walls. I'll always remember what it looked like, when they took off the lid—"

He began to cough, softly at first, then harder and louder; a thick, wet sound. He spat into his palm and saw blood there, and wiped it on the embroidered sheets.

Nura's eyes were wide. "Pul, let me call the physician—"

"No!" he said, and this set off a fresh storm of coughing and wheezing. The wine-goblet flew from his hand, spattering deep crimson across the rugs, as he coughed a spray of blood across the bedsheets. His eyes widened at that, but he clenched his fist and brought his breathing under control.

"No," he said, more quietly, in a tired, thin voice. "Every time that little bastard visits me, the gossip starts up again. The plotting. Everyone in this palace is waiting like hyenas, darting in to pick at my bones before I'm even—" He coughed again, harder than before.

She could only watch, trying to keep her breathing slow and rhythmic. *Even in motion, I am still.*

"Please, Pul, don't try to talk," she said when the coughs had quieted and he lay wheezing next to her. She filled a fresh goblet from the pitcher on the table and made him drink it all. "Just lie still. Nothing's going to happen tonight. Lie still and sleep."

The emperor nodded, and his eyes slowly closed. After a while, his breathing became more even, and he began to snore. She closed her eyes, too, though she thought she might never sleep again. But even as her thoughts swirled, they gradually slipped into dreams.

Some time after that, he woke her again, whimpering gently in the dark. He twitched and yelped, and made little frightened noises, and she wasn't at all sure what to do. But the emperor seemed to be in great distress so she gently shook him awake. He kept whimpering and twitching; murmuring a name—*Ishkara*. She shook him more firmly, and he gasped and his eyes opened and he looked around wildly, remembering where he was.

"Pul," she said softly. "You were having a bad dream."

He was breathing in gasps, his eyes wide.

"Does this happen often?" she asked.

He shook his head. "I do not know. No one has woken me like this before. Was I screaming?"

"No, my lord," she said. "Only whimpering—" She hesitated, just for an eyeblink: was it wise to mention the name he'd muttered? "And crying out a little," she finished.

He nodded. "Perhaps the guards never hear," he said. "Perhaps the other women are too afraid to wake me."

"It may be as you say," she said.

"But every night," he said. "Almost every night, I have these dreams."

She stroked his hair gently. "What dreams, Pul?"

He was silent for a long time, staring emptily into the darkness. "They're hard to talk about," he said, finally.

She nodded and ran her hand along his bearded cheek. "Perhaps it might help," she said, "to talk about them, just a little. Sometimes putting a thing in words..."

"We were out in Elam," he said after a moment. "This was years before Apli was born. I had nineteen, maybe twenty summers—about the same as Apli had, come to think of it, when the Elamu army cut him down. He shook his head. "We were putting down a rebellion. Always another Elamu rebellion. Every few years they had some new chief who declared himself king and refused me my taxes."

He laughed softly, without humor.

"And we, well we were the nastiest bunch of bastards on earth, back then. Riding to the fight in our chariots with the whole army at our backs, kicking up dust and the drumbeats thumping, making the sacred signs in the air with our hands, screaming, 'No mercy when we ride.' A band of young, stupid killers, half-mad on wine and spinplant. Ready to die."

This was the first she'd ever heard him talk about his youth. Was he boasting? Or was he, perhaps, telling the kinds of stories he'd always been expected to tell? She suspected he might be right on the verge of opening long-locked doors to her, if only she spoke the right passwords.

"It sounds as if you enjoyed it," she said.

"Enjoyed it?" He humphed. "It felt strange to me at the time. Feels just as strange to look back on it now. The boy in that chariot... I'm not sure he was ever me. I wasn't even first choice for the throne, you know. My brother was. He always led the charges. Before father packed him off to Babili, that is."

She held her expression calm and even, even as her heart leapt. *He unlocks the door!*

"But I played my part well enough." He sighed. "And I won't lie: I loved the parties afterward. Draped in gold and furs, throwing handfuls of jewels in the air, watching them rain on the women as they danced the dances they were only supposed to show their husbands. But they showed me. Oh yes. They showed me."

She suppressed a shiver at that. "It must've been an exciting life," she said, her tone as soft as air.

"It wasn't the excitement I loved," he said after a moment. "It was the respect. To feel like a *man*, if only for a night."

She favored him with a carefully chosen expression; just the right balance of sympathy and worship. "But you've always been a great man," she told him. "Even if it took time for others to see it."

He laughed drily. "If they saw me at all. I spent so much of my youth shut away in libraries, copying out poems and divinations under my master's whip-rod..." He shook his thick-bearded head. "Perhaps I would've made a better scholar than a king."

After that, he fell into silence. She stroked his hair, listening to his labored breathing. He'd just told her more than she'd ever expected to learn from him and invited her closer than he'd let anyone get in a long time, she guessed. She decided to take a wild gamble. If she judged this moment wrongly, it could cost her life. But if she judged rightly—

"Pul," she asked softly. "Who is Ishkara?"

He gasped, startled, his eyes suddenly wide. "Where did you hear that name?" he whispered.

She drew back, afraid she'd gone too far. "You were calling for her," she said, voice light as a feather. "In your dream."

He sat up slowly and leaned back against the cushioned headboard, dark eyes gazing at some phantom only he could see. His lower lip trembled; whether from fear or sadness she could not say.

"Some nights, I still wake up expecting to find her next to me," he said, so quiet she could scarcely hear. "She had the most beautiful smile. A rather plain face, perhaps. But that smile... she'd take my head in her hands, and smile like that, and all the world's roar would just—fall silent."

Nura watched him wordlessly, feeling as if she were gazing on a traveler on some far shore, across a great sea.

"She didn't even want me, at first, if you can believe that," he said at last. "It made no difference that I was a prince of Ash'shûr. She was—how did she put it?—'saving herself for the right man.' Oh, how I chased her. Until at last, one night, she appeared at my chamber door, in nothing but a silk blanket. 'I've been thinking about you,' she said. Smiled that smile. From that night on, we were inseparable. I bent the rules for her. Broke them. Fixed it so she never had to wear the veil, not in this palace or anywhere else. Walked with her in the garden every day the sun shone. Even brought her into the throne room, once Father was gone and I took the crown. She sat right there on the throne-dais, by my side, like no queen before or since."

A strange jealousy welled up in Nura's belly. Not the envy she'd feel for another concubine favored by the emperor, but a deep, certain knowledge that she would never be welcome in this sanctum of his thoughts. No matter how close she grew to the man next to her in this bed, she would always be a stranger to the man in these stories.

"I made three children with her," the emperor said softly. "Three beautiful boys. But it was never about that, not with her. We were reshaping the world together. Building our own little empire, just for us."

The question burned in Nura's mind: *What happened to her?* But to ask it outright would be to snap this thinnest of threads she had strung out for him to follow. "That sounds like a beautiful empire to live in," she said at last.

The king sighed deeply. "Then my brother made war on me, and everything began to change."

"Your brother—?" Nura said. "How did you two come to hate each other so fiercely?"

The emperor grunted ruefully. "I never hated him, though I'm sure he believed I did. I suppose it all started when he fell out of Father's favor. Acting a bit too much like an emperor when he didn't yet wear the crown. So father made him king in Babili, and named me his successor. Well, Father's body was scarcely cold before my brother brought his army north. Marched onto my land. Started burning villages—ah, no wonder you don't remember. You'd have been no more than a child then."

With those words, he shattered the illusion; the place outside of time they'd shared for those few moments when only true stories mattered. Now time had begun again; age rushing back with it. The king looked old, suddenly. Older, perhaps, than he had looked a few moments ago.

"I sent my brother dozens of letters," he went on. "Begging him to stop. Telling him I'd give him anything he asked. But he ignored my pleas. At last I had to march my army down to Babili and lay siege to it. The most sacred city in the world, the center of civilization, and there I was, hurling rocks at its walls like a barbarian. Shameful."

"You did what had to be done, I suppose," Nura told him.

The emperor grunted again. "He'd conspired with an Elamu king. Did you know that? My own brother. He and that son of a whore made a secret pact. Refused to pay my taxes."

She stroked his hair in the dark, saying nothing.

"So I took my army to Babili, with Apli, my firstborn, by my side. It was supposed to be a quick strike, but it turned into a siege, as these things so often do. Two months we sat outside those walls, trying to climb over them or dig under them. Anything to just be done with it, so I could return to Ninua, and to her..."

He paused and shook his head. "I never found out who did it. Poison, they said. But I was so far away. Two weeks' march to the east. Could've been anything. Anyone."

Nura's eyes went wide. "No!" she whispered. "How could anyone—?"

He shook his head. "Enough people had reason to hate her, Heaven knows. An unveiled woman in the throne room, always by the emperor's side, whispering Heaven-knows-what in his ear. Well." He huffed softly, a sound that was neither a sigh nor a dry laugh. "Kind things. That's what she whispered in my ear. She saw kindness in me that no one else could see, or wanted to. She made me think—" the emperor wiped at his eye. "She made me believe that things could be different."

Nura wrapped her arms around him, and held him. He shook, silently, scarcely breathing.

When at last the storm faded, he wiped his eyes, and gently extracted himself from her arms.

"I never found who did it," he said. "Not for certain. Whatever the truth was, it soon drowned in a sea of confessions ripped from men on racks and crosses. I hope her poisoner was among them. That, I truly hope." He licked his dry lips. "I made it back to Babili just in time for my army to scale its walls. While I marched up the Processional Way, my brother doused himself in oil. Put himself to the torch. He knew it was a kind death, compared to what I'd do once I got my hands around his throat."

Nura rolled onto her side, eyes fixed on his, though his were far away.

"And when I was done with my brother," the emperor said, "I marched east, to Elam, to settle that little problem. That was where I lost Apli. Up in the hills, on a scouting raid. I didn't even send him on that assignment. He volunteered. Insisted on it. So I let him go."

He ran a thick hand down his face and over his beard. His jaw tightened.

"Then," he said, "the morning we finally arrived at the walls of Shusha—that was the day they sent me the clay jar. Apli, or what was left of him, packed in like so much meat. I didn't cry. Didn't yell. Just called for my horse, and rode out for a parlay. And that impudent little Elamu king climbed up on the parapet, and shouted that I was a mad dog whose time had come to be put down. Well," he said. "I showed him who the dog was."

Nura licked her dry lips and waited.

"On the evening we stormed the city," the emperor went on, "I had that king brought before me. Had him stripped naked. Made him open his mouth. He was screaming. While I forced his mouth open he was begging, pissing himself, saying he'd do anything, that I could take his daughters, I could take his wife, just please, no."

He drew a deep breath and let it out shakily. "All I told him was he made me sick. I'd show him what it was to be a dog. And I held his mouth open and I ran an iron spike right down through his jaw. And I had a chain attached to that spike, and I told him to get down on all fours, and I dragged him back to his cage."

Nura's breaths came quickly now. "What happened to him?" she asked.

"I kept him in that cage, in my banquet hall," he said. "I pointed him out to my guests, and we laughed at him. He lay there while we feasted, so thin you could see his ribs, chained by the jaw, lying there in his own filth, and we *laughed* at him, Nura. Sometimes we'd throw him scraps and laugh even harder when he scrambled for them. And one day I looked in the cage and he was dead." The emperor took a deep breath again, and sighed. "And that," he said, "was the end of the would-be king of Elam, who dared to call the King of Kings a dog."

Nura managed to get her breathing under control. At last she said, "It was a terrible thing, it's true. You know that. And the fact that you know that, now, means you are no longer the same man."

"I am the man who did that thing," he said. "And so many more like it."

"No," she said. "That isn't true. You *were* that man, yes. But you are not him anymore. And she—" Nura caught herself before her words crept into that sanctum; the place only he could enter. "There is kindness in you, Pul. I see it."

"Kindness," he said, as if he did not believe it. "Tell me, Nura, what else do you see in me?"

She chose her next words with great care. "You are a wise emperor who has assembled a great library—the greatest the world has ever seen, with copies of every written work in mankind's history."

He looked at her sharply. "Do you know why I work so much on these tablets, Nura?"

"You search for secrets. Perhaps something hides in these tablets from before the Flood."

The emperor snorted a soft laugh. "If only my purpose were so thrilling." He sighed. "No, Nura. I created this library because no one remembers the important things. Where we come from. What we've accomplished. It's all chaos now, these immigrants from the western lands; their strange writing: *aleph*, *bet*. If you'd told me thirty years ago that this would be the fate of my empire—the empire of my father, and his before him... Well." He shook his shaggy head. "I'd have branded you mad, I suppose. Or worse."

"It's said that you and your father and his father marched many peoples from distant provinces across the world," she said. "Uprooted them and settled them in cities foreign to them, so they might forget their homelands, and only remember being citizens of your empire."

He grunted and nodded. "It is so."

"Surely you realized," she said, cautiously, "that this was like stirring a vast mixing-bowl. Even when the ladle stops stirring, the soup keeps swirling."

"Well said." He hummed approvingly. "But what is the soup we have stirred? I wonder. The old ways are dying, and we along with them. If we're lucky, some prince in the far future may dig up this place, and find these tablets we dug up from the ruins in Eridu and Kish. Who knows? Perhaps they'll even rediscover the trick of reading Shuméru." He shook his head. "Or perhaps now I'm just talking nonsense."

"It's not nonsense," she said. "I think it's noble. That's Ash'shûr's own truth."

"Sometimes I feel like I'm writing letters to them—these people I'll never meet. Like the motto we engrave on our tablets: 'For the Sake of Far Distant Days.' Came up with that myself. Maybe the only writing I ever did. I wonder if anyone will ever read it. My sons certainly won't."

"Someone will," she said. "Someday."

"I am a glorified secretary," said the emperor.

"And a fair governor," she said, "who has lowered taxes and promoted education. And a diligent priest, who has performed each of the holy rituals with exacting care, year after prosperous year."

He raised an eyebrow.

"And," she said, smiling, "you should know better than to fish for compliments."

He chuckled at that, and ruffled her carefully plaited hair. They lay back down together, entwining among the cushions.

"Close your eyes, Pul," she said softly, and he did; and she began to hum a tune, something from far away and long ago, in her village in the Silver Mountains. The melody was sweet in a sad way, and after a while the emperor's breathing began to slow, and she lay down next to him to return to sleep.

But then his eyes opened, and he said, "I see them, Nura." He heaved a shaky sigh. "Every time I close my eyes, I see their faces. Ishkara and my sons, and all the rest."

She stroked his hair softly. "That's all part of it," she said. "Part of what we carry with us."

"You know what I did to the first Elamu war-chief I killed?" he asked. "I had his head brought here to Ninua, packed in salt. Mounted it on a pike in my garden. It stayed there under the palm trees for weeks, those dead eyes and that gaping mouth turning purple and falling apart under the sun. Flies and birds picking at it while we picked at our roast duck and sipped our honeyed wine. The ladies complained about the smell, but I refused to take it down. It felt—satisfying, somehow, to look at it. No, not satisfying. That's the wrong word. Correct, perhaps. A small beacon of correctness in an incorrect world. Finally it was nothing but a dry skull, picked clean."

Nura tried to swallow, but her throat was dry. "I did hear of that," she managed to say.

"His name was Teumann," said the emperor. "This chieftain. He had a son, too, whom he loved very much. I made him watch when I beheaded that son. When he tried to close his eyes, I had his eyelids cut off. Then I had a man hold his head in place, to make sure he'd see every detail. I brought down the sword myself." He sighed. "To my mind, this was a mild punishment. A mercy, really. Many of my enemies suffered worse."

Now she was breathing quickly again. She tried to quiet her breaths but it wasn't helping.

"I had these deeds recorded, you know," he said. "Had them written down and engraved carefully, precisely, by expert scribes, all over the walls of this palace. Just as my father did, and his father before him. In the throne room, in the hallways. All those inscriptions you can't read, that just look like precise little markings to you. That's what you're walking past. That's what they say. That I pierced a man's jaw with a dog chain, cut off a man's eyelids so he'd watch me behead his son. A hundred things like that. A thousand, maybe. Thirty years of them. That's who I am. You know the songs."

"You mean 'The Lion and the Dog,'" she said, quietly.

"'*Hear the howling of its king, a dog in chains,*'" the emperor recited. "*Who weighed his worth against a lion.*" That's about what I did to the Elamu, you know. And long before that, years before you were born, my father and I did the same at the Ulai River. The Elamu claimed that river for their own, and we drowned them in it—just as my firstborn son and I did, half a lifetime later. As my young son will do again someday."

"It's only a song," Nura said. "Just words."

"There are many others like it," the emperor replied. "This is who we are."

She chose her words next words with great care. "All nations tell stories of themselves, to themselves. The story and the people are not the same."

"Still," the emperor said, "songs do not come from nowhere." He drew a deep breath and sighed. "And now with the Elamu kings gone, others are coming to take their place. These," he gestured at the air, "these Mída. Parsa. Horse-people and mountain savages. Which means one of two things: either my sons will have to do the same things I did, or—"

She waited, but he said nothing. "Or—?" she asked.

"Or it will be the end of the great cities of Babili and Ninua, and of all of this." He sighed. "And I don't know which of the two is more likely."

She reached up to stroke his head, but found it hard to touch him. He was staring blankly, not seeing her or anything here.

"And when I close my eyes," he said, "there they are. My brother, and the dog-king of Elam, and Teumann on his pike. All of them."

She sat next to him, saying nothing, not moving, until her heart ceased pounding and her breath came more evenly.

When she felt calm enough to speak again, she said only, "Pul."

"Yes," he said. "That was my name. That was what my mother called me."

"Your mother," she said. "She must have loved you very much."

"I wanted to read in the library," said the emperor. "I liked the stories. I wanted to read them."

She reached up and stroked his beard, and his hair. "And now," she said, "you can. You can read all the stories you want."

He laid his head against her chest, and for a long time they lay together like that in the dark, him shaking softly against her, his beard smelling of salt and warm breath.

"Will you come with me?" he asked at last.

"Come with you?" she asked. "Come where?"

He sat up. "To the library. Will you come to the library with me?"

"Of course," she said. "But it's the middle of the—"

"Guards!" He was already shouting for them, clapping, and they came running into the bedchamber, bowing. He commanded the lamps to be lit. It was done instantly. He commanded more lamps to be brought, and for guards and lamp-bearers to escort him and Nura to the library.

The guards and the lamp-bearers arrived in moments, and soon their small nocturnal troupe was making its way through the dim inner gardens of the palace; some of the alcoves empty and pitch-black, others lit by guttering lamplight that cast flickering shadows on the sprawled bodies of sleeping women from all corners of the empire.

They walked past all this, the guards and lamp-bearers stepping carefully over wine puddles and bodies and spilled plates of fruit; the emperor shuffling in his sumptuous purple robes, making no effort to be quiet or to dodge anything, kicking absently at any sleeper who half-awoke and cast an arm or a leg across his path.

Out from the inner chambers they walked; out through the thick barred door and into the palace complex's labyrinth of hidden hallways; Nura averting her gaze from the reliefs and inscriptions telling of the people the emperor had tortured and humiliated and slaughtered. She stared only at the floor ahead of her as they walked down long narrow corridors, then turned and walked down broader ones, winding across the expanse of the complex, never crossing the path of another living soul. Nura had never guessed the maze extended so far! But onward they walked, until at last they emerged at the enormous wooden door of the Great Library.

Two guards stood at attention on either side of the door, and they snapped to even tighter attention as they saw the emperor and his retinue approaching. Without waiting for a password, they unbolted the heavy doors and swung them aside, grunting quietly with the effort.

The lamp-bearers hurried inside to light the lamps within. Nura watched as lamps deeper and deeper within the room caught fire, casting their glow farther and farther back through rows behind rows behind rows of shelves as tall as the ceiling, all of them filled with stacks of scrolls and tablets. So many writings—more than she'd ever imagined could exist. Yet here they all were, all the epics and poems and histories and proverbs that ever were, in every language of mankind, from every corner of the earth; all gathered here, in this one place in all the world—the mighty city of Ninua.

"Come," said the emperor. "There's something I want to show you."

She followed him into the library. They walked past dozens of shelves of wood tablets with wax surfaces, scratched with squares and hatches, lines and curves of many strange scripts; past alcoves filled with scrolls of inked papyrus and parchment; past drying-racks filled with clay tablets, their surfaces freshly pressed with precise clusters of triangular markings.

At long tables amid the racks, five men labored by the light of many low-burned candles, shackled to the benches by iron chains. At first Nura took them for ordinary slaves—but as she looked closer, she saw that two were bald-headed priests swathed in white Nile linen, carefully inking papyrus scrolls with line upon line of curvilinear script. Two blue-robed men of Babili inscribed wax tablets with densely packed triangular characters. A lone pale-skinned scholar, clad in a fringed toga, scratched his own peculiar markings onto a tablet of his own.

She paused to watch, listening to the soft clinking of their chains as they worked.

"The two in white are priests from Misr," the emperor said, drawing close and following her gaze. "The blue-clad pair are Babili astronomers. The lone oracle is from Khatti. I have many more like them, but these will remain here until they finish the day's work."

His words invited an obvious question, so she obliged him: "What work do they do?"

"They are copying down every word they can remember of their peoples' prayers, histories, songs and spells," he said with evident pride. "Someday, this library will contain them all."

"Lifetimes of knowledge," she said. "Thousands of lifetimes."

"And each page more valuable than gold," he replied. "Those two Misru priests speak barely a word of our Aramaya, but they know spells older than the Pyramids. And that Khatti oracle may very well be the last of his kind. No one wants to learn the words of his old sagas. Not anymore."

"No one but you," she added.

He grunted in agreement.

Their little lamp-lit party wound their way onward into the labyrinth. As the slaves raised their lamps, the soft glow illuminated a vault that seemed without limit, whose far reaches and highest shelves vanished into distant shadows. Thousands upon thousands of tablets and scrolls filled shelves from floor to ceiling, every one arranged and tagged by age and origin and language; so the emperor told her. They trod down long aisles lined with tall shelves of older tablets, their surfaces faded and slightly cracked. She couldn't begin to guess at which languages they held, or how far they might have traveled to arrive here.

"This must be everything that's ever been written," she whispered gazing up at the towering shelves.

"Not quite. The emperor smiled gently. "But that is what I dream of."

They navigated down more aisles, around more corners. Still deeper into the vaults, where mosaicked alcoves held pale, cracked tablets set delicately on wooden stands. Other niches held bundles wrapped in cloth, or boxes of polished wood.

The emperor reached up and took down one of the wood boxes. It was about the size of a jewelry-box, and its top bore a series of triangular-clustered characters, engraved cleanly and precisely into the dark, sweet-smelling cedar.

"Do you know what this says?" the emperor asked her, tapping the writing.

"I'm afraid I never learned to read," she said, eyes downcast.

"This inscription," the emperor said, "is in Old Akkadu, a precursor of the ancient tongue of Babili. This box is more than a thousand years old."

"Very old indeed," Nura said.

"This?" the emperor huffed a laugh. "This is nothing. This box is as old as this morning's fresh-baked bread, compared to what it contains."

"What does the writing say?" she asked.

He smiled, tracing the inscriptions lines with a fingertip. "It says, 'This box holds a tablet from old Eridu. The most far-ancient writing in the world.'"

The emperor opened the box with great care, as if it might shatter under his touch. The box was lined with the softest fox fur, and inside sat a parcel, wrapped in the finest purple silk.

"No one," said the emperor, "is allowed to touch this box, or even to open it, without my express approval, and my direct personal supervision. The penalty for defying this command is death by flaying."

Nura nodded.

"But no one has ever committed that crime," he said. "No one cares to. Few even know this box is here."

He set the box on the shelf, and lifted out the parcel as if it were a newborn kitten. He unfolded one edge of the fabric, then another, then gently unrolled the package; until in his hand, on a bed of that soft silk, lay a small square tablet of the palest clay.

Nura was afraid to even breathe on it.

Its surface was inscribed with a few simple symbols—pictures, really. A foot. A hand. Something that looked like a head, and another that might be a staff of grain. Aside from that, it was bare, worn smooth by time, and spiderwebbed by tiny cracks.

The emperor looked up at her, fixing her with those dark, sharp eyes. "Do you know of old Eridu, Nura?" he asked.

She forced herself to meet that piercing gaze. And although she knew he already knew her answer, she said, "I'm afraid I do not know of it."

He nodded. "Few know of that place, aside from priests and scribes—and mad old kings, of course." He chuckled, holding back another fit of coughing.

"Where is it," she asked, "this Eridu?"

"It once lay far south of Ninua," said the emperor. "In the marshes of old Shumér. One of the very first cities of man, in those misty days when Heaven talked with Earth, and Earth talked with Heaven."

"And it is gone?" she asked.

"Only a small town remains there now," said the emperor. "A ghost of the city that one stood in that place. A thousand years before the first crude temple was raised in Babili, that city had already crumbled into the marsh."

She stared at the tablet a while longer, trying to memorize all its markings, certain she would never be allowed to see it again.

"What does it say, Pul?" she asked softly, using the special name he'd given her permission to use.

He smiled sadly and shook his head. "I do not know. No one knows. Not even our wisest scribes, who have studied Shuméru all their lives."

"Surely they must have some idea."

"The symbols are simply too few. They do not seem to form words. And we have no other writing from old Eridu, nothing to compare it to. Some scribes believe the language is not ancient Shuméru at all. It may be something even older."

He carefully wrapped the tablet back in its cloth and set it gently amid the fur inside the box, then closed the lid and returned the box to its shelf.

She reached up and stroked the beard against his cheek. "I can see you are most troubled by this tablet, Pul."

He sighed. "What is it, Nura, that my sons do not understand?" Tears rose in his eyes. "What is this that I cannot make them see?"

She wrapped her arms around him, and he around her, and they stood that way for some time in the lamplight, among shelves upon shelves upon shelves of thousands of tablets from every language and time and corner of the earth, all stacked and arranged and labeled neatly. She could see he drew comfort, in some small measure, from the thought that he could read and decipher at least a few of the mysteries inscribed on their worn surfaces.

Then he called and clapped for the guards and the lamp-bearers, who came and extinguished the lamps in the great library, and walked with Nura and the World-Lord back down the subterranean corridors and narrow hidden passages, beneath the palace's porticoed administrative buildings, among the alcoves of the inner gardens. Back through the vaulted doorway of the keep, to the heart of emperor's vast bedchamber. The slaves and eunuchs bid the emperor the most restful sleep and the sweetest of dreams, and bowed as they retreated, clearly longing for sleep.

As one of the lamp-bearers moved to extinguish a torch, the emperor raised a hand.

"Wait. Come closer," he said.

The lamp-bearer stepped into the lamplight, head bowed.

"Are you—" the emperor raised a hand unsteadily, as if seeing a ghost. "Are you of the Kalshu people?"

The man's eyes widened. He nodded mutely.

Nura searched the emperor's face and saw only perplexity and sadness there.

"Look at me," the emperor commanded in a soft voice.

The man looked up, hesitantly meeting the emperor's eyes. He wasn't Ashûru, Nura could see. His skin was strangely colored, almost reddish; his eyes the color of emeralds.

"By the Seven Stars," the emperor whispered. "Your people were once lords of Babili."

The man only shrugged and pursed his lips slightly.

"Lords of nothing, now," he said.

Nura glanced from the emperor to the green-eyed man. Something unseen was passing between them; something even she could not catch.

"You were brought here as a slave?" the emperor asked.

The green-eyed man nodded. "My family were all slain at the Battle of Iluna," he said, his voice barely more than a whisper. "And in the—cleansing, that followed." His eyes remained on the floor, but his jaw trembled and clenched.

"Let this man be set free." The emperor waved a gold-ringed hand at the guards, who nodded in acknowledgement. "Let him be given food, and a donkey, and allowed to go where he pleases."

The slave was shaking his head. "I am honored, lord," he said. "But I have nowhere to go. No one to go to. My place is here now."

They watched each other for a long moment: Nura, the emperor, and the slave. At last the emperor nodded, and the green-eyed man returned to the group of lamp-bearers near the door.

The guards bid the emperor goodnight, then exited the bedchamber with the slaves, all bowing one final time.

The King of Kings lay among tasseled silk pillows. Nura lay her head against his chest, and felt him breathing softly against her cheek. As his eyes drifted closed in the lamplight, she tried to picture the pale clay tablet he'd shown her—the one from primeval Eridu, wondering what mysteries its strange, simple inscription might contain.

Beneath her, the emperor lay still, eyes open in the lamplight. She knew that despite his hours poring over tablets and scrolls in the library he loved, what he saw each time he closed his eyes was a man with an iron spike through his jaw, gnawing bones in a filth-smeared cage in the royal banquet hall; and another man with his eyelids sliced away, weeping and cursing the Great King Ash'shûr-bani-apli, Emperor of the World, Lord of the Horizons, who stood proudly with sword in hand, adjusting his stance to behead that man's son before his eyes.

And so the World-Lord lay with eyes open, as though his own eyelids had been sliced away, and breathed softly beneath the woman drifting off to sleep atop his chest. She began to snore softly, while the emperor gazed out among the shadows of the royal bedchamber. Morning was still a long way away.

𒐀𒐀

When at last dawn cast the first shafts of dim sunlight through the windows, guards knocked softly on the bedchamber door, and Nura and the emperor rose, yawning and rubbing at eyes that had hardly closed all night. They dressed in silence, each movement feeling heavier than usual.

Slaves came to drape the emperor's outer robes over his shoulders, careful to conceal the bandage on his arm with a thick sleeve. They buckled golden belts and jeweled clasps about his person and draped a necklace of rubies and emeralds around his neck. Nura watched all this from behind her black veil, saying nothing. When the emperor's embroidered boots were laced and tied, he took her hand, and they walked down the long hallway, out into the city-within-a-city of the palace complex.

Surrounded by guards, trailed by an ever-growing train of slaves and attendants, they wound their way through the harem gardens, past the empire in miniature, wine-stained water and half-eaten plates of fruit amid women from every corner of the world. They passed the wall reliefs of the emperor's great deeds in war and the hunt, then through the gateway with its guards and statues of strange fish-tailed Shuméru gods, whose stone features watched silently over the hall.

Through the outer gardens, where already a few barons and dukes strolled, conversing quietly, dropping abruptly into low bows as the emperor and his entourage passed by. Past the topiaries and trimmed fruit trees and ponds of fish beneath the waterlilies. Past the towering door of the throne-room, past the dining-hall and the reception chamber and the small rooms for private audiences.

Out into the complex's great public courtyard, to the amphitheater where rows of steps and stone benches rose behind a smooth stone wall taller than a man. Nura and the emperor ascended the steps to their private box at the center of the seats, a sweeping balcony of white limestone flanked by towering stone bulls with the heads of long-bearded kings.

Pillowed couches awaited them there, along with a few dozen minor nobles already seated, black-veiled ladies at their sides. All of them waiting, gossiping, clearly having somehow caught word of the executions already, in the hours while Nura and the emperor had snatched their meager sleep. Kitchen-slaves materialized as they entered, setting a long, low table with plates of fresh figs and flatbread, boiled eggs and honey-wine. Nura didn't feel like eating.

When they were settled on their cushions, the emperor called, "Bring them out."

Four guards marched Ilani and the burly attacker out onto the sand at the bottom of the amphitheater, their hands bound behind them. Both wore expressions as stony as those of the fish-god statues. Another four guards marched out Duke Nusku and Baron Harshu, hands also bound, but still clad in all their finery—minus the daggers and the lavish jewelry, Nura noticed.

"Read out the charges," the emperor called.

A eunuch walked out onto the sand, and stood near the prisoners.

"For the crimes of high treason and conspiracy against the Crown," the eunuch proclaimed, "The Grand Duke Nusku and the Baron Harshu will suffer the harshest punishments."

The emperor nodded and gestured for the eunuch to proceed.

"For the crimes of high treason," the eunuch continued, "for violence against the Crown, and for the attempted murder of His August and Most Exalted Majesty, the King of Kings...

Ilani, son of Ash'shûr-bani-apli, Emperor of the World. And Burak, son of—" The eunuch conferred briefly with a gaggle of other eunuchs who stood nearby. "Son of an unknown slave," he continued, "will also suffer the harshest punishments."

Nura glanced at the emperor, who hesitated a moment before nodding again.

"These crimes are far more than simply offenses against the law," said the eunuch. "They are more heinous, even, than crimes against nature. No, conspiracy against the World-Lord, and violence against his person, are nothing less than the most profane sacrileges against the God Ash'shûr himself!"

A murmur rippled through the crowd of onlookers. The eunuch grinned subtly, relishing his moment at center stage.

"The penalty for these most hideous impieties," cried the eunuch, "is death by flaying and burning at the stake!"

The crowd's murmurs grew louder, more excited.

"What punishment," the eunuch asked, "does the Exalted One decree for these foulest of sinners?"

The crowd fell silent, every eye looking to the emperor; Nura's eyes included. The emperor sat for what felt like a long while, staring down at his son, ignoring the other criminals.

At last the emperor shifted his gaze, calling out, "Have you anything at all to say for yourself, Grand Duke Nusku?" He rubbed at his forehead. "It's been many years since we rode out on the hunt, hasn't it? Remember those days? Seems you've grown bored in your old age, Nusku. Decided to stage a new kind of hunt."

The two conspirators glanced at each other. Harshu, the young one in yellow, was visibly shaking.

"He gave me no choice, my Lord Emperor!" the young man blurted. "I implore you, grant me mercy! You know that I have always—"

"Serpent! Coward!" Nusku howled, launching himself at the younger man, even though his hands were bound behind his back.

The guards pulled the men apart.

"We made a plan. The plan failed," Nusku was shouting. "Own up to it! These are the consequences."

Nusku turned to the emperor, his half-bald head covered in sweat and dust. He turned to look up into the old man's eyes. "This is the way of things, O King," he said, calmly but loudly enough for the whole arena to hear. "You know the stakes as well as I do. All the kingdoms in the world, and more. I had to place my bet, as all of us have to. I chose the wrong number, and I lost the throw. In my place, you'd have done the same, Pul. It's the throne or the grave. You know this. Do what you must."

The emperor was trembling; whether from rage or from holding back another coughing fit, Nura wasn't sure.

"Death," he said, just loudly enough for everyone to hear. "A slow death by flaying and burning, for both of them."

A roar went up from the crowd; the kind of sound that might come from a pride of lions gloating over their prey. An animal revel.

The emperor raised a hand, and the crowd fell silent.

"And Ilani," he said. "Have you anything to say for yourself, my son?" His voice cracked slightly on the last word.

Silence hung for a moment. Then Ilani barked a harsh laugh.

"Ha! Your son, you call me!" Ilani cried. "What does this word mean to you: 'son'? A pawn in your great game on the world-board? A clever dog, to be called to heel when you want distraction? What son of yours, father, has ever meant half as much to you as those dry old tablets in your library? You could never bear to see a single crack on one of those tablets—oh, but today, you will flay and roast your own child, like a boar on a spit. This is what the word 'son' means to the World-Lord. Such an emperor is no lord of mine."

The eunuchs and the crowd gasped, and the eunuch standing nearby shrieked, "Enough of this blasphemy!" A guard bashed an armored fist into Ilani's head. The young man fell to one knee, spitting blood onto the sand.

Nura looked at the emperor. Tears were falling from his eyes. He wiped them away quickly, grimaced, composed himself. A moment later, his face was as hard as the stone of the arena.

She felt a panic claw up from her belly; not only for what was about to happen, but for what it would mean. For the nation, for this family—most of all, for Pul, after everything they'd talked about last night. She felt herself slip by instinct into the slow eshéru breathing exercise, repeating the words in her mind: *I move as the world moves. The world moves as I will.*

"Pul," she whispered in the emperor's ear, keeping her body perfectly still so no one would notice. "Remember the library. Remember the tablets."

Every lord and veiled lady in the crowd, and every eunuch on the sands, was looking up at them again, waiting for an answer.

The emperor nodded. "Death," he said, just loudly enough for everyone to hear. "Flaying and fire."

The crowd roared again, louder than before.

A cough escaped the emperor's lips, and his face turned red as he held it back. His body shook once, twice. Then he wiped his mouth with the back of his hand, drew a deep breath and sat still.

He leaned toward Nura. "You don't have to watch," he whispered.

"I am at your side," she whispered. "Always, I am at your side."

"This is how things are, Nura," he said quietly. "Any action against the throne must be answered with absolute ruthlessness. Instantly, without mercy. This is what holds the world together. This is all that separates us from savages."

I move as the world moves. The words came to her, unbidden.

Guards brought out tall wooden stakes and tied the four conspirators to them. The brute Burak only stared dumbly, but Ilani continued to bark out curses, laying blame on his father for every wrong in the world, until at last the eunuchs stuffed a rag in his mouth. Baron Harshu was weeping like a child, and

Nura saw a wet stain spread downward along his emerald robe. The Grand Duke Nusku held his head high, refusing to break eye contact with the emperor.

The guards did the flaying first; all four of the criminals at the same time. When they made the first cuts, the doomed men only gritted their teeth. But as the guards began to rend the flesh from arms and legs, all four cried out, their screams becoming inhuman; bestial.

Somewhere up in the stands, a troupe of musicians plucked lyres and tapped drums, while singers chanted the low, baleful verse of "The Lion and the Dog," which all assembled knew by heart:

"Weigh your worth against me," the false king howled,
Atop his high wall, across the rushing river.
"You are no lion," he cried, "And I'll never bend my knee."
"Never will my warriors kneel before a dog."
Now look: see their scattered bones along the riverbed.
The current cleansing the city's stones.
Hear the howling of its king; a dog in chains,
Who weighed his worth against a lion.

By now, the crowd was drifting away, some of the nobles looking pale and sick.

And then, though it seemed utterly pointless, guards brought torches and set branches aflame at the feet of all four of the dead men. Flames licked upward, blackening the criminals' skin and obscuring them in thick columns of smoke.

The emperor remained there through it all, not speaking, not crying; simply watching. Never taking his eyes away.

Nura remained at his side.

And when at last it was all finished, and four charred skeletons hung from the stakes beneath the harsh mid morning sun, the emperor rose slowly from his cushioned couch. Nura rose with him. He began to cough again, his body shaking with the effort.

They walked the long, silent way through the winding halls of the palace, past the gardens and the harem-chambers and the great stone statues and wall-carvings, back to the emperor's bedchamber, where slaves helped him remove his embroidered boots and robes. He dismissed the slaves and guards, and he and Nura sat side by side on the gold-trimmed mattress of the curtained bed.

And only then, in the dark, did the emperor allow himself to weep.

289 YEARS EARLIER
920 BC

Their cities I burned with fire.
The heavy yoke of empire I imposed on them.
I taught them to worship Ash'shúr, my Lord.

— The Chronicle of Tukúlti-apil-Esharra

Y

Around sundown, Mama and Kepha heard noises coming from the far edge of the field. Mama glanced up from the fish she'd been gutting, knife clutched tightly in hand, and poked her head out of the cloth-covered doorway of their reed hut.

"Men," Mama said.

Kepha grabbed his spear with the long iron tip from its place next to his bed-mat. He slipped out the door-flap and peered eastward across the sea of tall brown reeds. In the distance, a column of dust swirled in the purpling dusk.

As Mama slipped out the door-flap behind him, Kepha saw reeds shaking as the men came closer. Sure enough, they ran along the path that Mama and Kepha had cut for them. Their cries split the still evening air as they fell through the reed mat Kepha had lain down, into the pit beneath, onto the spear-points jutting up from far below.

Mama said to slow down and let the men's blood finish leaving them. Kepha walked nice and slow, like Mama said. All the way to the pit, they listened to the men screaming, and by the time they got there, the men had lost a lot of blood, just like Mama said they would. Mama looked down at the pale, dying men in the pit, and smiled, and told Kepha he was a good boy.

"The Gods in the iron are good to us today," she said.

One of the dying men had fallen on an iron speartip that pierced his lung. He was coughing up bright red bubbly blood that mixed with the dark drying blood from his stomach where other speartips had gone through. The other man was already dead.

Mother and son stood on the edge of the pit and watched. The dying man called to them in his language, which sounded like the language of K'nan. Mama and Kepha didn't understand a word of it. Kepha guessed he must be begging for his life, or maybe for a drink of water, or maybe for them to kill him quickly.

"Do him quick, baby," Mama said. "Careful, though. Keep your distance."

Kepha kept his distance. He and Mama ran their spears through the man's chest and stomach and lungs. He gasped and snarled, and fresh blood came from his lungs and stomach. At last he stopped breathing and went limp.

"Good boy," Mama told Kepha. "Such a big strong boy."

Kepha smiled and blushed, not knowing what to say.

Once they were sure the man was dead, they climbed down into the pit to strip the two bodies of armor and weapons and look for trinkets and other prizes. The men wore the armor of

Ashûru soldiers, but Kepha didn't think they were from the Ashûru lands, because they didn't have dark skin, or the long black woven beards those men usually had. Their skin was pale; almost pink. One had brown hair; the other's was black and curly.

"Where do you think they came from?" Kepha asked Mama.

"They look like men of House Dawíd," Mama said. "From Shomron in the west."

"How do you think they came by this Ashûru armor?" Kepha asked.

Mama shrugged. "Nobody's safe in the countryside these days."

Kepha guessed she meant they'd killed some Ashûru men and taken their armor and weapons, just like now he and Mama were taking those things from them. *Except these men had to win their gear in battle*, Kepha thought, *while we just killed them with our pit. That makes us cleverer.* The idea made him smile.

The men wore good armor: tight-woven strips of leather and wood and bone, round-pointed helmets of iron lined with hard leather; good sharp iron swords, straight, two-edged and tapered to points, with short round hilts and pommels, and tough leather sandals that laced all the way up to the knee.

The red-haired one—the one who died first—also had a talisman carved with an image of some bearded God Kepha didn't recognize. The other—the one with brown hair—had a bag of copper coins, a little pouch of dried meat, and a copper necklace set with a stone.

"Sige will trade us two sacks of barley for that stone," said Mama, eyeing it appraisingly.

Mother and son dragged the men's bodies up out of the pit, then laid the reed mats carefully back over the opening, and hid them with dirt. Then they dragged the bodies to a muddy pool nearby and threw them in, like they'd done with all the others. By the time they made it back to their hut by the river, Kepha was sore and tired. He lay down on his mat and slept while Mama went to Sige to trade the swords and necklace for barley.

By the time Mama came back to the hut, it was dark, and Kepha and Mama were both ravenous. In the dark, Mama lit a fire and boiled the barley in water. When it was soft, they sat by the fire scooping up the barley and eating it with their hands. Once Kepha had eaten his fill, he felt sleepy again, and so did Mama. They lay down on their mats and slept.

ᛉ

THE MORNING WAS hot when Kepha woke. Black smoke was pouring into their hut, and Mama was coughing and pushing Kepha outside. All around them the tall reeds were on fire, a big hot orange and red blaze throwing sparks everywhere and sending dark smoke to the sky.

They ran from the heat and fire and smoke, like rabbits dashing one way and another, looking for anywhere that wasn't burning or filling with smoke that choked them.

"Why are the Gods in the fire so angry at us?" Kepha asked Mama as they coughed, eyes watering.

"Not now, baby," she said, coughing hard. "Now it's time to run."

They stumbled out into an open place they'd cleared a few weeks before: just bare dirt. Nothing to burn. They gasped, catching their breath.

"The fire came from the direction of the road," Mama said. "We should run the other way."

"What will happen to our house?" Kepha asked.

"Forget about the house, baby," said Mama. "We've got to keep moving."

Now they could hear shouting and the sound of iron on iron. Men were fighting not far off. Kepha saw their speartips above the burning reeds. They were coming closer, running from the fire.

"Mama, look!" Kepha pointed.

The men heard him and began shouting in their Ashûru tongue. Mama and Kepha turned to run, but the Ashûru men were bursting out through the reeds now and into the clearing, two of them: one fat and gray-haired, the other young and thin; both in copperscale armor and pointed iron helmets, bearing long spears, their thick muscled arms and legs covered in cuts and burns.

Kepha screamed. Mama grabbed his hand and pulled him away into the reeds, but the Ashûru men were too fast. One ran and took hold of Mama. She screamed and beat at him, but he didn't even seem to feel the blows. The fat gray-haired Ashûru man caught Kepha by the collar and yanked him back, got an arm around his neck, and squeezed. Kepha fought as hard as he could, but soon his sight went blurry and black crept in around the edges, and he fell.

The younger man was tearing off Mama's tunic, even though she was screaming and beating him with her fists. He only laughed. Once he'd stripped her, he took a rope from his belt and bound her hands behind her back. Meanwhile, the man who held Kepha was doing the same.

Soon they were marching off through the reeds, away from the fire, the men chattering in their guttural tongue, Kepha and Mama stumbling as the soldiers pushed them faster, arms bound tight behind their backs, ropes choking their necks.

The men marched them a long way. Kepha thought the two must be father and son. Their faces were of similar cast, thick-nosed and shallow-chinned. The gray-haired one guided the younger with a mix of help and admonishment, praise and sudden violence.

The four of them walked all morning, out of the reeds and across a big flat place with dry grass. They walked all afternoon and evening, up into a hilly place with lots of rocks and little bushes. The men talked to each other all the time in the Ashûru tongue, and Kepha understood nothing they said.

When night came, the man and his son stopped and laid down their packs. They tied Kepha and Mama to nearby trees, and spoke words Kepha didn't know. One made a cutting sign on his neck, though, and Kepha understood that.

The man and his son made a fire, took some dried mutton from their packs, and gave a few strips to Kepha and Mama. They untied one of Kepha's hands, and one of Mama's, so they could eat the meat with their fingers. The man and his son drank water straight from their waterskins, and poured a little into Kepha's and Mama's mouths.

"Can you pull your other hand out of the rope?" Kepha whispered while the men were eating.

She shushed him, glancing nervously at the men. "Be patient," she whispered.

The man and his son sat around the fire and drank beer and sang strange songs for a long time.

Late in the night, when Kepha was starting to fall asleep, the younger man came and untied Mama from the tree, and dragged her away. Kepha cried out, but the man kicked him, hard, in the stomach, and he fell back gasping for breath.

A little while later, he heard Mama screaming, and he cried out again, straining against the knots as hard as he could, but they were good knots and the rope was strong. He heard Mama kicking and fighting, screaming at the men, and shouting "Don't look, baby!" to Kepha. He turned his head to look anyway, and saw that the man was holding her down on her stomach with her hands tied behind her back. "Baby, please," Mama cried, tears streaming down her face. "Don't look."

He looked away. The older soldier got up, laughing, and said something to Kepha in the tongue of Ash'shûr. Then he walked over to where Mama was, and she cursed at the men, and spat. Kepha wanted to look, but looked only at the grass by his feet. He tried to think about their house, and their field, and the little lake where they fished, but it was hard, because the man and his son were laughing and grunting, and Mama was crying very loud.

After a while, it was over. The two men walked off to sleep, laughing together, and Mama crawled back to where Kepha was tied to the tree. She was bruised and bloody, and crying softly, and Kepha wanted to put his arms around her, but he couldn't, because his hands were tied.

"Mama," said Kepha. "Please don't cry." But he was crying too. They cried together, tied to that tree, until they fell asleep on the hard dirt.

THE NEXT MORNING, the man and his son untied them from the tree and dragged them onward. The four of them marched all morning, up into the hills. Then they marched all afternoon, into higher places where there were only rocks and hard brown dirt. All day under the hot sun, in the wind, with those jagged rocks under their feet, Kepha and Mama marched.

Kepha's feet were bleeding on the rocks, and his legs and his back hurt from sleeping on them the night before. Mama could barely walk at all. She was bruised and bloody all over, so Kepha felt bad for feeling sorry for himself. He tried to give Mama his shoulder to lean on, but the younger man kicked him and snarled something in Ashůru. Kepha tried to fight the man, but the other one stepped in and knocked Kepha to the ground, and then both men kicked him in the stomach and legs and arms and chest and face, all over, until he cried and begged them please to stop. After that he didn't try to fight them anymore.

A few times, Kepha told Mama it was going to be all right. She didn't answer or even look at him. She just took slow steps, and more slow steps, staring down at the ground, or at nothing.

At sunset on the second day, they climbed to a place in the mountains; a cold windy place where only tiny brush and weeds grew, and a great stone wall rose thick and rough and brown above the rocks. The wall seemed as tall as a mountain to Kepha. But unlike any mountain he'd ever seen, this wall's surface was a flat expanse of rock and brick, broken at intervals by stone-crowned towers, where men in pointed copper helmets clutched long wood bows, and gazed down suspiciously to track the newcomers' approach.

Groups of Ashûru men in armor jogged back and forth outside the wall. Some rode horses, or swung swords at one another, though Kepha could see no battle.

Some men nearby were leading long lines of slaves, naked, chains around their necks, covered in bruises and blood like Mama, with that same dead look in their eyes. The men whipped the slaves, and the slaves didn't flinch or cry out; just stumbled and then kept walking, like Kepha did. The men were leading the slaves to the same place Mama and Kepha were going, inside the great stone walls.

They passed beneath a towering arch, where suspicious men asked questions of the soldiers who had Kepha and Mama. When the soldiers were satisfied, they opened a small door in a tall iron gate to let the man and his son through, dragging Kepha and Mama behind them.

Soon they were walking through in a marketplace of wood stalls, where men in rough-spun flax tunics argued in their strange tongue, debating over the black loaves, onions, turnips and plucked birds strewn across their tables. Legless beggars raised their hands to the passing column, scooting across the ground amid mangy, bone-thin dogs that snarled and snapped over discarded bones. Some of the beggars were missing hands, or arms. One was missing both his eyes. He keened a low, pleading wail, mouth gaping beneath hollow flesh-covered sockets.

Farther up the narrow street, blacksmiths hammered red-hot spears and swords on great iron anvils, splitting the chill air with clangs and sparks. Packs of dirt-caked orphans chased one another among the legs of the crowd, the younger ones tugging on the tunics of passersby while others skillfully pilfered onions and apples from the carts of distracted farmers.

As Kepha's eyes, ears and nose adapted to the reek and clamor, he realized that something seemed especially strange here: everyone seemed to be male. Could there really be no women in this city? But as Kepha examined the people more closely, he saw that many passersby wore black blankets that covered them from head to toe, except for a tiny slit for the eyes. Most of them wore black veils over their faces, too. The eyes behind those veils glanced at Kepha suspiciously—women's eyes. He caught the eye of one black-veiled woman, but a man grabbed her roughly and slapped her about the head, and pulled her away, scowling at Kepha as if he'd committed some offense.

At last they came to a place where many starving, naked men and women were shackled together, shivering in the cold. A fat man with a long beard came and talked to the man and his son who held Kepha and Mama. The gray-haired man pushed his son forward, clapped him on the back, and bid him speak. The son spoke hesitantly at first, until the fat man laughed in his face. Then he spoke more boldly, angrily, as Kepha had often seen Mama argue with Sige over the price of fish or arrows. Soon the son and the fat man were gesturing and pushing at each other, shouting in the strange thick tongue of Ash'shûr.

After many grunts and insults, the fat man threw back his head and laughed happily, and clasped arms with the son. The gray-haired father clapped his son proudly on the back, as the fat man drew a little purse out of his belt and handed over some coins. Then father and son slipped away into the crowd.

Kepha was glad to see them go, though he wished he had gotten a chance to kill them.

Big, strong men grabbed Kepha and Mama from behind and dragged them up onto a broad wooden platform at the center of the market, where a lot of other slaves were chained together, some of them naked, some in rags, some halfway between. All of them bruised and bloody and covered in dirt with matted hair. Kepha wished his hands weren't tied so he could swat the flies.

One of the chained slaves, a little boy, started to sing a song in a tongue Kepha didn't recognize. A man came over and slapped his face, hard. The boy stopped singing.

The man who had Mama said some last words to the fat man, and turned and dragged her down off the platform.

Kepha began to scream. "Mama! Mama!"

Mama didn't look up at him. Her eyes were dead, seeing nothing. She shuffled down off the platform at the end of the rope.

"Mama!" Kepha screamed again and again, pulling and trying to get out of the rope. "No! That's my mama! You can't take her!" He howled and kicked at the slavers. "Please, Mama, look at me!" he cried. But she didn't. She wasn't looking at anything.

Someone dragged Kepha away down off the platform, where a fat man with a greasy beard and greedy eyes was waiting with coins in his palm. A long line of other gaunt slaves lay chained on the ground nearby.

Suddenly, another man grabbed the arm of one of the men who was dragging Kepha away. This new man was a soldier. Kepha could tell by his copperscale armor and the short sword on his belt.

Kepha didn't know why, but at that moment he started thinking about how many sacks of barley Sige would trade for that armor and that sword. Then he felt stupid, because he knew he was probably never going to see Sige again.

The soldier said something in Ashûru to the men who had Kepha. The fat greasy man looked very upset and began shouting, and then all the men were shouting. The soldier drew his sword and called out to some other soldiers who stood nearby. They drew their swords, too. The fat greasy man backed away, snarling and spitting curses, his eyes bright with hate.

The soldier put his hand on Kepha's shoulder.

He spoke a tongue that sounded like how Babili-men spoke: "*Akkadu dababuka? Hakamukani? Adini?*"

When Kepha didn't answer, he shook his head and spoke like a Khatti-man: "*Neshili sakinusi? Eh?*"

Kepha still didn't answer.

Then the soldier spoke in words Kepha understood perfectly: "How about Aramaya? Are you from Aram?"

Those words sounded so strange coming from the mouth of an Ashûru man. The only people Kepha had ever heard speak Aramaya were Mama, and his sisters and brothers, who were all dead.

"I understand," Kepha muttered, barely looking the man in the eyes.

The soldier smiled and clapped Kepha on the shoulder. "Good. So you're from Aram. D'you like to fight?"

Kepha shook his head. "No," he said. "I hate fighting."

"Do you know how to kill a man?" the soldier asked.

"Yes," Kepha said, not looking at him. "I've killed a lot of men."

The soldier threw back his head and laughed. "See?" he said to his comrades. "I told you I've got a good eye." He turned to Kepha and looked him in the eye. "Listen," he said. "What's your name, giant?"

"Kepha," Kepha said.

The soldier smiled again. "All right. Listen, Kepha. This man wants to buy you as a slave." He nodded toward the fat greasy man, who was glaring at Kepha and the soldier. "You're a big fellow, which means this man will probably send you to work in the mines. If you're lucky, the mine will collapse and crush you to death. If you're not so lucky, you'll break rocks in the dark until you waste away from exhaustion. Do you want that life, Kepha?"

Kepha shook his head.

"Of course you don't," said the soldier. "That's why I'm offering you a choice. We can use you in the army—the army of Ash'shúr. The greatest the world has ever seen. You can fight and kill for us. This will bring you honor. If you fight well, you'll get to take gold and horses and women from the cities we conquer. Now, doesn't that sound like a better deal?"

"I guess so," Kepha said.

The soldier laughed. "Of course it's a better deal. But we only want you if you're ready to fight for us. To kill for the great God Ash'shúr. Are you ready to do that?"

Kepha didn't know what to say. He shrugged and said. "All right."

The soldier pointed at the fat greasy man and shouted something triumphant in Ashúru-tongue.

"I told them," he said to Kepha, "That you are a great bull, and are going to impress us all. I'm sure of it."

He took a few gold coins from a pouch at his belt and tossed them to the fat man, who tried to catch them but dropped a few. The fat man slapped and snarled at the slave-boy at his side, who bent down and picked the coins up off the ground.

The soldier took a key from one of the slave-sellers who'd been dragging Kepha, and unlocked the chains around his neck and hands. Kepha's whole body felt lighter as the chains came off, and he rose to his full height. The heads of these short, stocky Ashúru men only rose as high as his chest. It made Kepha feel good to be so tall again.

The soldier slapped his back. "My name's Esho. It's good to meet you, Kepha."

Esho was waiting for Kepha to say something. "You too," he said.

The soldiers took Kepha to a tavern, where they bought him fresh roasted mutton and dark crusty bread and beer. Kepha ate and drank all of it, gazing curiously at the men at other tables. Not one woman to be seen anywhere. Almost all the men seemed to be soldiers: muscular, scarred, bearded, wearing tattered tunics, leather belts, swords and various bits of armor. They laughed and joked together in Ashûru, which Kepha didn't understand a word of.

"How did you end up here, Kepha?" Esho asked while Kepha ate.

"Some men set our field on fire," Kepha told him through a mouthful of mutton and bread. "Mama and I tried to kill the men, but they were too fast and they caught us."

One of the other soldiers raised his eyebrows. "Have you killed Ash'shûr-men before?" he asked Kepha.

Kepha nodded and took a big gulp of beer. It felt so wonderful in his mouth, down into his throat and belly, and made him want to smile and talk. "Mama and I killed all kinds of men," he boasted. "Ashûru men, Khatti-men, Phryges-men—even Kush-men, whose skins are so brown they're almost black. They all pass by our field when they're going to the wars, or running away from them. We kill them all and take their armor and swords and little special things. Then we take the prizes to Sige, who trades us barley and fish and other good things to eat."

Esho looked at the other soldiers, then looked back at Kepha. "How did you and Mama kill so many men, Kepha?"

Kepha smiled, proud of what Mama had taught him. "We dug a pit, and put iron spears in it. We made a path through the tall reeds, right to the pit, and we hid the pit with reeds and dirt. All kinds of strong men fall into our pit. If they don't die right away, we hear their screams, and then we go kill them and take the prizes." Kepha smiled. "Mama says I'm very good at it."

All the soldiers were watching him now, their faces full of fascination. Kepha was starting to feel better than he had felt in a long time, with so much meat and beer in his belly.

"Do you want to find Mama?" Esho asked him. One of the other soldiers put up a hand to stop Esho, but he brushed the hand away.

Kepha nodded excitedly. "I want to kill the men who took Mama. I'll put so many spears in those men, and they'll scream and die, like in the pit. Then Mama and I will go back home."

Esho stroked his beard. "We'd like to help you get your mother back," he said. "But first you need to help us, all right? We're going to train you to kill with skill. To be a great killer of men. Then you won't have to use any tricks, like your pit. You'll be able to find those men and kill them with your bare hands, if you want."

Kepha was smiling and nodding. "Yes!" Kepha said. "That's what I want. All right, I'll help you. What do you want me to do?"

Echo reached out and patted him on the shoulder. "Just come with us, back to the camp," he said. "The training will take a while. But by the end of it, you'll be the toughest, meanest bastard on the face of the earth."

Kepha asked if he could have more food and beer, and the soldiers laughed and bought him another helping of everything. When Kepha was very full for the first time in as long as he could remember—and a little wobbly from the beer—they led him along many tight-twisting roads, out to the edge of the city of Ash'shûr, through a great gate in the wall, back to the place where the men rode horses and swung their swords.

Around a cluster of long, low wood houses, the men were doing all kinds of strange things. Some pretended to fight each other with wooden swords. Others ran in long lines behind a man who chanted rhymes. Still others clambered to the tops of tall piles of wooden beams, then down the other side, while a man on the ground yelled at them.

Some of the men even stood in big groups, all of them wearing helmets and copperscale armor, carrying big square shields, holding long iron-tipped spears. When the man at the front shouted, they thrust their spears forward, all as one. When he shouted a second time, and they'd all pull their spears back. A third time, and they tipped their spears forward. A fourth time, and they'd thrust them out low. It was like watching one man slowly fight the air, except all the men were fighting as if they were one man; as if all their bodies were bound together by invisible cords. Kepha had never seen anything so strange.

Kepha and his new friends walked past these men to a large hut, where an old scar-faced man sat behind a low table, talking with other old men. A few soldiers stood around, too, running off on errands or bringing news.

Esho and the other soldiers bowed low before the old man, and made Kepha do the same. Esho spoke with the old man in Ashŭru, and he stood up and examined Kepha, lifting his lip to check his teeth, and slapping and pressing on the muscles of his arms and shoulders. He barked a question at Esho, and Esho laughed and answered him. At last the old man huffed, shrugged, and gestured toward the door.

"What happened?" Kepha asked as they walked back outside.

Esho chuckled. "That was the regiment commander," he said. "He didn't want to let you in the corps, because you're not Ashŭru. Purity and all that. But I told him how strong you were and how many men you'd killed, and he agreed to try you out."

"What's a regiment commander?" Kepha asked.

Esho laughed. "He's your new god, Kepha."

Kepha didn't understand. "Mama and I know many Gods," he said. "Gods in the iron and the reeds, and in the water and fire."

Echo shushed him, glancing around nervously. "Forget all that, Kepha. From now on, you know only one God. The true God, Ash'shŭr."

"But I thought you said the regiment commander—"

"I was joking, for Godssakes," said Esho. "Seriously, don't let anyone around here hear you talk about other gods."

"Why not?" Kepha asked.

"Just don't," said Esho. "Now come on. We've got to find you a bed in the barracks."

They hurried to the barracks—a long, low house full of many sleeping-mats: mere piles of cheap flaxcloth on the floor. Esho talked with the men in the barracks, and found a bedroll that Kepha could use for the night.

Then, all of a sudden, Esho was in a hurry to be somewhere else.

"Dinner's at sundown," he explained to Kepha. "The men will show you how to get to the slop-place. Then at dawn, you'll start training with the rest of your company."

"What's a slop-place?" Kepha asked. "What's a company?"

Esho shook his head. "Do you always ask so many questions, Kepha?"

Kepha shrugged.

"Just follow orders," Esho said. "That's all you'll need to worry about from now on."

"When will you come back?" Kepha asked. "When will we go find Mama?"

Now Esho looked annoyed. "I don't know, Kepha." He sighed. "I'm in the army too, you know. I have things to do. This was supposed to be my leave day, actually. I should be in a bathhouse right now, full of wine, groping on some pale whore from the mountains—anyway, listen. I'll come see you soon. We'll go looking for your mother, all right?"

Kepha didn't know what to say. "All right," he said.

"Good." Esho smiled. "Just do as you're told. Work hard. You'll be fine."

He hugged Kepha tightly, then hurried off toward the barracks door.

"Esho!" Kepha called after him.

Esho half-turned. "What?"

"Thank you," Kepha said. "For being my friend."

Esho smiled and rolled his eyes, then disappeared out the door.

Kepha sat on his bedroll for a long time, hoping someone would come and say hello, but none of the other men showed him the least attention. They all lay on their own bedrolls, swapping private jokes in Ashŭru.

For the first time in days, Kepha had time to think. He thought about Mama, of course, and the field, and their house. He wondered if anything was left after the fire, and how long it would take to build a new house after he found Mama and they went home. He didn't know.

As the sun set, the men began to stand up and walk toward the door in groups. Kepha approached one of the groups of men, shyly, and made a sign for "eating," bringing his hand up to his mouth again and again.

The men laughed and said things to him in Ashŭru, and Kepha laughed too, though he didn't know what they were saying. They clapped him on the back and walked with him to a place outside, where fat, sweaty men were slopping dark porridge out of great iron pots, into cracked clay bowls that they handed out to the men.

He waited in line with the men, got his clay bowl of porridge, and joined the men sitting on the ground. He ate the porridge with his fingers and finished it after just a few handfuls. He got up and walked back to one of the sweaty men with the pots, and gestured for another helping. The man laughed, said something in Ashŭru, and shook his head when he saw Kepha didn't understand. He dropped a second helping of porridge into Kepha's bowl. Kepha smiled and nodded to say "Thank you," then went and rejoined the men.

They couldn't talk to each other, but they shared some things with signs. Kepha learned their names—Hawail, Yomadan, Marodeen. All such strange sounds. He told them his name, too. They pointed to themselves and then off toward the horizons, saying the names of Ashŭru places Kepha didn't recognize—Arbela, Kalah, Arrapakha—and he pointed to himself and said "Aram." They nodded and smiled. Then they made signs for breasts and woman-parts and tried to ask him things about women. He didn't understand most of what they asked, but he tried to tell them about Mama. They didn't understand, or didn't care. Finally he shrugged and gave up, and they went back to joking in their thick Ashûru tongue.

He didn't feel like they were his friends, exactly. But they seemed to accept him. He walked back to the barracks with them after they had finished talking, and he managed to fall asleep on the scratchy flax-cloth bedroll.

𒐋

At dawn, a man stood yelling in the barracks. He was older than the other men, and wore polished armor with a bright red plume on his helmet. Kepha didn't understand a word of what the man was yelling, but all the other men were hurrying to get up and put on their boots and swords, so Kepha hurried to get up too. All the soldiers stood straight-backed next to their bedrolls, and Kepha did the same.

The man who had yelled began walking up and down along the barracks, inspecting each of the men and bedrolls from head to toe. Sometimes he would scream suddenly in a man's face, and the man would flinch back slightly, but never fight back. Many times they yelled the word *sayid*, which Kepha thought might be the yelling man's name.

At last the angry man approached Kepha. He yelled at Kepha for a long time in Ashûru. He yelled so long, and Kepha understood none of it, and Kepha found this very funny. Kepha started to smile, though he knew he shouldn't.

The man punched Kepha hard in the stomach. Kepha doubled over, clutching at his belly, gasping for breath. The man yelled at him more. Kepha couldn't understand anything he was saying, but he kept repeating two words over and over—*Annu sayid!*—then glaring at Kepha, waiting for him to respond.

Without knowing what to do, Kepha began shouting out the words the man was yelling at him: "*Annu sayid! Annu sayid! Annu sayid!*" he yelled again and again.

The man stepped back, smiled slightly, and nodded. He said something approving in Ashûru, then walked down the line to yell at the next man.

When the *sayid* man had finished yelling at everyone in the barracks, they all ran out to a dirt path, and the man made them all run together, slowly, in rhythm. The man ran next to them, singing out little phrases which the men sang back. Kepha started to learn some of the sounds, and sang them back as best he could.

After they ran like that for a long time, the man made them do all kinds of other things. They climbed over tall piles of wood beams. They held their bodies low over the grass, and pushed themselves up and down, up and down, over and over again. They fought each other with wooden swords, which Kepha had no idea how to do. He got hit many times with the wooden sword. His partner went to complain to the *sayid* man, who screamed very loudly and angrily until Kepha's partner slunk back and began to fight with him again.

This was how Kepha's days passed. He woke at dawn to the yelling man, ran and fought and climbed all day, ate bowls of dark porridge in the evening, and slept on the barracks floor for a few hours each night.

Each day they did some different things, too, which meant Kepha was never too bored. Most of the things were easy; except the sword-fighting, which was always hard. He couldn't seem to move fast enough to avoid the blows.

As the days and nights passed, Kepha realized, to his shock, that he was beginning to understand a few words of Ashûru. The word *annu* meant "yes." *Adini* meant "no." *Patru* was "sword." It was still very hard to understand most of what the men said, but every day Kepha felt he was getting a little more of the sense of it.

Sometimes he would even try a few words in Ashûru, and the men would usually laugh and slap him on the back. One night at slop-time he held out his empty clay bowl and said "*Eli, addaniqa*," which meant "More, please," to the sweaty man behind the iron pot. The man threw back his head and laughed, and said something too quick for Kepha to understand. But the man gave him a heaping fresh helping of porridge, and Kepha felt very proud of himself. He thought Mama would tell him he was a very good boy right now. But thinking of Mama made him sad, so he tried not to.

Another evening, Esho came to visit Kepha during eating-time. Kepha ran to Esho as soon as he saw him. He threw his arms around his old friend and squeezed, until Esho gasped and pushed Kepha away, laughing, saying, "You're going to kill me, Kepha. Good God."

Kepha introduced Esho to all his new friends in the company, showing off some of his newly learned Ashûru words, which made Esho laugh and clap him on the back even more. Some of the men in Kepha's company knew Esho already, and greeted him with back-slaps and cheek-kisses. Kepha had never done a cheek-kiss, but he knew all Ashûru men did it. He hugged people instead, because he was afraid he'd get the kiss wrong.

"When can we go find Mama?" Kepha asked Esho while they ate.

"Soon, Kepha," Esho said through a mouthful of porridge. "You're not allowed to leave the camp during training."

"Why not?" Kepha asked.

Esho laughed. "That's just the rule. You need special permission from an officer. And you won't get that until you finish your training."

"When will that be?" Kepha asked.

"Good God, you ask a lot of questions," Esho said. But he was smiling. "A few more months, Kepha," he said. "Then we can go look for your mother."

Kepha considered this, and nodded.

"Esho," he asked. "What does '*sayid*' mean?"

Esho laughed again. "It's a title of respect."

"What's a title of respect?"

"It's something you say to someone who outranks you. Who's above you."

Kepha tried to understand, but he didn't, and Esho could tell he didn't. Kepha felt ashamed.

"Look," Esho explained. "You respect your mother, don't you?"

"I love Mama very much." Kepha nodded.

"Of course you do," Esho said. "But you don't just love her. You obey her, right? You do as she says, because she knows more than you do."

"Mama is very smart," Kepha agreed.

"Well," said Esho, "the officers here deserve your respect, too. You obey them because they know so much more than you do."

Kepha considered this. "I've learned some new things from them," he said, scratching his cheek.

"Exactly," said Esho. "And to show your commanding officer how much you respect him, you don't call him by his regular name. You call him by this special word, '*sayid*.'"

"I call all the officers '*sayid*?'" Kepha asked, more confused than before.

Esho drew a deep breath, then let it out and rubbed his forehead. All the others were laughing softly, and Kepha felt stupid again. He was glad none of them understood Aramaya. There was that, at least.

"'*Sayid*' is just a word, Kepha," Esho said at last. "It's a word you call your superiors to show that you respect them. All right?"

"All right," Kepha said.

He ate in silence a while longer, listening to Esho make jokes in Ashûru with the other men.

"Esho?" he said when the conversation seemed to be quieting down.

Esho rolled his eyes.

"Just one more question, Esho," Kepha said. "I promise."

"What is it?" Esho asked.

"Esho, why are there no women here?"

Esho groaned and threw down his clay bowl. The remains of his porridge spilled on the hard dirt. One of the men asked him what was going on, and he explained in Ashûru. Now all the men in Esho's company were laughing at him. He wanted to sink right down into the earth and disappear.

"You want a woman, Kepha?" Esho asked. "We'll find you some women soon enough. For now, just focus on your training."

Kepha looked down at the ground, not feeling hungry anymore. "All right, Esho," he said.

The men all began talking and joking together again, and Esho joined them.

"Esho?" Kepha said.

His friend turned to him, with a look somewhere between pity and despair. "What is it, Kepha?" he asked.

"I'm sorry for asking so many questions," said Kepha, quietly.

Esho's expression softened. He lay a hand on Kepha's shoulder. "There's nothing to be sorry for, Kepha. I'm sorry. We all get a little stressed around here, you know?"

Kepha nodded.

"We'll find your mother soon," Esho said. "We'll find you a woman, too, if that's what you want. All right? Just get through these last few months of training. Then you'll be a regular in the Ashûru army corps. You know what that means?"

Kepha shook his head.

"It means no man on earth will be able to mess with you," Esho said, looking Kepha square in the eye. "You hear me?" He smiled slightly, his eyes menacing. "No one."

Then Kepha smiled a little, too. "All right, Esho," he said.

THE MONTHS OF training seemed to pass more quickly after that. Kepha was understanding more Ashûru words every day, which meant he could follow the officer's instructions quickly, accurately, without messing up and getting punched in the stomach and yelled at. He learned to shout, "*Annu, sayid!*" which meant, "Yes, sir!" in response to every command, then do it as quickly and accurately as he could.

His body ached less than it had in the beginning, and he found he could run faster and farther than ever in his life. It felt good to run so fast in the morning, the wind whipping his hair and brushing his face, with so many of his friends around him, all of them singing out the marching songs in chorus with the officer:

Ash'shûr handed me a needle; told me, "Weave a web;
Thread it with your foeman's guts, and weight it with his head."
Shields will shatter! Spears will splinter! Iron-bound, I stride!
Weave the web for Ash'shûr, with my brothers at my side!

Oh, how the marches and songs filled Kepha's heart with joy!

He learned to block attacks from the wood swords, though he still moved too slowly to dodge most of them. In the final weeks of training, he and the other men of the company were given real swords—thick, well-hammered Ashûru shortswords, like the swords he'd taken from the men in the pit so long ago, but sharper and shinier.

All the men were encouraged to name their swords, and Kepha named his *Shinnu*, which meant "Fang" in the Ashûru tongue. Kepha loved Shinnu almost as much as he loved his friends. He learned to use her to thrust, chop and parry; to find the weak points in a man's defense and to slip through those gaps into the quick-kill places—the heart, the neck, the lung—or, if opportunity presented itself, into the slow-kill places: stomach, liver, thigh.

The armorer had to make special big armor and a giant helmet for Kepha, because the regular armor was too small to fit him. Some days he'd put on his special armor and helmet, and he and his friends would take up their shields and their long spears, and they'd march out to an open field in a big huddle. There, they learned to fight as one man: shields up, spearpoints down, *thrust*! "Hai!" they shouted. Then spearpoints back, shields up, *step forward*! "Hoh!" they shouted. Then shields up again, spearpoints down, and "Hai!" *Thrust*! Quick-kill! It felt good to know how to do something so well; to do it with all his friends, who did it just as well as he.

After Kepha and his friends had passed many days and nights in this way, a morning came when they all put on their full armor, strapped on their swords, took up their spears and shields, and marched out an open field before the city gates. Many men were waiting for them there: footsoldiers and commanders in copperscale armor and plumed helmets; rich men in robes of purple and crimson and emerald, sitting in cushioned seats atop tall boxes of wood. A few black-veiled women, sitting still and silent next to their men. Bright crimson banners and ribbons snapped in the chill mountain wind.

Kepha and his company marched in a neat line to the center of the field. Many other companies were marching the same way; more men than Kepha could ever hope to count.

A commander called, "Stop!" All the men stopped at once. All was silent.

The officer shouted, "Shields up!" Thousands of men raised their shields, all as one man.

"Points down!" The officer shouted, and the men lowered their spears in perfect unison. A strange excitement ran up Kepha's spine; a thrill at being a part of something so perfect.

"Hai!" cried the officer, and all the men thrust their spearpoints forward, then drew them back, in perfect synchrony.

"Points up!" the officer shouted, and the men turned their spearpoints to the sky.

"At ease," said the officer, and the men relaxed just slightly, letting the bottoms of their shields and the butts of their spearpoles touch the ground.

It was a cool morning, and the wind whispered against Kepha's bare skin. His special armor didn't feel hot or heavy at all.

A tall, bearded man, scarred and thick with muscle, rose from one of the cushioned seats atop the wood boxes. His square black beard and curling hair were plaited and bound with gold rings. He wore a short-sleeved robe of deepest crimson, belted with a thick leather strap from which two iron daggers protruded—no mere ornaments, these, but blooded weapons, their blades scored and notched with scars of combat, like the man's skin. Atop his robe he wore a type of armor Kepha had never seen before, like copperscale, but forged of dark iron, polished to a gleam so bright it hurt Kepha's eyes; all wrapped in a loose toga of bright indigo, fringed with shaggy fur that rippled in the wind. Upon the man's head sat a heavy wrought-iron band adorned with ingots of gold and turquoise.

When he stood to speak, all fell silent.

"All praise be to Ash'shûr, God of Gods," he intoned, spreading his hands, turning his palms upward to the sky.

"Ash'shûr alone is God of Gods," the crowd answered, turning their own palms upward.

Kepha had heard a lot about this God Ash'shûr during training, but he still didn't understand. Whenever he asked where this strange God was, or what he looked like, the men only laughed, or got annoyed with him. One time, when he'd asked what Ash'shûr was the God *of*, Esho had told him Ash'shûr was God of everything. It was all very confusing.

"Today," the iron-crowned man was saying, "you complete your training in Ash'shûr's battle school. This school has molded you into the deadliest fighting force the world has ever seen. I should know. I designed it."

He smiled, and a low laugh rippled through the crowd.

"A great work is beginning here," the man continued. "The Land of Ash'shûr is awakening. For years—nay, for centuries, our people have lain asleep, dreaming of our lost empire, of those golden days when an Ashûru king sat the throne of Babili. We have dreamed, oh, how we have dreamed of a return to that ancient glory."

The man paused to take a breath. The crowd was watching him intently.

"Throughout the long centuries since our first mighty empire was destroyed," he said, "our people have endured every humiliation. Our lands and wealth have been snatched by infidel armies. Our women carried off as slaves. Our children ripped from our arms as our cities burned."

His voice grew quieter now. He spoke out above the whistling wind:

"And what did our generals do?" He shook his head. "Nothing, of course. Only called the armies back, hoping to save lives—and meanwhile, brave men of Ash'shûr, in their tens of thousands, turned their backs and bent their necks for the sword. Because that is what they were ordered to do."

He was clenching his fists now, looking almost as if he might cry.

"But I am here today," he said, "to speak to you not of the silver days of our past, but of the golden days soon to come! Our struggle has spanned generations, as you all know. It was our great-grandfathers who trekked north into the highest mountain passes, to establish the routes to carry copper and iron down to Ash'shûr. It was their sons, our grandfathers, who traveled to pharaohs' courts in Misr, buying the finest war-stallions to strengthen the bloodlines of our horses. And it was their grandsons, our fathers, who studied the iron armies of

Khatti, sacrificing themselves and their men to learn the ancient secrets of combat, so that we might improve upon them."

He spread his muscled arms, eyes wide with triumph.

"And now, where are the great empires of Misr and Khatti? Where are Mitanni and Babili? Ha! All the great beasts have fallen silent at last. All, of course, save for Ash'shúr."

He paused a moment, his whole body trembling with excitement.

"And as I stand before you today, men of Ash'shúr," he cried, "I tell you that you will not have to wait for your sons to finish the great work begun by our fathers. It is *this* generation, it is *us*, here, who will strike the hammer-blow of Ash'shúr upon our enemies!"

The crowd leaped to their feet and roared, clapping their hands and cheering.

"Look to your left," the man said, gesturing wildly, clenching his fists. "Look to your right." Kepha did as the crowned man said. "The men you see beside you are the most precious prizes you will ever know. The mighty men of Ash'shúr. The holiest, most perfect men in the world. It is for *these* men that we all fight! For our supreme race, and for the one true God Ash'shúr, who created our people to serve as the iron hammer of his will!"

The crowd roared. A chill ran through Kepha's whole body; a rush of wind and ice and fire all at once. He felt almost as if he could see the God there before him, shining more brilliantly than the sun. Warm tears rose in his eyes, and he found he was trembling.

"The true God speaks to me every day," the man cried. "He tells me our time is come! All that is left is to submit to his divine will! To give in, to obey—to reap the harvest that waits for us!"

Now Kepha was cheering too: a wordless roar that thundered up from somewhere deep inside him. All the men around him were cheering, too.

"Ash'shûr!" The man was shouting again and again, pounding his chest twice on the first syllable, then thrusting forth his fist on the second. "Ash'shûr! Ash'shûr!"

At the foot of the platform, men began to beat great deep-voiced drums in time with the chant. Kepha joined in, pounding his heart twice with his spear-hand—"*Ash*"—then pumping his spear into the air—"*Shûr!*" He and his friends shouted the name until it lost all meaning; yet the sound felt so wonderful in his throat, and it made him feel strong to chant it as he pounded his chest and the drums thundered and he pumped his spear and howled it again and again: "*Ash-shûr! Ash-shûr! Ash-shûr!*"

After everyone had cheered and shouted for a long time, and all the men had received the divine blessing of the God Ash'shûr and the king, Kepha and his friends Hawail, Yomadan, and Marodeen walked back to the armory. They locked away their armor and spears, washed themselves with cold water from the well, put on clean crimson tunics, and walked up the road, through the great gate in the city wall.

⚹

THE FIRST TIME Kepha had entered the city of Ash'shûr, he and Mama had been slaves, naked and terrified. Now, just a few months later, he strode proudly with his friends, wearing the crimson tunic of the Ashûru army. The guards at the gate greeted him and his friends as equals, and let them through with salutes and smiles. It filled Kepha with pride, but also made him sad in a way that was hard to understand.

Passing heavy-burdened merchants, howling beggars and a few black-veiled women, they strolled the muddy streets until they found a tavern. When the man cleaning mugs behind the bartop saw their crimson tunics and their swords, he leaped over the counter and embraced them all as brothers.

"Hail Ash'shûr," he said as he clapped Kepha on the back.

All of them echoed the greeting, smiling.

The man brought them tall clay cups of beer, refusing to take anything in return. "The men of Ash'shûr's army always drink free in my house," he assured them. "You're welcome anytime."

Once they'd settled in at a table with their foaming mugs, slaves brought plates heaping with mutton and figs and dates, along with stewed chickpeas and barley porridge. Kepha devoured huge helpings of all of it, until his stomach felt wonderfully heavy and full, and he would've been happy to lie down and sleep right there on the sawdusted floor.

But the men were dragging him up, crying out that the night was only beginning

"Where are we going?" he asked.

"To claim our real reward," Hawail said, grinning cryptically.

They wound their way down a few narrow alleys between dark stone houses and shops, in the dim light of sparsely placed torches. They got lost a few times on the way, the men shouting and pushing each other good-naturedly, too gleeful to start a real fight.

At last they arrived at a door that looked, to Kepha, just like all the other doors on the block. One of the men knocked twice, then once, then three times, and a tiny window in the door slid open.

"Password," said a gruff voice behind the door.

"Rose petal," said Hawail, grinning.

The tiny window closed, then the door swung open.

"Four of you, eh?" said a squat, plump man in a tattered tunic. He pursed his lips and nodded. "We've got quite a crowd tonight already, but we should be able to find something for you."

The squat man stepped aside and gestured for them to enter.

"Welcome to Paradise, brave warriors," he said with a chuckle.

Kepha and the others descended a narrow staircase, lit by dim flickering lamplight from below. At the bottom of the stairs waited a low-ceilinged chamber, where soldiers and women lay entwined on low cushioned couches. These were the only unveiled women Kepha had seen in Ash'shûr, he realized. They wore thin, transparent dresses, some already hiked high on their thighs as the men groped eagerly upward. Other men accepted sips from cups of wine or vials of joyplant milk, which the women lifted for them to drink.

In one corner, a bored-looking musician plucked out a languid melody on a lyre. Smoke thick with sandalwood and myrrh drifted up through the humid air, wrapping the room in sweet-smelling clouds. A few of the women lay by themselves on couches, inspecting the newcomers with looks of vague curiosity.

Kepha's friend Marodeen rubbed his palms together eagerly. "Now this," he said, "is what we trained for." The others laughed.

The squat man had joined them at the bottom of the stairs. "Take your pick, gentlemen," he said. "Each of our ladies has her own particular gifts, of course. But you'll find all to be equally satisfying."

"They all look the same with the lights off, don't they?" Yomadan laughed.

"Oh, but my friends," said the squat man, raising his hands in protest. "You'll find that each of our girls has quite unique talents! Why, Yasemin here was known as the Bull-Rider of Mari—"

"I'm sure they'll all do fine," said Hawail, patting the man on the shoulder, already headed for a black-haired girl on a couch nearby.

Kepha's friends split off, each of them settling in next to a girl that caught their eye, whispering into her ears even as their hands began probing up her legs, down the top of her scant dress.

For a frantic few seconds, Kepha looked around the room in utter confusion. At last he chose an empty seat on a couch in the far corner, next to a small, slightly plump girl who stared emptily at the swirling smoke.

The squat man came rushing over. "Brother," he said, "I beg your pardon, but I'm certain I can find a partner with more—eh—stamina, for a great bull such as yourself." He grabbed Kepha's hand and tugged at it. "This one has been having, well, slight problems of late—"

"This one is fine," Kepha said, brushing the man's hand away.

The man took a moment to compose himself, then snapped at the girl. "Yasha, rouse yourself, for Godssakes. See if you can't make me some money for once." He reached out to slap her across the face.

Kepha caught the man's hand.

"Don't do that," he said. "Please, leave us alone."

The man backed away, muttering darkly.

Kepha and the girl sat next to each other in silence for a few moments, neither of them moving except to breathe softly. She really seemed to be somewhere else. She scarcely even blinked.

Some of the women on the other couches began to stand up, pulling their men with them. The men's faces glowed eagerly as they followed the women out of the room, down hallways where Kepha heard distant giggling and moans.

He turned to the girl. "Your name is Yasha?" he asked.

She only stared silently into the swirling lamp-lit smoke and steam.

"I'm not from here, either," he said. "I'm from Aram. My name is Kepha. Mama says it means 'Rock.'"

Her eyes turned toward him slightly. She drew a deep breath and sighed.

"I had a mama once," she said. "Far away."

Kepha nodded. "I'm from far away, too," he said. "The Ashûru men brought me and Mama here."

She turned to face him. The look in her eyes was still empty, far away. But she seemed to see him now, at least.

"What happened to her?" she asked.

"I don't know." Kepha shook his head. "They took her away, the slavers, on our first day here. Soon I'm going to go find her, and kill those men who took her."

"How will you find her?" she asked.

He'd never thought about that before. He felt stupid for never having thought about it. "I'll ask the slavers, I guess," he said, knowing as he said it was a stupid idea. "Or maybe my friends and I will hunt through the city. Ask everyone until we find someone who knows."

"It's a big city," she said. "Lots of people to ask."

Kepha nodded and sighed. "I know," he said. "But I'll find her."

For the first time, Yasha's eyes seemed to focus on his. "You love her a lot, don't you?"

He felt hot tears rise in his eyes. "Yes," he said. "I do."

Suddenly she looked at him oddly, as if realizing something. "If you're not Ashûru," she asked, "then why aren't you a slave?"

The question surprised him. He'd been thinking about Mama. "I—" he stammered. "My friend Esho took me from the slavers. He took me to the army place, and they let me be in the regiment, and trained me to fight for Ash'shûr."

"Do you like doing that?"

Still feeling the tears, he smiled a little. "Yes," he said. "I'm very good at fighting. I can use a sword, and a spear and shield, and I do all the drills exactly right."

She nodded, and they fell back into silence for a while. He glanced across the room and saw that the squat man was eyeing them suspiciously, almost angrily. She seemed to see him too, and a look of fear crossed her face.

"So," she asked, putting a hand on his leg. "Are you going to fuck me?"

He nearly jumped, he was so startled. "Am—am I *what*?"

She laughed, showing a smile that might have once been beautiful, before her teeth had been chipped and broken. She quickly closed and covered her mouth. "You're a bit of a shy boy, aren't you?" she said.

That made him blush. "No," he said. "I'm not shy."

"So what's the problem then?"

"Problem?" he asked, feeling more confused. "What problem? There's no problem."

"Don't you want to fuck me?" she ran her hand up his leg, but the look in her eyes was still distant.

"I—" he stammered again. "I want to do what I'm supposed to—"

She sat back, gasping. "Oh my God!" she whispered. "You've never—!" Then she covered her mouth and said, "Sorry. I'm so sorry."

Now he was really embarrassed. He felt confused and humiliated, all at the same time.

"How old are you, anyway?" she asked.

"Sixteen," he said. "I think."

She smiled, covering her mouth again. "You think?"

He shrugged. "Mama says she's not sure what month it was when I was born. She was running from bad men every day and night, and had to hide in all kinds of scary places. I don't like to ask her about that time, because it makes her sad."

"I understand," Yasha said. "I had to run and hide a lot, too."

"But they caught you," he said.

"Yes," she said.

"They caught us, too," he said.

He watched her for a few breaths, looking into her eyes. He thought she was very pretty, and he wanted to be closer to her, but he didn't know how. Mama had never told him about this, or shown him what to do. He felt confused again.

"Hey," she said. "Akhiqar is giving us the evil eye again."

Kepha glanced over at the squat man, who was watching them intently. "I'll close those eyes of his," Kepha said, beginning to get up, a dark expression spreading across his face.

"No!" she gasped, grabbing the hem of his tunic. "If you do that," she said, "he'll only beat me worse as soon as you leave. There's a better way."

"What way?" he asked.

"Come on," she said, getting up and taking his hand. "I'll show you." She stood barely as tall as his chest, and her hand was tiny inside his.

She led him down a narrow hallway, pas rooms with locked doors, with giggles and shouts and cries behind them. In the dim, flickering lamplight and the smoke, the scene seemed almost like a bad dream; the kind with endless hallways and invisible moaning things always just about to catch up.

At the end of the hallway, she unlocked a wooden door and led him into a small chamber with a cheap wooden bed and a small dressing table. She locked the door behind them, brought him to the bed and sat next to him on the stained, straw-stuffed mattress.

She took his hand again. His breathing quickened. He sat absolutely still, feeling excitement gather deep in his abdomen; tense between his legs.

"Yasha," he asked, his voice shaking.

"Yes?" She ran her hand up his thigh, toward the tenseness.

"Why—" he let out a soft gasp. "Why are there no women in Ash'shûr? I mean, why are they all hidden?"

"Because," she leaned closer, stroking his chest, "they are afraid of us." He could feel her breath on his face. His heart was pounding. "They fear our power over them. They fear that we will soften their rage, and drain away their will to make war. And do you want to know a secret?"

He gulped softly, feeling her hand tighten around him. "What?"

She smiled. "They're right."

Her hand on his chest pushed him gently back onto the bed. He lay back and she straddled him. Everything else faded away—the long hallway with its moans, the room of scented smoke, the camp and regiment, the pride that swelled when during the drills, the hatred of Ash'shûr's enemies, the fear that lived beneath it all never really went away; even Mama herself—all of it disappeared as Yasha moved above him, looking down into his eyes. As she slipped him inside and they both began to move together, for a few minutes that filled all time, there was nothing in the world except the two of them.

Afterward, as she lay on the bed next to him and softly stroked his chest, all these things came rushing back to him, and he began to cry, softly.

"You poor boy." She smiled gently and placed her hand against his cheek.

They lay there together for what felt like a long time, until his tears began to subside.

Someone was pounding on the door, shouting, "He'd better either be dead or paying you extra!"

"Time to go," she said, a sad look crossing her face.

She rose from the bed and adjusted her translucent dress. She took his hand and pulled him upright.

Kepha wrapped his arms around her and hugged her gently. She rose on tiptoes and kissed his neck, which was as close as she could get to his cheek.

She unlocked the door. The squat man, Akhiqar, was standing there, a furious look on his face. That look softened as soon as Kepha met his gaze.

"I hope you had a nice time, soldier," he said, doing a poor job of hiding his disdain.

"If you lay a hand on her," Kepha said calmly, "You won't live to see the sunrise."

Akhiqar gulped and stood aside to let them brush past, back into the hallway. He threw Yasha a glare as she passed, but kept his mouth shut.

※

Kepha's friends were waiting for him, sprawled on couches, sipping wine and joyplant milk, looking dazed and happy. Hawail rose and clapped Kepha on the back as Yasha returned to her couch in the corner.

The drunk soldier laughed triumphantly. "Feels good to be a man, doesn't it, Kepha?"

Kepha shrugged and took a seat near his friends on the couch. A few women in scant dresses sat near them, perhaps hoping for a second round. Most had drifted off to approach fresh customers.

"So," said Marodeen, leaning toward Kepha, spilling some of the wine in his cup. "How was it? Did she, eh—you know—do everything? Any special tricks?" He cracked up laughing, though Kepha didn't get the joke, as usual.

They were all looking at him expectantly. "It was very nice," he said after a moment.

His three friends looked at him like he'd betrayed them.

"'It was very nice'," said Hawail at last. "Well, I'm sure it was." His expression softened into a glazed smile. "Come on, maybe some wine will loosen your tongue." He poured a cup from the pitcher on the table and handed it to Kepha, who took a gulp to be polite.

"Well," said Yomadan, in a mock-conspiratorial tone, "mine had a *very* loose tongue. I'll tell you that for free." All three of them broke up laughing. Kepha laughed with them, so he wouldn't look stupid.

"That Yasemin," said Hawail. "They don't call her the Bull-Rider of Mari for nothing. She knows how to keep hold of the horns." They laughed at that, too. Kepha took another gulp of wine.

"How about yours, Big Kepha," Marodeen said. "What corner of the earth was she from?"

Kepha glanced over at the couch where Yasha sat. She was staring emptily at the smoke again.

"From K'nan, I think," he said. "She said they brought her a long way."

"And did she, eh—" Yomadan winked at him. "Bring you a long way?"

Kepha didn't understand, but he tried to hide it. "She brought me to her room," he said, forcing a smile.

"For Godssakes, Kepha," Hawail laughed. "You look like you've just been to a funeral. At least tell us she showed you a good time."

Kepha smiled as best he could. "We were very happy," he said. "It felt really good."

"Ha!" Hawail exclaimed. "There, you see! Women really *are* good for something."

"Oh, God, these priests," Yomadan moaned, running his hand down his face. "They'd say sex itself was a sin, if they discovered some other way to make children."

"The priests want to close down all these places," Hawail explained to Kepha, gesturing around the room. "The really strict ones do, anyway. 'Men should speak with no woman but their own wife,' the holy men say. 'We must give our seed only to pure-blooded Ashûru women.'" He adopted a stiff, absurdly formal tone, "'Impregnate them only in the one, proper, utterly boring position, for the sole, holy purpose of making new Ashûru soldiers!'"

All Kepha's friends were booing and hissing, throwing dates and nuts at Hawail, telling him to shut up. Women and men on the other couches glanced over in mild irritation, then got back to their business.

Kepha had no idea what they were talking about. He tried to think of a question that wouldn't make him look completely stupid.

"Do women have evil powers?" he asked when they'd quieted down a bit.

His friends all laughed, and he figured he'd asked a stupid question. But Hawail appeared to really be thinking about it.

"I don't believe they're evil," Hawail said, refilling his cup from the wine-pitcher, "though some of the holy men really do seem to think that." He shrugged. "They're just different. That requires no special belief. Anyone can look at them and see it's true. Not just their bodies, which is obvious. They're more—" He gestured in the smoky air, searching for words. "More emotional. Weaker. And what happens once every moon? They bleed like wounded animals. One minute they're sad, the next, they're angry, then hungry, then ready to fuck." He shrugged.

Kepha wondered if Hawail might be right about that. He remembered that Mama bled for a few days every month, even when she wasn't wounded. When he was little, those bloody days had frightened him, especially because Mama was moody during that time; lashing out at him without warning when he tied the fishhook wrong, or slipped and dropped a bucket of water. She always apologized afterward, but he knew to give her extra space during those days.

"I don't trust anything that bleeds for three days and doesn't die," Yomadan proclaimed, and all the men laughed. Kepha got the joke this time, though, and he didn't think it was true or funny. Mama bled every month, but he trusted her more than anyone. So he didn't laugh.

Hawail sensed the change, and said, "All we're saying is that women are bound to the earth, to the flesh, in ways that men aren't. Women's bodies obey Sín, the moon-god. They can't help it. When they have sex, they make a baby. And when we look at them, *we* think about sex." He smiled. "And sometimes, like tonight, that's a good thing. But most of the time, it's not. When we look at a woman, we start thinking about sex when we should be thinking about our city and our God, focusing our will on making war, so we can build a better world."

"Not to mention the problems that rise up when we look at another man's wife or daughter," Yomadan added.

"Right," said Hawail. "We can't help our thoughts. It's natural. That's what men and women do. And with whores and foreign slaves, of course, it's perfectly fine. That's what they're there for. But for Ashûru women, especially other men's wives and daughters?" He spread his hands. "That's why they cover themselves with modesty. It's for their own protection, as much as ours."

"Exactly," said Marodeen. "We *value* Ashûru women. We prize them highly—*in their proper place*."

"That's it," said Hawail. "It's very simple."

Yomadan and Marodeen refilled their wine-cups and began to drink again.

"So if women didn't wear those black coverings," Kepha said, slowly, "you'd all do what the men did to Mama, every chance you got."

His friends stopped smiling and fell silent.

"Kepha," Hawail said, putting his hand on Kepha's arm. "We're sorry about what happened to your mother. It was horrible, we know."

"You *don't* know!" Kepha cried, startling the women and men on the other couches. Tears were rising in his eyes again. "You don't know," he said, more quietly. "You don't know what it was like."

They had all stopped drinking. They were staring at him, as if afraid he'd tear them apart at any second. He didn't want to tear them apart. They were his friends. But he didn't like the things they were saying. He didn't feel like crying, either, but now tears were running down his cheeks.

"I don't think those things," he said. "The things you say. I don't want to do those things when I look at women. Not even when they're almost naked. And I don't want anyone to do those things to Mama. Not to anyone."

He slammed his wine-cup on the table, hard; the clay cracked, and wine began to leak out onto the stained wood. "I'm tired of listening to this," he cried. "And I'm tired of waiting. I've waited a long time, and no one wants to help me. I'm going to find Mama."

As he rose from the couch, he cracked his head against the low ceiling. He crouched, rubbing the spot where it hurt, and looked over to where Yasha sat. She was staring up at him now, wide-eyed.

"Let's get out of here," he said to her.

She didn't move; only looked mutely at Akhiqar. The proprietor glared at her, practically shaking with rage.

Kepha reached out and took her tiny hand in his and pulled her gently from the couch. They walked toward the doorway to the stairs.

Akhiqar rushed to block their way. "Boys!" he howled up the staircase. "We've got trouble! Get down here!" He turned to Kepha. "I swear on Ash'shûr's arrows, I don't care who you are, or how big. There are laws. She," he pointed furiously at Yasha, "is *my* property. If you so much as—"

Kepha cut off the man's words with a tight grip on his neck. Akhiqar spluttered and choked as Kepha lifted him off the floor. Hawail and the others were leaping up from the couch, yelling at him to stop, but he barely heard them.

A guttural roar escaped Akhiqar's throat. Kepha smashed him head-first into the stone wall, and the roar turned to a hiccup. A spatter of blood ran down the wall. Kepha slammed Akhiqar against the wall again and heard a crunching sound. Yasha had turned away, looking like she'd be sick.

Two big, cruel-looking men came running down the stairs, shouting curses at Kepha. He barely heard them. Hawail and his other friends were pulling on his arms, managing to bend the treetrunks of muscle behind his back. But the work was done. Akhiqar's body slid to the floor like a ragdoll, rage and shock still on his wide-eyed face.

Even the cruel-looking men were stunned. And though they were tall and muscled, Kepha dwarfed them. He lunged at one of them, snarling, and both of them backed away.

The Cradle and the Sword

Kepha took Yasha's hand. She didn't resist his pull. He scooped her small frame into his arms and ran up the staircase, leaving his friends' shouts behind.

He shoved open the wood door and stumbled out into the dim flickering light of the torchlit alley. He careened down side-streets, Yasha bouncing in his arms, with no idea where he was or where he was headed, looking about wildly for a place to hide, anywhere they wouldn't suspect.

Past mud-brick apartments and canvas-cloaked shopfronts; past knots of drunk revelers stumbling home for the night. He ran, and turned at random, and ran again. Once he passed a night patrol; two soldiers in crimson tunics and copperscale, carrying spears. They shouted after him but he'd already ducked down another alley. They didn't seem to care enough to give chase.

At last, when he'd run out of breath and his legs were burning, he came to a stable; a long building with many horses in stalls, and a place where hay was stacked into a tall pile. He slipped through the door and shuffled quietly past the horse-stalls, hearing a few horses whinny as they caught his scent; but none of them panicked.

The place with the hay-pile was quiet and pitch-dark. He was too tired to run anymore. He set Yasha down carefully on the soft hay, then lay down next to her. Her breathing was quick. She rolled over and laid her head on his chest. He wrapped his arms around her and she clung tightly to him.

"Yasha," he whispered after a while. "I'm sorry."

"For what?" she whispered.

"For everything," he said.

She laid a finger on his lips and said, "Shh. You're a good boy."

Kepha smiled there in the dark, though he knew she couldn't see it. But she felt it against her finger and repeated, "You're a very good boy."

He felt like he might cry again then, but he was too tired. He wanted to tell her so many things; things about Mama and what they'd been through, and about the army and his training, and about life back in the field so long ago, with the pit of spears and the cozy little hut where he and Mama lived; and about the things he felt when she was near him. But it was hard to think of the words for all those things, or to know which things to say first, or which were most important. While he worked in his mind to figure out what to say, he drifted off to sleep.

▼▼▼
▼▼▼
▼▼▼

Yasha woke him when the first hints of pre-dawn light crept through the cracks in the stable's walls.

"We should go," she whispered.

Kepha stood up, feeling hunger gnaw in his belly. For a moment he thought about eating some of the hay, or looking for an apple or something in one of the horses' stalls. But she was tugging on his arm, telling him they needed to keep moving; and he knew she was right.

At Yasha's urging, they took an old black blanket from one of the horses. Kepha tore a hole in it so she could see, and draped it over her. It looked absurd draped over her, and it smelled like a horse. Kepha almost wanted to laugh, but he didn't. At least they wouldn't attract too much attention this way.

Out on the winding streets, they tried to walk as naturally as they could; this towering crimson-tunicked man and the tiny black-blanketed form next to him. The few early risers they passed—groggy traders, mostly, and merchants dragging their carts of onions and radishes to market—saw right away that he was a soldier, and gave him wide berth.

As he led them deeper into the city, Yasha grew more nervous. "We should be heading for the city gate," she whispered. "We have to get out of here."

"Not yet," he said quietly. "Not until I find Mama."

"Kepha," she said, "your mother is probably—"

He stopped and turned to her. "She's probably what?"

Yasha searched for words, knowing she'd never find the right ones. "She's probably going to be very hard to find," she said at last.

Kepha nodded. "I know. But I'll find her."

She shuffled by his side as they found their way back to the slave market, where Kepha and Mama had been split up and sold all those long months ago. The market was mostly empty this early in the morning, when the first light of dawn was just beginning to light up the square. But Kepha saw one man he recognized, chewing an apple near the wood platform where slaves were auctioned off.

"That's him," he whispered to Yasha.

"Who?" she asked.

"The man who took Mama and me apart."

She raised a hand to stop him, but he was already marching across the square. The man looked up, and his eyes went wide as Kepha approached.

"I'm not going to hurt you," Kepha told him, "if you tell me where she is."

"I—" the man gasped, dropping his apple to the stony ground. "It's really you! I remember you. The giant."

"Who took my mama?" Kepha asked, leaning over the man.

"You're a soldier?" The man was stammering. "How did you become a soldier?"

"Answer me!" Kepha snarled.

The man glanced around the square and saw that no help was coming. He sighed. "Hell," he said at last. "You know what? I'm happy to tell you. It was Nisroch, that Aramean bastard. Paid a paltry sum for her, too, not that one can expect much for such an old—"

"Where did he take her?" Kepha asked, squeezing the man's shoulder.

"How should I know?" the slaver exclaimed. "Back to Aram, for all I know. South to K'nan, maybe. Who knows if he even remembers her?"

Kepha thought for a moment. "Where is he, this Nisroch?"

"Oh, I'll tell you that for free," said the slaver. "He's always holed up at the Bowman's Inn, out near the city gate. You didn't hear it from me, though."

Kepha released him, and he backed away, rubbing his shoulder.

"Do not call the guards," Kepha said.

"It would help me," the slaver said, "if I could tell people you had to beat it out of me."

Kepha looked at him quizzically.

"Hit me," the man said, gesturing at his face. "Come on. Just one punch."

Kepha shrugged and threw a hard hook into the man's jaw. He dropped to the hard ground, senseless.

Yasha gasped. Kepha hurried back to her, saying, "He told me to hit him. What a strange man."

"Did you find out where she is?" Yasha asked.

"The Bowman's Inn, near the city gate," said Kepha.

They rushed down more back-twisting streets and narrow alleys, heading in the direction of the gate. Every street seemed to lead to a blind alley or a turnaround, or end in an apartment courtyard. By the time they'd found their way to the inn, the sun was already high in the sky, and people were beginning to watch them suspiciously. Any moment, Kepha knew, someone would recognize them and summon the guards—maybe even the army. Kepha didn't know what the punishment was here for killing a man, but it wasn't hard to guess.

The inn squatted between two apartment blocks, a half-wreckage of wood planks and mud-bricks. A plaque hung above the door; a crimson-tunicked soldier was painted on it, drawing a bow.

The Cradle and the Sword

Kepha found a place for Yasha to hide in a nearby alley, then burst through the door of the inn.

"Where is he?" he demanded of the first man he saw, a beer-gutted, balding fellow. "Where is Nisroch the Aramean?"

"Just who in Ash'shûr's name do you think you are?" the beer-gutted man exclaimed, but Kepha was already pushing past him, through the door to the central courtyard, where cloth-curtained doorways led to the inn's rooms.

He flung aside the curtain of each room, finding a half-naked merchant on a bedroll in one; a furious old man in another; two men and many wood trunks in a third.

Then he threw open the curtain to the fourth room. There, on a low wood bed, lay Nisroch. He would've remembered the man anywhere; that fat, greasy-bearded man who'd torn Mama away from him so long ago. Things were so different now. He'd passed through army training, made many friends, become a soldier of Ash'shûr, and even found a women to love. But here, now, as he stared into Nisroch's beady eyes while the man sat up and glared at him in the shadows of that room, Kepha felt like that terrified little boy again, and had to fight the urge to run away.

Two thin young boys, both naked, covered in bruises, lay chained to an iron ring in one of the room's walls. They barely looked up at him. And there next to them—he could hardly believe his eyes—was Mama. She was also naked, thinner than he'd ever seen her, with bruises on her arms and legs, and angry red welts across her back. He didn't care. She was here. Real. Alive.

He saw all this in a flash of an instant. Then Nisroch was leaping from the bed, snarling, drawing a sharp iron dagger from beneath the blankets.

⟨

For a fat old man, Nisroch was lightning-quick with the dagger, and Kepha was slow. In an instant, the fat man had Mama by the throat, the blade pressed against the vein in her neck: a quick-kill point.

A smile spread across Nisroch's lips. "What now, you great ox?" he asked, gold teeth gleaming in the shadows. "Choose your move, if you can."

Kepha hesitated. He looked into Mama's eyes and saw nothing in them. She wasn't even looking back at him.

"Mama," he whispered.

Her eyes moved a little.

"Mama!" he said again.

She opened her mouth, slowly, and released a long, low groan. Her teeth were gone.

"Boys!" Nisroch bellowed, his dagger still at Mama's throat.

There was nothing for Kepha to do. He knew he'd be too slow. He might have a chance in a moment if he waited for it, but there was nothing to do until then.

Nisroch was shouting for his "boys" again and again, and at last Kepha heard them hurrying into the inn's central courtyard behind him. One of them slipped behind Kepha, pressed something sharp against his liver: a slow-kill point.

"There, now," said Nisroch, smiling again. "Now we're all together. A happy family."

"Please," said Kepha. "Don't kill her. Kill me instead."

Nisroch threw back his head and barked a laugh. "You're in no position to make a deal, Ox." He turned to the men behind

Kepha. "Agdar, go summon the city guards." He looked back at Kepha. "You're in a world of trouble now, boy."

"My name isn't 'boy,' or 'ox,'" Kepha said. "It's Kepha."

Nisroch rolled his eyes. "I don't give a good damn what your name is. You're an upstart slave, and you're about to die for it."

The man behind Kepha pressed the dagger-tip deeper into Kepha's back. He felt the fabric of his tunic rip, and a small trickle of blood run down his hip.

"We each have our place in the world, Ox," said Nisroch. "This is the order of things. It is what the God Ash'shûr ordains: God, king, man, woman—and slave." He turned Mama's head slightly and gazed down into her empty eyes. "Your mama had some trouble learning her place, too," he said. "Didn't you?" The slaver looked into Kepha's eyes. "But she learned her place in the end."

A roar tore up from Kepha's throat, exploded from his mouth. Howling, he charged at Nisroch. The slaver's eyes widened in shock. He pressed the dagger-point into Mama's throat. Blood ran down her neck. But Kepha was on him, gripping him by the throat, hurling him across the room. The slaver hit the far wall with a crack and dropped to the stone floor, twitching.

His guards were already hurling themselves at Kepha. He was too slow to dodge, and they pierced and sliced at him many times with their knives. But there were only two of them, and Kepha hardly felt the wounds. He gripped one by the head and cracked his neck, then dropped the man to the stone floor. The other guard backed away, pleading; but Kepha hurled a punch square at his face. It snapped his head back, and he dropped to the floor too.

Kepha ran to Mama, knelt next to her, examined the wound in her neck. She was gasping and wheezing; bubbling bright-red blood pumped from the cut with every breath.

"Mama, please," Kepha heard himself crying over and over. "Please stay! Please stay with me!"

But Mama's eyes rolled back. Her head lolled on her neck; her body went limp. Kepha kneeled on the floor amid the wrecked bodies of Nisroch and his guards, holding Mama in his arms, not caring about the blood that ran in thick rivulets down his arms and legs, staining his crimson tunic.

"Please, Mama," he whispered again. "Please come back. Please."

"Kepha!" a familiar voice shouted from outside the door.

Kepha looked up. There stood Esho; not armored, but clutching his shortsword, backed by five copperscale-armored men Kepha didn't recognize. Four of them held bows, drawn back with nocked arrows trained on Kepha; while the fifth one held Yasha, decloaked, clad only in her translucent dress. She was crying, and the man held a dagger to her throat.

Kepha stared up at his friend, too confused and terrified to know what to say.

"Lay her down, Kepha," Esho said quietly, in Aramaya, walking slowly and carefully toward Kepha, his palm upraised. "There's nothing you can do for her now."

"Esho," said Kepha, through the sobs that shook his body. "You're my friend."

"Yes, Kepha," Esho said. "I am your friend. Lay her down."

Kepha gently lifted Mama from his lap and laid her on the stone floor.

"Good," said Esho, nodding. "That's very good, Kepha. Now come to me."

"Why?" Kepha cried. "Why should I go with you?"

"Because," Esho said, "I'm your friend, remember?"

"You're not my friend!" Kepha howled. "You're just like everyone else!"

"Kepha, I helped you," Esho said. "Remember? I saved you from this man." He gestured at Nisroch's shattered body, sprawled against the room's back wall.

"You didn't save Mama," Kepha said. "Mama was the only one who loved me."

"That's not true!" Yasha cried from out in the courtyard. The soldier who held her pressed the dagger-tip harder against her neck, and a small trickle of blood ran down her collarbone, staining the thin fabric of her dress. "That's not true, Kepha," she hissed through the pain.

"Listen," said Esho, sinking to one knee next to Kepha. "You've done some bad things, Kepha. The kind of things they kill people for."

"I know," said Kepha, wiping at his tears.

"But you're in the army of Ash'shûr, which means I may be able to help you."

"Help me do what?" Kepha asked. "There's nothing left to do."

"Look, Kepha," Esho said. "Do you want to die right here, today, or do you want a chance at an actual life? A good life, maybe, with honor and meaning. It'll be hard, but I'm on good terms with a few commanding officers. I can probably get you a frontier post. Something on the border. It'll be rough, but—"

"I don't want that," said Kepha. "I don't want anything."

Esho swallowed, searching for words. "Listen. I don't say this to many people, Kepha, but I like you. I care about you. I want you to be all right. I think you're a good man, and you'll make a good soldier."

"You don't care about me," Kepha said.

"Yes, Kepha, I do," Esho said. "You may not believe it, but I do. And I know you care about her." He pointed back at Yasha. "You want her to be all right, don't you?"

Kepha wanted to say he didn't care about her—about anyone—but he glanced up and saw her, so small and afraid with that dagger-point at her neck, and it made him angry and sad, almost as upset as he'd felt about Mama. He could hardly believe it, but that was how he felt.

"I can make sure she's all right," said Esho. "You won't be able to take her with you to the frontier, but I can make sure she's well taken care of. And when you come back—"

"Liar!" Kepha screamed, leaping to his feet. The archers pulled their bowstrings tighter and aimed for his head and chest. "You're a liar, Esho. You lied about finding Mama, you lied about being my friend, and now you're lying about Yasha! I hate you! I hate Ash'shûr! I hate everything about this place! And I hate your God Ash'shûr!"

The soldiers gasped.

"Kepha," said Esho. "You don't mean that."

"You know what you taught me?" Kepha said. He moved quicker than he'd ever thought possible and snatched Nisroch's dagger from the floor. "See how well I learned?" He grabbed Esho and pressed the point to the man's neck.

"Kepha, no!" Yasha screamed.

"You do it, she dies!" shouted the guard with the knife at her throat.

"So do you," said Kepha.

He ran the dagger through Esho's neck and the man collapsed, clutching at his throat, coughing blood. Kepha raced toward the archers. They loosed their shafts. Arrows lanced into his neck, his chest, his stomach. They went deep at such short range, but he stumbled on, reaching for the man who held Yasha. Coughing, gasping for breath, he grabbed her captor and threw him aside and gripped the dagger in the man's hand, broke his arm, and plunged the dagger into the man's heart. The soldier gasped his last, a look of astonishment on his face.

The archers were on top of him now, and he could feel his strength fading.

"Run," he gasped to Yasha. She shook her head. The men piled on top of him, drawing their swords. "Run," he rasped again.

But she took the dagger from the dead man's hand and leaped on top of a man on Kepha's back, screaming, driving the blade down again and again between his shoulders.

"Get help!" one of the men was shouting. "Get the others!"

Another of the men broke off and ran back through the inn, calling for reinforcements.

The soldier Yasha stabbed slipped down off Kepha's back, slumping to the courtyard floor, blood pouring from a dozen wounds in his back and neck.

Kepha was too tired to stand up now, but he gripped one of the two remaining soldiers by the throat, leaned his weight down hard and forced the man to the ground, all of Kepha's body weight pressing down through one clenched hand, onto the man's neck. His eyes bulged as he slashed frantically at Kepha's treetrunk arm as he fought for breath.

Yasha dueled the other man like a wild beast, slashing out madly with the dagger, scoring shallow cuts across the soldier's thighs and arms each time he tried to move in closer with his shortsword.

The man beneath Kepha's hand thrashed one final time and lay still.

Arrow-studded, summoning the last wisp of strength in his muscles, Kepha lifted the sword from the hand of the man he'd strangled. He heaved his arm up, lunged to the side, and plunged the blade into the thigh of the man Yasha was fighting. The man howled and leaped back, tripping over Kepha's leg, hitting the stone floor with a grunt.

Kepha had no breath left, but he looked up into Yasha's eyes and nodded.

She fell on the man, screaming, pounding the dagger into his chest with both hands, ripping it out, plunging it in again and again.

Then, at last, Kepha collapsed. Arrows protruded from his neck, his shoulder, his chest and back. The shafts looked almost small, sprouting from such a giant. He and Yasha were soaked with blood and scored with cuts. The bodies of the five soldiers lay shattered all around them.

Yasha lay down next to him and pressed her body tight against Kepha's. His eyes were half-open, slipping closed. He tried to draw breath, but it hitched and he coughed, blood dripping from the corner of his mouth.

She took his great head in her hands and pressed her lips to his.

Soldiers poured into the courtyard, arrows nocked, bows drawn. Five of them, then ten, surrounding the pair of lovers curled up on the ground.

"Don't move!" one of them shouted. That almost made her laugh.

She looked into his eyes one last time. She thought she saw something there. Something that was hard to put into words. She'd seen it when they lay on the bed together, and she thought she saw a hint of it, just before his eyes slipped closed. She pressed herself closer against him.

"Move and we shoot," said the soldier. Every arrow was trained on her.

A silent laugh escaped her lips. She raised her head.

"Do it, then," she snarled.

The archers loosed their arrows, all as one.

296 YEARS EARLIER
1216 BC

Like a boat without anchor, I drift in the wind.

— Shuméru poem

Y

They called the boat *Zaham*. Raman, one of the oarsmen, said the name meant "Shining One" in Akkadu. Raman was the only one of the crew who spoke Akkadu, or claimed he did. In any case, it was a good name for the boat, because the *Zaham* carried a lantern at her bow, and without that light they'd never have been able to see in this forest to pole and row the flat-bottomed craft amid the mudflats and clumps of cattails that lined the riverbanks.

The day's last patches of cloud-filtered sunlight flickered on the muddy water, and on the leaves and branches that clawed inward on her shallows from every direction, from the gnarled oaks and elms whose roots tangled along both riverbanks, and spread their crowns of leaves against the cloudy sky, and from the willows that hung low over the half-stagnant water. Even as a breeze blew through, the air lay humid and close over the river, condensing into an evening fog.

Nahro wiped sweat from his forehead, peering into the shadows between knotted treetrunks, watching for some flicker of movement. He glanced at the others on the boat—Mekdem, the navigator, a Kush-man with skin the color of dark earth, sweeping the boat's long wooden pole back and forth in the muddy water, tapping its tip against the riverbank when the craft drifted too close to shore. Tewolde, dark-skinned as Mekdem, barely old enough to wield the sword he sat sharpening. Lanky Raman lazily pulling one oar, opposite Mutallu, gray-haired, arms crisscrossed with scars, pulling the other. And Aregastes, pale-skinned, black-haired, silent as always, lying back in the stern with closed eyes.

This wasn't the crew Nahro would have picked, but it was the crew that had come with the boat, and with the orders he was carrying upriver, into the forest.

Just three days ago, he'd been lying drunk in an army-issue bed in a supply post on the western shore of the Dark Sea. A full two months' march northwest from Ash'shûr, at the back end of nowhere, on the edge of a mist-shrouded forest of towering pines and oaks and willows.

He misliked this forest. So many trees in one place were unnatural. There were no wide-open spaces here; no sprawling plains or clear mountain air. Only shadows beneath the dense netting of tangled branches—shadows that seemed to glower out at the squat wooden shacks of the supply post, refusing to disclose their secrets. By night it was even worse: strange songs and howls echoed in those depths. Sometimes Nahro glimpsed great dark shapes skulking just beyond the edge of the circle of torchlight.

For weeks Nahro had waited in that maddening place, lying on the bed in that tiny log shack, gulping down mug after mug of cheap Khatti wine, rationing his last few vials of joyplant milk. He'd been on the verge of giving up hope he'd ever receive an assignment again.

One night he lost patience and downed all his vials of joyplant, and a few bottles of army-ration wine besides, and leaped around the room throwing punches at the air, visions of slain enemies dancing before his eyes—blue-painted warriors from the western campaigns, wrapped in furs and wielding bronze axes; men of Mitanni in copperscale armor, leaping from their chariots with arrows notched on bowstrings; Khatti shock troops brandishing heavy iron spears. He drew his sword and slashed at them, throwing himself against the walls of the chamber, staining the plaster red with wine and blood until at last he collapsed in exhaustion next to the bed, weeping, convulsing in frustrated rage, certain that he would fight these ghosts here forever.

But the next morning, two crimson-cloaked Ashûru soldiers had come for him in the bright sunlight and dragged him outside and plunged his head beneath the frigid water of the well until he'd come up gasping for air and helped him dress and buckle on his sword, then half-led, half-carried him to the largest cabin in the supply post. He stumbled into the shadowy, dust-moted room, blinking his eyes as they adjusted to the dimness.

A general sat in a chair at the room's far end, adorned in polished copperscale armor, his feathered helmet resting atop the table before him. A nasty-looking scar ran across his right cheek, and Nahro saw cold focus in his pale blue eyes. To one side of the general sat a scribe at a table, stylus and lamp at the ready. Nearby stood a younger man of indeterminate rank—but clearly military, judging by the sword and boots—and clearly important, judging by the gold rings in his plaited hair.

Nahro took all this in within an instant. He dropped to one knee and bowed low. His head ached and his vision swam, but he held the pose.

"Captain Eriba-Adad," the general said, using Nahro's warname. "Stand up and come join us. Lunch is about to be served."

Nahro stood and joined him at the table, pulling up a stool.

"Overseer," said the general, beckoning to the young man by his side, "would you please tell the captain a little about what's been happening up in the forest?"

The young man cleared his throat and addressed Nahro. "Are you aware of our supply posts and mining depots up the North River?" he asked.

Nahro looked carefully from the general to the overseer. Was this a test of some kind?

"I am... aware that we have supply depots in the north," Nahro said, slowly.

"We have supply depots in many active war zones," said the general. "Of particular difficulty are the mining posts up the North River."

"Yes, *sayid*," Nahro said, not sure what else to say.

A chorus of insects thrummed in the humid morning air.

Two slaves knocked and entered, bearing plates of dates and olives, and fresh-roasted mutton, and wine. Silence fell until the slaves had departed and closed the door behind them. The general smiled, tore off a piece of mutton, and began to eat.

"Our military has a longstanding agreement with the kings of Khatti not to instigate combat in the Tribal Lands," said the overseer, as if there'd been no interruption. "However, we have no such agreement with the local tribes."

"Savages," said the general, taking a gulp of wine. "By the way, captain, feel free to join me here."

"Thank you, *sayid*," Nahro said, and took a few olives to be polite.

"Most of the chiefs pose no serious problems," said the young overseer. "We give them good Ashûru bronze. They keep the wilder tribes in line for us."

"Each time we lose a soldier," the overseer added, "the rebels lose a whole village: every man, woman, child and dog. We salt the fields. The problem has been—containable."

"Until recently," said the general, looking Nahro in the eye.

The general returned his attention to the mutton, while the overseer watched Nahro oddly for a few moments. Nahro met his gaze, waiting for him to continue.

"Six months ago," said the overseer, "we began having problems with one particular tribe, at a depot far up the river. A collection point for iron and gold from the mountains. We'd been using local slaves to mine the metals, which we shipped downriver. The garrison reported near-daily attacks from a particularly primitive tribe. A tribe that paint their skins ash-gray, and fight not with spears or arrows, but with clubs and sharpened rocks. Brutal, relentless. Attacked every night. The tone of the reports became—panicked. Then they ceased entirely."

"As did the gold and iron shipments from that depot, obviously," said the general with a mouthful of mutton and dates. He took a gulp of wine and continued. "We assumed the natives had destroyed the depot. Killed the slaves and military personnel. So we sent a commander up the river, deep into tribal territory, to remedy this problem. His war-name was Ash'shûr-rim-nisheshu, personal name Rabail, son of Awiseen. Have you heard of him, captain?"

"No, *sayid*," Nahro said.

"Damned good soldier," said the general. "Served under me in the Mitanni campaigns. Graduate of the palace's battle school. Excellent tactician." He looked at Nahro intently. "We trusted him implicitly."

"Rabail filed no reports at all during his first three weeks at the depot," said the overseer. "At first we thought he'd been killed, like the others. We were preparing a larger garrison to take back the depot. But then the damndest thing happened. Shipments of gold and iron started coming in again. More every month, in fact."

"He was shipping us more metal than any other two depot commanders put together," said the general. "Extraordinary."

"That," said the overseer, "was when the documents began to make their way to us."

They both looked at Nahro, clearly waiting for a response. A gust of wind whistled through the wood planking of the walls.

"The—documents, *sayid*?" Nahro asked the general.

The general gestured at the scribe, who'd been sitting in silence throughout this conversation. "Would you please read that letter?" he asked.

The scribe cleared his throat and read without inflection: "Letter from Commander Ash'shûr-rim-nisheshu, Overseer of the North River Tribal Sector, to General Ninûrta-apal-ékur, High Commander of the Northwestern Tribal Territories."

"All right, just skip all that," said the general, waving a hand dismissively.

The scribe nodded. "*Small things testify to the influence of this place,*" he read. "*The oaks and willows, the chorus of frogs piping at sunset. The stones and moss. All wear a strange aspect. A face unknown to mankind. A deliberate, calculating purpose all their own.*"

He paused, and the general nodded for him to continue.

"*The bodies wear the marks, the same marks found in the sand along the riverbank. We hear their songs at night. Beautiful songs, and lately I have taken to singing them, too. They leave bones out for us, and now we leave our own for them. Soon I will go up to the caves and speak to them.*"

"That's enough," said the general.

All three of them watched Nahro carefully, as if waiting for him to understand something. Outside, the insects sang over the wind.

"Clearly," said the general, "Commander Rabail is mad."

All three of them were still staring at Nahro, as if in a dream.

"Clearly, *sayid*," Nahro said. "Entirely mad."

"And the tribe," said the overseer. "They also must be—removed."

"Removed, *sayid*?" Nahro furrowed his brow. "The entire tribe?"

The overseer bent down and retrieved a hand-sized stone from a leather satchel by his feet and placed it on the table. It was obsidian; black and polished. Two sides chipped to razor-sharp edges, converging onto a point.

"We received this—item—in the package containing the latest of Rabail's letters," said the overseer.

Nahro bent closer, and saw that the stone's sharpened edges were speckled with dried blood. "Is it some kind of a threat, *sayid*?" he asked.

"We're not sure what he intends it to mean," said the general. "But it does indicate that he's in contact with this tribe that lives far upriver. The tribe with ash-gray skin."

"A tribe that, we are informed, has no name," said the overseer.

They watched Nahro again, waiting for a response.

"No name, *sayid*?" Nahro asked.

"They have no name because they have no speech," the overseer said. "Rabail writes that they whistle sometimes. Make the sounds of birds and wild dogs. They don't build houses. Don't farm. Don't make fire."

"Barbarians," said Nahro.

"Not barbarians," said the overseer. "Animals. Beasts with no Gods. This is what Rabail writes. Or rather, what he *wrote*, before he went up into the hills to join them."

"No Gods," the general repeated.

"They live up in the caves," the overseer said, "Near some of the richest veins of gold. Who knows why. They don't seem to have any use for metal."

"And you believe Commander Rabail has—joined with this tribe," said Nahro.

"Joined, allied with, enslaved, what does it matter?" said the general. "He is somehow operating in conjunction with these—beasts. These cave-dwellers."

The general and the overseer watched Nahro for a few moments.

"There is a reason we have these trading posts and mining depots," the general said after a moment. "We're not shipping gold and iron thousands of leagues, back to the heart of Ash'shûr, just so rich men can build nicer houses."

"Of course not, *sayid*," said Nahro, though he wasn't sure what the general was getting at.

"Give us the room, scribe," the general said.

The scribe rose from the table, rolled the clay tablets in cloth, placed them carefully in a small wooden box, and left the cabin.

They waited until the scribe had closed the door behind him.

"Who would you say rules the world today, captain?" asked the overseer.

He looked at Nahro, waiting. The insect chorus sang on.

"No one, *sayid*," said Nahro after a moment. "That is, no single king or kingdom."

"Well said, captain. Very well said." The general took a plump date from the plate and nibbled at it. "The world is tugged and torn between many great empires. Dogs who just will not let go of the bone. The pharaohs of Misr, swimming in gold. The emperors of Khatti, secure in their mountain fastnesses. The Mitanni kings. The old noble houses of Babili. The island lords of the Great Western Sea. All the hundreds of client-kings who nip at their heels."

"And the Empire of Ash'shûr, of course," Nahro added.

"Most certainly," the general agreed. "And on that point, captain—the feeling at High Command is that this state of affairs cannot sustain itself forever. Even the most lavish banquet, as we all know, is only ever a few courses away from the sweets. And this banquet—" he laughed softly to himself, gesturing at the sheep-bones and olive-pits scattered across the plates. "Well, the high lords of Babili and Misr have been eating one main course after another, and now the good meat's running out."

Nahro furrowed his brow. "You mean some sort of a..." He shook his head, unsure of the proper word. "An end is coming."

"A weak pharaoh here. A lost battle there. A sunk shipment of gold over there..." the general waved his hand and shrugged. "The world walks a tightrope, captain. And for far too long, the Ashûru people have been just one empire among many. The domains of Khatti and Mitanni, the Kingdoms of Misr and Babili—are we really no different from them? What would be your opinion on that, captain?"

"My opinion, *sayid*," Nahro said, very carefully, "Is that Ash'shûr is a different kind of empire."

"A wise opinion," said the general. "That's why we're building a different kind of army. More ruthless, more perfectly trained than any before it. A force that will terrify our enemies. Put an end to these wasteful little wars we keep fighting. Impose order. Law and civilization."

"A noble purpose, *sayid*," Nahro said after a moment. "One that is," he paused to choose the right words, "very clearly undermined by Commander Rabail's behavior."

"Clearly," said the general, "Commander Rabail must be removed from his post."

Nahro nodded.

"Use every means at your disposal, captain," said the overseer. "Whatever is necessary."

He stared into Nahro's eyes as if looking for something.

Nahro refused to look away.

"We'll be sending you upriver tomorrow morning," the general said at last, breaking the silence. "With a boat crew who have a good deal of experience handling small tribal incursions. This trip will be a bit rougher than they're used to, but—well, that's war, isn't it, captain? When you're finished with Rabail, you will assist the boat's crew in cleaning up the rest of this—infestation."

"Yes, *sayid*," said Nahro, visions of the painted warriors already rushing up into his mind, making his thoughts clearer, sharpening his senses.

"That's all, captain," said the general. "Get a good night's sleep. May the God Ash'shûr watch over you."

"Thank you, *sayid*," said Nahro.

He bowed, left the chamber, and walked across the courtyard, back to his room. The assignment filled him with a cold, vague tension. It was a feeling he'd learned to savor.

ΥΥ

Now, watching the others in the boat, the *Zaham*, as the sun crept behind the tangled trees, Nahro mulled over what the general had said about Rabail. A great commander. Graduate of the palace's battle school. How did a man fall from such heights into such confusion? What temptation had pulled at him?

A deeper question, though, lurked at the center: Why did Command want this man dead? Rabail had been sent upriver to handle a problem. He'd handled that problem, one way or another. Gold and iron were coming downriver again, in even greater weights than before. The man was unhinged, certainly—but that could be said of plenty of soldiers, especially this far out in the Tribal Lands. Something was missing from this story. What had Rabail done to sign his own death sentence?

Nahro watched shadow and light play on the oak leaves, as if they might contain some clue of an answer. But they kept their silence, like all else here except the choruses of evening insects.

Something itched on Nahro's arm. A mosquito. He swatted it and watched fresh blood—his blood—pool around its crushed body.

"Captain," said Mekdem, the boat's earth-skinned navigator, keeping his eyes on the water ahead.

Nahro looked up.

"It's too dark to keep pushing tonight," Mekdem said. As always, one of his calloused hands clutched the tiller, pumping the long oar back and forth like a fish's tail, pushing them upriver and deeper into the forest. "There's a garrison post just around the next riverbend. We can tie up there for the night."

"Just so long as we get moving before sunup," said Nahro.

Mekdem pumped the tiller in silence for a few moments, watching him.

"Just how far up this river are we going, captain?" he asked at last.

"That's for me to know, navigator," said Nahro.

"Because a few leagues beyond this garrison post," said Mekdem, "we'll be entering an unpatrolled area."

All the others had looked up, now, and were watching them.

"That's not Ashûru territory," Mekdem continued. "That's nobody's territory."

"It's somebody's territory," said Nahro.

The others looked at him suspiciously, but nobody made a move. They all knew the penalty for questioning a direct order from a superior officer. And while none of them had seen how quickly Nahro could draw his sword and put it to use—or make use of the various other small blades hidden in the folds of his cloak and tunic—they had a fairly good idea of those things just by looking into his eyes, and at the carefully casual way he leaned on the *Zaham*'s bow. He made sure they all got a good look, then turned his gaze back to the river.

They arrived at the garrison post shortly after that. It wasn't much—just a few squat huts surrounded by a low palisade wall of outward-pointing tree trunks, sharpened to points. Mekdem eased the *Zaham* up alongside the shore. The men jumped out onto the root-tangled riverbank, threw ropes around two nearby trees, and tied the boat up for the night.

By then, two tattered-looking soldiers had stumbled out of one of the huts to watch. They wore tunics and helmets, but no armor. Short-swords dangled from their belts.

"You're a long way from home, aren't you?" asked one. His black hair and beard jutted out in all directions.

"Who's in charge here?" asked Nahro, marching up toward the palisade wall.

"In charge?" the black-haired one looked at his companion, and they laughed.

"Eilram's in charge, *sayid*," said the other one, gangly and cinnamon-skinned, probably from somewhere in the Zagros Mountains far to the east.

"You should address your commander by his war-name," said Nahro.

"We don't know it," said the tan-skinned one. "He makes us call him Eilram."

"I see," said Nahro. "And where is Commander Eilram now?"

"Been gone for about three days, *sayid*," said the black-bearded one. "Took most of the men up onto the ridge there," he nodded vaguely into the forest beyond the camp. "Village up there's been making raids on us whenever a boat comes in. Eilram decided he's had enough."

The others had finished tying up the *Zaham*, and joined Nahro in front of the wall.

"We'll be laying up here for the night," said Nahro.

"Fine by us, *sayid*," said the black-bearded one, spreading his arms wide. "One good thing about this garrison post: we've got plenty of beer to go around. I'm Footsoldier Tamzi. This here's Footsoldier Dawa."

"Welcome to the end of the world," said Dawa.

Tamzi and Dawa swung open the heavy tree-trunk gate in the palisade wall, letting Nahro and the rest of the crew inside.

Night had fallen by now, though only a scattered few stars shone in bits of cloud-covered sky Nahro could glimpse through the forest canopy. The two guards walked around the camp's perimeter, lighting torches and checking traps, and then started a fire in the firepit. They brought out bowls of stew from one of the huts, and cracked open a clay vessel of beer, and passed around mugs for the men, who pulled up wood benches around the firepit.

They ate in near-silence, listening to the forest, hearing only chirping insects, night-birds hooting, and occasionally a twig snapping that made them all look up from the fire, searching for a sign of movement in the shadows. But they saw none.

Tamzi drained his mug, wiped beer foam from his beard, and asked, "Do you lot have any joyplant?"

Raman the cook threw back his head and laughed. Nahro didn't see what was so funny.

"We drank the last of it down on the seacoast," grunted Mutallu, the scarred, gray-haired one. "Holed up in that naval post for three weeks."

"Three whore-less weeks," muttered Tewolde, the young Kush-man. He took a gulp from his mug. "You weren't much for sharing the joyplant, either."

Nahro's mind ran back to his last night in his room in the trading-post, alone, downing all the joyplant at once and fighting ghosts in the dark. "I'm out, too," was all he said.

"Got mushrooms, though," said Aregastes, the pale-skinned one. He'd hardly spoken all day, but he was grinning now.

"I knew it!" cried Tewolde. "Pass the bag around."

"We'd take some mushrooms," said Dawa.

"We've only got a little bit left," Aregastes said. "Not enough to see Gods or anything. They'll keep you up, though."

He produced a small leather bag from the folds of his tunic, loosened its tether and passed it around. Tewolde and Raman eagerly took small handfuls of the dried reddish caps and chewed and swallowed. The guards Dawa and Tamzi followed his example. Even Mutallu took a few handfuls.

"None for me tonight," said Nahro, when the bag came around to him. "Not with Commander Eilram and most of the garrison off in the forest."

Tamzi snorted, then remembered himself and straightened up. "*Sayid*, with all due respect," he said, then started to laugh again, "Eilram eats more mushrooms than anybody."

Now Dawa was laughing too, and the rest of the men joined in. Except for Nahro, who watched the men carefully, trying to decide how to manage this; and Mekdem, who kept his eyes on the treeline.

At last, Nahro took a few dried mushroom caps from the bag and chewed, forcing himself to swallow the bitter, slimy pulp. He extended the bag to Mekdem, who refused.

They sat for a while, looking up at the trees, watching tiny dancing insects light up like shooting stars amid the branches. A chorus of crickets sang high-pitched from somewhere deep in the shadows. From the riverbanks rose the piping of frogs, some voices slow and low, others fast and rasping. Though no wind disturbed the thick, close air, the reeds and willows seemed to dance softly of their own accord, to some rhythm only they could sense. A mist rolled in, seeming to rise from the ground, chilling Nahro's skin with tiny droplets of water that mingled with his own cold sweat.

A strange excitement rose in his belly, as if the rhythms of this ceaseless sound and motion might unweave him somehow. His breathing quickened, and the dancing lights seemed to swirl with many colors—deep greens and reds and blues; and the songs of the crickets and frogs seemed to pulse in rhythm with his breath: loud and high, then soft and low, in and out, back and forth like the soft waves that lapped against the riverbanks.

He felt, in a way he could not explain, as if he were doing something wrong, somehow—as if he *should* belong here, as part of the branches and reeds, and the moss-covered stones, and the fog and insect-song; he knew he belonged to it but could not find the rhythm of it.

He glanced at the faces of the others: dark-skinned Tewolde, pale-skinned Aregastes and scarred Mutallu, the camp guards Dawa and Tamzi; all of them grinning like fools, or laughing, tracing invisible patterns in their air with their fingers, humming strange little tunes from home. More rhythms he could not find, or fit into. Despite the warmth of the night, he felt cold sweep over him, and shivered.

Only Mekdem, who had taken none of the mushrooms, continued to watch the trees in silence, as if expecting—what?—a surprise attack? The return of the garrison? Or for some faceless force to rise from the shadows and expel them from this place?

But nothing came from the trees that night. As Nahro struggled to control his breathing, the others drank more wine and joyplant, and joked and laughed until they grew too tired to sit up straight, and stumbled back to the huts and fell asleep on mats on the floor. Mekdem didn't drink, but he finally lay down on the ground outside one of the huts, and closed his eyes.

Nahro sat up for a long time after they fell asleep, watching the shadows of the trees playing in the moonlight. He didn't feel tired, but he must've drifted off at some point, because he felt someone shaking him and opened his eyes and the sky was softening into dawn.

ψψ

Mekdem stood above him. Nahro sat up and looked around the camp. No noise, no movement.

"I'll wake the others," said Mekdem.

Nahro shushed him. "Do you hear that?" he asked.

"What?" Mekdem whispered.

Deep in the woods, the cracking of branches. The pounding of feet. Someone was running toward camp.

Nahro stood up, scanning the treeline with Mekdem.

Out of the trees and fog burst a savage—a pale, wild-haired man covered in dried mud, naked, feathers in his hair, blood spattered on his chest and hands.

Mekdem started for his bow, which was propped next to one of the huts. Nahro drew two throwing-daggers from his tunic.

The savage made it about halfway from the treeline to the palisade wall.

An axe spun through the air, out of the trees, thunking into the back of the savage's head, spraying blood. He went down face-first, arms splayed, eyes wide open in shock.

All this in the space of two breaths.

Three soldiers came sauntering out of the trees in the predawn light, their shadows playing strangely behind them in the mist.

"Not a bad hit, through the trees," said one to the soldier who'd apparently thrown the axe. He bent down to yank it from the split head of the dead savage.

"I could've hit him from farther," said the third.

"If we'd have waited any longer, he'd have split off to the right," said the one who'd just retrieved his axe. "The bet still counts."

Now the first man caught sight of Nahro and Mekdem behind the palisade wall. "What's this?" he shouted. "We've got visitors."

"Visitors from a faraway land," said the one with the axe, wiping the blade on his tunic.

"Hey, Kislev Company," the first soldier called back into the forest. "Don't be rude—come meet our guests."

A voice thundered out of the trees: "They'd better have beer and boats!"

More soldiers emerged from the shadows and fog beyond the trees, in groups of twos and threes. Among them strode an officer—copperscale armor buffed to a golden-brown shine, helmet topped with a horsetail dyed bright yellow, long beard and hair precisely plaited. Short but muscled, with the stride of a giant.

"Get those wak bastards up here," the officer called back into the woods; "wak" being the preferred military slur for the wild people of these forests.

Two infantrymen emerged from a knot of elms and pines, scrambling over moss-covered stones, pulling a string of bound captives between them. Every one of the savages was caked from head to toe with mud; many stained with blood. All were bound hand and foot, clamped in bronze shackles. They shuffled silently, exhausted.

"Wak sons of bitches killed six of my men," the officer shouted; though Nahro was getting the sense this was simply his normal speaking voice. "Six good Ashûru soldiers—can you believe that? We got ten of them, though, minus the one that Footman Gadatas just expertly axed. Congratulations on winning that bet, Gadatas."

Now the rest of the *Zaham*'s crew had woken up, along with Tamzi and Dawa, who stumbled toward the palisade gate, calling out greetings to the rest of their company.

The officer waved at Nahro and Mekdem. "How many of you are there?" he shouted as he stomped the gate in the palisade.

"Just six of us, *sayid*," said Nahro as the officer shook his hand.

"Garrison Commander Eilram," the officer said. "But please, call me Eilram. Everyone does."

"Captain Eriba-Adad," Nahro introduced himself using his war-name. "You can call me Nahro, *sayid*, if that's how you do things here."

"Nice to meet you, Nahro," said Eilram, grasping arms with him. "And who's this?"

"Mekdem, *sayid*," said the Kush-man. "Navigator."

"Navigator?" Eilram fairly shouted in Mekdem's face, beaming. "You brought me a boat? We can use more boats! Wak sons-of-bitches burnt my last boat."

"Actually, *sayid*," said Nahro as the garrison marched past him, captives in tow, "we just camped here for the night. We're headed upriver."

"Upriver?" Eilram cried. "That's wak country, captain. Ain't any garrison post upriver from here."

"Yes, *sayid*," said Nahro. "I'm aware of that."

But Eilram had already turned away. He was clapping Mekdem on the shoulder and shouting, "Where you from, sailor? You fish on the Nile?"

"I'm from Men-nefer, *sayid*," said Mekdem.

"Men-nefer?" Eilram howled, then turned to his men. "Shabaka! Nedjeh! Come over here."

Two Kush-men in full ironscale armor came running up from the wall, beads of sweat shining on their deep brown skin.

Commander Eilram clapped his hands as they approached, and called out, "This here is Navigator—sorry, what's your name?"

"Mekdem."

"This is Mekdem, from Men-nefer," Eilram bellowed. "Mekdem, meet Shabaka from Medewi, and Nedjeh from Napata. Three Kush-men, come all the way from the Nile just to enjoy our company. Welcome to the north end of nowhere."

The Kush-men exchanged disbelieving hugs and arm-grips and greetings in their tongue. Although all three of them wore the crimson of Ash'shûr, they looked as if they'd stepped into this dim forest from another world—a sun-scorched land of dark-skinned men who walked on desert sands—only to meet here, swathed in rolling fog, dressed in the foreign garb of Ashûru soldiers, in the shadows of oaks and pines at the far end of the earth.

"These two can fish like nothing you've ever seen," Eilram was declaring with a raucous laugh. "The monsters they've pulled out of this river. Incredible. What kind of bait do you use in muddy water like this, Mekdem?"

"Commander," Nahro tried to interrupt him.

"I haven't tried to fish this river too much, actually," Mekdem was saying.

"We caught a fish as long as both my arms a few weeks ago," Nedjeh told him. "Scales like armor."

Meanwhile, the younger Kush-man Tweolde had come running over, drawn by the sound of his mother-tongue. Shabaka was apparently halfway through a joke in the tongue of Kush, which already had Mekdem and Tweolde smiling.

"Must've been half-dragon, that fish," Nedjeh went on. "Nearly took my hand clean off."

Eilram turned abruptly back to Nahro. "Who's your commander, captain?" he asked.

"I'm not at liberty to disclose that, *sayid*," Nahro said.

"If you want Kislev Company to escort you into wak country, captain," said Eilram, guiding Nahro a few steps away, "I suggest you find yourself the liberty to disclose a little more."

"Escort—" said Nahro. "We're not asking for an escort. I've got a full crew—"

Eilram was roaring with laughter now. "If you plan to get half a league further up this creek of shit," he howled, pointing at the river, "you're damned well going to need an escort. Now where's your authorization, at least?"

"I don't have any documents, *sayid*," said Nahro. "This trip is not—"

Eilram turned to the men who had hold of the captives, and were making them kneel near the firepit, as most of the boat's crew looked on impassively, except for Tewolde, who looked as if he might be sick at any moment. "Not there!" he shouted. "March them out in front of the wall, so the ones in the woods can watch."

The soldiers lifted the captives back onto their feet, and frog-marched them back out the gate, to the bit of open weedy ground between the palisade and the treeline.

"Like I was saying," Eilram said, turning back to Nahro, "We can get you about a league upriver, that's all. But if I lose men on this trip, I need to know what to say in my report."

Nahro thought for a moment as Eilram shouted more orders to his men. "There's an installation upriver," he said quietly. "A mining depot."

Eilram looked at him sharply. "What do you know about that?" he asked.

"I know it's a depot for gold and iron, from the mountains," Nahro said. "I know it was under heavy attack, presumed to be wiped out. Until a few weeks ago."

"Four of his barges have docked here over the past few weeks," Eilram said, watching Nahro with a strange expression. "So much gold and iron, they could barely float. Never seen the like."

"*His* barges?" Nahro asked.

The commander shook his head. "Incredible man, isn't he?"

Nahro raised an eyebrow. "You've met him?"

"He's spent a few nights here," Eilram replied. "As much poet and priest as warrior. The only sort that can put the leash on a place like this. Course, back at High Command, they couldn't figure out what to do with him." The commander laughed. "Killed a superior officer, did you know that? Back when he was only a unit commander. His regiment was getting hammered hard in some border skirmish again the Khatti. General called for a retreat. Well, he wasn't having it. Slit the officer's throat. Took command and won the battle. Minimal casualties. Unless you count the officer, of course."

"So they promoted him and sent him up the creek," Nahro said.

"What else can you do with a man like that?" Eilram said. His eyes narrowed. "Actually, that's a good question, captain. What happens when you find him?"

"My orders are to keep heading upriver until I find this depot," said Nahro.

"And the rest is secret." Eilram shook his head. "Well, I'll tell you something for free, captain. If you mean him any harm, you won't get within ten steps of him. Plenty of men have tried, believe me."

"As I said, *sayid*," Nahro said. "My orders are to locate the depot."

Eilram looked at him for a long time. At last he shrugged. "All right, Nahro," he said. "I'll get you about a league upriver. After that, you're on your own."

"Thank you, *sayid*," said Nahro.

"Don't mention it," Eilram said with a smile. "Now," he shouted at no one in particular, "let's go watch my hard-working men slay some waks who thought they could put a fear in Kislev Company!"

Nahro and his men followed the garrison soldiers out to the open ground, under the pale light of the cloud-hidden dawn. The men of the garrison had forced the captives to kneel. Most of the mud-painted warriors now understood what was about to happen, and a few began weeping openly, tears streaking the mud and blood on their faces as they pleaded with their captors in their strange rolling tongue. Most, though, only glared silently at the soldiers, or stared off stone-faced into the forest.

Eilram turned to the treeline and shouted into the forest. "I know you're watching, you wak pieces of shit," he howled. "This is you, next! You hear me? Next time, this is you!" He turned to the men. "All right, do it. Quick and clean, men. This isn't a dog-pit."

The men slaughtered their captives one by one—lopping off heads, mostly; sometimes running swords through hearts. After the first two or three, Nahro turned away, along with the Kush-men Mekdem and Tewolde. Tamzi and Dawa watched eagerly, as did the rest of the garrison men. Eilram watched, too, although he didn't seem to be enjoying it. He watched as if he felt compelled to.

By the time the executions were done, dawn had turned into morning. Mekdem and Tewolde were already down by the riverbank, doing their best to balance on the knotted roots as they untied the boat's ropes from the treetrunks.

As Eilram supervised the cleaning of blood-coated weapons and the tossing of bodies and heads back into the woods, Raman and Aregastes negotiated quietly with Tamzi and Dawa, swapping small leather pouches—the last of their mushrooms, presumably—for other pouches and vials from the soldiers. Mutallu was taking one last walk around the palisade's perimeter, his scarred face unreadable.

Commander Eilram noticed Nahro heading for the boat, and strode toward him, plumed helmet under his arm, bellowing, "You boys really are in a hurry, aren't you? I respect that."

Tamzi and Dawa ran by, cackling. Eilram snapped his fingers at them, barking, "Hey! Hey!" and the two disheveled guards rushed to their commander's side. He motioned for them to hand him the satchel, took it from Tamzi and took out a few of the red-and-white-speckled mushrooms. He chewed them thoughtfully as he handed the satchel back.

"We'll go up the riverbank on foot," Eilram shouted. "Keep pace with your boat." He made a round-up gesture to the rest of his men, who were mostly finished with the bodies by now. "There're a few wak villages up that way, but nothing we can't handle."

"Thank you, *sayid*," said Nahro, watching the rest of the crew—Raman, Aregastes, and Mutallu—converge on the riverbank and climb into the boat.

"Course, after a league or so," Eilram was saying, "you'll be on your own. I mean, captain, that's forest. I mean *real* forest. The bad country."

"I know, *sayid*," said Nahro.

He hurried down to the boat, where Mutallu and Raman had already taken up oars, and Mekdem stood ready to push off from the bank.

"We taking this trip or not, captain?" Mekdem asked.

"That's a hard man to break off a conversation with," Nahro answered with a grin, and that broke them all up with laughter. All except for Mutallu, who was watching the river and the woods.

ONCE THEY WERE in the water and moving, the chatter settled down to an odd word here or there, then dwindled to nothing. Commander Eilram and his men vanished into the woods. Nahro caught sight of a cloak or the flash of a helmet among the branches now and then, but mostly the soldiers kept pace with the boat without giving any hint of their presence.

As they pushed upstream away from the camp, the river turned marshy, its banks choked with reeds and mud-stained ferns and willow bushes. The bushes grew as large as trees with spines that swayed and bended to strange rhythms in the current and the wind.

Waves of shadow swept across the canopy of trees; over the branches of knotted oaks and elms, and the straight-necked white birches and spearlike pines, their leaves and limbs running wild in the thick air, their roots knotted among vast gray stones cloaked in moss. Bigger trees, too—tall cedars, their red-brown bark cracked like calloused skin, their arms spreading so high above that flocks of birds darted among them.

And always the voices of the insects and the frogs, and the cries of birds, and the lap of the muck and water against the riverbanks, and the drifting mist in the humid air.

Even in its near-silence, the forest seemed awake, as if all this unchecked growth was chattering or singing in some key just outside the range of human hearing; a song whose first verses had swelled long centuries before the first man opened his eyes, and whose final chorus would hum long after the last man's bones sank into the mud. The faceless lords of this place wore bark for skin and leaves for crowns, and the men who scrambled over their roots and branches were ants here.

Nahro couldn't say why he felt these things, but he knew them as one knows things in dreams. He mentioned none of this to the others; only watched the water and the riverbanks, waiting for some sign yet to come.

Around mid morning, Raman spoke up out of the silence: "How can people like that exist?"

"You mean the waks, or Kislev Company?" Aregastes asked.

"I mean, how can places like *this* exist?" Raman said, dragging one lanky arm in the muddy water. "We all come from civilized places. I grew up in Babili, for Gods' sakes. Center of the world."

"Here we go," said Aregastes, rolling his eyes.

"I was studying Akkadu," Raman said. "I wanted to be a scribe. I liked poetry."

"Now you're a rower on a riverboat," said Mutallu.

"Lesson learned: don't recite Akkadu poetry to a governor's daughter," said Raman. "Especially not when you're both naked."

"We all wanted to be something else," said Mekdem, watching the river, churning the mud-brown water back and forth with the great oar at the boat's rear.

"What did you want to be?" Raman asked him.

"I was a fisherman," said the navigator. "On the mother Nile. That was all I ever wanted to be. Sun and sand, open sky. Fresh fish every day, and my wife's soft brown skin every night. If that's not paradise, I don't know what is."

"The Nile," said Tewolde. "Now that's a real river. Not like this muddy mess of a forest stream."

"All it takes is one night," said Mekdem. "One wild night and one too many beers, and a few bad bets on the dice, and the next morning you wake up and it's thank the Gods you're in the Ashûru army now!"

Tewolde howled with laughter, but nobody else was smiling. Not even Mekdem. Tewolde stopped.

"What about you, Nahro?" Aregastes asked. "How'd you end up fighting for the great Ashûru war machine?"

"I could ask you the same question," Nahro said. "How'd *you* end up fighting for us? Where are you from, anyway? Phrygía? Kaptara?"

"Me?" Aregastes said. He took his rough leather cap off his black hair and ruffled it. "I was born not too far from here. Parents didn't want me, apparently. Grew up on the streets. Did it for myself. Soon as I was old enough to draw a bow, I joined up. Three meals a day and plenty of foreign cunny. That answer your question, captain?"

"I guess it does." Nahro nodded.

"So I return to my earlier question," Aregastes said. "What about you?"

"Me?" Nahro said.

They were all watching him.

"Well," he said, "You're never going to find out who you are on some farm in Tunip." He snorted. "Hell, I don't know."

Aregastes rolled his eyes again.

Mutallu was leaning on the rail, watching shadows in the trees.

"What about you, oldtimer?" Nahro asked him.

"I joined up for the same reason most young men did," Mutallu said. "See the world. Kill savages. Except I'm not sure what 'savage' means anymore."

They all looked at him.

"What in the Seven Stars are you talking about?" Raman said.

"I've killed men like these," Mutallu said, "mud on their skins, feathers in their hair, stone axes and arrows—I've killed them here and killed them in the southern marshes and got scarred up by the ones in the Silver Mountains, where even the Khatti shock-troops won't go. They're all around us. It's like we, all of us—Ashûru and Khatti and Babili people, all our cities and lands and everything—we're all in a sort of a big boat together. And from inside our boat, we point out at the forest and we say, 'That's where the savages are.'"

Raman looked at Mutallu oddly, trying to fit those words into sense. "That's quite a speech," he said after a moment. "What's your point?"

"You go back far enough," said Mutallu, spreading his hands, "there was no boat at all. Just the river and the forest. Just this."

Raman grunted. Mekdem was stroking his chin.

"There are two great rivers in our land, too, you know," Mutallu said. "Imagine paddling up the Swift or the Slow, long years before anyone dreamed of Babili. Before Urim and Kish, even. Before Eridu."

"There were no boats before Eridu," said Tewolde. "Just the Gods, and the eternal seas." He spread his arms prophetically. Everyone laughed. "Abzu and Tiamat, locked in battle, forever and ever."

"Let him tell the story." Aregastes pushed the boy down.

"I'm not telling a story," said Mutallu. "I'm just saying, back then there were no farms or watercourses, you know. Just forests where the farming-plains are now. Look at the old carvings. You can see our lands used to be all tangled with trees. Not so different from this, right here, to tell the truth. Imagine paddling up that river, maybe right next to the places where Urim and Eridu would someday stand. But back then, there was just the river and the woods. Shadows. Fog. The songs of insects. And then out of those shadows come the arrows and the spears—"

He trailed off. No one was smiling anymore.

"I saw a map once, back in Babili," said Raman. "A map of the whole world, with the sacred city at its center. The priests said it was copied from an even older map—one from a long time ago. And the map had all these strange places on it: 'The Island Beyond the Flight of Birds.' 'The Place Where the Sun Is Hidden.' I didn't even know if those places were real or not, but I felt a kind of pull from them. Like I wanted to go find them."

A silence fell over the boat, broken only by the singing of insects in the trees.

"Where are all those magic islands now?" Raman said after a moment, as if to himself. "There's no place left beyond the flight of birds. No place where the sun is hidden."

"And yet," said Tewolde after a moment, "here we all are."

"I don't think I want to go looking for those places anymore," Raman said. "I mean, you tour with the army for a while, you find out we've mapped most of the world by now. Hell, half the world's serving in this army. You meet bastards from everyplace, from the Silver Mountains to the Spice Islands." He gestured at Mekdem. "Navigators who sailed all the way from the Nile to this dungheap forest."

"No more magic on the map," said Aregastes.

"There are some places, still," said Mutallu. "But they're not on that kind of map."

Raman looked at him. "What in the Gods' names is that supposed to—"

A spear arced out of the forest. Thunked into the boat-deck. Two more, thudding into the hull.

Someone yelled "Shit!" and then the spears were all around, raining onto the boat from both sides of the river, thudding into the deck from all angles. Stone-tipped.

The men scrambled for shields and bows, ducking tight against the deck, holding their shields above them. Raman was making a high-grayed keening sound, halfway between a scream and a howl of pain.

"Are you hit?" Nahro yelled to him.

"Gods damn us!" Raman screamed. "Gods damn us all!"

Nahro caught sight of a few mud-coated warriors up on the riverbank. He notched and loosed a quick series of arrows, and watched two of them thunk into the head and chest of a warrior, who tumbled into the river.

More of them were crowding down onto the banks, shouting and chattering in their strange tongue.

From up in the trees came Commander Eilram's voice: "Free-fire! Kill anything painted brown!"

The men of Kislev Company were running down to the riverbank, loosing arrows through the trees, mostly scoring hits. The mud-painted fighters fell quickly, but more were pouring out of the trees on the other side of the river.

"Pull!" Mekdem was screaming at Raman and Tewolde. "Get on those oars and pull!"

The two men took the oars and pulled frantically, and the boat began moving again.

Mutallu and Aregastes were also loosing arrows, slaying man after man with quick, professional accuracy. Aregastes dropped an archer out of a tree with an arrow straight to the forehead. Mutallu used a big Khatti compound bow, nearly as tall as a man, launching thick-shafted bolts that hurled men's bodies back into the trees.

Commander Eilram strode along the riverbank, barking orders to his men almost at random: "There's a big one, up in the tree there! Down by the water, two with spears!" He walked proudly, upright with his helmet under his arm, arrows and spears missing him by hairsbreadths but never grazing him. He caught Nahro's eye, smiled, laughed.

Nahro dodged as a spear hit the deck where he'd been an instant before. He loosed an arrow at the thrower, who stumbled off into the woods clutching the shaft in his bloodied shoulder.

The Kislev Company archers mowed down the attackers, who tumbled into the water by the dozen, arrows bristling from their chests and shoulders. They seemed to be losing momentum. A desperate young man charged down to the riverbank, hurled his two spears in quick succession, and caught an arrow in the eye from Aregastes. A burly warrior wearing a boar's-skull helmet leaped into the water and swam toward the boat, but a thick bolt from Mutallu threw him back against the roots on the shore and pinned him there, stunned and coughing blood.

"Blood and mud!" Eilram was howling, still standing chest-out on the riverbank. "Blood and mud! Look at these colors, men! Look at these beautiful colors!"

The spears and arrows slowed to a light hail, and finally ceased. Nahro chanced a look up over the deck, and saw the Kislev Company soldiers finishing off the last of the attackers with arrows, spear-thrusts and throat-slits.

"Listen, captain," Commander Eilram bellowed from the shore. "It's been a pleasure, but this is where we leave you. It only gets worse from here."

"Understood, Commander," Nahro called back, saluting.

"You mad bastard," Eilram shouted, beaming. "If I had ten men like you, I could conquer this whole Gods-damned forest! You hear that, men? If I had ten of you like Captain Nahro there—"

But Tewolde and Raman were dropping short-oars over the boat's sides, pumping hard as they fell into rhythm. The boat careened out of hearing range, rocking and pitching wildly until at last, not even Eilram's booming voice could cross the distance. Nahro looked back and saw him wave joyously from the shore, then turn and march back into the forest.

Nahro realized something. "Where's Mutallu?" he said.

The man's gray-haired body, pinned to the deck by a spear, answered that question. Raman was snarling a string of curses, tears streaming down his cheeks. Mekdem watched impassively, but his eyes were watery. Aregastes was muttering curses in his own tongue, loosing arrows into the forest at random.

"Stop that," Nahro snapped at him. "You're wasting arrows."

Aregastes spat a few words in his language, but sat down and dropped his bow beside him.

"Help me get his body overboard," said Nahro.

"Gods!" Raman cried, rocking back and forth like a child as he pulled the oar. "Gods shit on this jungle!"

"Pull it together, soldier," Nahro told him, as gently as he could.

"All due respect, fuck you, captain," said Raman.

Nahro grabbed a fistful of his hair and yanked. "You want to die too?" he asked.

Raman laughed wildly.

"You want to die?" Nahro repeated. "Because that's what's going to happen if you don't shut up and keep rowing. You're going to end up in that river, like him."

Aregastes and Nahro heaved Mutallu's muscled body over the side. It splashed into the muddy water and floated away behind the boat.

"We're all going to end up in this river," Raman said. "We're all going to die on this Gods-forsaken mission, and we don't even know what this mission is!" His voice rose to a scream. "We don't even know why we're here!" He panted, his whole body shaking.

Now everyone was looking at Nahro.

"It would be nice, captain," said Mekdem, "to have some idea of where I'm taking my boat."

Nahro looked away into the forest; but when he looked back, all eyes were still on him.

He sighed. "There's a mining depot upriver," he said.

Mekdem nodded once. "I've heard of it. Gold and iron."

"A savage tribe has taken control of the depot," Nahro said. "We have reports they're assembling a large attack force." That part was a blatant lie, obviously, but—"We have reason to believe that a rogue Ashůru officer is leading them." Close enough.

The men still breathed tensely, but their eyes seemed slightly less accusatory.

"Does that satisfy your curiosity, navigator?" Nahro said.

Mekdem's dark brown eyes watched Nahro for a long moment.

"Orders are orders," said the navigator at last, and turned back to the river.

"Indeed they are," said Nahro.

The Cradle and the Sword

THEY PICKED THEIR way along, running into shoals and mudbanks, jumping out of the *Zaham* to probe the knee-deep water with wood poles, looking for the next channel, the next opening in the flow, any space of water that would permit the boat through.

The short-oars were useless for paddling now. Tewolde and Raman used them like poles, pushing them into the mud as Mekdem pumped the tiller in the sludge behind the boat. Several times they all had to get out and haul the boat over a mudflat, trying to keep quiet as they spat and cursed and stumbled in the muck. Then they'd haul themselves back on deck, panting and gasping and soaked with reeking green-brown slime, picking leeches off their necks and backs, hurling them into the water. Then they'd keep pushing upriver.

This became everything, this picking, searching, pushing. As if nothing else existed but muddy waterways leading deeper into the shadows.

Then they reached a place they couldn't cross. A wooden bridge had crumbled into the river, blocking the way with timbers angled like whalebones.

Men clambered over the boards, putting out fires, shooting arrows into the foliage. Spears flew in from the shadows, but they only plunged into the water.

Mekdem maneuvered the boat as close as he could get it.

"Who's in command here?" Nahro called out to a nearby soldier crouched on the bridge, loosing arrows into the trees.

The soldier laughed.

"Footsoldier!" Nahro shouted.

The man looked up, dazed.

"I need to speak to your commanding officer," Nahro said.

"Commanding officer, *sayid*?" the man replied.

The remaining timbers buckled, groaned, and collapsed into the muddy water. Mekdem poled the boat over to a pile of shattered beams occupied by a troop of soldiers, all of them taking gulps from wineskins, slurring obscene variations on traditional Ashûru battle-songs.

"Who's in charge here?" Nahro asked them.

"In charge?" one of them said, looking up, bored.

"What's this bridge?" Nahro asked. "Who controls it?"

"Controls it?" another of the men said. They all started laughing. "Seven Stars!" he shouted. "Every morning we build it. And every afternoon these savages tear it apart." He threw his head back and howled like a wolf: "*Howoooo!*"

Another segment of the bridge collapsed, sending up great muddy waves that rocked the boat and splashed over the men clinging to the pile. They howled and cursed and laughed, and something in Nahro wanted to join them at that moment to suck wine from the wineskins and laugh and curse the river.

"We can push through there," said Mekdem, pointing at the place where the segment had fallen into the water.

Tewolde and Raman began to row again, and the boat pushed through the mud-red water, between the creaking, collapsing sections of the great bridge as more tumbled into the river. Spears and rocks continued to fly out of the forest. Shouts and curses, too, in an unknown tongue. The soldiers clinging to the bridge hurled back their own obscenities, in the languages of a dozen homelands.

The *Zaham* slipped past a mess of planking, half sucked into the mud. Three soldiers stood on it, whipping slingstones off into the trees, in the direction of each shout they heard.

Nahro tried one last time. "Hey footsoldier," he called out.

One of the slingers looked up.

"Do you know who's in charge here?" Nahro asked.

The soldier laughed and laid a stone in his sling. "No *sayid*," he said. "I don't. Is it you?"

He turned away and whipped his slingstone into the forest. Up in a tree, something thunked, and a cursing voice fell silent.

The boat slid through, leaving the bridge behind, slipping deeper into the woods.

The trees seemed to be growing more densely up here. Taller, more expansive. Even in the afternoon, only hints of sunlight filtered down through the dense canopy. Luminous insects danced among the branches. As if the stars had come out during the day.

Nahro guessed it was sunset when the man stepped into the water and hailed them.

The man wore only a tanned loincloth. His skin was pale; pinkish, almost white, painted with spirals and snakes of dark ochre. Long red hair, bound up into an elaborate knot atop his head. Green eyes. Nahro couldn't remember the last time he'd seen green eyes.

Knee-deep in water, illuminated palely in the lamplight from *Zaham*'s bow, the man raised his hands to show he was unarmed. He spoke calmly, slowly, in a language none of them understood. Was it the same language the other tribe had used? Nahro thought maybe, but he wouldn't have staked a bet on it.

Aregastes nocked an arrow, but Nahro raised a hand to stop him.

"What in the Gods' names is this, now?" asked Raman, on the verge of panic.

"You speak Ashûru?" Tewolde called out.

The man shook his head, made a clicking noise that sounded disapproving. He spoke words that sounded vaguely familiar to Nahro.

"Seven Stars," Raman muttered, then said something to the man in what sounded like Akkadu.

The pale man answered, also in what sounded like Akkadu.

"What's he saying, footsoldier?" Nahro asked.

Raman laughed; a wild, high-grayed sound. "He says—you're not going to believe this—he says he's glad we're here."

"Stop the boat," said Nahro.

"You sure that's a good idea, captain?" Mekdem asked.

"No," said Nahro. "I'm not." He turned to Raman, who was chattering away with the man in Akkadu. "Ask him who he is," Nahro said.

After a few quick words, Raman replied, "Says he's headman of the Daka people. Says they used to trade, uh," he clarified a couple of words with the man, "trade wine and copper with us."

Nahro turned to Mekdem. "You know anything about this?"

The navigator shook his head. "No, captain. I don't."

"He says they'd be honored to have us for dinner," Raman said, his expression somewhere between bewilderment, relief, and fear.

"Not a good idea, captain," said Mekdem, before Nahro could even open his mouth.

"Tell him," Nahro said, "to ask his people to show themselves."

Raman conveyed this to the red-haired man, who smiled, laughed, and shouted something in his own language.

The riverbank was suddenly full of pale-skinned men, women and children, all nearly naked, adorned with feathers and leaves, beads and painted patterns. Oldtimers, too, their reddish hair gone gray; some looking barely able to walk, but happily wading into the water, leaning on walking-sticks, waving at the men in the boat, squinting in the lamplight beneath the shadowy canopy and the flickering insects.

Aregastes was beaming, and Tewolde was catching a smile too. Raman was laughing as if he might be going mad. Mekdem scanned both banks of the river, looking almost angry that he found no signs of an attack.

"Let's tie her up," said Nahro. "It's about that time of the evening anyway."

The crew brought out the ropes and tied the *Zaham* to some thick-trunked trees, of a species Nahro had never seen before. Ten men could barely have encircled one of their trunks. Their leaves were broad, waxy, and arrow-shaped, as long as a man's forearm.

Tewolde and Aregastes leaped out onto the shore, sidling cautiously up to the Daka people. Raman talked excitedly with the red-haired headman, who kept pointing back into the trees.

Mekdem stood leaning on the boat's tiller.

"Come on," Nahro said to him.

"I think I'll keep an eye on the boat," Mekdem said.

"They've got women," Nahro said.

"They have any that aren't pink?" Mekdem asked.

"What?" Nahro raised an eyebrow.

Mekdem laughed without smiling. "I'll stay with the boat," he said.

***

The Daka people led Nahro and the rest of the crew up the shore and into the woods. After a short walk they arrived at a wide crescent of wood huts surrounding a neatly cleared patch of ground with a firepit in the center. The largest huts were at least twice as tall as a man—great triangles thatched with neat weaves of leaves and branches, their wood planking painted with bright red-and-yellow patterns of dots and curving lines.

Nahro and the others sat on strangely patterned animal skins around the fire, and the Daka men and women brought them a sort of stew of meat and spices, spooned atop the waxy leaves of the great trees that rose all around them, and carved cups filled with a sweet, milky liquid that tasted faintly like wine.

Raman and the pale-skinned headman kept up a steady stream of Akkadu banter. Nahro hadn't spoken Akkadu since his battle-school days. But the sound of that ancient language wasn't so different from modern Ashůru, once Nahro got used to the complex tones and word-endings. He was surprised to find that snatches of the conversation began to make sense, especially as the drink warmed and relaxed him.

"We are the most civilized of all the tribes here," the headman was saying.

"Most people say this is uncivilized territory," Raman replied.

The headman looked disappointed. "Is this place not civilized?" he asked. "We bring you food and drink. We treat you as proper guests. We offer to trade. What is uncivilized here?"

Raman laughed, a bit drunkenly. "Nothing, my friend," he said. "Nothing is uncivilized here. Do you like joyplant?"

"No joyplant tonight," Nahro said in Ashůru.

The headman clearly caught his meaning. "Why no joyplant tonight?" he asked in Akkadu.

"We're too far upriver," Nahro said. "It's not safe."

"Not safe?" the headman looked stunned. "Not safe? The Daka people have kept this riverbend safe since the time of my grandfather's father. We taught civilization to these savages."

"What savages?" Nahro asked.

"All the tribes around here." The headman counted on his fingers. "The Gita. The Skudra. The Moesi people, who used to eat dogs before we came. Disgusting."

Raman was laughing.

"Don't laugh," said the headman, though he was laughing too. "It was horrible, in my grandfather's father's time. But you and me? We are brothers, of course. Civilized men. We taught civilization to all the barbarians we found. Taught them to build villages and grow fruit. To gather valuable things and trade. Ended the stupidity. The killing."

"What about the tribe with no name?" Nahro asked.

The headman stopped smiling.

"What do you know about the tribe with no name?" he asked.

"I'm looking for them," said Nahro.

The other Daka people were watching their headman, now, as the *Zaham*'s crew were watching Nahro.

"No one looks for that tribe," said the headman. "There is no reason to look for them."

"I have a reason," said Nahro.

"What reason?"

"I'm looking for a man who lives with them."

The headman frowned and looked away. Then he turned back to Nahro, sharply, and said, "Why do you look for that man? He is not a good man. Here we are good people. Stay with us. Trade. Be glad. It is a good night."

"I'm not here to trade," said Nahro.

"Then go back where you came from," said the headman.

"I need to find that man."

"No," said the headman. "You do not."

"Where are the caves?" Nahro asked.

The headman looked away again, up into the shadows of the trees. He drew a deep breath, held it, and sighed.

"I will make a deal with you," he said to Nahro. "We will drink your joyplant milk together, and we will smoke some of our spinplant, and I will tell you a story about the tribe with no name. Then you will tell me whether you still want to find this man."

Nahro took a long drink from his carved cup. "All right," he said. "We're sleeping here anyway."

Raman and the headman muttered together, then the headman laughed and announced something to the Daka people, who also began to laugh.

Men and women got up, and got the men of the *Zaham*'s crew up, and moved them into a small round hut with no hole in the roof. The hut was just barely big enough to hold the boat's crew, the headman, and the five other Daka men and women who sat inside.

Some Daka people handed in bundles of spinplant: five long leaves on each stem, like green fingers, and plump buds covered in tiny hairs. The headman threw the bundles into the fire, and the earthy scent of spinplant smoke began to fill the hut.

Raman and Aregastes returned with small satchels. These turned out to contain small vials of joyplant milk, and the last of the mushrooms, both of which the Daka men and women took eagerly.

Men and women began to fall together, running their hands along each others' arms, legs, chests, downward. Tewolde was kissing a Daka girl, grabbing her desperately, laughing. They stumbled to their feet and left the smoke-filled hut together.

Nahro sipped a little of the joyplant milk, making sure the headman saw him. The headman nodded and sipped from his own vial.

Raman and Aregastes laughing in the background. Sounds of wind and swirling colors and spinplant smoke. Someone was tapping a rhythm on a drum. Others joined. The drumbeat tapped on and outward, and the other people got up and stumbled out of the hut.

Now there were only Nahro and the headman, and the low fire and the smoke.

"Do you want to hear the story?" asked the headman.

"What is your name?" Nahro asked him.

"My name does not matter now," said the headman. "Do you want to know of the tribe that has no name?"

"Yes," said Nahro.

The headman nodded.

"In the beginning," he said, "there was only the forest. The forest was always here, of course."

Nahro watched the fire. It seemed to dance differently here.

"Then came the animals. The birds and fish, and the little lights that fly."

The headman was also gazing into the fire. It danced on his pale-skinned face.

"And finally came the first people. They were like animals too. They had no language. No houses. But they had sharp stones."

Thick smoke drifted across Nahro's face.

"But the Daka people came from the river. In the time of my grandfather's grandfather. The river taught us many things. How to grow fruit. To build houses, and make bows and spears and paint."

Nahro watched the headman speak into the fire.

"Many people wanted to learn civilization from us, and we were glad to teach them. The river was generous with us, so we were generous with all the wild tribes we met. We taught them to fish in the river, and to make bows and arrows for hunting birds. We showed them how to tan skins and build huts. We explained the way to form a village, and to create laws, and to make trade with other tribes. All these things we taught them."

Now the headman looked into Nahro's eyes, firelight dancing on his face through the smoke.

"One tribe, however, did not want these things. They hated our huts and villages and trade. They hated fish-hooks and bows. They even hated names and speech."

The headman spoke quietly now.

"They did not want to be people. This was the way they lived: the strong ones decided when they would hunt. They would hunt birds or fish, or other men and women. It was all the same to them. When they grew angry, they would fight, and one would kill the other. When they wanted a woman, they would take a woman, even if it was their own sister. Even their own mother."

Only the sound of the fire now. Sparks and smoke in the air.

"What tribe has ever lived this way? Even the people we found here. Even the most base savages who could not make fire before we taught it to them—even those people understood: 'This is a bird for food; this is a man.' 'This woman is a wife; this one is your mother.' All people know these differences. Even birds and wolves know them. Every creature that can see, sees these things."

The headman shook his head gently.

"No," he said. "These people made a choice. To be worse than animals. To be something the forest and the river did not create. Something that does not come from the world."

The fire crackled. The last of the spinplant burned into smoke.

"That," said the headman, "is the story of the tribe that has no name."

Nahro and the headman stared into the fire for a long time.

"I'm here to end that tribe," Nahro said.

"You want to die?" asked the headman.

Nahro looked at him. Watched the firelight dance in his green eyes.

"Well," said Nahro. "No man learns who he is by staying in his own village."

"You're wrong," said the headman. "That's the only place where a man learns who he is."

Nahro got to his feet and ducked out the door of the hut. "I'm going to those caves tomorrow," he said.

"I know," said the headman.

"You're going to show me where they are," said Nahro.

"I'll tell you where they are," said the headman. "But I will not go near them."

"Why not?" asked Nahro.

"Because," said the headman, "I know what kind of man I am."

WHEN THE FIRST light of dawn pierced in slender shafts through the canopy of the forest, Nahro walked down to the riverbank to check on Mekdem.

The *Zaham* had been cut loose, and was gone. The torn remains of the ropes still hung from the trees, but no sign remained of the navigator and the boat.

Nahro ran back through the woods, stumbling over tangled roots and vines, sending birds and insects scattering. He burst into the hut where the headman still slept and shook the pale, sleeping man awake.

"The boat's gone," he said. "So is my navigator."

"What are you talking about?" the headman muttered, rubbing his tired eyes.

"Someone cut the ropes," Nahro said.

"Who would do such a thing?" asked the headman.

"That's what I'm asking you," Nahro snarled, drawing a dagger from his toga and placing it against the man's neck, grabbing him by his long hair.

The headman struggled and cried out, bringing a few Daka men and women running. Raman and Aregastes came with them.

"What the hell's going on?" Raman asked as he ducked in the doorway of the hut.

"Mekdem's gone," Nahro said. "Someone cut the boat loose."

Aregastes moaned.

The Daka people were yelling and calling out to the rest of the tribe now. The headman was frantically trying to explain something to them in their own language, and they tried to press into the hut, but Raman and Aregastes held them back, drawing their own swords.

"We should never have gotten out of the boat," Raman cried, laughing wildly.

"Either of you seen Tewolde?" Nahro asked, his knife still at the headman's throat.

"Not since last night," said Aregastes.

"All right," said Nahro, yanking the headman up and marching him out of the tent, knife on throat. "We're going to go find my men now. Understand?"

"I don't know where your men are," the headman shrieked. "I don't know who did this!"

All the Daka people were gathered around the hut now, two dozen of them at least. Many of the men had stone axes and bows with arrows tight against the strings. They had Nahro and the men surrounded.

Nahro paused a moment, looking for a way out. He saw none.

"Tell them what's happening," he whispered in the headman's ear.

The headman spoke a string of quick syllables in the Daka language. The people cried out and chattered, but no one charged.

One Daka man barked a short reply, louder than all the rest.

"What did he say?" Nahro asked the headman.

The headman tried to shake his head in refusal, but Nahro pulled his hair and pressed the knife closer to his neck.

"Ajavu says," the headman said, "that he knows who took the boy. He does not know about the boat."

"What happened to the boy?" Nahro asked the Daka man who'd shouted.

The man replied in clipped syllables.

"He says," the headman said, "that the girl went missing this morning too."

"What girl?" Nahro asked.

"The girl that your boy went off with last night," came the answer.

"Where did they go?" Nahro asked.

The Daka man, Ajavu, raised a bladed black stone in the air and said something in his language. The Daka people gasped and cried out.

The headman released a moan of despair.

"What did he say?" Nahro snarled.

"He found that stone in the woods at dawn," said the headman. "Two sets of footprints leading to it. Four sets leading away."

"What is that?" Aregastes asked.

Raman was shouting "Who are these people?" over and over.

"They always leave one of their stones, so we know it was them," the headman was saying. "They know we will not follow. You should not follow. It's death."

"It's death for them if we don't, right?" Nahro said.

He let go of the headman, who stumbled into the arms of his people. Then he looked at Raman and Aresgastes, who were clearly in no condition to fight.

"You don't have to come with me," Nahro said.

"Come with you where?" Raman shrieked. "What the hell is going on?"

"I'm going to kill the man I was sent here to kill," Nahro said.

"And if we don't come with you?" Aregastes asked.

Nahro shrugged. "Start building a boat, I guess."

Raman put his head in his hands. Aregastes looked around wildly, as if a solution might present itself.

"Which way are the caves?" Nahro asked the headman, who pointed off into the forest.

Nahro nodded. "Thank you for your hospitality," he said, and marched into the foliage.

A few moments later, he heard Raman and Aregastes following.

The forest soon began to slope upward, and they were fighting their way through vines that seemed to grip their ankles and pull them down. Through thin shafts of cloud-dimmed sunlight, they watched the bushes shake with hidden motion as they passed. Every tree seemed to loom with a mass larger than itself, as if strange, half-seen shapes hid in the shadows, always at the edge of vision.

They climbed without speaking, tearing each breath from the suffocating air. A mist rose, and every cough and exhalation sent out more creeping tendrils of it, to join and mingle with the dancing shadows that surrounded them, slipping in from every side.

At last the wine-choked forest floor gave way to hard dirt, then to bare rock. Dense green trees yielded to shriveled brown ones whose dry canopies dropped rains of dead leaves on their heads as they passed. They saw the sun again, for the first time in days, but it hid behind thick gray clouds, giving off only a dim, almost moonlike light.

When they reached a narrow pass between two tall cliffs, Nahro raised his hand for a pause.

"They'll be waiting," he whispered.

Raman and Aregastes nodded, wiping sweat from their soaking faces.

"I'll go in first," he said. "If I shout, come in ready to kill. If I make no sound and I don't come back—"

He trailed off, but they were watching him, waiting for him to finish the order.

"Don't come in after me," he said.

They nodded again.

There was nothing else to say. Nahro drew his sword, and stepped quietly between the cliffs.

The passage was narrow, barely wide enough for him to slip through. He glanced up at the clifftops above. No sign of movement. He pressed through.

He came out onto a small basin; a sort of natural chamber in the rock, open to the cloudy sky. Another fissure, broader than the one he'd passed through, leading deeper into the cliffs. Still no sign of anyone.

"Come through," he called back through the passage, as quietly as he could.

After a moment he heard their footsteps and saw them emerge out of the narrow fissure between the rocks. They scanned every inch of the deep crater around them, but saw no hint of movement and heard no sound, not even a bird-call.

"No birds," said Aregastes, as if hearing his thoughts.

Nahro nodded. "They're here."

Aregastes pulled an arrow back against his bowstring. Raman drew his sword, and a short dagger from his belt.

Nahro led the way into the next chasm, trying to keep his eyes on everything at once. Only silence around them, and rock and sky above.

The ground rose upward again, and they scrambled up an embankment toward the entrance of a cave, whose wide, open mouth receded far back into shadow. Nahro backed against the rock wall, out of instinct more than anything. Raman and Aregastes caught up with him, panting and catching their breath in the cave's yawning mouth.

Something came flying out of the darkness, connecting with Aregastes's head, which fountained blood. He dropped instantly, blood already pouring from his shattered skull. Next to him lay a heavy black rock, sharpened to a point.

"Oh Gods no," Raman was howling.

Nahro grabbed him and ran back out of the mouth of the cave, toward the embankment, but something dropped onto them from above. Silent. Like a man but huge, thick and muscled, painted ash-gray from head to toe.

A huge hand gripped Nahro's head and smashed it against the rock wall. All went black.

HE AWOKE WITH a throbbing pain in his head. He opened his eyes, and at first saw only dark. Then thin shafts of light and vague shadows. His arms and legs were unbound, but he was packed inside a small room. An outlet in the rock. Thick wood bars. He kicked at them. They didn't budge. He kicked harder. Not even a vibration.

The sound brought one of them. Maybe the same one from outside in the cave; hulking and gray-painted. It—he?—peered into Nahro's cage. Smaller ones, children, also painted gray from head to toe, gathered around the big one's legs, hid behind them, peered curiously between the bars.

"He will see you," said the big one, in thickly accented Akkadu.

"Where is he?" asked Nahro.

The big one didn't seem to understand. Or maybe he did and just didn't care. "Soon," he said.

"Where are my men?" Nahro asked, coughing through a parched throat.

The big one only turned and walked away, taking the little ones with him.

"Water," Nahro croaked. "Please."

But they were gone.

He had no idea how long he waited in that shadowed place. Thin shafts of daylight; narrow slivers of moonlight. Sleeping and wakefulness, waking and dreams. Caves and the forest, the boat and gray-painted people of the tribe without a name. Maybe some came to peer in at him, as though he were a curiosity; an animal. Or maybe those were just dreams. Someone brought water at some point. Nahro gulped it eagerly. When it was gone, no one brought more. More dreams. More thirst in the dark.

One morning, a face appeared between the bars of Nahro's cage. Its features were hard to make out, but Nahro could see that its skin was the sandy color of the Ashûru people, and that it was shaved bald, and wore a trimmed black beard.

"It doesn't really matter what I say, does it?" said the face.

Nahro watched the face and tried to focus on it. His eyes were tired. Too long in the shadow. Too long without water.

"Whatever words I speak," the face said, "this part of the story will play out the same."

A hand reached out, holding a wood cup filled with water. The hand tipped the cup into Nahro's mouth, and Nahro drank. He swallowed the water in gulps, every mouthful tasting perfect. The face became a bit easier to see.

It was the face of a man of Ash'shûr. Middle-aged. Handsome, but bony. Sunken cheeks. Pale gray eyes that seemed to pierce Nahro every time they looked at him. Nahro willed himself not to break the man's gaze. He held it.

"Do you think," asked the man with the gray eyes, "that you know who I am?

Nahro held his gaze steady. "You're Rabail," he said.

The man ran a thick hand down his face and through his beard. "And do you think you know who you are?" he asked.

"I am Captain Eriba-Adad, Fourth Regiment," said Nahro.

"What is that name?" asked Rabail. "Is that what you call yourself, inside your mind? Is it what your children call you?"

"I have no children," said Nahro.

"That's a shame," said Rabail. "I have many children. You can see them, all around here. Playing."

Rabail pressed his hands to his face and held them there a long time.

"I know what they say about us," he said. "About my people. That we eat each other. Fuck our own mothers. Why do you think," he picked at something in his teeth, "they would tell stories like that, captain?"

"Because they're true," Nahro said.

Rabail leaned back, vanishing into shadow. When he leaned forward again, his eyes were locked on Nahro's.

"I have skinned the flesh from men's bones," he said. "And I have eaten it. What does this make me?"

He watched Nahro, waiting for an answer.

"I don't know, *sayid*," Nahro said. "But I know it means you're a criminal."

Rabail barked a laugh. Tiny voices giggled around his ankles.

"Criminal," Rabail said. "That's a word they've called me. They have a lot of words for me. For us. For the way we live."

"'Insane,' commander," Nahro said. "Another word is 'insane.'"

Rabail looked at something far away. He stared at that distant point for a long breath. He turned back to Nahro.

"What happens, captain," Rabail asked, "When the nation of Ash'shûr goes to war?"

Nahro closed his eyes.

"Open your eyes, Nahro!" Rabail howled.

Nahro's eyes snapped open. Rabail was staring into them, as if trying to tear through them to see something inside.

"Two roads," Rabail said, "diverge from this place."

Nahro watched Rabail's eyes, twin pits of black in clouds of pale gray.

"One road leads back," Rabail said. "Back to the place we came from. The place where a host of Gods wear the trees and the stones and the water like clothes. The Garden where a thousand tribes speak a thousand tongues."

Rabail dipped the wood cup into a bucket of water and put it to Nahro's lips again. Nahro drank eagerly.

"The second road," said Rabail, "leads forward. Along this road, Gods shatter and turn to ash. Words are forgotten. Men become hounds. Women become cattle. A boot presses on a neck."

Nahro sucked up the last of the water. Rabail took the cup away.

"Which of these two roads," Rabail asked, "do our gold and iron build?"

The last of the water slipped down Nahro's throat, but his tongue was still dry.

Rabail took hold of the wood grate, untied a knot outside, and opened Nahro's cell.

"You're free to come and go as you please," Rabail said. "You'll be watched, of course. Lay a hand on any of my children, and I'll kill you."

Nahro sat perfectly still, watching.

Rabail turned away and laughed at some private joke. "When you do it," he said, turning back to Nahro, "I don't want to know about it. You understand? I don't want to see it coming." He smiled. "Surprise me."

Then he turned and walked away, the gray-painted children following at his heels, laughing and playing.

⁂

SOME TIME LATER, Nahro crawled out of the crevice in the rock. He stumbled into blinding daylight, shielding his eyes. All around him rose gray cliffs overflowing with bushes and trees, vines and ferns spilling across the boulders; waterfalls of leaves and petals. From every ledge and crevice, the gray-painted people watched—men, women and children, all dark gray, except for the gleaming eyes and teeth.

He ran through corridors of rock, climbing boulder-strewn hills, peering into caves, looking for—what? For Rabail? The man was nowhere to be found. Nor were any of the men from the boat. For a way out? No such thing, except back the way he'd come, and that was guarded by grinning gray-painted men with watchful eyes and sharp stones in their hands.

Sunset came, and then night began to fall. No one lit a fire. The stars came out, and a half-moon behind the clouds. Shadows and pale phantoms. Men and women ran and laughed in the dark, howling and chirping like beasts.

Nahro stumbled over roots and branches. Where was he going? Back to the cave where he'd slept before, for all those thirsty days. That was at least a place he knew. But in the dark, he couldn't find it. He fell asleep in the bushes, curled up like a child.

In the morning, he wandered again. And the morning after that. He lost track of the wordless days; the nights without fire.

When he thirsted, he found a pool. When he grew hungry, one of the gray-painted ones approached him and offered a bit of meat. He didn't want to take the meat, because part of him knew what the meat most likely was and knew that Rabail had arranged for him to starve until he would eat this meat. So he refused it. Refused it for many days—who knew how many days—until at last he had passed beyond hunger into a world of shifting shapes and muscles that would no longer move. Water but no food. Only the meat, offered each day by shining white smiles in ashen paint.

He tried eating other things. The plants made him sick. There were no fish in the pools. The gray-painted people laughed at him.

One morning he woke with hunger clawing up from his belly so loud he screamed, and he ran to the gray-painted people and took the meat from their hands. He gnawed the meat with tears in his eyes, feeling the juices dribble down his chin, and he was grateful for it. He wept because he was starving, and because the taste of flesh was perfect.

When he had eaten, he slept for a long time. He did not want to wake up.

But in the night, he felt a heavy hand shaking him awake.

"How did it feel, Nahro?" Rabail asked. "How did it feel to taste what you are becoming?"

"You're insane," Nahro said, refusing to look into the man's eyes.

"And you are joining me there," said Rabail. "At the place where God and animal become one another."

"You killed them," Nahro said. "All my men."

Rabail shook his head softly. "Not all of them," he said.

Nahro rolled over and scanned Rabail's bearded face. Nothing there. A blank.

"You'll see one of them at dawn," Rabail said.

He rose to his feet and strolled away.

Nahro got up and followed him. Rabail walked calmly, serenely, never glancing behind. He took a path Nahro had never found, a winding trail that led up between the caves. A few of the gray-painted people were following, but so few of them were here. There used to be more.

Rabail's path took them out onto a grass-covered hilltop. The whole forest spread around them, an ocean of mist-shrouded green in every direction. No wind blew, but the trees were alive with a motion all their own.

All the gray-painted people were gathered on the crest of the hill, around the circle of tall stones that stood there, every stone taller than a man, carved with strange markings.

Rabail strolled to the center of the stones. He turned to Nahro and smiled.

Then, slowly and deliberately, he turned his back.

The people were chanting; a rhythm too complex to follow, or perhaps not a rhythm at all. It seemed to match the movements of the trees and the shadows.

Rabail was talking intently to the gray-painted people now. A group of women, fox skulls on leather straps around their necks, were embracing him, weeping, tears streaming down their ash-dark cheeks. He was smiling, reassuring them, whistling and chirping to them. No words. Only sounds.

Nahro came up behind Rabail. Here in the open, he knew his intent must be obvious, but no one made a move to stop him. He reached for one of the daggers in his tunic. They all watched him silently, sad expressions on their gray-painted faces. Rabail continued to coo and mutter to the women. He moved down the line, spending time with some others.

Closer. Nahro could smell Rabail; earth and meat, sweat and bark. He drew the dagger and raised it. Rabail embraced a gray-painted woman, kissing her forehead. The men watched intently, but none moved. Their eyes wanting him to do it. Willing it.

He brought the dagger down hard into the side of Rabail's neck. The man gasped and clutched at air. The gray-painted people watched, wept, but did not interfere.

Rabail fell to the ground, pale robes spilling around him, blood spurting from his neck. Nahro brought the dagger down again and again, severing the artery, spraying bright blood across the grass, onto the tall stones. Rabail's eyes rolled back. He twitched, gasped, lay still.

Nahro rose slowly to his feet. The gray-painted people watched him.

He walked into the crowd, back in the direction of the caves.

They fell to their knees around the body of their fallen lord. Every man, woman and child. With faces solemn and pious, they raised their razor-sharp rocks above the body—then brought them down, and began to carve.

Just as Nahro began to turn away, one of the worshipers looked up. It was Raman, painted ash-gray from head to toe. He smiled.

⟨

Nahro ran to Raman, pulled him up, dragged him through the crowd, who parted to let him through, utterly absorbed in their labors. They stumbled back down the hillside path, Raman yelling, "Hey, what are you doing? You did it!" as they stumbled across boulders and over vines and roots, back down through the caves and through the cliffs, where two huge gray-painted men stood guard. They raised their sharpened rocks.

Nahro drew his sword. Faked left, stepped right and ran the blade up through the lung of the first guard, who went down coughing and spitting blood. Whirled, slashing the other guard across the chest. Not fatally, but enough to slow the man down.

They ran down through the fissures between the cliffs, through that rocky chasm barely wide enough for a man to pull his body through, but they pulled themselves through it, out and over the moss-covered hills, tripping over tangled roots and rocks onto the leaf piles of the forest floor, and down the slope until at last they came to the riverbank.

Where Nahro went, Raman followed. They ran through the forest-filtered dawn and into the morning, hearing the shouts and whistles of the tribe behind them. But the calls grew fainter, and by the evening the only sounds were the insects and the birds and the wind.

They did not sleep that night. Nor did they speak of what they'd seen and done in the hills. If Raman had asked, Nahro could not have put into words why Rabail had hidden himself among those hills; why he had taken the tribe with no name as his children, and eaten of their flesh; why he had spared the two men who sought him and bent his neck for the dagger. Nahro had no names for those hungers, though his heart knew them well. *For this is what war is*, he thought: *men devouring one another.*

In the morning, they built a boat. The best they could do, lashing together branches and reeds into a rough sort of canoe. But it floated, even when they stepped into it. They took branches for push-poles. They didn't need oars. They were heading downriver this time.

The current carried them beneath the towering cedars and the shifting shadows of the willows, the knotted trunks of the oaks and pines, and the ferns and the tall pale birches, crowding out the sunlight, holding the mists and the thick air close to the ground.

All around them, the forest seemed to press in. Nahro kept his eyes on the river. It would take them out of this shadow, out to the sea—or to someplace other than this forest.

As long as we have a boat, Nahro kept thinking.

Just as long as we stay in the boat.

118 YEARS EARLIER
1334 BC

No king becomes powerful all on his own.

— Akkadu proverb

Y

Two lithe black horses bounded through the royal forest, dodging branches and leaping over roots, their riders close on the trail of a wild leopard.

Crown Prince Hardash took the lead, black-braided hair bouncing behind him as he steered his sleek night-black horse between the oaks and elms. Even at seventeen, he already sported the start of a full beard, and his muscles rippled beneath his tanned skin—sure signs of his mother's Ashûru blood. He wore a short-sleeved robe of white linen, embroidered with a mosaic of pale blue sapphires, topped with a loose leather vest adorned with polished beads of turquoise. Two bronze daggers gleamed in his broad leather belt.

On the prince's heels galloped Indash, the king's bastard son, paler and lankier than his half-brother, and a year younger, but every bit as sharp-eyed on his own quick stallion. He was clad in a robe of coral-colored linen, sewn with round yellow flowers; and a leather hunting-belt, in which two daggers lay tight against his ribs.

Behind the prince and his half-brother trotted a gaggle of knights, barons and childhood friends, ostensibly aiding the hunt, but really here to see and be seen in their embroidered linens and gold girdles.

The prince caught sight of the leopard's dappled hide, slipping into a thorn-bush beneath the branches of an old oak. He signaled silently to his half-brother and used his legs to guide his horse around the other side of the bushes as he slid an arrow from the quiver on his back.

As the prince tore around the bushes, Indash swung his own horse around, raising a hand to stop and silence the nobles behind him. Obligingly, they halted their mounts and cut the chatter to whispers. Then he turned his horse back to the bush and drew his own arrow as he crept in.

Despite the prince's effort to keep silent, some movement startled the leopard, which burst out the far side of the bushes in an explosion of twigs and leaves, the muscles beneath its spotted hide shifting in the forest-filtered sunlight.

The beast leaped up at Prince Hardash, snarling and baring its claws. The prince loosed an arrow straight down the leopard's throat. It choked and fell back, scraping its claws down the side of the prince's horse, scoring the animal's side with bloody gashes. The horse tumbled to the forest floor, whinnying in panic, as Indash crashed through the bushes to the prince's aid, loosing arrow after arrow into the leopard's side, aiming for the soft spot between its shoulders.

Hardash half-leaped, half-crawled from under his collapsing stallion, drawing both bronze daggers from his belt. The beast was severely weakened already. It stumbled and gasped as it clawed at the horse, trying to raise itself up, its spotted fur bristling with arrow-shafts, running with fresh red blood.

Indash, still seated on his own horse, knew better than to fire the killing shot. He watched his half-brother rear back before the leopard as it snarled and stared into his eyes with what looked like raw hate. The beast swiped at Hardash with one shaggy clawed paw, then the other. The prince dodged, hooting and laughing, daggers raised. Indash heard soft applause from the nobles behind him. He rolled his eyes.

The leopard reared back, aiming to launch itself bodily at Prince Hardash, and that was when he struck, plunging both daggers straight through the beast's neck. His blades burst out behind the leopard's head, spattering blood on the treetrunks and bushes.

As the leopard collapsed, a wreckage of arrows and blood, the nobles applauded louder, sending up whistles and cheers. The prince withdrew his daggers from the beast's neck, wiping the blood from one blade, then the other, against the embroidered sleeve of his white robe.

Hardash slid his sword back into its jeweled scabbard, then looked up at his half-brother, beaming like a child.

"Sometimes I wish they'd fight a bit harder," he said.

Indash grinned down at the prince. "Perhaps next time I won't fire so many arrows," he said.

Hardash laughed. Now the nobles were converging on them, sending up thick clouds of perfume and flattery: "A fine kill, my prince," said one; "A warrior as great as his father," said another. On and on it went, as slaves materialized to hang the great beast from a tree, bleed it dry, then take its skin back to the palace, where the prince would tumble upon the spotted fur with palace concubines as he bragged of this hunt.

Just a moment ago, such fierceness in those eyes, thought Indash.

Prince Hardash, meanwhile, was staring sadly down at his horse.

"Broken leg," the prince called to his half-brother, looking genuinely pained. "And he's lost a lot of blood."

"He's a damned fine horse," said Indash.

"You were," said the prince to his horse, bending down to stroke the fallen stallion's cheek. "The finest I've ever ridden." Then he plunged one of his own daggers into the beast's soft-furred neck. It twitched and lay still. Indash thought he might see a hint of a tear in his half-brother's eye as the prince strode toward him. But Hardash quickly shook off the feeling and recomposed the half-smirk he usually wore.

Indash climbed down from his horse, offering it to his half-brother.

"Thank you, brother," said the prince as he swung himself up into the saddle.

"Half-brother," Indash corrected him, "though you're welcome all the same."

The prince waved a hand dismissively as he settled himself atop his new mount. "You'll always be a brother to me," he said, looking down at Indash. "I won't hear a word to the contrary."

"Will your brother have to walk back to the palace on foot?" Indash asked.

The prince laughed again. He looked back at the nobles and snapped his fingers. "You there," he said. "Baron—eh—"

"Nazibugash," replied the baron, a plump middle-aged in a brocaded blue toga. "Son of Kakrime, of—"

"Yes, yes," said the prince. "My brother put ten arrows in a leopard today, Nazibugash. What have you done for me?"

"I, eh—well, I—" The baron stammered, drawing quiet chuckles from a few of the other nobles.

Hardash looked at him as if he were astonishingly stupid. "Get off your horse!" the prince cried. "Seven Stars, it's like speaking to an infant."

The plump baron rushed to dismount from his dun-colored mount, his face glowing red. He got an ankle tangled in his stirrup, and barely managed to stay upright as he stumbled to the forest floor in a storm of fallen leaves. Now Indash was laughing, too, though he also felt bad for the poor man. He made a note of the baron's name, fully expecting to hear it in a less pleasant context before the year was out.

As Nazibugash waddled off in search of a spare horse to mount, Indash swung himself up onto the man's saddle. His tan, black-maned horse was shorter and stockier than the lithe stallions of the royal stables, but the creature accepted Indash without comment. When he gave it a slight nudge with his heels, it trotted obligingly toward the prince.

"Well," said Prince Hardash. "I don't know about you lot, but I'm thirsty."

A chorus of agreement went up from the entourage, and the prince galloped off with a cry of "To the palace!" Indash kicked his dun horse softly, and it sped off in pursuit of the prince, surprisingly nimble amid the tangled roots and branches.

They broke out of the wood, onto the grassy plain just south of the city of Babili, whose stone walls sprawled for miles, like vast arms wrapped around the treasure-hoard at the center of the world. At the city's heart towered the glistening blue-and-gold walls of the royal palace—and, taller still, the great ziggurat, a mountain of polished white sandstone, its pinnacle nearly piercing the clouds.

𒈫

Their horses thundered across the flat plain, Indash's mount catching up with the prince until the two stallions galloped side-by-side, hooves pounding in lockstep. Indash drew a deep breath of the warm spring wind that sent his long hair flapping, like the black mane of his horse. Prince Hardash whooped and laughed, urging his sleek night-colored horse to gallop harder, faster, kicking up clouds of grass-specked dust as they tore across the flat earth.

As the riders approached the city, farmers and trinket-sellers dodged aside on narrow dirt roads amid low mud-brick shacks: the suburbs outside the city wall, where children played beneath tall palm trees, and packs of goats and sheep roamed between patches of grass.

Beyond these outlying neighborhoods, the tall sails of barges plied the serene current of the Slow River; and in the gaps between them darted rowboats and small rafts, poled by traders and messengers carrying parcels into the city. Babili's mud-brick walls towered on the other side of the river, their intricate brickwork broken only by the crenellated towers from which helmeted guards watched the broad pontoon bridge that led to the city's great western gate.

Indash and Hardash trotted beneath the gate's vast arch, the heat of the day turning to cool shadow as the guards parted to let them through, along with a stream of sandaled men in colorful togas, and wool-kilted shepherds leading their flocks among merchants' donkey-drawn carts.

The young men's horses galloped down broad flagstone-paved avenues, past the striped awnings of market stalls, around corners where pale mud-daubed shops and apartments jutted wildly into the streets. Scarved old women watched from rooftops, beneath umbrellas decorated with intricate colorful patterns. In the shadows of the brick apartments, children kicked leather balls and pursued one another through the alleys, squealing with laughter, chasing away the city's wild cats, who sulked away around corners.

Near the heart of the city, the riders passed beneath a second, much more tightly-guarded gate: the portal that divided the sacred temple and palace precincts from the rest of the city. Wary guards eyed them carefully, until at last Prince Hardash snarled, "You know very well who I am," and the spearmen stepped aside to let them through the imposing inner gate, into the manicured outer gardens of the palace complex, where bright-robed, coiffed courtiers strolled with their friends among the short-palms and flower bushes.

As they trotted through, Hardash glanced up at the towering ziggurat behind the painted columns and porticoes of the palace outbuildings: a stepped pyramid of painted blue and gold, its tip seeming to pierce the clouds. Around its lower steps, sumptuous green vines and flowering bushes spilled from terraced platforms, accented by palms and topiaries; a garden in the sky, rising to greet the sun above the topmost painted towers of the palace.

When at last the young men and their retinue strode into the palace's entrance hall—sweaty and dusty after their long uphill gallop through Babili's labyrinth—Hardash and Indash made straight for the inner garden, calling for the slaves to bring pitchers of beer and wine.

But the garden was already occupied. King Burnaburiash the Second, Protector of the Kalshu People, Exalted Majesty of the Kingdom of Karduniash, paced around long shallow pools, trailed by a small group of his closest confidants. The burbling of fountains and the chirping of birds in the trees masked the men's quiet conference, as they strolled beneath overhanging green leaves accented with oranges, lemons and sweet-smelling flowers of purple and white. Their soft slippers padded on a floor mosaicked with constellations of bright blue and yellow tiles, amid walls adorned with faience-glazed bas-reliefs and carvings of Gods and kings and wild beasts devouring their prey.

The king stood out clearly at the head of that company: a burly, thick-shouldered man of middle age, his long black hair and square beard tightly curled and trimmed, the bright blue linen of his short-sleeved robe sewn with tiny flowers in the finest gold thread, his loose outer toga dyed deep red, fringed in gold, its front panel embroidered with a towering golden palm tree outlined in green, attended by kneeling golden bulls and lions, the sigil-beasts of Babili. Gold rings set with emeralds dangled from his ears, and a stole of brilliant blue linen hung about his shoulders, beneath a headband of hammered gold, in which rubies and sapphires glimmered in the afternoon sun.

"Father!" Hardash ran to embrace the king.

The king looked up from his conversation, irritated. "What is it?" he barked. As he recognized his two sons, his expression softened, just slightly, beneath his vast gold-clasped beard. "Ah, back from the hunt. Success, I gather?"

"I killed a leopardess," Hardash said, embracing his father, kissing him on the left cheek, then on the right, then on the left again, as was proper from a son to his father. "A big one."

"It is a good omen," said Shagarakti, the palace vizier, at the king's ear. The jewels dripping from his earrings and necklaces clinked softly with each tiny movement he made. He was draped in a deep blue robe embroidered with gold flowers, encircled by an ascending fringe of white tassels. His hair was curled and coiffed far more ostentatiously than that of the king, but the gold band atop his head was simple and unadorned.

"We're in need of good omens these days," grumbled the king, embracing Indash more brusquely, kissing him once on the forehead.

"We were just going to have a drink to celebrate," said Hardash, turning to bow out of the conversation and the garden. "We won't trouble you, father."

"No," said the king, placing his hand on the prince's shoulder. "Stay, son. It's good for you to see how these conversations go."

"Oh, father, I'm sure I'd only be a bother," said the prince, clearly thinking of the wine and women he was already missing.

"Nonsense," said the king, his expression hardening again. Then he smiled, stroking his son's braided black hair. "Look at you, already a man. How quickly time passes. I should have brought you into these conferences years ago." Then he turned to Indash. "And you," he said, smiling slightly. "Stay silent, follow behind us, and listen. One day soon, you may be the only man my son can trust."

"I'd be honored, Father," said Indash, noting the disapproving expressions on nearby faces, and the prince's look of surprise. He'd learned to enjoy moments like this, and he made sure he enjoyed this one, while it lasted.

"Good," said the king, resuming his pacing around the garden fountain. "Now, where were we?"

They walked together, the king and his advisors and sons, talking quietly beneath the multicolored canopy of flowers, wines and trees, their words obscured from unwanted listeners by the calls of birds and the bubbling of the fountains.

"The Empire of Khatti does not pose an immediate problem, Majesty," one of the advisors, a stocky scar-faced man named Gidar, was saying. Indash recognized him as the palace's master of arms, field-commander of the Kalshu armies and—if the stories were true—slayer of hundreds of warriors. Instead of an ornate robe he wore only a simple tunic of pale green linen, belted with a leather strap in which two bronze daggers gleamed.

"I should hope they don't, Gidar," said the king. "Not if my daughter is doing her job in the Khatti emperor's bed."

"The emperor is quite happy with the marriage, I'm told," said Maruttash, the palace's master of spies, who looked utterly unlike a spy in his loose-sleeved brown robes, devoid of jewels or gold, the face beneath his clean-shaved head always wearing a neutral, mild expression. Indash supposed the man's very blandness made him so effective at his work—or perhaps it was merely an act.

"In that case," said the king, "Elam should pose even less of a problem."

The mention of the eastern Kingdom of Elam sparked a chain of memories in Indash: afternoons spent playing in the palace yards with his half-sister Princess Napirasu, a plain girl, but sweet and clever, who'd been married off to the Elamu king as soon as she showed her first blood. As she'd prepared to depart with the foreign king's caravan, she'd told Indash that her aunt had been married to the previous Elamu monarch, and was still, presumably, living in the royal palace of Elam; a former queen without a husband. The princess had hoped to find a second mother in her aunt when she arrived in Elam. But Indash knew from many stories how things generally went between old discarded queens and fresh new ones. That was the last he'd heard of his half-sister.

"Has our little sister sent word lately?" Hardash asked, giving word to Indash's thoughts.

The king turned to the prince as if suddenly remembering him. "She is well," he said, glancing at Maruttash for confirmation.

"It is... a happy marriage," Maruttash assured the prince, his face wearing the same neutral expression it always did. "The lord of Elam treats her well."

"Moving on," said the king, cutting off a questioning look from the prince. "What does the young pharaoh of Misr say of the greeting-gifts we've sent? And our letter of protest about this nonsense with the Ashûru king?"

Kadashman, the palace's master of scribes, chose his words carefully. "We have not," he said, "received a reply from the land of Misr, as of yet."

"Impudent little pharaoh," the king snarled. "Even more arrogant than his heretic father."

"Perhaps the messenger has been delayed," Kadashman offered.

"Like our last messenger was 'delayed' for two whole years?" snarled Gidar. His expression contorted the scar that ran down his jaw and neck; an old relic of the Khatti Wars.

"What madness runs in these Misru bloodlines?" the king exclaimed. "First a sun-worshipping father who thinks he can trick me with impure gold. Now his effeminate, half-lame son, this boy-king... Tut-ankh-amon," the king spat the strange name, "who receives the king of Ash'shûr—*my* vassal—at his court as an equal."

"The world is crumbling," said Shagarakti, the palace vizier, with a soft shake of his perfumed head.

"More than a thousand years have passed since the days of Misr's great pyramids and mighty pharaohs," Kadashman commented. "Kingdoms are like generations of a family: the first one builds. The second expands. The third falls into decadence."

"What my long-winded friend means to say, I believe," said Gidar, "is that the bloodline of Misr grows weak in its old age. Perhaps in a few years, they'll be ripe—"

"In a few years, this Ashûru war-chief will be pharaoh!" The king slammed his palm into a nearby treetrunk, shaking the branches and sending up a panicked flutter of tiny birds.

The others watched him while he took a few deep breaths and got his breathing under control. "If not in name, then in influence," he said, more quietly. "The idea beggars belief, but we all know it's a fact. It's time to face up to it."

The prince stared wide-eyed at his father, clearly feeling out of his depth. Indash felt the same, but he tried to piece the story together as best he could: The old pharaoh had died; his son was seen as effeminate and weak, and was hosting his father's vassal, the king of Ash'shûr, at his court. What would this mean—war with Misr? With Ash'shûr? With both? Indash held his tongue, hoping the prince would be astute enough to ask.

"Father," said the prince, "Isn't Ash'shûr just a weak little tribe? Why don't we punish them for this insolence? I could lead—"

"Ash'shûr isn't just a small tribe anymore, boy," Gidar cut him off.

"It turns out they're damned good at trade," Kadashman explained to the young prince. "They've grown wealthy, Gods damn them—and we let them do it, right under our noses, fools that we are. Now they've got a web of ships and wagon-trains stretching from Ninua to the Great Sea. Every year they grow richer. Every day they're snapping at my heels, acting less and less like the vassals they are."

"Not just wealthy, but cutthroat," the king snarled. "I fear no army of Khatti or Misr, but these Ashûru—" He shook his shaggy head. "Wouldn't trust them as far as I can spit. They don't play by our rules, my son. I've seen them burn whole villages to the ground over some imagined insult. Decorate leagues of roadside with crucified enemies."

"And now they strike deals with pharaohs behind our back," said the prince, his expression darkening.

"Perhaps," Shagarakti put in, "the princess—?"

"Princess?" The king whirled on the vizier, wrinkling his brow. Then a smile crossed his face. "Ah yes," he said, turning to Hardash. "How fares your wife Sherua, my son?"

The prince was already shaking his head. "She has no influence with her father," he said. "Typical Ashûru king. Doesn't even read her letters—or at least, he doesn't answer them."

"Then what in the Gods' names was the point of that marriage?" the king snarled.

"If nothing else," Shagarakti put in, "she may serve as leverage. Prince Hardash is, after all, half-Ashûru himself. And Princess Sherua is the eldest daughter of the House of Ash'shûr. "

"And a boring bed-companion," Hardash muttered under his breath as Indash hid his smile.

"What was that?" the king snapped at him.

The prince stiffened. "I only said, father, that my wife is clearly of little importance to the Ashûru king, eldest daughter or no."

"Speak with her anyway," said the king, tightly. "Ruling is not all hunts and battles, my son. More often, it means whispering sweet words in the right ears. Whisper some to your wife tonight, and bring me news by morning."

As Prince Hardash turned away from his father, Indash wanted desperately to ask more practical questions: how Ash'shûr's military might stood in comparison with Babili's, and where each side's weak points might lie—but he bit back his words, as the king had commanded, and followed the pacing group for another circuit of the garden fountains.

"Surely," said the prince, "my upstart father-in-law can't pose a threat to us here."

The king snorted. "That must've been what that old Khatti emperor thought, too."

"Old Khatti emperor—?" the prince asked, but Indash knew what the king meant.

He remembered the story from his lessons: a century or so ago, the city of Babili was a possession of an overextended Khatti emperor far in the west, who struggled to control the far-flung empire he'd wrenched from the ancient First Dynasty of Babili. The city was ripe for the plucking then, like a bright purple fig on a low-hanging branch. The crown prince's ancestors—the army of Kalsh, led by the king's own forefather Ulamburiash the Great—swept down from the eastern mountains to pluck that ripe fruit.

The rest was a beloved family tale. Ulamburiash had encamped his forces outside the city, and dispatched a messenger to the Khatti emperor with a simple offer: *Fight a costly war you cannot win, or turn Babili over to me and accept me as your ally.* Overwhelmed and under-supplied, the emperor had capitulated, ordered his forces to stand down—and a triumphant Ulamburiash had paraded into the jeweled city without so much as drawing a sword or a bowstring. The noble line of Kalshu kings had ruled Babili ever since.

"History," King Burnaburiash said to his son, "is a long list of mistakes not to repeat. Pay attention to your lessons."

"I don't have lessons anymore, Father," said the prince, a frown crossing his bearded face.

The king humphed. "I'll assign you some new ones."

By the time they'd finished another circuit of the gardens, and the king had dismissed the two young men, Prince Hardash wore a deep scowl.

"Oh, cheer up," said Indash as they hurried toward the dining-hall, in search of their hunting companions. "Your father did you an honor by including you in that little stroll."

The prince let out a sigh. "And if my wife won't give me an answer he likes, what then?"

"Welcome to kingship," Indash said. He cracked a smile. "It's not all hunts and battles, you know," he said in his best imitation of the king's bass-toned voice.

Then they were laughing again, stumbling into the dining-hall to the surprise of their friends, who greeted them with shouts and embraces, at a table weighed heavy with roasted rack of lamb, and suckling pig roasted in honey and cumin, with almonds and sprigs of fresh mint; fish stewed with peppered lentils; salty goat's cheese, and flaky sweetbreads rolled with pistachios; honeyed pomegranates, bunches of plump grapes, oranges, candied figs and dates, and pitchers spilling with sweet wine and foaming beer.

Indash and the prince fell into comfortable cushioned chairs, grabbed bits of fresh-baked barley flatbread and used them to tear chunks of tender, steaming meat from the pig and lamb. They filled their silver cups with wine, and their mugs with beer, and their bellies with meat and cheese and fruit. And for a few hours, they forgot all about Ash'shûr and the pharaoh, and thought only of the cups in their hands and the concubines in their laps.

Late in the evening, when the candles had burned down to low mounds of wax, Indash glanced across the room to see Nazibugash, that pouty nobleman Prince Hardash had removed from his horse this morning. The beady-eyed man looked at him for an instant, then turned back to his companions. Indash thought of alerting the prince, but decided against it. The night was growing old already, and it seemed a pity to ruin this feast for the sake of so small a disruption.

ψψψ

Hours later, Indash woke from a dream in the dark of the dining-hall, his mouth sour and sticky with the dregs of wine. Someone was whispering a little way off, at the other end of the long table, where his half-brother sat. The room was too dark to see much more than shadows. Thin shafts of moonlight lanced down from the tiny high-set windows, casting dull blue light amid the shadows of tables, chairs and sleeping revellers.

Through bleary eyes, Indash saw movement in those shadows, and heard more whispering. On instinct, he remained absolutely still, keeping his breathing slow and regular, like a sleeper's.

"The Ashûru are here," a gravelly voice whispered. Indash recognized it as Shagarakti, the palace vizier. The man had apparently removed his jeweled necklaces, for he walked in silence.

Nazibugash, the plump baron whose horse Indash had borrowed this afternoon, half-woke with a grunt. He pushed Shagarakti away.

"Their army is massed outside the city as we speak," whispered another voice—Maruttash, the master of spies, unless Indash missed his guess.

Movement; the sliding of a chair. "I'm still drunk," Nazibugash muttered. "We'll do it in the morning."

"The king will be awake by then!" hissed Shagarakti, startling Indash, who shifted slightly in his chair. Shagarakti looked up. "Who's there?" he whispered.

"No one's there," whispered Nazibugash.

"I saw something," said Shagarakti. "Someone moved."

Nazibugash rose slowly from his chair, scanning the room with the other two men. Indash remained absolutely still.

"Just someone twitching in a dream," Nazibugash whispered.

After a tense few moments, Shagarakti whispered, "We can't wait any longer. The sun will be up in a few hours. We must move now, before the palace wakes."

"I told you," whispered Nazibugash, "I'm too drunk."

"You don't have to do anything," Maruttash hissed. "You just have to be there. In the room. The rest is already done."

Nazibugash seemed to think about this, then whispered, "All right. I'm getting up." He heaved himself up from his chair, stumbling across the dining chamber.

Indash waited for them to leave the dining-hall, then quietly rose from his chair. He didn't want to believe what he'd just heard, but the implication was obvious. By the time the king woke at sunrise, the people of Babili would be bending their knees to an Ashûru conqueror. The thought made sickness rise in Indash's belly.

He hurried out the door of the dining-hall, across the audience chambers and sitting rooms, to the towering stone doorway that divided the palace's public areas from the royal apartments. Two spearmen stood guard there, and saluted when Indash approached.

"Come with me, quickly," Indash said to them. "I must speak with the king."

One of the guards put out a hand to stop him. "Slow down, boy," he said; and for a moment Indash felt a flare of jealousy, knowing a guard would never address his half-brother the prince that way. "The king will still be here in the morning."

Indash knew this would go much easier if he simply explained what he'd heard. But his instincts also told him not to hurl accusations carelessly, especially about such high-placed officials, let alone the prince himself. What was he to say?

"I—I think there's a plot against the king." He settled for a half-truth. "I saw a suspicious-looking man creeping around the palace tonight."

The guard huffed and grinned. "No assassin got by us tonight, I can assure you."

"I think he climbed up on the roof," said Indash, piling lie upon lie now. "Come on, we have to hurry!"

He pushed past the guards and raced down the hall, past the tall ornate doors that led to the apartments of the queen and the prince, past the royal nursery and the long hallway that led to the royal harem, past the royal baths and interior gardens, all closed off or deserted at this time of night.

At last he arrived at the foot of the staircase that led up to the king's bedchamber, where two more guards stood at attention.

"The king is in danger," he gasped, out of breath.

These guards must've seen the terror and desperation in his face, because they rushed with him up the stairs, to the locked cedar door of the king's bedchamber. One of them slammed his fist against it.

"Exalted Majesty," the guard called. "So sorry to wake you, but—"

The door swung open, just wide enough for King Burna-buriash's head to peek out.

Indash's guts turned to water: he was already too late.

"What is it?" hissed the king. "What's the meaning of this racket?"

"Majesty." The guards bowed.

"Is all well?" asked one of them.

"Is all well?" The king furrowed his brow angrily. "What is this madness? I finally manage to get to sleep, and next thing I know I have guards banging on the door. Does that sound all well to you?"

"We received a report, Majesty," said one of the guards, gulping.

"Report?" snapped the king. "What report? From who?"

"From me," said Indash, trying to push past the guards. But they weren't budging. "I just need to speak to you alone, just for a moment."

Realization dawned in the king's eyes. "What is it, boy?" he asked. "What have you seen?"

The guards glanced at each other, then at Indash.

"Please, Father," Indash said. "It'll only take a moment."

The king stood aside to let Indash into the room behind him. Only a few candles lit small sections of the vast bedchamber in flickering amber light. Indash could make out the king's thick-posted cedarwood bed, draped in hangings, filled with cushions.

"What is the meaning of this?" the king demanded as Indash closed the door behind him.

"Father, you have to listen," Indash said, and suddenly the words were tumbling out of him. "An Ashûru army is massed outside the city walls."

The king's brows lowered. "Already? They were supposed to be days away." He huffed. "Well. They'll keep till morning."

Indash shook his head. "Shagarakti and Maruttash came and woke Nazibugash in the dining room tonight."

The king's brow furrowed. "Nazib—who?"

Indash shook his head. "He's a minor baron. It doesn't matter. The point is, they thought I was asleep, but I heard every word. They've ridden out to meet with the Ashûru commanders while you sleep."

A dark look crossed the king's thick-bearded face. "These are deadly serious accusations, Indash."

"I know," Indash agreed. "But I heard what I heard. What else could it possibly mean?"

"What exactly did you hear?" the king demanded.

"Shagarakti said, 'The Ashûru have arrived.' Then Maruttash said, 'It has to be done now. Tonight.' Nazibugash said he was too drunk to do it, and asked to wait until morning. But Maruttash said, 'The king will be awake by then!' Those were exactly their words, Father. I swear it by all the Gods. Then Nazibugash got up and they all left together."

"Left to go where?" the king asked.

"I—I'm not certain," Indash admitted. "I think they were headed for the stables."

The king stroked his beard. Deep furrows creased the skin between his bushy brows.

"Guards!" the king cried suddenly, making Indash jump in surprise.

The door swung open and four guards instantly appeared in the room. "Exalted Majesty," said the captain, bowing low.

"Assemble the army," the king ordered in a quiet voice. "Every man, horse and chariot in the city."

The captain of the guard paused, confused. "Majesty, if I may have until morning—"

"Not in the morning." the king barked. "Now!"

The guards froze.

"I'll be dressed and ready in a few moments," the king said to no one in particular. "When I come down to the courtyard, I expect a horse to be saddled and ready." He glanced around at Indash and the guards. "Well? What are you waiting for? Do it!"

Indash hurried from the room on the heels of the guards. His belly churned with a strange mixture of fear and excitement. Fear, because he knew that the situation in Babili would look very different by sunrise this morning. And excitement because, for the first time in his life, he was to play a part in the doings of the king.

THE NIGHT SKY above the forest softened into the pale blue of pre-dawn. Indash sat his horse next to the king, who gazed out over the horsemen arrayed in a neat line extending outward to his left and right along the edge of the royal wood, an hour's ride to the north of the city. Though it was too dark to see much more than shadows, Indash knew that hundreds of horsemen waited with them now, and behind the horses, lines of spearmen and slingsmen checked and rechecked their shields and weapons.

Throughout the night, messengers had criss-crossed the fields and forests outside the city, bringing word that thousands of men, horses and weapons were being assembled north of Babili, on both sides of the Ashûru camp. Indash and the guard-captain had managed to talk the king out of an immediate surprise attack, while the guards sent urgent messengers to every barracks and camp within an hour's ride of the city. Now they all waited for sunrise, when their trap's jaws would snap shut.

As a soft golden glow brightened the horizon, Prince Hardash returned from scouting, his horse trotting up from a winding side-trail to approach the king.

"How many men do they have?" the king demanded.

"We counted five hundred supply tents," said Hardash. "Each supply tent usually holds weapons and food for twenty fighting men, which would make ten thousand, against our five."

The king blew out a long, slow breath, his eyes wide. Indash could see nervousness there, but he kept silent.

"They've been known," Indash said slowly, "to bring more tents than they need, and light extra fires by night, to inflate their numbers. Or so I have read."

"Indeed they have." Hardash nodded, throwing his half-brother a cold glance. "Unfortunately, in the darkness it's impossible to say for sure."

"Gods-damned scorpions," the king snarled. "Why can't they fight fairly, with honor?"

"Such is the perversion of the Ashûru mind, Father," Prince Hardash said. "They believe victory to be more important than honor."

The king huffed, unimpressed. "Ready the men, my son. Shamash's sun-chariot will soon break the horizon."

As the sun crested the hills behind the Ashûru camp, the king nodded to the captain, who drew a great curving horn from his saddlebag and blew it once, twice, thrice.

Suddenly all was gallop and thunder. Indash spurred his horse, joining the rush downhill. On every side, horses' hooves pounded the earth, kicking up grass and soil as they picked up speed. Beside him, the king drew his bronze blade from its scabbard, the rubies and emeralds on its dragon-headed hilt glimmering as they caught the first light of dawn. Far below, hundreds of pointed Ashûru tents stood in neat rows, their silhouettes stretching off to the right like rows of fangs.

Even as he hurtled toward the battlefield, Indash was suddenly beset by thoughts of what the Ashûru were known to do to those they defeated: Crucify them. Flay them. Impale them. The enemies of the Ashûru died slow deaths in the salt-mines, crushed by falling rocks or choked by vapors in lightless caverns. He searched his memory for any tale of an Ashûru commander showing mercy; a hint of clemency toward an enemy who proved especially brave or honorable.

But there was no such tale, so far as he knew. He was charging either toward victory, or toward torment, mutilation and death. They all were. There would be nothing in between.

He drew his sword and spurred his horse faster, charging headlong toward the front ranks of horsemen, eyes wide for the first Ashûru archers or spearmen to emerge from their tents. But as he swept through the camp, he saw only the burning coals of campfires; empty tents with flaps snapping in the morning breeze.

A few women and old men stumbled from some of the tents: cooks and whores and camp-followers, shielding their eyes from the dust and sunlight. Not a single man of Ashûru to be seen.

"Where are they?" someone was yelling. "Where in the Seven Stars are they?"

Indash rode from tent to tent, leaning down from his horse to peer inside each one. Empty. Not a weapon or shred of armor. Other contingents of horsemen were wheeling around, crashing back through the tents and fire-pits, riders calling out to each other in confusion.

A sickening thought rose in Indash's heart. Suddenly he knew where the armies of Ashûru had gone. He spurred his horse and hurried across the camp in search of the king.

He soon ran into a congestion of horses and men, at whose center he could hear Prince Hardash's booming voice demanding answers. A circle of the king's foot-soldiers held a knot of terrified slaves at spearpoint. The slaves cringed and raised their hands, pleading, weeping.

Prince Hardash was shouting at them. "Tell us where your masters went! Tell us now and you'll keep your lives."

"They didn't tell us, my prince!" one of the slaves howled. She was an old, scrawny woman, clad in the tatters of a stained wool shift that had been half torn away.

"A loyal slave! Hah!" The king barked a humorless laugh, reining up his horse as he entered the circle. "Loyal to the Ashûru, no less."

"Why would they tell us their battle-plans?" the woman howled. "My prince, look at us! We are slaves, not soldiers."

A green-cloaked Babili soldier thrust his spear-tip into the woman's face. "You are addressing Burnaburiash the Second, King of Karduniash! You will address him as 'Exalted Majesty,' or 'Perfect One.'"

The old woman cowered, raising her hands above her head, begging forgiveness.

"Please, O Perfect One," cried another slave, a bearded old man so thin his ribs showed through the flesh of his bare chest. "Take us with you! We will work in your tanneries, build your palaces—"

A sharp thwack from a soldier's spear cut off his words. "How dare you address the king?" the soldier snarled. "Speak when you're spoken to."

"Enough." The king raised his hand. "Captain, round up all the slaves you can and take them back to the city. The first hundred belong to me. After that, each man may sell or keep the ones he finds."

The slaves raised a cheer of relief, raising their hands and blowing kisses to the king, who mounted his horse and rode away from them, toward Indash.

"Father!" Prince Hardash called. "I think I know where the Ashûru army went."

"Quiet!" the king hissed. "I'll not have you starting a panic. I've sent out messengers. Any moment we'll know for sure. Then we'll move. Ah—here comes one now."

A soldier armored only in hard-boiled leather rode up on a thin horse, its lips frothing with white foam. Man and horse were both gasping for breath.

"Majesty," the messenger panted.

The king's hand gripped his reins, ready to turn and ride. "Where are they?" he demanded.

"The city," the rider gasped. "They're inside the city!"

Prince Hardash's eyes went wide, his mouth half-open in shock. "What do you mean, *inside* the city?"

The messenger reeled back, glancing around in panic. "The—the north gate is open, Majesty. Someone must've opened it! Opened it for them, somehow, and—"

The king roared; a great bestial howl of rage that seemed to shake the very soil beneath then. Men and horses glanced up, turning to look for the source of the sound.

"To me!" the king screamed, "All of you!" yanking his horse's reins fiercely, turning southward. "To the city, now!" He kicked the horse's sides so hard the beast leaped into the air, tearing across the camp at a dead gallop.

Indash spurred his own horse, racing to catch up with the king. All around him, the other horsemen were doing the same, churning up great swirling clouds of dust as foot-soldiers scrambled out of the way of kicking hooves.

In the midst of this thunder-cloud of horses and men and swords, Indash hurtled south toward Babili. The vast arch of the north gate stood wide open, its thick doors of oak and brass swung wide; a gaping hole in the towering stone walls that girded the city.

Through that open wound marched the army of Ash'shúr: three long columns of men in crimson tunics covered by dark bronzescale armor, long sharp-tipped spears pointed at the sky, flanked by two columns of horsemen; a thick-bodied red serpent winding straight into the heart of Babili.

THE COPPER CHAIN hung heavy around Indash's neck, chafing at the skin beneath. Manacles glamped his wrists and ankles, and dragged along the pavement before and behind him. The chains bound him to the king, who marched before him, and the captain of the guard, who marched behind; along with a long line of other captured soldiers that stretched behind them, down the length of the Processional Way.

They had arrived too late. As soon as the king had caught sight of the Ashúru army marching through Babili's north gate, he'd led his cavalry galloping down to the east gate, hoping to catch the Ashúru by surprise before they reached the palace. But the company of horsemen had arrived to find Ashúru guards already installed at the east gate—and at the west gate, and every other gate along the city walls.

"They're here!" the Ashúru guards called down to their commanders below. Soon Indash, the king, Prince Hardash, and the rest of Babili's expeditionary force found themselves surrounded by Ashúru cavalry, knocked from their horses at spearpoint, and clamped in chains.

As Indash tramped along the flagstones of the Processional Way, he looked up to see Ashúru archers lining the roofs of the flat-topped houses along both sides of the broad street. The crimson-tunicked men stood stone-still, arrows notched and ready on the strings of their heavy recurved bows. No sign of civilians, or of the green-clad men of the city watch. Only cold-eyed men in red tunics and dark bronzescale armor, staring down at them from every roof and in every unshuttered window.

A blood-caked body lay in the street, its green cloak marking its late owner as a man of the palace guard. A pair of thick-jowled Ashûru dogs tore at the corpse's legs and back, yanked back on their leather leashes by a black-bearded foot-soldier who laughed each time they lunged at the body, snarling with red-stained teeth. A small company of other Ashûru soldiers massed around the scene, pointing and calling out encouragement.

"You there!" Something hard cracked against the back of Indash's head. He stumbled forward, chains clinking, bright colors dancing in his eyes. He turned to see the frowning face of an Ashûru warrior, the butt of his spear upraised for another strike.

"No stopping," the soldier grunted at him in a thick mountain accent. "Keep walking."

Indash turned away from the scene around the body, his stomach twisting in knots. He forced himself to take another step forward, and another, and another.

Soon they were marching though the wreckage of Babili's noble quarter. Outside a burning tavern, a terrified young baronet clutched a wooden sword, dueling for his life against an Ashûru swordsman's bronze blade while a circle of soldiers pushed and jeered. On the front steps of a manor-house, soldiers divided up the sons and daughters of a wealthy family, dragging them apart as elders wept and children wailed.

Beneath the shade of a fabric stall's awning, an Ashûru commander in a feather-plumed helmet bent a howling woman over a barrel, her skirts tossed up over her back, while a clump of spearmen watched and waited their turn. The woman locked eyes with Indash, and he turned away as she split the morning air with a sound beyond a scream; a high-pitched animal wail that stretched on and on, dissolving into weeping.

Indash yearned to break free and rush to help her; to stop those screams and punish the men who wrenched them from her. But fear held him in place as much as the chains did. He swore to himself that, if he was ever freed from those chains, he would offer the people of his city as much comfort as he could; though, at this moment, he could scarcely imagine what shape that comfort might take. Meanwhile the woman's voice continued to echo through the street, following him, pleading. That voice echoed in Indash's ears long after they'd passed out of hearing range.

Some time later, they arrived at the great gate of the royal palace. Ashûru soldiers ran back and forth in droves, carrying vases of gold and silver, necklaces glistening with rubies and sapphires, fine linens and embroidered carpets, piling all of it into mule-drawn wagons like so much offal.

Other lines of captives marched near them, driven by soldiers cracking whips and shouting threats. Indash recognized some of them: dukes and serving-girls, cooks and counts and generals, all chained together indiscriminately, marched half-naked across the flagstones. If any man or woman in that sad assembly recognized Indash or the king, they gave no sign of it.

The soldiers marched the prisoners down stone stairs, into the torchlit dungeons beneath the palace. They unchained Indash, the king and a few other men from the rest, and kicked them onto the soggy straw lining the floor of the cell. They did the same with the rest of their captives, then took the torch with them and marched back upstairs, leaving the prisoners in pitch darkness.

⁂

Just before sunrise the next morning, someone rattled the door of their cell.

Indash rose from the straw, rubbing the sleep from his eyes, and opened the door. A lone guard stood outside.

"The coronation begins at sunup," said the guard, gruffly.

The guard escorted them, still in chains, to the royal audience chamber, just as the sun-God Shamash was casting his first rosy rays through the room's tall windows.

A large crowd was already gathered—dozens of noblemen and women whom Indash barely recognized, all of them packed in tightly beneath the room's high ceiling, muttering in low tones amid the tapestries and wall-carvings showcasing the king's great deeds in war. No sign of Maruttash or Shagarakti, or that strange nobleman Nazibugash.

Just as the first gold sun-rays slipped through the windows, a horn blew, and the Ashûru delegation marched out from behind the twin thrones. Unlike the nobles of Babili, every one of the men wore two broad-bladed daggers in his belt, a fact that was already attracting nervous stares and whispers from the crowd. The highest-ranking among them wore polished armor and helmets of burnished bronze, adorned with peacock feathers.

At this column's head marched a straight-backed Ashûru man with cold gray eyes. He wore a robe of finest crimson linen embroidered with intricate patterns of vines and flowers, its fringe of leopard-fur held up by two slaves, their heads bowed reverently as they shuffled along behind him. His long black hair and beard were plaited in neat ringlets, and gold hoops dangled from his ears.

Behind this imposing figure walked a line of figures draped in black from head to toe, as if they were in mourning, only their eyes visible through thin slits in the black veils that covered their faces.

"His wives," Indash heard someone whisper.

When the Ashûru generals and the remaining nobles of Babili had arrayed themselves on both sides of the thrones, the horn sounded again, setting off a chorus of slow, triumphant music, low-pitched flutes and harps led by drums beating out a stately rhythm.

A group of royal priests, astrologers and augurs approached the throne, their shaved heads gleaming in the dawn light, their hands clasped prayerfully amid folds of gold-fringed robes; except for the ones who carried the crowns of Babili—a tall gold cap resembling an ornately carved column for the king, and a slightly smaller one for the queen—on plush red pillows; and the acolytes who carried the gold sceptre, and the jewel-encrusted vase of sacred anointing-oil, on pillows of their own.

The high priest of Marutúk, supreme God of the city, took his place next to the throne, clutching his golden sceptre against a breastplate studded with the eight sacred jewels, representing the eight gates of the city; his head capped by a tall helmet decorated with images of the robed God traversing the heavens.

A pair of Ashûru guards led Prince Hardash's wife Sherua up to the throne-dais. The princess, though she was Ashûru by birth, wore an embroidered emerald robe in the style of Babili, the city she'd called home all her life. Her eyes were red, her cheeks stained with the tracks of scarcely concealed tears.

Shamash sent his bright rays through the window behind the throne, touching the usurper-king's head with a shaft of golden light. The music swelled triumphantly, its timing perfect. The high priest lifted the crown from its pillow.

The musicians fell silent.

"Eternal Marutúk," intoned the high priest, "son of our father, the God Énki, Lord of the Abzu, I beg that thou bear witness unto the crowning of thy son Akhabbu, son of Akhiseen, commander of the First Army of Ash'shúr, as King in Babili."

The priest was speaking in a very old dialect of Akkadu, a mostly dead tongue that Indash hadn't spoken since his school days. But the words were so formulaic, and the names so familiar, that he was able to follow most of the ritual.

"March thou on the king's right hand, Lord Marutúk. Assist him on his left..." It went on in that vein for some time, as the sun rose behind the throne and even Indash had to fight to hold back a yawn.

After what felt like an hour, the high priest reached for the vase of sacred oil. The priest who held the vase removed its carved gold stopper. Akhabbu knelt as the high priest raised the vase above his head.

"With this sacred oil," chanted the high priest, "blessed by the seven high priests of the seven highest Gods, I anoint thee, Akhabbu, son of Akhiseen, King in Babili." He tipped the vase, and a thin stream of thick liquid flowed down onto Akhabbu's head, running down his brow and into his eyes. He wiped his face, but remained still.

The high priest took the tall golden crown from its pillow. "I crown thee," he cried, "Lord of the City and Lands of Babili!" And he placed the helmet gently atop Akhabbu's head. Then he took the gold sceptre, held it before the king, and said, "With this sceptre, the supreme God Marutúk grant thee lordship over the city of Babili and its people. May he guide thee in its right usage." The high priest handed the sceptre to Akhabbu, who accepted it with a nod of his head.

The high priest turned to the crowd. "Long live the king!" he cried. "Long live the king!" the crowd returned. Indash shouted it too, in case anyone happened to be watching, which he assumed someone was. "Long live King Akhabbu!" the priest cried. "Long live King Akhabbu!" the crowd repeated. "Long live Akhabbu, King in Babili!" the priest shouted, and the crowd returned it: "Long live Akhabbu, King in Babili!"

The new king sank onto his throne, gold crown towering atop his head, gold sceptre in his hand, his red leopard-trimmed robes settling about him. The music fell silent again, and the throne room fell into a nervous stillness.

"Where are the traitors?" Akhabbu demanded, his voice reedy and rasping, like claws on stone.

Sounds of struggle echoed across the throne room, and the crowd behind Indash parted to make way for Maruttash, Shagarakti and Nazibugash, stumbling as a contingent of crimson-cloaked Ashůru guardsmen drove them toward the throne with rough shoves.

Akhabbu rose, his movements swift and efficient as those of a leopard.

"Well," the usurper said. "What have you to say for yourselves, my proud little traitors?" He studied the three traitors as a hunter might study a wounded stag, his pale gray eyes cold and empty.

The prisoners glanced at each other nervously, none willing to be the first to speak.

"Speak up," snapped Akhabbu, glancing absentmindedly around the room.

Maruttash stepped forward, bowing low before his new king. His eyes were sunken and sallow, his robe wrinkled, hanging askance.

"In one sense," the master of spies said, his voice quavering, "we are traitors, it is true. But our treason was against a king who no longer sits on the throne of Babili."

Next to Indash, a deep growl rumbled in the throat of King Burnaburiash. Indash glanced over, and saw tears rising in his father's eyes. Deep as Maruttash's betrayal stung him, he could scarcely imagine what the former king must be feeling, watching this Ashůru warlord perform the royal rites.

"We have done all that was asked of us," said Shagarakti, the palace vizier. He looked almost as bedraggled as Maruttash, in his stained linen robe. Indash could see an ugly purple bruise on the man's neck, caked with dried blood. "And," he added, "we will continue to do the same for you."

Nazibugash, the minor nobleman, stood with his hands clasped before his embroidered robe, saying nothing. His gold jewelry had disappeared, but he seemed otherwise unruffled.

"And you?" Akhabbu asked him, eyebrows raised in mild curiosity. "Have you nothing to say?"

Nazibugash gave a slight shrug, as if it scarcely mattered one way or the other. "A useful tool serves its function, Majesty," he said, his voice calm. "When it is no longer useful, one throws it away. Until such a time comes, throwing away a good tool would simply be wasteful."

The Ashûru usurper nodded, stroking his beard. A hush fell over the nobles, soldiers and prisoners assembled in the throne room, as they awaited his next words.

"All three of you have been useful," Akhabbu said at last. "But a traitor is a traitor. He who betrays one king may as easily betray another."

Maruttash and Shagarakti fell to their knees, prostrating themselves before the new king, begging for their lives. Nazibugash, for his part, remained still, his hands clasped before his belt as he watched the Ashûru usurper calmly.

"Quick deaths for all three," Akhabbu said to the general beside him, as if asking for a glass of wine. "Beheadings, preferably. Dawn tomorrow."

Guards converged on the three conspirators, dragging Maruttash and Shagarakti up from their prone positions on the carpet stretched before the throne. As they dragged the two of them away, a third pair of guards gripped Nazibugash's arms. He turned calmly, as if departing with old friends.

Akhabbu cocked his head, as if listening to someone unseen. After a moment, he nodded.

"Wait," he said.

The guards and conspirators froze, halfway between the throne and the doorway at the opposite end of the chamber.

"This one stays with me," he said, pointing at Nazibugash.

Fresh pleas and wails of despair went up from Maruttash and Shagarakti. Nazibugash remained still, though Indash thought he could detect a hint of a smile crossing the man's lips.

"An unscrupulous man can be useful, when used properly," Akhabbu muttered, as if speaking to himself. "Are you an unscrupulous man, Nazibugash?"

"I am but a tool, Exalted One," the man replied, bowing slightly.

"Put him in a room somewhere," said Akhabbu. He turned to the high priest. "On to the next item. Where is the unseated king? Where is the prince?"

Guards gripped the chains that bound Hardash and the former king and dragged them out of the crowd and onto the carpet before the throne.

"Do what you will with me, you scheming swine," the old king spat at Akhabbu, froth forming in his great black beard. "I am king of Babili. I know it, and so does everyone here. I've never feared death, and I won't start today."

The Ashûru king nodded appreciatively, a slight smile playing on his thick lips. He sauntered to the edge of the throne-dais, and smoothly squatted on his haunches to gaze down on his prisoner with hawk's eyes.

The king stood his ground, meeting the predator's glare.

"These are brave words for an unseated king," Akhabbu said after a moment. "If they are true, then you will die with bravery, which is more than many men do."

Burnaburiash leaned forward carefully and spat on the steps to the throne. A guard thwacked him in his fat stomach with the butt of his spear, and he stumbled back, coughing and gasping.

"You may not fear death," Akhabbu told him. "But you may find, before all is finished, that you fear the road to it."

He cocked his head in that strange way again, as if listening to a voice from another room.

After a moment, he turned to one of the generals at his side. "Crucifixion and flaying," he said without inflection. "And give him a few days to reflect."

The old king's lips tightened in a grimace, but he did not cry out or beg mercy. Instead his voice came quiet and stern, though audible to all in the chamber. "Oh, I'll fear that cross," he said. "Be sure I will. And I'll scream when the nails are driven in, and when the knives come down on my flesh." He paused, glancing around the room at all those who had once sworn fealty to him. His eyes settled, at last, on the usurper-king Akhabbu, at whom he glared with hatred hot as bronze in the forge. "But I will never—*never*—bend my knee to an Ashûru serpent like you. That I swear."

A thin smile crossed Akhabbu's lips. "We will meet again soon," he said.

"I look forward to it," said the king, flatly.

At a gesture from Akhabbu, the guards dragged Burnaburiash away. He did not look behind them, only marched, in chains, back straight and head high, as if he still ruled in this throne room.

"And you, prince," the usurper said to Hardash, once the king was gone. "Have you anything interesting to say?"

The young prince licked his lips. He was trembling, but he held himself steady and firm. "Would it make a difference?" he asked.

Akhabbu raised his eyes to the throne room's high ceiling. His mouth worked silently, as if muttering in conversation with some hidden advisor.

"Depends what you say," he told Hardash at last.

"I'll not bend my knee," the prince said, his voice quavering. "But I beg you not to execute my father—or at least give him an honorable death. A soldier's death. Do that, and I'll promise not to raise an army against you the first chance I get."

A faint smile slowly crossed the new king's lips, though it never touched those gray eyes of his. "In case you haven't noticed," he said, "you're in no position to bargain. Perhaps now might be a good time to start begging."

"I cannot do it," the prince said. His whole body was visibly trembling now. "I cannot beg."

Akhabbu tilted his head, mouthed a few silent words, and nodded.

"Crucifixion," the new king said. "At dawn. Next to his father."

The prince turned pale and collapsed limply to the carpet before the throne. Guards lifted the prince by the armpits and dragged him away, his slippers scraping limply against the polished stone floor.

After a long moment of tense silence, the high priest glanced at Akhabbu nervously, and whispered instructions to the drummers, pipers and lyre-players arrayed around the throne. The musicians struck up a new melody: a wedding prelude. A chill ran through Indash's limbs.

"At this well-omened hour," intoned the high priest, "we shall now celebrate the new king's marriage to Princess Sherua—"

A collective gasp erupted from the crowd, as Princess Sherua bowed her head, fresh tears streaming from her dark eyes.

The high priest read out the rest of the princess's formal titles: "Jewel of the Sublime Crown, daughter of His August and Most Sacred Majesty Ash'shûr-ubállit, King of Kings, Commander of Commanders, Lord Emperor of Shumér and Akkad."

More murmurs rippled through the crowd at these titles and claims. The Ashûru had been a small vassal state just a generation ago. Now their king was claiming supreme rulership over all the kings of the Riverplain. The claim was shocking in its absurdity; and yet, like many of those assembled in that throne-room, Indash wondered if it might be coming true today.

"In view of the fact that the princess's husband is to be executed at dawn," the high priest continued, "it is right and fitting that she take a new husband as soon as possible." He turned to Sherua, extending a hand. "Jewel of the Crown, if you would be so kind."

Weeping, the princess stepped forward and exchanged hurried vows with the new king, her whole body trembling as she wept. She promised to obey her new master in all things, to care for him in sickness and health, to bear him many sons. The king, for his part, promised to provide for her, to protect her, and to sire sons with her. They clasped hands, and the priest poured hot wax atop their fingers, sealing the contract.

When it was done, Akhabbu raised a hand sternly. The crowd fell silent, watching him with intent nervousness, wondering who might be the next to receive a death sentence.

"Is there any other business?" he asked.

Before he could stop himself, Indash found himself stepping forward onto the carpet before the throne. The whole room seemed to focus in on him. Suddenly he felt present; real, in a way he hadn't for a long time, as if he'd half-forgotten he was a character in this tale, only to find himself suddenly at its center. He looked down at his hands and saw they were trembling.

"The people of this city are distressed, Majesty," he said, trying to keep his voice steady.

Akhabbu turned to a nobleman at his side. They held a brief whispered conference.

"Indash," Akhabbu said, turning back to the crowd. "The king's bastard. Why should I pay heed to you?"

Indash licked his lips, forcing himself to look the Ashûru king in his pale gray eyes.

"I have always served my king," he said. "But more than that, I love and serve this city."

Glancing around the throne-room, he saw smiles cross the faces of a few nobles; but they were too terrified to raise a cheer.

"Though I hold no claim to Babili's throne," he continued. "I love her with all my heart. And though I mourn the death of the king, and of many people I've known and loved, I would do anything in my power to help those who still live."

The Ashûru king stroked his beard, eyes darting around the ceiling. He nodded once, then once more.

"Yes, how very strange," he said. After a moment, he nodded again. "Very well, you shall have all the work you desire." He turned to a nearby general. "Throw him in the mines. Somewhere deep."

All feeling seemed to rush out of Indash's limbs, and he had to fight to keep from collapsing to the floor. He felt blackness clawing in at the edges of his vision.

"What an interesting morning this has been," Akhabbu said, his eyes darting about the throne room's ceiling and walls.

But Indash scarcely heard the words. He collapsed onto the carpet before the throne, and the room's colors and sounds faded away to black.

ᛪᛪᛪ
ᛪᛪᛪ
ᛪ

"Who'd you kill?" whispered the slave chained next to him.

For the past seven days, Indash had sat chained in the back of this mule-drawn wagon, jolting and bouncing along pot-holed back-country trails, watched through very moment of his waking and sleeping by bored-faced Ashûru guards.

Every few days, the wagon-train halted at mud-brick villages and scatterings of reed huts, where scrawny men in tattered clothes dragged out their thieves, rapists and murderers; those they'd chosen to cast out from their midst in return for a handful of clipped coppers. The guards dragged the condemned men and women onto the backs of the wagons, clamped them in fetters, and rolled on northward, out of the grassy plains of Babili and up into the rocky foothills of Ashûru territory.

This time of day, around sunset, the guards tended to doze, and the captives took the opportunity to exchange what snatches of gossip they could.

"Well?" whispered the slave again. "No point hiding it now. Who'd you send to the Underworld?" He was a squat man of ruddy complexion, his face bristling with a week's growth of beard.

"I didn't kill anyone," Indash whispered back, keeping his eyes fixed on the dusty road unrolling behind them.

"Stole some jewelry?" the other slave persisted. "Must've been something pricey, if they sent you to the mines. I'd guess... gold necklace?"

"I'm not a thief either," Indash replied.

The man only huffed. "I'm Bulludhu." He raised a hand as high as he could, pulling his chains tight. "They call me Bulludhu Wolf-Slayer, because that's what I do, any time it needs doing. And you are...?"

Indash grasped wrists with Bulludhu as best he could, chains clinking. "I'm Indash," he said. "What'd you steal, Bulludhu?"

"A young girl's virginity," Bulludhu whispered with a chuckle. "Only problem was, she was my brother's bride-to-be." He snorted a conspiratorial laugh.

A scene from Babili flashed in Indash's mind: that woman in the shop, bent over a barrel by an Ashûru commander as his men waited their turns. A feeling of disgust churned in his belly.

"The penalty for that crime," Indash told Bulludhu, "is that the rapist must take the deflowered woman to wife, and provide for her until the end of his days."

"So I hear," replied Bulludhu, with a shrug. "But I'm no rapist. She came to my hut in the dark of night, whispering my name. To *my* hut she came. I'll swear on it till the day I die."

"How soon do you think that'll be?" Indash mused.

Bulludhu threw him a sour look. "I don't expect you to believe me. No one else does." He sighed deeply. "Anyway, what do they do with a rapist who has no property, not a single goat or sheep to call his own?" He shrugged. "Send him to the mines."

Indash shook his head. "That makes you happy, does it? Feeling like you've gotten away with it? In case you haven't heard, mine-slaves aren't known for long lives."

Bulludhu just rolled his eyes. "Has anyone ever told you you're not much fun to talk to?"

A small laugh burst from Indash's throat. "Is that what life should be? Fun?"

Bulludhu shrugged. "Why not? Any day you could wake up chained, bound for a death in the mines, or worse. Best enjoy what the Gods give us, 'fore they snatch it away."

"The Gods are capricious," Indash agreed.

Bulludhu's brow wrinkled. "They're what?"

"Impossible to predict," Indash said. "One day you're king, the next you're hanging on a cross, and they're sharpening the flaying-knives."

Bulludhu's eyes widened. "That what you were? A king?" He burst out laughing. "My apologies, Exalted One."

"No, never exalted." Indash shook his head. "Just a bastard, who picked a side and lost the toss."

"Do you regret it?" Bulludhu asked. "Taking the side you did?"

"No," Indash said. "I regret not taking it sooner."

A few hours before sunset on the tenth day, the wagons began lumbering up a series of switchbacks ascending the side of a great mountain range. The air grew cold and windy as they ascended, but no one offered them blankets. Indash shivered, clutching himself to keep warm, shifting to keep the cold metal of his chains from chilling his skin.

At last they reached a flat yard of dead gray soil. A great pit yawned at the center of this place, ramps along its sides spiralling down into vast darkness beneath the earth. Thousands of half-naked men and women climbed down into the pit along

The Cradle and the Sword

one narrow set of ramps, empty reed baskets on their backs, while an equal number clambered upward along other ramps, bent and straining under heavy loads of copper and iron ore.

A crimson-cloaked guard yanked at the chain around Indash's neck. He stumbled from the back of the wagon, legs weak and half-numb after more than a week of disuse. Bulludhu stumbled out behind him, followed by a line of ten other slaves, all of them shackled together. Other soldiers were pulling dozens of slaves from the other wagons, every man and woman exhausted, shivering, chained to the ankles of the others.

"Move," said the guard, pointing toward a group of stone huts across the yard. "Go get your numbers. Then you can eat and sleep."

Indash was too exhausted to argue. In the last ten days, he'd eaten nothing but cold barley gruel spooned into his hands from barrels lashed to the sides of the wagons, and had drunk only stagnant water from village wells. The thought of a hot meal, more than anything else, pushed him onward toward the huts.

Outside one of the low stone buildings, a bored-looking Ashúru soldier sat behind a battered desk, sorting stamped clay tokens into crates. Indash could see the smoke of a cookfire rising from the building's chimney. Though his tongue and throat were parched from thirst, the smell of boiling fat made his mouth water.

"Number?" the soldier at the desk drawled as Indash the line of prisoners clanked toward him.

"I don't have a number yet," said Indash. "My name is—"

"Go over there, get your numbers," barked the soldier, jerking his head in the direction of a three-sided outbuilding where a smith pounded red-hot bronze over a forge.

"We're starving!" cried Bulludhu. "We've had nothing but cold porridge for—"

"Get your numbers," the guard cut him off. "Don't make me tell you again. Numbers first. Then you eat."

Other soldiers were approaching, pulling nine-tailed whips from their belts and cracking them experimentally. "Do we have a problem here?" one of them asked.

"No problem," Indash told him. He turned to Bulludhu and the others chained behind him. "Come on. Let's just get our numbers, then we can eat."

"I want a sip of water!" Bulludhu persisted. "My throat's dry as a desert! Just one—"

A soldier's fist struck him dead in the face, knocking him to the gravelly soil. His chains tugged at Indash and the others as they stumbled to steady themselves.

"Son of a whore," Bulludhu spat at the guard. "Take these chains off, jackal. We'll see who the big man is then."

The guard hit him again, harder. Blood poured from Bulludhu's nose and mouth. He spat out a tooth on the rocky ground.

"Try me again, dog," snarled the guard. "We can do this all day."

"Bulludhu, enough," Indash said. "It's useless."

"Piss on you, too, then." Bulludhu sneered at him. "I'm Bulludhu Wolf-Slayer, and I bow to no man."

The guard's whip cracked across Bulludhu's face and chest, tearing gashes in the man's hairy skin, spraying blood onto the gravel.

"You," the guard said, cracking the whip again, "are no one." Another crack, and a fresh spatter of blood. Bulludhu howled. "You are a slave," said the guard. Another crack, another scream. "You are the property of the army of Ash'shûr." Again the whip cracked. "And you bow to me."

"Enough!" An older soldier with a scarred face was striding up, his bearded lips twisting with annoyance. "Leave it, footsoldier."

The soldier with the whip looked up, his face a mask of offended fury. "He insulted me, *sayid*," the blood-spattered soldier protested. "Called me a son of a whore!"

"I don't care if he buggered your grandmother," snapped the commander. "If he can't work tomorrow, I'm taking it out of your pay. Don't make me tell you again."

The soldier opened his mouth to protest, but the commander was already turning to Bulludhu. "What's your number?" the scarred old warrior demanded.

Bulludhu mumbled unintelligibly through a mouthful of blood and shattered bone.

"We haven't gotten our numbers yet," Indash told the commander. "We just arrived."

The commander spread his hands. "I step away for a piss, and when I come back, I find anarchy," he snarled at the soldiers nearby. "Wake up!"

The men snapped suddenly to attention, carefully averting their eyes from the scene.

"Bronze-smith," the commander called across the yard.

The soldier hammering bronze by the forge froze in mid-strike, his leather-gloved hands half-buried in the red-hot coals.

"Give these new arrivals their numbers," the commander told him. Then, to the other guards: "You there! Make sure they sit still."

Crimson-tunicked soldiers hustled to obey, as the commander looked on with a look of sharp disappointment. They lifted Bulludhu from the ground, and frog-marched the line of chained slaves over to the bronze-smith's forge.

"Give me a number," the smith called across to the soldier behind the desk.

The desk-soldier strolled over, fishing a clay token out of a small wood crate under one arm. "Four-three-six-two," he read out.

The smith retrieved a bronze staff from his workbench and fitted its tip with four small metal chits, each molded into a cluster of sharp-pointed triangles signifying a numeral. Once he'd fitted the four chits into place, he plunged the end of the staff into the red-hot coals. Before Indash could pull away, another soldier grabbed his head with a pair of thick-fingered hands, holding him in place. After a moment, the smith drew the red-hot brand from the fire, and pressed it into Indash's forehead with a smooth, practiced motion.

For an instant, Indash felt nothing. Then hot knives seemed to slice into his flesh, digging deep beneath the skin of his forehead, gnawing into the muscle and sinew beneath. He bit his tongue, willing himself not to cry out. Tears rose in his eyes. The smell of his own searing flesh reached his nostrils, and bile rose in his throat. He gasped and struggled, but the guard's hands clamped his head like a vice.

At last the smith pulled the brand away, and Indash released a breath he didn't realize he'd been holding. All the other slaves were staring at him, eyes wide with horror. The flesh of his forehead stung. His head spun as if he'd had too much beer. His stomach churned emptily, and he thought he might be sick. He could smell his burnt flesh in the cold air.

"Four-three-six-two," said the desk-soldier again, double-checking the marks burned into Indash's forehead. He nodded, satisfied, and tossed the clay token into a nearby box.

"Next," called the bronze-smith. Bulludhu's eyes bulged with fear.

After every slave in the chain-gang had been numbered and branded, the guards marched them to the stone house that smelled of food, where a fat cook ladled a thin stew of stringy goat-fat and sinew into filthy clay bowls. They each received one bowlful, and a clay cup of metallic-tasting water, just enough to reawaken their hunger and thirst without satisfying either.

By then the sun had nearly set, and they were marched to another low stone building, where they were thrown onto a floor covered in cold straw, and told to sleep.

"This'll be the last good sleep you get," a soldier told them. "Best enjoy it."

An hour or so later, another line of chained slaves came tramping in, then another, and another. Soon the floor was packed with gasping, moaning, complaining bodies. Men and women of every age, from young girls to wrinkled old men; every one of them filthy, with skin so pale it was almost white. Some of them were so thin that Indash could see their ribs protruding through the flesh of their backs.

He thought he'd never be able to fall asleep in this place.

And yet, next thing he knew, a guard was stomping through the straw, kicking at the slaves, barking, "Up, all of you! Breakfast time!" The sky was still dark and starry, the predawn air so cold his breath steamed before him.

There was no stew or clay bowls for breakfast, only a thin flavorless gruel spooned into each slave's upraised hands, and a clay cup of strong sour wine. Indash's head felt swimmy again after he'd choked this down, which made the morning trip to the sewer-ditch slightly more tolerable.

As he squatted at the ditch with the rest of the chained slaves, gagging at the sounds and odors, he expected to be sick any moment—but strangely, a sort of calm had permeated him. He felt as if he had reached the bottom of the lowest pit. There was nowhere deeper to sink. He took an odd sort of comfort in that.

But as the chain-gang marched out to the vast yawning pit of the mine-shaft, Indash realized his descent had scarcely begun. Fumes of sulphur, thick with the reek of rotten eggs, rose up to choke the slaves as they inched their way down the ramp. All those thousands of pale, bony bodies with empty reed baskets on their backs, pushing downward into the noxious darkness.

The stench grew more intense. Not only the old-egg smell of sulphur, but the heavier stink of rotting meat. Indash soon saw its source: a pile of bodies heaped carelessly in the open air, flies buzzing and swarming over every dangling arm and shattered ribcage. As Indash and the others marched past this wreckage of flesh, a pair of slaves came trotting up out of the darkness, carrying the lifeless remains of an old woman between them. They hurled her onto the pile, scattering the flies into a black cloud, which resettled after a moment to resume feasting. The two slaves turned around and trudged back into the mine shaft.

When Indash and his companions reached the mines' main entrance, a contingent of guards handed some of them copper pickaxes from nearby barrels. The smallest and weakest among them got smaller hand-picks, while those with a bit of muscle received heavy hammers.

Indash took his pickaxe and followed the others into the dim cavern. His chains clanked along with the chains of the slaves before and behind him; these things that were once men and women, now property of the Ashûru army.

And like the rest of them, he knew, he would break stones in that darkness until he died.

Time lost all meaning in that place. The days and weeks ran together, a ceaseless cycle of trudges up and down ramps, cold gruel, sips of water, dreamless sleep, predawn shouts, sewage trenches, and immeasurable hours choking on fumes in dim cramped mine shafts, chiseling rock from the walls and passing it to the hammerers to be shattered, or clambering up the ramps with a basket full of fragments veined with iron or copper. Their skin grew pale and pink in those sunless depths, and the sulphurous fumes bleached it almost white.

They spoke, sometimes, Indash and the rest of the slaves chained to him. Some told sad tales of home, of sons and lovers never to be seen again. Others sang songs, which the rest learned if they were easy, and fit the rhythm of their stone-breaking.

Bulludhu Wolf-Slayer worked in sullen silence, even after the swelling on his face abated. He scarcely glanced up to meet the guards' eyes anymore. Something deep within him had been shattered. The others were scarcely more talkative, but Indash learned about them one scrap of conversation at a time, through the long lightless days in those chasms.

A young woman named Seri, three slaves down the chain, had grown repulsed by the attentions of her fat, drunken husband, and had leaped on him with a dagger one night. Gray-haired, gangly Utuaa had stolen twenty cows from his village's wealthiest family. Full-hipped Damkina had seduced a married nobleman and made a child with him. Kishar had burned down his beloved's house in a fit of jealousy. Aya had stolen eggs to feed her fatherless daughters. Their crimes held to no theme; no overarching rightness or wrongness. Some of their stories brought tears to Indash's eyes. Others revolted him.

Some nights, bedded down in the wet straw of the sleephouse, chains would clink in the darkness as the slaves crawled together to join in couplings: Damkina with Kishar, Aya with Seri, men with women or with other men, with any warm body that opened for them in the darkness.

"Tell me of your village," Seri whispered as she climbed atop him one night.

"I grew up in Babili," he told her. "A great city."

Indash could not say how many of these pairings were forced, and how many voluntary. In this place of broken will and sapped strength, the distinction blurred; and in the morning, none spoke their complaints aloud. Some nights the Ashûru guards came; some for men, others for women. They took their partners roughly, with grunts and kicking. Indash heard cries of pain in the darkness, and sobs afterward. But he lay still and made no sound, though he hated himself for it.

Tonight, though, no guards had come. Only Seri, whose company warmed him like a small flame in this freezing place.

"What was your city like?" she asked him, rocking back and forth above him, chains clinking.

He tried to find the words, any words to tell of the mighty walls and the gardened towers and the temples like mountains, but such descriptions were beyond his power. Here on the cold damp straw, Babili seemed unreal, a place he'd once dreamed of. A phantom of a world that had never been.

"Was it beautiful?" she asked.

"Yes," he said. "I think so."

She spoke no more after that; only rocked atop him until she sighed and trembled, then rolled over next to him and began to snore. He lay awake for a long time after, trying to recall the face of his father the king, or of his half-brother the prince, or of any of his sisters. But images would not come to him. He remembered only names: Burnaburiash and Hardash, Maruttash and Shagarakti—and Nazibugash, who betrayed his king. In the morning, even those names faded away.

One by one, the slaves in the chain-gang perished. Kishar chiselled into a pocket of noxious fumes; the vapors seared his eyes and lungs, and he died gasping. Utuaa caught a stray blow from another slave's pickaxe one afternoon, deep in the darkness of a cramped mine shaft. He leaped upon the other slave in fury. But by the time guards arrived with torches, the old man lay strangled on the floor, dead as the stones around him. The other slave was dragged away, gibbering madly in an unknown tongue.

Aya grew ill from a moldy batch of porridge, her pallor obvious even through her bleached-white skin. She vomited her breakfast onto the stone floor, and collapsed. A soldier came and beat her, but she could not rise, no matter how Indash and the others pleaded with her. At last the soldier gave up and slit her throat, muttering his annoyance. Two slaves came to carry her away and throw her atop the rotting pile outside.

Each time a body was carried away, the soldiers broke the chains of the dead, hammered the chains of the living together, and sent them back to work.

At last, only Indash, Bulludhu and Seri remained. No other slaves had been chained to them, though this was the usual practice. But the guards, apparently, could not be bothered. Or perhaps they expected all three survivors to perish at any moment. They were certainly weak enough, wasted away almost to naked bones. Even a short trudge from one mine shaft to another left them gasping, shaking, short of breath. Seri seemed to be growing sick, especially in the mornings, when she often vomited up her gruel. Indash guessed they had weeks left to live; a month or two, at most.

At another time, this might have frightened him, or made him furious. But here in the mine-shaft, he felt nothing at all. His life had not belonged to him for some time, and soon it would be done. The thought filled him with a strange relief.

But a change had begun to come over Seri. Her appetite returned, but she began to complain of aches and pains. Her small breasts started to swell. A few weeks later, her growing belly had become impossible to hide, even with a loose tunic.

"You there," one of the guards barked one morning, as the three of them were approaching the main pit, preparing to descend the ramp.

Seri glanced at Indash, who shook his head silently.

"I said you!" snapped the guard, craning his neck to read the number branded on Seri's forehead. "Four-seven-four-two. Come here. Now."

Seri's eyes widened. Two Ashůru soldiers came tramping over, scowls on their thick-bearded faces.

"Are you deaf, you stupid cow?" one of them demanded.

Seri stared up at him, her whole body taut with fright.

"Must think I'm stupid, too," the guard laughed to his companion. He leaned in toward Seri. "Think I've never seen a girl with child before?"

"I—I'm sorry," Seri stammered. "There's no one—I don't have the herbs to stop it. I— "

"I—I—I," the first soldier mocked her, his tongue hanging stupidly. "Seven Stars, even for a slave you're stupid."

"What would you have her do?" Indash spoke up.

"Am I speaking to you?" the soldier whirled on him.

Indash shut his mouth, glaring silently at the man.

"Don't look at me like that," the soldier snapped at him.

Indash said nothing; only glared steadily into the man's dark eyes.

The second soldier's fist cracked across Indash's jaw. He stumbled, but held himself upright, blood pouring from his lips.

The first soldier was chuckling coldly. "I see. It's yours, isn't it?" He bent and rubbed Seri's round belly. She winced and pulled away. "Your own little slave baby."

The other soldier laughed. "Your own little family, right here in the mines."

Indash glared at both of them.

The first soldier gripped Seri's arm, pulling her toward him. She struggled weakly, chains rattling.

"We're going to deal with this here and now," the soldier said. He turned to his companion. "Hold her arms." He took a step back, swinging his arm experimentally.

"No," said Indash. "You can't!"

The soldiers looked him up and down, snorting with laughter. "What do you think you're going to do?" he laughed.

"Nothing," said the second soldier. "He'll do nothing."

Indash glanced over at Bulludhu, who had dropped into a fighting stance. He slowly lowered himself into readiness, eyes locked on the first soldier.

"I'm warning you," the first soldier told him. "Stay back, or as Ash'shûr's my witness, I'll throw you down that pit myself, and I'll take the cut to my wages with a smile."

The second guard grabbed Seri's arms and pinned them behind her. She began to weep, tears coursing down the filth that coated her cheeks.

The first guard took a half-step back, raised his fist level with her swollen belly, and prepared to swing—

"No!" Indash howled, leaping for the soldier's throat. The man stumbled back, startled. To his right, Bulludhu launched himself at the second soldier, slamming into him and knocking him to the stony ground.

"Help!" the tackled soldier howled.

Bulludhu's fist crashed into the soldier's face, again and again, until his cries turned muffled.

Indash faked left, dodged right, and wrapped his chain around the first soldier's neck. The soldier's eyes bulged. He fought furiously, thick muscles flexing beneath the dark skin of his arms. Indash managed to hold on as the soldier bent and lurched, lifting him from the ground, yanking Seri's chain. She tripped and fell, hitting the gravel hard.

Meanwhile Bulludhu pummeled the soldier beneath him. The man's limbs twitched, and Bulludhu pressed his thumbs into the man's eyes, leaning down with all his weight. The soldier flailed wildly, but Bulludhu rode him like a wild bull, his muscles taut, his eyes afire.

Other soldiers were running toward them now, shouting— at least ten furious crimson-tunicked men. Still more were pouring over the ridge into the yard.

Indash pulled the chain tighter around the soldier's neck. The man fell to his knees, arms grasping at the air, face bright red. Indash somehow found the strength to pull tighter, squeezing thin streams of blood from the soldier's neck-flesh. A moment more and the man fell on his face in the dirt. He twitched and thrashed, then lay still.

Bulludhu Wolf-Killer looked up into Indash's eyes, his face contorted with rage and exhaustion—and with something else, relief, maybe. He slipped the bronze short-sword from the dead soldier's belt, and pried open a link of the chain that bound the three slaves together.

"Go, you bastard!" he snarled at Indash.

Indash stumbled away, sliding the metal links out of his collar and shackles. Bulludhu was still working on the chain that joined Seri to him. He pried furiously, face red with the effort, but the copper chain-link would not bend.

"Don't be a fool, Indash!" Seri cried. "Run!"

A soldier leaped upon them, bronze blades flashing in the cold morning air. Seri screamed. Indash raised his blade, the bronze clanging as it clashed with the soldier's sword. Another was behind him now, closing in.

Seri screamed; a long, high, animal sound, like the woman bent over the barrel in Babili, so long ago in another life. Indash dodged and slashed, blocked and parried. Behind him one of the soldiers raised a foot and kicked Seri backward over the edge of the pit.

He saw her face, as if frozen in time, contorted in helpless terror.

The chain caught the soldier's ankle. His eyes widened—and together, he plunged with them over the edge, into the darkness that yawned below.

Hating himself more than he had when he'd heard the woman's screams in Babili, more, even, than he'd hated himself as he'd watched his father carried away to be tortured, Indash turned and fled across the yard, ignoring the dozens of crimson-cloaked reinforcements who poured over the embankments, screaming and pointing their swords.

He ran to the edge of the yard, and scrambled up the steep piles of boulders until he was hidden among that ruin of cracked gray stone. He clambered through chasms and ravines of dead rock, where no flower or blade of grass disturbed the silence. As the sun crested its journey across the heavens, he stumbled down through a scree of dust and rubble, through foothills of pale brown dirt. And as the evening sky turned angry red, he trudged down hillsides among charred black things that had once been trees.

When at last the sky roiled like a purple bruise, and the air grew so cold he could scarcely feel his fingers or toes, Indash crawled into a hollow among the gnarled roots of a dead tree, and covered himself with soil to keep warm. There, shivering and starving and half-mad with thirst, he fell into a half-sleep, pursued not only by Ashûru guards, but by the ghosts of Seri and Bulludhu, and all the others he had left behind.

SOMETHING WAS SHAKING him. He opened his eyes, recoiling from the kick coming any moment—

But he was not lying in the wet straw of the sleep-house. He lay beneath a blanket of dry leaves, in a wood of gnarled junipers. And it was no Ashûru guard who stood over him, but a short, stocky woman in a filthy tunic, her eyes shaded from the bright morning sun by a broad-brimmed hat of woven straw.

"Where am I?" Indash asked, his mouth so dry he could scarcely speak.

The little woman's thick eyebrows shot up in surprise. "You're in my wood," she said. "I've never had a ghost in my wood before."

"I'm not a ghost," Indash said.

The little woman shrugged. "You look like one."

Indash glanced down at himself and realized the woman was right. His hands had become so white they were almost translucent. His arms and chest had withered to little more than bone; his eyes grown so accustomed to darkness that he could only walk by night. Even his hair had turned frail and fallen out.

"What's that mark?" the little woman asked, pointing at Indash's forehead.

He'd almost forgotten the brand he wore. He stroked the scarred flesh with pale fingertips. "It's my number," he said.

"Aha!" the woman exclaimed. "You were a slave. I knew it!"

"Yes, I'm a slave," Indash replied.

"If you're a slave," said the woman, "then where's your master?"

The face of the Ashûru soldier flashed in Indash's mind. He remembered the way the man's eyes had bulged as he'd pulled the chain tighter around his neck—

"I escaped," he said.

The woman seemed to ponder this. "How you do that?" she asked.

"I killed the guards," Indash told her.

The little woman nodded, satisfied. "Just as I thought." She rose and put out a hand. "I'm Rubati. They call me Rubati Quick-Hands."

"Who calls you that?" Indash asked.

Rubati shrugged. "Just people. Shall I call you by your number, or do you remember your name?"

"Indash," he said, reaching out to clasp arms with the little woman.

"Well, Indash," said Rubati. "Now that the formalities are done, I suppose you'll be on your way."

"Please," Indash gasped. "Where can I find water?"

Rubati produced a waterskin from beneath the folds of her tunic and passed it to Indash, who gulped eagerly until his belly felt as if it might burst.

"I suppose you'll be wanting food next," Rubati said as Indash wiped his lips and passed the waterskin back.

The very thought of food made Indash's stomach rumble. He'd eaten nothing but roots and sour berries since he'd escaped. "Yes," he said. "Anything. Even cold gruel."

Rubati pulled a disgusted face. "Why would I eat cold gruel? I trapped a rabbit last night. Come. I've got a bit of stew left at camp."

Indash tried to remember the last time he'd had rabbit stew, and found he couldn't. It must've been years ago. At least, he felt sure it'd been years since he'd been exiled from Babili. The thought that he might live to see home again—however remote the possibility—filled him with agonizing hope; a desire so fierce it brought tears to his eyes.

He followed Rubati through the wood, between the red-barked trunks of pines and firs, and the gnarled arms of wide-crowned junipers and tall elms. Their bare feet crunched on the dry leaves that carpeted the ground among the stones. A cool wind whistled against their faces. Somewhere, birds were singing. Perhaps Rubati was right, he thought: maybe he was a ghost after all; one who'd crawled up out of the grave to rejoin the living world.

"Tell me," Indash asked the little woman, as they leaped from rock to rock across an icy stream. "Who is king in Babili?"

Rubati looked back at him as if he'd told a bad joke. "How should I know such a thing?"

"What about in Ash'shûr?" Indash persisted. "Who rules in that city?"

"What do I care for the names of kings?" Rubati frowned. "They rule, then they die. Then another man with the same name rules in their place. Ah! Here we are."

A tent of tanned goat-hide was stretched between two trees, its entrance supported by a wood pole stuck upright in the soil. Just outside its doorway, a circle of rocks surrounded the ashen remains of a cook-fire. Mushrooms, onions, and bulbs of garlic hung drying from lines of sheep-gut strung between the branches of nearby trees, where stoppered clay pots sat nestled in the heights.

"No matter how far one roams," Rubati said, "nothing feels quite like coming home." She rubbed her hands eagerly, smiling at the scene. After a moment, she clambered up the trunk of a nearby tree, returned with a clay pot, and unwrapped the line of sheep-gut that bound its cloth stopper tight.

As soon as she removed the cloth, Indash smelled meat and garlic, and his mouth began to water. Rubati smiled and handed over the vessel. For the second time this morning, Indash nearly wept for joy.

"If you're going to stay a while, you'll need to earn your keep," the little woman told him as he sat by the fire-pit, devouring handfuls of savory rabbit-and-onion stew. "Especially if you keep eating like that." She laughed; a surprisingly light, delicate sound. "Trapping isn't a hard trade to learn," she told him. "Just takes patience, is all."

"I'll just finish this," Indash said between mouthfuls. "Then I'll be on my way."

An offended frown crossed Rubati's face. "After I invite you into my home and share my food? It'd be rude not to stay the night, at least, and tell me your story." She grinned. "Haven't heard a good story in ages. And yours is an epic. One look at you is enough to tell me that."

They spent the afternoon setting traps in the woods. Rubati knew many kinds of traps and snares by heart, and she proved to be a strict but patient teacher. She showed him how to weave many sticks together into a long cone, and place it in the stream to catch fish. She explained the way of finding a branch young enough to bend but still strong enough to recoil, and how to secure a loop of sheep-gut to the end of such a branch, and bend that end to the ground and notch it in a crevice of a nearby tree, so it would snap upward and pull the loop tight when triggered.

She also showed Indash how to craft bigger traps for the leopards and black bears that prowled these woods. She taught him how to conceal a pit full of sharpened wood spikes beneath a lattice of twigs and leaves. And she showed him how to lash a sharp blade, scythe-like, against the end of a flexible branch, and how to bend the branch back and notch it against a tree, tied with a tripwire of sheep-gut concealed along the ground.

At each stop she plucked onions and garlic-bulbs from the soil, and harvested fresh green leaves of mint and coriander, and retrieved fish and rabbits and squirrels from the traps she'd set on other days. Indash had never seen such a bounty outside the halls of the royal palace. He realized, with embarrassment, that he'd never thought to ask how the palace cooks obtained the meat they served. He'd walked the streets of Babili, of course, and seen the rough bread and gruel that the poor and slaves ate—but had never considered that wild forest folk might dine on fresh meat, like kings and queens.

"Course, you can't set traps like these further south," Rubati told him as she extracted a rabbit from a loop-trap, and snapped its neck with a quick, efficient motion.

Suddenly, Indash realized why he'd never seen trappers like Rubati in the royal woods. "Because kings own those forests," he said. "They'd call it poaching."

Rubati shrugged. "No one owns the beasts or the trees," she said. "No one but the Gods. But kings like to claim they do, and they've got the swords and gallows to make life hard for a poor woman like me."

"Doesn't anyone claim this forest?" he asked her.

"First one king, then another," she said, shrugging again. "But this wood is too cold and distant for anyone to bother much. Sometimes a hunting party comes in the summer. I just pack up and move high into the mountains until they're gone."

She pointed to the purple mountains that towered above the trees in the distance. The sun had begun to dip behind their snow-capped peaks, casting long shadows behind the trees in the soft golden light of later afternoon. As they broke through a stand of thorn-bushes to arrive back in camp, Indash realized they'd been cutting a great circle around this area of the forest. Rubati must know every tree and stone like the rooms of her own house. A brighter, roomier house than any wealthy nobleman possessed, Indash thought.

"Best get started on the firewood," she told him.

He took a dented copper axe from beside Rubati's tent, and gathered a bundle of kindling, along with some thicker branches to keep the fire burning. By the time he returned to camp, Rubati had skinned and cleaned the rabbit, and was chopping up onions and herbs and garlic for their stew.

"Wash up before dinner," she told him as he arranged the kindling in the fire-pit. "There's a stream just that way. The water's mighty cold, but you're covered in dirt and you smell like death. I'll not have your stench spoiling my appetite."

The stream's water was just as frigid as she'd warned; so cold it seemed to bite into Indash's skin and suck away all the warmth inside him. But that biting cold felt right, somehow, as if it were purifying him; making him new. He scrubbed at his face and head, and all his crevices; and was surprised to see his skin turn even whiter as the water sluiced away the black dust of the mine, carrying the filth downstream in whorls of ugly gray, streaked with the brown of dried blood.

As he stumbled back into camp, shivering in the red glow of sunset, Rubati fetched a shaggy sheepskin from the tent. She wrapped him in the warm wool, tutting like a nursemaid as she dried his head and back. He felt a smile spread across his face—the first smile in longer than he could remember. Rubati grinned, something in her eyes saying she, too, understood how it felt to smile again after so long. When he was dry, she gave him a tattered, hooded robe of black wool, which hung loose about his gaunt frame.

They ate in silence, by the hot glow of the fire. The stew was so delicious it nearly made Indash weep. And though Rubati brushed away his compliments, she blushed at the flattery. After the stew came mugs of old wine, a bit strong and sour, but perfect for warming the chest and relaxing the limbs. By the time he reached the bottom of his mug, Indash wanted nothing more than to stretch out and sleep. But Rubati was watching him intently.

"Where do you come from, Indash?" she asked, the firelight dancing in her eyes.

He stared into the flames, hesitant to speak.

"You've a Babili accent, unless I miss my guess," she said. "Quite high-born, too."

He glance up into her eyes, and could see she meant to have an answer.

"Yes," he told her. "I grew up in Babili."

She nodded, satisfied. "A noble, were you? Son of a baron?"

He shook his head. "No, nothing like that. I was—" Even now, the word was hard to bring to his tongue. "I am a bastard. Eldest bastard of the king, who took me into the royal household as a boy, when I began to show my strength."

Her eyes widened slightly. "Son of a king," she muttered.

"Son of nobody," he replied. "That king is long dead."

"And the king's son," she asked. "Was he not fond of you?"

Indash looked at her sharply. "I never said he had a son."

She met his gaze for a long moment. "He must've had a son," she said at last, waving a hand dismissively. "Every king must have a son."

Indash nodded, wondering whether he'd imagined that strange glint in her eye. But as he began to speak of what had befallen his family, he found the words hard; these words he'd spoken to no one, not even to himself, since the day he'd been cast out.

"The king and his son, both, were slain by a new king," he said at last. "An Ashûru king, who had them flayed and crucified."

Rubati spat into the fire. "Kings are cruel men," she said.

"My father was a good king, I think," he said, "But the Ashûru are cruel as demons."

"All kings are cruel to their enemies," she replied. "Some are cruel to their own people. I wonder, this father of yours— how would he have treated me, had he caught me on land he claimed as his own?"

Indash found he had no reply. His father had often ordered poachers' hands cut off for their crimes—and had been called merciful for it. Perhaps some of those poachers had been Rubati's friends.

"Well," she waved a hand dismissively, "I never judge a man by the cruel deeds of his king. Otherwise we'd all be at each others' throats, and there'd be no peace at all in the world." She chuckled softly.

"But some men," he answered, "inflict cruelty in the name of their king. Revel in it."

"This is true," she said. "Those men, I judge differently."

"There are many such men among the Ashúru," he said. "In the mines, they treated me as less than a man—less than an animal. That was the cruelest thing of all—not the darkness or the fumes, or the cold or the pain, but the knowledge that those men had *changed* me. Forged me into something I did not want to be. Even if they let me go, I knew I would always carry that with me."

She watched him for a long time, shadows dancing across her face in the flickering firelight.

"A piece of copper, perhaps, does not want to be a blade," she said at last. "And yet—" She drew her sharp copper knife from her belt and speared a piece of meat from the stew, pointing it at him.

"And what about me?" he asked after a moment. "What have I been forged into?"

She opened her mouth to answer when they heard a sharp crack and a cry of pain from the forest—not an animal yelp, he knew at once, but a man. After a moment, more loud crackling sounds split the night, followed by more howls of agony.

"The traps," Rubati whispered.

They crept through the moonlit shadows beneath the pines and junipers. Rubati seemed to know every rock and branch from memory, stepping neatly over crevices and stones without need of a torch. Indash stumbled many times, trying his best to keep up with Rubait without making too much of a clamor.

Soon they reached a place where two thick-trunked fir trees grew close together, the needles of their pointed crowns intertwined in the heights. A soldier was pinned against one of those trunks by a knife lashed to the end of a branch. The knife had pierced him through the lung, and he gasped for breath, dark blood running down the front of his crimson tunic.

"He's Ashûru," Indash whispered.

"He's an intruder." Rubati shrugged. "And he'll be dead in a moment."

The pinned soldier raised a trembling hand to point at Indash, his eyes alight with recognition. His bearded mouth worked frantically, though only a thin wheeze escaped his lips.

"Come on," Rubati said. "Let's check the others."

Another Ashûru soldier had fallen into the spike-pits nearby. In the second pit lay two huge Ashûru hunting-dogs, their chests and legs pierced by the spikes, jowled lips hanging open senselessly, their dead eyes staring at nothing.

"Give him up," the impaled soldier called up to Rubati. He lay in a tangle at the bottom of the pit, sharp wooden spikes running through his arms and legs. "He's an escaped convict. A murderer. There's gold in it for you."

Rubati glanced at Indash, pursing her lips appreciatively. "Murderer, you say?"

"Killed two soldiers of Ash'shûr," he told her.

"What is the penalty," Rubati asked the soldier, "for killing a soldier of Ash'shûr?"

"Death, of course," said the soldier. "A slow death by crucifixion."

Rubati nodded, considering this. "I've killed a soldier of Ash'shûr tonight," she told the man in the pit. "Or rather, one of my traps did. So it seems there's not much in it for me either way."

The soldier's eyes bulged with rage. "He is a slave!" the impaled man howled, spittle flying from his thick lips. "A slave who killed my brothers!"

"Your brothers," Indash snarled, "invaded my city. They condemned my father and brother to be flayed upon crosses. They enslaved my people, branded us like cattle, sent us into the mines, to die miserable deaths in the poison dark. When we collapsed onto the straw to catch a bit of sleep, your brothers entered in the night and had their way with us. And when a woman and I found a few moments of happiness, your brothers dragged her aside, to—" He found he could not speak of what the soldier had tried to do to Seri; to the child in her belly. "To destroy the child within her," he choked, tears rising in his eyes.

Rubati was staring at him strangely, as if seeing him for the first time.

The soldier in the pit glared up at him with open disdain.

"And now that I've fled," Indash said, his voice trembling, "you hunt me down with dogs, as if I were a wild beast, to drag me back to that place and inflict more torments on me." Tears blurred his sight, and he felt hot rage rise in his chest. "What kind of men are you?" he screamed at the man in the pit. "What madness is in your hearts?"

The soldier in the pit was laughing at him. "One way or another, slave," he said. "You will know the fear of Ash'shûr, and you will tremble and piss yourself like a dog." He glanced at Rubati. "You too, traitor. I only regret I won't be there to watch."

Indash reached out and snatched the filleting knife from Rubati's belt. He clambered down into the pit, fighting off the soldier's protesting hands. He gripped the man's head by its thick black hair, and pulled back.

"Prepare a place for your brothers," he told the soldier. "They are coming to join you."

He drew the blade across the soldier's throat, feeling hot blood run down his fingers as the man gasped, twitched, and fell still.

Rubati watched him, eyes her eyes wide in the moonlight, a hint of a smile on her lips, as he wiped the blade on the wooly black sleeve of his robe, and handed it back to her. She was nodding slowly, as if considering something.

"I don't just set my traps for bears and leopards," she said after a moment.

"You were expecting them," he said, more a statement than a question.

"Them, and many others," she replied, her grin widening. "But I was not expecting you."

"I'd kill them all if I could," he said.

"I know you would." She nodded. "Stay until morning. I want you to meet a few of my friends."

⟨

THERE WERE THREE of them, all clad in the light copperscale armor and green tunics of Babili's regular army. They stood beneath the canopies of pines and firs and cedars, casting long shadows in the early morning sunlight.

"I'm Hunzu," said one of them as they clasped arms, stepping forward and extending his hand to Indash. He was tall and thickly muscled, clad in a rough brown tunic, with four battered blades slid through his belt.

"This here's Seluku," Hunzu nodded toward his stocky companion, "and Ubar," he nodded toward the heavyset one with the burns. They both reached out to clasp Indash's arm.

"This is Indash," Rubati told them. "Returned from the dead."

"And to look at you now," said Seluku. "I'm not so sure you aren't. Dead, that is."

Suddenly Indash remembered his appearance again: a gaunt, bald figure of palest white, bald and robe-clad, with strange symbols scarring his forehead. He scarcely looked human anymore—more like a vengeful spirit from a fireside tale. In a way, he supposed, that was what he'd become.

"You're quite the unexpected guest," Hunzu told him. "After that performance of yours in the throne room on coronation day, we all expected—"

"Performance?" Indash asked.

Rubati chuckled. "You were the only man in Babili who refused to bow to that Ashûru swine," she said. "We all thought you were dead for certain."

Indash turned to her. "I thought," he said, "that you cared nothing for the names of kings."

She only grinned. "I had to make sure of you first," she said. "Now I have."

Indash scanned the soldiers' faces, looking for any sign of familiarity. "You were there in the throne room that day?" he asked. "I don't recall seeing any of you."

"We weren't there in the room, no," said Seluku, the stocky, pockmarked one. "We're just humble soldiers. But everyone in Babili and far around knows the tale of Indash's bravery."

"Bravery?" The word sounded alien to Indash. "I've done nothing brave. I failed to prevent the invasion, or the deaths of my family. I accepted slavery in the mines rather than join my father and brother in death. And I—" Images of Seri and Bulludhu flashed in his mind. How they'd plummeted into the pit as he'd turned and run for his life. "I am a coward."

All three of the soldiers were smiling now.

"Bravery doesn't always mean attacking," Hunzu told him. "Sometimes, letting go of a lost cause is the bravest thing a man can do."

He placed his hand on Indash's shoulder and squeezed.

"When I heard that story," Seluku told him, "you know what I said? I said, 'That's the man who deserves to be king.' That's what we all said."

They all watched him intently, as if expecting him to say more. But what was he to say? He had no claim to the throne. No army or wealth. Not so much as a sword to call his own.

"I am no king," he told them at last. "Only a ghost."

"Come on, ghost." Hunzu grinned. "We've got something to show you."

They led him deeper into the woods, to a towering tangle of branches where sunlight barely penetrated. There, in the shadows, he clasped arms with dozens of soldiers: old war-veterans and young recruits; swordsmen and spearmen and bowmen; blacksmiths and arrow-fletchers. He lost count at thirty; there must have been a hundred of them, or more, all spending their leave-time here, in miserable shelters built of knotted branches, laboring in secret night after night.

At the center of the camp stood a great elm tree. From one of its thick knotted branches hung the bodies of ten Ashûru soldiers. Arrow wounds pierced the dead men's chests and necks. Someone had removed the arrows. Only patches of dried blood remained.

"Seluku's a crack shot with a bow," Hunzu said. "We catch them scouting out here sometimes. Take 'em down before they know what hits 'em."

Indash raised a hand, inspecting the dandling boots of one of the dead soldiers. "These uniforms," he said. "They're different from the regular Ashûru troops."

Hunzu grinned tightly, nodding. "You've a good eye. They're not regular footsoldiers. They're Protectors."

The word was new to Indash. "Who do they protect?" he asked.

Seluku grunted. "Who do you think? They walk the streets of every city where the Ashûru have planted their boots. Protecting the peace, so it's said. Lurking around every corner, more like. Stealing meat, guzzling beer and groping our women."

Indash's mind flashed back to the thing he'd seen, that day he'd been marched up the Processional Way in chains: the terrified man outside the tavern, defending himself with a wooden sword. The woman in the back of her shop, bent over the barrel, screaming. He shuddered.

"I knew a baker's wife who refused a loaf to one of them," said Ubar, his voice quiet. "The swine ran her straight through with a spear, right there in front of her husband. When he sought out the captain of Protectors to plead his case, they slew him, too."

"I was leaving a tavern one night," Hunzu said, "when some drunk bricklayers started shouting at them, calling them red-cloaked swine and goat-lovers. Next morning I walked by that tavern, and those men's heads sat on pikes right outside its door. Blood half-dried and running down the wood."

"Any man or woman can tell you these kinds of stories," Rubati told him. "Everyone knows someone who's died at their hands, or suffered awfully. No one walks outside anymore without good reason. Not even in broad daylight. Just isn't worth the risk. They stay indoors and keep the shutters closed."

"Babili herself, made frail and nervous." Ubar shook his head. "Like a great burrow of timid mice."

"That," said Seluku, "is why I slay every one of those swine I see."

"They'll send more," said Indash. "They'll never stop hunting you."

Ubar raised an eyebrow. "Unless…?"

"Unless we take back the city," said Indash. "Throw off this Ashûru yoke and put a new king on the throne."

They watched him for a long moment. He looked across the group, meeting each man's eyes. Though he could never be their king, he knew the city of Babili as well as any man. And if these soldiers were willing to fight for Babili, even die for her, as they claimed…

"How many of us are there?" Indash asked.

Ubar grinned. "The whole army of Babili wants this, from top to bottom. Three thousand men who wear the green, all ready to do their duty when the moment comes. We even have supporters in the palace itself."

Indash nodded. "Then let us show these Ashûru how Babili conquers her conquerors."

⟨Υ⟩

A CRESCENT MOON hung over the city and the plains that night. In the shadows of the tall palms, Indash led ten hooded, black-cloaked soldiers toward Babili's southwestern gate. They exchanged hushed words with the gate guards, who let them in through a small door.

Once inside, the soldiers split up into two groups of five, hurrying along streets and alleys, past covered shops and markets, mud-brick houses and teetering apartment complexes, making their way silently up the hill toward the palace.

At the outer wall of the palace complex, the guards proved less cooperative. One of them ran to sound the alarm, and a skilled bowman took him down with an arrow through the jaw. The other guard panicked, and opened the gate to let them through. Indash and his five men held the gate, as their five companions rejoined them, vases of oil in their arms.

"Will you join us?" Indash whispered to the guard who'd let them through.

As the trembling man opened his mouth to sound an alarm, Hunzu ran a sword through the back of his neck. The blade burst forth from his throat, and he fell to the pavement, a dark stream pouring down his tunic.

"We asked him a week ago," Hunzu whispered. "He said no."

The ten fighters hurried toward the wooden sprawl of the hastily constructed barracks where the Protectors slept. Indash took a vase of oil, uncorked it, and sloshed the thick liquid along the wall of the barracks, as all the others uncorked their own vessels and did the same.

Hunzu drew out a length of flax-rag from his satchel, soaked it in oil, and laid it out from the barracks to the far side of the yard. Then he trod across the palace's outer yard, portioning out loops of rag on the street with each step. Indash and the other fighters walked alongside him, watching carefully for Protectors or other surprises, but none came.

As the moon rose high in the starry sky, they reached the far side of the palace complex. At a nod from Indash, Hunzu produced two spark-stones from his satchel, struck sparks, and set the cloth alight. Flames rushed down the rag. They waited, tensed and listening.

The barracks erupted in a blaze, searing the night air with a wave of heat. Indash and the others watched as Protectors came stumbling out the burning wreckage, screaming, flailing frantically at the flames on their arms, in their hair, on the bedsheets wrapped about them. The barracks began to collapse, sending up sparks and smoke into the night sky.

An alarm bell sounded from deep within the palace. Ashûru footsoldiers and palace guards came pouring out of the inner keep. But the army of Babili was rushing inward along sidestreets and alleys now, hundreds of fighters rushing up toward the palace hill. The Ashûru screamed with rage, trying to form up into a line against the attackers. But amid the flames and shouts, they formed only disordered groups. Indash watched as the fighters of Babili cut them down in the dark, man by man.

Ubar found Indash and clapped him on the back. "This was a good plan," said the tall, burn-scarred soldier, smiling eerily in the flickering flame-light.

"It is not finished yet," Indash told him.

Even as he said this, Indash saw new skirmishes breaking out by torchlight in the dark streets; bursts of flame, people screaming, and the clash of metal on metal, all across the city, as the fighters of Babili's army battled the Protectors in every alley and courtyard.

"Go," Ubar told him. "Find the ones you seek."

Indash tore his gaze from the battle unfolding across the city. He turned and raced into the palace, heading for the royal apartments, following the groups of green-clad army soldiers who battled Ashûru royal guards in the tapestry-hung halls and chambers, knocking over braziers and lamps, sending flames dancing up the ornately carved stone walls. Corpses of soldiers lay scattered like discarded dolls, spattered with blood, gashed deeply across their chests, backs, heads. Some of the bodies wore the green tunics of Babili, but most wore Ash'shûr's red.

He burst into the throne room to find a crowd of terrified noblemen and women, their faces lit by softly flickering lamplight. As he scanned those faces, he recognized many of the men and women who'd knelt here just weeks earlier, to bend their knees to their usurper-king. A few of the noblewomen wept softly. Most of the men trembled embroidered nightgowns, casting their gazes from shadow to shadow, eyes wide with fright.

Indash threw back the hood of his black robe, exposing his pale white flesh and the brand on his forehead. A few of the nobles gasped—whether because they recognized him, or took him for a vengeful spirit, Indash could not say. Some extended their hands to him, pleading for mercy.

"Where is Akhabbu?" he demanded. "Where is the Ashûru usurper?"

For a long moment, they only gaped at him in silence.

At last, one nobleman spoke up. "The—eh, usurper slipped out a back passage and escaped," he said in a voice as thin as thread.

"What of the others?" Indash asked. "Nazibugash. The conspirators who murdered my father."

"Indash," a voice echoed from the crowd of nobles. "I beg the honor of placing myself at your service."

Indash turned to search for its owner.

Nazibugash, the once-minor nobleman, stepped forth from the crowd, his robes bright blue and sewn with flowers.

With a few strides Indash closed the distance between himself and the traitor. "It is time," he hissed, gripping the man by the shoulder of his robe, "for you to tell me the truth."

Nazibugash smiled ever so slightly. "I could not agree more, my prince," he said calmly. "But might I suggest somewhere a bit more private?"

"No," said Indash, "Here. Now. Why did you conspire, Nazibugash, to murder my father, the king?"

A soft gasp went up from the nobles.

Nazibugash nodded his acceptance. "While I alone did not plot the murder of your father," he said mildly, "I did participate in the conspiracy that arranged his death."

The nobles began to mutter.

Indash glared into Nazibugash's imperturbable eyes. "You conspired against my father, and my brother. And against Babili herself."

Nazibugash made a "more or less" gesture. "Many of us did," said the baron. "And the old king was less clever than he seemed."

Indash tightened his grip on the blue-robed baron. "Look what's come of your selfish little plot," he said. "An Ashûru king on the throne. His soldiers terrorizing the city. Half of Babili burning."

Nazibugash sighed. "My prince," he said.

"I'm not a prince," Indash snarled. "Now answer me!"

Nazibugash's eyebrows rose ever so slightly. "Indash, then," he said, after a moment. "Surely you cannot think these things would *not* have come to pass, had we not ended the late king's reign."

Indash paused a moment. His pale brow furrowed.

"Your half-brother Hardash would have taken the throne in a few years anyway," Nazibugash said, "even more destroyed by drink and whoring than he already was. Ash'shûr would have had time to grow even richer and more powerful, and would have invaded Babili with its full army. All that has come to pass would still have come to pass, except it would have been much worse."

"Liar!" shouted Hunzu, marching into the room. "Traitor! Murderer!" The nobles whirled to watch him draw his sword, striding toward Nazibugash. "Indash, let us silence this serpent's tongue once and for all!"

Nazibugash turned to look at the approaching swordsman, unflustered. "What word have I spoken," asked the baron, "that is untrue? Tell me."

"Every word from your mouth is a deception," snarled Hunzu. He pressed the point of his blade against Nazibugash's neck.

Indash put his hand on the man's arm. "Wait a moment," he said. "He is a great deceiver, it's true. But before he dies, I must hear the confession from his own lips. The reason he did it."

Nazibugash smiled. "Have you ever heard the Shuméru word *zíd*?" he asked Indash.

"I never had lessons in Shuméru," Indash said. "Father didn't feel it was necessary. It's been a dead language for a thousand years."

The plump nobleman inclined his head left, then right, as if the answer wasn't so certain. "Perhaps so," he said. "Nonetheless, it is good for you to know this particular Shuméru word."

"Very well," Indash said, his grip still tight on the baron's robe. "What does it mean?"

"It has no exact translation in our Kalshu tongue," said Nazibugash. "It means, roughly, 'One that functions correctly.' One that does what it is supposed to be doing."

"'Effective,'" said Indash, "is the word you're looking for."

"Perhaps," said Nazibugash. "But the word applies equally to people. A Shumérû priest-king who performed the correct rituals, who appeased the Gods and brought about good harvests, who led his people to victories in war—such a lord would be called *zíd*."

"I see," said Indash, drily.

"My point," said Akhabbu, "is that at the end of his long reign, your father was no longer *zíd*."

Indash blinked, letting go of the baron's robe. "What are you saying? He wasn't ruling correctly—?"

"Not at all," said Nazibugash, brushing the wrinkles out of the cloth at his shoulder. "He did everything correctly. But correctness is not enough. The job of a king is not merely to be correct. It is to solve the problems no one else can solve. To see the solutions no one else can see."

"You're saying he was growing weak." Indash's brow furrowed.

"No," said Nazibugash. "Not weak. Just short on solutions. Our Ashûru vassals were growing in wealth and power. Your father found no way to check that growth, until at last the pharaoh of Misr himself was entertaining the king of Ash'shûr at his court. Your father failed to prevent this, or to exact so much as an apology from the pharaoh. Solutions to these problems must have existed. The Gods knew what those solutions were. A *zíd* king would have seen them, too. But your father did not."

"Times change quickly these days," said Indash. "We all struggle to keep up."

A smile crossed Nazibugash's face. "Exactly," he said, nodding. "All of us, but not the king. The king must be *zíd*, always, without fail. That's why he is king. That is what a king is for. And what is *zíd* one year may no longer be so in the next. Do you see?"

"I see," said Indash, "that you calculate coldly, and that you never had any love for my father."

The smile vanished from Nazibugash's face. "I have love," he said, "for whatever is *zíd*, and for nothing else."

"You call this *zíd*?" Indash asked, gesturing around them at the nobles who cowered in the lamplight. Outside, the screams of soldiers still rang out above the roar of the fire.

"No," said Nazibugash. "I do not. But out of these ashes, something *zíd* will rise."

Indash stepped back. "Nazibugash," he said, "I think I will give you your wish after all."

The baron gave him a questioning look.

"Now, at the moment of your death," said Indash, sliding his bronze sword from its scabbard, "you will meet something undeniably *zíd*."

Hunzu grasped Nazibugash by the shoulder and forced the man to his knees on the embroidered carpet before the throne.

"See for yourself," said Indash, "how *zíd* is a sword of Babili."

His blade swept clean through the baron's neck.

A horrified gasp went up from the nobles as the traitor's head tumbled across the floor, spurting blood onto the polished tiles. It rolled to a stop at the base of the throne-dais, its eyes wide with surprise, as if even now, it could not believe its fate.

⟨𒐖

"It isn't hard," a calm voice echoed through the throne room, "to slay a cringing little baron like him."

Indash and the others whirled. The Ashûru usurper Akhabbu strolled into the lamplight from behind the throne. His pale gray eyes scanned the fighters. The gold band of kingship rested atop his plaited black hair, its emeralds and sapphires glimmering in the lamplight. As he approached, he drew his bronze longsword from its scabbard—an ornately carved sheath of polished ivory, tipped by two snarling lions' heads. He sliced at the air, feeling its weight.

"I wonder, bastard," he said, "Can you slay a king with a sword in his hand?"

"You're no king of mine," Indash said, turning to face him. "And this battle is over. You've lost."

Akhabbu tilted his head side to side, as if considering this. "Perhaps so," he said. "Still, at least one of us will die an interesting death in this room tonight. I wonder whether we'll be allowed to finish this ourselves, or whether you'll command your footsoldiers to do your chores for you."

"They're not mine to command," Indash replied.

"Just say the word," Hunzu snarled, "and I'll run my blade through his neck."

The Ashûru usurper glanced at Hunzu, eyebrows raised in mock surprise. "And I wonder," he said to Indash, "whether, before the end, you will piss yourself and beg for a quick death, as your half-brother did."

Indash wiped his sword on the shaggy sleeve of his sheepskin robe, as Akhabbu sauntered toward the throne-dais, muscles rippling beneath his dark skin in the shafts of pale moonlight from the windows high above. His eyes shone sharp and cold. *Leopard's eyes*, Indash thought.

"Or perhaps," Akhabbu said, "you will scream and weep as my blade scores your flesh. That was the parting gift your father gave me." He nodded to himself, balancing his sword on the palm of his hand. "A death like that would be most interesting. Most people die far too dully, don't you think? But perhaps dramatic deaths run in the family—!"

Akhabbu lashed out on the last word, bronze blade singing as it sliced the air a hairsbreadth from Indash's chest. Indash leaned back slightly, letting Akhabbu step forward; but the Ashûru usurper did not stumble. The two of them fell into slow, circling steps: the black-bearded, crimson-robed usurper-king with the dead grey eyes, and the gaunt, ivory-skinned slave with branded forehead and black wool robe. Hunzu, Ubar and the others spread out across the throne room, watching every step and feint.

"No king becomes mighty all on his own, you know," Akhabbu said, dodging backward to escape a thrust from Indash, dancing on the balls of his booted feet. "He must surround himself with companions, and he becomes like them, whether he intends to or not. His companions make him greater, or lesser than he could be. For example, I am king here in

Babili, yet I swear fealty to the Lord Emperor in Ash'shûr. His greatness makes me greater. In that I am lucky."

Indash parried a chop, then a thrust from Akhabbu's sword. His robe was beginning to weigh on him, making him feel heavy in comparison to the usurper-king, who seemed almost to float on air.

"And you, bastard," Akhabbu said, leaping forward to slash at Indash's sword-hand, dancing back to escape the riposte. "With whom do you surround yourself? How many men do you require to achieve your aims tonight? How many will you need before this fight is finished?"

Indash lashed out and scored a cut across Akhabbu's sword-arm, drawing a gasp from Hunzu and the other fighters. The Ashûru king only nodded appreciatively, switched his sword to his left hand, and continued to dance and feint around his black-robed adversary.

"As for me," Akhabbu said, "I have not only an emperor, but a dragon whispering in my ear."

He lunged low, sweeping his blade at Indash's knees. Indash dodged too late, caught the edge against his right leg, and limped back, clutching the upwelling of blood inside his robe.

"Tiamat, the Great Salt Sea, sings to me." Akhabbu said. "She sings of a world scorched down to bare rock." The usurper drew a deep breath and let it out in a long sigh as he feinted and parried. "Empty. Silent. Scrubbed clean. Is this not a lovely song?"

He lashed out quicker, slicing gashes across Indash's white cheek, his forehead, his hand. The gray-eyed man did not laugh, or so much as grunt, but only inhaled sharply with each blow, as if he could scarcely contain his fervor.

Indash was moving slower now, limping, the carpet and floor around him dotted with drops of fresh blood. But he held himself upright, his eyes never moving from Akhabbu's.

The usurper lunged forward again, dropping almost to a crouch to thrust at Indash's neck. Indash spun sideways, gripped his blade with both hands and drove it down into the meat of Akhabbu's thigh. The usurper threw his head back, wincing, but still made no sound apart from a choked gasp.

Indash wrenched the blade forward, hard, tearing a gash down Akhabbu's thigh. The usurper's leg buckled. He dropped onto the floor, rolling onto his side.

And though such a thing seemed impossible, all those in the throne room swore that at that moment, a wreath of flame flashed and danced around Indash's head, as if a trick of the light transformed him for a moment into the vengeful spirit he so resembled.

Indash straddled Akhabbu, gripping his shoulder to roll him over. The usurper drew a needle-knife from within his robe and lashed out, leaving a shallow gash across Indash's bleached-white cheek. He struck again, quick as a scorpion, eyes widening with anger as Indash dodged and parried each blow.

Indash thrust his blade deep into Akhabbu's belly, hearing the tear of flesh and feeling hot blood run down over his fingers. The usurper's cold gray eyes gazed up into his. Akhabbu's thick brow furrowed, his lips contorted in a grotesque imitation of a smile. His pale gray eyes glimmered, wet with tears, darting around the room's ceiling. He muttered and nodded, as if in conversation with something unseen.

"Like salt," whispered the usurper-king. "It tastes like salt—like you, my lady. I come to you... gladly..." His lips twisted in a strange smile.

Indash wrenched the blade upward and felt it lodge in the dense flesh of Akhabbu's heart. Gouts of blood poured from the king's mouth; from his chest and belly, down Indash's hand and arm as Akhabbu twitched and writhed on the carpet before the throne. A few moments later, he lay still, eyes and mouth still agape with wonder.

Every eye in the room fixed on Indash as he stumbled to his feet, his short-sword dripping with the deep crimson blood of the slain usurper.

For a long moment, all stood silent; the only sounds the distant roaring of fires and the shouting in the streets. Unmoving, they watched him wipe his sword again on the sleeve of his robe.

At last, Hunzu bent over Akhabbu's corpse, wrenching the gold band from the usurper's blood-stained hair. "All hail the savior of Babili!" he shouted as he raised the band aloft for all to see. "Long live his exalted majesty, King Indash!"

All around him, the dukes and duchesses, the guard captains and spies, the tattered freedom fighters dropped to one knee, bowing their heads low. Men unsheathed and upraised their swords, speaking oaths of fealty to their new king.

This time, Indash did not flee. He sank to his knees, and let Hunzu place the crown upon his head.

197 YEARS EARLIER
1531 BC

*The Great Prince shall send his chariots,
And he shall slay his enemy.*

— Treaty between Khatti and Misr

Y

The long bronze dagger gleamed under the noon sun. Prince Balathu faked left, dodged right, and struck inward to the left again, straight for Duranu's lung.

Duranu stepped sideways out of the blade's path, then lowered his own dagger to parry the strike. Balathu spun round, swift and silent, slicing toward Duranu's neck. But Duranu's blade was there first, blocking the strike.

Balathu's leg slipped back, tripping Duranu, who stumbled back, almost falling. Balathu leapt on him, pressing the blade of his dagger to his opponent's throat. As he did this, he felt a sharp sting at his thigh, and looked down to see that Duranu held the point of a dagger there.

"You win by cheating," said Balathu, holding absolutely still.

"Wars aren't won with honesty, Son of the Crown," said Duranu.

Balathu smiled. "No. They certainly aren't."

Duranu drew back his dagger, and raised himself back up to his full height, as Balathu sheathed his dagger in the jeweled scabbard that hung at his belt. The crown prince of Babili adjusted the plaits of his thick square beard, smoothed his embroidered satin robes, and drew out the gold necklaces he'd tucked inside.

"You plan to wear those baubles on the battlefield?" Duranu asked, raising an eyebrow.

"Of course not," Balathu replied with a smirk. "I'll march out naked, like a good honest soldier."

Duranu was about to reply when a messenger slave, panting with exertion, crossed the top of the ridge.

"Crown prince," he gasped, sweat soaking his rough tunic.

"Catch your breath," said Balathu, tossing the slave a skin of water. "Whatever it is, it can't be that urgent."

"Thank you, my prince." The runner gulped down a few mouthfuls of water, then said, "but if it please your lordship, the matter is urgent."

"Well?" Balathu rested his hand on the pommel of his dagger.

"Your father, the king, requires your presence at dinner tonight."

Balathu smiled wryly. "Don't you mean he 'requests' my presence?"

The slave shook his head. "'Requires,' my prince. Those were his exact words. He made me repeat it twice. If it please your lordship."

"It does not particularly please my lordship." Balathu turned to Duranu, sighing. "But all the same, we'd best not disappoint the Crown."

𐤉𐤉

Six young initiates in white wool kilts knelt in a circle, facing one another. At the center knelt the high priest with one shoulder wrapped in a long white toga; his long grey beard a contrast to the wispy black half-beards of the acolytes.

Thin shafts of sunlight shone through the narrow windows of the high-ceilinged chamber, casting patches of light on the young men's bald heads. Smoke rose in delicate tendrils from the braziers of myrrh and sandalwood. One of the priests played a slow, solemn melody on a low-pitched reed pipe, while others softly beat goblet-shaped *lilis* drums and clinked the counter-rhythm on hand-cymbals. The acolytes swayed in synchrony, humming, eyes closed, their faces expressionless.

Ekurzakir could see none of this, kneeling with eyes closed in the circle next to the high priest. He knew it was not *zíd* to picture the material world during chants, but the pictures came to him anyway. The high priest had told him not to push these images away or to dwell on them, but simply to let them come and go as he chanted. So he let the scene play out behind his closed eyes as he swayed and chanted with his brothers.

"Lord Marutúk, maker who devised the celestial discs," chanted the high priest, his haunting melody woven intricately among the sounds of the reed.

The others sang the response, a countermelody: "Architect of mountains, sculptor of land and sea."

"Decider of destinies, knower of inmost hearts," chanted the high priest.

"Shrouded one, keeper of the hidden gates," sang the others.

The high priest chanted a complex wordless melody of open ohs and ahs, his chant seeming to stretch out for the space of many breaths. He followed the melody of the musicians, played upon it, and danced around it. On and on his melody went, until Ekurzakir's thoughts dissolved inside it, and he felt he was the melody, and the melody *was* the God Marutúk, and there was nothing more of him, only an empty space that the God now filled—an ecstatic peace that Ekurzakir wanted never to end.

And with that wanting, the peace slipped away, and he was just a priest again, kneeling on his soft pillow on the hard temple floor, breathing smoke of sandalwood and myrrh, listening to the chanting.

He opened his eyes for a moment. The scene was exactly as he'd imagined it. Exactly as it had been before he'd closed his eyes.

Something whacked him on the back of the head, hard.

He glanced over at the high priest, who knelt, eyes closed, on his pillow, clutching a reed in one hand, chanting his ever-varying melody in one long breath, as if his lungs never ran out of notes.

Thwack! Eyeblink-fast, the reed struck Ekurzakir's head again. Then the high priest sat utterly still, eyes closed, chanting.

Ekurzakir closed his eyes. He tried to concentrate on losing himself, on seeing the God, but this only made it worse, as always. He followed along for the rest of the chant, but he was only singing the words. At least he didn't get thwacked with the reed again.

When the prayers were over, the priests opened their eyes, and nodded to each other as if in greeting, as if they'd all just returned from someplace far away. Perhaps the others had, Ekurzakir thought, but not him, at least not today.

As he rose from his pillow, feeling the familiar pain surge outward from his knees, he caught sight of a messenger-slave waiting nervously in the temple's outer chamber. The boy's head was bowed. Knowing better than to stare into the prayer chamber during a service, he caught Ekurzakir's eyes and threw him a pleading look.

Ekurzakir padded over to him, careful not to step on the threshold with his bare feet.

"What is it, my son?" he asked, smiling gently.

"Y-your father, my prince," stammered the boy.

"My father is the God Marutúk," said Ekurzakir. "And I am no prince. Only a teacher."

The boy looked utterly nonplussed. "Yes, teacher," he said. "Yes, of course—"

Ekurzakir patted the boy's head with a thin, veined hand. "Relax, my son," he said. "I was just playing with words."

"I see, teacher," said the boy, though he now looked more hopelessly confused than before.

"What does my father say?" Ekurzakir asked.

Now the boy was back in familiar territory. "The king—I'm sorry, teacher, but he insisted I bring you his exact words—he requires your presence at dinner tonight."

Ekurzakir smiled, raising his eyebrows. "Did he say anything else?"

"That was the entire message, teacher."

"He requires me, does he?" Ekurzakir stroked the rough tangle of his beard.

The boy nodded. "Those were his words, if it please your—eh, I mean, teacher."

"Funny," said Ekurzakir, "how he never required me before."

"Teacher?" the boy gave him an inquisitive look.

"Nothing," he said. "Nothing at all. Tell my father I'll see him tonight."

The boy hurried out of the temple, trembling with nervousness. But he wasn't so rushed that he forgot to pause near the entrance, at the basin of water—a reminder of the sweet waters of the lake called Abzu. He dipped two fingers into the water, dabbed a splash on his forehead, then hurried out the door.

Ekurzakir remembered the first day he'd crossed that threshold to take his vows. He couldn't have been much older than that boy, and every bit just as terrified of entering this holy place, even as the third-born son of the king of Babili. "A wise prince fears the Gods," so the saying went, though Ekurzakir hadn't felt wise then, nor did he now. He wasn't supposed to be thinking of the past, anyway.

He wasn't supposed to think of the future, either. But he couldn't help wondering what trap Father planned to spring tonight.

𐎛𐎛𐎛

THE MERCHANT KNELT before Nicanuur, his face a mask of despair.

"My prince, the guards you sent with our caravan—"

"Were my own men," Nicanuur finished. "Yes, you've reminded me."

"Yes. Yes, so I did," the merchant stammered.

Nicanuur reached out from his seat on the plump wool cushions, took the cup of water on the low table before him and raised one finger for patience while he drank a long series of gulps. The merchant held his tongue.

"As you were saying," Nicanuur said, gesturing for the merchant to continue.

"As I was saying, my prince," the merchant said, as Nicanuur stroked his neatly trimmed beard. "You assured me that your Kalshu guards were the best."

"I assured you," Nicanuur corrected him, leaning forward, "that they were the best *fighters*. Not the most loyal."

"They turned on us!" the merchant cried out, sending spittle flying onto the cushions. "Made us stop on a road in the wilderness, to wait for their friends—oh yes, their friends lay in wait for us and came at us in chariots, loosing arrows from every direction—we had no chance!"

The green-eyed guard behind the merchant laughed, a toothy grin splitting the beard on his almond-skinned face. Nicanuur shot the man a sharp glance. He snapped back to attention, arms clasped before him like a statue, trying hard to suppress a smile.

"How much did you lose?" Nicanuur asked, in the tone of a parent reproving a child.

"All of it!" the merchant cried. "Every barrel of beer, every bolt of cloth! You must hunt these Kalshu traitors down and punish them! You must—"

"Tell me again what I 'must' do!" Nicanuur snarled. The merchant bowed low, his head nearly touching the floorboards, his shoulders trembling.

When the man raised his head, Nicanuur favored him with a sympathetic smile.

"I will tell you," said Nicanuur, "what *you* must do."

"Please, my prince, I—"

Nicanuur raised a hand. "You will repay me half the value of the goods you lost."

The merchant's eyes widened. "Half a silver mina! I'd have to sell my house, my oxen—"

"Half a mina is more than fair," said Nicanuur, "given the value of what you lost."

"Merciful prince, I beg you, for the sake of my children—" Tears were rising in the man's eyes now.

Nicanuur leaned forward, looking deep into those eyes. "How many children do you have, merchant?"

"Th-three, my prince." The man's jaw was trembling. "A little girl and two beautiful boys."

"Well, then," said Nicanuur. "For the sake of your children, I urge you to bring me—hmm. A quarter of a mina of silver, before the end of the month."

The man leaped up and kissed Nicanuur's ringed fingers. "Thank you, merciful one! Oh, thank you." He looked up at the guard, joy and relief on his face. "Is he not merciful?"

The guard smiled. "He is, indeed."

Nicanuur accepted the man's gratitude, then bid him good day, reminding him to deliver the silver before the month was out.

When the merchant was gone, and the door closed behind him, Nicanuur summoned the guard to his side. The tall, thick-shouldered man knelt next to his master's cushions, the tiny links of his bronze-scale armor clinking as he moved.

"So, all told, Shuriash," Nicanuur asked, turning to the Kalshu guard. "How much is our profit?"

Shuriash smiled. "Twenty bolts of cloth, ten barrels of beer, and a chest of bronze jewelry. Plus the quarter of a mina you so mercifully charged our client. All told, nearly three silver mina."

Nicanuur smiled, satisfied. "That makes a mina and a half for you, my friend."

"My thanks." Shuriash bowed his head, tapping his forehead to show respect. "You know, of all the employers I've worked for, Nicanuur, you are by far my favorite."

Nicanuur grinned, plucked a silver wine-goblet from the low table, and filled it from a nearby pitcher. "I enjoy our work every bit as much as you do, my friend. Believe me."

Shuriash took a seat next to the prince, filling his own goblet. "But," said the burly man as he sipped his wine, "there's something I've been wanting to ask you."

"Ask away, old friend," said Nicanuur, spreading his hands. "My thoughts are as open as a temple whore's legs."

"Why do you do it?" Shuriash asked. "That is—well, you're the second-born son of the king. Your family sits atop wealth beyond dreams."

As Nicanuur opened his mouth to answer, a slave-boy burst into the room, his face sweaty with exertion. "My prince," the boy panted.

Nicanuur's brow furrowed. "Seven Stars, boy! However did you find me?'

"Your father the king told me," the slave replied, wiping sweaty hands on his rough tunic.

"Indeed?" said Nicanuur, eyebrows raised. *Seems the old man hasn't gone totally blind after all.*

The slave-boy only stared at him, his face a mask of nervousness.

"Well, spit it out," Nicanuur said at last. "What does the old man want?"

"The king—these are his exact words, my prince—the king requires your presence at dinner tonight."

Nicanuur's expression hardened. "And what if I'm busy tonight?" he snapped.

The boy backed away, terrified. Shuriash chuckled softly.

"It was only a joke, boy," said Nicanuur, grinning. "Of course I'll come. Tell the old man it'll be my absolute pleasure." He smiled, showing all his teeth.

"Yes, my prince," said the boy, bowing frantically, backing out the door. "Thank you."

"Sure you don't want to stay for some cake?" Nicanuur called after him. "Joyplant? We've got joyplant!" He shook his head. "Do my eyes and ears deceive me, Shuriash, or is this new generation painfully thick?"

"If so, you've got nothing to fear from them," said Shuriash. "Your father and brothers, on the other hand..."

"Quite so." Nicanuur nodded. "And only a few hours till dinner." He sighed. "I'd best take some time alone to collect my thoughts. Your evening is your own, Shuriash."

The Kalshu fighter grinned. "Enjoy your plotting, old friend."

"I always do," replied the prince, as Shuriash gulped down the last of his wine.

"That's an Adnanu vintage, you know," Nicanuur said, scowling in mock-offense as Shuriash wiped his beard. "Finest grapes west of the Silver Mountains."

Shuriash belched. "Tastes like grapes, sure enough." He plunked the silver goblet on the table and rose to his feet, dipping his head and tapping his forehead as he ducked out the chamber's low doorway.

"Oh, and Shuriash," Nicanuur called after him.

The burly man glanced back.

"In answer to your question," Nicanuur said.

"My question?" Shuriash asked.

"Why I do this," Nicanuur reminded him. "Why I scheme and cheat merchants, when my family already has all the wealth and power in the world, and I have only to ask for anything I desire. Well, there's your answer."

Shuriash folded his scarred arms. "I can hardly wait."

"I've never had to work for anything in my life. I do this to test myself, Shuriash. To see what I'm made of. To see for myself, perhaps, how I might rule, someday."

"An interesting test," Shuriash answered, bowing again and stepping out into blinding daylight.

When the man was gone, Nicanuur poured himself another goblet of wine.

"But Father's tests," he muttered to himself, eyeing the dark liquid, "are always the most interesting of all."

Sa'amsu-Ditana, eleventh king of the First Dynasty of Babili, sipped his wine suspiciously. He fidgeted against the hard cedar-wood of his ornately carved, gold-leafed chair, the linen of his brilliant blue robe itching against his sensitive skin. He reached for his jewel-studded goblet, and the white tassels of his sleeve dipped into the wine. Those tassels would be stained red forever. The king humphed. Tracing his finger along the delicate gold inlay of his plate, he eyed his three sons, who sat on gold-plated chairs around the long heavy table of polished cedar.

"At least one of you," the king said in a creaking voice, "is plotting to kill me."

Nicanuur put out a hand. "Father—"

"Don't 'Father' me!" the king snapped. "I don't know if it's you, or one of you," he glanced at Balathu and Ekurzakir. "Or all of you. But you're plotting."

Household slaves had already cleared away the previous courses: cucumber and olives in tart vinegar; lentil stew spiced with black pepper; rack of lamb roasted in honey and cardamom; plump duck and suckling pig baked with onions and turnips, and a selection of soft and crumbly cheeses baked in flaky pastry. In this lull before the next courses, only fruit adorned the table; candied dates and figs, and a silver plate heaped high with oranges, grapes and pomegranates, most of them untouched.

The king turned to his latest wife, Arinna, who sat at his left hand. She had the milky skin and reddish hair of a Khatti princess, both of which stood out sharply above the deep red linen of her low-necked dress. Her eyes gleamed with a strange old wisdom, as if the soul behind them was somehow aged beyond the body containing it. She'd arrived at the palace three weeks ago, a friendship-gift from the Khatti war-chief Murshili; and she'd done little since then but whisper in the king's ear. All three of the king's sons watched her with open distrust, through the wafting smoke of candles and braziers of myrrh.

"Which of them could it be, my beloved?" Arinna asked.

The king's eyes shifted across the table to Balathu, his eldest son, seated at his right hand. A broad-shouldered lad, he'd had his long beard braided with golden rings tonight, to match the gold hoops in his ears; and had decked himself in a robe of dark green, its chest embroidered with leaping gold stags, its sleeves short and trimmed with gold flowers. *The better to show off those absurd muscles of his*, the king thought.

When Balathu made no response, the king glanced at Nicanuur, his second-born, seated next to the eldest, draped in a robe of deep gray, adorned with an intricate maze of stars and flowers. Always wearing that hint of a smirk, Nicanuur was. Always watching with those slightly narrowed eyes, as if he'd just remembered a joke in which you were the punchline. No answer there, either.

On the young queen's opposite side sat Ekurzakir, who hadn't even bothered to change for dinner, still clad in the simple habit of the temple, its white flax sleeves nearly covering his hands. The young priest kept his own silent counsel. Not that the king expected much else.

"In recent weeks," the red-robed queen Arinna said, "my husband has grown suspicious of your murderous intentions."

Before any of them could answer, the king pounded the table with a fist. "As of tonight, I am utterly convinced!"

A tense silence reigned.

"Do you want to know," asked the king, "how I became convinced?"

His sons looked from him to his young wife, silent accusation in their eyes. This only confirmed the king's suspicions.

"First," said the king, "the season is ripe for an assassination. My hair and beard have long gone gray. That damned Ashûru arrowhead in my shoulder means I couldn't draw a bow or lift an axe, even if my arms still had the strength."

"Father," said Ekurzakir, the priest, "I'm sure the Gods still have many years in store—"

"Shut it, boy," snarled the king, drawing a muffled laugh from Balathu.

The king's anger whirled onto his eldest son. "What are you laughing at, you great shaggy beast?"

The smile vanished from Balathu's face.

"Second," the king continued, "most of our family's wealth is piled up right here in the palace. A hoard of gold and jewels amassed by my great-great-grandfather, Lord Ammurapi himself, and by all the kings of Babili before him. Convenient. All a man has to do to claim that hoard is to ascend the throne, so long as he has the bloodline. And all three of you, though you seem barely aware of it, carry noble blood that reaches back to the founding of our dynasty, when our Amurru ancestors swept out of the western deserts and captured a village called Babili, three centuries ago.

"It is good to remember our history, Father," said Ekurzakir, smiling like a proud schoolboy. The king didn't bother to insult him. This was exhausting enough already.

"Third," he said, "And most perilously of all, I am tired." He sighed. "Not only by battle, but by kingship itself. By these," he gestured vaguely in the air, "endless parades of quarreling nobles and feuding tribespeople, with their pleas and disputes and lies to be sniffed out. I know you can all see the exhaustion in my limbs, in my eyes. And all three of you remain," he coughed, "invigorated, by your unceasing campaigning, looting, drinking and whoring."

Ekurzakir gasped at the last word. "Whoring? Father, I really must protest—"

"You mean to say you're still a virgin, Zaki?" Balathu guffawed. "After all these years?"

"Shut up, both of you!" the king bellowed, triggering a fit of coughing.

When he'd caught his breath, he said, "I could have lived with my knowledge of all these things, and still held onto some some small shred of trust in you three. You are, after all, my sons. Gods know that ought to count for something. Then again, I raised you all to fight like me. To be ruthless. Calculating. Cruel, even, when circumstances demand cruelty. Don't think for a moment that I regret those lessons."

He met the eyes of each of his sons in turn, looking for any side-glance, any shift in expression, that might hint at the culprit. Perhaps they were plotting something in concert. Or perhaps each of them was simply waiting for the opportune moment, scheming for himself alone. The king knew not. But he knew the moment would come, and that it would arrive sooner rather than later.

"I could execute all three of you, of course," the king said, abruptly, enjoying his sons' careful efforts to hold neutral expressions. "Perhaps you, Ekurzakir? No, but it wouldn't do to execute a priest, would it? 'A wise king fears the Gods,' as the old saying goes. And believe it or no, I've still got a few scraps of piety wrapped around these old bones."

He turned to Balathu. "Or you, Balathu? You've made no secret of your desire for my throne."

"The throne is my birthright, Father," said the brute. "But I do not claim it yet."

The king huffed. "And what of you, Nicanuur? Always watching everyone with those sharp little eyes, saying nothing, as though we're unworthy of your wisdom."

"Your will be done, Father," said Nicanuur, in that same half-mocking tone he'd always used, ever since he'd first learned to sneer at slave-girls.

"No," said the king. "I will not have you executed. And do you know why? Because those are the very traits that make you each so valuable. Piety. Brutality. Cunning. All vital traits in any man who takes the throne."

"Why, Father," said Nicanuur. "I'm touched."

"Don't go all soft and lovey just yet, boy," snarled the king. "There's a reason I've called you all here tonight, and it's not just to insult you. Much as I enjoy that pursuit."

He paused to catch his breath and take a long guzzle of wine.

"It's to tell you that I have chosen my successor." The king smiled wolfishly. "But I do not yet know which of you it will be."

All three of them stared at him. Young Arinna looked equally surprised. The king smiled, letting their minds whirl for a few moments.

"Please explain, Father," said Ekurzakir at last, spreading his hands, looking every inch the mild-mannered priest.

"Bring in the scribe!" the king barked.

A nervous, bald-headed man appeared, clutching a small writing-bench in one hand; a reed stylus and a cloth-wrapped parcel in the other. He set the bench on the floor in the corner, and unwrapped the cloth to reveal a wax tablet.

"Let it be recorded," said the king, "that whichever of you brings me the head of the Khatti king Murshili will take the throne when I die!"

Arinna gasped aloud, then covered her mouth.

The king's gaze whirled on her. "Yes, my love. And let me tell you why. I know your father is gathering armies in the hills northwest of here. I know he plans to march on Babili before the summer's out."

"It isn't true, my beloved," she said, stroking his sleeve, trying to keep her voice even.

"I don't know if you're lying, or just ignorant," said the king. "And frankly, I don't care. I've got spies in your father's army, as I'm sure he has spies here." He grinned, eyes gleaming like a wolf's. "Oh, but you mustn't think I'm upset, my dear. Your father has provided me exactly what I need: a convenient way to keep three scheming sons busy while I enjoy my old age. Or whatever's left of it." He clapped his hands. "Scribe, you may go."

The scribe finished a few final scribbles on his wax tablet and wrapped it hastily in its cloth, then gathered up his bench and tools.

"Tell them to bring in the food," the king called after him. "If it hasn't gone cold."

"Father," Ekurzakir spoke up. "Surely you know that priests don't march in battle."

"Nor do they take the throne," the king shot back. "Not even if they kill the king in his bed. There's a solution neat enough for a mathematician."

Two young slave-boys entered, bearing silver trays of fresh river-fish sauteed in butter and coriander, surrounded by boiled red crayfish and crabs. Even as the king and his sons dug into the river-food, more slaves brought in a vast platter of honey-glazed ducks, smelling of roasted dates and almonds, garnished with sprigs of mint and sweet caramelized onions and leeks. Along with these came plates heaped high with steaming wheat flatbread, sweet and soft, and fresh flagons of beer and pitchers of wine, chilled with blocks of ice carted down from distant mountain peaks.

"I'll do it," said Balathu through a mouthful of duck.

The others looked up from their meat and goblets.

"I'll ride out and kill this Khatti warlord in single combat," he said.

"And what do you think would happen then?" Arinna asked, running her finger along the rim of a golden goblet.

He turned to her, glaring, saying nothing.

"The army would appoint a new war-leader," she said, "and then they would march on Babili."

The king smirked at her. "I thought you said there was no Khatti army marching for my gates."

She didn't even flinch. "I was speaking only in possibilities, O Perfect One." Her voice was as smooth as her milky skin. "*If* a Khatti army were to appear at your gates, and *if* your eldest son were to defeat that army's champion in single combat—"

"Was this your idea, concubine?" Nicanuur interrupted her. He popped a date into his mouth and looked at her, chewing behind his smile.

She stopped for a moment, nonplussed. "I assume you mean this succession trap, which your father has just sprung on all of us. No, I had no part in it. How could I, when I knew nothing of this approaching army?"

"A very good question," said Nicanuur. "But by any road, it was you who convinced Father that we're all scheming to end his life."

The king pounded the table. "I don't need a concubine to tell me you want me dead."

"I'm not a concubine!" Arinna shrieked, startling them all into silence. A long moment passed. After a few heartbeats, she composed herself and said, "I'm a daughter of the king of Khatti."

Nicanuur smiled mildly. "'King,' is it, now? Last I heard, your father was no more than a glorified war-chief. And what of your mother?"

"What of her?" Arinna snapped back.

"My point exactly," Nicanuur answered.

"Enough of this bickering," snarled the king.

He settled back onto his cushions, looking up at the mosaics that lined the walls: the king in his chariot, the king hunting lions, the king receiving gifts from foreign nobles, the king making offerings to the Gods. Everything rendered in delicately carved tiles of marble and turquoise and lapis lazuli, with accents of gold. Perfect, frozen. The idea of a king and kingdom that never were, and never would be.

"I've told you my decision," he said. "The rest is up to you. Now shut up and let me enjoy my wine."

"THIS SCHEME, YOU realize, is not set in stone." Ekurzakir adjusted the fine linen blanket about his shoulders, wishing he had a simple wool one. But fine linen was all the palace had.

Nicanuur strolled next to his younger brother in the shadows of the palace gardens. At this time of the evening, the only light came from the oil lamps hanging from posts where the mosaicked paths crossed, leaving the long corridors between the palms and topiaries in shadow; perfect places for a nighttime chat.

"You mean, if we really do end Father's life," Nicanuur mused.

Ekurzakir looked at him with disgust. "Are you mad?" he asked. "We'd have a succession war like Babili hasn't seen in centuries, and an invading Khatti army to handle at the same time."

"Which is precisely what Father has handed us anyway." Nicanuur shrugged. "And what we'll still have to deal with, if Balathu dies in this absurd single combat he's dreamed up."

Ekurzakir stopped and listened. "Someone's here," he whispered.

A topiary rustled. Arinna stepped out from behind it, shrouded in a long dark hooded robe. She stood amid the shadows for a long moment, utterly still, watching them.

"You know," she said at last, "I'm not your enemy."

Nicanuur strolled toward her. "You're a—"

"Yes, I know. I'm a Khatti concubine," she cut him off, standing her ground. "Or whatever you want to call me. That doesn't mean I want the Khatti to take Babili."

This gave Nicannur pause for a moment.

"Explain that," said Ekurzakir. "If you please."

She threw back the hood of her robe, letting the dim moonlight cast her face in blue and gray. "How do you think I was treated in Khattusha?" she asked. "I wasn't a concubine, but I wasn't much more. I'd never set foot outside the women's quarters until I went to marry your father. Here I'm a queen—in name, at least." She saw their expressions darken, and added, "No disrespect to your mother, of course. I would've been honored to know her."

"You would've been blessed by the Gods," said Ekurzakir, "to meet her even once."

She nodded respectfully.

"By any road," she said, "I think we can make common cause."

Nicanuur laughed quietly. "What common cause? Your queenship ends with Father's life, no matter which of us takes the throne. You must know that already."

She shrugged. "I've no desire to be wed to any of you."

"Out with it, then," said Nicanuur, a knowing smile spreading across his lips. "What do you want?"

"Én-priestess," she said, matter-of-factly. "Highest rank in the temple. Here in Babili, or in Níppúr. One of the wealthy cities. Put me out of the way. You'll never hear a word from me. Not so much as a scratch on clay."

Ekurzakir's brow furrowed. "Surely Father could give you that now—"

"Don't be dense, Zaki," Nicanuur said. "Father wants her in his bed." He smiled at Arinna. "I would, too, if you weren't who you are."

"I'm flattered," she said drily. "Do we have a deal or not?"

"You still haven't told us what you're offering," said Nicanuur.

"I'd have thought it was obvious, my prince," she said, smiling right back at him. "I have your father's ear. And other parts of him, as well."

Nicanuur snorted a laugh.

"I will convince him," Arinna said, "to make a slight modification to his scheme: he will declare as heir whichever son delivers Babili from my father's army, through combat or any other means. Negotiation, I think, would be preferable."

"So your father's head remains safely on his shoulders," said Nicanuur.

"I could give a damn about my father's head," she hissed. Then, more softly, "Once a scribe has recorded the change, I will tell you the next step of my plan."

"I think you should tell us now," said Nicanuur.

"I think I have no reason to tell you," she said mildly.

Ekurzakir raised an accusing finger at her. "When Father finds out about this—"

"He will thank me," Arinna interrupted, "for proposing a scheme that doesn't spark the wrath of the Khatti, and that doesn't place that oaf Balathu on the throne. I bear your father no ill will. Nor either of you. And I would prefer not to see this beautiful city sacked by the Khatti. And I'd rather die old and plump, in a temple, than young and screaming under the knife of some Khatti prince."

"Well said, concubine." Nicanuur nodded.

"So do we have a deal or not?" she asked.

"I think we do," said Nicanuur. He put out his hand, and she clasped his palm in hers: a formal embrace of agreement.

"Go on, brother," said Nicanuur. "Clasp her hand."

Ekurzakir hesitated, but found himself unable to refuse. He put out his hand and clasped hers.

"Good," she said. "Now I'm off to your father's bedchamber, to put our plan in motion."

She threw her hood back over her head, and vanished into the shadows among the bushes.

᛭᛭᛭

"I SAID NO." Balathu raised his arm and pushed Arinna away, firmly and none too gently.

She stumbled back a few steps, looking up at the great bearded face of the king's eldest son, lit from below by the flickering candlelight in his bedchamber. He stood fully dressed in ankle-length robes, belts, and sandals. He'd removed only his cloak, and thrown it carelessly across the cushions of the bed. Arinna, by contrast, wore only a thin shift, which she now adjusted to let it hang more loosely around her shoulders.

"I have already been of much use to your father," she said sweetly.

"That's exactly why I'm not interested," he said, turning away from her to take his scabbard from the bed.

"And I know my father well," she said. "He may be king of Khatti, but he's far from immortal."

"No man is immortal," Balathu grunted. "The Gods know the day of his death, same as any other man."

"The Gods," said Arinna, "have also seen fit, in their wisdom, to grant each man certain strengths and weaknesses."

"Get to the point," said Balathu, strapping his bronze breastplate around his thick stomach.

"Among your brothers," she said, "you alone are at home on the battlefield. You alone command the loyalty of Babili's armies."

"That's why the throne will be mine," he said, glancing impatiently at the door behind her.

"Unless," she said, letting the word hang between them.

She had his full attention now. "Unless what?" he asked, his eyes narrowing beneath his bushy brow.

"Unless," she said, "one of your brothers finds another way to turn the Khatti army away from Babili, and talks your father into modifying his terms."

He moved closer to her, backing her against the wall, looming over her as he stared down sharply into her eyes. "You'd best stay out of this game, witch," he growled.

"Surely I'm not so frightful to you." She looked up boldly at him, eyes wide as an innocent child's. "I have no spells to cast, my prince. I simply report what I see and hear."

"And what exactly," he brought his shaggy face close to hers, "have you seen and heard?" She could smell the garlic and onions on his breath.

"I heard your brothers plotting against you and your father, in the garden," she whispered, bringing her hand up to softly touch his chest. "Surely that's no surprise."

"No surprise," he grunted. "Were you discovered?"

She smiled cunningly, bringing her face a bit closer to his. "I may be young, Son of the Crown. But I'm no fool."

"And what," he asked, "is their plan?"

"It is as I've said," she whispered, her lips almost touching his. "They've a scheme to rout my father's army before it reaches Babili."

He slowly raised his hand and placed his meaty fingers around her neck. "Tell me this scheme of theirs," he whispered.

"First," she whispered, her lips brushing against his, "tell me what is to be done with me."

She ran her other hand down his abdomen and began to stroke. He lifted her up bodily, spun her around, and tossed her onto the piled cushions of the bed.

But instead of leaping upon her, he sneered and pointed a thick finger at her. "I don't know who you think I am, girl," he snarled, "but I'm not that stupid. No, don't bother to look so shocked and offended. I know what you're about."

Her expression went from mock innocence to sharp cunning in an instant. "Then hear me well, Prince Balathu," she said, her tone cold and hard. "Everything I've said is true. Your brothers are planning to rout the Khatti army, and Nicanuur plans to claim the throne."

"Amateur!" Nicanuur's shout echoed through the bedchamber. Arinna and the crown prince both looked up, eyes wide with surprise.

A great hanging tapestry on the far wall was thrown aside, and Nicanuur strolled out from the shadows, a triumphant smirk on his face.

"It's the oldest play in the world," he said, sidling up to her.

"What are you doing in here?" she asked, too shocked, for the moment, to find words to lash him with.

"You must think we're all three of us new to this game," Nicanuur replied, still grinning. He'd drawn a bronze dagger from somewhere, and twisted its tip against his finger as he talked. "Really, girl, if this is what they call scheming in the palace of Khattusha, I'd say we have little to fear from Khatti."

He turned to Balathu. "And what do you say, brother of mine?"

Balathu glowered at him. "I say I'm tired of you sneaking about, jumping out of shadows."

Nicanuur smiled indulgently at his older brother. "But that's my way, Balathu. I'll never be as talented as you on the field of battle. I must use what talents the Gods have seen fit to give me."

"The Gods gave you a serpent for a tongue," Balathu said, eyeing his brother warily.

"A poison one, no less." Nicanuur smiled and turned back to Arinna. "Surely, dear girl," he said, "you didn't think I'd simply follow your scheme on trust." He laughed.

She stared daggers at him from the bed.

"Seven Stars!" he exclaimed. "You—did you actually think to play us against one another?" He turned to Balathu and clapped his unamused brother on the back. "*Us*? The royal sons of Babili? We who've been scheming to cut each other's throats since before we could walk?" He laughed in astonishment. "You know what? I admit it. Father's right. She *is* entertaining. I see now why he keeps her around."

Balathu shook his younger brother's hand off his back. "All the same," he said, "I haven't heard you deny it."

Nicanuur looked up at him. "Hmm?"

"What the witch claimed," Balathu said. "That you've a scheme to rout the army of Khatti, and lay claim to the succession."

Nicanuur sighed. "That scheme has been promised me by our witch here." He favored Ashultu with a smirk. She returned a scowl. "But whatever it is, I'm sure we can work it together."

Balathu grunted. "And Zaki?"

Nicanuur waved his dagger dismissively. "Oh, you know Zaki. All he wants is to go back to his temple. It was like pulling teeth just to get him here tonight."

"Is he still here?" Balathu asked.

Nicanuur shrugged. "I believe so."

Balathu's eyes narrowed.

Nicanuur sighed in mock exhaustion. "Yes, all *right*, he's here. He's in the bathhouse, soaking, alone, as usual. Ask your own whisperers if you don't believe me."

"Whisperers?" Arinna spoke up, recognition dawning on her. They both turned to her, annoyance on their faces.

"Yes, dear?" Nicanuur asked. "How may I be of service?"

"'Whisperers?'" she repeated. "You mean you've both got spies all over the palace?"

They both looked at her, incredulous.

"Well," said Nicanuur, "yes." He suppressed a laugh. "You mean you don't? Truly?"

She only glared back at him.

"Oh dear," he said. "Oh, my dear. Didn't they teach you *anything* in Khattusha?"

"No one taught me," she said, staring daggers at him. "I had to teach myself."

"Well," Nicanuur clapped his hands together. "At least you're learning now."

Suddenly Balathu stepped between the two of them.

"What's the witch's scheme, Nicanuur?" the bearded giant asked, looming close to his brother's face.

"I'm not a witch!" Arinna snarled.

"She hasn't told me, yet." Nicanuur shrugged mildly. "She promised me a clever plan to rout the Khatti and snatch the succession from you, if I agreed to make her én-priestess when I took the throne. And I must admit, I am curious to hear the plot."

The brothers turned to Arinna. Balathu's eyebrows were lowered in undisguised mistrust, while Nicanuur wore that infuriating smirk of his, as if he already knew what she was going to say, and was enjoying drawing the moment out, like a cat toying with a wounded sparrow.

Arinna met the brothers' gaze and held it as long as she could.

"There was no secret strategy!" She threw up her hands at last. "Hasn't your brilliant mind figured that out by now? The only strategy was this one, here: to turn the three of you against one another before my father's army arrives."

Balathu glared at her with utter contempt, while Nicanuur grinned with mild amusement. She glared back at them, heart pounding with rage, and with a growing fear of what was to come next.

"I know." Nicanuur chuckled softly. "I just wanted to hear it from your lips."

"Did Father put you up to this?" Balathu demanded of her.

"Of course not," Nicanuur sneered. "Father may be old and frail, but a scheme this idiotic? Not even on his worst day. Think before you speak, brother of mine, for once in your brutish life."

Understanding dawned in Balathu's dark eyes. A smile crept across his thick lips, and he cackled a coarse laugh. "So, this is the mastermind our Khatti enemies send into our midst?" The crown prince spat at Arinna's feet.

Her lip trembled, and her eyes were fire. "You are cruel," she hissed. "Both of you. Cruel and wicked, petty little boys."

"Not as cruel and wicked as our father," said Balathu.

"We may never live up to his example," Nicanuur sighed. "But we do try."

"So what now?" Arinna asked, her voice cold and bitter. "You'll kill me?"

Nicanuur laughed, his eyes wide with surprise. "Kill you? Why would we kill you? Father loves you! And now, so do we both. Is it not true, brother?"

"Whatever you say," Balathu grunted, eyeing Arinna with open revulsion.

"No," said Nicanuur, a gleam in his eye, "I think we show her how the experts strike deals."

"We've had enough of deals for one night," Balathu said, pushing past his brother, aiming for the door.

"Oh, but I think you'll like this one very much," said Nicanuur. "The proposal is this: Father appoints you, Balathu, his one and only successor, as is right and proper."

"I'll be his successor anyway," Balathu replied, "when I ride out with the army and bring back the Khatti king's head." But his tone said he suspected a trap.

Nicanuur nodded thoughtfully, pacing closer to his brother, still twisting that dagger against his fingertip. "You'll be successor, yes," he said. "But king—well, there's a long way from successor to king."

"A fine threat," Balathu said, his voice sharp as a blade, "from the little brother who could never land a blow."

"No. That's why now I pay people to land blows for me." Nicanuur looked almost bored. "Come now. I have no interest in threatening you. In fact I have no interest in the throne, or in commanding the army. I don't even like this city much, if I'm altogether honest. Surely you must know this by now."

Balathu nodded, understanding spreading across his face. "I see. You step out of the way. I get Babili and the crown. You get the country estates. Is that it?"

"Simple." Nicanuur spread his hands and smiled.

Balathu grinned. "And when you've gathered enough silver to storm my gates with your own army?"

"That's *years* away, brother." Nicanuur waved a hand dismissively. "We'll worry about the future when it comes."

Balathu nodded slowly, then suddenly spit in his palm and held it out to his brother. Nicanuur spit in his own hand, and the two clasped palms tightly.

"Done," said Balathu. "Now I'm off to win father's war."

"Oh, do be careful," Nicanuur said. "One never knows what might happen on those battlefields."

"Or in the corridors of the palace." Balathu shoved his brother aside and stormed out the door.

When he was gone, Nicanuur turned back to Arinna.

"There now," he said. "A deal well-struck. What did you learn?"

She stared at him, eyes still afire with hate and distrust. "I learned that you and your brother are both serpents. And even serpents can strike deals with one another."

Nicanuur nodded, a look of genuine satisfaction on his face. "Not bad, actually. You may make a fine pupil yet."

"I will never be your pupil," she snarled.

"My dear," he said. "Surely you can see you already are. And now it's time for you to be useful to me. I have a message for you to carry to a Kalshu friend of mine."

He smiled then, a hard, sharp smile. Arinna did not like the look in his eyes.

"And when you're done doing that," he said, "I have another message for your father."

THEY LAY TANGLED among the white linen sheets; Ekurzakir and Siduri, one of Father's bath-slaves. His hand stroked her long black hair absently, and her fingers played across his bare chest. They were spent, not happy, really, but exhausted enough, for these few moments, not to care.

"You hardly visit me these days, Akku," she said, using the special name she'd used for him since they were children. It meant "owl," and no one else knew of it.

"I hardly leave the temple these days," he said, smiling softly. "I've only ascended the third of the Seven Pillars."

"How many times have I ascended yours?" she put a finger to her lip in mock thoughtfulness.

He hit her with a pillow, and she squealed and laughed.

"It's hard work, Siduri," he said, though he was laughing too.

"All the more reason to come here for some distraction," she replied.

His expression soured. "I hate it here. You know that."

She looked crestfallen.

"Not you, Siduri," he reached out to stroke her cheek. "Please don't look like that. But all this plotting, scheming, striking, creeping in the shadows. I've always found it distasteful. There's something... undignified about it."

She smiled and pressed her hand against his cheek. "That's why I've always loved you, Akku. Of all the king's sons, you are wisest."

He drew a deep breath and let it out in a long sigh. "Not wise enough to turn this overgrown village into a true city," he said. "Just five generations ago, Babili was little more than an outpost on the edge of the desert. On nights like tonight, it still feels like some wild chieftain's town of tents."

"Not chieftains," Siduri said. "Kings. Your ancestors. Your family."

"Our people, the Amurru," he said, "are barbarians from the desert. That's all we've ever been, at heart."

"Until King Ammurapi," she replied, her voice soft and gentle.

"Yes, the great Ammurapi," Ekurzakir smiled faintly. "Builder of Babili. Creator of the sacred law code. How tired I am of that name. And what of his descendents?"

She grinned at him. "One of them, at least, is an acceptable lover."

"Acceptable?" he hit her with the pillow again, acting outraged.

She put her hands up in surrender. "A great lover! I meant 'great!' Please forgive me, my prince!"

"No, not a prince." He sat up. "Just a monk, I told you."

"You'll always be a prince to me." She kissed his neck, his cheeks, his forehead. "My prince."

He leaned back against the pillows. "Not even son of a king, if these Khatti capture Babili."

She moved nearer to him and stroked his arm softly. "One does not capture Babili," she said. "Babili captures her conquerors. You told me that."

He shook his head. "I hope it's true."

She raised an eyebrow. "Akku. I know nothing of war, but surely you're not afraid of this Khatti war-chief."

"I'll always remember the first time I saw Khatti writing," he murmured, as if to himself. "It was the final year of my scribal training at the temple. Master Apli brought in a Khatti tablet, to show us how inferior their culture was. And do you know what I did? I laughed at it. The characters looked so childish and sloppy. Such an obvious, clumsy imitation of our scribal arts." He shook his head. "I suppose we all expected their armies would be similar."

"Are they not just mountain people?" she asked. "Everyone calls them savages."

"I saw a man, once, who survived a battle against the Khatti," he said, speaking to the far wall, not really looking at her. "Soldiers carried him to our temple, seeking a physician for him. He was badly wounded. Bristling with Khatti arrows. Shafts as thick as my thumb, piercing him straight through." He shook his head. "The muscle it must take to draw those bowstrings."

"Akku, there've always been enemies. When I was a girl, it was the Elamu. Then the Ashûru. They're only men, after all—"

He shook his head. "I heard the other soldiers talking of the Khatti, while their comrade lay dying. They spoke of tall, lean horses, like the wild ones up in the mountains, pulling fast, light wagons with only two wheels. These wagons can fly as swiftly as the horses can run, and the men upon them can rain arrows from every direction, wheeling and swooping like birds about the battlefield."

He was trembling now, even as she caressed his cheeks, his bald head. "Like monsters from a tale," he whispered.

She licked her dry lips. "These Khatti-men have strayed far from what is natural," she said. "The Gods will punish them, surely."

"Their armor, too, is iron," he cut her off. "It cannot be pierced, it is said. Not even by stone."

"Nor can their arrows pierce stone walls," she said, quietly. "I shouldn't think."

"I would have agreed with you, once," he answered, stroking her soft hair. "Now I am not so sure. Babili's walls have weathered all sorts of storms. But never one like this. This is different. I think of these Khatti-men, and my bones sing strangely. Like rain is about to fall."

She watched his face turn even paler in the glow of the lamps.

"There must be hope, surely." Her voice was almost a whisper.

"For Babili," he said, "perhaps you're right. Maybe our city will capture her conquerors, as you say." He paused and swallowed with a dry throat. "But my family?" He shook his head. "The day I saw that man, bristling with Khatti arrows, and heard what the Khatti can do—on that day, I swore I'd never serve in the palace or the army. I came home that very night and told Father I would dedicate my life to the Gods."

She ran her fingertips across his shaved-bald head. "If one place in Babili is safe from a conquering army," she said, "it's the temple. I'd say history has been clear on that point."

"And if history changes?" he asked.

"History often changes," she replied. "But the Gods? I think they'll always be here."

He kissed her then, with much more confidence than he truly felt.

BALATHU RODE OUT from Babili's great western gate, at the head of the royal army. Behind him towered the city's crenellated walls, baked mud-brick atop a foundation of stone; so thick that men could walk three abreast atop their ramparts. Before the army, far across the plain west of the city, lay the army of Khatti—still unseen, since the morning was cool, and a mist hung low over the plain.

No matter, thought Balathu. *It means their archers are blind, too.*

The footsoldiers of Babili rode in ponderous chariot-wagons of the time-tested Shuméru style: squat boxes of timber with tall forward bows and four thick-planked wheels, their sides strapped with shields of hammered copper and boiled leather. Each was was manned by a driver, a spearman and an archer, drawn by a pair of trotting donkeys.

Behind the lumbering wagons marched tight lines of spearmen and archers: Babili's corps of professional soldiers, more than three thousand strong; a forest of long bronze-tipped spears and wood bows and polished helmets. Before them marched a great mass of peasants levied hastily from farms and estates and taverns: men in ordinary cloaks and tunics of every color and cut, carrying bronze-headed maces and axes, hammers and slings, cruel-looking homemade weapons of their own design, bristling with nails and blades. Most of them would die before the battle really started; they must have known this, yet they marched eagerly, joining the troops in war-songs and chants.

At a signal from Balathu—and much whipping and cursing from the drivers—the great boxy wagons drew to a halt: a wooden wall standing between Babili's infantry and the front line of Khatti chariots: vague shadows in the swirling mist.

Balathu checked the wind. He tightened his grip on his spear and whispered a quick prayer to Marutúk. After a moment, he nodded.

"Shields up!" he cried, drawing his sword and raising it high in the cool morning air.

"Shields up!" echoed commanders up and down the line. Across the plain, three thousand men raised their shields. Knuckles tightened on spears and swords, on maces and bows.

"These Khatti like to close the distance quickly," muttered Duranu, dropping the wagon's reins for a moment to slide his plumed bronze helmet over his long plaited hair.

Balathu eyed the fog. "They'll shatter against our wagons," he said. "If we keep pushing forward, their line will break. That's how this always works."

Duranu glanced up and down Babili's line of wagons and auxiliaries, doing a poor job of hiding his apprehension.

Better get them moving, Balathu thought.

He'd just opened his mouth to call for the charge when the first arrows came lancing out of the mist. First just two, thudding into the grass, too far out do do any damage. Then more—dozens; hundreds of thick-feathered shafts arcing out of the fog-shrouded sky, rolling closer—

"Shields high!" Balathu howled, raising his heavy bronze shield above his head. All up and down the line, thousands of men did the same; but even as they ducked beneath their shields, he heard the first screams. Men were dying, and still no one had seen the enemy.

"We need to move!" Duranu cried.

"Forward!" Balathu bellowed. Donkeys brayed and bucked as panicked drivers cracked whips and snapped reins. Across the plain, the line of wagons lumbered slowly forward atop their thick-planked wooden wheels.

"Archers ready!" Balathu called. As the wagons rolled forward beneath the hail of arrows, archers under cover of shields notched their own shafts to bowstrings.

Balathu gazed into the mist, searching for any sign of the Khatti line. He heard the thunder of approaching hoofbeats; the rattle of wood on wood. *How much farther can they be?*

Then he saw them.

Chariots burst forth from the mist like birds on wing.

The small, light carriages rolled atop thin spoked wheels, each drawn by a pair of tall, lean horses, the plumes in their headdresses bouncing as they galloped and leaped in formation. They broke off to the left and right, swarming out along the line of lumbering wagons—hundreds of them, each with an archer loosing shafts at frantic speed as the vehicles fanned out across the plain.

Even in his horror, Balathu's eyes widened in awe, to see such a thing. *It is as if they fly*, he thought.

YYY
YYY
YYY

EKURZAKIR WATCHED FROM the wall above Babili's western gate as the Khatti chariots hurtled toward Babili's front line. They sped as if borne on wings, leaving trails behind them in the fog. Even knowing what he knew about them, Ekurzakir's stomach leaped, to see them fly so quickly. From up on the wall, they looked like a storm blowing in from the desert: a wave of motion converging on the city, a dustcloud in its wake.

Balathu shouted for his army to press the attack. Babili's line of wagons rolled forward, the teams of donkeys trotting, pulling the great wood boxes with all their might, barely exceeding walking-speed.

The infantry spread out between the wagons, pushing the peasant troops up to the front line, where they fell like wheat trampled beneath a stampede of hooves, screaming as they died, transfixed with dozens of iron-tipped arrows.

Meanwhile the line of Khatti chariots, fast and nimble as the horses that pulled them, unfurled like two great wings around the army of Babili. From up here, the unfolding looked almost leisurely; but Ekurzakir knew the chariots must be flying faster than a man could run.

Even as they hurtled across the plain, the Khatti riders raised their bows and loosed arrows at Babili's front lines. Balathu and his men raised their shields, catching many of the shafts; but many others struck home, knocking drivers from wagons, dropping infantrymen where they stood.

And still the Khatti wings unfolded. The wave descended. The two armies would come to grips at any moment. Already the flanks of Babili's army were dropping into combat positions, lowering their shields and spears, preparing to meet the crashing wave—

But at the last second, the wave became a whirlpool. The wings of Khatti chariots coalesced into a great spiral; a vast wheel whose axle was the army of Babili. As the wheel began to rotate, the Khatti archers let loose a hailstorm. Arrows rained into the center of the wheel, thick as flies on fruit; so thick they hid the army in shadow.

The Babili infantry raised their shields high and arrows sprouted from the hide-covered bronze, appearing as if by magic. Commanders screamed at their men to keep shields high, to hold spears steady, to advance—and many units did. Ekurzakir could see them, thick knots of hide and bronze, plodding slowly out toward the edges, where the auxiliary troops fell like scythed corn, their bodies already turning the field into a marsh of blood. And still the Khatti arrows rained.

Ekurzakir had never imagined men could loose arrows so quickly. Each time his eye tracked one Khatti chariot-archer, the man's arms seemed to move in a blur, plucking arrows from the quiver at his side, pulling them back against the bowstring, loosing the shafts. The instant one arrow flew, another was already on the bowstring; as one arrow struck home against an infantryman or horse, dozens more flew toward new marks.

Each archer in a every Khatti chariot loosed arrows like this; like a many-armed monster, tentacles and missiles whirling. A thousand chariots, a thousand archers, swirled like slingstones around Babili's ranks. The great storm-wheel rotated, a hail of sharp-tipped iron raining ceaselessly into its center.

BALATHU COUGHED IN the dust and fog, ducking low in his wagon, his shield held tightly over his head, tight against the cart's wood walls. Duranu crouched next to him, shield covering the other half of the wagon. The undersides of both their shields bristled with iron arrowheads.

Their archer had died in the first moments of the attack. They'd pushed his wreckage of his body from the wagon. Their donkey was undoubtedly dead. Arrows still fell like hail from every direction, their iron tips piercing through their shield every few moments.

How had it happened so quickly? The Khatti should barely have had time to reach them. Still, they couldn't keep this up forever.

At last, the rain of arrows thinned. It didn't cease, but it slowed.

"All right," Balathu grunted. "It's time."

He reached for the great horn beneath his feet; a ram's-horn as long and thick as his arm. Raising it to his dry lips, he blew with all his might. The horn's low song rumbled across the plain, more felt than heard, humming in the bones of every man who still lived. Balathu blew the horn a second time, then a third.

⟨Y

EKURZAKIR HEARD THE horn-blast, even from up on the wall.

And as the morning fog began to lift, he saw them riding in from the edges of his vision: Twin wings of fast light chariots, pulled by tall strong horses that galloped with the speed of the wind. Out of the forests they rode, from both sides of the Khatti at once.

For a moment he was terrified that the Khatti had sprung a second surprise—but then he saw the banners of Babili flapping above them: gold dragons on green backgrounds. Looking closer, he could see that the new attackers weren't Khatti: they wore a confusion of tunics and capes, many of rough wool and fur. Where had they come from?

A moment later, the racing newcomers crashed into both sides of the whirling wheel of Khatti chariots, loosing arrows; striking out with spears. They fought without the discipline of the Khatti, without the speed and lightning movement. Instead, they careened through the whirl of chariots, throwing them into disarray.

As the Khatti wheel began to break—first at one point, then at many—they hurled long thick spears against horses and chariot-drivers alike, sending chariots end over end, impaling drivers and archers against their own chariots, or pinning them to the ground.

The Khatti whirled away with astonishing speed, like a school of fish, dodging out of the path of the attackers, who chased them down, knocking them from their chariots, leaping upon them with bronze axes and short-blades as they hit the dirt. These new attackers fought like alley-brawlers. But it was working. The great Khatti wheel was breaking apart.

At a horn-blast from Balathu, the tattered remnants of Babili's army pressed the attack. Most of the chariot-donkeys had died under the rain of arrows, as had most of the auxiliary troops. But the infantry marched forward, their ranks swelled with spearmen and archers from the chariots.

Babili's spearmen thrust up at horses, impaling them, knocking riders from chariots, to be finished off by spear-thrusts and axe-blows of anyone who happened to be nearby. The fighting had turned savage, at close-quarters; a riot. Khatti corpses fell atop those of Babili's auxiliaries and infantry, which already littered the ground.

Soon the field was a ruin of blood and torn flesh; men and horses and donkeys torn to pieces, scattered like meat under a butcher's knife. The spectacle was drawing a black cloud of vultures and crows, swirling high overhead in their own great wheel.

The Khatti were retreating. Ekurzakir could hardly believe it—they still had the clear advantage of numbers—but their chariots were turning about, fleeing wildly back to the Khatti camp in a chaotic jumble. No more Khatti arrows fell. It was an absolute rout.

The charioteers on Babili's side gave chase, but the Khatti horses were faster. The fleeing enemies soon outstripped their pursuers, hurtling back the way they'd come in a churning cloud of dust and lifting fog, tinted red by the mist of blood.

⟨𒐊𒐊⟩

BALATHU WATCHED THE Khatti chariots speeding away; a riot of horses and spoked wheels vanishing into a retreating cloud of dust. Even after everything; all the planning, the promises he'd made and the assurances Nicanuur had secured from the Kalshu chieftain, he could hardly believe they'd fulfilled their promise. Still more, he could scarcely believe it had worked.

He raised his short-blade high in the air, shaking droplets of blood from its bronze shaft. He drew in a deep breath, and let out a deep, throaty cry of victory. The men around him took up the cheer, and soon all the survivors were pumping their spears in the air, cheering, chanting "*Bab-i-li! Bab-i-li!*"

"Marutúk be thanked," he whispered, panting with exhaustion, dripping with sweat and caked with half-dried blood.

A Kalshu chariot wheeled up beside him. Nicanuur stood tall in its carriage, next to Shuriash, that Kalshu fighter who always seemed to be at his side. Both wore gleaming bronze-scale armor, and helmets with plumed crests—an almost absurd contrast against Shuriash's rough wool tunic.

"Against all odds, dear brother," Nicanuur said, leaping down from the chariot. He seemed to wear not a scratch. Not even a blood-stain. "We triumph."

Balathu eyed his brother and the Kalshu fighter. "I see, now, that there was more to your plan," he said. "You wanted to charge in and save the army. Get them on your side."

"I saved Babili, didn't I?" Nicanuur grinned, surveying the charnel-house around them. "You weren't exactly covering yourself in glory out here."

"I remember you saying you had no interest in war," Balathu replied. "Or in the throne."

Nicanuur shrugged. "I changed my mind. One should always leave oneself the option, I think, to change one's mind."

"Wouldn't be hard kill you, you know," Balathu said. "Right here. Right where you stand."

"True enough," Nicanuur agreed. "But you wouldn't live long after murdering the savior of the army."

Balathu laughed humorlessly.

"But as you say, brother," Nicanuur went on. "I have no desire to be king." He gestured to Shuriash, who stepped down from the chariot. "What are you waiting for?" Nicanuur gestured for Balathu to take his place. "Finish the battle. You've got them on the run, brother of mine."

With a suspicious glance at Nicanuur and his silent Kalshu companion, Balathu climbed onto the chariot. "Just what I was thinking." He snapped the reins. "Go give those Khatti bastards a taste of Babili bronze."

For a moment, the horses didn't move. Balathu snapped the reins harder, and the horses whirled, leaping forward into a gallop that nearly sent Balathu tumbling backward out of the chariot. He held on tight, getting a feel for the rhythm. Even through his fog of blood and exhaustion, he couldn't help feeling impressed, feeling the whole vehicle maneuver around him. As the horses turned, the chariot turned; as they sped forward, so did the carriage, smooth and light on its twin spoked wheels. They flew, a swift boat sailing over the land.

"When this is all over," he said, smiling, "I'll build a thousand of these."

⟨𒁹𒁹𒁹

FROM HIGH ATOP the city walls, Ekurzakir watched the Kalshu chariots form up amid the wreckage of the battlefield. They'd taken few casualties. They massed in their hundreds, chasing the tail of the receding Khatti cloud.

Babili's exhausted infantry stayed where they were. Even from up here, Ekurzakir could see the bronze-helmeted men rallying around their commanders. They waited, watching the chariots of their Kalshu allies pursue the enemy.

The Khatti chariots were far away now. They'd halted up in the hill country at the far side of the plain—still a long way from their camp. They were beginning to turn around, facing back toward the battlefield. Their line began to spread out again, forming into two wings as before.

But the Kalshu chariots flying Babili's flag were swiftly closing the distance.

Ekurzakir cried out, "No! Stop!" but of course he was too far away. He understood then why Nicanuur had declined to pursue the fleeing Khatti chariots. He knew why his brother had encouraged Balathu to climb aboard one and charge the enemy. Because he remembered another thing those soldiers had said, in the temple, on that morning so long ago, as they'd watched the man bristling with Khatti arrows die slowly on the bed.

The Khatti flee at the slightest danger, the soldiers had said. *But it is a false flight.*

He watched, powerless, as the Khatti chariots slowed— and reversed course, their archers turning and loosing a fresh avalanche of arrows at their pursuers.

The chariots flying Babili's flag slowed, then stopped and frantically began to turn about, as their drivers recognized the trap they'd charged into. But they were too late. The Khatti chariots were already upon Balathu and the others, a wave crashing down from the hills; a pair of wings enfolding the cluster of Babili flags; encircling the chariots and raining a storm of iron arrows on them from every side.

Horses wheeled, bucked, and fell to the ground, bristling with arrow-shafts. Kalshu warriors leaped from chariots and fought back with spears and daggers and bows; but they were only a few hundred to the Khatti's thousands. They drowned in the flood, swallowed by the dust and iron.

And far away, back on the battlefield, amid piles of the blood-drenched dead, Ekurzakir saw Nicanuur standing still, watching impassively, Shuriash by his side. Ekurzakir knew his brother couldn't laugh yet, of course; not surrounded by Babili's army as their commander charged to his death. But

Nicanuur would laugh later, tonight, alone in the palace. The thought twisted a cold knife in Ekurzakir's belly.

Babili's infantry were massing into a long line, their backs to the city's western wall. Even after the losses they'd sustained, enough had survived to form a line two men deep, stretching the width of the Khatti chariot-cloud that now descended on them. Not enough to mount a defense.

Nicanuur cut one of the few surviving donkeys free from its ruined wagon. When the donkey stepped free, Nicanuur climbed onto its back. Nearby, Shuriash was doing the same with another of the donkeys. The beasts bucked and complained at their riders, but finally accepted the burdens. Nicanuur and Shuriash tapped the beasts with the flat of their daggers, and they set off, alone, toward the descending Khatti stormcloud.

⟨𒐕⟩

THE KHATTI SLOWED when their leaders saw Nicanuur and Shuriash riding out alone. The cloud of dust they'd raised swept before them across the plain, choking him. He coughed and waited for the dust to clear.

When Nicanuur could see again, he saw that the Khatti line had formed up at the edge of the plain, well out of arrow range. The line of tall, handsome horses parted to permit a chariot through. This was no ordinary vehicle, but a great gleaming conveyance, drawn by a team of four white-maned stallions.

As the great chariot drew closer, Nicanuur saw that its carriage was fronted with reliefs of hammered gold, in which twin eagle-headed Gods supported a shining sun. Its rim was topped with sculptures of long-horned bulls, and a round, fringed sun-shade embroidered with many-colored flowers sat atop a pole at its rear, throwing its passengers into shadow.

The chariot approached Nicanuur at a stately pace. He sat atop his donkey and waited. At last its four steeds trotted to a halt before him, and two passengers disembarked. One was a soldier in a pale blue tunic and a helmet of hammered bronze, wearing a long shirt of heavy copperscale, carrying a thick recurved bow nearly as tall as he was.

The second man to disembark was clearly a king: broad-shouldered and almond-skinned, with a thick square beard and a long drooping mustache. He wore a loose tunic of deep purple, embroidered with white suns; and a gold-tasseled shawl banded in purple and black, fringed with tiny bronze bells that jingled as he walked. A shirt of glimmering ironscale armor hung almost to his knees, cinched by a broad white belt; and his point-toed shoes were of polished leather. Towering plumes of white horsetail sprang from his gleaming bronze helmet.

Nicanuur removed his own helmet, slid his dagger from his belt and dropped it to the dirt. Shuriash did the same.

The Khatti lord pulled off his horsetail helm and shook out his long black hair. He strolled casually toward Nicanuur with a bow-legged gait, holding out a scarred hand, speaking words in his own tongue, in a deep, rolling voice: "*Utu'shi Murshili hassátaras Khattushilias, salli hassu udnē Khatti, su kínun ésha Babílias.*"

"You have the honor," the translator said, "of addressing the Sun-King Murshili of the line of Khattushili, King of the Land of Khatti. And now Lord of Babili."

Nicanuur put out his hand and grasped forearms with the Khatti king, who spoke a few more words in the Khatti tongue: "*Parā handātar a'siwatti.*"

After a brief conference with his translator, the Khatti lord spoke again, and the soldier gave Nicanuur his words: "My lord wishes to thank you for your help in eliminating your brother, as well as his Kalshu enemies."

Nicanuur offered a shallow bow, tapping his forehead respectfully. "Tell him he is most welcome."

The Khatti king was gazing strangely at Shuriash. After a moment he asked another question of his translator.

"My lord wishes to know," the translator said, "how your Kalshu friend feels about sending an army of his own people to their deaths."

Shuriash sneered. "My own people," he said, clapping a hand on Nicanuur's shoulder, "never treated me half as well as this man."

The translator conveyed this to the Khatti king, who seemed to ponder it for a moment. At last he clapped his hands together and spoke a long string of words in his tongue.

"The terms of our agreement will remain as agreed upon," the translator said. "But Babili will pay seventy mina of gold to Khatti every year."

"Seventy mina—!" Nicanuur scowled, but Shuriash put a hand on his arm. The Kalshu fighter shook his head sternly, and Nicanuur fell silent.

The Khatti king saw this, smiled, and spoke more words to his translator.

"Babili is the wealthiest city in the world," the soldier said. "We know you have the gold."

Nicanuur drew a deep breath and let out a long, tired sigh. "Very well," he said. "Seventy mina each year."

"Should even a single payment fall short," the soldier continued, "or should any lord in Babili rebel or contradict the word of King Murshili in any way, our army shall return. And we shall not be so merciful next time."

"Understood," said Nicanuur.

The Khatti lord murmured something else to the translator.

"And," the soldier said, "Babili shall not build any fast chariots, or breed any mountain-horses."

Nicanuur's face fell. The Khatti king smiled through his thick beard. Nicanuur stared up into the man's pale blue eyes for a long time, but he saw no mercy there. Only the gleam that a man's eyes get in victory. He knew that if the Gods had favored Babili's army today, his eyes would have gleamed the same.

"Do you accept these terms, prince?" the translator barked.

Nicanuur nodded. "I accept."

"Good," the translator said.

The Khatti king rode up before Nicanuur, drew his bronze sword, and extended its point delicately to tap Nicanuur on the forehead, muttering an incantation in his strange tongue.

"As agreed," the translator said, "The Lord of Khatti appoints you, Nicanuur, king in Babili—and a subject oathbound to his lordship—from this day forward."

"Convey my thanks to him," Nicanuur replied with a curt nod.

The Khatti king demanded something of the translator, who asked, "My lord wishes to know, where is his daughter, Arinna?"

Nicanuur thought about this for a moment. "She is safe and well, in the palace."

The translator conferred again with his Khatti lord. "My king expects his daughter to be well rewarded for the service she has provided," he said after a moment, "in carrying your plan to his ears."

"Oh, she will be well rewarded, indeed." Nicanuur smiled. "Now that I am king, she will have what was agreed upon: she will be én-priestess in the city of Unúg."

After a whispered conference, the translator asked, "My lord wishes to know, is this Unúg a great city?"

"Of course." Nicanuur nodded solemnly, concealing his smile. "It is one of the greatest and most ancient cities in all the empire, as any priest will tell you." *They'd also tell you Unúg's priests haven't held any political influence for centuries*, he mused. *If I hadn't paid them to say otherwise.*

The Khatti king spoke again with the translator, who said, "You made a wise choice today, King Nicanuur."

"Wise?" Nicanuur said. "I don't know about wise. I made the only choice I had."

"The king does not refer to your surrender," the translator clarified. "He means your choice to keep your younger brother out of the fighting altogether."

Nicanuur's eyes widened. *How can he know—?*

The Khatti king smiled. So did the translator.

"King Murshili knows many secrets," said the translator, "in his own land and in the lands of his enemies. Surely this cannot surprise you, O King. Surely your own spies are everywhere."

"Everywhere in Babili," said Nicanuur. "But not in Khatti."

"Well then," said the translator. "That's one difference between you and us."

The Khatti king donned his plumed helmet and leaped back into the carriage of his chariot. His translator joined him beneath the shade of the tasselled sun-shade. The driver flicked the reins, and the four white-maned stallions whirled about before the gates of Babili, casting up a cloud of dust. The line of horses and chariots trotted forward to join them.

Nicanuur climbed back onto his donkey. With Shuriash at his side, the new king rode before the line of Khatti chariots, to tell Babili of his surrender.

HIGH UP ON the wall, Ekurzakir watched his brother ride the donkey back toward the shattered mass of wagons, soldiers, and arrow-studded bodies piled about Babili's western gate. The line of Khatti chariots rolled close behind.

Soon they will be within our walls, he thought, feeling tears well up beneath his eyes.

He found a nearby staircase and descended from the wall, unable to look the guardsmen in the eye. What remained, now? Balathu was dead. Nicanuur was king. Arinna, the Khatti concubine, was now én-priestess, leaving Father to wither into his dotage somewhere in the bowels of the palace—or to fall beneath an executioner's blade as Nicanuur looked on, smiling that horrid smile. Ekurzakir wasn't sure which thought sickened him more.

Babili would remain much as she had always been, he knew. Daily life would change little. He would still pray with the priests in the temple, and attend the festivals on the holy days. And on warm summer evenings he might still go to meet Siduri in the bathhouse. Men and women would still shout bargains in the markets, and drink good Babili beer in the taverns, and transcribe old Shuméru poetry in the schools.

But something would be different from now on. After these Khatti would come other conquerors; brash men sweeping in and out of the city like a brothel bed, taking what they wanted and leaving their stains behind. And over the centuries, plundered by one horde after another, her ancient temples and palaces and gardens would slowly crumble into disorder, then at last into ruin.

The golden days of Babili, he knew, had reached their end at last.

351 YEARS EARLIER
1882 BC

Now listen: the hands of these people are destructive.
Their features are those of monkeys.
They do not show reverence.
They are an abomination to the dwellings of the Gods.

— The Marriage of Martu

𐎂

"My father grew up in a tent, in the desert of K'nan," said Én Yahdun of Babili. "I grew up in the slums, in the ancient city of Urim, south of here. Playing with rats in the alleys. My son, well...."

Yahdun gestured vaguely at the office around them, which displayed all the magnificence of the young city of Babili: his desk was engraved with dragons and bulls, leafed in gold, surrounded by tapestries and reliefs of old Shuméru kings and priests, clad in long one-shouldered togas fringed in white and gold, like the én behind the desk. Two men sat in gold chairs on the other side of that desk—Nasir, the én's son, and Ashtamar, son of Warad, who had just made a very serious request of him.

"My son's son?" Én Yahdun continued as Ashtamar watched him. "I'm not so sure. What we have here is..." he shrugged and stroked his thick black beard. "Fragile. It depends on all of us."

Nasir wondered where his father was headed with this story. This was how the én liked to persuade people: by telling tales.

"Do you know why I took the title of én, instead of headman, or governor?" Yahdun asked suddenly, looking from his son to Ashtamar.

"Because," said Ashtamar, stammering, "because you are the boss."

"Anyone can be a boss," Nasir interrupted him.

Ashtamar glanced at Nasir, annoyed, but Yahdun gestured for his son to continue.

"Gather up some men, if you want to be a boss," Nasir said. "Go out and rough up the locals, steal their barley and gold, rape their women. Men will fear you. They will call you 'boss,' as long as you keep providing barley and gold and women. But a boss adds nothing to the world. When he dies, no one will remember his name."

"Growing up in the slums of Urim, I saw many bosses rise and fall," Yahdun agreed. "I did not want to be another boss. So when I came here to Babili and took the crown, I did not call myself a headman, or a governor. I called myself 'én.' This is not an Amurru word. It is not from our language. Do you know where this word comes from?"

"I know it's an old word," said Ashtamar, casting confused looks at Nasir and Én Yahdun. "Very old."

"Not just old," Yahdun said. "Ancient. It goes back thousands of years, to the first dynasties of old Shumér. An én is a man who goes between the Gods and other men. Interprets and executes the Gods' will. A holy administrator."

"Like a high priest," said Ashtamar.

"No!" Yahdun slammed his palm on the desk. "Not like a priest. What does a priest do? Hides in his temple, thinking secret thoughts, performing rituals, accepting offerings. No, an én leads his city. Guides his people. Fights for them. Provides for them."

"The head above all other heads," Nasir said.

"When my father brought me here to Babili," Yahdun said, "it was little more than a village. But I dreamed that we, the Amurru, would finally build our own great city here—a city like those of ancient Shumér and Akkad; a city as magnificent as old Urim itself. That was what I dreamed. Do you know what I saw here instead?"

Ashtamar bit off a reply and shook his head.

"I saw dozens of bosses," Yahdun said, "all fighting, killing, stealing, trying to hold onto one little street. One tiny piece of turf. I put an end to all that. Now no man is slain without my permission. If one of my people steals food from another, I have that man's hands cut off. If one of my people rapes another man's wife—well, you know my laws."

"They are good laws, Én Yahdun," said Ashtamar. "Which is why I ask you—"

Yahdun raised a hand, cutting him off. "But do you know what else I saw, growing up on the streets of Urim?" the én asked. "I saw people whose only dreams were to live in the ruins of houses others had built, and to fight for food and women. My people were living in a magnificent city, but they had no capacity to appreciate it. No desire to learn its history. To understand the great and ancient culture that created it: the Shuméru people, who built Urim two thousand years ago. Those same people whose distant descendants still live here among us in Babili today."

The én looked up, meeting the eyes of his son, and of Ashtamar, searching for a glimmer of understanding there. When he'd satisfied himself that they were following his words, he continued.

"The Shuméru people," he said, "took the mud and reeds that still grow along the banks of the Two Rivers, and they baked the mud and reeds into bricks. And brick by brick they built houses and temples and sturdy walls, and carved their stories and songs into the brick, and painted beautiful frescoes on it, and crafted delicate images of the Gods to dwell inside it, and carefully planned each season's harvest so everyone would have enough to eat. And kept the peace around their city so traders would bring exotic jewels and spices from faraway lands—all this, they built out of the mud and the reeds of the riverbank."

"That's quite an achievement, Én Yahdun," said Ashtamar, after a silence.

"And when our fathers, the Amurru people, first came out of the western desert and entered Urim, and drove out the eastern Elamu warlords who'd invaded and occupied it," the én sighed and shook his head. "Those ancestors of ours had no wish to understand that city, or how it had been created. And because they had no understanding of the past, they had no dreams for the future."

Yahdun paused and smoothed his beard.

"Here in our new city of Babili," he said after a moment, "I have changed all that. I have taught our people the old ways of Shumér and Akkad. And in showing them the past, I have given them the idea of the future. Our future. This is why I had the bosses put to death. Why I decreed that there would be no more bosses, why I set up headmen in their place. Men who report to *me*. Who serve not their own self-destructive interests but *our* interests, the interests of our people, of the future we are building together. This is why I took for myself the title of én. Do you understand, Ashtamar?"

"I think so," Ashtamar said.

"Good," said Yahdun. "I'm glad you understand."

The én leaned back in his chair and took a long drink of water from a carved tamarisk-wood goblet on the desk.

"Now," said Yahdun. "Ashtamar, son of Warad. You come to me today. It pleases me that you should visit my house, that you receive my attention. So I invite you into my home. And I ask you what you would ask of me. And what is it that you ask of me?"

"I—I have already explained, Én—"

"Explain again," said Én Yahdun. "Now that I have explained these things to you, and you have said you understand them. With those things in mind, Ashtamar, explain to me, again, what it is that you ask of me."

Ashtamar licked his lips. He opened his mouth, paused, licked his lips again, and tried a second time.

"I believe in what you are working to achieve here, Én Yahdun," he said. "I, too, am glad to see the end of this pointless killing, cousin against cousin. Like you, I dream of a better future for our people, here in this Babili we've built. When you appointed me headman of the Riverfront, you tasked me with preserving the peace in that neighborhood. And I have worked every day, hardly stopping to sleep or to eat, making sure your laws are enforced. Never hoping for any reward, except that my children, like all others, would live to see peace. To live some kind of life beyond just tents and sand. To grow up in a city, where they could—could make something of themselves."

Tears were forming in the corners of his eyes.

"So when Simaal of the Western Clans came to me, wailing and beating his chest, demanding to know why my children were encouraging his children to abandon the worship of our Amurru Gods, to burn incense and make sacrifices at the Shuméru temples—when he came to me howling about this, I told him what you told me: that these children were our future. Ways are changing, I told him. Our children will not live in tents like we did. Their lives will be different. Better. We should teach them to respect our Gods, too, of course. But we are no longer a band of desert tribes. Now we are city people—like the Shuméru, as you say. And so, here in Babili, I told him, it was fitting that our children should make sacrifices to the Shuméru Gods, too."

He took a deep, shuddering breath and tried to speak again but uttered only a soft sigh. Then, with tears welling in his eyes, he made himself continue.

"Men came to my house that night, while my family slept. They stole away my wife, and dishonored her in the alley. All of them, together. I found her the next morning, weeping, covered in blood, unable to speak. And my daughter and grandchild—"

The last word came only as a soft breath.

"They are gone, Én Yahdun. Until this morning. The baby. I found him in the river. What was left of him. My beautiful daughter—she is nowhere to be found."

He paused. Took a few long, deep breaths. Wiped his eyes.

"And so I ask you. Beg you, as your faithful servant. Give me justice, for me and my wife, who cannot speak, and for my children, who will never speak again. This is all I ask. Justice."

Én Yahdun stood, walked around his desk to Ashtamar, placed his hand on the man's shoulder. Bent to kiss his head. Ashtamar trembled and wiped his eyes.

"Ashtamar, my faithful servant," Yahdun said. "You have done well for me on the Riverfront. And what Simaal has done is beyond excusing. I will deal with him. Have no doubt about that. But the justice you ask for, Ashtamar, is desert justice. It is the justice of barbarians."

Ashtamar burst into fresh tears.

"Look at me!" Yahdun snapped, causing them both to jump.

Ashtamar looked up into Yahdun's eyes, terrified.

"Justice will be done here. But I will not have men prowling the streets, pulling people from their homes, taking blood vengeance on the families of murderers. On their children. This is not civilized. We do not kill in the heat of anger. When we execute criminals, we do it calmly. Coldly. In public. In such a way that all the people can see we do it not from anger or pride, but because it is the law. This is the justice of the city.

This is the justice I will deliver to Simaal, and to whoever these men were who helped him. You have my word on this."

Nasir watched Ashtamar carefully. After a moment the man nodded, slowly, then stood and embraced Én Yahdun, kissing him on both cheeks.

Én Yahdun took Ashtamar's head in his hands, kissed him on the forehead, and gave him a little shake, as if to steady him.

"Be patient, Ashtamar," Yahdun said.

Ashtamar nodded mutely. Én Yahdun put his arm around the trembling man, and led him toward the door of the office.

When Ashtamar was gone and the door was closed, Én Yahdun took his place behind his desk, and steepled his fingers.

"How should we handle this, my son?" he asked Nasir.

Nasir shook his head. "It's disgusting," Nasir said. "The whole thing makes me sick."

Yahdun made a vague gesture, as if this went without saying. "This is part of living in a city. So many of us pressed up against each other. Akkadu people, Kalshu, Elamu, Amurru. Shuméru too, though they're rarer than they used to be. Who knows how many dozens of other tribes. There will always be disgusting people, doing sickening things."

"I don't want any part of it," Nasir said.

Yahdun raised his eyebrows. "You don't think Ashtamar deserves justice? You don't think his family does?"

Nasir stood, walked to the window, looked out over the awnings and the mud-brick and the pavement. Kids kicking a leather ball. A fancy woman gliding by in gold and purple, attended by guards.

"There's no way out, is there?" Nasir said. "One way or another, someone's going to kill someone because of this."

Yahdun nodded. "We thought we'd left the desert. But we brought it here with us."

Down in the street, a woman followed a trail of sandy footprints around a corner, catching a naked boy who'd run away in the middle of his bath.

"What if there were a way," Nasir said, "to find out exactly what happened?"

"But we know what happened," said Yahdun.

"But I'm talking about being absolutely sure," Nasir replied. "Who did it. When it was done. How it was done."

"And what would that accomplish?"

"We would bring the murderers to court," Nasir said. "We would read out their deeds before the people. We would punish them according to what they had done."

Yahdun stroked his beard and nodded slowly.

"No street vengeance," Nasir said. "No blood feuds. No killing of children."

"No killing of innocent men," said Yahdun.

"Exactly." Nasir nodded.

"It would need to be done quickly," Yahdun said. "Ashtamar won't wait long."

"I'll start tonight," Nasir said.

"Start now," said Yahdun. "Take a few men with you. Men you can trust."

Nasir embraced his father and hurried out of his office. In the reception room Nasir found Samsu, Yahdun's most trusted enforcer. Nasir explained the plan to him, rushing through the details but sketching the general outline as best he could.

"I'll start in the taverns," said Samsu. "Someone will be gossiping."

"We should take someone else," Nasir said. "Someone who understands the tongues they speak on the Riverfront."

The Cradle and the Sword

"I think Isidu is doing sums in the account room," Samsu said.

Nasir ran down the hall and burst into the account room. Isidu looked up from behind a tall stack of clay tablets on the desk, scratching his bald head with his reed stylus.

"Isidu," Nasir said, "Father and I need your help."

"I'm—I'm right in the middle of a land deed," he said slowly.

"Are you sure he's the best man for this job?" Samsu asked, coming up behind Nasir in the doorway, folding his muscled arms thoughtfully.

"I'm not sure any of them is the best man for this job," Nasir said.

"What job?" Isidu asked.

Nasir ran through the basic idea again.

Isidu scratched his long beard. "We'll want to start with the local busybodies," he said. "Anyone who likes to gossip."

"Good," Nasir said. "Samsu, head for the taverns, like you said. Isidu, let's start down at the Riverfront."

They parted ways at the front gate, agreeing to meet back home at sundown. Isidu and Nasir hurried through the tangled shadowy alleyways, past filthy children and dogs and women grinding grain, making their way to the marketplace by the river. They burst out into the sunlight and the overpowering smell of fish, pushing through the mass of people—Amurru people in long robes and striped headscarves, arguing the prices of fruit and sheep; Ashûru traders from the merchants' colony on the outskirts of the city, clad in splendid purples and blues, gold rings and plaited beards; dark-eyed Elamu-men laughing at a troupe of Kalshu acrobats in colorful pantaloons. A band of red-haired Khatti-men inspected bronze-tipped arrows.

Isidu and Nasir pushed through the crowd, looking for anyone local to the neighborhood. Everyone seemed to be from someplace else.

A little way off, Nasir caught sight of a tiny old woman in a brown robe standing beneath the shade of a brick arch, watching them. He tugged at Isidu's sleeve and pointed her out.

"Let's go talk to her," he said. Nasir looked at him. "As good a start as any." He shrugged.

She eyed them suspiciously from beneath a ragged shawl as they approached. It was mercifully cool down under this arch, but it smelled of dead fish and worse things. Two rats were fighting over a melon rind in the gutter.

"Do you speak Amurru?" Nasir asked the old woman.

No answer. She scratched her back, sniffed, and looked away.

"Akkadu? Elamu?" Nasir shook his head. "Shuméru?" he asked, half-jokingly.

She spat a dry, toothless laugh, and rattled off a long string of syllables: "*Agín shágzu gúrra, ímde nízu muésunsun.*"

Nasir felt the hair on his neck stand up. *Did she just speak fluent Shuméru?* Everyone knew there were still Shuméru people living in Babili—but their ancient language had lain in its grave for hundreds of years. Hadn't it? Except for temple rituals, and maybe scribal schools—

"Isidu, do you speak any Shuméru?" Nasir asked.

"I remember a little from school." Isidu shrugged. "I think she just called you arrogant."

"Tell her we just want to ask her a few questions," Nasir said.

Isidu addressed the old woman haltingly, one careful Shuméru syllable at a time.

She laughed in his face, shook her head, then turned to Nasir and said something very slowly, in the most condescending tone possible: "*Éne zuani, lutúr. A'ázu zuani.*"

"She says she knows who you are," Isidu said. "She says she knows your father."

"Who are you?" Nasir asked. Isidu translated.

The old woman cackled again and addressed Isidu in the same condescending tone. It went on for a while.

The Cradle and the Sword

"She says—" Isidu paused and nodded while the old woman threw in a few more words. "She says it doesn't matter who she is, but she knows why you're here. She says if you want to know who's making all the trouble on the Riverfront, it's no secret. It's the—how did you call them?" He asked her in Shuméru, and she snapped a response. "Right. The Hook Temple people."

Nasir looked at him. "What in the Gods' name does that mean? Hook Temple? What people?"

Isidu rushed to translate all this as best he could, but the old woman had already caught Nasir's tone. She laughed, coughed raucously, spat something thick and wet on the ground, barely missing his feet.

"She says—" The old woman added a few more words, and Isidu sighed. "Yes, all right. She says if you didn't spend so much time up in your fancy house, you'd know what's been happening on the Riverfront."

Nasir felt a sudden urge to scream at this old woman, or worse, but he held himself back. "If she would be so kind," Nasir said to Isidu, "as to please forgive my ignorance, and inform me what's been happening on the Riverfront."

Isidu did his best to translate this. He must've conveyed a fair idea of Nasir's tone, because the old woman looked at Nasir and laughed, wide-eyed. She explained something to Isidu, gesturing broadly at the marketplace around them.

"She says just look around you," Isidu said. "It's a mess down here. All these people, all these tongues. All these different Gods. Something like this was bound to happen sooner or later." He looked at Nasir and shrugged. "That's what she says."

"Yes, but what does she mean about this Hook place?" Nasir asked.

Isidu started to ask this, but the old woman drew herself up and shook her head abruptly, looking at something behind them. They turned to look, and saw a small group of men walking toward them, serious expressions on their faces. Nasir suddenly wished they'd brought Samsu, and about three other big men. When Nasir turned back to the old woman, she'd slipped away into the crowd.

The men were close now. Five of them. Dockworkers, probably. Knots of muscle and tattoos.

"We should go," Isidu said.

"No." Nasir shook his head.

He let the five of them approach. They didn't try to encircle him and Isidu but just stood between them and the marketplace. Nasir hoped that was a good sign.

"I know you," said the one in the front, evidently the leader.

He stood a head taller than Nasir. His greasy hair was pulled back, tied with a headscarf, and his beard hung long and thick to his chest. Atop his faded red robe was draped a leather apron spattered with dried blood and fat. An array of clean bronze knives were thrust through his belt. A butcher; Nasir didn't have to guess.

"That's what everyone's been telling me today," Nasir said. "I suppose you have me at an advantage."

The butcher nodded, looking around at his cohorts, as if Nasir had just said something he appreciated. "I suppose I do, son of Yahdun. I suppose I do."

"You have the pleasure," said the stocky one with the scarred face, "of addressing Simaal of the Western Clans. Who I recommend you address as '*sayid*.'"

"Very well, *sayid*," Nasir said to Simaal, keeping his tone just on the neutral side, "What can I do for you?"

"Is this what Én Yahdun sends?" asked the lanky one with the scraggly beard, and the sailor's tattoos of ocean waves and stars down his arms. "The heir and an errand-boy?" He barked a laugh, looking to the others for a reaction. "Honestly, who does he think he's dealing with?"

"That's what I was hoping you could tell me," Nasir said, looking Simaal in the eye.

Simaal spread his hands. "We have no secrets here." He reached back and prodded a young man forward. "This here's my son, Eshuh. He's training at one of those fancy temple schools. Knows how to read and write, don't you, boy?"

"I'm learning," said the boy, quietly. His head was shaved bald, as a temple acolyte's usually was, though he was too young to have to shave his first wisps of beard.

"Speak up, now," his father told him.

"I'm learning to read and write," Eshuh said, slightly louder.

Simaal patted the boy on his bald head. "But I took him out of school today. Brought him down here on the Riverfront to learn some of his father's trade."

"He doesn't need to be here for this," Nasir said.

Suddenly Simaal was in his face with a pointing finger. "I decide what my son needs to see," he snarled. "I, and no one else. Is that clear?" He grabbed Eshuh's chin and tilted it up to face him. "You watch this closely, boy."

"Yes, father," said Eshuh.

"As you wish, Simaal," Nasir said. "Do you represent the Hook Temple?"

Isidu whispered something nervous in his ear, but Nasir waved him away.

Simaal scratched his cheek and licked his lips, as if formulating an argument. "When you look around the Riverfront, *boy*," he said, emphasizing that last word, "What do you see?" He raised his eyebrows and looked at Nasir expectantly.

Nasir glanced out at the marketplace, immediately cursing himself for breaking the man's gaze in a moment like this. His father would've smacked him upside the head for that. He met the butcher's eyes again and said, "Commerce. Traffic. People from many lands and cultures."

Simaal nodded, as if Nasir had just said something intriguing. "So many lands and cultures. So many languages, and Gods. A babble. A confusion." He flicked his hand at each of these words, as if he were throwing them at Nasir. The men behind him were nodding in agreement.

"Babili is a big city," Nasir shrugged. "Someday it may be called the center of the world, the elders say."

"The center of the world." Simaal repeated, shaking his head. "The center of a sewer, more like. All the sewage flows downhill, doesn't it?"

"I'm not sure I follow," Nasir said, though he was fairly sure he did.

"What Simaal is saying," said the lanky sailor, "is that this place is full of lamis and horsebacks, and gugurs, and a dozen other breeds of animals from Gods-know-where."

So they don't like Elamu-men and Khatti-men. Or Shuméru people. Or any other race, apparently. Én Yahdun had ostensibly outlawed the public use of ethnic slurs, but how does one enforce that? Maybe everyone was spouting them down here.

Nasir decided to push his luck. "What does that have to do with Ashtamar and his family? They're Amurru, like us."

Simaal wore a thoughtful expression. "Were they?" he asked.

"Of course they were," Nasir said. *Is he all-but confessing to the crime, right here and now?*

"Tell me, son of Yahdun," Simaal said. "When an Amurru family abandons the worship of the true Gods," he paused, as if gathering his thoughts, "to worship these gugur animal gods—when their children stop speaking the Amurru tongue, to speak gugur slang, and when those children," he paused and drew a deep breath, "mix with these gugur children, making half-breed babies—after all that, can you really say they are still Amurru?"

Was that what this was about? Not the worshipping of Shuméru Gods, but—

"What half-breed babies?" Nasir asked.

Simaal laughed, looking around at his comrades, who chuckled with him. "Papa didn't tell you that part, did he?"

"The child they found in the river—?" Nasir asked.

"What did Ashtamar tell you? Did he tell you that was his full-blooded grandson? An Amurru child?" He glanced around angrily, as though looking for something to punch. "Lying snake."

"You're saying the baby was half-Shuméru." Nasir said, keeping his voice even.

Simaal looked at Nasir like he was stupid. "Yes, that's what happens when you let your slut daughter take a gugur boy to bed."

"And the daughter—?" Nasir pressed.

"That problem is solved now too," Simaal said flatly.

"But why the wife?" Nasir asked. "Why Ashtamar's wife, as well as the daughter?"

Simaal snorted. "Have you seen that woman? Flirting shamelessly with every gugur animal at every tavern on the Riverfront. How can you call that kind of woman a 'wife'?"

"I call her a whore, same as the daughter," said the sailor.

"And so, what, then?" Nasir said. "'Get rid of the children and the problem stops?' That's how the Hook Temple takes care of the Riverfront's families?"

Simaal's expression hardened. "The Hook Temple," he said, putting a finger in Nasir's face, "is none of your damned business. But those children had to go."

Nasir kept his expression neutral. "What's this Hook Temple?" Nasir asked. "A temple for the old Amurru Gods? Nobody's saying you can't worship them."

"You're damned right nobody's saying that," Simaal said. "Specially not around here."

"So why keep it a secret?" Nasir asked.

"I told you, *boy*," Simaal snapped. "We have no secrets."

"As you say." Nasir took a step back. "Then perhaps I'll stop by the Hook Temple sometime."

The sailor and a few of the others moved as if to make a grab at Nasir, but Simaal waved them down.

"I've got no quarrel with your father, boy," the butcher said. "You can tell him that. No bad blood between Én Yahdun and Simaal of the Western Clans." He stepped closer and looked Nasir deep in the eyes. "And you can visit the Temple any time you like." He pointed behind him. "We're there every night, praying to the true Gods. Just up the alley there, on Grain Street." He tapped a finger on Nasir's chest. "Coming inside, on the other hand," he said, "is a very different story."

"We'll see," Nasir said.

"No," Simaal said, "You won't."

He turned and clapped the sailor and the stocky one on their shoulders. "Gentlemen," he said, and they turned and strolled off into the crowd.

Nasir shook his head. "My father wouldn't be happy with that," he murmured. "Letting him get the better of me."

"I'd say you stood up pretty damned well," said Isidu, who Nasir had almost forgotten had been standing there the whole time.

"I have to say," Nasir said. "I wasn't sure what to expect, but I wasn't expecting a voluntary confession."

"In all but name," Isidu said, scratching his beard. "Shame I didn't have a tablet and stylus with me. I could've taken down his admission of guilt, and we could go to court right now."

Nasir coughed a laugh.

"So what now?" Isidu asked. "Get a glance at this Hook Temple?"

Nasir nodded. "If we can do it without looking too obvious. We've still got a few hours before sunset."

They strolled around the market, trying to look casual, which was always hard when one tried to do it purposefully. They questioned a few other people; in Amurru or Akkadu when they spoke it; Isidu doing his best with Elamu or Khatti when they didn't. A few times they had to give up on a sail-

The Cradle and the Sword

or or shopkeeper who didn't speak a word of any tongue they knew—or pretended not to, anyway.

Those willing to talk with them were surprisingly frank about some facts and frustratingly evasive on others. The Hook Temple was just around the corner, on Grain Street. Everyone agreed on that point. The Temple had been enacting justice on the Riverfront ever since Én Yahdun's men refused to take care of the problems. What problems? Too many different races here, obviously. A confusion of tongues. Mistrust, betrayal, lying, cheating, hatred. Outbursts of violence—unreported, of course, because Yahdun's men would prevent the enactment of real justice.

Strangely, though, no two people could seem to agree was which group was the problem. Most everyone hated the Shuméru, who were called "gugur," apparently because of the way their language sounded. The Shuméru and Akkadu families, oldest natives of Babili, feared the Amurru, whom they called desert savages, illiterate apes, killers, rapists. The Elamu lived in fear of the Amurru, too; but they also distrusted the Akkadu, who, they said, had rigged the city's markets and schools to put their own people at an advantage, and cheat all the other tribes out of an education.

And on the topic of the crime they were investigating, even the loosest tongues suddenly stopped moving, and talkative foreigners abruptly lost their ability to understand questions in any language.

ᛉ

AFTER A FEW hours of fruitless interrogating, Isidu suggested they make a pass by the Hook Temple before they went to meet

Samsu. The Temple was right where Simaal had said it would be; up the alley near the stone arch, on Grain Street. They walked past grain merchants, stall after stall of them in the shadows of mud-brick apartment blocks, their baskets and sackcloth bags overflowing with barley and wheat, their eyes watching the newcomers suspiciously as they passed. A few stray cats chased the mice that nibbled bits of spilled grain.

They came to an old stone doorway about halfway down the alley. No way to walk by it casually—everyone was staring at them now, and the alley was narrow. Above the doorframe, someone had carved a few lines of symbols in complex spike-and-slash writing.

"Can you read that?" Nasir asked Isidu.

Isidu squinted up at it, in the dim light of the alley. "Looks like Elamu writing," he said. "But it's not—" he broke off.

"Not what?"

"It's just a list of names. 'Sarpátinum, Nabu, Sín, Marutúk.'"

"The old Amurru Gods." Nasir gasped with recognition.

"Desert Gods," Isidu said quietly.

"How's that?"

Isidu shook his head. "Nothing. I've just always thought—"

A burly old man appeared opened the door and leered out, startling them. He snarled as they hurried away down the alley, taking the stares of grain-merchants and customers with them.

Once they were back in daylight and had caught their breath, they began pushing in the direction of the Moon Quarter and Én Yahdun's manor-house. They fought their way through the crowds and clamor, even louder now that sunset was approaching and the merchants' stalls would be closing soon.

After a long uphill push, they managed to escape the rush, and made their way onto quieter side streets. Nasir realized he was growing hungry.

"What was that you said about desert Gods?" Nasir asked Isidu as they walked, to take his mind off his stomach.

"Hmm?" Isidu shrugged. "Nothing important, really. It's just, I grew up here in Babili. I'm Akkadu, you know. From one of the old families. Grandson of the grandson of—you get the idea."

Nasir nodded for him to continue.

"I grew surrounded by all kinds of Gods. The old Shuméru Gods like Énlil and Énki, and Inanna, whom we Akkadu folk call Ishtar. Gods like Humban and Nahhunte, from Elam in the east, and who knows how many hundreds of little Gods in the rivers and the stones. Whenever new Gods came to Babili, our people made them part of the family."

"So this makes the Amurru—what, in this family? Wild uncles from the desert?" Nasir smiled. "Careful with your next words, Isidu."

He grinned. "What I was going to say is, every tribe of Gods have their own ways of solving problems. In the old stories, I mean. You know, Shuméru Gods tend to sort things out with trickery and sex, which I suppose is the most fun. In my family's tales, the Akkadu Gods love their noble contests and feats of strength. And with Amurru Gods—well, it's eye for an eye, mostly. Do to others what they did to you. Desert justice."

Nasir walked in silence for the space of several heartbeats, stroking his beard.

"I sometimes wonder if there's something to that," he said at last. "Desert justice."

Isidu's brow furrowed. "How do you mean?"

"I know what my father is trying to build here," said Nasir. "I've heard it all my life. All of us living together, cheek by jowl. Letting each tribe resolve its own problems in its own ways. This is how one keeps a city intact. So my father says."

"You don't sound so sure," Isidu said.

Nasir licked his lips. "I try hard to believe it," he said. "And then I talk to someone like Simaal, and..." He shook his head. "Something claws at me. A strange pride. To think that my ancestors in the desert were such fierce, proud people. Hard and sharp as bronze. Sometimes I feel... it sounds mad, but I feel as if it will erupt from me. From my very hands, against the confusion of this city."

He was trembling. Isidu put out a hand to steady him.

"Is it in my blood, Isidu?" he asked.

"If so," said Isidu after a moment, "then it is in your father's blood, too. And he has fought it."

"He has fought it with laws," Nasir replied. "With restraint and tolerance. And I wonder, is that enough? What the Hook Temple did to those children, it's…" His face contorted into a snarl. "It demands an answer, does it not?"

"Answering desert justice with more desert justice," Isidu said. "Before long, we'd all be living in tents again."

Nasir glared at him for a moment, then fell back against the wall, rubbing his face with his hands. "What are we to do, Isidu? What am I to do?"

Isidu thought for a moment, choosing his words with care. "Desert justice cannot be brought whole-cloth into the city," he said at last. "At least, not in the same ways it was applied in the desert. It sows terror and hatred. But that doesn't mean it can simply be stamped out, either. Attack it in anger, and it draws nourishment from the violence. Meet it with love, and it thrives on that, too."

Nasir threw up his hands. "So what do you suggest?"

Isidu's eyes grew wide and he shook his head. "They're here, and they're not going anywhere," he said. "And if they're going to stay—which they are—then they have to learn to accept their place in the family. Adapt a little. Learn that there are certain things one does not do in the city, regardless of what the old laws say. And the rest of the family, meanwhile, has to avoid stepping on the newcomers' toes. It's what we've been doing around here for as long as anyone can remember."

Nasir thought about that for a few moments.

"That's quite a speech," Nasir said. "For an accountant."

Isidu rolled his eyes.

They started walking again, in silence this time. They made their way through the winding alleys and tangled streets, back up the hill to Nasir's father's house. But as they asked the guards in each room, they found that no one had seen Samsu, their other agent, since this morning.

"He must be at one of the taverns," Isidu said.

The sun was setting now. They hurried down to Tavern Street, asked in at a few places, and finally found Samsu at a beer-house on the corner, slouched in a booth with his head hanging low over a big clay bowl full of sweet-beer.

"Good Gods, this is all we need right now," Isidu moaned.

Samsu looked up with an "Ehh?" He cast his gaze around blearily until it settled on Nasir and Isidu. "Where've you two been?" he asked, surprisingly clearly. "It's after sunset. I was getting bored."

"You were supposed to meet us back at the house," Nasir said. "Remember?"

Samsu chuckled like he'd just remembered something funny. "Oh, right," he said. "Well, anyway." He bent and sucked the reed straw in his bowl, gulping down more beer.

They sat down opposite him in the booth. A barmaid came over to ask what they wanted, but they waved her away.

"What did you find out?" Nasir asked in a low voice.

He laughed softly. "It was them all right," he said. "Simaal and that bunch. Everyone knows it."

"We know it too," Isidu said. "We ran into him down at the Riverfront and he bragged about it."

"What else did you find out?" Nasir asked.

Samsu raised his eyebrows and made a *hmm* sound. "Not much. Something about a temple. Fishing Temple or something."

"Hook Temple," Isidu said.

Samsu pointed a shaky finger. "That's the one."

"We know," said Isidu. "Is that really all you found out?"

Samsu spread his hands sarcastically. "Well I'm sorry I didn't have the good fortune to run into the murderer himself, when he happened to be in a mood to confess. Though I have to wonder why, in that case, he's not here in chains right now."

"There were five of them," Isidu said. "Two of us. What exactly were we supposed to do?"

"All right," Nasir said. "This isn't solving anything. We need a plan."

"I say we go back to the Hook Temple," Isidu said. "Tonight, when they won't be expecting it."

Samsu nodded. "Bring more men this time."

"Can't bring you, though, Samsu, can we?" Isidu said under his breath.

"I'll be just fine, thank you," Samsu said. "I'll go back and round up Kirku, Turum, a few of the big fellows." He sucked up the last of his beer and stumbled up from the table.

"Wait," Nasir said. "What happens when we get to the Hook Temple? We go in cracking heads, and Simaal and his crew—if they're even there at all—slip out the back door. No, we need something better."

They all sat and thought for a while. Samsu tried to wave down the barmaid for another beer, but Isidu stopped her from bringing it, and ordered cheese and bread for himself and Nasir. They sat and thought while they waited for the food to arrive.

"What if," Nasir said at last, "We grab someone on the way into the Temple? A regular. Rough him up a bit, talk him into going inside and lure them out. And we're there waiting for them with ten or twelve strong men, blocking their escape. No chance of escape. Grab them all at once."

Samsu was nodding slowly. "Could work," he said.

The barmaid brought a woven-reed board of rough brown bread and dry cheese, which Nasir and Isidu attacked with relish.

"A lot of ways for it to go wrong," Isidu said through a mouthful.

"Either of you have any better ideas?" Nasir asked. "Any way we might stand a good chance of catching them without putting our lives in immediate danger?"

The Cradle and the Sword

They thought for a while as they finished off the bread and cheese. At last, they all admitted they had no better plan than the one Nasir had proposed.

"Well then," Nasir said. "Let's go tell my father."

BACK AT ÉN Yahdun's house, Nasir and Isidu stood waiting outside the office door. At last it opened and a few headmen from the Hillside district strode out, eyeing Isidu suspiciously, but bowing slightly when they recognized Nasir. When they were gone, Nasir knocked on the doorframe and stepped into the office. His father looked up.

"The seekers return," said Yahdun, smiling tightly. "Come in."

He kissed both of Nasir's cheeks, and kissed Samsu and Isidu lightly on their foreheads. Samsu quietly closed the office door, and they settled into the chairs in front of the én's desk as Yahdun took a seat behind it.

"So," said the én. "What's the report?"

Nasir took a moment to gather his thoughts. "It was Simaal. He runs some kind of gang down on the Riverfront."

"That old fanatic," said Yahdun.

"You know him?" Nasir's eyes widened.

Yahdun sighed. "He's been causing trouble down by the docks since the day I arrived here in Babili. Back when he was just waist-high, he used to catch the little Elamu boys and girls, and beat them black and blue. For not being Amurru."

Nasir's face contorted in disgust. "Well now he's running a sect. The Hook Temple. Or working for it. We're looking into it."

"And what interest does the Hook Temple have in my friend Ashtamar, and in his wife and children?" Yahdun asked.

Nasir glanced at Isidu, whose face was unreadable.

"Ashtamar didn't tell us the whole story," Nasir said after a moment.

Yahdun gestured for his son to go on.

"What happened to his wife and daughter is real enough," Nasir said. "Simaal confessed to it, right on the Riverfront."

Yahdun's eyebrows went up. "You talked with him?"

"Truer to say he talked with me," Nasir said. "But yes."

"And he confessed to the crimes?" Yahdun asked.

Nasir nodded. "Yes—"

"Not in so many words, Én Yahdun," Isidu cut him off.

Yahdun turned to the scribe. "What exactly did he say?"

"He said the Hook Temple handled it," said Isidu.

"And he also said," Nasir added, "that the infant child wasn't Ashtamar's full-blooded grandson."

Yahdun nodded slowly. "Foreign blood," he said.

"Shuméru blood," Nasir said. "Babili blood."

Yahdun sighed and shook his head. "It makes me ill," he said, after a moment. "Not just the violence, but this—this proud ignorance. This lack of any desire to understand."

"Perhaps Simaal and his people feel they're the ones who aren't understood," said Isidu.

After a moment, Yahdun scratched his beard and said, "Maybe so. But this," he gestured around them. "This is not how understanding begins."

Isidu humphed and said, "No, this is how something else begins."

"What do you plan to do?" asked Yahdun.

"We'll go to the Hook Temple tonight," Nasir said. "A big group of us. Get hold of a priest—an acolyte. Whoever we can. Persuade him to lure the conspirators outside. Snatch them up and bring them here."

"And if your bait fails to be persuasive?" Yahdun asked.

"We'll just have to take that risk," Nasir said. "Unless you can suggest a more foolproof plan."

Yahdun shook his head. "Short of trapping them inside and setting a fire, no," he said. "And I'd prefer you not set a fire on Grain Street."

"I'd prefer to avoid that too," Nasir said, a bit shocked that such an option had crossed his father's mind so quickly, when it hadn't crossed his own at all. Here was a man, Nasir reminded himself, who had clawed his way up from utter poverty, killed off all the local bosses, and established a grip on every neighborhood here in Babili. He was a kind father; but he was also—to many—the most terrifying man in the city.

"Good," Yahdun nodded. "Take Turum and the others. They're loafing around here somewhere, probably playing dice. Hopefully they're not too drunk."

"Just one final question, Father," said Nasir.

Yahdun looked at him expectantly.

"I didn't mention that the Temple was on Grain Street," he said. "How did you know that's where it is?"

Yahdun smiled. "You've got a sharp ear, my son."

Isidu looked at Samsu, then at Yahdun. Something silent was passing between them.

"That place has been there a long time," Yahdun said after a moment.

"You mean Simaal isn't the one running it?" Nasir asked.

"Oh, I'm sure Simaal is behind these particular crimes," Yahdun said. "They have his scent all over them. But the Temple—oh, that goes back to my childhood days, or further. The first Amurru in this city. A safe place for savage old Gods."

"'Sarpátinum, Nabu, Sín, Marutúk,'" Isidu quoted.

"That's them," Yahdun agreed.

"Why didn't you destroy it, then?" Nasir asked. "When you were putting an end to everything with the bosses, and the old practices?"

"Destroy the Hook Temple?" he asked. "You misunderstand, my son. The Hook Temple isn't a building. It's not a place. It's a sect. A set of beliefs—a creed." He sighed. "By any road, I thought they were gone. I burned down the last one, back when you were a boy. But I can't burn down ideas."

"But you can arrest the people who carry them out," Nasir said. "Bring them to justice."

"Some of them, yes," Yahdun said. "These men, for sure. These men, you will catch, tonight. But the Hook Temple? Every time I think it's gone, it comes back. Members die and they recruit new ones. Attack in new ways." He sighed again. "And besides," he said. "I have a feeling that even if they somehow wiped the whole sect out, something even worse might rise to take its place."

"That's a grim view of humanity," Nasir said.

"It's a grim view of the worst in us," Yahdun replied. "Which is, I think, a reasonable one."

Nasir found he had no response for that.

"Well," Yahdun said at last, "only so many hours in the night."

Nasir and Isidu rose from their chairs. Én Yahdun kissed their cheeks and heads, and muttered a blessing over them.

As the door closed behind them, they split up to track down as many trustworthy fighters as they could find around the house. Nasir located two low-level enforcers in the kitchen, flirting with a slave-girl. He'd worked with both of them on small jobs where a bit of violence had been required, and knew them both to be quick with a knife. Isidu managed to find two of his own, and insisted on coming along, himself.

Samsu, for his part, returned five muscled, face-scarred thugs he said he'd fought with before.

"Turum here gave me this," he said, nodding at a sneering fellow in a stained green tunic, and tracing a puckered scar on his arm.

"Back before he worked for your father, of course," Turum added.

That made twelve of them, all told. They'd have to suffice.

▼▼▼
▼▼▼

THEY MARCHED DOWN to the Riverfront, all twelve of them in a tight clump, none of them looking particularly friendly. Children scurried into the shadows, then crept out to follow them at a safe distance. Merchants and wives closed their shutters. Men eyed them suspiciously.

Perhaps word has already spread, Nasir thought grimly. After his talk with Simaal this afternoon, and then his visit to the Temple, of course everyone on the Riverfront would be chattering. Nasir cursed himself silently, wishing he'd thought about that earlier. Too late now. Simaal and everyone at the Hook Temple must be preparing for them even now. Or if they weren't already, someone was surely running to tell them.

"They'll be expecting us," Isidu whispered, as if reading Nasir's thoughts.

"And if we don't strike tonight," Nasir replied, "Ashtamar and his friends will. I promise you that. Then we'd have a blood feud on our hands."

"Maybe so," Isidu said. "I still wish we'd had more time to plan."

"And what could we have done differently?" Nasir shot back, looking Isidu in the eye. "Other than hesitate and waste time we'll never get back?"

Isidu looked at him strangely, then shook his head. "Let's just be done with this," he said at last.

By then they'd reached the edges of the Riverfront market. All the stalls were closed for the night, their goods carted away to safe places and thick sackcloth blankets tied over the awnings. Rats ran in the gutters, chased by scrawny cats.

They made their way down to Grain Street. No grain-sellers around at this hour, though someone slammed shutters closed as they approached.

The group halted at the entrance to the alley. Nasir peeked down the narrow corridor between the mud-brick apartments. Dim reddish light fanned out onto the street from the doorway of the Hook Temple. A man and two women were loitering outside, talking quietly in excited tones.

"I'd be the bait, but they'd recognize me," Nasir said. "And Isidu too, most likely." He turned to Samsu's friend with the green tunic. "Turum," he said. "Take one other man you trust, and get them to let you inside the Temple. Lure Simaal and his crew out the back if you can. We'll be waiting for them. If not, come back and tell us what you saw."

Turum nodded, grabbed the arm of a heavily scarred man with a short black beard, and headed up the alley toward the glowing light.

Nasir left Samsu and two more of the men near the entrance to Grain Street, out of sight but in a good position to catch sight of anyone coming back the way they'd come. They'd catch anyone who tried to slip out the Temple's front entrance.

That left eight of them, including Isidu and Nasir. Nasir led them around to the other side of the apartment block, where they found the tiny side-alley that led out from the back of the Temple.

Not a single person walked the street. Not even a stray cat. They sat on empty wood boxes and waited.

A long time passed. They heard nothing from the side-alley.

Nasir sent one of the men around to Grain Street. He didn't come back.

"They're taking them one by one," Isidu said.

For a moment, Nasir had the sickening feeling that he'd lost his bearings. Should he run home with the men he had left, gather up a larger force, barricade everyone inside the Temple and set it ablaze? Or should they charge in now, the seven of them who were left?

Just then, Samsu came stumbling out of the side-alley, naked, covered in bruises and blood-caked cuts, gasping for breath. His left arm looked broken. So did some of his ribs.

"Gods above," snarled one of the men, as they all leaped up and hands went to daggers.

"Quick," said Samsu. "They think I'm dead. Or too hurt to move."

"What happened?" Nasir demanded.

"We waited a long time, me and Kirku," he said. "When Turum and Eru didn't come back, we slipped up Grain Street to see what'd happened. That was when they jumped out and took us."

"Who?" Nasir asked. "Simaal's crew?"

He shook his head. "I'm not sure. They were too quick. All wearing these masks, painted red."

"How many?"

"At least six," he said. "And more inside. Maybe fifteen, twenty men. Turum saw women, too."

"Shit," someone said.

"Beat me till I blacked out," Samsu said. "When I woke up, I heard screams. I think they're—ah, Gods, I think they're sacrificing them."

Nasir was already moving up the side-alley, Isidu and the others behind him. "Stay here," Nasir told Samsu. "You're too hurt to fight."

"Fuck that," Samsu said, falling into step behind them. "Those are my friends in there."

The side-alley was dark, but it was a short way to the back door. One of the men kicked it down, and flickering red light poured out onto them.

The fighters inside were waiting.

The man who'd kicked down the door—Nasir never learned his name—caught an axe blow to the face. He went down with a grunt and lay still.

The next two were already leaping over his body, daggers out, stabbing expertly at the shirtless men in red wooden masks, bodies painted in angular red designs. The one with the axe went down, blood pouring from his chest and stomach. Another caught a blade in the leg, dropped his dagger, fell to one knee. Nasir lopped his head off with a single stroke, spattering blood on the mud-brick walls.

But more were coming. Nasir backed up against the blood-stained wall, letting Samsu and the other fighters fan in around him.

Samsu took a dagger and an axe from the dead men. "Come get me, you bastards," he snarled, naked and blood-drenched in the doorway.

Two more of them came through the door, too quick to stop—all in red wood masks, half-naked, painted in strange patterns of shapes and lines. As they clashed with them, Nasir heard a scream next to him and turned; another three redmasks had come in the back way, from the side alley. One of Nasir's men was already down. Just six of them still standing now. More were coming.

They fought like wild beasts. Like lions in a trap. Samsu hacked and stabbed and parried with two of them at once, screaming like a madman, sending them stumbling back clutching severed arms and bleeding stomachs. Isidu dodged and slashed with a long dagger, getting in some hits, but taking more. They backed him up against the wall.

Nasir tried to fight his way to Isidu, but three of the woodmasked men had surrounded him. Someone grabbed Nasir from behind, pinned his arm behind his back, and took his dagger. He lashed out with naked fists.

Something hard hit him on the head and he fell, black mist at the edges of his sight.

Then nothing.

The Cradle and the Sword

NASIR WOKE WITH an aching head. He tried to lift his arm to touch it, but the arm wouldn't move. He opened his eyes, tried to look down at his arm, and couldn't. He felt ropes tight against his forehead, around his wrists and ankles. He was tied to something hard and splintery. He was naked, a sack over his head, letting in only pinpoints of reddish light.

Someone came close, lifted up the bottom of the sack, forced his mouth open, poured something bitter down it. Nasir choked and spluttered, but fingers gripped his nose tightly until he swallowed. Then the fingers released, and Nasir sucked in breaths of stale, humid air.

"Do you know why you are here?" asked a voice.

Someone ripped the sack from Nasir's head. He saw blank mud-brick walls lit by dim firelight. A few red-masked, painted men and women standing a safe distance away. Some holding drums. Others holding hooks—the kind fishmongers and grain-farmers used.

The voice's owner stepped into view. He wore a wood mask like the others, but painted yellow instead of red, and a long robe dyed the color of saffron. Atop his head towered a pointed crown of polished tamarisk-wood, flecked with gold.

"I asked," said the man in yellow, "if you know why you are here, son of Yahdun."

"I'm here because you murdered an innocent girl, and her child," Nasir said. "Raped an innocent man's wife. I look forward to dying here. My father won't stop until you and everyone you love are dead."

"A bold prediction, son of Yahdun," he said.

"Take off the mask, Simaal," Nasir said.

"Simaal?" he asked, puzzled. "Simaal is right here."

The butcher strolled into view before Nasir, half-naked and red-painted. He lifted off his mask so Nasir could see it was him, then returned it to place. Beside him stood a small masked figure: his son, Eshuh.

"In any case," said the yellow-robed one, "Your response is incorrect. You are here not for any reason of your own, but because the old Gods brought you here."

"Sarpátinum, Nabu, Sín, Marutúk," chanted voices all around Nasir.

"Damn your Gods," Nasir heard Samsu shout from behind Nasir, clearly in pain.

"Our Gods?" said the yellow-robed one. "What a strange way of putting it. For they are your Gods too, of course. The true Gods of the Amurru. The supreme Gods of the desert, and of the world."

"They're not the Gods of this city," Nasir said, trying to keep his voice calm. "This kind of savagery is outlawed here. And once my father hunts you down, this barbarism will die with you."

"This 'barbarism,' as you call our faith, will never die," the one in yellow answered calmly. "You, on the other hand, will die here, tonight. But before you die, you will see the Gods of your ancestors—of *our* ancestors—and you will know they are the true Gods."

"Is that why you forced your drug down my throat?" Nasir laughed. "So I'll dream your desert Gods? These Gods who kill women and infants? I'll never worship such Gods, not even if they dance before my eyes."

"Oh, you'll worship them," said the yellow-robed one. "For to sacrifice yourself to them, body and mind, is the supreme act of worship."

He spread his hands, and drums began to beat all around them. Someone lit a fire behind Nasir's back. Nasir felt the heat begin to sear the backs of his legs and arms, even through the board he was tied to.

Samsu was screaming again. Nasir also heard Isidu's voice shouting blasphemies and threats, and the voices of a few others. It sounded like only about four of them had survived, all tied up, back to back, around this bonfire.

The yellow-robed one was chanting in a dialect Nasir didn't know; some dead speech of the desert. The drumbeats intensified, and now the others were chanting too. The room hummed with their voices. The fire was growing hotter.

As the yellow-robed one finished his chant, he approached Nasir, mask close to his face. Nasir could see his eyes behind the mask's hollow ones. Deep black-brown eyes, sharp and focused.

"Now, son of Yahdun," he said quietly. "It is time to meet the true Gods."

SHARP PAIN ERUPTED in Nasir's stomach. The yellow-robed man was twisting something inside it. Warm blood ran down his abdomen and down his legs. Nasir forced himself not to cry out. The man twisted the hook again.

Behind Nasir, Samsu and the others were crying out too. Fresh screams every few moments.

Nasir's vision swam. The yellow-robed one looked into his eyes. Twisted the hook. Hot flames licked against Nasir's legs and back, searing his skin. Strange colors and shapes were forming in the shadows behind him.

"Do you see the Gods, son of Yahdun?" the man in yellow whispered.

"I only see a dead man," Nasir snarled.

Suddenly the man in yellow yanked out the hook and stepped away. Someone stepped in from the side and threw a sack over Nasir's head again. Everything went dark.

And there in the blackness, amid the drumbeats and the chanting and the pain, the swimming shapes and colors began to take on form.

Nasir felt as if he were sinking into the ground, down below the mud-brick buildings and the pavement, into deep many-pillared caves far beneath the earth. Halls that extended for countless leagues beneath desert and city alike, catacombs with steps leading ever downward into buried vaults where no light from above penetrated and no man had ever walked.

Downward he sank into those vaults, and into the vaults beneath them, until he lost all sense of time and space. Until he reached a chamber deeper than all the rest, where he heard strange drumbeats and looked out into the shadows among the towering stone pillars. A procession was approaching.

He shrieked and tried to turn away, but he had no head to turn or eyes to close in this place. He was powerless to move, or to do anything but watch as they shuffled closer, these things that had once been men and women but had long ago grown dry and desiccated. Remains that should not have been able to walk, that shambled even as they fell apart, along the endless floor of the vault—dozens of them, hundreds, in lines that stretched away as far as he could see, all converging on a great circular pit in the center of the chamber.

It was as if he were above the pit, looking down into it now. Nasir saw that as even it plunged deeper into the earth, it somehow looked out upon the sky—a sprawling desert sky, full of stars but empty of moon or clouds. In the depths of that great pit, among the cold stars, forms coalesced and took shape—forms made of desert snakes and crawling scorpions, bleached bones and gnashing teeth and the wings and heads and blood-stained beaks of vultures; all grasping and stinging and devouring one another as they put out squirming feelers and shapes like arms and heads, rolling and twitching and pulsing in that deep among the stars.

The things turned to look at Nasir, though they had no eyes. He felt them gazing into him. Seeing the desert, the same things they were made of, within his heart. He felt those things—bones and scorpions and vultures—stirring in his belly, and knew they had always been there. They gnawed him from the inside, churning and clutching in anticipation, carrying him up toward those stars, deeper into the pit—

Nasir screamed, though he had no lungs or mouth. He screamed with his whole being; a wail of terror and rage.

The pit and the stars and the vaults fell away; the pillars beneath the earth shaking free of their foundations. Dim firelight flooded back in, and he realized he was screaming, there in the Hook Temple with the sack over his head and the fire searing his back. He screamed again and drew a deep breath, then screamed again, each new howl pumping fresh blood down his belly and legs.

Behind Nasir, Samsu was screaming too, even louder. With a roar that seemed to shake the stones, Nasir heard the powerful man strain until he tore the ropes that bound him. A gasp went up from the worshippers. The drumming stopped.

Samsu roared again, and Nasir heard him tear his other hand free from the board. Something clattered in the fire behind Nasir, and he saw an explosion of sparks and coals fly across the room, burning the men and women who cringed against the wall.

"Samsu!" Nasir shouted, and suddenly the big man was next to Nasir, cutting the ropes that bound his hands and feet. Nasir stepped away from the fire and turned to face him.

Half of Samsu's face was a wreckage of blood and cuts. He seemed to be missing an eye. Blood pumped even now from a deep, wide gash in his abdomen. In the instant in which Nasir took all this in, the huge man was already at the fire again with his board, scooping up great piles of coals and flames, hurling them around the room in blind rage. His howls sounded inhuman. Mad.

The colors still swirled from the drug, and the edges of Nasir's vision swam, but he turned to the fire with a board and imitated Samsu, scooping up flames and flinging them at everyone who approached. Smoke poured upward through an opening in the roof.

Flames were leaping up all around them now. People were fleeing, screaming, garments ablaze. Smoke poured up around his nose and mouth and into his eyes. Red-masked men were trying to reach them with hooks, but the fire was out of control now. Nasir looked for the yellow-robed one, but he was gone.

Nasir pushed through the blaze to the place where Isidu and the other man were tied up, but they were both unconscious, eyes closed, heads slumped on chests. He found a knife on the floor and cut Isidu free. Samsu was doing the same to the other man, a burly fighter whose name Nasir had forgotten. Nasir lifted Isidu over his shoulder and pushed toward for the back door. Samsu tried to heft the other man over his own shoulder, but a gout of blood poured from his stomach, and he collapsed on the floor with a grunt.

The smoke was choking them. Nasir carried Isidu out the door, through a few tiny rooms where they met no resistance, and out through the side-alley. He lay the scribe upright against the wall, and tried to run back inside for Samsu and the other fighter, but the fire seared his face, and smoke sent him coughing back out into the side-alley again.

"Isidu," Nasir repeated the scribe's name, slapping his face, shaking him, but no response. He shook him, hard, a few more times, but nothing. No breath from his mouth. No pulse in his veins.

Something else had to be done here. But there was nothing left to do. He'd failed.

He heard movement at the entrance to the alley, and glanced up, expecting to see red-robed men and women with hooks in hand. Instead, he saw a small knot of scarred, thick-muscled fighters in tunics and headscarves. He blinked through the smoke, hardly able to believe his eyes. These were his father's most trusted men. The ones who guarded the inner sanctum of the house atop the hill.

Silently, one of them put out a scar-hatched hand, and helped Nasir to his feet.

"Isidu." Nasir coughed, pointing back at his fallen companion. "We have to—"

"No time," the man grunted. The others took up positions around the burning alley, sharp eyes scanning for any threat.

A great wail went up from Nasir's throat, and he felt himself collapsing again. "Eleven good men are dead in there!" he cried. "Killed for no good reason, except..." He trailed off, gasping for breath. "It should've been me. I should've been the one..."

"Enough," grunted his father's fighter.

The scarred man ripped a robe from one of the fallen bodies and threw it around Nasir's shoulders, then took him roughly by the arm and pulled him out of the mouth of the alley. Even as they left the place behind, Nasir glanced back to see the Hook Temple's roof collapsing in a shower of smoke and flame.

His father's fighting-men marched him up the market street, then through the empty markets of Riverfront, sending cats and rats fleeing as they rounded each corner. The pain from the wound in his belly was burning now. It was hard to breathe. He ignored it and kept marching, through blocks of closed stores and shuttered apartments, up to Hillside, through the gates of his father's great house, past stunned guards who parted to let them pass.

It was only when he reached the house's entryway that Nasir looked down at himself. He was naked, apart from the cloth around his shoulders. Covered in blood and bruises. A seeping wound in his abdomen. He collapsed on a couch in one of the sitting rooms. The swimming colors came back again, but he fought them away, even as he felt blackness pressing in at the edges of his vision.

ᵞᵞᵞ
ᵞᵞᵞ
ᵞᵞᵞ

Nasir woke in daylight, lying somewhere soft. He reached up to touch his head and felt bandages there. Bandages around his abdomen. Everything clean and white.

Thoughts of Isidu and Samsu flooded back to him. The fire-lit room. The red-masked men and women. The one in the yellow robe. Tears rose behind his eyes. Even this sunlit room seemed swathed in shadow.

Én Yahdun came in to check on his son when the sun was at its peak. Nasir sat up to greet his father, wincing with pain. The én waved at him to lie still.

"The physician says your wounds will heal," Yahdun said, taking a seat on the bed next to his son. "If you don't move about too much. That means you're staying in bed until he says otherwise."

"Did you find the others?" Nasir asked.

"Samsu and Isidu, and the rest?" Yahdun said. He shook his head. "It's all ash now, my son. Most of Grain Street. Took the locals all night to put the fire out."

"And the Hook Temple?" Nasir asked.

Yahdun inclined his head. "Moved on to some other back alley of the Riverfront, I'd say."

"But I saw so many of them die..." Nasir trailed off.

"All of them?" Yahdun asked.

"Not all," Nasir admitted. "There was one—a man in a yellow robe. He slipped away during the fighting."

Yahdun nodded. "And even if that man died," he said, "another would wear the yellow."

A strange thought came to Nasir. "Father," he said.

Yahdun looked into his son's eyes, waiting.

"You were once part of it," Nasir said. "The Hook Temple."

Yahdun scratched his beard. "My father was. Wanted me to be."

Nasir nodded. "But you refused."

Yahdun drew a deep breath, let out a long sigh. "He took me along with him one night. It wasn't by the Riverfront back then. Most of the Amurru still lived out in the slums. The Temple lit their fire in a trash dump, at the edge of the city."

The én paused for the space of a few heartbeats, gathering his thoughts. "My father insisted I come along one night," he continued after a moment. Then he paused again and shook his head. "No, that isn't true. I wanted to go. Strange how a father's beliefs always seem right at the time. How his ways seem like the right ways."

Nasir thought back to what he'd said to Isidu in the alley. He wanted to tell his father what he'd told the scribe. How hard he sometimes found it to believe in the patient, tolerant justice of the city. How he sometimes felt a strange pride at the hard sharp fierceness of the desert, clawing up from a place deep within him. The thrill he'd felt when that sharpness erupted from his hands in the smoke-choked darkness of the Hook Temple. But at this moment, the words would not come.

"There was a sacrifice that night," his father was saying. "An Elamu boy of no more than ten summers. He screamed when they put the hooks in and he saw the desert Gods. My father made me watch. Wouldn't let me turn away. Then he made me drink the draught, too."

"You saw..." Nasir's eyes widened.

"I don't know what I saw," Yahdun said. "To this day, I don't know. I try not to think about it. But I never want to see it again. I never wanted you to see it, either."

Nasir's brow furrowed. "But you let me go to the Temple anyway. You let me take eleven men to their deaths—"

"The deaths of those men are on *your* head, my son." Yahdun fixed Nasir with a hard gaze. "Don't you ever forget it. You made the plan. You took the men. Remember what they did for you."

Nasir's eyes fell. For a long time, he sat in silence, drawing shallow, trembling breaths.

"You knew my plan would fail," he said at last, in a quiet voice.

"I didn't know they'd put the hooks in you, make you drink the draught," Yahdun said. "Some things, not even an én can foresee."

"But you sent those men to get me out," Nasir persisted. "To make sure the Temple burned."

"The Temple was going to burn, one way or another," Yahdun said.

They sat in silence for a while.

After a time, Nasir said, "I felt something, when the drug took me."

Yahdun's eyebrows rose. "Hmm?"

"I was screaming," Nasir said. "Terrified, at these—these things. Whatever they were. Desert things. In the pit. In the sky. And I felt," Nasir stopped, tried to wet my lips with a dry tongue. "I felt things like them, inside me. Like they'd always been there. Trying to come out."

The én nodded slowly.

Nasir felt hot tears welling up in his eyes. "I know it's not right. Those things have no place in a city. No place in an én's son."

Yahdun stroked his beard, thinking. At last he said, "Those things are in all of us, I think. When we pretend they are not, we throw cover over the traps our minds lay for us. We leave ourselves vulnerable to the very disease to which we claim we are immune."

Nasir didn't know what to say to that. Én Yahdun bent and kissed the top of his son's head.

"Bless you, my son," he said. "Bless you for staying alive, and for coming back to me."

The Cradle and the Sword

"What will happen to Simaal and the others?" Nasir asked.

"If they're not dead, they soon will be," said Yahdun. "I've got every man in five districts hunting him down."

"But after all you've said, about city justice—?"

"That man tried to kill my son," said Én Yahdun. "He killed children. He'll face whatever kind of justice I choose." Yahdun kissed the top of his son's head again. "And he tried to kill something even greater."

"You mean this city," Nasir said. "What we're building here."

Én Yahdun looked at Nasir for a long time. At last he sighed. "The world is full of great cities. Sacred places with famous temples and histories. But here in Babili we have everything. Do you understand? Every sort of people. Every art and idea since the creation of the earth, all in one place. This could be more than just a city. It is like a—a cradle, in which a new kind of world begins to grow. Imagine it," he whispered. "A thousand years from now, poets still singing of Babili."

Nasir smiled slightly. "It is a good dream, Father. But as you say, here in Babili we have everything. The noblest and the most savage. We may tear ourselves apart before those songs have a chance to be written. Or—"

Yahdun looked at his son inquiringly, gesturing for him to finish.

"Or when they sing our name a thousand years from now," Nasir said, "it may not be for reasons we'd like."

Én Yahdun nodded slowly, stroking his beard. At last he rose from the bed, kissed his son's head one last time, told him to get some rest, and left to take care of other business.

Nasir lay in that bed for the next three days, drinking water, eating meat, regaining strength. During the day he'd talk with his father from time to time, and with other men who eyed him suspiciously, and told him they forgave him for the deaths of their friends. But their eyes told him they did not mean what they said.

At night, though, Nasir mostly fought off sleep. Whenever he slipped down into dreams, it was as if he was slipping downward into those vaults beneath the earth again, and he heard strange voices chanting and calling out to him, and saw movement at the edges of his vision; and though he always covered his eyes and turned his head away, he knew that if he dared to look, he would see them again, those desert things among the stars, and things in him would cry out to join them.

When he felt he could resist no longer, and the crawling desert things were pressing inward, clutching at his eyes and heart, he would scream and howl until he woke panting in the moonlight, covered in sweat. And he would try to tell himself that none of it was real; that those things could not be waiting inside him, hungry for the chance to burst forth.

That was what he kept telling himself. But in his heart, he was never sure he believed it.

209 YEARS EARLIER
1991 BC

Tree planted in the Abzu,
Rising over all lands
In hollows in the hearts of hills,
In green places unvisited by man...

— Énki and the World Order

When the god-king's messenger came for Nisaba, she was lying on the grassy shore of the great Slow River, watching the sun set behind the distant palm trees and mud-brick shacks on the horizon.

The river's deep blue water scarcely seemed to stir beneath the reddening sky. Out among the muddy waves, Nisaba caught glimpses of the gleaming scales of great river-carp, revered since the most ancient days as sages of the deep, attendants and messengers of the God Énki himself, keeping their own silent counsel. Only a soft, warm wind whistled at this hour, when the last of the day's barques and rowboats lazily sailed for home, and evening birds descended to hunt for singing insects amid the tall rushes of the riverbanks.

Nisaba was remembering a discovery she'd made one afternoon when she was a child; a discovery she'd told no one about—not even her beloved Amnanu—of a tiny door in the wall behind her family's house. The door was scarcely big enough for her to squeeze through, but she pushed it open as wide as she could, and managed to slide through the opening. On the other side she found a garden where all the plants glimmered with lapis lazuli and carnelian and emerald and amber, and strange birds sang haunting songs in human speech. Even as she gazed wide-eyed at these marvels, she felt sure that if she ever left this place, she was never like to find it again. All the same, she had to share it with someone. She scrambled back through the door and ran to tell her mother, but when she returned to the place where the door had been, she found only a tangle of vines with solid wall behind them.

Nisaba never found that door again—and as time went by, she came to believe she'd imagined the whole episode. Still, her memory of the garden was vivid, one of those strange childhood recollections that one can never quite get out of one's mind.

The messenger boy coughed behind her, startling her back to the present.

"How in the world did you find me here?" she asked him, sitting up, brushing grass off the folds of the toga draped about her thin arms.

The boy, panting with exertion, said, "Ishme said you liked to come here and watch the sunset."

She rose to her feet, sighing. "Ah, yes. The royal vizier makes it his business to know mine, doesn't he?"

The messenger only shrugged. "If you'll follow me, your ladyship?"

Nisaba laughed. "Ladyship?"

The boy cocked his head, furrowing his brow in confusion. "Aren't you a lady of the court?"

"Do I look like a lady to you?" she asked him.

He shrugged again.

Nisaba snorted. "I'm a scribe," she said. "Well, a poet."

The boy's eyes widened.

"Well, come on, then," Nisaba told him. "Let's go see what his majesty has to say."

She turned as she rose, facing the tall brick walls of the city of Urim: barriers of baked mud the color of bone, stretching to the horizons, severing the wilderness from the city; their flat expanse interrupted only by crenellated towers where guards in round copper helmets scanned the grassy banks of the river, and the farm-plains beyond. As Nisaba and the messenger boy passed under the great stone gate back into Urim, she had the strange sense of leaving something behind.

The boy, for his part, had little else to say throughout their long walk through the maze of Urim's streets, beneath the awnings of market stalls packing away the last of the day's fish and bread; past troupes of acrobats and musicians folding up their mats and instrument-cases as the crowds dispersed homeward; along the polished, palm-tree-lined flagstone avenues of the city's finer neighborhoods, where the mud-brick buildings were plastered in finer white, painted with fanciful geometric designs in red and black; where coiffed poets and bureaucrats in long linen togas paraded with their ladies, in search of an evening's diversion at the theater, or the manor of a wealthier friend.

She parted ways with the little messenger when she passed through the towering inner gate of the palace, through the open-roofed royal gardens with their sprawl of vines and flower-bushes entwined around date-palms and cedars; through corridors lined with colorfully glazed bas-reliefs of priests and gods in conversation, to a vast doorway guarded by two stern-looking soldiers in traditional sheepskin kilts and leopard-skin cloaks. They crossed their spears before the doorway as she moved to enter.

"Stop that nonsense and let her through," called a voice from deep within the lamp-lit room beyond.

The guards uncrossed their spears, admitting Nisaba into the sweet-scented vastness of the royal dining-hall. The gazes of thirty or more noblemen and women locked onto her as she strode toward the king, along an ornately carved cedar table set with roast fowl and fish, baked dates stuffed with almonds and pistachios, honeyed apples and pears, barley-cakes and flatbread, and innumerable golden flagons of beer and wine. Sandalwood and myrrh smoked in braziers around the table. In the hall's far corner, a group of young women in white tunics stroked a gentle melody from their lyres.

At the head of the table sat the royal person himself, Shúlgi of Urim, God-King of the Third Dynasty of the Second Shuméru Empire, his long black beard trimmed square, plaited and clasped with gold; his head shaved shiningly bald like that of a priest, his divine person draped in a one-shouldered toga of emerald-dyed linen, fringed in white, embroidered with intricate floral patterns in fine gold thread. Jeweled rings of gold and silver glimmered on his hand as he raised it for her to kiss.

"My favorite poet!" the god-king smiled gently. "Come, sit." He made a "get up" gesture at the fat nobleman who sat nearest him—a duke named Etum or Etirum, Nisaba seemed to remember.

The duke rose from his gilded chair with a barely disguised grumble, brushing back the ringlets of black hair that encircled his plump face. "My dear Nisaba," the man remarked in the driest tone imaginable. "How lovely to see you."

As the duke shuffled off in search of a more welcoming table-companion, Nisaba took her seat next to the god-king, offering him her most polite smile. On the god-king's other side sat Ishme, the royal vizier, his thin face motionless as stone as he watched her from beneath his bushy brows.

"We have read your latest piece, Nisaba," said the god-king, "and we find it to be your most beautiful work to date. Several of our most lettered barons have also read it, and their opinion is the same."

Shúlgi glanced down the table at a few smiling noblemen and women, who nodded in agreement.

"That's very kind of you, Majesty," said Nisaba.

"What was it you remarked to us, Lady Belessunu?" the god-king asked a woman sitting a few chairs down. "Something about 'utter honesty'?"

"Quite so, Sublime One," replied Lady Belessunu, favoring Nisaba with an eager smile. "Nisaba, your characters speak just as ordinary people do. Why, I could have sworn some of your dialogue came straight out of my own life."

Nisaba smiled. "Have you much occasion to speak with ordinary people, Lady Belessunu?"

A tense hush fell over the table. Some of the nobles actually froze, morsels of food halfway to their mouths.

Shúlgi threw back his head and guffawed, filling the room with deep laughter. All the nobles joined in. "Utter honesty!" the god-king wheezed, wiping a tear from his cheek. "Just as we said. We expect nothing less from our most treasured poetess."

Nisaba smiled politely.

"Oh!" Shúlgi exclaimed suddenly. "You must forgive our atrocious manners." He snapped his fingers at a troupe of nearby serving-slaves. "Plates of fowl and fruit for our poetess, at once. And wine. Or beer? Would you prefer sweet-beer?"

"Wine would be lovely," Nisaba replied, as the slaves served her heaping plates of spiced duck, apples and pears and dates and a variety of steaming breads, and replaced the duke's half-empty goblet with a clean one, filling it with deep red wine.

The table fell back into its usual rhythm; nobles chatting quietly and laughing with half-covered mouths as they picked at their food and sipped from their goblets. Nisaba joined them and found that the duck tasted exquisite, delicately spiced with cinnamon and cumin; and the fruits and sauces, and of course the wine, and even the breads, carried taste and texture to levels of perfection she'd hardly dreamed possible.

While she dined and drank, various dukes and duchesses, barons and baronesses, offered their compliments on her poetry. A few of their insights were surprisingly astute—"That line about the dead sapling was a reference to the death of the hero's son in the first act, was it not?"—but most of their comments were platitudes about her majestic descriptions of the Gods, the sweeping landscapes she conjured, the tragic nobility of her heroes. A few of the commenters had clearly never read any of her poems, but she acknowledged their compliments all the same.

As the slaves replaced the meat and fruit with plates of honeyed pastries, candied nuts and crushed mountaintop ice flavored with syrup, the god-king raised a hand for attention, and the nobles fell silent.

"The reason we have asked you here tonight, Nisaba," Shúlgi said, "is not simply to heap praise upon you. Though, as the Gods themselves know, you certainly deserve it."

A murmur of agreement rose up from the nobles.

"We have invited you here," the god-king continued, "to make you an offer we have never made before."

Nisaba's stomach clenched with excitement. In normal circumstances, she supposed her mouth would've gone dry with nervousness—but these were far from normal circumstances, and this exquisite wine seemed to be going to her head.

"We would commission," Shúlgi told her, "a great new poetic cycle. A cycle worthy of this new flowering of society, this height of culture in which we now live. An epic that—like this kingdom of ours—preserves and protects the majesty of ancient Shumér, while also presenting the innovations of our new empire."

Nisaba licked her lips. Perhaps it was the wine, but the god-king's description made her a bit dizzy. "That is quite a project, Perfect One," she said, slowly. "I'm not sure I—"

Shúlgi raised a hand firmly, cutting her off. "Your humility does you credit," he said gently. "But we have read the writings of many of Urim's most praised poets and poetesses, and we would entrust this great work to none other than yourself."

All down the length of the table, noblemen and women were watching Nisaba expectantly. She took another gulp of wine. Perhaps the god-king was right, she thought. She often found contemporary poets' work disappointing; stiff, formal and repetitive, all but devoid of boldness or creativity, so unlike the wild, adventurous epics of the great Shuméru poets of centuries past.

"What would be the topic of this poetic cycle, Exalted Majesty?" she asked.

Shúlgi spread his gold-ringed hands. "Why, whatever you wish, of course!" He smiled. "That is to say, whatever the Gods inspire. It is our will that you work without restrictions, without fear of judgment or threat of poverty. We expect the full vibrancy of your creative gift. Nothing less."

A wave of vertigo swept over her. It wasn't an altogether unpleasant feeling; it felt like a sudden drunkenness. Yes, she must be drunk: on the fine wine, on the heaping praise, on the atmosphere and, most of all, on the fact that the king, who had already been her unseen patron for the past several months, had just summoned her to the royal palace and commanded her to write whatever she pleased. In this thundering euphoria, self-doubt felt foolish—no, almost blasphemous. Who was she to naysay?

"I will be glad to start work immediately," she told the god-king.

A broad smile spread across his bearded face. "We shall install you here in the palace complex, in an apartment suitable to your station." He nodded to his vizier Ishme, who nodded back in acknowledgment.

"Where do you lay your head at present?" Ishme asked her.

The question struck Nisaba a bit off guard. "Eh—the Two Lions Inn. It's on the far side of the city, in a less-reputable—"

"I know the place," Ishme said in a clipped tone. "I will have your things fetched at once."

She could never tell if this man disliked her, or was just utterly cold. For the past months, he'd served as her only contact with the palace, collecting her tablets of poetry and delivering her payments from the royal treasury. She'd always found him vaguely frightening—but now, seeing him here among the nobles, she wondered if he simply behaved this way with everyone, and if that might be precisely the reason why the god-king trusted him so.

"And now," Shúlgi raised his goblet, "let us celebrate the commissioning of this great new work. May our poet's namesake, the Goddess Nisaba the Scribe, bless this endeavor."

A chorus of agreement rose from the nobles.

After that, Nisaba began to lose track of the goblets of wine, the exquisite desserts, the lyre-songs that gave way to fast, pounding rhythms on *bala* drums and *zamzam* reeds—rhythms that drew her and the nobles and even the god-king up to dance, as slaves hurried to clear the table and chairs away; first, several dances lately fashionable at court, whose strange steps left Nisaba stumbling over her own feet; then the old familiar folk-dances with lines of men and women weaving and circling elaborately back and forth across the polished floor, like bees in a hive, or fish swimming in oceans of wine and beer and the thick smoke of myrrh and sandalwood.

She lost track of herself, and whom she danced with, and what words were whispered in praise and promise that night.

But her last thought, as her head hit the pillow, was, *I will be remembered.*

𒌋𒌋

THE WAX TABLET sat on her desk. Blank, damn it all. She sat with her head in her hands, staring down at the tablet's dull yellow surface, watching its color slowly lighten as it dried in the afternoon air. Soon the wax would begin to harden, then to crack.

She carefully waved a burning lamp just above the tablet's surface, keeping the wax soft and supple. Ready to receive an inscription that wouldn't come.

Her vast new rooms in the palace felt so unlike her cozy mud-brick room at the inn. Her writing desk was fine dark oak; its legs and feet carved to resemble the forelimbs and paws of lions. Its surface was polished to a perfect shine. She almost feared to drip any wet wax upon it. Maybe that was the problem: this desk, and this whole room, were too clean, too gleaming with obvious wealth. She never struggled like this sitting at her shabby little writing-table at the inn.

"Three days," she sighed to herself. That was how long she'd been mulling over possible first lines, characters, scenes; anything to get the story started in her mind, and move her hand to put her stylus to the wax. Nothing was taking shape.

Yesterday morning, she'd walked all the way up to the temple, bought a few pieces of overpriced fruit and butter from the hawkers in the outer courtyard, and offered the gifts as sacrifices to her namesake, Nisaba, Goddess of scribes and writing. As she knelt before the Goddess, chanting prayers, she thought she almost caught a whiff of a story. But when she tried to take hold of the idea, it slipped through her fingers like water.

Writing had never been so impossible before. It wasn't always easy, to be sure. She'd struggled many a time with a troublesome line or an uncooperative character. She'd even faced blockages like this, and overcome them. But never a blockage that lasted three straight days. Never an absolute blank like this one.

The morning after the god-king's banquet, she'd woken in her spacious new chambers in the palace; head throbbing, limbs aching, mouth dry and sour-tasting; and a powerful terror had washed over her. Why had she agreed to this commission? She'd never be able to complete it—or if she did, the work would fall far short of the god-king's expectations. But she couldn't exactly go running to the throne room and inform the god-king she'd decided not to take the job after all. She had no choice but to begin the work.

So she began, the same way she always began: by gathering her stylus, her erasing-rag and a water dish, and a fresh tablet of wax, and settling in at her writing-desk. And there she'd passed most of the last three days.

A knock sounded from her chamber door, making her jump.

"Nisaba?" called a familiar male voice. "Is this your room?"

She pushed herself up from the table and walked across the sunny chamber's polished stone floor. As Ishme the vizier had promised, all her belongings had been delivered here from the inn: a box of clothes and a small parcel containing her writing supplies, all of which still lay half-unpacked by the wall next to her lion-footed cedarwood bed.

"Thank the Gods you're all right!" Amnanu exclaimed, bursting into the room and throwing his arms around her.

She returned the kisses of her beloved, trying to pull back and talk at the same time. "Of course I'm all right. Love, what are you—?"

"You have no idea how *worried* I've been." He gripped her shoulders, shaking her as one would when scolding a child. "I've had half the slaves in my father's household out scouring the city for you. I went to the inn, where that swine of an innkeeper made me shell out five copper obols before he'd tell me a thing. Then he suddenly remembered some men from the palace who came to take your things."

A sinking feeling spread outward from the pit of her stomach. "I'm so sorry," she said, taking his head in her hands. "These past three days have been madness, just absolute insanity—"

"You didn't think to write?" he cried.

The irony of those words made her double over laughing before she could stop herself. She got a grip on herself, threw her arms around his neck, and stroked his cheek, which was now red with fury. "That's all I've been trying to *do*, sweetlove," she said. "For three straight days. Just trying to write one single line."

Amnanu looked like he might cry, or explode with rage, or collapse with relief. Perhaps all at once. "You could've sent a messenger," he said.

"Yes," she agreed, planting kisses on his lips. "I could have. I'm sorry. Please forgive me."

"Three days, Nisaba," he said, between kisses. "Three days. Mother and Father told me to stop worrying, but I couldn't rest until I knew you were safe. I've been in a panic."

"I know," she agreed, kissing him harder. "So have I."

"Clearly not for the same reasons I have."

"Shh," she whispered. "It doesn't matter now. You're here. I'm here. That's all that matters."

She pulled him to the cushioned vastness of her bed, and unbelted his toga, and began to do some of the things he liked. His complaints turned into surprised moans, then into eager grasping. As he slipped her dress up over her head, she wondered if maybe this was the piece she'd been missing all along. Maybe once they'd both released, she'd finally be able to write.

But when they were both finished and exhausted, lying sweaty amongst the linen sheets and tasseled pillows, she combed through her mind and still found no hint of a story, no hook from which to hang a first line. She rolled over and sighed.

"What's wrong, my love?" Amnanu asked, running his fingers through her tangled hair.

"I've never been so empty of ideas," she said, rolling over to face him. "I can't think of a single line worth writing down."

"What's the poem about?" he asked.

She realized, suddenly, that her betrothed knew nothing of her new assignment. How could he? She told him, briefly, of the banquet she'd attended, and the god-king's commission.

"The god-king gave you this assignment?" Amnanu exclaimed. "Shúlgi himself?"

"Yes, I had dinner with him. But that's not the point," she said. "The point is—"

Now he was laughing at her, his whole body shaking with mirth.

"What's so funny?" she demanded.

"Sweetlove," he said. "Sometimes you truly amaze me. The god-king invites you to dinner—invites you to sit next to him at the head of his table, in fact—lavishes praise on your poetry, installs you in a suite in his palace, and tells you to write whatever your heart desires. And your response is to coop yourself up in your room for three days, lashing yourself with abuse."

She began to form a reply, but bit it off.

"You're astonishing." He shook his head, smiling and ruffling her hair. "Do you not see what's being offered to you? Even my father would give his right hand for an opportunity like this."

She huffed. "You know I have no interest in playing courtly politics, or attending some stuffy—"

"I'm not talking about whispers and curtsies," he said. "I'm talking about the vast field of options the god-king has given you. What is it you want? To consult rare ancient texts? Go to the royal library, demand they open the vault for you. Want bards and tale-tellers and from distant lands? Send for the best. Get a private performance."

Her eyes were widening now. He was making a very good point, she realized. Perhaps this baron's son, who'd grown up with bards and poets at his beck and call, was better equipped to see the possibilities than she was.

"Our god-king has commanded something enormous of you," he said, gently. "No question about that. Something unprecedented, truly. But he's also given you unprecedented power, Nisaba. The archives and stages of the world—of all history—lie open to you. Their keepers await your whim." He smiled. "*Use* that power. Wield it. Create a work like no one's ever seen before. Like a great tree with many branches, each bearing wonderful fruit."

She kissed him. "That's a lovely thought. But right now, you've made me feel the calmest I've felt in three days. And I'm falling asleep."

Cuddling up next to him, she nuzzled against his neck, closed her eyes, felt the long, slow rhythm of his breath, and slipped into sleep.

In her dream, she was deep underwater. Not swimming, exactly, but floating and flying downward, drawn by some unseen force. Silvery schools of fish swirled past, and tiny tentacled things whose skins danced with flickering multicolored light. They seemed to fill the depths, these tiny dancing lights, a sky of whirling stars all around her.

As she drifted deeper, she sensed a great presence nearby—something that seemed to comfort and terrify her at the same time, filling her belly with dread even as it lured her deeper amid the swirling colored lights.

Then a shape loomed up from far below, vast as an island rising from the depths; shadowy and many-formed, it seemed to resemble a fish and a man and a goat all at once, or perhaps some combination of all these. It was a God.

You have called me, hummed the voice of the God, deep within her bones.

In a flash, she recognized this God: it was none other than the primordial God Énki, Lord of the Abyss, dweller in the deep, keeper of the arts and gifts of civilization.

She opened her mouth to answer, but it filled with water. A thought flashed in her mind: *This is the kind of dream that only happens in stories.*

And yet, the God's voice answered, *here you are.*

In his left hand, Énki held a bowl that somehow overflowed with water, even in the depths of the sea. In his right hand, he held a branch, or perhaps a tree, with seven branches—three on each side of the trunk, and a seventh crowning branch sprouting from the top—each tipped with a fruit that looked like a star.

What does it mean? she asked in her mind.

This Tree is what you have sought, said the God. *It is the world. It is all that has been, and is, and is yet to be.*

I don't understand! The thought erupted in her mind, unbidden.

And as she looked at the tree, her mind filled with ten thousand sights and words: the deeds of great kings and heroes; the journeys of Gods through the heavens and the underworld; the crafts of farming and building and brick-making; the tricks of writing signs and crafting verse; the creation of speech and the naming of all the things in the world; the rising of the first men and women from the churning mud; the primeval war between Abzu, the eternal freshwater sea, and Tiamat the salt sea—all these things and many more she saw, as if she herself was living through them, had already lived through them, and held them all in memory.

Then the ocean and the God were gone, and Nisaba was walking in a temple courtyard she did not recognize, amid tall palms and jasmine-bushes blossoming with tiny white flowers. Next to her strolled a woman in a long skirt and mantle of white linen, pleated like palm fronds. She was almond-skinned, her eyes outlined in blackest kohl, a round crown of wool resting atop her black hair, coiffed and set with pins of gold. A high priestess, by the look of her; one of the old Akkadu Empire.

"I've been so curious about you," said the priestess.

"Who are you?" Nisaba asked.

The priestess only smiled. "When I compose poems, I write for the Goddess Inanna, and for myself. Never for a king. Tell me, what is it like to live in such a poetic time?"

"This isn't a poetic time," Nisaba said. "The days of real epics are dust."

"So they say about your time, in many others," the priestess replied. "I suppose the past always seems romantic."

"So *who* says?" Nisaba asked.

"All the others, of course." The priestess smiled again. "The ones who read you. Imitate you."

Nisaba's eyes widened. "But I haven't written my poem yet."

The priestess laughed softly. "And yet," she said, "you already did, long ago."

Nisaba sat up in bed, gasping in the dark, covered in cold sweat. Amnanu snored softly beside her.

Wrapping a blanket around her shoulders, she rose in the pitch-blackness of the chamber, felt about for tinder, managed to strike a spark and light a taper, and start a flame in the oil lamp on her writing desk.

It was still too dark to see much of anything, but she trusted her hand with a stylus, even in this shadowy room.

She waved the flame carefully above the surface of the the tablet, softening the wax without melting it. Then, for the first time in days, she picked up her stylus and began to write.

ᛉᛉ

Nisaba knelt before the god-king's throne. She'd been kneeling here for several minutes now. Beneath her skirts, her knees were beginning to hurt, pressed against the polished stone floor. They hadn't even given her a pillow to kneel on.

This was the pose she'd dropped into as soon as she'd finished reciting a stanza of her poem. No one had given her permission to rise, so here she stayed, wondering if they'd forgotten all about her.

Shúlgi was whispering with a black-robed man at his side. *A baron? Another poet?* She had no idea. A tax official? She occupied herself with funny guesses for a few seconds, until a smile started to spread across her face, which she was suddenly at pains to hide.

"Your verses are both lovely and profound, as always, Nisaba," boomed the god-king's voice, pulling her back to the here and now.

"Thank you, Sublime One," she said, still kneeling.

"What are you doing down there?" He gestured for her to rise. "This isn't an execution hearing."

"I'm sorry, Majesty," she said, clambering to her feet, pain exploding outward from her knees. "I don't really know much about the etiquette—"

"Nisaba, you are much loved here," Shúlgi said gently, favoring her with a smile. "My friend here tells me we are blessed by the Gods to have a poet of your talents."

Nisaba had no idea who the bearded, robed man at the god-king's side was; but she smiled and curtseyed, and he replied with a polite nod and smile of his own.

"However," the god-king continued, "the three of us could not agree—tell us, when you say, '*In that seaside land did Énki plant the tree,*' are you referring to trees in general, or to a specific tree?"

She licked her lips, racking her mind for a response that would satisfy the god-king without breaking the poem's magic. She'd never enjoyed explaining her poetry; it was like unweaving an elegant piece of cloth to search for bits of elegance in its individual threads. But now she had no choice. All eyes in the throne room were on her. The god-king waited patiently.

"The Tree is a symbol," she said at last, "which can mean many things."

Shúlgi gestured for her to continue.

"Well, for example," she said, "the trunk of the Tree upholds the world, just as pillars uphold this palace. Its branches and leaves reflect the multiplicity of living things on this earth: birds, beasts, fishes, men and so on. Just as a tree springs forth from the ground, this world springs forth from the Abzu. The abyss. The eternal and unknowable Mind."

Now the god-king was smiling. "Most eloquently put, Nisaba." The god-king clapped lightly, and all the nobles in the throne room joined in.

The man standing by the throne was looking at her in a way she didn't like at all.

"Tell us," Shúlgi continued. "Now that you have completed a few stanzas, what shape does the work take in your mind? We are most eager to know its theme and scope."

"It will be—" Nisaba hesitated. Despite her feverish bouts of writing over the past few days, she still had no overarching tale; nothing to tie the passages together. "It will be a series of interconnected episodes, Exalted Majesty. Some of them set in our day; others in earlier ages of the world. Together, they will tell a story, not of any single hero or quest, but of *us*. The story of Shumér. Of our people and our land."

The whole throne room had fallen silent. Nisaba could her her own blood rushing in her ears.

Shúlgi was smiling, tapping a tightly clenched fist against the arm of his throne.

"Yes," he said. "*That* is a poem worthy of this court, of our majesty, and of the glory of Shuméru culture."

The god-king rose from his throne, casting his gaze around the throne room, meeting the eyes of various nobles. "Do you see this woman?" He gestured at Nisaba. "Do you hear her words? Every one of you should hold yourself to such a standard. Kings in faraway lands will hear of this poem, of the splendor of our court. And they will turn their eyes to Shumér in longing, as they did in days long past."

He descended the polished marble steps of the throne-dais, and took Nisaba's hand. "Write us this great epic, Nisaba," he said. "Plant the Tree of Énki in our land once again."

She had to suppress an urge to point out that the meaning of the tree was actually quite different from what he'd just said, as the throne room erupted into rapturous applause. She could only smile and curtsy again, as the god-king favored her hand with a soft kiss.

Then Shúlgi returned to his throne, and to important matters of state, and suddenly it was as if the moment had never happened at all.

As she pushed through the crowd of nobles, seeking the door out of the throne room, she felt a hand on her shoulder. She whirled, surprised to see the bearded face of the man who'd stood at the god-king's side.

She raised a hand, politely, to stave him off. "I'm honored that you enjoy my verses, lord, but I'm afraid I can't discuss—"

"This isn't about the poem," he cut her off, in a voice carrying a subtle accent; not quite Akkadu, but similar... "Come," he insisted. "Somewhere quiet."

He placed a hand softly against her back, and guided her out through the crowd, down a dim hallway, and into a small alcove where a narrow window looked out on the palace's interior garden.

"I don't appreciate being shoved around," she said, turning about to look him square in the eyes. "Who are you?"

He turned his back without answering, shielding her from the view of inquisitive courtiers passing in the hall.

"You're some sort of priest, aren't you?" She could see by the look in his eyes that she'd guessed rightly. "Not an ordinary temple priest, but—"

"Where did you hear that?" he cut her off. "About the Tree?"

Something cold clenched in her stomach. "The tree—?" She shook her head, as much from genuine confusion as fear. "It's just a symbol. I—I invented it, for my poem."

He took her by the arm, roughly. "We both know that's a lie." he hissed. "I warn you, girl, don't play games with me."

"I warn *you*, priest. Don't touch me," She snarled in reply, shoving him away.

Nearby nobles were beginning to turn and stare.

"Since you know of the Tree," he said, barely above a whisper, "you know one does not speak of it. One does not write of it."

"How dare you threaten me!" she snapped.

"I'm not threatening you! I'm—" He paused and took a breath. When he spoke again his voice was softer, more pleading. "I'm trying to warn you. You're opening doors you can't close."

She gazed at him, noting the tension in his eyes. No, not just tension; fear, scarcely concealed. How could he know of her dream; of Énki and the Tree? It was impossible. Then she remembered what Amnanu had said to her, just before she'd drifted off to sleep: "Create a work like a great tree with many branches, each bearing wonderful fruit..."

"I swear to you," she said, keeping her voice and her gaze steady, "I don't know anything about any secret trees. It was just something my—" she stopped. It was better not to mention Amnanu or the dream. "—something a friend of mine said. I was struggling with inspiration, trying to write this poem and he said, 'Write something great. Plant a tree with many branches.' Something like that."

His eyes narrowed. "And who is he, this... 'friend' of yours?"

"He's—nobody," she stammered, suddenly caught off guard. Furious with herself, she quickly regained her balance and drew herself up to her full height, lancing him with a sharp gaze. "And he's none of your business," she finished curtly.

Before he could say another word, she dodged around him and hurried off down the hall, letting the crowd of curious nobles close like curtains behind her. Already humming with speculation, no doubt.

Even amid her confusion and fear, she found room to savor the moment. *Let them speculate about the intrigues of their mysterious poet*, she thought.

Yet at the same time, she was thinking, *How could he possibly know? How could either of them know about the Tree?*

⁂

AMNANU WAS WAITING in her chambers when she returned. Sprawled across the bed, just as she'd left him this morning, before she'd headed off to her audience with the god-king.

"How was your royal audience?" he asked her, sitting up.

"Not half as interesting as the conversation I had afterward," she said, fixing him with a sharp stare. "A gentleman asked me how I came by this idea of a tree, and you'd better thank the Seven Stars I didn't give him your name."

He looked at her blankly. "What gentleman? What on earth are you talking about?"

"That's exactly what I'm asking you," she said. "Where did you hear about the Tree? Why did you tell me to write about it?"

"I didn't tell you to write about any tree, Nisaba." He threw up his hands. "I said write about whatever you want. That's all I said."

She raised a finger. "No, you said, 'Create a work like like a tree with many branches, each bearing wonderful fruit.'"

He smiled like a child. "I did say that, didn't I? Perhaps I should try my hand at poetry."

"Listen to me!" Nisaba snapped.

His smile vanished, and his face went pale.

She sat next to him on the bed. "Who told you about the Tree, Amnanu? I need to know."

He spread his hands, stammering. "Nisaba, I swear by all the Gods, I have no idea what you're talking about. I don't know anything about any tree."

She stared into his eyes for a long moment. He wasn't lying, or holding anything back. He always looked up and to the left when he tried to dodge a question, but right now he was looking her square in the eye, genuinely frightened.

"What happened to you?" he asked.

She shook her head. She herself could hardly believe it. "A man cornered me. Some kind of priest. I don't know. Told me it's forbidden to write about the Tree."

"What tree?" he exclaimed.

"I don't know!" she cried. "The Tree of the world. It's some kind of a holy symbol or something, and apparently these priests want to keep it a secret, and somehow I happened to use exactly the same symbol in the stanza I read to the god-king today, and now this priest thinks I'm trying to pull back the curtain on the mystery, and he—he threatened me, or warned me, to stop writing about it."

The words were pouring out of her now, and she felt ashamed of it, like a frightened child who couldn't get a grip on herself.

Amnanu leaped up from the bed and took her by the shoulders.

"Someone threatened you?" He looked fiercely into her eyes. Even in the midst of everything, she felt a sudden desire for him well up inside her.

"He didn't threaten me, exactly." She furrowed her brow. "It was more like a warning. As if he were afraid what might happen to me."

"Who was he?" Amnanu demanded. "Did you get his name? If you could recognize him again, my father could—"

"My love," she pressed a hand gently against his chest. "Getting your father involved is the last thing I want to do. I'm in enough trouble as it is." She extricated herself from his arms and dropped onto the bed with a sigh. "Besides, this priest stood at the god-king's right hand today. Not even your father wields that much influence at court."

"Actually, what I was going to say," Amnanu said, "is that my father may know this priest. Which means we can find out what he wants."

"I already know what he wants." Nisaba shook her head. "He wants me to stop talking and writing about this Tree."

"What tree?" he asked, thoroughly confused.

She locked eyes with him for a long moment, debating how much to tell. At last, she decided she had to trust somebody, and he was the most trustworthy person she knew right now.

"Amnanu, I..." she trailed off, unsure where to begin.

"What, sweetlove?" His eyes were so earnest, she almost wanted to laugh. "Whatever it is, you can tell me."

"Last night," she said, "after you said that thing about the tree... I had a dream. I sank deep into the ocean, and I—I know it sounds mad, but *I met Énki*. I'm certain of it. That it was really him, I mean. In one hand he held a bowl overflowing with water, and in the other hand he held a Tree with seven branches. He told me the Tree was the world, and then—somehow I saw my whole poem. All the Gods and kings and heroes of Shumér, as if I'd lived all the tales myself. Then I walked with another poet, a priestess. She seemed so strange, and yet so familiar. And then I woke up and began to write."

He stared at her, wide-eyed, for an uncomfortably long time.

"Amnanu, I swear I'm not going mad—"

"Énki spoke to you," Amnanu breathed.

"Yes!" She nodded, laughing with relief that he believed her. "Yes, I'm certain. And I've been writing ever since."

"And he showed you this Tree, whatever it is."

"I think I might understand it," she said. "It's sort of a symbol for everything that's real. Everything that crosses over from imagination to reality. And everything that ever has, or will."

Suddenly Amnanu was smiling, like he'd had an idea.

"I've seen it," he said.

She shook her head. "Seen what?"

"The Tree!" he cried. "I'm sure you've seen it too, without knowing it. It's in all the murals in the temples, the ones where the Gods bring forth creation. And I've seen it on wax seals. It's everywhere. It's just—most people don't know what it means.

It's some kind of a code, or something, that these priests use." He was gesturing wildly now, pacing back and forth in front of the bed. "The question is, why are they so afraid of the truth getting out? What are they protecting?"

"I don't think the Tree itself is the point." She shook her head. "Temples thrive on mystery. Putting the idea in words takes the mystery away. Like when you have to explain a joke, and suddenly it's not funny anymore."

He looked disappointed. "But what if they're hiding a secret?" he persisted. "Forbidden knowledge, passed down through the ages. Don't you want to know for sure?"

"What I want right now," she said, "is to finish my poem. And I can't write about the Tree."

He gaped at her. "So, what, you're just abandoning this mystery? How can you just look away?"

"I'm not looking away." She raised a finger to cut him off. "In fact, I think this Tree may be the perfect way to tie my whole epic together—especially if it runs as far back through history as this priest seems to think it does. Maybe I can write *around* it." She chewed a fingernail. "And I'm wondering, now, if perhaps other poets have done the same."

"That's brilliant." He stroked his short beard, dropping onto the bed beside her. "Surely you're not the first to run up against these priests, whoever they are. There must have been others."

"And they must have their own poetry and songs, whether written or not," she said. "Rituals, and—I don't know—prayers, maybe, that reference the Tree indirectly."

"In ways only the initiated would understand!" He was nodding now. "The verses may have been all around us our whole lives. But since we didn't know which Tree they were referencing—"

"—they would've seemed like ordinary songs and poems," she finished. "Exactly."

He gazed at her excitedly, almost like a child. "Where will you start?"

"The Royal Library," she said. "They've got hymns and chants from every period. It's worth a try, at least."

"And I'll ask my father about this priest," Amnanu said. "If he's as afraid as you say, that may give us some leverage over him."

"Or a clearer view of our real enemy," she said.

Locking eyes with him, so intent and excited, she couldn't help but smile.

And then, at last, she gave into the part of her that wanted to leap atop him and unbelt his toga again, and work out all the morning's fear and excitement amid the sheets.

When it was all finished, she kissed him again, rose and dressed, and set off for the Royal Library.

"I'M NOT QUITE certain what you mean," said the royal librarian, an owlish priest with the nervous habit of picking at his fingernails.

Nisaba gazed up at the seemingly endless rows of wood shelves, where lamp-cast shadows danced around thousands of stacks and bundles of baked clay manuscripts. Even now at midday, the vast windowless vault felt gloomy as midnight.

"Surely you must have some hymns here that refer to trees," she said to the librarian.

On her way here, she'd pondered how to ask the librarian about trees without arousing his curiosity, or even his anger, if he happened to belong to the same brotherhood as the priest who'd warned her in the palace hallway. But this man seemed to have heard nothing about her throne-room oratory, or her tangle with the priest in the hallway—or even to have any clear idea who she was. She counted herself lucky. The last thing she needed was another suspicious set of eyes on her.

"Oh, we certainly have some such poems," he answered, tapping his bearded chin thoughtfully. "I can recommend a few."

"Isn't there some sort of list you can check?" she asked.

"A topical list, you mean?" The librarian shook his head apologetically. "We maintain scrupulous records of each document's city and dynasty of origin... but a list of all the thousands of topics in every written work we possess? Why, that would be the work of a lifetime. A dozen lifetimes."

"So my only choice is to read every poem in the archives?" Her shoulders slumped as she glanced into the depths of the vault again.

"Or to obtain the titles of specific poems." He looked genuinely saddened.

"Where can I obtain those?" she asked.

He shrugged. "From someone who knows the poems in question, I would presume."

This line of inquiry was going nowhere. "You said you can recommend a few poems that refer to trees?" she asked with a note of hope.

The priest nodded eagerly, relieved to be back on safe ground. "I certainly can. Trees are mentioned in several popular praise poems I know of, and... hmm... yes, also in the *Genesis of Énki and Ninkhursanga*, I believe..."

A chill ran up Nisaba's back at the name "Énki," but the librarian didn't seem to notice; he was already puttering off toward one of the nearby stacks, oil lamp in hand.

The texts he brought her turned out to be quite a mixed bag. Two of the poems mentioned trees only in passing: "*Lions are abundant under the canopy of trees*," "*My Nibru, where black birch trees grow*," and so on.

Another was a praise hymn that contained the intriguing lines,

There stood a single shady tree at that place.
Its shade was not diminished in the morning,
Nor at midday or in the evening.

But the poem offered no further explanation of this singular tree.

The most promising hints, by far, came from the well-known *Genesis of Énki and Ninkhursanga*, in which Énki's divine seed miraculously caused the Goddess Ninkhursanga to give birth to eight plants—the first of which was a tree—in the garden paradise of Dilmun. Still more curiously, the poem also described the God Himself as a tree:

Father Énki, tree planted in the Abzu,
Rising over all lands;
Great dragon who stands in Eridu,
Whose shadow covers Heaven and Earth,
A grove of vines extending over the land...

The hairs on Nisaba's neck rose up. How had she never noticed the symbolism before, in all the hundreds of times she'd heard this epic sung? This was proof, surely, that she wasn't the first poet to reference the Tree explicitly. Perhaps this very poem had been composed by an initiate of the secret priesthood, or had made the reference obliquely enough to satisfy the priests. Or perhaps the tale itself was even older than the tradition of secrecy. What a fascinating thought.

Still, the text offered more questions than answers. She recognized the name of Dilmun from her scribal-school days: an island far to the east, whose history lay shrouded in myth. Kings of Dilmun still traded with Shumér even now, so it was said. But legend held that the ancestors of the Shuméru people themselves had once dwelt there, too—walking with the Gods in a garden paradise, long before they came to live in the Land Between the Rivers. If Énki had planted the Tree in the Garden of Dilmun, then perhaps the Tree was just as lost as the paradise.

Could that be why the priests wanted the Tree kept hidden? What if they knew of some ancient means of access to the

God Énki Himself? That'd certainly be a secret worth guarding—a secret that'd make Nisaba, who'd spoken with the God directly, a clear threat to their order.

"Did you find what you were looking for?" the librarian asked as she returned to the front desk.

"I'm not sure," she said. "Do you have any texts about Dilmun?"

"Dilmun?" He seemed surprised. "Why, of course. I'm quite certain I gave you *Énki and Ninkhursanga*. Or didn't I? My mind seems to be in a thousand pieces these days."

"Yes, you did," she said. "That poem is the reason I want to know more."

He hummed thoughtfully, picking at his fingernails again. "Well, Dilmun is mentioned in quite a number of poems, as you may well imagine. Not to mention innumerable trade and transport records—dry stuff, really, and centuries of it. What in particular do you wish to know?"

She shrugged, not quite knowing where to begin. "When are our people supposed to have lived there? Why did our ancestors leave?"

"Excellent questions!" He grinned mirthfully. "I'd very much like to know the answers myself."

"Surely there must be some record of that time," she said. "Something definite."

He barked a laugh. "If such a record were discovered," he said. "Its very existence would be a cause for celebration. By the time our ancestors learned how to write, Dilmun was but a distant memory. We recall it only in story and song, as much tall tale as truth, I should say."

She furrowed her brow. "What about the people who live there now? Haven't they preserved any tales of that time?"

The librarian shrugged again. "I suppose you'd have to ask them. I know of no such text."

But now she was smiling. "That's it!"

"That's what?" he asked.

"Written texts only go back so far," she said. "But oral traditions go back much further."

He nodded thoughtfully. "Such tales may still exist, it's true. One can often find them in remote villages, or perhaps among certain nomad tribes."

And I, thought Nisaba, *have the authority to summon all of them here, to Urim.*

"My dear," the librarian was saying, "I'm so sorry, my dear. What was your name?"

Telling him the truth was too risky, she realized.

"You may call me Ninti," she said. It was the name of Énki's daughter in the epic: "Lady Life."

"Yes, Ninti," the librarian muttered. "If you do happen to discover such an ancient song, would you be so kind as to bring the singer here, to the library? I should very much like to record his words. For posterity and all that, you understand."

"I'll do my best," Nisaba told him. "Thank you, again, for all your help."

She left him there at the desk, still studying the same text he'd been poring over when she'd entered, by the unchanging light of lamps in the shadows.

⋎⋎⋎
⋎⋎⋎

THAT NIGHT, A local bard from Urim came to Nisaba's chamber, in answer to a summons she'd sent out throughout the city, for any tale-teller who knew the very oldest stories.

The bard sang the great epics, more eloquently than she'd ever heard them sung before. He sang the hero Gilgamesh's journey to the forest, and to the bottom of the sea, to seek the plant of immortality. He sang of Én Merkar of Unúg, who sent the Lord of Aratta too many angry messages for his herald to remember, and so was forced to invent writing to record his myriad complaints. The bard sang of Inanna, who seduced the God Énki, Lord of the Abzu, and sailed away with the *mhé*, all the attributes of civilization, in her Boat of Heaven—and who, in another tale, was imprisoned in the Underworld for three days and nights by the Goddess Erishkegál.

All these old tales, and many others, the bard sang to her; some stories she recognized and many she'd never heard before; songs of heroes and long-dead kings, Gods and Goddesses, monsters and floods and journeys into the heavens and beneath the earth. She wrote nothing down, but held it all in her memory, letting the characters and the rhythms of the songs churn in her mind.

When the sun began to rise above the walls of Urim, the bard left her, and she slipped smoothly into a sleep rich with dreams.

That afternoon, she rose and began to write of the ancient days of Shumér, when great kings and heroes did battle with monsters, and the Gods themselves laid the bricks of the first cities.

But as she wrote these tales, a feeling of boredom, even numbness, began to creep over her.

"Every word I'm saying has been written before!" she cried to Amnanu when he came to visit.

He picked up a freshly inscribed tablet from the shelves next to her writing-desk and scanned the intricate lines of tiny symbols covering its surface.

"But this is wonderful!" he exclaimed. "You write of Én Merkar and the Lord of Aratta as if you knew them yourself."

"I did know them," she said. "In my dream."

"By the way," he said, "I've done some asking around about that priest. His name is Misharam, and he comes from somewhere to the east. Apparently his whole family died in some calamity."

Her face fell. "I can't even imagine such grief."

Amnanu nodded in agreement. "They say he wandered the countryside for years, until he arrived here and managed to secure a place at court. He must be quite the orator. Everyone agrees he has the god-king's ear, night and day."

That didn't tell her much. "And the secret brotherhood?" she asked.

He shook his head. "Everyone agrees Misharam works alone. Eyes are everywhere at court, but no one's ever so much as seen him enter a temple, or speak with another priest."

"Perhaps he's not a priest at all," she mused.

"Or once was," he said, "and is no more."

She bent over her desk again, cradling her head in her hands. "Still no clue about why he's so protective of the Tree. Or what other libels he may be whispering about me at this moment."

He wrapped his arms around her from behind, cradling her as she slumped in her writing-chair. "Sweetlove," he cooed in her ear, "the god-king is going to adore your poem. I know it."

She turned to face him. "I'm sure he will," she said. "But it's not the poem I want to write. Every line of it has already been inscribed by a hundred other scribes on a hundred other tablets. All in the same symbols. Isn't that strange? So many who believe they've tricked the very same characters into saying something new."

"Beautifully put," he said, planting a kiss on her lips. "But isn't that the whole point—to tell what everyone knows, in a way they've never heard it before?"

She rose from the chair, running her hands through her tangled black hair. "I feel like a bird in a golden cage," she sighed. "Everyone's waiting for this brilliant poem, but I can only write in certain ways, about certain things. It's not just that I can't speak directly about the Tree. I can't even write of the amusing flaws and weaknesses of ancient kings, which I saw and heard in my dream. Instead, I must imitate the style of poets a thousand years in their graves."

"And yet," Amnanu said, planting kisses on her forehead, "Our Shumér is not the Shumér of old. It has passed through the fire, through the great Dark Age after the fall of the Akkadu Empire. Ours is a Shumér reborn."

"Reborn," she asked, "or simply dug out of its grave?" She bit her lip. "You know, they say that in the time before the Flood, great fish would come out of the Two Rivers and whisper mysteries from the depths. Teach people how to write, to compose songs—"

"—and how to invent wheels, and build the first cities." Amnanu nodded, rolling his eyes. "We all grew up with those stories. But do you really believe that's where the great old poems come from? Out of the mouths of fishes?"

Nisaba sighed deeply, her shoulders slumping. "Who knows? But even if not, doesn't a story like that speak volumes about the people who invented it? The earliest poems have such a..." She closed her eyes, grasping for the right words. "...a *playfulness*. As if all the world's a game."

"But surely poetry didn't die with old Shumér," Amnanu said softly. "I've read Énheduanna's poems from the Empire of Akkad. They're haunting. You can feel her agonies across three hundred years, as if she's whispering in your ear."

She nodded against his neck. "And even in the depths of the Dark Age, Gudea of Lagash wrote poetry that feels so *human*. So honest and real. I know. But that stuff is all so terribly *grim*."

He chuckled softly. "Surely our priests and poets love the old, playful Shuméru poetry, too."

"They claim to love it," she chewed the inside of her cheek. "But do they, truly? Have they ever taken the time to read the old poems on their own terms, to understand what they're really about? I think our scholars love their own idea of old Shumér—the great old kings. The inventors of the wheel, and of writing. The first mighty cities on earth."

Amnanu raised an eyebrow. "Aren't they right to love those things?"

She sighed. "Maybe so, but—you don't invent new things by acting so glum and serious all the time."

"No, of course not." He nodded solemnly. "Ideas like those can only come from the mouths of wise river-fish."

She grabbed a pillow from the bed and threw it at his smirking face, fighting the smile that crept across her lips. "I'm not saying our scholars don't love the old Shuméru poetry, in their way. But they've loved it so fiercely they've crushed it to death. Embalmed it like a fruit preserved in wax: too delicate to touch, too bland to eat."

"Oh, I'll show you what it means to love fiercely," he said, and reached out to tickle her stomach. Soon they were falling onto the bed together, laughing wildly; and for a while Nisaba forgot her troubles.

But as Amnanu slept beside her that night, dissatisfaction crept over her again. The true wellspring of Shumér—the *meaning* of this culture, and the root of any truly great Shuméru epic—must lie further back in the past, before the days of kings and cities, when men and Gods walked together in the Garden.

And so it was that a week later, amid the curling smoke and glowing candles, a woman-bard from the ancient city of Unúg traveled to Urim to sing to Nisaba. The woman sang of older things; stories hinted at in the first bard's tales, and in the tales of Nisaba's childhood, but seen from other points of view.

The bard sang to Nisaba of the great Flood that had washed over the Shuméru lands in ancient times, when Heaven talked with Earth, and the Gods commanded a wise man to build a strange floating vessel to save his life, rewarding his obedience with immortality. She sang of the first men, whom the Gods had formed from clay when the great abyss called Abzu clashed with the salt sea called Tiamat, and churned up the land of Shumér in frothing mud.

She sang of the Garden that grew far to the east in Dilmun, and of the Seven Stars that reigned over that place, and of the Watcher who was placed at the Garden's gate to guard against nameless things from outside. She sang the secrets whispered into women's ears by a serpent in a Tree: the ways of tilling

The Cradle and the Sword

the soil, and of caring for wheat and sheep and olive trees, and of making clothes to keep warm, and houses and hearths and cookfires. All these things, and many more, had women taught men in the Garden of Dilmun.

For the snake had come from the Tree, the woman sang, and the Tree had come from Énki, Lord of the Abzu, dweller in the deep, keeper of the arts and gifts of civilization. All who had knowledge knew Énki, the bard sang, and all who knew Énki knew the Tree.

As the sun rose the next morning, Nisaba thanked the bard and embraced her warmly. Instead of lying down to sleep, she went to her desk and began to write, casting her mind back to those far-distant days before kings and palaces and walls, when the ancestors of the Shuméru people dwelled in a garden tended by kind, wise-eyed women. She did not write of the Tree, but she wrote words that whirled around it, hinting at the secrets whispered from its branches, and the manifold meanings and becomings that unfolded endlessly from among its leaves.

But as she wrote of the Garden and the Tree, and the women who ruled in that peaceful place, she felt scratchings at the back of her mind—for even these antediluvian songs contained hints of stories still more remote, clawing at the fringes.

***

THE GOD-KING Shúlgi stared down at Nisaba from his throne, wide-eyed and mute.

She stood before him, fresh-engraved tablet clutched in her arms, and waited for him to pronounce sentence. Perhaps it was just her fear talking, but he looked horrified; as did the priest Misharam, who stood at the Shúlgi's side, black-robed and even more disdainful than before, whispering softly in the god-king's ear.

"My dear Nisaba," said the god-king as the priest turned away.

A chill ran through her limbs.

"This is a most... unusual direction for your poem to take, is it not?"

She bowed her head. "That was only a single stanza, Perfect One. The epic will, of course, include all the famous tales of kings and heroes—"

"Of course it will." Shúlgi stated flatly, in a tone that commanded even as it agreed. "Of this I have no doubt. Yet it does seem—does it not?—that your poem becomes less the great Shuméru epic that was promised, and more a history of faraway foreign lands."

"But it's not—!" she blurted.

A gasp went up from the crowd of nobles lining the aisle. Nisaba softened her tone.

"Exalted Majesty," she tried again, more demurely. "Is it not true that our own ancestors once dwelt in Dilmun across the sea? Is it not true that Énki and Ninkhursanga planted the first garden there?"

"Dilmun," said Misharam in his strange accent, "as you yourself must know, dear poetess, is in fact an actual country to the east, inhabited by distant cousins of the Akkadu folk. And though it produces excellent cedar-wood, it harbors no magical gardens. Nor is it the Shuméru people's homeland, or the home of the God Énki. It is nothing more than a common poetic *allegory* for lost innocence."

In truth, Nisaba hadn't known that. She cursed herself for not realizing it sooner.

"But is it not said," she retorted, "that Dilmun was the place where the sweet waters of the Abzu and the salty sea called Tiamat churned together to create the earth, and the first people? Do you not agree that the Shuméru people are the first people?"

A murmur rumbled through the audience chamber; more excited than angry. Her blow seemed to have landed, because even Shúlgi himself had turned to the priest expectantly.

If Misharam was flustered, he showed no sign of it. "It is true," he agreed, "that Abzu and Tiamat crashed together to create the Shuméru people from the mud. But it is well-known that this creation occurred *here* in the land of Shumér, on the shore of the sweet lake called Abzu, where the world's first city, Eridu, still stands today.

"For as you know, it is written of old:
When skies above were not yet named,
Nor earth below pronounced by name,
Énki and Ninkhursanga mixed clay upon the Abzu,
Fashioning the Shuméru people;
And laid the bricks of cities,
The first of which was Eridu.

"Are these not the words of the Gods themselves?" Misharam demanded. "Either the Gods created mankind in some garden in Dilmun, or on the shore of the Abzu, here in Shumér. It cannot be both. As for me, I trust in the Gods' word."

The crowd of nobles murmured their approval.

Nisaba fought back a momentary panic. What poem was Misharam quoting from? The words sounded familiar, but she couldn't quite place them.

Drawing herself up, she answered, "The Garden of Dilmun is not my invention. The simple fact that we all know the tale serves as proof that it is an ancient Shuméru tradition. How mankind could be created both in Dilmun and in Eridu, I do not know. I admit this is a mystery to me, as are many things about the Gods. But whether the Garden is real or simply an allegory, I believe it is necessary in any tale that tells the full and complete story of our people."

Some nobles in the crowd hummed in agreement, while others humphed in disapproval.

"But if Your Sublimity wishes it," she concluded, turning her gaze to the god-king, "I will remove Dilmun from my poem."

The crowd fell silent. The god-king locked eyes with Nisaba, his catlike gaze seeming to pierce her flesh and examine her very thoughts. The two of them watched one another for a long motionless moment.

"You," Shúlgi said at last, "are the poet. Not I. If you will not bend on this, I will trust your intuition."

A gasp of surprise erupted from the crowd. Misharam was glaring at her.

"However," the god-king continued, "since you have chosen to pursue this path, I charge you to discover the truth about Dilmun, and about Eridu and the Abzu, or to intuit this truth as best you can, and to write these truths clearly and beautifully, as befits a great epic of our new Shumér."

The crowd applauded softly as Nisaba bowed before the king, scarcely able to hide her triumphant smile.

But as she expected, Misharam cornered her again on her way out of the throne room.

"You want to end us all, is that it?" he demanded.

She made no move to escape this time; only stood her ground and stared up at him boldly. "Just because your life was destroyed, Misharam," she said, guessing at a likely weak spot, "doesn't mean you must try to destroy mine. I have no fear of you, or of the secret brotherhood."

He looked utterly baffled.

"Secret *what*? Brotherhood?" He shook his head. Then recognition dawned on his face. "Is that what you think I've been warning you about? Some sect of priests out to protect the Tree? There is no such sect, Nisaba. There is only me."

Now it was her turn to be perplexed. "Then what were you warning me about? What are you so afraid of?"

Misharam glanced up and down the hallway, drawing curious gazes from nearby nobles.

"Let us talk somewhere more private," he whispered.

She shook her head. "I've no interest in going anywhere with you."

He winced. "Nisaba," he said, "I beg you. No one must know what I'm about to tell you."

She looked into his eyes and saw fear there, and despair, but nothing else. He wore the look of a sick man, resigned to his own death.

"The library," she said at last. "We won't be disturbed there. But if I shout for help—"

"Very well." He nodded. "Let us hurry."

"Oh! Brought me a bard already, have you?" The librarian leaped up from his chair with a grin, owly eyes bulging, sending his reed stylus clattering on the chamber floor.

"I'm afraid not," Nisaba replied. "This gentleman and I need a moment to talk in private."

The librarian spread his hands, indicating the gloomy room around them. "You won't find a more private place in all the palace complex. Most of the time it's just me down here."

"Do you have a reading alcove, perhaps?" Misharam asked. "Someplace out of the way."

"Down past the first stack, to your left," the librarian answered. "Take a lamp."

Nisaba grabbed one from the table, lit it, and stepped aside to let Misharam pass in front of her. Watching him carefully in the soft lamplight, she followed him down the length of a tall stack of wood shelves stocked with rows upon rows of baked tablets, each bundle labeled with tiny plaques of wood attached delicately with bits of string. She wondered, not for the first time, how many more trees and gardens one might discover here, if one had the time and patience to search.

A squat wood door in the left wall swung open to reveal a tiny reading alcove, stocked only with a desk and a single chair. Misharam sank into the chair, while Nisaba remained standing, holding the lamp. As nervous as the priest seemed, she wasn't about to take any chances.

"Well?" she demanded. "What's the secret within a secret that no one else in the palace may hear?"

Misharam stared down at his slippers for some time, his hands folded in the sleeves of his robe. When at last he spoke, it was with the voice of a man exhausted with worry.

"I had a daughter, Nisaba," he said, his voice cracking on the last word. "She'd be about your age, now. We raised her to become a priestess, my wife and I."

"Where was that?" she asked, already beginning to suspect she knew the answer.

He looked up, locking eyes with her for a long moment. "We lived in Dilmun," he said. "In those days, I was only a temple acolyte, not even an initiate yet. But I served the Gods well, as best I knew how."

"Dilmun," she breathed. "What was it like?"

"Not an enchanted garden, if that's what you're asking. It is a small country, spanning two islands and a strip of desert coastline. Many boats from East and West dock at its quays, where merchants grow rich by shipping cedars to Shumér and other places. It is a land not so different from yours, in truth."

"Is that why you're so protective about it?" she asked. "Simply because you know what the real Dilmun is? But then why try to keep the Tree a secret—?"

He raised a hand, imploring her to wait a moment. "It's not simply because I come from Dilmun," he said. "It's because of what I discovered there. The thing that—may the Gods help me—I shared with my daughter, thinking such a divine gift would ensure the high priesthood for her. But I did not understand what it was that I offered her, or what terrible things it would demand in return. And if you write that the Tree is still to be found in Dilmun, and if others go in search of it—"

"What divine gift?" she interrupted. "What terrible things, Misharam? What are you talking about?"

"It is real!" he hissed, glancing around as if someone might be listening from some corner of this cramped alcove. "The Tree stands in Dilmun. It has always been a symbol, yes, of course, of the God Énki and the whole of creation. But it is also a real tree, hidden deep within the forest. A tree that has stood for unnatural eons, and that—you'll think I'm mad, but it speaks to those who pass. Speaks in a voice that hums in one's bones, offering passage through the ocean of all that might be and all that has not yet been. Knowledge of the Abyss." His eyes flicked up to hers; his face a mask of open fright. "Do you understand, Nisaba?"

Her breathing had quickened. She took several deep breaths, willing the breaths to slow. "What is it?" she asked. "What is the Tree?"

He shook his head. "I don't know. Perhaps it is Énki Himself. Perhaps an impostor, or one of the trees he planted at the world's dawn. Or perhaps it is something older, something that grew in that place before even the Gods arrived. Something that deceived and captured them, too."

"And you've seen this—Tree, for yourself." She could hardly believe the words as they fell from her mouth.

"Saw it," he said. "Spoke to it. Was afraid to enter that Abyss myself. But when I returned home, my daughter could see in my eyes that something had changed in me. She pressed me for days, until at last I gave up the secret. Foolish creature that she was, I loved her with my whole heart. Next morning she had vanished. I pretended to search for her, frantically, wailing and running about the whole city. But I knew where she'd gone."

"And your wife?" Nisaba asked.

"Crippled by grief." His voice was scarcely more than a whisper. "Tied stones about her ankles and walked into the sea. On that day I left my home and wandered west, alone."

"To warn people about the Tree?"

He humphed softly. "I'd hoped never to hear of the Tree again. I did my best to put it out of my mind. I came to Urim's court as a trade advisor, in truth, an expert on the eastern shipping routes. When you read your poem in the throne room that day, my blood ran cold. As if a dead hand had reached up from the grave..."

She watched him, silently, for a long moment, stunned that she could ever have been frightened of such a frail, broken old man. She felt sorry for him now, wanted to wrap her arms around him, as if he were her grandfather, and tell him everything would be all right.

"I won't write about the Tree directly," she said at last. "I can't complete my poem without alluding to it, but I've no need to tell the tale you've told me."

"Thank you," he breathed.

"As for the Garden of Dilmun, though," she said, "I need to learn the truth. If not for my poem, then for myself. Doors have been opened in me that cannot be shut so easily."

"I beg you," he said. "Do not seek the Tree."

"I seek only the truth," she said. "Whatever I may say or conceal in my poetry, I have to begin with what I know. And I need to know where our people come from."

"I wish I could help you there," he said. "But truth is, I'm as ignorant on that score as you are."

She sent out messengers, seeking storytellers from the villages and the mountains; throat-singers from the tribes of nomadic herders who lived at the edges of the desert; toothless grandmothers who whispered by firesides in reed huts in the inmost swamps; bearded hunting-bards from the mountain forests.

They all came at her summons, night after night, lured by the god-king's limitless gold; and she listened to their stories night after sleepless night, ears alert for any crack in the wall of myth; any thread on which she might tug to unravel these opaque layers of folklore and peer through to some clear memory beneath it all.

Some of the tale-tellers brought strange instruments, and invited her to join them in tasting plants that produced visions. She swayed to the wild drumming of a white-robed mystic from Elam, breathing the smoke of the sacred *haoma*, hearing tales of cold mountain passes where the earth belched smoke and fire, and swirling mists swallowed men whole. She drank a bitter oily brew with a long-bearded Guti man in tattoos and furs, who played a deep-voiced flute and sang of shambling antlered things that whistled in the forest on moonless nights. A squat, pale-skinned marsh-woman gave her the leaves of a vine to chew, and sang of a place in the swamps where cats refused to hunt; where on certain evenings the frogs would fall silent, and voices could be heard chanting in a strange tongue, and something like a voice would bleat in answer from deep within the trees.

She pressed every one of the singers to tell more. And though at first they pretended to be guarding primordial secrets, each one of them revealed at last that these were only tales passed down from grandmother to grandson; whispers of things not seen or heard for centuries, if they had ever been at all.

Sleep fled from her. She wrote frantically, scarcely caring for the structure of her verses, feeling only the rhythm of the words, the eerie whirl of the imagery. But the well was running dry. She could feel it.

And so it was with a feeling approaching despair, wracked by weeks of waking dreams brought on by the strange draughts and plants and music of the bards, that she sat to hear the song of the a frail, pale-skinned man in a brown robe.

"And where are you from, singer?" she asked him.

"I am of the Ayya nomads," he said, in a voice like wind through reeds, as his slender form darkened her chamber doorway. "Who walk the plains of Dilmun."

Nisaba's blood ran cold. *Dilmun!* At last she'd discovered a bard who might know the truth. She fought back her exhaustion and stood to greet him, trembling with anticipation.

"I heard you are looking for old stories," he said, still unmoving.

"I've heard quite a few old stories," she said. "I'm looking for the things the stories are hinting at. That they will not say directly. Do you know those things, bard?"

He stepped forward into the light, rough brown robes swirling about him. "I know many stories. I know the secret whispered by the snake—"

"Yes, by the snake in the Garden," she interrupted, barely able to keep her eyes open. When had she last slept?

"Then you already know the secret of the Tree," he smiled slightly, sending spiderwebbed wrinkles across his mottled skin.

"I've been writing about the damn Tree for weeks," she said. She rubbed her eyes, leaned forward and fixed her tired gaze on him as best she could. "I want to know what it truly is."

The nomad was laughing. Shaking with mirth, his dark eyes gleaming in their sunken pits. *How old is he?* She wondered.

He took another step toward her, nodding slowly. "That's what you want, isn't it? Nisaba, daughter of Etel-pisha."

She started. *What kind of parlor-trick is this?* Her father's name—? How could he possibly know such a thing? But she held herself calm, refusing to let him see her off balance.

"We singers don't just tell tales for pampered ladies like you," the nomad said. "We trade stories everywhere we travel. And every tale-singer from here to the Spice Islands is telling tales of you, Nisaba."

The thought had never occurred to her. But it was absurdly obvious, she now realized. She'd summoned every bard her messengers could reach; of course they'd all been trading tales of her. She cursed herself, again, for failing to think beyond the palace walls.

"I know the stories you seek, child," he said, stepping still closer to her, in a way she didn't like at all. "You should have asked for me sooner. I could have saved you time."

"What stories are those?" Her eyes narrowed. "Concoctions dreamed up to please me?"

"Plenty of those tales are floating about, it's true," the nomad said. "But I think you'd recognize them for what they are."

He had a flair for flattery; she had to give him that.

"No," he continued, settling himself cross-legged on the carpets. "I bring you the *old* tales. The tales of my people, the Ayya, who have followed our herds across the edge of the desert since before the dawn of your world."

Her brow furrowed. "Your people claim to be older than the world?"

"That is not what I said." He raised a bony finger. "I said we are older than *your* world. We dwelled in Dilmun long before the seas rose and sundered it from this land. In those far-distant days, the seas sat lower; and the sweet and salt waters, Abzu and Tiamat, mixed freely in a forested swamp that stretched for many leagues. In those days, the Two Rivers became one in Dilmun, which was the name of the land we shared—your people and mine."

She drew a sharp breath. If this nomad spoke the truth, then both creation stories spoke of the same place! *So Misharam is wrong, and both stories are indeed true...*

"Your ancestors dwelled with mine in Dilmun long before they trudged west across the swamp to build Eridu," the nomad said. "And I assure you, the world was doing quite all right before that."

Nisaba raised a finger in protest. "But the poem says, *'Before the land of Dilmun yet existed, the ziggurats of Unúg and Eridu—'*"

"Yes, I know." The nomad cut her off, smiling. "That's from *Én Merkar and the Lord of Aratta*, is it not? Quite a famous poem—composed, of course, many centuries after the seas had risen to separate Shumér from Dilmun, and your people had long forgotten what the Garden truly meant. Let alone what had come before it."

She sat up. "You're saying you know stories from *before* the Garden?"

He nodded slowly. "Yes." A strange smile crossed his thin lips. "But they are forbidden stories."

She had to keep herself from rolling her eyes. But he seemed to sense her feeling all the same, because he raised a hand to forestall her.

"I do not say this to evoke some cheap sense of mystery," the nomad said flatly. "It is the simple truth. When your people moved west and established Eridu, they called this land Shumér, and declared it separate from Dilmun, the place where the Shuméru people were created, and have always dwelled, and always will dwell. But this is a lie. Your people sought to forget the Dilmun that once was, where our peoples mixed and wandered freely, and there were no cities or kings. But my people have kept the ancient ways, and those ways have always frightened you, because they are older than yours."

Nisaba frowned. "You say 'are,' not 'were.'"

The nomad smiled thinly again. "Indeed. For, as many of your tales hint, we still practice the old ways—albeit in secret. Our world remains as it has always been." A stern sneer crossed his thin lips. "And our hearts were glad when you departed from it."

She smirked. "For a man in the heart of Shumér, you don't speak of us with much respect."

He made that same noncommittal shrug. "Such is not our way. I speak only the truth. Slay me if you wish. Another will replace me."

Coming from any other man, this would have sounded like empty bluster—but from this still, cold-eyed nomad, it felt like a simple statement of fact. One might as well threaten a stone, she thought.

The Cradle and the Sword 533

Nisaba paused and took a breath, willing her body to dispel some of the tension that had built up since this strange man had entered her chamber.

"I have no wish to harm you, nomad," she said. "I only want to hear your stories."

"Very well." He nodded. "Then I will begin by telling you the truth about the Garden and the snake."

And so he did. He drew a long-necked instrument from his bag, plucked at its strings, and sang to her of the world before the Garden, when men and women walked naked in the shallow swamps near the desert's edge, stone-tipped spears in hand, following great herds of gazelle and ibex and oryx. He sang of the years of crippling famine, when many tribes of nomads were forced inward into the forests, away from the open sky, to root for vegetables like pigs.

He sang of a clever shaman named Énki, who had first learned the secret of making Gods from a clan of enchantresses in that forest: women who wove serpents into their hair, and were said to turn men to stone with the merest gaze. The nomad sang of how Énki, drunk on the knowledge he had gained from the women, had tried to teach the men of his tribe many mysteries they did not understand; so that they twisted Énki's words, believing that if they clothed their nakedness they could put on the splendor of the Gods themselves, and that if they tore down the trees and churned the land they could create a new world, as Gods did. All wars and strife among men, the nomad sang, had begun on that day—and the Ayya people had cursed women and serpents ever since.

For the truth, the nomad sang, was that men had made the Gods in their own image. In the time before Énki and his tribe came to live in the Garden, there were no Gods, for no one had dreamed them yet.

In those far-distant days before the famine and the Garden and the Gods, the nomad sang to Nisaba, before the seas had risen to sunder Dilmun from Shumér, humans and animals mixed freely and without distinction; and the earth was filled with creatures neither animal nor human: the old folk of the forest, squat and thick-bearded, who knew the secret of putting on the flesh of the bear.

The nomad sang the tragedy of the virgin woman who envied this secret, and walked alone into the woods and offered her body to the males of the old folk, who repaid her by teaching her the way of becoming a bear. But the wily old folk tricked the woman; for once she had changed to a bear, they refused to tell her the secret of becoming a woman again; so that the woman's lover, believing the old folk had taken and slain her, gathered hunters and went into the forest and killed a bear—which was his own woman, of course, gasping her lover's name with her last breath as he fled in horror, driven mad by the deed he had done.

The nomad sang of many formless shambling things that walked in the forest, and in the desert, and in the high mountain passes. He sang of the keeper of the herds, a thing that wore no single shape, which kept all the world's cattle and gazelle and oryx hidden in a cave; until hunters disguised as sheep sneaked inside the cave and wounded the keeper, and freed the great herds to wander across the grasslands forevermore. He sang of immortal serpents that possessed powers of speech and flight, who dwelt in lakes and rivers, and would rise up and whisper the cure for any illness for the price of a maiden's lifeblood. He sang of women who gave themselves freely to the lusts of forest-things with hooves and goatlike eyes; who sometimes give birth to daughters, but other times carried offspring they nurtured in secret, which might pass for men when they walked upright on cloudy nights.

And he sang, at last, of the Tree, which had pierced the sky from the depths of the sea, uncounted eons before Gods or men came to the place that would one day be called Dilmun. The Tree had always stood in that place, he sang; and it would stand there long after this world had crumbled back into the seas, and Abzu and Tiamat warred again, casting up generation after generation of strange worlds and creatures without end. Through it all, the Tree had sung and would forever sing to those who wandered within reach of its voice, promising passage to the eternal Abyss of things unformed and yet to be.

The Tree's voice did not lie. As men had always known, one who entered the Tree would indeed pass over into the Abyss of the Unformed, to hurtle endlessly through the trackless night between worlds; the womb where nothing was; where all things forever became.

As the sun rose and the nomad packed away his instrument, Nisaba sat silently, staring into the rosy sky, seeing not the clouds or the palace walls, but the world behind them; the world of the unformed and the becoming; the Abyss where Énki dwelled, and would dwell forever.

⟨

AMNANU HAD NEVER stood in the royal audience chamber before; much less held the full attention of the god-king Shúlgi. He was well-bred enough not to tremble or flinch, but his heart was racing.

"What do you mean, she *left*?" Shúlgi demanded.

"As I said, O Sublime One," Amnanu replied, careful to keep his voice steady. "Nisaba barred me from her room for weeks. She spent many nights with strange bards and tale-tellers from many lands. I learned of this only by rumor. Last night, she summoned me to her room. I hurried there, and she greeted me eagerly. Told me she was very close to completing her poem."

Misharam lifted a wax tablet from the stack next to the god-king's writing-desk and scanned it appreciatively. "She's certainly given us a lengthy epic," he mused.

"She worked all through the night last night," Amnanu continued. "And when I awoke this morning, she was gone. Now you know as much as I do."

The god-king frowned, but said nothing. He looked at Amnanu, and at Misharam, who averted their eyes. He scanned the tapestries and reliefs adorning his private audience chamber, but these held no answers either.

For the first time in his long and illustrious rule, there seemed to be nothing in the world to say.

〈𒐖〉

Nisaba stood atop a cliff, the evening wind whipping her cloak around her, as it tossed the dense-leafed canopies of titan oaks and pines at the forest's edge.

This had to be the place. For the past three days, as she'd climbed hills and scrambled over boulders, the humming had grown stronger in her bones. When the ship from Urim had first docked at the quay of Dilmun, she'd scarcely felt it at all; just the tiniest tremble in the back of her mind, so subtle it could've been no more than her imagination.

But as she'd made her winding way through the streets of Dilmun's towns, passing suspicious-eyed merchants and fisher-folk, the men with dark skin and long black beards; the women veiled and bedecked with gold rings, the humming had grown a bit stronger; a soft thrumming beneath all her thoughts, guiding her away from the city, out through the suburbs where mud-brick shacks squatted amid palm trees and patches of grazing-grass, so like home, and yet so different.

The humming had grown even more insistent as she'd trekked beyond the last of the reed huts, up into the rocky country where she met only sheep and goats, up through the tree-line, into a world where elms and oaks and cedars crowded out the sky, reaching out to clasp limbs in the distant heights where brightly-colored birds danced.

Now the humming drowned out all else. It thundered in her, pulling at her, as if along a track, to this clearing high in the hills, where cold streams splashed among pale gray rocks, and the oaks gave way to pines and firs and pale striped birches.

Before her stood the Tree, its upper branches piercing the sky.

It could be nothing but itself. Its roots clutched the earth like giants' fingers knotted among the stones. Its trunk vanished into the clouds, so thick at its base that one could build a small town inside it. What seemed to be tiny branches sprouted all along its gnarled bark—but Nisaba realized these were smaller trees; ordinary trees, dwarfed by the impossible size of the Tree from which they took root.

She stepped forward, across a clearing that seemed to grow in size; or perhaps the scale of the Tree distorted all sense of the scale around it. She walked among birches and pines, closer to the source of the humming, where a labyrinth of roots spread outward across the rocky earth like veins in a hand.

Nisaba found a space between those roots, a doorway as tall as a palace; a gap among the network of tangled bark and leaves where the Tree met the earth. She stepped across the threshold, into the space between the roots, where vines glimmered with lapis lazuli and carnelian and emerald and amber, and the voices of birds sang to greet her.

Come to the Abzu, they sang. *Enter the place where all things become.*

158 YEARS EARLIER
2149 BC

The Guti, a race who know no order,
Descend from the mountains…
Like a plague of locusts they scour the land.

— The Curse of Agadé

Tirigan sat on the hillside, watching his goats graze beneath the setting sun.

They were a beautiful little herd. The females' udders swelled with milk; the males sported long curving horns and pelts of sleek white hair, perfect for sewing into kilts. The kids played around the hooves of their elders, charging and leaping, butting heads and letting out high-pitched bleats. One smaller female grazed too close to a senior male. He lowered his head and half-charged at her, and she fled to the fringes, bleating an apology over her shoulder.

Tirigan stood stiffly, glancing toward the sun that was now almost low enough to touch the horizon. He stretched, leaning back to relieve the ache in his back, rolling his head around on his shoulders to ease the tightness in his neck. He hoped tonight would be quiet, and that no one would come to disturb his family's sleep. But the tension in his back, and in his limbs told him otherwise, like joints aching just before a storm.

When he whistled, Pel came running, barking, tossing his furry head as he herded the goats back toward the house. Tirigan leaned down and ruffled the dog's fur, then followed him at a leisurely walk.

The house was scarcely more than a hut: four walls of tightly woven branches daubed with clay; but with the fire his wife had lit crackling in the hearth, it felt like a palace. The warm glow cast golden light on Kara's blond hair. Tirigan watched her prodding the coals around the roasting vegetables with a stick. When she was finished, he wrapped his arms around her shoulders and held her tightly.

Before he could do more, the twins burst in: Jaka, the boy, and Aji, the girl, both of them barely knee-high, green-eyed like their mother, and bursting with energy as always. They chased each other around the fire. Kara pulled away from Tirigan and reached out and grabbed the twins' arms.

"Don't run around the fire," she scolded them. "You'll burn yourself."

They pouted. "What's for dinner?" Jaka asked.

"What do you think?" Kara replied. "Onions. Carrots. Radishes." She grinned at the twins. "Maybe even meat from one of the goats?"

Aji squealed in horror. "No! I love the goats."

"We only kill goats on special occasions," Tirigan assured her.

"On a holy day," Kara explained gently, nudging the roasted vegetables out of the fire with her stick. "Like the longest day of summer, or the shortest day of winter."

"The days when the Gods listen to us most closely," Jaka said.

"That's right," Tirigan replied, helping Kara pile the vegetables on a clay plate decorated with a simple black-paint design: frolicking goats, chasing each others' tails in an endless circle. "On those days, we spill the blood of a goat out of respect for the Gods. They accept it as tribute," Tirigan said, "and reward us with healthy baby goats, and new patches of onions and radishes."

"Do the Gods eat the tribute?" Aji asked.

Kara smiled. "Not exactly. A tribute is something you give someone when you want something from them," Kara told the girl. "Like how I'm going to give you these vegetables to make you stop asking questions."

The twins pouted, but Tirigan fell back laughing.

After dinner, when the day's stories were told and the soft songs had been sung around the dying fire, Tirigan lay with Kara on their rough straw bedroll, while the twins snored softly at the other end of the house's single room.

"Do you think they'll come tonight?" she whispered to him, running her fingers along his bare chest.

"I don't know," he said, though he was fairly sure he did.

She heard the little lie in his voice. "Is there nothing we can do?" she asked.

"We have nothing left to give them," he said. "Unless they want radishes and goats."

"Promise me," she whispered. "Promise me if they try to take me, you'll do what's necessary."

He shook his head. "I'm not going to think about that."

"You have to," she said. "I need to know you're ready to do it, if the time comes."

"I'm not going to promise you that," he said.

But as he drifted off to sleep beside her, he wondered what he really would do, if it came to it.

Later, the farm lay in silence beneath bright stars, attended only by the songs of night insects. Tirigan and Kara lay snoring on their sleeping-mat, her arm draped across his chest; him, traveling in dreams, unaware of the weight of her arm. Aji and Jaka slept curled on their mats nearby, blinking and moving softly as they ran through unseen countries. Around them, all was still.

Then, amid quiet rustling, shadows crept out of the dark—phantoms striking tinder and lighting torches whose dancing orange glow flickered across their scarred faces and chests. Illuminated by torchlight, the phantoms gained substance to become four men wearing tattered wool kilts dyed in the blacks and blues and reds of cities they'd never sworn allegiance to, with mismatched leopardskin army cloaks and boiled leather vests, and burnished copper daggers in their belts, each hilt carved with the sigil of some man who'd thought to challenge them, and would never raise a challenge again.

The four hurled their torches at the house. Tongues of fire leaped up, licking at the walls, roaring and devouring the dry reeds.

In shadow, the men stood watching silently as flames engulfed the walls and roof.

Tirigan and Kara came out stumbling and coughing, him clutching Jaka, her carrying Aji.

"What do you want?" Tirigan shrieked.

The men grinned, brandishing dented daggers and chisel-axes that glinted in the firelight. The leader wore an eyepatch, and a scraggly gray beard that hung almost to the belt around his tunic. Around his neck was a necklace strung with what had once been men's and women's ears, more than a dozen of them, dried and dirt-covered until they'd turned black and shriveled like unwholesome fruit.

"Take it!" Tirigan cried. "Take the goats and leave us in piece."

The thieves looked at each other, laughing at Tirigan's foolishness.

"Goats!" cried the leader. "We don't want your goats."

Meanwhile, two of the others were creeping closer, muttering "Easy now," reaching for the weeping, terrified children in Tirigan's and Kara's arms. Jaka and Aji pulled away, screaming. The thieves reached out for the fleeing children, sweeping them up in their scarred arms before they could run away.

"Take me!" Kara shrieked suddenly.

The thieves froze. The leader looked Kara up and down, his face a craggy, shadowy landscape in the firelight.

She walked toward him. "Please," she said. "Take me, but not my children."

"Aye, we'll take you," the leader said, stepping toward her.

"Kara, no!" Tirigan howled, running to get between her and the leader. But the fourth thief was too quick. He slipped around behind Tirigan, who felt something hard and heavy crack against the back of his skull.

The last thing he heard before all went silent and dark was his wife screaming "No!" above the shrieks of his children.

Énsi Gudea, governor of the city of Lagash, was dreaming. He knew he was dreaming, because the walls of his palace were moving oddly, and he traveled from room to room without walking. People he knew—priests and courtiers and minor nobles—appeared, spoke nonsense, and turned into other people. Yes, this was most certainly a dream.

Not everyone knew how to realize when they were in a dream, but Gudea had learned the trick of it from the priests who'd been his tutors, back when he was only a boy—before he'd come into his inheritance and accepted the Shepherd's

Crown: governorship of the city and land of Lagash. Like any leader who journeyed between Gods and men, he had to know when he was in a dream, so he might be alert and ready for any signs the Gods might send him.

Now, in his dream, Gudea stood outside the palace of Lagash, in a stone quarry where many men were laboring hard under the hot sun. Their master was whipping them, but they worked slowly, sending up wails of complaint.

Then another man stood next to the slave-master. The other man was wise and serene, wearing the pure white robes of a priest. The wise one stopped the slave-master's hand, took the whip, and tore away its leather lashes, replacing them with soft tufts of sheep's-wool. Then he handed the whip back to the slave-master, who began to call out happy words to the workers, praising their workmanship and reminding them of the great house they were building. Instead of whipping them, he tickled them with the wool, making them laugh. And in their joy they worked much harder than before, singing triumphant songs to the heavens.

Now Gudea stood alone with the wise man in white. Sometimes he seemed like a man; other times like a wise-eyed serpent. At last Gudea recognized him: this was none other than Ningishzida, his personal God.

"My lord!" Gudea cried, prostrating himself on his knees, exposing his shaved-bald head to the God. "I did not recognize you. I beg you to forgive my impiety."

"There is nothing to forgive, old friend," Ningishzida said softly, helping Gudea to his feet. "You need not be so formal with me. Have we not known each other well, these many years?"

"We have, lord," said Gudea, smiling, brushing dust from his loose one-shouldered toga. How wise and kind the God's eyes were. Gudea wanted to tell the wise-eyed one everything; to unburden himself of all his sins.

"I bring you a message," Ningishzida said. "From a higher God, one of those who dwell beyond the Gates of the Heavens."

"A message," Gudea repeated. "Which of the Gods finds me worthy?"

"None other than Far-Seeing Ningirsu," Ningishzida said. "The winged lion, son of Énlil, the South Wind, wielder of the enchanted mace named Sharur the Smasher-of-Thousands, farmer and healer, destroyer of demons, ancient protector of the city and lands of Lagash."

The list of epithets sent trembles through Gudea's body, even deep within this strange dream. "I beg you, old friend," he said to wise-eyed Ningishzida, "tell me what message the God Ningirsu sends to me."

The white-robed God smiled. "Ask him yourself."

Gudea found himself standing before a vast throne. On the throne sat a being radiant with light, filling the room with a blinding golden glow. Terrified, Gudea prostrated himself before the throne, pressing his forehead seven times against the carpeted floor.

"Arise, Gudea," rumbled a voice like a lion's roar, "my faithful servant."

Scrambling to his feet, Gudea still had to avert his eyes, the God's radiance was so overwhelming. Gudea recognized this radiance as the *melammu*—the splendor worn by all the high Gods, which made them impossible to look upon. Without the intercession of a personal God like friendly old Ningishzida, the slightest brush with a high God's *melammu* would incinerate any mortal, body and soul.

Thankfully, with the help of Ningishzida's intercession on his behalf, Gudea was able to kneel in the presence of this God, though even now he was unable to look directly at the *melammu*. Its radiance filled him with primordial terror, and at the same time, with an overpowering love and comfort, as if the God saw through him clearly as water, and understood and accepted all his sins and secrets, and loved him all the more for them.

A pair of lions, one male and one female, sat at the left and right of Ningirsu's throne, which was formed of purest gold, and adorned with rubies, emeralds, carnelian, lapis lazuli and many other precious stones. The radiant God held in his hand a mace, its handle as long as Gudea was tall. Its head was that of an eagle, cast in bronze, looking about and snapping at the air like a living bird.

"Far-Seeing Ningirsu," Gudea stammered. "Mighty lion, roaring south wind—I am unworthy to kiss the dust beneath your feet."

"I have a task for you, Gudea," Ningirsu spoke like thunder. "A great undertaking for the city of Lagash."

"I am a tool in your hand, Eternal One," Gudea said. "I await your command."

"Ningishzida," Ningirsu spoke to Gudea's personal God, who appeared white-robed at his side. "Open the gateway."

Wise-eyed Ningishzida took Gudea's right hand, smiling. A pair of serpents emerged from the friendly God's shoulders. In his left hand he now held a bowl, overflowing with water, the clear stream pouring onto the floor, forming a pool around their feet. The pool grew as large as a lake, and too deep for Gudea to see the bottom through its dark fathoms, though he and Ningishzida remained standing atop the water, hand-in-hand.

Gudea recognized this deep water: it was the Abzu, the great freshwater sea from which all life and creativity arose. Home of the great God Énki, Lord of the Abyss.

"My Lord Énki," spoke radiant Ningirsu from his golden throne. "Wise in all the arts, teacher of language and of tricks, crafter of tools and cities, keeper of the *mhé*, the attributes of civilization: I ask you to teach this man Gudea how to build my house."

Gudea's mind was reeling. He had been introduced not only to the high God Ningirsu, one of the most ancient and magnificent of all deities. But Ningirsu himself was calling on Énki, one of the eternal primordial Gods, one of the Seven Gods who Decree, one who dwells in the Ocean of Being itself, who brought the world forth from chaos. A God who had not spoken with mere humans since the days before the Flood, in those faraway years when Heaven talked with Earth and Earth talked with Heaven. Even in the dream, his whole body hummed with excitement and terror.

Gudea gazed down into the Abzu, and it was as if his mind was as vast as all the world. He saw his city of Lagash, not as a man standing in the city, but as if he were able to see every part of it—the inside and outside walls of every house and temple, every stone of every street, the watery depths of every well and the green-leafed top of every palm-tree, every man and woman and child, every barrel of grain and rack of meat, every disease, every act of lovemaking, every birth and murder and celebration and sacrifice and prayer—at the same time, at once, as part of the same united whole.

A deep voice hummed from the depths of the Abzu, soft and comforting, wise beyond words.

Behold your city of Lagash, a voice thrummed in Gudea's bones. Every word seemed to unspool chains of thought that branched into webs of meaning without end.

Long ago, the voice hummed within Gudea, *I showed men how to build this city for Ningirsu.*

Gudea could find no words to respond. He filled his heart with affirmation, knowing the God would understand.

"The land lies in ruins!" Ningirsu thundered from his golden throne. "What has become of the Sons of Szarrukín? Woe to Akkad's noble houses, who proclaimed themselves Gods, then squabbled until their empire crumbled to dust. Now worms gnaw their gold-crowned heads!"

Gudea recognized these names and saw before him the long-bearded face of Emperor Szarrukín, head of the most powerful family of the land of Akkad, who had ruled all the lands between the Two Rivers more than a century ago, claiming to have subjugated the entire earth, welding all civilized lands into the first world-spanning empire in history. Shumér had been the jewel in that empire's crown—but then the Shuméru cities had rebelled, one after another, while Akkad's noble houses brawled like starving dogs over scraps of land, until their empire tore itself to shreds. All this Gudea saw.

"The ancient cities have reverted to barbarism," Ningirsu bellowed. "They lash out at one another like vipers, spurred by petty chieftains who desecrate the sacred places. The common people live lawlessly, slaying one another over stale crusts. Barbarians ravage the land, raping and stealing like wild beasts!"

"Who is king? Who is *not* king?" squawked Sharur, the God's eagle-headed mace.

"Shumér whores herself to a hundred madmen," Ningirsu bellowed, "each naming himself governor or lord of some stretch of river."

Yes, all things come to pass, Énki's voice thrummed in Gudea's bones. This simple statement seemed to carry a thousand other meanings; poetry that slipped through Gudea's mind before he could grasp its sense. It was as if all this cacophony was beneath the ancient Énki's notice somehow, too small and petty to merit the Lord of the Abzu's attention. As if even the resplendent God Ningirsu was petitioning Énki, begging for help like a child upon his father's knee.

"You alone, Gudea, have remained a faithful servant," thundered Ningirsu. "You will build me a new house in Lagash, and preserve Shumér in her purity."

Yes, Énki's voice hummed. *A house.*

Then Gudea saw the house and was within it, observing every part of it at once: a great temple, towering to the sun. At its top, a sanctuary, a holy-of-holies where Ningirsu would make his dwelling-place on earth. But when the God spoke of a "house," Gudea now realized, he meant not only a temple but a whole city; a new Lagash, purified and cleansed, organized and efficient, clean and well-constructed and proper in every way—not only in the stones of its streets and walls and houses, but in the laws of its courts, the rituals and ceremonies to be observed, the dress and conduct of its citizens, and the distribution of its grain and beer and sheep. All this was to be the new house of the God Ningirsu, Lord of Lagash.

"I..." Gudea pleaded. "O Ningirsu, I do not understand all this!"

Do not try to understand, Énki's voice hummed comfortingly. *Only see.*

And Gudea did see. He was looking not at the city now, but at a glade of junipers and elms. He thought he recognized it; the woods northeast of Lagash. Legend held that the glade had once been the site of a great temple; but now, in this age of darkness, only wild beasts made their dwellings there. Among the roots of the trees he saw a tablet of white stone, with a strange design engraved upon it.

"This," said Ningirsu, "is my house."

Then blinding white light erupted; a *melammu* more radiant and terrifying and beautiful than Gudea could stand. He felt his head burst and fill with brightness—

—and awoke in bed, sweat dripping in beads down his bald head and clean-shaven face. He sat up and saw that the light was the first rays of dawn, lancing through the high, narrow windows of his simple mud-brick bedchamber.

Next to him, his wife Ninalla stirred and rubbed her eyes, waking and rolling over to him. Her eyes widened in fear when she saw his look of terror, and the sweat rolling in rivulets down his pale face.

"My love!" she gasped, placing a soft hand against his smooth cheek.

"It's all right," he whispered, staring into the distance with visions of strange new things still whirling in his mind. "I had a dream."

She sat up. "Did you speak with a God?" she asked.

At last he turned to look at her. "Ningishzida spoke to me," he said. "For the first time in months."

"You are blessed," she said, smiling.

"He brought me before the throne of Ningirsu," Gudea continued.

Ninalla made a sacred gesture of protection, looking wide-eyed at her husband.

"And the Lord Ningirsu..." Gudea trailed off, unable to speak the words, almost unable to believe them.

She placed her hand against her heart. It was racing.

"The Lord Ningirsu," Gudea said at last, "bid Ningishzida to open the gateway to the Abzu. I went into its depths, and there..."

She stared into his eyes, rapt and waiting.

"There I met with Énki, who spoke to me."

Ninalla gasped. "Énki has spoken with no man since before the Flood," she whispered.

"Énki and Ningirsu spoke to me," Gudea said, "of building a house."

"A house?" she looked at him, puzzled. "You mean a temple."

"Not only a temple," he said. "Many things. I did not understand it all. But I must obey. But I need an interpreter."

"Your sister Nanshe," Ninalla replied. "She interprets dreams at the temple."

"Yes, of course." Gudea nodded. "I'll pay her a visit this very morning."

"Oh, my love, can this really be true?" Ninalla wiped away tears. "The God Énki Himself?"

"It is true," Gudea said. Then he remembered something the God had said to him. "All things come to pass."

Ninalla's brow furrowed. "What do you mean?"

Gudea shook his head. "I'm not sure. But I think there may be hope for Shumér after all."

ᛉᛉᛉ

THE WILDERNESS FROZE Tirigan at night and scorched him by day. Beneath the angry face of the noonday sun, he trudged through the dry grass and across baked riverbeds of cracked clay, or hid himself in bushes and palm-groves, drinking water from stagnant puddles and pools when he could find them, eating any berries that were safe to eat, digging up edible roots where their stubby green leaves sprouted from the hard dirt. He moved by night, by the light of the moon and stars, not knowing where he was going, or what he was looking for. Only that he must keep moving.

He'd lost count of the days since he'd woken next to the ashen ruin of his family's home, head aching, vision blurred. The first time he'd tried to stand, the world had swum like water, and he'd lost his balance and collapsed to the charred grass, head ringing even worse than before, tears of despair and rage coursing down his cheeks.

At last, though, hunger drove him back to the wreckage of the house, where he dug a few half-charred radishes from beneath the blackened dirt. He found the shattered clay plate, painted with goats; and a toy he'd made for the children: a little wooden donkey on wheels. Hot tears rose in his eyes. He forced himself to his feet, and set off in the direction from which the raiders had come.

That afternoon, as the red sun dipped behind the distant mountains, he stumbled past a dead juniper tree. Three bodies hung from its branches, scarcely more than bones, picked clean and shimmering in the heat. Something big had been at the legs; the bones lay scattered on the ground, cracked and pale.

No stone stood to mark this place, for none was needed. Cruel Nergál ruled here: God of pain and war, and of the harsh noonday sun. Tirigan cursed that God, and walked on.

He paused only when hunger or thirst compelled him to devour roots and leaves and sour berries, or when sleep collapsed him, or when the noonday sun beat down too fiercely for him to move. At all other times he was on the march, day after long hot day, night after cool shadowy night.

A network of wood-and-clay channels had once brought water here from the faraway river, branching out neatly to feed each furrow with cool streams. Now those aqueducts lay in shattered ruins atop the dead grass, a few of them splashing water stupidly into stagnant pools amid hillocks of mud, turning the field into a churned-up wreckage of moss and buzzing flies.

Herds of bony cattle, freed by raiders and left to wander the countryside, stood listless among the hard brown bushes, chewing mouthfuls of dry cud, tails swatting at the flies that swarmed around their mangy flanks.

When Tirigan caught sight of a rising dust-cloud, he found a hiding-place and let the travelers pass. Sometimes they were only cattle or sheep, shaggy and starving, questing for green grass they would never find. But other times the dust was raised by bands of thieves or raiders, though he never saw the men who'd taken Kara and the children.

One evening, just before sunset, he was hiding in a stand of thorn-bushes, watching a small troupe of slavers trudge across a weed-tangled field. A doorframe of gnarled wood stood alone at the edge of the dead grain-stalks, amid piles of worn clay and palms. The sole surviving remnant of a clay house dissolved back into the earth.

The slavers stomped and splashed past the doorframe, dragging a pair of women on ropes behind them—the younger one small and slender, the other tall and lean with muscle. Both women seemed to be too tired to struggle. They followed unwillingly, dragging their feet, mud staining their legs and the remains of their rough-spun wool togas.

The men dragging them appeared to be father and son, or perhaps brothers: a middle-aged man with long, scraggly black hair, wearing only a ragged fleece kilt and a necklace of men's bones, his rattling fingers pointing wildly as he trudged. The other, a lanky young red-haired boy, wore a tunic that had once been red, now stained and muddy.

As Tirigan watched from the bushes, the smaller woman stumbled and fell into the mud with a splash. The boy dragging her was jerked back by his grip on the rope. He fell backward and splashed to the ground near her. The taller woman turned and hid a chuckle. The boy scrambled up and grabbed her roughly by the neck-rope, yanking hard.

"You think that's funny?" he snarled.

He slapped her and knocked her to the mud. Then he whirled and began to beat the small woman furiously; first with his hand, then with a leather ox-goad he pulled from his belt. She screamed, making Tirigan wince from his hiding place. Blood ran down her neck, her back, and her shoulders, where his strikes tore flesh and fabric.

"Enough!" shouted the older one. "You stupid fool. She would've fetched twenty coppers from a brothel-keeper; now she looks like that, we'll be lucky to get five."

"She laughed at me!" the boy retorted.

"They'll all be laughing at us now," the older one said, "marching into Lagash with this bloody mess."

The taller woman glanced into the bushes, and locked eyes with Tirigan. She gasped in astonishment, but quickly hid it. The look in her eyes, though, was clear: *Help us.*

The man and the boy were still arguing, absorbed in their quarrel. Now was the time to strike. *But strike how?* Tirigan wondered. *And with what?* He was only a poor farmer, and he carried no weapon but his small copper dagger, which had never tasted any blood but that of a fresh-caught fish.

And yet, that look in her eyes. So terrified, yet so full of hope.

Suddenly Tirigan found himself leaping from the bushes, racing across the muddy swamp toward the arguing man and boy. The man looked up, eyes wide with surprise. Tirigan slammed into him, knocking him hard on his back with a great splash of mud.

Tirigan pounded the man's face and wrestled the ox-goad from his grip, and then whipped him with it. The man drew a battered old dagger from his belt. Tirigan ripped it from his grasp and plunged it into the man's bare chest, again, then again, until the mud around them ran red with blood and the long-haired man lay still.

It had all taken no longer than the space of ten breaths.

Tirigan rose to his feet. The tall woman had seized the opportunity to wrap her rope around the red-haired boy's throat, and pull it tight. Now all three of them were staring at him. None made a move to attack, or to run.

"Go on, then; finish him off," Tirigan said to the woman.

The red-haired boy burst into tears. "I didn't even want to take them!" he pleaded. "Wartu said he'd kill me if I didn't. Please don't kill me." Tears were streaming down his mud-stained cheeks.

Tirigan watched him for a moment. "Do with him what you like," he said.

He turned to leave.

"Wait!" the slender woman cried out.

Tirigan half-turned, looking back at her.

"We'll travel with you," she said.

He huffed a dry laugh. "I'm not going anywhere you want to go."

She shrugged. "Where are you going?"

"To find the men who took my wife and children." It was the first time he'd actually said it aloud, and he found the words alien in his mouth, as if they held no meaning.

"Where are they?" she asked.

"I don't know." He sighed, pointing in the direction he'd been walking. "That way, I think."

"I can help you find them," the boy blurted. "I'm an excellent tracker. I can find sign in grass, in the woods—" The woman cuffed him on the head and he shut up.

But he'd caught Tirigan's attention, and he saw it. His eyes pleaded.

"I can fight," said the tall woman. "Keep me alive and give me a knife and I'll slit the throat of any man you tell me."

"Don't you have homes of your own?" Tirigan cried. "Families?" But he could see in their eyes that none of them did.

He bent down and lifted the dead man's chipped bronze dagger from the mud and wiped off a bit of the blood. He tossed it to the tall woman, who caught it with her free hand, wiped the rest of the blood on her tunic, and slid the knife into her belt. "I'm Vaya," she said.

"Tirigan," he told her.

"Aji," said the slender one.

"That's my daugh—" the words caught in his throat. They were all watching him. "My daughter's name," he finished quietly.

Vaya released her rope's choke-hold on the boy's neck. The boy swallowed, rubbing the skin, and said, "I'm Kurum."

Tirigan nodded to all three of them.

"Well," he said, "if you're coming, then come on."

The four of them splashed through the mud, in the direction Tirigan had pointed.

JUST AFTER SUNRISE, Gudea burst through the gates of the temple courtyard, his toga hiked above his knees, sandals clacking on the paving-stones. His head was shaved bald, like that of a priest. He wore no ornaments or embroidery—only a simple one-shouldered toga, its flax dyed deep green, fringed in white.

Nanshe, Gudea's sister, looked up from her prayers. Her movement drew surprised glances from the other priests who knelt around her in the small sanctuary, palms upraised in prayer before the statue of Ningirsu, God of war. Even in mid-morning, the interior of the temple was gloomy; windowless, apart from a small hole in the high roof to let out the smoke of burning sandalwood, and of the candles that flickered on the mud-brick walls.

Gudea signalled to Nanshe, but she shook her head and remained kneeling, following the other priests through the remainder of their long, low chant:

Lord Ningirsu, resplendent as the sun.
Fearsome in battle, he roars like a storm...

As they chanted in chorus and counterpoint, old Abuwaqar, the én-priest, solemnly waved the sandalwood before the God Ningirsu's altar, his eyes downcast in humility.

Gudea reflected that the God really had preserved the city of Lagash through many battles. Bands of barbarians—usually some ragtag tribe of the foreign people known as the Guti—had tried to storm the walls several times, but the brave fighters of Lagash had always driven them back. In this age of darkness, when warlords ruled most of the ancient cities and bands of wild barbarians ravaged the countryside, Lagash truly was an island of civilization unto itself.

When the chant was finished, Abuwaqar performed the final ritual gestures and blessing with the other officiates. As the gray-bearded én-priest shuffled back to his chambers, Nanshe strolled toward the temple courtyard where she knew her brother would be waiting for her.

She paused at the basin of water near the entrance—memorial of the bottomless depths of the Abzu, on whose banks the world's first city, Eridu, had been raised at the world's dawn—and splashed a few drops on her forehead.

Nanshe found Gudea among the dilapidated pillars of the courtyard; still and serene as always, hands clasped in front of his simple one-shouldered toga, shaved head gleaming in the morning sun. As he turned and caught sight of Nanshe, a grin spread across his face. He remained exactly where he was, however, not shifting in the slightest.

"Sister dear," he said, smiling warmly.

"Én Gudea," replied Nanshe, bowing to kiss her brother's hand.

Gudea waved her off. "I'll have none of that 'én' nonsense, Nanshe. I've told you, I'm no king or high priest, simply an énsi, a humble city-governor, whom the Gods have seen fit to put in charge of their city of Lagash. 'Brother' will also do."

"As you say, brother," Nanshe answered with a smile.

Gudea clasped his hands around Nanshe's forearms and kissed her on both cheeks.

"So, Gudea," said Nanshe, smiling. "What brings you to our temple today?"

"The Gods," said Gudea, as if musing on some unspoken idea. "Yes, it is they who've sent me here."

Nanshe's eyes widened. "Did a God visit you again?"

Gudea wrapped his arm around his sister's shoulders. "Can we talk in private?"

"Of course." Nanshe led her brother to a nearby alcove in the temple garden. Though nearby priests eyed them curiously, no one dared approach.

"My personal God Ningishzida came to me in a dream last night," Gudea whispered.

Nanshe was silent for a long time. When at last she spoke, her voice was hushed and cautious. "What did he tell you?"

"He brought me before the throne of Ningirsu himself," Gudea said.

Nanshe made a holy sign of protection. "What did Ningirsu command?"

Gudea's voice was almost a whisper. "He showed me the Abzu."

"You spoke with—with Énki?" Nanshe gasped. "Directly? How—?"

"I heard his voice. He spoke to me about building a house for Ningirsu, but I didn't understand."

"A house," Nanshe ran a hand over her face. "You mean a temple?"

"A temple, yes," Gudea said. "But not only a temple. It was as if I saw a whole city, all at once. This is why I came to you. What can it mean?"

Nanshe's brow furrowed. She closed her eyes, and was silent for the space of many heartbeats.

"The God means means for you to build a new Lagash," she said at last, her eyes opening. "A citadel of scholarship and correct governance, whose culture will give birth to a new Shumér."

Gudea took his sister by the shoulders, eyes afire. "The end of this age of darkness," he gasped.

Nanshe nodded her head. "It's a beautiful dream, Gudea. And if Énki himself has commanded it, of course we must try. But—"

Gudea smiled. "It sounds impossible, I know. But I must do what I can to bring it to pass. This afternoon I'll go and talk with the nobles."

"I am ever at your side, of course," Nanshe said. "But—"

"I know you are, sister of mine." Gudea said, embracing Nanshe, kissing her on the forehead. "Now I must go on a brief expedition. I will return soon."

"An expedition—?" Nanshe shook her head in confusion.

"That was Ningirsu's other command," he told her, already turning to depart. "I must go to the forest northeast of the city, and bring back what I find there."

"Gudea," Nanshe said, "take some soldiers with you, at least. The barbarians are everywhere."

"They are indeed," Gudea replied. "But I won't be long. I know precisely where I'm going."

※

Tirigan squatted in the bushes with the women Vaya and Aji, and the red-haired boy Kurum.

"Yes, that's them," he said. "I'm sure of it."

They were watching four men counting plunder in a rough camp, on the far side of a field. Tirigan recognized the leader: the man's long gray beard and eye-patch marked him beyond any doubt as the one who'd taken his Kara. The others looked vaguely familiar; he'd only seen them by firelight on the night they'd taken his family. Yet here they were, rifling through sacks of grain and tools with their leader around a rough round tent of animal skins.

"What do we do?" Kurum whispered.

"It'd be foolish to attack now, in broad daylight," Aji said.

Tirigan nodded. "There's no cover, just an open field. Four of them, three of us. We'll only win if we surprise them."

"After dark, then," said Vaya.

"When they've fallen asleep," Tirigan agreed.

As they settled into their hiding-place to wait out the rest of the afternoon, a deep unease settled over Tirigan: Kara and his children didn't seem to be in this camp. The men had probably sold them as slaves to some nearby tribe. But that raised a host of fresh questions: Where were they now? How were their new masters treating them? Would there be more battles before he had them back?

After a while, Vaya gave voice to those thoughts. "Tirigan, I don't see any captives."

"Slaves aren't convenient to carry," Kurum pointed out, and both women glared at him. He spread his hands defensively. "I'm just saying, men like these would rather sell captives than keep dragging them from place to place."

"You think they sold them?" Tirigan asked quietly. "Not—?"

Kurum's eyes went wide. "Oh, no! Very unlikely. Why would they go to the trouble of taking captives, then—well, throw away the profit?"

"He's right." Vaya placed a hand softly on Tirigan's shoulder. "It would make no sense."

Tirigan nodded. "Then we must take them alive, and make them talk."

When night fell, they crept from the bushes: Tirigan and Vaya sweeping widely to the left of the bandits' camp; Kurum and Aji sweeping to the right. They moved across the field in near silence, focusing on the lone sentry propped up drunkenly next to the bandits' fire.

The man turned slowly toward Tirigan, a look of horror on his face. Then Aji came from behind him, neatly slitting his throat with one stroke of her bronze dagger. She stood, wiping the blood on her dress, exchanging grim smiles with Tirigan.

Two others lay sprawled on the ground, a little way from the fire. Vaya fell on one of them, wrapping a rope around his neck and pulling it tight, while Kurum leaped atop the other, plunging his own dagger again and again into the man's chest. But the man Vaya was strangling kicked and bucked, making a lot of noise. Tirigan heard muffled shouts and movement from inside the leader's tent.

The eye-patched leader burst out, bronze axe in hand, leaping at Tirigan, who stumbled back, falling to the ground, grabbing a long dagger from one of the dead men. The leader swung the axe. Tirigan raised the dagger to block it, but the warrior was stronger than he looked. His axe-blow struck the dagger from Tirigan's hand. He leaped at Tirigan, snarling.

"You want her?" the eye-patched fighter hissed. "I can tell you where she is."

Tirigan's eyes widened. Vaya, Aji and Kurum had the leader surrounded, but Tirigan raised his hand to stay them. "Tell me," he said. "Tell me where they are."

"First, promise you'll spare my life," the leader said.

"I'll promise no such thing," Tirigan said. "But I promise I'll make your death a quick one."

"Not good enough," said the leader, and leaped at Tirigan with the axe. Tirigan leaped to the side, but the leader pivoted, sweeping the axe-blade low, barely missing Tirigan's chest as he jumped back.

Meanwhile Kurum had ducked into the leader's animal-skin tent. A moment later he ran back out, eyes wide with horror. "Tirigan—!" he cried, and Tirigan knew without doubt what he'd seen, because now the bandit leader was grinning cruelly.

"Well," said the leader. "Now you know where she is."

Tirigan roared. He threw himself bodily at the leader, knocking him backward into the campfire, which licked up around his legs. The leader shrieked, flailing wildly with his axe. Tirigan stepped back, watching the grey-bearded man stumble out of the coals. After just a few steps, though, a blade suddenly protruded from his neck, spilling blood down his chest as his eyes widened in shock.

Kurum stepped from behind him, withdrawing the blade. The leader collapsed to his knees, gurgling, clutching at his neck, even as his feet and legs continued to smoke and smolder from the fire. A moment later he lay dead on the dirt.

"You shouldn't have done that," Tirigan said to Kurum, panting.

"He wasn't going to tell us anything," Vaya said.

"But my children—" Tirigan protested.

"I know the towns and tribes around here," Kurum said. "If your boy and girl still live, we'll find them."

"In the meantime," Aji said, "You have to make sure it's really her, in the tent."

Tirigan looked up at her, his face a mask of despair.

"If you don't look now," Aji said, "You'll never be sure."

Tirigan nodded slowly. He rose, and made himself light a torch from the fire, and open the animal-skin flap of the leader's round tent. There, by the dim light of the campfire, lay a woman's body. Tirigan raised the torch, and saw that it was her, his Kara, bruised almost beyond recognition; motionless. Throwing the torch away, he fell atop her, shaking her, crying out prayers to every God he knew. But even as he howled, he already knew it was too late.

A long while later, he emerged from the tent to find Aji, Vaya and Kurum seated quietly around the fire, staring into the flames, chewing a bit of bread and vegetables they'd found. They all looked up as he approached, but none of them said anything. They only rose, and put their arms around him, and held him tightly while he wept violently.

Finally exhausted, he lay down next to the fire.

"There's still hope," Vaya said quietly as she draped a blanket over him, but he wasn't sure he believed her.

"Plundering the wilderness like a barbarian now, are we?" Nanshe grinned mischievously.

Gudea laughed, loudly and deeply, his slender body shaking in the dim light of the palace's meeting chamber. "I must be the strangest man in all the world, Nanshe," he said, wiping tears of mirth from his eyes, "for I have no interest in gold or cattle, but only in digging up what others throw away."

"And little interest in preserving your own life, it would seem," said Nanshe, in a mock-chiding tone.

The nobles they'd summoned were watching this conversation with narrowed eyes, as if unsure what to make of this pair of siblings. They picked at imaginary dust-motes on their one-shouldered togas, or in their long plaited beards. But none dared say a word.

Gudea waved a hand dismissively. "What is one man's life, really, in the sweep of history?"

"You speak not just of *any* man's life," Nanshe chided, "but of the life of the énsi of Lagash."

"All the same," said Gudea. "The Gods have already decided the day of my death. They know who my successor will be. In the meantime, I try to do as they command." He turned to the nobles. "In this case, they commanded me to go to the forest northeast of Lagash, and to bring back what I found there."

"And what did you find?" Nanshe asked.

Gudea smiled, at her and all the assembled nobles. "Let me show you."

The énsi led them to the room where slaves were depositing their leather-wrapped bundles. Sunlight streamed in through the high, narrow windows, casting shadows around all the piles of packages. Gudea bent and untied the ropes that bound one of the parcels, and gently unfolded the leather.

He lifted out a small plaque of white stone, carved with an intricate geometric pattern: squares within squares; rectangles stacked on rectangles. He held it high, his eyes ablaze. The sun gleamed on the tablet's smooth surface.

"Do you know what this is?" he asked, his voice nearly a whisper, his eyes darting restlessly.

Nanshe stepped closer. "I have seen tablets like this," she said, "in the temple archives."

Gudea smiled. "Then you know what it means."

"I do." Nanshe smiled back and nodded.

"Tell them," Gudea said, gesturing to the assembled nobles.

"It represents a temple," said Nanshe, "as seen from above."

"Exactly," said Gudea. "First, because this is how the Gods see the temple, from Heaven. Second, because it is not yet a temple, but the plan of one." The énsi smiled, retrieving another artifact from the parcel: a tablet of gleaming black obsidian, carved with tiny triangular symbols. "Have you ever heard," he asked the small crowd, "of Szarkalisharri?"

"It sounds like an Akkadu name," said one of the noblemen, a stout fellow in a white-fringed toga clasped with silver rings. Irarum was his name, Nanshe remembered.

"It is indeed." Gudea nodded, smiling. "Szarkalisharri was the last ruler of the Empire of Akkad. I have had the histories of his empire read out to me, these last few days."

Because the God Ningirsu spoke of that emperor in your dream, Nanshe thought. *Though I'll keep that truth to myself.*

"I have learned," Gudea was saying, "that Akkad's empire ruled the Land Between the Rivers for nearly two centuries, before it fell to the Guti barbarians fifty years ago."

"And good riddance," huffed Kuwari, the city's lugál: warchief and boss of Lagash's guard forces. Tattoos of lion-headed *anzú*-birds wrapped their wings about the scarred fighter's bare arms, and his shaggy fleece kilt was dyed yellow and black: Lagash's military colors. "Now that those Akkadu despots are dead and gone," he said, scratching his thick black beard, "we Shuméru are free again."

"Are we?" Gudea's brow furrowed. "Perhaps not so much as we think. There are advantages to empire. Trade flows freely, as does knowledge. Lords grow fatter, it's true—but so do libraries."

Irarum, the stout nobleman, merely humphed.

"Surely," Nanshe said to him, "You have heard of Szarkalisharri's great-great-grandfather, Emperor Szarrukín of Agadé."

"I have... heard that name," said the nobleman.

"Szarrukín forged the first empire in all the world's history—so the old poems tell us," Gudea said, clasping his hands gently in the manner of a teacher. "His armies conquered all of Shumér and Akkad, and beyond, east into Elam, west to the Great Sea, and even far north into the mountains, where the wild savages of Ash'shúr raise stone altars to their blasphemous gods. His sons expanded the empire even further: into Aram and K'nan, into the high plateaus east of Elam where horse-tribes gallop over unfarmed steppe, and even into the great Southern Desert, where nomads dwell in tents upon the swirling sands."

"You make it sound so—poetic," said Irarum, drily.

"All things grow poetic with age," replied Gudea, serene as ever.

"Even so," Lugál Kuwari put in, "surely it's better for Shuméru cities to be ruled by Shuméru governors."

Gudea spread his hands. "Before the emperor Szarrukín rode out and unified the Land Between the Rivers, things were not so different from today: each Shuméru city-state ruled by its own petty lord—a mob of éns and lugáls all squabbling for control of tiny parcels of land and small stretches of river. That's where this boundary-stone of the ancient lugál Eannatum comes from, in fact," Gudea said, gesturing at a weathered pillar inscribed with images of long-gone battles. "Eannatum won a border dispute against the lugál of Umma, and gained control of a valuable riverbend, for a time."

"I take your point," said Kuwari. "Those lords were petty and greedy. But at least they honored the Shuméru Gods, and protected their cities. Not like these barbarians who infest our land today."

"Indeed not," Nanshe replied. "In the days since Szarkalisharri's empire crumbled, the Land Between the Rivers has fallen into anarchy and war. Where are Shumér's old noble houses now?"

"One house remains," said Irarum, pointedly, looking at Gudea.

The énsi smiled gently. "I am no king," he said. "I claim no great lineage. I am merely the servant whom the Gods saw fit to appoint, in these days of chaos."

"And what of the rest of our cities?" Nanshe added. "Warlords and criminal families have seized Urim, Eridu, Unúg, Kish—even sacred Níppúr itself. Their armies war endlessly for control of the rivers and the farming-plains. The art of writing is all but lost, as are many ancient tablets of literature and prayer. Our land is ruled by small, ignorant men, who know nothing of the past, and dream of no future—and by the hordes of the Guti, these savages who care nothing for Gods or writing or civilization, and hunger only for plunder."

Gudea nodded in agreement. "What my sister says is true. We live in an age of darkness. The Gods alone know if civilization will ever be reborn. But I hope it will, someday. And I believe we must do what we can to preserve it."

"The barbarians are *here*, even now," Nanshe added. "At our very gates—"

"And we will sweep them aside," Gudea replied. "Do not fear, sister of mine. The night is ending. Soon, a new day will dawn."

Brother and sister fell silent, meeting the eyes of each man in the crowd.

At last, Lugál Kuwari nodded. "Then... we will need a greater army, énsi," he said.

"Yes." Gudea said, his hand balling into a fist. "A great army. All the mercenaries we can hire."

"And new weapons," Nanshe added.

"The sharpest, strongest bronze in the land." Gudea smiled.

"I will alert my fighters," Kuwari said.

"And your bricklayers," Gudea added.

"My—bricklayers, énsi?" Kuwari's brow furrowed again.

"For the new temple." Gudea spread his arms. "Construction begins at once. I have already drawn up the plans. We shall need as many strong men as you can spare from the city watch."

Kuwari bowed low. "As my énsi commands." He turned to go.

"Kuwari," Gudea called after him.

The lugál turned back.

"Thank you," Gudea said. "For not calling me mad."

"That is not my place, énsi," Kuwari replied. "I command in war, and you command in peace. Such is the way of things." The lugál nodded brusquely and hurried out the chamber door.

After the noblemen had dispersed, Gudea and Nanshe strolled together beneath the tall palms of the palace garden. As they walked along tiled paths among bushes of flowers and pools of brightly darting fish, Nanshe tried to catch her brother's eye; but the énsi walked in silence, his bald head bowed as if in prayer, though his eyes were open.

"What do you think, sister?" he asked suddenly. "Am I indeed mad?"

Nanshe walked beside him, choosing her words with care. "If you are mad, Gudea," she said after a moment, "then so am I. For I, too, have met the Gods in my dreams."

Gudea smiled. "And what did they tell you?"

"That they would send a new énsi," said Nanshe. "One who was *zíd*."

Gudea nodded thoughtfully. "And am I?" he asked. "*Zíd*?"

"That is not for me to decide, brother dear," said Nanshe. Then she smiled. "At least, not yet."

Then Gudea smiled too, and nodded as he always did when something became clear to him.

ONE NIGHT THEY bedded in the woven-reed barn, on a farm not so different from Tirigan's. The gray-haired farmer brought them a few stale crusts as they lay on the straw that carpeted the barn's dirt floor.

"I do wish you'd stay more than one night," the old man told them. "The taxmen will be along any day now. Wouldn't be so bad if they came once a year, but lately it's every week."

"What taxmen?" Vaya asked.

The old man shrugged. "How should I know? In the old days, my grandfather paid taxes only to the énsi of Lagash. But now we deal with green-kilts from Umma, too, and men from farther afield. And then there's Asak and his band, always demanding goats and barley and Gods-know-what, in exchange for 'protection.' Pah!" He spat on the ground by Tirigan's feet. "Last time they took my four best goats. All we've got left is the old nanny-goat now, and she hardly makes milk anymore."

"This Asak," Tirigan asked. "What does he look like?"

"My eyes aren't what they used to be," said the old man, "but I know he wears an eyepatch."

"That man is dead," Tirigan said.

"How do you know?" the old man asked.

"Because," said Kurum, "he died by my hand."

The old man's eyes widened at that. "In that case," he said, "you will sleep in my house tonight. The barn is no place for heroes like you."

Tirigan waved off the invitation. "We'll be fine here in the barn."

"Speak for yourself," said Aji, getting up from the clay. "I haven't slept on a proper bedroll in weeks."

Vaya and Kurum were rising, too. At last Tirigan sighed and heaved himself up from the straw.

After hot bowls of gruel and a soft bedroll, all four of them slept soundly, for the first time in weeks. But when the sun rose the next morning, they were off again.

They traveled mostly by night, sleeping through the day's hottest hours in forests and bushes, cutting a wide path around any bandit encampments they spotted, and hurrying off the road and out of sight when they heard a raiding party approaching.

One afternoon, they watched from the bushes as a whole troop of professional soldiers, outfitted in the yellow-and-black kilts of Lagash, carrying copper-tipped spears and shields, clad in gleaming helmets and leopardskin cloaks, marched lockstep along a road, chanting military songs. As the lines of marching men stomped by Tirigan's hiding-place, he counted more than five hundred of them—more men than he'd ever seen in one place.

"They're headed for Umma," Aji whispered as they hid behind a sun-baked boulder.

"Yet another quarrel between rich old men," Vaya said.

"Kish and Umma once fought a battle near my family's old farm," Kurum told them. "I think it was over some farming land, or maybe for the stretch of river where we fished. I climbed up a hill to watch, but I was too far away to see much of anything. The men looked like ants."

"Ants," Tirigan said. "That's what we all are, to these Shuméru lords. Their armies fight like giants, and all we can do is try to dodge their footsteps."

"My family lost a farm, too," Vaya said, placing a hand on his shoulder. "First the army of Lagash captured it, then Kish, then Umma. By then all the aqueducts were shattered and the farms dried up, until the land wasn't worth fighting over anymore."

As they traveled, they carefully skirted the fields and outlying towns under the protection of the great cities and their army garrisons. They stuck mostly to open country, woodland and field and heather; places too desolate or too out-of-the-way to draw the attention of armies.

One day they met a group of women, clad roughly in gazelle-skins, fishing and washing clothes on the bank of a long band of a river, which ran with muddy water.

"Where do you come from?" the oldest of them, a gray-haired crone, asked Tirigan.

"Nowhere you'd know," he replied.

"Headed to the village?" one of the younger ones asked.

Tirigan scanned the horizon. "What village?"

The woman laughed; a sound strange to Tirigan's ears. "The village," she said, as if this name explained itself. "You're Guti, like us. I can tell by the look of you. And you look as if you could use a hot meal and a bed."

Next thing Tirigan knew, he and his fellow travelers were following the women past a palisade wall of wood stretched with hardened animal-skins, accented by sharpened wood stakes, surrounded by a moat of muddy water. Guards in wool kilts stood at the gate, and let the women through with friendly hugs and smiles.

Within the wall sat a conglomeration of reed huts, and brightly painted tents covered with the skins of sheep and goats and gazelles. Many people walked to and fro among the houses, while the women sat chatting and grinding grain; the men butchered sheep and gazelles, while children ran squealing among their legs. Tirigan looked for his Jaka and Aji, but didn't see them.

The women brought him and his companions to a tall house built of wood and reeds, decorated with the deep black oryx pelts, accented with ribbons of green and red.

As Tirigan's eyes adjusted to the house's dim interior, he saw a fat, jolly woman seated atop a pile of furs and skins, draped in leather and furs, sipping from a drinking-horn and talking with a group of men who sat and stood nearby. When the women entered, leading Tirigan and his companions, all the men fell silent and turned to them. The plump woman raised her eyebrows inquisitively.

"We met these guests by the river," one of the fisher-women said. "They have traveled a long way."

"Have they?" The plump woman beckoned Tirigan closer. "Tell me, traveler, where do you come from?"

Tirigan stepped forward. "I come from many days' walk to the south of here."

The plump woman gave him an odd look. "How many days' walk?"

"I—I'm afraid I don't know," Tirigan said. "We've been walking—I've been walking—ever since—"

"Some bandit bastards took his wife and children," Vaya cut in, stepping forward. "We helped him hunt them down and slay them."

The plump woman smiled appreciatively. "Did you now? And what did these bandits look like?"

"The leader had a long gray beard," Vaya said. "And an eyepatch. He's gone from this world now."

Now the plump woman smiled broadly. "Then you are certainly guests in my house, for that was Asak One-Eye, who caused my people no end of trouble."

She gestured to the fisher-women, and the men around her. "Come, make room for my new friends. Fetch them fish and beer. What did you say your names were?" She thumped her chest. "I am Jirazi, and this is the Village of the Long Riverbend. Welcome."

Tirigan took a seat on a pile of furs nearby. His companions did the same. Women and men from the village brought plates of fresh fish, and roast vegetables, and horns of beer. Tirigan ate ravenously. He'd forgotten how wonderful food and beer could taste. By the time they'd all eaten their fill, the chief's house was filled with gawking men and women, and a mass of children huddled around their legs.

Jirazi spoke many more words as they ate, and Tirigan tried to follow them, but the children drove his thoughts back to his own little Jaka and Aji. His eyes fell as he remembered their faces.

At last Jirazi noticed. "You're thinking of your boy and girl, aren't you?"

Tirigan nodded. "My thoughts never leave them."

"Then I'll delay no longer." Jirazi turned and whispered to a group of men by her side. They nodded in reply, and disappeared through a doorway in the back of the house.

Jirazi turned back to Tirigan. "It's shameful," she said, "what men like Asak One-Eye did to us." She sipped from her own drinking-horn. "Another pack of Shuméru wolves, preying on the Guti people."

Kurum looked at her oddly. "What people?"

Jirazi spread her arms, laughing. "The Guti people, of course! *Our* people. Can you not see we're all of the same stock here?"

Tirigan looked around the room, and saw she was right. No one in this village resembled the black-haired Shuméru soldiers, or looked like Asak One-Eye and his men. Everyone here looked a bit like Tirigan and his family, and like his companions: almond-skinned, with eyes of glimmering green and blue, and hair in many shades of gold and red.

"I've heard that word 'Guti' before," Kurum said to Jirazi. "My mother used to tell me tales of the old Guti heroes, when I was a boy."

"And there will be Guti heroes still to come." Jirazi laughed. "Gods know there are plenty of Guti people on the Riverplain these days. We need to stop fighting each other. Work together." She turned as the door-cloth rustled. "Ahh! Here they are."

Tirigan couldn't believe his eyes: the men had returned with his own Jaka and Aji, looking more plump and healthy than ever. They ran to him, and he wrapped them in his arms, crying for joy.

"Thank you," he said to Jirazi through his tears. "Thank you, Jirazi."

Jirazi gestured to a nearby group of men. "Thank *them*," she said. "They were hunting in the western fields when Asak One-Eye and his boys passed through. Traded a fresh gazelle for these two."

The words barely registered with Tirigan, but he stood and embraced each of the men in turn, telling them, "Thank you. Seventy times seven, thank you all. How can I ever repay you?"

Jirazi smiled. "Good question. As it happens, I do have something in mind."

Tirigan looked her in the eye. "Anything."

"Well," Jirazi grinned. "You've already demonstrated your talents on Asak One-Eye and his band. There's a town up the stream—a Shuméru town, next to a stream the Guti should own."

Tirigan struggled to find the words. "Jirazi, I owe you my children's lives—"

"Indeed you do." Jirazi nodded.

"But I'm no warrior."

"Oh," said Jirazi, "but you are. You most certainly are. You've proven that."

"I'm sorry," Tirigan told her. "There must be some other way. Anything else."

Jirazi's eyes narrowed. "Do not make me say," she said quietly, "that your children belong to this village. Tirigan, I like you. Do not force me to put it in those terms."

Vaya leaped up. "How dare you—!"

But Tirigan waved her down. "No, Vaya," he said. "Jirazi is right." He reached out his arms for Jaka and Aji and pulled them close again. "Her men saved my children's lives."

"Not just saved," Jirazi reminded him. "Cared for as our own." She spread her hands and spoke the next words carefully, to make sure her meaning was clear: "And we will continue to care for them, one way or the other."

Tirigan nodded slowly. "All right," he said. "On one condition."

Jirazi smiled. "You have but to name it."

"If my companions are willing, I'll have them by my side." He looked to Vaya, who nodded once; and to Kurum, who also nodded, as did Aji.

"Oh, but you'll have many more than just these three by your side," Jirazi said.

And it was then, in that moment, that Tirigan fully understood what she intended.

"You'll have fifty of my best fighting-men," Jirazi said. "And anything else you require."

Despite everything, a strange excitement rose in Tirigan's chest. Anticipation, a sense of joy he'd thought he'd never feel again.

"And what am I to do with all these warriors, my chief?" he asked.

Jirazi grinned. "Pay these Shuméru tyrants back," she said, "for what they've done to the Guti."

Gudea glared down at the judge who knelt before his throne. Nanshe had not seen her brother so enraged since they were children. He had given his life to the Gods, spent countless days and sleepless nights in meditation and prayer, and the Gods had rewarded him with a peace that could not be broken; an impenetrable calm that was almost eerie. But today his cheeks were flushed, and venom dripped from his tongue.

"What do you mean, you gave her land to her younger brother?" Gudea roared at the terrified judge, who cowered beneath the folds of his ornate robes, kneeling on the hard stone of the audience chamber's floor.

"That—my énsi, that is the law established by the Akkadu governors," the judge stammered. "When the father dies, all land goes to the oldest male relative."

"Stand up," Gudea snapped.

The judge hesitated, then rose slowly to his feet.

"You don't have to look so frightened," Gudea said with a sigh. "I'm not going to execute you." He extended a hand and helped the judge to his feet. The plump man breathed an audible sigh of relief.

"I need you to understand something—what is your name?" Gudea asked.

"Ubara," the judge answered. "Son of Dubara."

"Ah yes," mused Gudea. "Dubara Snake-Eater. Or 'Cake-Eater,' as we knew him in his later years."

"I—I can assure you, Énsi Gudea—"

"Yes, yes; you're nothing like that greedy old swine," Gudea waved him off. "I'm sure you aren't."

Ubara gulped. "I'm truly not, your highness. I hated him."

"A man ought not to hate his father," Gudea said. "No matter what the old man has done."

The judge cringed again. Gudea placed a gentle hand on the man's meaty shoulder.

"Ubara," said the énsi. "Walk with me a while."

Nanshe followed them at a distance as they strolled out of the audience chamber and into the palace courtyard. It was the cold season, the winter month of Nisan. Most of the elms and junipers had withered to little more than trunks with bare branches, casting shadows on dry brown bushes beneath a cloudy sky. A shiver ran through Nanshe's body, prickling her skin.

"I have no wish to be a great lord, Ubara," Gudea was telling the judge as they strolled across the courtyard's flagstones. "I am no king. No lugál or even an én. I have no wish to impose new laws. Only to restore the proper laws which the Gods gave us in old times."

"Is that so, Énsi Gudea?" The judge raised a thick eyebrow.

"It is so," Gudea said. "I'm well aware that in the Akkadu laws, men were accorded greater rights than women. Many other things in the Akkadu laws also differed from ancient Shuméru custom: punishments were harsher. Taxes were higher. More gold flowed to the palace, less to the temple."

"All this is true, énsi," Ubara agreed. "I am simply enforcing the laws in which I've been trained all my life—"

"Akkadu laws!" Gudea exclaimed, stopping and turning to the judge. "Not Shuméru laws. Not *our* ancient laws. Not the laws given to us by our Gods at the world's dawn, when Heaven talked with Earth and Earth talked with Heaven."

The two men stared into each others' eyes for a long moment.

"No, énsi," Ubara said at last. "Not those laws."

Gudea looked past the judge, strolling slowly toward the slumbering skeleton of a great oak tree. "I am cleansing this city, Ubara," he said, as if to himself. "I am letting a purifying fire loose over it."

"I have heard of your purges," Ubara said quietly. "The expulsion of all who were ritually unclean."

"Lepers and plague-bearers have no place in Lagash," Gudea replied. "Some may call this cruel. This dead man's son, who will not receive the inheritance promised him under Akkadu law, will also call the Gods' judgment harsh. His older sister, however, will certainly see the matter differently."

"Yes, énsi," Ubara agreed tentatively.

"The Shuméru lands have fallen into ruin," Gudea said, "because they became impure, contaminated with foreign laws and customs. But Lagash, as you know, is already growing back into greatness."

"I have seen the new buildings, énsi," Ubara said. "The new canals and roads."

Gudea smiled tightly. "And more is to come, Ubara. Much more. If you will trust me, and preserve the ancient customs of Lagash, and of our Shuméru Gods."

Ubara bowed low. "It will be done, énsi."

Later that afternoon, Gudea and Nanshe were walking together along the waterfront. Lugál Kuwari strode a few paces behind them, hand resting on the pommel of the dagger in his belt, his sharp eyes inspecting the crowd of laborers rushing to and fro among the docks.

They strolled past wool-kilted porters bearing baskets of figs and honeycombs, and shipbuilders caulking their boats with vats of fish oil bubbling in copper cauldrons. Nest-hunters extracted ducks and pigeons from tangled nets; thick-shouldered oxen shook their heads beneath the yokes of wagons, while harnessed donkeys brayed in annoyance, bearing loads of flour and malt for brewing; vessels of sweet-beer and clarified butter and flower-scented honey. In pens and reed cages, long-fleeced barley-fed sheep, plump pigs and fattened geese waited to be loaded onto barges, bound down the Slow River to the great salt sea, for trade in distant lands.

Flat-bottomed cargo ships from far up and down the Two Rivers were tying up along the shore, unloading titan trunks of red cedarwood from the Silver Mountains; sparkling quartz and sweet-smelling tamarisk wood from K'nan; amber and copper from the Great Southern Desert, gold and turquoise from the lush riverbanks of Misr; timber of cypress and oak from faraway Dilmun and Magan; even rare blue stones from Meluhha, whose mountains ringed the distant rim of the world, beyond the edges of maps.

Most of these fine woods and stones were bound for Lagash's new temple; a half-finished ziggurat that already towered far above city's highest houses, its upper levels a bonework of scaffolding and rope. It would be years, still, before the sacred house was complete; yet every day it seemed to grow taller.

Far out on the water, hundreds of workmen stacked the stones of a half-finished quay; a great bar of piled stone bestriding the point where the Two Rivers met in a whirling vortex of mud and foam. When this quay was complete, it would provide moorage for dozens more ships, doubling the hoards of goods from far-off lands flowing to Lagash, to build her new temples and manor-houses, palaces and parks. Even from here on the shore, Nanshe could hear the stone-layers' work-songs ringing in the afternoon air.

"How long has it been, sister of mine," Gudea asked, watching the sailors unload their cargoes, "since ships from such distant lands have docked in the Land of the Two Rivers?"

Nanshe shook her head. "Before we were born, I suppose," she mused.

"Long before," Gudea agreed. "A century, at least. Perhaps two. Long ages of poverty. Provincialism. Ignorance in a sea of more ignorance." Gudea drew a deep breath of river air, sighing and smiling. "And now the new quay is nearly finished. When I look out on these ships, I see an end to our agony."

"And a new birth for Shumér, I dare to hope," Nanshe said.

"Or for Lagash, at least," Gudea replied. "I pray the Gods will let me live long enough to see this city restored, even if the rest of the work is fated for my descendants to complete."

A messenger came running up the road, his wool kilt stained with dirt. He stumbled toward Gudea, gasping, panting, dust falling from his body with every step.

Lugál Kuwari stepped forward, half-drawing his dagger. "Who are you?" he demanded. "What business have you with the énsi?"

Gudea pushed past the lugál, waving him down. "Let him pass, Kuwari. He clearly has something important to say." He looked into the messenger's eyes in that deep, penetrating way of his. "Well, speak up," he said. "What is it?"

The messenger took a moment to catch his breath, then delivered his news.

"Another raid, énsi," he said. "On five villages northeast of here. They've destroyed your canals."

Something cold tightened in Nanshe's stomach.

Gudea turned away, running a hand down his face. "Those canals were just finished!" he hissed. "We worked for months—!"

"The barbarians also carried off many cattle and sheep," the messenger said quietly. "And the people."

"The people—?" Gudea whirled on the messenger, who cowered back. "What of the people?"

"They... left, énsi," the messenger said. "With the horde."

"What do you mean, they left?" Gudea demanded, his voice tight and quiet.

The messenger wore a look of hopeless confusion and fear. "I know not! They seem to have... packed up and moved away," he said. "There was no sign of battle. No dead. The people are simply... gone."

Gudea's eyes were empty. His mouth worked wordlessly.

Nanshe stepped forward, placing her hand on the messenger's shoulder. "This is the same horde that has committed so many other acts of destruction against our villages," she said, "is it not? These impious Guti barbarians, year after year."

The messenger nodded. "But now there are more of them." he paused, looked fearfully from brother to sister. "Shuméru villagers as well. Our own people."

Nanshe nodded slowly, licking her lips. In a carefully controlled tone, she asked, "Tell me, messenger, what is your name?"

The messenger's eyes widened.

"Do not be afraid," Nanshe smiled tightly. "I only wish to know with whom I speak."

"Igi," the messenger said. "Igi, son of Kalam."

Nanshe nodded again. "Igi, son of Kalam, tell me what else you know of this horde."

Igi the messenger shrugged. "It is said that they are led by a man named Tirigan. A Guti man, son of a nobody."

"And where does he come from," Nanshe asked, "this Tirigan, son of a nobody? Where is his family?"

"They say he comes from a Guti town to the north," Igi said. "A place called the Village of the Long Riverbend."

"Lugál Kuwari," Gudea spoke up. "How many men can we spare from the construction works?"

"Spare?" Kuwari spread his hands, pleading. "We cannot spare any! The men are working double shifts as it is, and—"

Gudea waved a hand gently to calm the man down. "I know, lugál. You're right. Now is not the time."

"Next spring, perhaps." Nanshe said. "Once the new quay is finished."

The lugál thought for a moment. "Yes." He nodded, stroking his beard with a scarred, tattooed hand. "Next spring. Before these barbarians have time to get their forces in order. Shall I deliver battle to them, énsi?" Eagerness shone in his dark eyes.

"You may," Gudea said. "Next spring, when the weather grows warm. Go to this Village of the Long Riverbend. Cleanse it of... impurities."

"Oh, I'll cleanse it, énsi." Kuwari smiled. "Have no doubt of that."

Nanshe watched her brother for a long time, waiting for some word of question or instruction. But Gudea only stood on the half-constructed quay, staring out over the water, his expression unreadable.

After a while, the énsi closed his eyes and raised his hands, palms upward, and began to whisper his own silent prayer.

Tirigan's band of fighters piled their wagons high with barrels of barley and beer, with sheepskins and leather, with copper and jewelry and anything else they could find as they ransacked the town's houses.

Fifty-odd Shuméru captives stood in a clump, ankles and wrists bound tightly; old men, young men, women and children, all with naked fear in their eyes.

"I make you an offer," Tirigan told them, pacing around the group to meet every pair of eyes. "Or rather, a choice. Join us today, now, and you'll have all your treasure back, and more besides. All we ask is that you leave your farms and come with us."

At first, only silence answered him.

"Why did you do this?" a woman's voice wailed. Tirigan scanned the captives and found its owner: a plump middle-aged woman in a stained wool dress, her three children clinging to her knees, staring at Tirigan with looks of utter horror. "We're only poor farmers. What have we ever done to deserve this?" Tears were pouring down her cheeks now, Tirigan saw as he approached her.

"Your farms," he told her, "have fed the nobles and armies of Lagash, while your own people starve. Come with us, and you'll never go hungry again."

"This is our land!" an old man cried. "And now you've brought the wrath of Lagash on your own heads. Their armies will be hunting you night and day now."

"This was Lagash's land," Tirigan answered him. "It was never yours. Now it no longer belongs to Lagash, either."

"And who does it belong to, then?" the old man demanded. "You?" He spat at Tirigan's feet.

Tirigan shook his head. "Not me. All of us. And it can be yours again, once Lagash is finished."

"Ha!" The old man barked a laugh. "You believe you can take Lagash with this band? Fool. They've a thousand men! You've got, what, a few hundred?"

"And fifty or so more, now," said Tirigan. "Thanks to you."

"You'll die dashed against those walls," the old man grumbled.

But a wiry man stepped forward. "I'll do it," he said. "I'll join you. Lagash's taxes have been starving us for years. Wouldn't mind putting a blade through a few perfumed necks."

The others watched in silence as Vaya cut the ropes around his wrists and ankles.

"He's right," said another, a short thick-set fellow with close-cropped brown hair. "Better to die in battle, with a full stomach, than starving on a dried-up farm."

More began to step forward: old men leaning on knotted canes, women with small children in their arms, farmers and millers, fathers and sisters and sons.

"Follow me," Tirigan told them, "and I will give you the Riverplain."

They trudged across the open fields, this ever-growing band, through the dry grass and along winding trails of packed dirt, pulling wagons piled high with barrels of trout and catfish, fattened sheep and goats, sheaves of barley and hulled wheat, bundles of green mint and coriander, vessels of beer and butter and fresh cow's-milk, baskets of onions and leeks, cucumbers and turnips, lemons and oranges and pomegranates packed in honey, copper scythes and chisel-axes and ploughshares, bolts of fleece and flax and softest linen. All the finest fruits of the countryside, shared freely.

Many afternoons they passed great roving flocks of unsheared sheep, herds of long-horned cattle attended by throngs of pigs and goats, trudging across the countryside wild and unfenced, free to gorge themselves on dry grass and sleep beneath the stars; for it was the belief of Guti people that animals gave the best meat and milk when left to wander freely. Whenever they came upon sheep or cattle in fences, they broke the gates down and chased the beasts out onto the open plains, whooping and laughing as hundreds of hooves thundered off toward the horizon in a cloud of dust.

They slept when the cruel God Nergál hammered the earth with his hot noonday sun. They dragged wagons of plunder until they were tired of dragging, and then they pitched camp under the stars, and drank beer from their barrels, and sang songs to the moon-God Nannár, and danced until they fell into sweet exhausted sleep.

Word was spreading, Tirigan knew. The governors of the Shuméru cities were dispatching armies to track down his horde and slaughter them. But the governors' efforts were clumsy, and were often at odds: two cities' armies meeting in the field were as likely to attack each other as to coordinate their efforts. Sometimes, when a small contingent of professional soldiers ran into Tirigan's band, they simply threw down their weapons and joined him.

So it was that Tirigan's band grew into a troop, and the troop swelled, over several summers, into a horde: five hundred fighting men and women, then seven hundred, then a thousand—farmers and fisherfolk, bandits and brigands, warriors of a dozen wild tribes, soldiers clad in scraps of raiment from a hundred villages and cities: fleece kilts, skirts of rough-spun flax, cloaks of leopard and oryx, armor of copperscale and boiled leather, dented helmets and shepherd's hats. They carried long copper daggers, chisel-axes, maces, spears, and homemade weapons that had no name. From their necks and belts hung trophies: dried ears and fingers and sun-bleached bones.

And each time wagons grew heavier and the horde grew greater, Tirigan called at last for a return to the village of the Long Riverbend. There among the the Guti people—his people—Jirazi would throw great feasts for his horde, who would dine and drink and dance until they could stand no more. And always there were his children, Jaka and Aji, grown bigger and stronger each time, plying their father for tales of his adventures in the wilderness, of the Shuméru armies he'd conquered and the wonders he'd seen.

Months passed in this way; how many, Tirigan could not say. Little Aji was blossoming into a young woman; Jaka nearly as tall as some of the fighters in the horde, and begging to join them on their next summer campaign.

"You can't make him stay in the Village forever," Vaya told him, one night by the fire. "Sooner or later, he's going to march out with the first army that takes him."

Much as Tirigan hated to think this of his son, he knew Vaya was right.

One fine morning, when the first warmth of spring was in the air, Tirigan's army found itself marching back toward the Village once again, wagons heaped with plunder. Tirigan was imagining how Jaka would react to the news of his enlistment into the horde as they caught sight of the Village's wood-and-hide wall on the horizon. Smoke was rising from the houses—too much smoke. Tirigan raised a hand for the horde to stop.

Kurum and the woman Aji approached on his other side. "Should I send out some scouts?" Kurum asked.

"Could be a good idea," said Aji. "Make sure no one's lying in wait."

Tirigan thought about this for a moment. "No," he said at last. "Let's walk in alone, just the four of us. As we always do."

They told the horde to lay camp a ways off, and explained they'd bring the plunder into the Village once they were sure everything was safe. Then they walked toward the hide-bound palisade walls of the Village of the Long Riverbend, just as they had on that spring morning, what felt like centuries ago.

As soon as he saw the half-butchered gazelles lying abandoned in the Village's central clearing, Tirigan's fears were confirmed. Something was wrong. He began to run. As he approached closer, he realized there were no people about. Not a soul anywhere in the Village.

To his right, Kurum gasped. Tirigan turned to look, and saw the grass strewn with bodies: men, women and children, their bodies covered with dried blood and flies.

They walked carefully through the burnt-down huts and tents, the smashed reed houses and scattered firepits. Bodies lay everywhere; almond-skinned men, women and children, their gold and red hair spilled across the dirt in pools of blood, beneath clouds of flies. A few starving dogs and rats had already begun to gather around the bodies, sniffing and nipping tentatively.

Tirigan searched frantically through one scorched ruin after another, dreading what he might find, yet feeling a small upwelling of relief each time he did not discover the charred bodies of Jaka or Aji. This did not mean they were not among the dead, of course; only that they were not among the dozens of bodies of other children strewn against the walls of half-collapsed reed huts. He felt he ought to weep over the fallen mothers, fathers, sons and daughters of Guti, but he found he could not, as if his body were drained of tears, and he had none left to shed.

As he, Vaya and Kurum tore themselves away from the scene of the massacre, they met a scrawny, long-bearded old man at the edge of the village. His wrinkled skin was almond-colored; his eyes sharp and green.

"Were you of the Long Riverbend?" the old man asked them.

"In a way," said Tirigan.

"Did you see it?" Aji asked. "When they did this?"

The old man nodded. "I was out in the fields. Saw them coming. Ran and hid in the bushes. I didn't watch but I... I could hear the sounds."

Why didn't you help? Tirigan wanted to ask, but he knew there was nothing one gray-bearded elder could have done against an army.

"They took a lot of people with them," the old man said, tears rising in his reddened eyes. "Women. Children. Anyone too weak to fight but strong enough to walk. Took them all as slaves."

"Who took them?" Kurum demanded, grabbing the old man by his tunic.

Tirigan tore the boy's hand away and pushed him back. "Enough." He sighed. "There was nothing he could do."

"But he saw them," Aji said softly. "You know who did this," she said to the old man. "Didn't you?"

He nodded tiredly and spoke one word: "Lagash."

⟨

Word of the approaching Guti horde was sweeping across Lagash like wildfire.

When the first of the messengers had stumbled into Gudea's audience chamber with the news, a week or so ago, Gudea had sworn the man to secrecy, forcing him to swear an oath binding his tongue in the name of Ningirsu.

One man could be silenced, but not a whole stream of reports pouring in from outlying farms, travelers, soldiers and village elders in the countryside around Lagash. The horde was too big to hide, and they appeared to be making no effort to do so.

Terrified witnesses reported a cloud of dust as large as the city itself, swirling around a mass of heavily armed men and women who were joined by reinforcements every day. All the Guti, it was said, had heard this horde was on the march, and all were coming for their share of the spoils.

"They may be many, but they have no idea how to lay siege," said Lugál Kuwari. The warleader stood next to Gudea, pointing out strong points on a cowhide map of Lagash, spread across a great wood table in the palace's war-room.

Nanshe scanned the lines of the map, remembering that afternoon, years ago, when her brother had brought back great stacks of stone tablets bearing architectural drawings for the city's new buildings. They'd had so little time to build their new city, their beacon of civilization at the heart of a Shumér gone mad; and soon all that work might be swept away into darkness again. Truly, the Gods' plans were strange.

"And what if they bring ladders?" Gudea asked calmly. "They may not be able to penetrate the walls, but they can scale them."

Kuwari's thick-bearded face contorted into a mask of annoyance. *The lugál is in charge now*, Nanshe wanted to whisper to her brother. *You've governed brilliantly in our years of peace, but now war is upon us. Step aside and let the war-chief deliver battle, as he has promised.*

She gazed up at the bas-relief of the war-God Ningirsu carved on the chamber's far wall. Flickering candlelight cast the image of the God—depicted allegorically, as a lion-headed *anzû*-bird flanked by eagles, rather than the way Gudea had told her he'd seen the real God in his dream—in sharp, foreboding shadows. Nanshe looked into the lion-God's eyes, whispering a quick prayer for wisdom.

"Lugál Kuwari," Gudea said softly. "Would you please give my sister and me a moment alone?"

With a sidelong glance at Nanshe, Kuwari slipped from the room, muttering sourly.

"Nanshe," Gudea said quietly, when the lugál had gone.

She looked up from the map, meeting her brother's eyes.

"I have prayed to Ningirsu," Gudea said, "and to my personal God Ningishzida, and I have received no reply I understand."

Nanshe tried to think of something comforting to say, but could find no truly honest word to speak. "My own prayers rarely receive answers, Gudea."

"Could it be because of the Guti slaves?" Gudea asked, his face perplexed. "I told the soldiers not to bring them into the city. Those slaves are ritually impure—and they have no wish to work on this great project of ours."

"Perhaps not," Nanshe said. "But soldiers always fight harder for the promise of women, willing or no."

"Women?" Gudea shook his bald head. "Some of those slaves are scarcely more than *children*, Nanshe. No, this is not what I dreamed."

"Yet, as you well know," Nanshe persisted, "we lack strong young workers. Lagash needs slaves, Gudea, as all great cities do."

The énsi gazed into his sister's eyes for the space of several heartbeats. "Can the Gods truly approve of this? They will not speak to me." Suddenly his eyes lit up. "Can you not intercede on my behalf?" he asked Nanshe. "Bring me an answer I can put to use?"

Nanshe hesitated, searching carefully for the right words. "Only a personal God can intercede with a higher God like Ningirsu," she said at last. "A personal God, or perhaps an én-priestess—"

She regretted the words as soon as she spoke them. She and Gudea had spoken, many times, of what the Gods did to overly ambitious men who overreached their fated roles.

But her brother was already smiling. "I declare, Nanshe, that you are now én-priestess of Lagash." He patted his sister on the shoulder.

Nanshe reeled. This was not what she'd wanted. The Akkadu emperors had tried to become as Gods, and the Gods now punished all Shumér and Akkad with an age of darkness. Gudea, by contrast, refused even to claim én-ship of his own city, and the Gods had rewarded him with a new Lagash, crown jewel of this dark age. The lesson was clear.

Slowly, Nanshe lowered herself to her knees before her brother. "I beg you, Gudea, do not force this role on me," she said, clutching the hem of Gudea's robe. "I do not want it."

Gudea reached down and raised his sister up. "That," he said, "is precisely why you are the right person for the job." He patted Nanshe on the back. "Besides, we both know that our én-priest grows old, and begs me to release him from his duties."

Nanshe nodded thoughtfully. "Old Abuwaqar would relish the opportunity to live out his days at home, it's true."

"So bring him word of his release." Gudea smiled. "And when you have assumed the mantle from him, speak with the God Ningirsu. Return and tell me how Lagash may be saved."

Nanshe did as she was told. She hurried to the temple and informed the priests of the promotion Gudea had just bestowed. None of them expressed much surprise—least of all old Abuwaqar, who consented to his replacement with relief, and insisted they begin the Ceremony of the Handing-Over of the Mantle with as much haste as his aged bones could muster.

As soon as the ceremony was completed, Nanshe ascended the seven hundred stairs to the very peak of Lagash's still-unfinished ziggurat, carrying a dove of the purest white.

As she laid the plump bird on the altar, Nanshe gazed out through the scaffolds and stacks of brick, across the sprawl of her city. This was the first time she'd climbed up here since construction had begun several years ago. When at last the ziggurat was completed, this peak would serve as the very point where Heaven met Earth. Only the most purified priests would be permitted to ascend it.

From this dizzy height, Nanshe could see the roof of every stone manor and mud-brick house; every marketplace tent and table; every banner snapping in the cool spring wind. Along the flagstone avenues stretching out from the temple in straight symmetric lines, rows of tall palms flanked gardens of flowering bushes and thick-trunked oaks, where birds sang their evening songs. Colonnades of polished sandstone, dotted with intricate geometric designs of red and white and black, stood sentry around stone-lined pools and fountains where glimmering fish darted to and fro.

Men in long one-shouldered togas of every color strolled in groups, or with long-skirted women, up and down the grid of clean-swept avenues, bearing baskets of fruit and grain, or tugging children along by the hand. Nanshe's eyes traced his people's myriad paths up the winding side-streets that spread out for leagues like veins along skin. The Swift and Slow Rivers split the city like cracks across an eggshell, their mighty streams meeting in a rushing torrent amid the great stone quays, where boats from a hundred lands unloaded their exotic cargoes.

Nanshe's eyes roamed all the way to the towering crenellated walls at the edges of Lagash; walls wide enough for men to stroll two abreast along their rim. Just beyond those walls, copper-helmeted soldiers patrolled along the palisade of sharp wooden stakes that surrounded the city, encircled in turn by a deep moat fed by canals from the rivers.

And further still, stepped farms sprawled on hillsides, each plot leveled and furrowed with dark red soil churned up from beneath the dry topsoil, edged by low walls of stacked stone, all the way to the edges of the pine forests that adorned the great flat-topped mountains in the furthest distance.

This is what we built, Nanshe thought, fixing the city in her mind. *If only for a short while, it was here.*

Then she drew a the sharp bronze sacrifice-dagger and slit open the belly of the pure white bird, and read in its entrails what was to be done to save this city, this Lagash built by a strange énsi named Gudea.

〈Υ

Tirigan sat on the hillside outside the great mud-brick walls of Lagash, watching a herd of goats graze beneath the setting sun.

They reminded him a little of his goats back home—the females' udders swelling with milk, the males sporting long curving horns and pelts of sleek white hair, perfect for sewing into kilts. The kids played around the hooves of the grown-ups, charging and leaping, butting heads and letting out high-pitched bleats. One of the smaller females grazed too close to a senior male, and he lowered his head and half-charged at her. She fled to the fringes of the group, bleating an annoyed apology.

He'd have been proud to own this herd, back in the old days, before everything had changed. There was a time, not so long ago, when Tirigan would spend whole days, from first light to the last rays of dusk, just watching his goats, observing their rhythms; their intricate wordless politics. It had a certain elegance, a completeness that one never found in war. Of course, back in those days, Tirigan had found the herdsman's life intolerably dull and had longed for glory and battle. One can never go back, he thought.

Two forms stirred at the edge of Tirigan's vision. Vaya and Kurum, of course, come to tell him they were ready. He dusted his grass-stained hands on his rough brown tunic and rose to his feet, feeling his back and knees creak, and raised a hand in greeting. He stood, and joined them in walking back to his tent.

The tent was cold. Tirigan huddled next to the fire, watching the flame-light play on the ox-hide walls. In the center of the tent, a brazier of spinplant leaves burned on the coals of the fire, sending thick earthy-smelling smoke throughout the tent. The smoke made him feel relaxed, but also tangled up in his thoughts, which turned inward, running down endless trails that seemed to lead nowhere.

"There are other cities on these plains," Vaya was saying, eyes languid with the effects of the smoke.

"Aye," said Tirigan. "But no other that may hold..." He trailed off, though they all knew the words he kept from his tongue: *my children*. "No other that holds our people as slaves," he said quietly.

They both stared at him, eyes wide with apprehension.

Kurum spoke first. "I lost friends in the Long Riverbend, just as you did. But you know as well as I do, we'll never scale Lagash's walls." He stroked the thin tangle of beard that had taken root on his face. "That city is a fortress," he said. "We'll be dead before we reach the ramparts."

Tirigan raised a finger. "That's why we'll take the little towns first. All of them. Every poorly defended plot of land on the Riverplain. Then we strike their heart."

Kurum nodded slowly. He scarcely looked a boy anymore, in truth. He was all knots of muscle now; a veteran hardened by years of near-ceaseless raiding. "Once we have the outlying towns," he said, "we'll control the roads. The trade-routes from one great city to another. We can cut off their lifeblood."

"Call it what you like," Tirigan said. "It could work."

"Even if you're right, Tirigan," Vaya said, "it'll take months to starve them out. Then we'll have to make make our demands..."

"Demands?" Kurum raised an eyebrow. "What demands— that they hand over their prize city to the Guti?" He huffed. "They'll die before they give up Lagash."

"Then we demand," Vaya said, "that the rulers of the Shuméru cities stop raiding the Guti towns. And that they let our people go."

"The governor of Lagash will never agree to those terms," Tirigan said. "They see us as beasts. Cattle, or worse."

They all fell silent at that, for they knew it was true. Tirigan watched the fire for a long time, gathering his thoughts.

"And in the meantime, our women and children are dying inside those walls," said Tirigan. *As are my children*, he thought. "Starving. Suffering unspeakable things." He drew a deep breath and let out a long, weary sigh. "We have no choice. We must set our people free."

Kurum huffed. "Suicidal foolishness. We didn't march all this way only die at the walls of Lagash."

Tirigan gestured outside the tent, where their horde of fighters lay camped, "*They* all came here," he said, "because I asked. They're here by their own free choice. And so are you, Kurum."

Kurum's brow furrowed. He looked from Tirigan to Vaya, frowning.

At last he sighed and said, "It's just the spinplant, making me talk strange. Come here." He gathered the two of them in an embrace.

"If we're going to strike," Vaya said, "We'd best do it now, before their army can assemble."

Tirigan nodded. "As soon as the sun's gone."

"Then you'd best go speak to your fighters," said Kurum, "while there's still enough light for them to see you."

He grinned, running his fingers along the worn handle of his bronze-tipped mace.

"I don't have much to say," said Tirigan.

"Speak to them anyway," said Vaya.

He followed them down the hillside, to the edge of the escarpment where they'd pitched their camp. They'd all gathered to hear him speak before they battle. Hundreds of warriors, packed in as far as he could see; men and women clad in rough leather and furs, with almond skin and long braided hair of gold and auburn, clutching spears and maces and daggers, and unnumbered other weapons they'd lashed together themselves or pilfered from the dead. They waited here eagerly, looking up at him, ready for the word to attack.

My herd, he thought, though he would never speak such words aloud.

"My friends," he said. Then, louder, "Are you hungry?"

The cheer went up, first from those closest to him, at the base of the escarpment, spreading backward through the masses until they'd all taken it up, raising their weapons in affirmation.

"Tonight," he cried, "while the Shuméru sleep, we take their city of Lagash!"

"Lagash!" They shouted the foreign word, so full of promise.

"Their walls are tall, and made of stone," he shouted. "But their people are small, and afraid."

He heard shouts and saw nods of agreement as his words spread backward through the crowd.

"They are farmers and priests," he cried. "Barely a warrior among them. The Shuméru cower behind their walls, keeping our brothers and sisters in chains. But tonight, their city will belong to the Guti!"

A cheer thundered up from the valley, accompanied by the clanging of weapons and the high-pitched cries of war.

"Tonight," he cried, "Lagash belongs to us—and our people will be free!"

They were in frenzy now, their eyes half-mad with battle-hunger. A dangerous thing, that hunger, he thought. A knife's edge. But tonight, he was balanced perfectly on it.

The sun had half-sunk beneath the horizon now, and he climbed down the escarpment with Vaya and Kurum at his sides. Holding his dagger high, he led the march eastward across the plain, the last of the sun at their backs, casting long thin shadows before them. They carried no tents, and no children. Nor did they bring wagons or sheep or oxen. Nothing to slow down the vast mob of warriors who marched against the walls of Lagash.

〈𒌋𒌋

THE BARBARIANS HAD arrived. From high up on the city wall, Nanshe watched their torches flickering by starlight, casting flickering orange glows across masses of long-haired heads, far out beyond Lagash's palisade of sharpened tree-trunks, and the moat beyond that. Out in the darkness they congregated—waiting for something; she knew not what. Their bodies were swathed in animal skins, or draped in fine fabrics stolen from cities to which they held no legitimate claim. They carried long daggers, spears, maces and clubs. Few shields, though. These fighters valued courage above prudence. *In all things*, she thought, *they honor the animal above the divine.*

The wind slipped Nanshe's mantle off her shoulder. She adjusted the white linen cloth, tucking its folds tightly into the place where the garment wrapped about her chest. Even beneath the mantle, her head felt cold in the night air, and a shiver ran through her, though her arms had no hairs to raise. She wished, not for the first time, that the Gods would allow her just a bit of hair, especially in a cold season such as this. She felt naked up here.

"The énsi still hasn't come forth from his house." Kuwari's rough voice started Nanshe.

She turned to see the lugál standing behind her. He wore a round helmet of beaten bronze, and vest of boiled leather and bronze-scale over his bare, tattooed chest. Two daggers were thrust into his belt, gleaming against the black-and-yellow of his shaggy kilt. Across his shoulders was slung a cloak of leopardskin.

"I wish you wouldn't sneak up on me like that," she said.

"Those barbarians will say the same of me, if the Gods will it," Kuwari replied, smiling tightly.

Nanshe looked back out over the wall; over the torchlights flickering in the blackness. "My brother said he'd come forth this evening, to watch your attack."

Kuwari nodded. "So he did."

Is there any chance he's coming forth now? Nanshe knew the lugál wanted to ask. But even had he asked, Nanshe would not have known what answer to give him. Her brother's ways were almost as mysterious as those of the Gods themselves.

As Gudea had requested, Nanshe had spent many nights at the temple, praying to Ningirsu for guidance. But despite the many doves she sacrificed, the war-God gave no clear sign. On the morning when she'd felt she could delay no longer, and must tell Gudea the truth, he had appeared in her doorway, trembling with the excitement of a new dream he'd had: a dream of barbarians dashing themselves against Lagash's mighty walls, drowning in a sea of bronze and boiling pitch. *I only hope*, she thought, *that I interpreted that dream correctly.*

"I have no doubt that Ningirsu will preserve Lagash," she told Kuwari. "As he always has."

It is I, your lugál, who'll preserve Lagash tonight, she could tell Kuwari wanted to reply. But the lugál kept his silence and only nodded curtly.

"Are the vessels ready?" she asked him.

"They are." Kuwari nodded.

Nanshe stepped to the edge of the wall, watching the torchlights converge out of the darkness. The barbarians were shouting, wailing, singing battle-songs in some guttural mountain-tongue, its harsh syllables so unlike the smooth sounds of civilized Shuméru. As they approached more closely, she saw that many of the fighters carried ladders of rough-hewn wood.

"Best get to safety," said Kuwari, drawing one of his daggers.

"I feel quite safe here," said Nanshe. "As long as you're in command."

Kuwari huffed and stomped off to confer with other leopard-cloaked soldiers who'd taken their stations along the wall. The men filled clay vessels with boiling black pitch, readying them to tip over the walls at the lugál's signal. Kuwari inspected each man and vessel as he strode along the wall, as he watched the approach of the horde far below.

"Énsi!" Nanshe heard the guards behind her exclaim. She turned to see her brother ascending the wall, the wind whipping the thin one-shouldered toga wrapped around his bony form. He strode toward her, deliberate as ever, eyes scanning the soldiers on the walls, and the torches flickering in the darkness.

"It will be as I dreamed, Nanshe," he said quietly.

"What can these savages hope to achieve?" she asked him, shaking her head. "They must know they'll never scale these walls."

Gudea gazed down into the darkness for some time, his face unreadable as ever.

"Each thing in the world fulfils its function," he said at last. "I do not know why these barbarians dash themselves against our walls tonight, any more than I know why a moth hurls itself into a candle-flame."

"And us, Gudea?" she asked. "What is our function?"

He turned to her, smiling softly. "To build houses for the Gods, Nanshe. To protect their songs and laws. To ensure that even in the darkest days, the bridge between Heaven and Earth does not completely shatter."

The barbarians' ladders clattered across the moat. Soon they were pouring over the water, down into the ditch around the palisades, up over the sharpened stakes and toward the city walls. If they were surprised at the absence of any soldiers to stop them, they showed no sign of it. Soon their ladders were thunking against Lagash's walls, swarming with warriors eager to ascend.

Kuwari came running, barking orders to his men as he approached: "Ready those vessels! Up high, now!" As he reached Gudea and Nanshe, his expression soured. "You shouldn't be up here," he said. "Could get messy."

"The whole world is a mess, Kuwari," Gudea said. "For once, I should like to see a bit of it cleaned up."

The lugál huffed. "Very well," he said. "Try to stay out of the way. Both of you."

Kuwari raised his arm, held it high, then dropped it. All at once, the soldiers dumped the boiling pitch down onto the attackers climbing the ladders. The barbarians screamed and fell, howling and writhing as the black tar boiled their skin.

"And now," shouted Kuwari, "for the killing stroke."

He took a torch from a holder on the wall, raised it, and waved it in a pattern: left twice, then right, then left twice again. Out in the woods around the city's outer moat, other torches answered with the same signal.

Soldiers poured out from among the trees, inward across the moat and over the palisade; dozens of leopard-cloaked fighters in black-and-yellow kilts, bursting suddenly into the shocked barbarians' torchlight from every side. They raised their spears and chisel-axes, stabbing and hacking at every fur-cloaked body they found.

It was hardly a battle, Nanshe thought. More of a slaughter. Like hogs in a pen, the barbarians fell beneath the slicing blades of the soldiers of Lagash. Trapped between the city wall within, and the palisade and moat without, they flailed wildly in their panic, even as they were cut down in their hundreds. Nanshe watched it all, relieved and faintly sickened all at once. She turned to Gudea, and saw that a faint smile played upon his lips.

Kuwari nodded in grim satisfaction. "This," he said, "is what separates men from beasts."

⟨𝗬𝗬𝗬

Tirigan lay on the cold dirt outside the walls of Lagash, wrenching each slow breath from the night air, feeling blackness creep in at the edges of his vision. Each breath came harder than the one before, sending fresh shockwaves of pain across his tar-scorched body. It hurt too much to sit up, or even to turn on his side. And so he stared up at the stars and waited for someone to come.

All around him, he could hear men howling curses, calling for their mothers, screaming with a ferocity that hardly sounded human. If he turned his head just slightly, he could see the fires atop the walls of Lagash. He wondered what the men beside those fires were thinking. If only Jaka and Aji could tell him what they'd seen within those towering walls, in a city where such abundance lay piled up.

That is, he thought, *if my children still live at all.* Now he would never know. And it was that realization that hurt worst of all, far more deeply than the burning pitch.

But despite the pain and powerlessness he felt, it was Kara who danced in his memory at the last; she and the children, Jaka and Aji as they were when they were young. Chasing one another around the farm, laughing by firelight, playing with the dog. Dancing beneath a warm evening sky.

It was very hard to breathe now. Up above, dark clouds devoured the moon and stars.

Tirigan closed his eyes and let himself fall away.

138 YEARS EARLIER
2287 BC

I approached the light,
But the light scorched me.
I approached the shade,
But I was covered with a storm.

— The Exaltation of Inanna

When Kitra walked the long, shadowed hallways of the palace of Urim, she did not see the bare mud-brick, or the sputtering torches, or the worn wooden doors, or the thin shafts of sunlight that lanced down through tiny high-set windows. As she walked, she closed her eyes This was what she saw:

Sunlight poured in through windows that were taller and wider than she was, each covered by a grate of delicate geometric bronzework. The glazed bas-reliefs on the walls gleamed green and blue and gold. Oil lamps hung from ornate stands at regular intervals, along with braziers where myrrh and frankincense smoked.

And she was not alone, walking this hall. Lords and generals turned to watch her pass, adjusting their embroidered togas and the gold rings in their plaited beards. Duchesses and countesses in brocaded dresses smiled at her, jewels glimmering in their necklaces.

She opened her eyes, and the shadows and mud-brick were back. No matter. It would soon look like the palace she saw when she closed her eyes. She was certain of that.

Footsteps behind her gave away the presence of Inu, her favorite of the Shuméru acolytes she'd been assigned when she'd arrived here at the temple of Urim. She turned, and Inu bowed low, wiping her hands on her wool apron.

"A thousand pardons, Your Radiance," said Inu.

Kitra smiled, went to her, raised her up. "None of this 'Your Radiance' nonsense," she said, as Inu lifted a ceremonial robe from a nearby chair, and opened it for Kitra to slip her arms through. "At least, not in private."

Inu's eyes widened. "How shall I call you, then?"

"When others are nearby," said Kitra, wriggling into the long robe's many tiers of flounced white linen, "I suppose 'my lady' will have to do. In private, call me Kitra. That is my name."

Inu bowed again. "As you will, Your R—I mean, Kitra."

Kitra grinned. "Thank you, Inu. Now, what did you come to tell me?"

Now it was Inu's turn to smile. "It's time," she said. "They're all waiting for you."

"How do I look?" Kitra asked, doing a full turn.

Inu smiled. "Lovely. Just one more thing." She drew a long white mantle and stole from a rack by the door and draped them delicately over Kitra's tightly bound hair, and around her shoulders. "There. Perfect."

Kitra followed Inu down the long shadowy passageway, up a stone staircase, around the bends of a much narrower hallway, even more choked with candle-smoke, that turned many corners and passed many doors, up a longer, steeper staircase that ended in a heavy locked wooden door.

Inu pounded on the door—twice, three times, then twice again. Kitra heard movement on the far side, and the door swung open, blinding her with sunlight.

Squinting her eyes, Kitra shuffled out into the brightness. She found herself standing on a long balcony overlooking the temple's central courtyard. Amid the purples, whites and greens of flowering bushes and trees, a crowd of Shuméru noblemen and women looked up in anticipation, shielding their eyes. They weren't looking at her, though; they were watching the man who'd just joined her on the balcony: her father, the Emperor Szarrukín.

Trumpets sang, and all the Shuméru nobles down in the garden craned their necks to see. Her father waved to them, smiling tightly.

The emperor wore a one-shouldered toga of fine linen, dyed deep crimson, patterned with tiny circular flowers of red and gold, fringed with tasseled gold thread, and a pair of point-toed leather boots laced up to his knees—all tokens of the luxurious Elamu style lately favored at court. About his shoulders hung a loose mantle dyed brilliant blue, its shaggy sheep's-wool fringe the only faint hint of the simple Akkadu toga he'd favored in his early years of conquest, before a host of exotic lands had lain their finest arts at his feet, and lent their strange flavors to the empire he ruled today. His ringed right hand clutched the gold sceptre granted him by the high priests of the holy city of Níppúr—the very sceptre which, it was said, the God Énlil himself had forged with divine power, when Kingship had first descended from Heaven in the mists of the world's infancy.

Every ring of his beard lay carefully plaited, his long black hair braided and looped into a tight chignon behind his head, crowned with a gold band. Kitra could see why they'd called him "The Hawk" back in the palace of Kish: his pale blue eyes and sharp aquiline nose gave him every appearance of a hunting-bird. *A hawk*, Kitra thought, *who's made the whole world his prey.*

At the emperor's elbow stood his favorite wife, Queen Tashlultum of Agadé, Kitra's mother—a huntress worthy of her beloved Hawk: eyes and cheekbones sharp, shining black hair wrapped in a tall bun, adorned with leaves of hammered gold strung on beaded chains of carnelian and lapis lazuli. She wore a long, straight toga of coral-colored linen, a stole of white leather draped about her shoulders, studded with the long black feathers of eagles from the northern mountains.

Before the royal couple stood Rimush, Kitra's elder brother, the very spit and clay of his father. The prince's beard had scarcely begun to grow in, but his long black hair was plaited and bound just like the emperor's, and his eyes were the same pale blue, and his toga a similar crimson. Instead of clutching a royal sceptre, his hand rested loosely on the jewelled pommel of the long bronze dagger at his belt.

And next to Rimush, Kitra's younger brother, Manishtushu, gazed out across the crowded courtyard. His toga seemed a bit showy for the occasion, as usual—soft linen dyed emerald green—and a pair of long-antlered stags, patterned in tiny silver beads, charged at one another across his chest. *He must've hired a new Elamu tailor*, Kitra thought, *at a price that would make Father choke.*

As the royal trumpets continued to sound, the emperor, smelling of sweat and sandalwood, leaned in close to Kitra's ear. "Enjoy this while you can, my dear." He smiled wryly. "The first time is always the most exciting. After that, it's just a ritual."

She covered her mouth and smiled. When she turned to look at him, he was already stepping away, raising a gold-ringed hand for silence. The trumpets stopped, and the nobles down in the garden looked up at them expectantly.

"We've come a long way," said the emperor. "Well, perhaps not all of us. I see the scions of most of Urim's noble families down there. From rich to richer, for many of you."

A few of the nobles chuckled, faintly embarrassed—or pretending to be.

"But you all know my story," the emperor continued. "Forty years ago, I was nobody. Just another orphan from Agadé, cast off on a reed basket in the river. Twenty years ago, I was cupbearer to the king of Kish, who feared I wanted him dead." The emperor paused, grinning. "He was right."

He laughed, and the Shuméru nobles laughed with him, nervously.

"Up north in Akkad," he went on, "we have no radiant holy city like Níppúr, no House of the Mountain from which the God Énlil can sanction and uphold kings, as he does here in Shumér. No, up north we've got strongholds and citadels. And when it comes to ruling, we've always had one way of deciding who's king: we fight it out."

He laughed, low and rueful. "And oh, how I've fought." His hawk eyes scanned the crowd: bald-headed priests, plump noblemen swathed in linen, women in gold headdresses, coiffed hair piled high. Not a warrior among them. "I don't think any of you were there with me at the Siege of Mari, or the Battle of Cedar Hill," he said. "But as Marutúk himself is my witness, you're all getting fat at my table." He barked a laugh. "Tell me I'm wrong! Trade flows freely from Meluhha to the Great Sea. You're wearing Elamu linen and Magannu jewelry. Tonight, unless I miss my guess, most of you will dine on fish and fowl seasoned with Meluhha spices, served on plates from the Silver Mountains. All the lands of this wide and varied world bring their treasures here, to the Land Between the Rivers."

"I say all this," the emperor continued, more solemnly, "to remind you that great things can come from small beginnings. From small beginnings in Agadé, to be more specific." He reached out an arm to Kitra and drew her close to him. "This is my Kitra," he said. "She's the firstborn daughter of my dear wife Tashlultum—" He wrapped an arm around the queen, pulling her close. "—and sister of my son and heir, Prince Rimush." He patted his son's bare shoulder, then turned back to Kitra. "But I should really say, this woman *was* Kitra," he went on. "For from this day forward, Kitra of Agadé is dead."

Someone behind Kitra whispered, "Kneel," and she did, carefully adjusting her skirts as she sank to her knees before the emperor.

The emperor extended his hand, and a priest approached with a sharp bronze knife, his bald head bowed in reverence. He took the emperor's hand, and neatly slit a small cut across the palm. As the blood began to well forth, Kitra also extended her hand, and felt a sharp sting as the knife bit into her own palm. The emperor extended his bleeding hand to her, palm up. Kitra took it, gently, as if they were about to dance. He looked her in the eyes, smiled, and squeezed her hand gently.

"Before the eyes of Marutúk and Énlil," the emperor said, "and of Nannár, patron-God of Urim, along with all the priests of this temple..." He smiled gently. "I confirm you—" He touched Kitra's head, "—as Én Hedu-Ana, Ornament of Heaven, High Priestess of the temple of Nannár, and én of the City and Land of Urim!"

A gasp went up from the crowd below, drawing a satisfied smile from the emperor. The emperor had chosen his daughter, a woman of only twenty-six summers, to serve as high priestess and governor of this holy city at the heart of the Shuméru world, for no greater reason than—what?—to tighten the threads that bound the old noble families of Urim to the upstart House of Szarrukín? Perhaps because her father saw, with those hawklike eyes, that he could rely on her. She hoped she wouldn't provide a disappointment.

The emperor accepted a vial of rose-scented oil from one of the priests, and poured a thin stream onto Kitra's head. The sweet-smelling liquid ran through her hair, and over her eyes. She suppressed a giggle. Down below, the nobles were applauding again. An important-looking priest came to place his hands on her head and mutter a ritual incantation.

Then came another priest, younger. Where the first priest had looked faintly bored, this one's movements seemed furtive, somehow. She looked up at him, and saw something in his eyes that terrified her: not hate, exactly, but a coldness.

He lunged at her, grasping for her hair with one hand as he raised a bronze dagger in the other.

She leaped back, and felt her mind snap into a different kind of awareness. All the motion around her seemed slow: the snarling assassin, the shocked priests, the stunned emperor, the guards lunging forward, drawing their long daggers. It all looked almost beautiful, like a dance. A thought came to her, unbidden: *I move as the world moves.* And she thought, *What a strange idea.*

Guards leaped upon the assassin, dragging him, kicking and snarling, away from her.

Her elder brother Rimush ran to her side, kneeling next to her. "You're hurt," he said, and she looked down to see that he was right: blood seeped through a small tear in her dress, near her hip.

"It's nothing," she said, knowing she should be trembling with terror, but she did not feel afraid. Only alert—and something greater, something beyond alertness. How very strange.

"Fetch a physician at once," Rimush was bellowing. In that moment, she saw a glimpse of their father in him. She saw that men would someday fear this boy, obey him, and kneel before him. But at this moment, no one else paid them any mind.

Guards had already surrounded the emperor and the queen, hurrying them toward a nearby door and out to safety. And where was the assassin? Spirited away to some lightless dungeon, no doubt. Moments later, only she and Rimush remained, attended by a small cadre of nervous spearmen.

"That man wasn't after the emperor," Kitra told Rimush and the guards who remained. "He came straight at me."

"Why would anyone want to assassinate you?" her brother asked.

"An Akkadu princess, ruling the mightiest city in Shumér?" Kitra winced, fingers pressing against her wound. "Think about that, Rimush. Think about what it means to these people. This cut is just the beginning."

𒀭

On the morning after the assassination, Kitra realized she had lost her name. As her father had said, she was no longer Kitra. She was Én Hedu-Ana, governor and high priestess of Urim—or she was Your Radiance, or Your Purity. But never just Kitra. Never again would she be Kitra.

Since the attack, she had seen and heard nothing of her father. A force of bodyguards appointed by the emperor had hurried her from the palace to her chambers in the nearby temple complex. Day and night they stood outside her door. She insisted on carrying a weapon, so Telal, the captain of her personal guard, presented her with a tiny bronze needle-knife. Scarcely longer than a finger, narrow and sharp as its name implied, the weapon was useless in a real battle, of course. But it was easily enfolded within robes, and deadly at intimate range.

Thus armed, filled with apprehension about the next attack, still not at all sure that she remembered her training, Kitra began her life as én-priestess of Urim.

Her day began before sunrise, when her attendant Inu woke her before morning prayers. There in the dark of her chamber, she washed her body with cold water, as Inu lit candles, murmuring the morning litanies to Nannár and Utu, the Gods of the moon and sun, with the taste of sleep still in her mouth, and its dust still in her eyes.

Once Kitra completed her ritual ablutions, Inu and a few other attendants dressed her in her inner robes, ornate with woven filigree and expensive dyes, then helped her put on her outer robes, which were embroidered and tasseled, fringed with gold. They plaited her hair and pinned it with jeweled pins, and then, after one final inspection to ensure that every thread and tassel was in place—and the needle-knife swathed deep in a fold of her robes—she walked down the dim, smoky hallway to the temple's inner chambers, where no guards were allowed to follow. She relished this short unaccompanied walk, until she reached the main sanctuary of the House of Great Light, temple of the sun-God Utu.

There, beneath the high ceiling of the cavernous chamber, she led the Ceremony of the Rising of the Sun, kneeling on a cushion, facing west, and raising her palms toward the softening pre-dawn sky. Every morning, she began the chant—

Utu comes forth, incandescent in light,
Rising from his palace to traverse the sky.

—verse after verse as she knelt there, knees going numb, arms feeling ready to drop with exhaustion. But the chant went on, the other priests following her melody, their counterpoint melodies adding depth and complexity to the song –

The stars turn away in awe
Before the face of their radiant lord.

—and the sun crept slowly higher, sending blades of dust-moted light through the sanctuary's west-facing windows.

When at last the morning prayer was over, she joined the other priests in the dining-hall for breakfast: boiled eggs and dates, fresh figs and grapes, and bread with good cheese and butter—all donated to the temple by farmers and shepherds and nobles alike.

For the rest of the morning, and most of the afternoon, she alternated between her audience chamber and her private office, hearing prayer requests, accepting donations, bestowing blessings, greeting diplomats, and reading and answering the clay tablets that piled up on her writing desk, no matter how many of them she answered and had packed away to the archives. Somewhere in the midst of all this, she sometimes found time to sneak a quick lunch of bread and fruit.

Evenings, at dusk, she made her way back to the main sanctuary, where she led the Ceremony of the Setting of the Sun and the Coming of the Moon, bidding goodbye to the God Utu for the day, entreating him to return next morning, and welcoming Nannár, God of the moon, in his nightly parade across the dome of the heavens.

In addition to these daily ceremonies, she was sometimes called on to officiate a special prayer to one of the Seven Gods who Decree—a request to Énlil, Lord of Breath, to restore the health of a dying duke; or an incantation to Ninkhursanga, Lady of the Mountains, for good fertility for sheep and goats; or a prayer to Énki, God of trickery and wise arts, to fill the emperor's head with clever plans for the coming campaign season.

Along with Kitra's name, her language was also gone. Though her native Akkadu was a common tongue on the streets of Urim—even this far south, in the heart of Shumér— it certainly wasn't spoken here in the temple. Every prayer and litany and ritual greeting was spoken in an archaic dialect of Classical Shuméru, a tongue that felt stiff and formal compared to the modern "city Shuméru" the people on the streets spoke.

She sometimes thought of the traveling priests who visited her hometown of Agadé when she was young. How she hid nearby and eavesdropped on their conversations, thrilled by how their language sounded: they were speaking Shuméru! She barely understood a word of the language—having grown up speaking Akkadu like everyone up north—but even so, Shuméru sounded exotic to her, courtly, the elegant tongue of priests and kings in the great cities to the south.

Sometimes, here in Urim, she thought back to those dreamy days in Agadé, wishing she could speak back through time and warn the younger Kitra away from this obsession.

Shuméru had a whole range of subtly different dialects, each considered right and proper for particular types of speech and song. Kitra had to be ready to use every one of them at a moment's notice. In her special prayers to the Seven, for instance, she had to remember to speak and chant in Emesal, so-called "thin-tongue Shuméru," a dialect with softened consonants and heightened vowels that priests had spoken since time immemorial to make sensitive imprecations and requests of the highest Gods and Goddesses.

Kitra secretly thought of Emesal as "pillow-talk Shuméru," a fact she shared with Inu one night as she climbed into bed.

"You mustn't let the priests hear you say that!" Inu said, tucking the billowing bedsheets around Kitra by the light of burnished bronze lamps.

"It'll be our little secret," Kitra told her, grinning.

"And the Gods?" Inu asked. "Surely they'll disapprove."

"If the Gods have time to disapprove of our little joke," Kitra replied, "They're having a boring night indeed. You really think Énlil and Inanna have time to eavesdrop?"

"They do sometimes," Inu said. "In the stories."

Kitra waved a hand dismissively. "You mean like Énki and the Boat of Heaven, and all that? Inu, those are just tales for children. The Gods aren't really like that."

Inu looked down, blushing, suddenly focused on arranging the bedsheets.

Kitra put out a hand and pulled Inu onto the bed. "I'm not making fun of you," she said. "Tell me, what do you think the Gods are like?"

Inu shrugged. "How should I know? I'm not a priestess. All I know are the stories."

Kitra nodded, looking into Inu's eyes. After a moment she said, "I hadn't thought about it that way. Here in the temple we debate the ultimate nature of the Gods. But to anyone who's not a priest, the Gods are simply those stories. No more and no less."

"I like the stories," Inu said. "The adventures, the miracles. Gives life some color. Like the whole world's a theater."

Kitra smiled. "I love that," she said. "You're cleverer than me by half, Inu. Maybe you should've been high priestess."

Inu gasped. "Don't say that! I don't know any fancy prayers. I can't even read—"

But now Kitra was laughing. She pulled Inu close to her and stroked her hair. "You don't have to be nervous," she said softly. "We know each other well."

Inu looked up, eyes wide. "You're the én," she whispered.

"I'm just Kitra," the én replied. "I told you the day we met. I'm just Kitra, and you're just Inu."

Kitra felt Inu's body relax. She slid a finger under the girl's chin, tilted her head up, and kissed her.

Inu gasped, but a moment later she was returning the kiss. As she undid Kitra's night-robe, she whispered, "Are you sure?"

"Only if this is what you truly want," Kitra whispered.

"There are laws," Inu said between kisses. "We must only do this on holy days. At the festivals."

"With men, yes," Kitra said. "But there are no laws about what women may do with women."

She felt Inu truly relax into the kiss; a kiss that ran up and down her body, until it sent tremors to the ends of her limbs, all the tensions that had been building exploding out from her. They tumbled onto the bed together, laughing, slipping from their robes.

𒀭

"What is the meaning of this?" cried the man who stood before her throne.

"The meaning of—what?" Kitra glanced around the assembly room. It was large and bright, with square pillars along the walls, painted in stripes of red and crested with yellow flowers, and murals of tall palms, lions, kings and Gods. Shuméru noblemen were seated on benches around the room, in long togas of bright red and blue, fringed with shaggy fleece. Nearby sat women of the old families of Urim, their hair pinned up with leaves and feathers of gold, their long striped dresses tasseled with white.

The nobles glanced at her, then at the newcomer, and Kitra sensed some unspoken exchange passing between all of them.

"Who are you?" she demanded of the man.

"You may call me Lugál Ané," he said, nodding his shiny bald head, sauntering up the central aisle between the benches. He was draped in the pleated sheepskin robe and mantle of a Shuméru priest. "Surely it's a name you know."

It wasn't, though, as far as she could recall. "You're the lugál of Urim?" she asked him. "In that case, I'm afraid I bring you bad news: this city no longer needs a warleader. It is protected by the five thousand trained fighting-men of the Akkadu Imperial Army."

For a moment, the lugál looked genuinely stunned that she did not recognize him. "Lugál Ané?" he prompted, waving his hands. "Of the Great House of Meshanépáda?"

That name rang a bell in her mind. "Meshanépáda, the ancient king of Urim?"

"The very same." He nodded, satisfied. "As you well know," he went on, "a man of my house has both worn the én's crown *and* carried the lugál's dagger here in Urim, going on four hundred years now."

Kitra hadn't known this. But she kept silent and waited for him to finish.

"Now, you all know I've got no quarrel with you Akkadu folk," he continued, glancing around at the nobles, nodding and receiving nods in return. "Got plenty of Akkadu friends, as it happens. The ones who work hard, please the Gods—well, they're just as entitled to lands and titles as any Shuméru, far as I'm concerned. But an Akkadu girl on the throne of Urim—?"

"I'm not a girl," Kitra snapped. "I'm your én." All eyes fixed on her as she rose from her seat, glaring down at Ané. "And yes, much is going to change in Urim. The old passes away. The new rises in its place.."

The lugál huffed. "You speak as if you know this city. As if you were not shipped here—"

"I speak," Kitra declared, so loudly her words rang from the throne-room's walls, "as the woman backed by all five thousand spears of the Imperial Army," she said, eyes fixed firmly on the priest's.

"However," she said, more gently, "I would much prefer to coax new fruit from Urim's soil, with warmth and light."

"If you have an offer to make, state it clearly," Lugál Ané grunted.

"As the én of Urim," she said, raising her voice almost to a yell, but holding her trembling tightly in check, "I need not make 'offers.' And I do not take orders from a priest under my command."

A gasp rippled through the assembly at that last word. Kitra cursed herself silently. Talk of commands and hierarchies played well in the proud, stiff courts of Akkad in the north but not nearly so well here in the marshes of Shumér, where loose, temporary alliances had shifted freely among the éns, énsis, and lugáls of a dozen great cities since time immemorial.

"All the same," she continued, keeping her voice even, "I am in a position to add significantly to the estates of any families who prove helpful during this period of transition."

She scanned the nobles again, seeing eyes widen with scarcely concealed yearning. Lugál Ané, for his part, looked less enthused. "Is that sufficiently clear for you?" she asked the lugál in a pointed tone.

"Clear enough, so far as it goes," Ané agreed. "But what, I wonder, will you ask of us during this—as you say—period of transition?"

Despite the man's snide remarks, Kitra could tell by the looks on the other nobles' faces that she'd sunk her hooks in them. "Little more than a few small administrative changes," she said breezily, carefully recalling all the terms her father had forced her to repeat until she could recite them perfectly, without hesitation. "From now on, copies of all your harvest and production records will be sent to the royal palace in Agadé."

"Your father's palace, you mean," Ané put in.

"Yes, that is the palace I mean," she replied flatly. "The palace administrators wish to have records of all lands in the imperial domain."

"How much more tax do we have to pay?" a nobleman shouted from the crowd. Other voices rose in a murmur of support.

"For the time being, no more than you pay now," Kitra assured them. "The difference is that the temple now pays tax to the Empire. If and when an increased tax is levied on your estates, I will do all in my power to keep it as low as possible. Second—"

"And what, precisely, is in your power?" Lugál Ané demanded.

She was growing tired of this. "Second," she snapped, cutting him off, "All new laws passed by this assembly must be reviewed and ratified by the regional governor before becoming law."

A more nervous murmur rose at this, tinged with growled phrases like "an Akkadu governor" and "making peasants of us all." Kitra raised her hand, gently, for silence.

"Only in very rare cases do governors actually intervene," she assured them. "Urim's government has worked beautifully for a thousand years, and I, for one, have no wish to fix what isn't broken." She smiled softly, but their expressions remained nervous.

This seemed a poor moment to introduce the third change—the most delicate of all. But if she didn't speak up about it now, it would doubtless prove even harder to implement later.

"As you say," Ané muttered, smiling snidely, "all things pass away eventually."

She chose to ignore the jab. "All things made by mankind, yes," she said. "But ritual—" She raised a thin finger, meeting the eyes of the assembly. "Ritual comes from the Gods. Ritual remains."

As she scanned the nobles, she saw some nodding softly and others gazing at her attentively, curious. A good sign, perhaps.

Ané licked his lips in annoyance. "What sort of... ritual did you have in mind, then?"

She nodded and took a deep breath. "For a start," she said, "no more little displays like—" She gestured at Lugál Ané. "—this, here. From now on, this assembly will conduct itself like the civilized court it is. Any man or woman who wishes to speak will rise, and speak clearly and respectfully, while the others listen."

The assembly murmured at this, but no voices were raised. Perhaps this wouldn't be so difficult after all, she dared to hope.

"Lugál Ané," she said, "if you would please take a seat." She gestured at an empty spot on a bench near the throne. "No more sauntering in here unannounced."

He bowed, low and absurdly exaggerated, but he trudged to the bench and duly took his seat, gazing at her expectantly.

"I also notice quite a bit of—shall we say—less-than-noble attire in this assembly today," Kitra said, taking care not to single out any nobles with her eyes. "You are all landed nobles, scions of ancient families, members of the great assembly of Urim. I know you take pride in those titles. Let your dress reflect that pride. Impressive as your family tattoos may be, I don't want to see them here. Men, no more fleece kilts or bare chests. Ladies, no more jewelled necklaces or flowery headdresses. This is a court, not a banquet hall."

She heard tittering from the assembly benches and saw many of the nobles turning and leaning to laugh at their more roughly attired peers. *Good*, she thought. *Let them laugh. They'll hold each other to our standards better than a legion of spears ever could.*

"And finally," she said, "from now on, we will all speak to one another properly, with correct honors and gestures."

The nobles laughed more loudly at this, aping outrageous bows and flourishes toward one another. She let them play for a few moments, then raised a hand for silence.

"You will address me as 'Your Radiance,'" she said, "and bend the knee when you enter my presence, or the presence of any high official."

The murmur rose to a roar. Her red-tunicked Akkadu bodyguards stepped tentatively from their hidden posts behind the throne-dais, round bronze shields and spears at the ready. She waved them back frantically, hoping none of the assembly had seen them.

"I, in turn," she went on, raising her voice to be heard over the assembly, "will address each of you by your rank and family name, which I am currently at pains to learn. I hope you will forgive any missteps on my part, as I will be glad to forgive yours."

Her eyes found Ané on his bench, smirking up at her like a hyena who'd found a fresh corpse. *Enjoy this moment*, she said to him with her gaze. *For it is about to end, and you will not see it again.*

"And now," she said loudly, raising her hand, "for the matter of your estates. Specifically, whose are to be expanded."

They fell silent at that. She allowed a thin smile to cross her lips.

"More than a few of you," she said, "will walk out of this chamber this evening with considerably more land to your names. Now tell me, who here agrees that a new field and a herd of cattle is worth a bit of curtseying and scribe-work?"

The looks in their eyes told her all she needed to know. One by one, she began to call their names.

KITRA'S MIND RAN back to that moment many times over the next three years. Each time a new royal year-name was assigned in the temple register, informing all scribes that this was "The Year the Emperor Destroyed Uru'a" or "The Year the Emperor Went to Simurrum." Each time another palace official arrived at the court of Urim, bearing news of some new tax or army levy. Each time she reviewed the tables of temple rations, and saw that many families would lack barley to feed their children this winter—on those occasions she thought back to the promises she had made in the assembly chamber that morning, and knew she had deceived them.

She often remembered that moment at the happiest times, too. At gatherings and banquets where Urim's people regaled her with sweet songs, and with their strange, playful poetry, so full of mystery and metaphor, line upon line whose meanings twisted and turned back upon themselves like cunning serpents.

That moment sometimes came back to her, too, in the midst of long nights of cheer-filled drinking at the temple brewery, of sampling beer from the sacred vats, as the brewers sang hymns to Ninkasi, Goddess of brewing. How these Shuméru loved their beer! Sweet-beer, dark-beer, thick-beer, tart-beer; more varieties and subtleties of flavor than she'd ever dreamed possible, every batch and barrel treasured like a first-born child by the men and women who'd crafted it.

And she remembered that moment most of all on quiet afternoons at the estates of the noblemen and women who'd become her friends—quiet, scholarly Beletum and his erudite wife Eluti; bright-eyed Gemekala, always quick with a filthy joke, and her husband Ahum, who'd built his estate up from a small farm; and his father, plump gray-haired Igmilum, widowed these many years, always as full of old stories as he was with ale.

"Have you heard the story of the fox and the wild bull's horns?" the old man asked her one day, as they sat sipping date-wine in his garden. He reclined in a chair carved with gazelle's hooves, his great hairy belly spilling over his fleece kilt, his wrinkled, tan skin baking in the afternoon sun.

"No, I don't think so," she told him, glancing at the mural on the house's wall: bulls with the faces of grinning, bearded men, frozen in place as they cavorted among green reeds, while fish splashed in the rippling waves of the river beneath.

"Not this story again, Pa," Gemekala rolled her eyes, running a hand through her wavy black hair.

"Oh, let him tell it," Ahum waved his wife's objection aside with a thick-fingered hand.

"I'd like to hear it," Kitra told the gray-haired man across the table.

Igmilum nodded, splashing a bit of sweet-beer across his hairy belly and rubbing into his flesh—*to keep my tan even*, so he liked to say. "Well," he began. "One day, a fox demanded that the God Énlil let him borrow the horns of a wild bull. 'The bull's horns are so tall and glorious!' the fox complained. 'I deserve to try them on, at least!' And after much begging and cajoling, Énlil agreed to the fox's request. But while the fox was wearing the wild bull's horns, it started to rain."

"We could use some of that rain around here," Eluti commented, shielding her eyes as she glanced up at the cloudless sky.

"That fox *raced* back to his burrow." Igmilum pointed sharply across the garden, as if tracing the fox's path. "But the bull's horns rose so high above his head that he couldn't fit through his own door!"

A smile spread across Kitra's lips.

"The storm kept up all night," Igmilum went on. "The wind was howling, and the rain was pelting, and oh! How that fox shivered in the cold and damp."

Gemekala made a windy *oooh* sound, miming the pelting rain with an impish wiggle of her fingertips.

"And when at last the rain ceased," Igmilum concluded, "and the fox had dried off, he stomped back to Énlil and gave back the bull's horns. 'I have no use for these horns!' he declared 'They belong with their rightful owner.' And that was the last time the fox ever mentioned the matter."

The old man spread his hands, as if to say, *there you have it*.

Kitra snorted a laugh. "Kingship can be cumbersome," she said. "Is that the lesson?"

Igmilum tilted his head side-to-side. "Crowns, sceptres, swords and fancy dresses," he said with a playful smirk. "Everybody loves to play with them. And there's no harm in playing, I suppose." He winked mischievously. "Until one day you find you can't fit in your own burrow anymore."

"Oh, stop speaking in riddles," Gemekala whacked her father-in-law's fat belly.

"You see?" the old man leaped up, clutching his belly in a pantomime of agony. "She rises against me! Even Énlil offers no protection from a daughter such as this!" Now they were all laughing, as father and daughter wrestled across the tiled porch.

But even as Kitra smiled, she couldn't help thinking, *up north in Agadé, we have no silly stories about the Gods. To us, the Gods are terrible, solemn beings, and we fear to take their names in vain*. All the same, the date-wine and the sunlight warmed her almost as much as these people did, and she laughed right along with the rest of them.

The official purpose of this visit, and a thousand others like it, was to gather information for the palace records. But in truth, very little record-scrutinizing got done. She went to Igmilum's farm just to wander among the olive and apple trees, and hear the songs of wild birds, and listen to tales of the Gods and heroes and monstrous beasts that had roved over the earth in days long past.

And in those first heady days of her én-ship, she refused an armed escort. She even dared to walk Urim's maze of streets unaccompanied, handing out apples and barley-bread to hungry children, offering blessings from Nannár and Énlil to every man and woman who paused to greet her.

That all changed the day of the second attack.

She was strolling in the temple garden. The low-hanging sun cast the short date-palms and flowerbeds in a golden glow. Tired in body and mind after a long afternoon of counseling feuding couples and counting wheat-barrel deliveries, Kitra felt her eyes drift closed. This was the first moment she'd managed to steal for herself all week. She stood, savoring the warm emptiness of the red glow behind her eyelids.

Then pressure landed on her shoulder, and she whirled to come face to face with a man in a sackcloth toga—the garb of a penitent—his face covered with a theater-mask: a snarling monster, its face a grotesque mass of wrinkles. The man struck at her stomach with a dagger, and she somehow stepped aside. Her attacker's weight carried him forward, and he stumbled past her for a step, startled.

She felt the moment that day on the palace balcony, when the first assassin had attacked her: everything seemed slower, clearer, inevitable as waves crashing against a riverbank. She saw where the knife was headed next. The attacker aimed to step behind her and push the blade up against her neck.

Even in motion, I am still. The words came to her fully formed, from nowhere—the same words she'd thought on the balcony. She took a step out of range of the attacker's arm and whirled to face him, drawing the bronze needle-knife from deep within her robes, slipping its ring-grip over her finger. And she did feel still, somehow, as though the whole world were moving. But because she moved with it, it felt effortless.

The attacker hesitated for the briefest eyeblink. She struck viper-quick, piercing the side of his neck with the needle-knife. Watching him stumble back, clutching his throat to stanch the flow of blood that pumped in small spurts from the tiny wound, she realized she'd struck the great vein. He turned and ran, a trail of red dripping to the pavement behind him.

"Guards!" she yelled. "Assassin!"

They came clattering into the garden several long breaths later—plenty of time, she reflected, for even the laziest assassin to finish his work. But now the world was speeding up again, filling with shouting Akkadu bodyguards and gasping priests, and she no longer felt still. She felt like a boat tossed in a storm.

The assassin hadn't gone far. His legs had given out as he'd reached the edge of the garden, and now he lay sprawled next to a jasmine bush, blood pooling on the polished flagstones. A guard knelt next to him, flipped the body over roughly, lifted the mask from the pale, lifeless face, and shook his head as he looked at its emptily staring eyes.

"Dead," grunted Telal, the captain of her personal guard; a scarred Akkadu warrior whose black beard and hair were going gray at the tips. "That was a fool thing to do, Your Radiance," he added quietly. "He may've had information."

Kitra prodded at the corpse with the toe of her slipper. "This man knew what he was doing. One more breath and I'd have been dead."

The captain sighed resignedly. "Who taught you to use that needle-knife?" he asked.

"Taught me?" she asked. "It's a simple principle. Wait for an opening, then strike. What's to be taught?"

He looked at her for a long time. "By Énlil's breath, I'm glad you're on our side," he finally said, shaking his head.

"And what side would that be, captain?" she asked, wiping blood from the needle-knife and slipping it back within her robes.

He raised an eyebrow. "The side of the emperor," he said. "Of course."

"That's a side not many share these days," Kitra said. "Tell me, captain, does your family have enough to eat this winter?"

"I'm afraid I have no family," the captain replied. "But the temple feeds me well enough. Now, if it please Your Radiance, we should get rid of this body before anyone—"

Kitra heard footsteps hurrying up a nearby corridor. She braced herself for another attack. But the acolyte who emerged was scarcely more than a boy; bald-headed and white-robed, looking as nervous as she felt. His eyes went at once to the body, and the pool of blood it lay in. His eyes went wide, but he asked no questions.

"Your Radiance," he said, bowing low. "The Crown Prince Rimush is here. He awaits you in the reception hall."

Her brow furrowed. "My brother—?" No visit had been planned. What could he want?

"Take care of this," she told Telal, nodding to the body. "And have my guards check any messenger leaving the temple complex. Someone will be waiting for word of success. I want to know who's carrying that word, and to whom."

Telal nodded brusquely.

Kitra bent to the young acolyte. "You understand, of course," she told him gently, "that Énlil and Nannár look very kindly on boys who keep secrets. Is it not so?"

He gazed up at her, wide-eyed. After a moment he nodded. "It is so, Your Radiance," he said, very quietly.

She rose and padded down the corridor, as quickly as dignity would permit. Behind her, she heard Telal barking orders to the other Akkadu bodyguards. In a few moments, no one would know the attack had happened. No one, of course, but those who had witnessed it—and a boy who, Gods willing, could keep a secret.

CROWN PRINCE RIMUSH was much changed since that morning he'd stood with her on the temple balcony, and saved her from that first assassin. He looked more like Father than ever—or, rather, more like Father had looked in the early days of his reign, back when the emperor's hair had shone black, and his belly had not yet begun to swell with roast pork and Shuméru date-wine.

The prince wore a linen toga dyed deep black, patterned with red flowers, and a crimson mantle embroidered with fine silver thread. His long black hair was braided and bound into a tight coil at the back of his head, crowned with a band of silver, set with polished turquoise and greenstone. His beard had grown in, thick and full; it was trimmed square, plaited and bound with rings of silver. It was his eyes, though, that gave away his age most surely. Their youthful shine had given way to a careful, penetrating gaze—the gaze of a man well-practiced in searching out secrets.

"Rimush, dear," Kitra called to her elder brother across the vast reception chamber. "What a pleasant surprise."

"Pleasant?" He turned to face her, his face cold and hard, without hint of humor. "No, not pleasant, I'm afraid."

She embraced him, kissing him on one cheek, then the other. He returned her kisses without enthusiasm, then turned away.

"Rimush, what is it?" she asked, a deep worry beginning to claw up from her belly.

"Are we watched?" he asked abruptly, eyes darting to the room's far corners.

"Watched? No, I don't think so—"

"Who might be listening?" He peered behind pillars, as if he expected a spy to leap out at any moment.

"Brother." She placed a hand firmly on his shoulder. "Tell me what's happened."

He turned to her and gazed deeply into her eyes for the space of several heartbeats.

"Father is dead," he said at last.

Her eyes went wide. "What?" she whispered.

Rimush nodded. "He has been sick these past six months. A festering rib-wound from the Battle of Uru'a, the physicians say. But it could be poison just as easily. He drank that beer sent from the temple at Kish, though I warned him not to. Those priests have never been our friends."

She scarcely heard his words. *Father, dead?* This could not have come at a worse time. The harvest records showed a shortfall, as usual; and perhaps whoever had sent today's assassin knew it. So this meant—

"You are emperor now," she whispered.

He gave the slightest of nods.

She sank to her knees, prostrating herself once, twice, thrice at his feet. She rose and took his hand and kissed its silver ring. "My Lord Emperor," she said.

"Careful who sees you doing that," he said quietly. "You'll notice I've come clad in silver, not gold. Akkadu kings aren't much beloved this far south."

"Nor Akkadu priestesses, either," she added. "I was attacked again today."

Something dark rose in his eyes. "I will double your guard," he said, lips tightening. "Give me the names of anyone you suspect. Anyone who might remotely—"

"Rimush." She placed a firm hand against his chest. "I have this under control. This city is dry tinder, and now is not the time to strike sparks."

"Sparks?" He gaped at her, incredulous. "Sister, I mean to put the torch to these dead trees. I mean to set a blaze Shumér will not forget."

She backed away slowly, shaking her head. "Rimush, it was only one attack—"

"One attack?" he threw her words back at her, closing the distance between them with a step. "Only one attack? Kitra, half these cities have sent knives against my tax collectors. My governors walk the streets surrounded by armed bodyguards, and sleep with daggers beneath their pillows. Kish and Umma have risen in open revolt. The heads of good Akkadu men sit on spikes outside their gates."

"Because there is famine, Rimush!" she cried. "Give them back their bread and beer, and—"

"Bread and beer." He snorted. "No, we've come much too far for that. That bread and beer feed our armies. Armies we cannot do without."

"Why not?" She glared at him. "Because you need them to fight the men and women you starve?"

He turned away, pacing restlessly about the chamber. "It's not just the food shortages, Kitra," he said.

"Famines," she said tightly. "Call them what they are."

"It's not just the *famines*, then," he said, more quietly, pausing and turning to face her. "You know that as well as I do. These Shuméru are too proud. Too in love with their temples and their family trees."

"Rimush, what are you planning—?"

"No more than needs to be done," he answered. "I promise you that."

KITRA SAT HER throne atop the high brick dais, surrounded by red-tunicked Akkadu guards in pointed copper helmets, bearing round bronze shields and long-tipped spears, gazing out at the crowd of enraged Shuméru nobles. She tried to remember how this assembly chamber had looked on that day when she'd first sat at its head; the day she'd promised too much to these people, far more than she could ensure they received. Trusting, they had not been. Naive? No, certainly not. But in those early years, some had surely held out hope that the House of Szarrukín might improve their lives.

She saw no hint of that hope in Urim's noblemen and women today. Snarling mouths, glaring eyes, pushing arms and grasping hands flowed before her as if in a dream, angry words roaring in torrents, like the waters of the Swift River rushing over stone. Her bodyguards held them back, but they pushed forward again—dear Beletum and Eluti from the farm; Ahum, and even Gemekala, whose teary eyes Kitra found she could not meet. She turned away, heart sour with shame.

"I have family in Kish!" someone was yelling. "Your brother slaughters our people in the streets!" someone else cried. "He burned down my cousin's farm!" She searched for the sources of these shouts, but could not find them among the mob.

"Be seated," she called to them, raising her hands. But the nobles pushed and shouted, spat and howled. She raised her voice, but the shoving and clanging of spears drowned her out.

"Shut up!" she finally shrieked. "All of you!"

They stepped back. To her shock, the room actually fell silent for a moment. She took a deep breath and let it out slowly.

"None of your estates are in danger," she told them.

"This isn't about estates," someone snarled.

She met his eyes. Palusum, his name was. Scion of one of Urim's oldest families. He wore a one-shouldered toga in the Akkadu style, but his proud, beardless face was pure Shuméru.

"You're right, Palusum," she said. "It's about much more than your estates. The cities of Kish and Umma have risen in open revolt against the emperor—"

"We swore allegiance to you and your father," cried Eluti. "Not to this butcher brother of yours." She clutched a stylus in her right hand and a tablet in her left, as if she meant to scratch these very moments into clay. "He has declared himself a *God*, Kitra. Who ever heard of such a thing?"

Kitra met her friend's eyes, searching for any hint of recognition there, and finding none. "It's not about who's sworn allegiance to whom," she said, more softly. "It's about building a Shumér we can all live in, together."

"A Shumér where *we* run the cities and farms," Palusum sneered, tapping his fingers against his chest, "while *your* family reaps the profits." He glanced at the nobles around him. "Is that the kind of Shumér we want?" Words of denial rumbled through the crowd.

Of course, Palusum himself, like most of the nobles in this assembly-chamber, had reaped plenty of his own profits over the years, but Kitra knew now was not the time to point this out. "A lot has changed over the past twelve years," she said. "I certainly don't deny it."

"Promises were made, Kitra!" someone shouted. On any other day, she'd have called for order and insisted on being addressed properly. But now was clearly not the time.

"Name one promise I haven't kept, that was within my power to keep," she said.

That silenced them for a few moments.

When at last a voice spoke up, it was not that of outraged Palusum or judgmental Eluti. It was the voice of the friend whose words she'd most dreaded to hear, because she knew those words would cut to the bone.

"Maybe you did keep your promises," Gemekala said, stepping forward into the chamber's center aisle. "All the ones you could keep, anyway. But we all know that isn't the point."

Kitra raised a hand. "Gemekala, I—"

The woman shook her head, licking her lips tightly. "No. It doesn't matter how many estates your family hands out, or how many times you reassure us that visits from Akkadu governors are just formalities. We're not stupid, Kitra. We all see what's going on here."

Kitra shook her head, eyes wide. "Tell me, Gemekala. Tell me, because I don't know. What is my family doing that's so horrible?"

Gemekala ran a hand over her forehead. "You're not *from* here. You've lived here for twelve years, I know. And you're one of my best friends—but you didn't grow up here. It's different."

"Different—?" Kitra's brow furrowed.

"Your father looked down from the mountains of Akkad," Gemekala said, "and he saw something beautiful. He saw Shumér. Maybe he truly loved this land. I don't know. Maybe he just wanted it for his own, as every king wants rare birds for his garden and lovely women for his bed."

The nobles watched her, transfixed by her words as she paced before the throne-dais.

"But if a man loves a woman," she went on, "I mean, truly loves her, then he realizes he cannot own her. That would destroy the very thing that makes her so beautiful. The instant a yoke is laid upon her neck, some spark inside her dies. And from that moment on, she is no longer the same woman."

Only the wind whistled in the narrow windows of the audience-chamber.

"So it is," she said, "with Shumér."

Kitra sat in silence for a long while. She thought to open her mouth, but her lips were trembling. No words would come.

"Hear! Hear!" someone cried from the benches.

Shouts of affirmation echoed through the chamber, punctuated by thumps on the benches and walls.

Lugál Ané rose from his bench and swaggered up the aisle, just as he had on that morning, twelve long years ago.

"This," the lugál crowed, gesturing back at Kitra, "is what you get when an Akkadu tyrant sits on the throne."

"Enough!" Kitra cried, rising from her seat. But the crowd of nobles were standing, *cheering*, shouting their agreement with the bald old priest. She raised her hand and nodded to her bodyguards. They pushed in from around the throne, spears raised.

"See how your tyrant deals with open debate!" Ané was shouting over the crowd's roar. "See how she fears the truth!" The old priest raised one hand, two fingers pointed at the ceiling. And he flicked that hand downward.

All at once, masked men and women swarmed in from all sides, leaping upon the Akkadu guards with daggers. Kitra screamed. Her bodyguards fought furiously, thrusting out with their spears, shields raised to block the blades. But they'd been taken by surprise. One by one, they fell before the assassins' knives. The crowd churned, some fleeing, others pressing closer to the melee.

"Your Radiance!" A voice called from below the throne. Kitra glanced down to see Telal, captain of her personal guard, extending a hand to help her down from the dais, as a small contingent of Akkadu guardsmen tightened around her, spears and shields upraised against the attackers. She took his hand and descended, raising her skirts so as not to trip.

"We must get you to your chambers," Telal told her.

"My chambers—?" She gazed at the hand-to-hand struggle unfolding only an arm's length from her. Another Akkadu guardsman fell fending off one assassin when another buried a blade in his neck from behind.

"Come on!" Telal snarled, tugging her arm roughly. Summoning her wits, she hurried after him, out the back door of the assembly hall. Two spearmen ran ahead of them, down the narrow hallways where acolytes leaped out of the way.

When they reached the door of her chamber, Telal and the rest of her surviving bodyguards dashed inside, scouting for hidden assassins. The captain emerged a moment later, nodding.

"I'll post guards outside the door," he told her. "This hallway is narrow, which makes it easy to defend. No one's getting in, unless they can break through a brick wall."

She hurried inside, and the bodyguards closed and barred the heavy wood door behind her.

"Telal," she called through the wood planks.

"Your Radiance?" his gruff voice called back.

"Thank you," she said. "For staying with me."

"Your father saved my life," the captain replied after a moment. "At the Battle of Cedar Hill."

"I didn't know that," she said.

He grunted, then changed the subject. "We'll get you out of here soon. Don't you worry."

And then he was gone, leaving her alone with her writing desk, and the locked door, and the distant sounds of battle raging up and down the halls of the assembly house.

WHAT COULD POSSIBLY be keeping him? Kitra wondered, for the thousandth time, pacing the floor of her chamber, back and forth, trampling a footpath into the sumptuous carpet beneath her writing desk.

She hadn't left this chamber since Telal and her bodyguards had locked her in here, for her own safety. That had been—what, three days ago? Four? She checked the clay ledger on the desk again. Yes, four days, during which her only contact with the outside world had been through Telal's guards, who brought her meagre meals of flatbread and wine, and carried away her chamberpot each morning to replace it with a clean one. Lock any sane woman in a room for four days, she thought, and a madwoman will emerge. Had she run mad yet? It didn't seem so. But she felt just on the verge of it.

She'd kept busy writing a diary of the events of the past few days. When she ran out of events to transcribe, she began writing her thoughts; snatches of conversation in her own mind, really. Over long mornings and afternoons at the writing desk, those thoughts had slowly coagulated into lines of poetry:

Ancient temple
Set deep in the mountain
Dark shrine
Frightening, red-stained place
Walls tall and thick
Like a trap.

What strange poems were these? She'd never read anything like them, in all her years of study. It was hard to imagine anyone would ever make any sense of them, much less want to read them. Still, she kept writing. What else was there to do?

She had been the én of this city, once. Yes, she could remember it, though those scenes seemed like tales from someone else's life. Now she waited on the words and acts of men whom she outranked—or had once outranked. What was she now? She had no way of finding out. That simple fact made her feel more powerless than all the rest of it put together.

A soft knock came at the door.

Kitra looked up from her writing. "Yes?" she said, a bit too quietly. "Who is it?" she tried again, trying to put a bit more confidence into her voice.

"It's me, Your Radiance," came Telal's voice. "I bring a message."

Kitra rose from her writing desk, scattering half-finished clay tablets, sending styluses clattering to the tiled floor. She rushed to the door and lifted its heavy bar with a grunt, then hefted it aside with the guards' help.

"Telal!" She ran to embrace him, despite herself, planting a kiss on each of his cheeks. He was the first person she'd seen or spoken to in days. "What's happened?"

His eyes fell, and his lips worked without forming words. When at last he raised his face to meet her gaze, he wore the look of a beaten man. "The news is... not good, Your Radiance. I am sorry to say."

She nodded solemnly, keeping her voice even. "How many of them has Lugál Ané swayed to his side?"

He licked his cracked lips. "I'm afraid the situation has... degenerated further than you know."

She stepped back, eyes widening, afraid to ask for the truths he was about to offer.

"The fighters of Urim have always been Lugál Ané's men," he said, too ashamed to look her in the eye. "They outnumber us ten-to-one, Your Radiance."

"But, my friends..." Kitra stammered. "Eluti and Gemekala—"

Telal shook his gray-haired head. "I do not know what has become of them, or which side they have chosen in this fight."

"Do not know—?" Kitra repeated, grasping for his meaning. "But surely the assembly—?"

Telal ran a thick hand across his beard. "The assembly meets in secret now, Your Reverence. We do not know where."

The room seemed to spin. Kitra wondered if she was going mad after all. "Surely they must come to the temple," she insisted. "They have to offer prayers and make sacrifices."

It was then, at last, that she saw how deeply beaten Telal was. He stepped back, shoulders hunched, his red tunic torn and frayed, caked with blood, dried dark red, stained with black smoke and the filth of the streets, as were his scarred arms and hands. He gazed into her eyes, as tears rose in his.

"We have lost Urim, Your Radiance," he said, more quietly than she'd ever heard him speak. "Lugál Ané's faction controls the army, the temple, the streets. We have fought tooth and claw to protect this assembly hall and its grounds. Dozens of my men..." He choked on the words, but forced them out. "Dozens of my men have fallen, to keep you safe, here, in this room. None regret their sacrifice, I assure you. But this city is no longer ours."

"No longer ours..." She found herself repeating his words again, as if this might make their meaning clear. "Then whose is it?"

"I suppose," he said, "that for the time being, Urim belongs to her own people again."

The way he phrased it, it almost sounded like a blessing. A logical choice. If one only forgot that this meant the exile of Kitra and her family—or worse, if Ané had his way.

"What do we do?" Kitra felt like an infant having to ask this. But, strange as it felt, she had to concede that at this moment, Telal understood Urim far more intimately than she did.

"As it happens," he said, his voice a bit firmer, "I've received a message. About your brother."

Kitra's eyes widened. *On today, of all days.* She felt fairly sure she knew what news the captain brought, but she could not bring herself to speak the words aloud.

"He's been..." she tried, and found she could not finish.

"Slain." Telal's eyes fell again. "In his palace, in Agadé," he said. "Some men of the court plotted against him, and..."

The earth itself seemed to be slipping loose from its moorings. Kitra was almost sure she could feel the world tilting, pitching wildly into a whirling, star-speckled void.

"He was gathering a new army," Telal went on. "Preparing to march on Kish, then on Umma and Adab. Half the cities between the Rivers were rising in revolt."

Kitra could find no words. The space within her felt empty, devoid of sound or light.

"There is a second part," Telal said. "To the message."

Kitra looked up, eyes far away. "A second part?"

"Your brother requests your presence at a great feast, in Agadé," Inu told her. "In a week's time."

Kitra shook her head. "My brother—?"

"Your *younger* brother," Inu clarified. "Manishtushu. He has accepted the throne."

Kitra's eyes went wide. "No," she stammered, as visions arose in her mind: her younger brother perishing, full of dagger-wounds, in some shadowy palace corridor, as Rimush had.

"The news is still secret," Telal said. "Your family's vizier entrusted it to me, for your ears only."

"Nine years," Kitra muttered after a moment. "Nine bloody years under that wolf. At last it's over."

"Kitra," Telal said gently.

She looked up, scarcely seeing the captain.

"We're going to get you out of here," he whispered, placing a hand softly on her shoulder. "Out of Urim. I've secured a wagon. We leave tonight."

She gazed back into his eyes for a long moment, seeing something else through the fog of confusion and grief. Something that glimmered, even now; a softness. As if he were waiting for something.

"Is Inu still here?" she asked, gently lifting his hand from her shoulder.

Telal hesitated a moment. "She has remained at the temple, yes," he said at last. "She asked that we send word as soon as it was safe—.

"Just a few minutes with her," Kitra said. "Then we'll leave this city. I'll go wherever you think is safest."

Telal bowed stiffly, knocked on the door, and plodded out.

Kitra paced for a time that felt as long as all the days before, until at last a soft knock came at the door, and the bar lifted, and Inu padded into the writing-chamber.

"You didn't leave," Kitra whispered, planting kisses on the young acolyte's head, as the guards closed and barred the door behind her.

"Of course I didn't," Inu smiled softly.

Kitra told her, quickly, of the news about her slain brother, and the younger one who'd risen to take his place.

When she was finished, Inu only said, "Come sit down."

Kitra furrowed her brow. "Sit down? Why?"

"Because he was your brother, Kitra," Inu said, guiding her to the chair and wrapping her arms about Kitra's neck. "Because you loved him."

"Inu, I'm..." Kitra extended a hand upward, tentatively, brushing Inu's cheek.

"I know," Inu said, reaching up to clasp Kitra's hand. "You loved them all."

Kitra pulled Inu close and wrapped her tight, and pressed her forehead against the younger woman's soft hair. Suddenly everything came crashing in on her—the attack today in the assembly chamber, and now this news of her brother. "Ah, Nannár!" she wept to the empty air. "Ah, Nannár, what will we do?"

They held one another for a long time, the én in her flowing white robes, and the young acolyte in her pleated wool gown. Hot tears poured down Kitra's cheeks—not for her brother; no, but for everything he'd cost her. This strange, enchanting, ancient land, which her family had loved so dearly they'd crushed the very air from its lungs.

"Telal has secured a wagon," Kitra said, after a long time. "To smuggle us out of the city."

"Tonight?" Inu asked. The thought felt strange to Kitra, too: twelve years of life in this city, all of it snuffed out in a flash.

"Come with me, Inu," Kitra said.

A look of anguish crossed the young woman's face. "Kitra, I cannot. The God Nannár is my husband."

"Your place is with me," Kitra whispered.

"No," Inu said, gently. "It's here, in Urim. At the temple. And when you return in triumph, Nannár and I will be here, waiting for you."

Kitra nodded mutely and turned slowly away from the young priestess. "Then what else is there to say, Inu?" she asked, after a long moment.

"I can stay," Inu said, running her hand along Kitra's back. "Just for a short while. Until the wagon comes."

"Please." Kitra took the young woman's hand delicately and pulled it away. "Just go, Inu."

Inu bit her lip, close to tears herself. But at last she said, "As you wish, Your Radiance." She bowed low and padded across the room, knocked on the door, and waited for the guards to unbar it.

"Kitra," she whispered as she crossed the threshold.

Kitra looked up, her eyes gazing at something far away.

"This isn't where this ends," Inu said.

When Kitra did not answer, Inu bowed again, out of habit, and padded away down the hall.

As Kitra leaned back into the soft chair behind the writing desk, she felt as if she were shrinking. As if this room, so cozy only days ago, now yawned monstrously around her; a looming beast that had slipped beyond her control. She lay her head on her arms, atop the writing desk, and waited for Telal to return to her.

HER LITTLE CARAVAN waited for her in the pre-dawn darkness, at Urim's north gate. She wrapped herself in a cloak, and climbed into the back of a covered wagon, drawing the flap behind her. Telal snapped the riding crop, urging the donkeys forward. The wagon began to roll, and soon they were rumbling north on the imperial highway.

The packed-dirt road gave a less bumpy ride than the potholed paving of Urim's streets. Imperial soldiers had been hard at work over the past ten years or so, clearing away the trees and bushes for several spans back from the edges of the road, making it near-impossible for thieves and brigands to lie in wait. Regular way-stations gave them fresh donkeys and hot meals, which she ate in secret, packed safely among her pillows in the back of the wagon.

After a week of this smooth, monotonous traveling, the imperial highway petered out into rocky dirt trails, until at last she was compelled to dismount from the wagon and walk with Telal and his men. The sun glinted on their bronze helmets, and their leather scabbards bounced against their woolen kilts as they trudged in silence on either side of her.

And so it was that they approached the town of Agadé, home of Kitra's family, and birthplace of the House of Szarrukín. The town hadn't been much to look at when Kitra lived here as a child; just a sprawl of mud-brick huts, market stalls and temples connected by dirt trails, lacking even a protective wall, since it held so little worth protecting in those days.

But the rise of Szarrukín had brought torrents of gold flowing back to the emperor's birthplace. A great mud-brick wall now surrounded the town, its foundations formed of solid rock; its crenellated towers attended by vigilant copper-helmeted guards, who demanded Kitra's name, and the names of her protectors, before standing aside to let her pass through the great arched gate.

Kitra could scarce believe her eyes. The grassy dirt tracks of her childhood had been transformed into flagstoned avenues. What had been squat hovels were now flat-roofed stone villas, where merchants sipped wine and nibbled dates beneath vast awnings. Humble market squares had become spacious plazas adorned with colorful statues and fountains, where traders haggled over treasures over the shouts of acrobats and the piping of musicians.

Among all this richness, the most enriched place of all was her family's estate, a cluster of gleaming keeps of polished stone atop the highest hill in town. As they approached, a second set of guards stood to attention outside a locked gate set in an inner mud-brick rampart; smaller than the city wall, but still so tall that Kitra could scarcely see over its top.

"Name yourself," a guard grunted, craning his thick neck to size up Telal and her other companions. A scar ran diagonally across the man's face, twisting his lip in a permanent sneer. Two others sauntered out from the gatehouse to take up positions on either side of him.

"Do you not recognize the daughter of Szarrukín?" Kitra asked, keeping her head high and her voice even.

"The emperor's daughter rules in Urim," he retorted. "Everyone knows that. Now state your true name and business, or be on your way."

Telal stepped forward. "If you had swifter messengers here in Agadé," he snapped, "you'd know that Urim has fallen to Shuméru usurpers, just as Kish and Umma have."

The guards' eyes widened. "Marutúk preserve us," one of the younger ones muttered.

"That's as may be," the older one grunted. "But even if it's true, it's no proof of your claim. How am I to know you are who you say?"

Suddenly, a cracked voice rang out from the other side of the gate. "Kitra!"

It was old Saduq, Kitra's great aunt on her father's side. The gray-haired woman came running, skirts hiked above her ankles.

Kitra looked the head guard in his eyes and held his gaze for the space of a few heartbeats. He looked from Saduq, back to Kitra, back to Saduq again.

"Well?" the old woman demanded after a moment. "Aren't you going to let her in?"

The guards heaved open the gate, and Kitra set foot within her family's estate for the first time since her childhood.

"Back so soon?" Saduq joked as they trod the paved road up the hill, toward the main houses. The old woman looked just as Kitra remembered her: gangly and gray-haired, with the same half-toothless grin that had looked down on her since she was a little girl. Had so little time passed in Agadé? It felt like years, yet somehow, it felt as if she'd never left. As if she was, indeed, back so soon.

"Urim didn't agree with me, auntie," Kitra said kindly. It felt such a relief to be speaking Akkadu again; simple, straight-sentenced Akkadu, so much clearer than Shuméru's dozen dialects, with their complex backward-twisting grammar.

"You'll always have a place here," Saduq said, though her eyes narrowed, just slightly, in a way Kitra might not have noticed before her days in the palace and the temple.

"I'd like to see Mother," said Kitra. "And my cousins. And everyone."

"They're all right where you left them," said Saduq. "Though your mother... well, you'll see."

As she strolled among the orchards and outbuildings of her family's estate, word of her approach spread. Soon cousins and aunts and uncles swarmed around her, asking seventy times seven questions about everything under the sun: What was Urim like? Did anyone speak Akkadu? What did they eat? Did they worship the same Gods? Did she say her prayers every day? Were the man handsome there? She did her best to answer the questions as quickly as they came, but of course they never ran out.

After a time, she begged leave from the endless questioning, and hurried to the long stone manor-house at the center of the estate. She'd grown up in this villa, yet it seemed so much smaller than she remembered it, as if the garden out front, and the olive and lemon trees, and even the doorways had shrunk in her absence. How strange.

Pushing aside the door-cloth, she ducked into the villa's dim entryway, letting cool interior air wash over her sun-baked skin.

"Mother?" she called, swatting away flies. "It's me."

There was no one in the empty dining room, where the couches and chairs sat empty, gathering dust. Not a soul pacing the central garden, where Father had loved to stroll around the pond with his closest confidants, scheming in the shadows of tall palms and tamarisk trees. Now that pond had gone green and foul; the trees dead and dry, clawing the empty air.

"Anyone?" she called again. Not even a servant appeared. The only sound was the whistling of the hot wind through cracks in the stones.

At the far end of the garden, she entered the villa's inner chambers, where she half-expected to hear her brothers' voices, as they chased one another with wagons on strings, or fought with wooden swords, urged on by Father's hearty cheering: *Yes, that's it, Rimush! Strike for the heart!*

But no voices echoed in these rooms today. Not so much as a footstep, aside from the soft padding of Kitra's boots on the polished marble floors. At last she reached the doorway to Mother's bedroom. For a moment she hesitated, her heart clenching in dread at what she might find within. *I move as the world moves.* The words came again, unbidden. Kitra drew a deep breath and stepped into the bedchamber.

The room was dark, unlit by even a single lamp. It smelled of old wine and sweat, and other, less pleasant things. At the chamber's center lay a great four-posted bed of ornately carved tamarisk, draped with curtains of thin linen. Amid piles of tasseled pillows and embroidered blankets sprawled a woman's form, unmoving and swathed in black.

"Mother," Kitra called softly.

The figure on the bed did not move.

"Mother, it's me," she persisted.

"Go away," her mother whispered, her face pressed against a pillow.

Hot tears rose in Kitra's eyes, though she tried to push them away. "Don't you want to see your daughter?" Her voice cracked.

The figure on the bed gave a long, low groan. "I have no daughter," Kitra's mother moaned. "I have no sons. I have no husband. The Gods have taken everything from me—!" The last word collapsed into a fit of shaking sobs.

Kitra ran to the bed and lay next to her mother, hugging her tightly and stroking her black-veiled hair, whispering kind words. But the woman on the bed did not speak again, or even turn her head to look Kitra in the eye.

How long she stayed there with this unmoving, black-shrouded shell that had once been an empress, Kitra could not say. She lay there, stroking her mother's hair and whispering to her, as the sun-rays lengthened in the chamber's narrow windows, and the light turned orange, then blue. Kitra's stomach began to ache. Her mouth turned dry and sticky.

At last she rose from the bed, and walked out past the dead garden, to the villa's front lawn, where all her aunts and uncles and cousins were waiting for her, with a picnic of dates and flatbread and wine spread on the grass. She ate, and talked with them, and answered seventy times seven more questions, and they asked her nothing about her mother, nor about what had happened in Urim. And for tonight, she realized, it was a relief to think of none of those things, for the first time in as long as she could remember.

She rose early the next morning, and walked alone among the olive trees of the family orchard, letting her thoughts focus on nothing in particular. In the afternoon she chatted more with her aunts and uncles, and played with her little cousins Zeri and Nazir. They were the ones who'd changed the most in her absence, both of them far taller and more thickly muscled than when she'd left.

Mother never emerged from the house, and the rest of the family carefully avoided the topics of her father's and brother's deaths. On the topic of her younger brother, Manishtushu, they also seemed reluctant to speak, as if worried they might inadvertently attract some curse with the mention of his name.

And so, in a strange way, she came to feel like a woman without a family, adopted into the fold of these strangers who shared her family's name, who took pity on her. So passed Kitra's first three days in the town that had once been her home.

Then, on the fourth night, her brother Manishtushu summoned her to dinner, at the royal palace at the center of Agadé.

As she crossed the great arched threshold of the palace's garden, all she could think was, *I've never seen so many men in one place*. Not in Urim's assembly hall, and not at the great seasonal festivals in the temple complex. Certainly not at any banquet her family had thrown before.

Beneath a starry sky, endless rows of palm trees stood watch over tables that stretched as far as her eyes could see. Braziers of red-hot goals churned the night air in shimmering waves of heat, casting warm golden light over boards groaning with roast pork dripping with honey, fattened duck stuffed with pistachios and soft cheese, piles of apples, pears and melons; plump dates and figs and bunches of succulent purple grapes.

At the head of the central table sat her brother, Manishtushu, wrapped in a soft one-shouldered toga of finest crimson linen, woven with tiny silver stars, tasseled in gold thread; a mantle made from a lion's mane draped about his shoulders; his hair tightly braided and bound in a chignon behind his head, topped with a gold band set with polished turquoise and amber.

Around him, at the long tables stretching the entire length of the garden, sat the men of every noble family in all Akkad, so it seemed to Kitra. Near her brother, enjoying pride of place, she recognized old Hamati and his son Tukul, of House Esznanak, pallid as ever, all elbows and cheekbones, their togas deep blue, woven with the long-horned goats that were their sigils. Along the left, she saw Iszkur, lord of House Gurúsz, grown considerably more corpulent since last she'd seen him, sucking on a juicy pork rib through his thick square beard. Those plump-bellied boys arrayed near him must be his sons; and the raucous gold-pinned ladies with them, their wives—or pleasure-girls, perhaps. Sharp-eyed Zinsu of House Szarubád scanned the assembly like a hawk, as did his wife Nidintu, gray-haired but alert as ever.

And those were just the beginning. At the next tables sat the green-cloaked sons of House Aharszi, long spears at their sides as always; the fork-bearded fighters of House Umardá, owls perched on their shoulders and arms; the seven daughters of House Ludana'at, grown to flower of womanhood since Kitra had last seen them, each attended by a husband handsomer than the last.

Kitra soon lost count of the familiar faces. As she scanned beyond the nearest tables, she guessed a full thousand men must be dining in this garden tonight—and with their wives, sons and daughters, the number was surely twice that.

"Sister!" A deep voice thundered.

Kitra whirled to see Manishtushu rising from his seat at the head table, beckoning her with open arms.

"My favorite high priestess in all the world." He beamed, planting a rather drunken kiss on each of her cheeks. "You've had a safe journey, I hope?"

She could think of a few choice ways to respond to that, but she held her tongue. "It was... uneventful."

"Well," he replied, guiding her to the chair next to his, "you're in luck, because this promises to be a most eventful night."

I've rather lost my taste for eventful assemblies, she wanted to say. "You're looking well, brother," she told him, in a tone she hoped didn't sound too sardonic.

He looked at her oddly, as if trying to decide her meaning. "And why shouldn't I look well? I am the emperor, after all."

"And long may you reign," she bowed her head. "Emperor."

Could that be what this banquet is about? she wondered. *Does he plan to proclaim himself a God before all the great houses of Akkad, as our fool of an elder brother did? How to prevent him from making that fatal mistake, if indeed he plans to make it—?*

"How long," she asked him, "do you plan to keep us in suspense about the purpose of this banquet?"

"'Purpose?'" He regarded her wryly, sipping wine from the silver goblet at his right hand. "Who says I need some secret purpose to roast some juicy pigs for our family's most faithful friends?"

A few nearby nobles cheered drunkenly at that, clanking their goblets on the wine-stained tabletops. Almond-skinned slaves in rough-spun togas—peasants from the eastern mountains, Kitra guessed—circled the tables with lowered eyes and chilled pitchers, replenishing wine in response to barked orders from Akkad's wealthiest lords and ladies.

"Tell me, dear sister," Manishtushu asked, sucking a bit of pork-fat from his thumb. "Are things really as bad as they say, down in Urim?"

What could she tell him? That she'd barely escaped with her life, and Lugál Ané had seized her throne? That most of her closest friends wanted her dead, or at least exiled? Any invasion the new emperor launched would only stoke the blaze. Of course, he'd find out for himself soon enough, as soon as his own scouts returned.

"Don't worry about spoiling my appetite." He nudged her, grinning. "I only want to know if any of these Shuméru nobles might prove useful to us, if we were to, say, expand their estates a bit more—?"

She pondered this for a moment, the faces of her friends reeling through in her mind. At last she said, "We passed that point years ago. At best, your bribes would go ignored. At worst, such offers could well anger them further."

Manishtushu grunted. "As I thought. Ungrateful swamp folk." He sighed and burped. "Still, it's just as well, I suppose. All the more reason to proceed."

A chill ran through Kitra's limbs. "Proceed with what?"

Her brother grinned and tossed her a mischievous wink. He burped again, and heaved himself up from his chair. He truly had grown to an impressive height; he was head and shoulders above Kitra, and most of the men around him.

"Friends!" he bellowed.

A few heads turned, but most of the revelers ignored him.

"Noble houses of Akkad!" he cried, louder and more thundering than before.

This time a few mean nearby fell silent. Whispers began to spread, and the wave of quiet grew slowly outward, silencing conversations and songs and tables further away, reaching the far end of the garden at last.

When the only sounds were the wind and the night insects, Manishtushu waved his hand and summoned a group of Shuméru scribes. The bald-headed men shuffled toward the head of the first table, linen robes swirling, as Manishtushu beckoned a few nearby noblemen and women to rise from their seats to make room. When the scribes neared Kitra's seat at the head table, they took seats in the empty chairs and set about arranging their styluses and clay tablets on the tabletop.

The new emperor drew a deep breath, and spoke with raised voice: "'Great things,' as my father liked to say, 'come from small beginnings.'"

For a moment, Kitra found herself back on the temple balcony in Urim, thirteen long years ago, with Mother and Father, and little Rimush and Manishtushu by her side. It seemed a world away and an eternity ago; a dream scene from some other woman's life.

"When my father made that boast," Manishtushu was saying, "he'd scarcely begun to understand what greatness truly is. He laid his yoke on all the lands from the Zagros Mountains to the Spice Islands, it's true—but his sons... well, his sons hold more land than he ever dreamed. My dear departed brother—" Manishtushu chuckled. "He became a God. If that's not the definition of greatness, I don't know what is."

Here it comes. Kitra winced.

"But I haven't summoned you all here tonight to declare myself a God." He laughed, as Kitra suppressed a gasp of relief. "No, I'll leave that up to all of you, after you hear what I've got to offer you."

Two thousand pairs of noble eyes gazed up at the emperor in rapt attention. He basked in it, reveling in the anticipatory silence for the space of a long breath, then two, until Kitra began to wonder if he'd forgotten the rest of his speech.

"As of this moment," Manishtushu declared, pointing a finger skyward, "each and every piece of land in the possession of any Shuméru city, temple, or family that has rebelled against the Crown... is hereby declared imperial property."

A soft gasp went up from the scribes. Manishtushu shot them a sharp glance, urging them with a jerk of his head to start inscribing. At last they did, like men compelled to move by levers beyond their control. Nobles at the nearer tables were also gasping and muttering. Whisperers at farther tables demanded confirmation; clarification. Most were certain they'd misheard, until nods and affirmations turned their whispers into exclamations, then into cheers.

Manishtushu smiled, turning to take in all the astonished stares. After a moment he raised his hands for quiet.

"The owners of this land will be compensated for their loss," he proclaimed, "at a cost of two years' estimated harvest."

A laugh rose from the nobles, spreading like fire around the more distant tables. Two years' harvest? What fool of a farmer would sell his family's land for such a pittance? But of course, they would sell it at that price, or be buried beneath their own soil, to fertilize the new owner's crop of barley.

"The total amount of the sale," Manishtushu continued, "has been calculated at—" He conferred briefly with the scribes. "Eight thousand, four hundred fields. And I am pleased to announce that, according to the most ancient records and erudite scholars—" He paused, looking to the scribes for confirmation, then nodded, satisfied. "Yes, this is the single largest land transaction ever to be executed, in all recorded history!"

A cheer resounded from the nearest tables, spreading like rolling thunder through the vastness of the crowded garden.

Manishtushu bent close to Kitra. "A transaction most befitting of our family name. Do you not agree, sister?"

She'd gone pale and could scarcely move her lips. "Most befitting," she echoed his words, and this seemed to please him.

"This land," he announced, raising himself back up to his full height, "will be parceled out evenly among the forty-nine Great Houses of Akkad who have served my family most faithfully."

Clamor erupted. The lords and ladies seated closest to the emperor—scions of the noble houses most obviously in his good graces—cheered and clinked their goblets, scarcely able to believe their sudden good fortune, while heirs of families farther away cried out nervously, debating with one another whether they'd receive a share of the prize, or could perhaps persuade one of the more favored families to part with a chunk of theirs.

"The lords of each family will, of course, be free to distribute this land among their own vassals as they see fit," Manishtushu was saying, though by now the cheering, yelping, arguing mob seemed scarcely to be paying attention. Kitra couldn't help but be reminded of the assembly hall back in Urim, and glanced around nervously for armed guards. A long line of spearmen stood at attention behind her brother, shields raised. None moved a muscle.

Manishtushu gestured to a group of stone-workers, waiting nearby around a heavy-laden wagon draped in a thick cloth. Grunting and cursing, they wheeled the wagon out before the head table.

"In celebration of this act," Manishtushu fairly bellowed over the roar of the crowd, "I have caused a great memorial to be carved, to stand forever in memory."

He nodded to the stone-workers, who whisked the cloth off the wagon, revealing a squat obelisk of black stone, its four polished faces carved with line upon line of intricate characters.

"I have commanded this obelisk to be inscribed," Manishtushu was saying, "with a proclamation of the names of each noble house, and the gifts it shall receive!"

Gazing closely, Kitra could see that the inscription was in a new script—the same familiar Shuméru symbols, but more formal, somehow; every line sharp and straight, and every square rigidly aligned. And for some reason, all the symbols had been turned ninety degrees, onto their sides. How strange!

As nobles approached to examine the gleaming monument, Manishtushu dropped into the seat at the head of the table, accepting congratulations from nearby friends, smiling and nodding, every inch the emperor. He glanced at Kitra, who stared back, looking much less pleased that he'd hoped.

"I can never go back now," she told him evenly. "Do you understand that? I can never return to Urim. They'll kill me."

Her brother gazed into her eyes, and she thought she saw some glimmer of compassion there. Perhaps she was wrong. "We are, each of us," her brother said, "like those fish-tailed Gods and human-headed bulls in the paintings, Kitra. Half human and half... something else. Don't you see? Mere humanity would be inadequate for these roles we play. And so the human in us must diminish."

She shook her head, hot tears rising behind her eyes.

He placed a hand on her shoulder. "Name a city," he said. "Any city between the Two Rivers. I'll make you én-priestess. Just say the word."

She tried to imagine ruling in Sippar, or in garden-encircled Mari—or even in Níppúr, the radiant holy city, where the God Énlil himself dwelled in the House of the Mountain.

Would the high priests of Níppúr even permit such a thing? She supposed it didn't matter. Her brother would command it, and it would be done.

But none of those cities would have her friends. None would have her favorite room, quiet and peaceful, high atop the stepped pyramid, or her writing desk, or the library she'd spent the last thirteen years assembling. None of them would have Lugál Ané, which meant she would never get revenge for the degradations he'd visited upon her.

And of course, none of those places would have Inu.

⟨

The days in Agadé turned into weeks, which grew into two long months. A rainy spring dried into a hot summer, then began to cool into a windy, dusty autumn. At last she sent Telal back on the imperial highway, to find out anything he could.

She spent more time at Agadé's temple, praying to the hard, stern Gods of Akkad: the sky-father Anu, the judge Marutúk, the passionate temptress Ishtar, who Kitra felt must surely be the same as Inanna, the Shuméru Goddess of love and war, with whom she'd come to feel a peculiar closeness during these past weeks.

As she knelt before the divine altars, the high priest might acknowledge her presence with a solemn nod. But he and his acolytes gave no other acknowledgement of her rank in Urim; a rank, she thought, that might very well have lost its meaning. To keep her mind occupied, she prayed the traditional prayers, and the ones she remembered from her childhood, and then she began to pray her own prayers. She didn't know where the words that spilled from her mouth came from:

Oh Inanna, I have been driven forth from my house,
Forced to flee like a bird in flight.
My life is devoured,
I walk among the mountain thorns.
Let your holy heart return to me!

She began to write some of these prayers down. The prayers became poems, growing longer, taking up stacks of clay tablets that piled up in the corners of her sprawling, echoing rooms in the family manor.

One night, she dreamed she was walking in the temple courtyard, back in Urim, in the shadows of the tall palms. But the buildings were much changed, their baked clay replaced by white marble; their geometric mosaics replaced by terraces of glimmering gold and blue. But among the broad flagstoned avenues, Kitra recognized the outlines of her own familiar temple, now crumbled to ruin and dust.

Another woman was walking beside her; a woman clad strangely, in a dress of shimmering fabric, embroidered with fine patterns of vines and flowers. The woman appeared not to notice her. Her eyes scanned the ruins of the ancient temple, as if searching for some sign there.

"There's a lot more down there than you can see," Kitra told her after a moment.

The woman glanced up, eyes widening as she took in Kitra's appearance. Kitra glanced down at herself and saw she wore the pleated wool mantle common for priestesses, along with a long, flowing *hursaj*-garment whose many-pointed fringe hung about her ankles. A bit formal perhaps, but nothing to occasion such astonishment. Perhaps the woman was simply surprised to have a visitor in her dream—though, as Kitra well knew by now, it was a common enough occurrence.

"The halls and chambers extend deeper than anyone guesses," she explained, nodding toward the temple foundation the strange woman was inspecting.

The woman jerked back, brow furrowed in confusion. "What is in those halls you speak of?" she asked, in a voice so quiet it was almost a whisper.

"Monsters, of course," Kitra told her. "The ones you most dread, and most yearn to face. The Gods in the Abyss."

Then the waters of the Dream-Sea swirled, and the woman was gone, along with her strange temple complex. Kitra sat up in bed, in the pale light of early dawn. She went to her desk, and took up a stylus, and began to write again.

The more she wrote, the more of her emotions came pouring forth, feelings she'd never suspected she had. Rage not only against Lugál Ané, but against the Gods themselves, and against a world that could allow such injustice. Dreams of vengeance and violence, and more hatred than she'd ever imagined she was capable of feeling:

I entered the temple at your behest, Inanna.
I was the high priestess—Én Hedu-Ana!
But now I am like a leper.
My mouth, which once spoke words so sweet,
Now speaks only confusion.
My beauty turns to dust.
What is he to me, this Lugál Ané?
Hear me now, Inanna:
One day, this woman will take his manhood.

Another night, as she drifted to sleep, she prayed to the Goddess Ninsunu, the Great Lady who sent dreams, to give her a vision that might tell her of these poems' fates; of who might read them and understand their meaning. There must be some reason, she prayed, why these verses rose within her mind and demanded to be written.

And that night, she dreamed a very strange dream. She watched as many wise-eyed women carefully retrieved clay tablets from the ruins of Urim's old temple—tablets inscribed with Kitra's words, and with the words of many other poetesses who were born long centuries after her. She listened as those poetesses talked wistfully of the long-ago days of Én Hedu-Ana, and of a poetess named Nisaba, who had composed a great Shuméru epic. Then she was in the room with this Nisaba, who cried out in frustration at the poetry of her own age, asking why her king would commission such impossible work, and why the Gods denied her the inspiration to write it, when Én Hedu-Ana had possessed the talent to write so beautifully.

At last those whirling scenes faded, and Kitra dreamed of walking in the temple courtyard in Urim again, amid tall palms and jasmine-bushes blossoming with tiny white flowers. Next to her strolled the young woman she'd seen a moment ago: Nisaba the poetess. She was clad in a strange garment; a sort of loose robe of pale purple, belted with a sash, hanging in pleats. Her long black hair was elaborately curled and coiffed, but pinned up messily with cheap copper pins.

Nisaba glanced about her, as if just now realizing where she was. When she saw Kitra, she started.

"I've been so curious about you," Kitra said, smiling warmly, hoping to put her fellow poetess at ease.

The woman gazed at her, perplexed, as if trying to recognize her. "Who are you?" she asked.

Kitra grinned. Since this dream had come in response to her prayer, she guessed the stranger must be a great poetess of a distant age; perhaps a connoisseur of fine ancient works. "When I compose poems," she told the woman, "I write for Inanna, and for myself. Never for a king. Tell me, what is it like to live in such a poetic time?"

The woman's brow wrinkled. She shook her head. "This isn't a poetic time," she said. "The days of real epics are dust."

Kitra found that idea strange. She'd prayed for a vision of future poets, not for complaints about a time when poetry had crumbled to dust. "So we say about your time, and many others," she replied struggling for words. "I suppose the past always seems romantic."

The woman woman gazed at her strangely. "So *who* says?" she asked.

"All the others, of course." Kitra smiled again, thinking of the scribes copying her work. "The ones who read you. Imitate you."

The woman drew back. "But I haven't written my poem yet."

That made Kitra laugh. Time could play funny tricks in dreams. "And yet," she told the woman, "you already did, long ago."

Then the woman and the temple were gone, and Kitra woke again in the bluish light of predawn, to return to her desk and write. She wrote feverishly, with trembling hands—for now she knew, beyond any doubt, that the Gods had given her these words for a purpose.

And so things went for many days, until the days became weeks. But on the day when Telal returned from his mission to Urim, Kitra could see from the look on his face that something had changed.

"Lugál Ané has made you an offer," he said.

⟨𒐖⟩

THE NEXT MORNING, they loaded up the wagon—her, Telal and three of the guards who'd come with them from Urim. The fourth had been promised a wife here in Agadé; he refused to leave.

Kitra's aunts, uncles and cousins said goodbyes through their tears; all except for Kitra's mother, who remained in the house, silent as ever. Most of the aunts and uncles were convinced Kitra was riding off to her death. Telal had warned her and Manishtushu of this, last night at the royal palace, when he'd explained the offer Lugál Ané had made.

"He's gotten the Shuméru nobles to agree to reinstate her as high priestess of Urim's temple," Telal had explained, "though not as én."

"Then what's the point?" Manishtushu snapped. "I've already taken that fat oaf's land. I'll take his city, too, if I have to."

"He promises," Telal continued, unshaken, "that he will put an end to the rebellion. That crops will be harvested as usual, and taxes will flow smoothly to Agadé again."

"And all he wants in exchange is my sister for a hostage," Manishtushu spat. "I won't have it."

"We all know this is a trap," Kitra said. "But I think I know a way to turn it to our advantage." She was thinking, too, of her poem—*Hear me now, Inanna: One day, this woman will take his manhood*—though she held back those words. "Lugál Ané knows that if he's to have any hope of preserving his position, he needs a go-between—someone who sees both sides of this war."

"He'll bargain for his position with a knife at your throat, Kitra!" Telal snapped, startling her with a sudden ferocity.

In the silence that followed, Manishtushu glared at her, wide-eyed. "How many more members of this family have to die," he cried, "before you learn not to trust these Shuméru savages?"

Kitra raised a hand, cutting him off. "Lugál Ané will try to use me against you, of course," she said, calmly. "We all know that. But I don't plan to let it get to that point." She drew a deep breath before she went on. "He also needs me cooperative, willing to argue his sides of cases to you, brother."

Manishtushu rubbed his mustache. He nodded for her to go on.

"I predict he'll threaten me first," she said. "Separate me from my guards, demonstrate his power over me, and over Urim, try to frighten me, even as he promises that things might go easier for me if I prove I'm on his side."

"If you go to his bed, you mean," Telal snarled.

Kitra nodded. "Perhaps so. But I'll move first in that dance. I'll invite him for some entertainment, rather than wait for his summons."

"He'll never agree to meet you alone," Telal told her. "As soon as he hears you're back in Urim, he'll send guards for you. He won't come himself."

"Surely he goes some places alone," Kitra said.

"And when you get him alone," Manishtushu demanded, "what then? Slit his throat at the moment of rapture? You're a politician, sister; not an assassin."

Something hot and fierce rose in Kitra's chest. "I am the right hand of the war-Goddess Inanna," she said, in a tone sharp as a blade. "I have survived two assassins, a scheming old man, and a burning city. I move as the world moves. And the world moves as I will."

Telal and Manishtushu were staring at her, as if seeing her for the first time. They watched her, still and silent, for a long moment.

At last, Manishtushu nodded. "Keep a close eye on her," he told Telal. "At the first sign of trouble, get her away from that place. I don't care if you have to tear down the whole temple to get her out."

"Lord Emperor," Telal said softly, "are you certain this is wise?"

"No," said Manishtushu, "I am not. Not in the slightest." He turned to Kitra and favored her with a tight smile; so much like Father's smile that it twisted a knife in her. "But I know better than to deny my sister a thing on which she's set her heart. Ride tonight, the both of you. Perhaps you may reach Urim before word of your approach arrives."

Telal bowed low, as Kitra wrapped her arms around her brother, kissing him on both cheeks.

"I will make this right, brother," she whispered in his ear.

"If anyone on earth can do so," he said, placing his rough palm against her cheek, "it is you, my dear."

The road back to Urim was much the same as the road to Agadé: hot, dry, smooth and uneventful. She slept in the wagon, hidden by blankets. The guards sneaked food out to her when they stopped at a caravansary for the night.

A week later, their little caravan reached one of the mud-brick villages on the outskirts of Urim, just a league from the city walls. No one here seemed to recognize them, or even care who they were. Any men and women not toiling in the fields lay under awnings in the heat of the midday sun.

Telal rented them a small room at a roadside inn. Meanwhile, Kitra summoned one of the other guards, and sent him into the city with a message to deliver at the temple.

The guard returned at sunset, bearing Inu's reply: "Come to the southeastern gate at dark."

Though she'd refused to entertain the idea that Inu might not be alive, Kitra still nearly collapsed with relief when she heard the guard deliver the response.

"And you spoke to her in person?" she asked the guard.

He nodded. "I'd know her face anywhere."

When the sun began to set, she hurried toward Urim's southeastern gate. Telal insisted on accompanying her as far as the wall. Inu was waiting for her.

"I thought you were dead," Inu whispered.

"Far from it," Kitra said, embracing Inu, kissing her forehead and her hair.

"What do you plan to do?" Inu asked as they hurried along the unlit streets, toward the temple.

"I plan to offer Lugál Ané an evening of pleasure," Kitra said. "And strike when he's at his most vulnerable. Do you know where I might meet him alone?"

"Of course," Inu said. "I've watched him like a hawk, just as you asked me to."

"Then where," Kitra asked, "does he take his entertainment?"

"In his own chambers," she said. "He has women brought from brothels in the dead of night."

"Then the Gods smile on us," Kitra said. "It's nearly the dead of night now."

The arrangements were made surprisingly easily. A few women at the temple remembered Kitra fondly, and were glad to let her accompany them on their nocturnal visit to the én. When his personal soldiers came to collect the women, Kitra joined Inu and the rest of them on their midnight walk to the palace, shrouded in a hood and cloak, just as when she'd left the city.

How different the palace had become in her absence! The walls were now decorated with mosaics; lions and dragons glazed bright blue and gold. Braziers of musk and attar and sandalwood smoked in chambers lit with beeswax candles.

The door to the lugál's chamber was easy enough to recognize: this had been Kitra's chamber not so long ago. How long had it been? Two months? Three? It felt like eons had passed since the morning she'd ridden out of Urim into exile.

The chamber looked so bare now. Just as when she'd slept here, the desks were piled high with clay tablets; poetry and literature, and of course reports from across the city. In the center of the room stood a great bed, covered in white sheets and pillows. The bed where she'd taken Inu, on that night that now seemed centuries ago.

The guards closed the doors behind her. For the first time in a long while, she stood alone.

Ané entered a moment later, looking exactly as she remembered him: fat, bald, draped in billowing white robes. But now he also wore the gold crown of Urim.

The lugál clearly recognized her, but showed no sign of surprise.

"So, the lost daughter returns," he said mildly. "Please, sit." He gestured at the bed.

Slowly, cautiously, attending to her breathing, she strode to the bed and sat. *I move as the world moves.*

"Some of the nobles want you back," Ané said bluntly, pouring himself a cup of wine from the tray on the bed.

She tried to conceal her surprise. "Urim isn't quite as easy to run as you'd thought, is it?"

He shot an annoyed glance at her. "Is that what you really think this is about? Me wanting to run Urim?"

Now she was more confused than ever. "I must admit," she said, "your seizing of the throne gave me that impression."

He drew a deep breath and sighed long and low. "I've enjoyed the privileges of rank," he said after a moment. "I won't deny it. And I deserved this throne before your father sat you on it, much as you never acknowledged that." He shook his head. "But none of those things, alone, would have driven me to plot and scheme as I did. Do you have any idea how exhausting that is? I had a delightful life, before you came. Cargo ships sailing in every day. Banquets every night." He whirled on her in sudden fury. "Why did your father have to poke his finger where it didn't belong?" He demanded. "Why try to fix what clearly wasn't broken?"

"I—" She'd prepared herself for a thousand variations on this conversation, but somehow she hadn't expected this. "What are you talking about? I never forced you to give up your comfortable life—"

"You still don't see!" The lugál spread his arms wide, eyes ablaze. "After all these years. I can't believe it."

She tried to catch hold of the reins of the conversation again. "What don't I see, Ané? Explain to me what I fail to see."

He glared at her in silence for a long moment. "Urim does not belong to your family," he said at last. "It never has, and it never will. *My* family rules here, and so it will always be."

"But you need my family on your side," Kitra replied softly. "To keep all you've worked so hard for, you need me, whispering sweet words in my brother's ear."

"Sweet words," he repeated. "Well, now's the time to whisper some to me. If you want that brother of yours to have any hope of seeing your lovely face again, then prove your love for Urim, and for its én."

Kitra's heart pounded in her chest. This was it. The moment she'd always dreaded had arrived.

"Come, my dear," the lugál said, sidling closer to her. "In times like these, we must all make hard bargains."

"I have no other choice, Your Radiance," she said softly.

He liked that. A soft purr rose in his throat as he leaned in to brush her lips with his. "And why should I believe you, after everything I've done to you?"

"You don't have to believe me," she purred right back. "I'll show you."

"Yes," he smiled, backing toward the bed. "Please do."

The indignity of it wasn't particularly hard to endure, after all the others she'd suffered. What was this, a great sweating block of flesh moving above her, after the long hard roads through the desert, and the long nights spent praying alone, hearing no answer? As he did his work, she let her mind tip into the other awareness, and heard only the words. *I move as the world moves. The world moves as I will.*

He didn't take long. When he was finished, he lay his head back on the pillow and said, "You may go."

"Go where, Your Radiance?" she asked.

"Anywhere you like." The lugál waved a fat hand dismissively. "The slaves can prepare you a room to sleep. Or go to an inn. When I want you again, I'll summon you."

"And I have your word?" she asked.

"Anyone in this city who lays a finger on you," he said tiredly, "will have me to answer to. Now go."

She went, and the next night, he summoned her again. She worked patiently, learning what he liked, what excited him, what made him trust her. They spoke little. She kept him entertained. He summoned her the next night, too. And the one after that. Six nights in a row he called her to his bedchamber, and six nights in a row she pleased him until he fell back snoring on the white pillows.

Before she went to him the seventh night, she knelt in her quarters and said a prayer to Inanna; the first prayer she'd said since her days in Agadé. The words mattered little. It was a prayer both of despair and of hope, a pleading for one chance to do what she had to do.

Last of all, she slipped a tiny bronze knife beneath her innermost garment, and went to him.

Their rutting had fallen into a comfortable ritual. Lugál Ané did not hesitate. He came at her groping eagerly, throwing her to the bed. She didn't resist. She fell smoothly onto the sheets, accepted him on top of her. He tore off her robes. She helped.

When he'd stripped her down to her inmost garment, she drew out the blade, and in one smooth motion she plunged it deep into his neck.

He fell back, gurgling, blood pumping in bright red gouts from his neck. She plunged the knife into his chest, into his belly, into a dozen more places. He stumbled up, trying to call for help, but she slipped easily atop him, placed a pillow over his face, and plunged the knife in again and again.

And when at last he stopped twitching, she reached down, and did what she had promised the Goddess Inanna she would do: she took his manhood.

Then she fled, through the back passages she'd learned over the past seven days, out into the back alleys, where Inu met her and hurried her away to an inn on the outskirts of the city.

𒌋𒁹𒁹

A FEW NIGHTS later, she was sitting in her old chambers atop the temple again. Most of her things had been brought back, transforming her room into a small island of comfort in the midst of a city that hid its face in fear.

As soon as word of what she'd done to Lugál Ané had reached the streets, Urim's people had flung themselves at one another in a maelstrom of hateful factions: the few remaining supporters of her father's empire fought knife-and-club against those who'd benefited from the lugál's rule, while half a dozen other groups wanted some other man or woman on the throne, or no én at all, or a new regime from some other city. For two weeks, screams and shouts had echoed in streets that ran with blood by day, and glowed gold at night with the heat of a thousand uncontrolled fires.

By the time Manishtushu's army had arrived, Urim had very nearly torn herself to shreds. Copper-helmeted soldiers had marched through streets thick with dried blood, spilled grain, and the bodies of the dead, rounding up offenders and putting them to the sword in public plazas, in full view of their weeping friends and families. Through it all, Kitra had remained here, locked in her chambers at the top of the ziggurat, hating herself for her cowardice, but terrified to venture outside.

When at last the war in Urim's streets had fallen silent, only her supporters dared to show their faces in public. She'd summoned them to the temple assembly hall, hardly surprised that Gemekala and Eluti and the rest of her old friends no longer stood in their midst. She thought of her brother's words, that night at the great banquet: *We are, each of us, half human and half... something else. Don't you see? Mere humanity would be in-*

adequate for these roles we play. And so the human in us must diminish. As she parceled out lands and titles to the Shuméru nobles who'd acquiesced to her family's reign, she wondered if Shumér had, in the end, devoured all that remained of her humanity.

Tonight, in her lamp-lit chamber at the top of the temple, she wrote by candlelight, a poem of praise to Inanna; a bittersweet requiem for the carnage of these past weeks: "*Devastatrix of the lands, you are lent wings by the storm. In the guise of a roaring wind, you charge.*"

She heard a knock at the door, and Inu entered.

Hours later, when the candles had burned down and they lay in the darkness, sweaty among the soft sheets, Inu rolled over and whispered, "What you were saying the other night. About the Gods."

Kitra groaned and threw an arm over her face. "What about the Gods?"

Inu stroked her hair. "You have a problem with the Gods, now?"

Kitra drew a deep breath and let it out in a long sigh. "All day long it's Gods and Goddesses. Week after week, month after month. Chants and litanies and rituals and blessings. All I want is one ordinary conversation with an ordinary human being. But here in the temple, there are no ordinary human beings. Only priests and attendants and acolytes."

Inu frowned. "Am I not ordinary?"

"You, my dear," Kitra said, reaching up to stroke Inu's hair, "are most extraordinary. You're the only true friend I've had, through all this. Perhaps the only one I have left."

"I can hardly imagine what you've suffered," Inu said, "But... surely you must love the Gods, still."

Kitra sighed. "Do we have to talk about this now?"

"Do you ever stop to think that others might have problems of their own?" Inu snapped.

Kitra sat up and looked at her sharply in the darkness. She was high priestess of Urim for an instant, and Inu cringed, ashamed. But Kitra's expression softened, and she reached out and took Inu's hand in her own, gently stroking the lines of the palm.

"What is it, Inu?" Kitra whispered. "Do you doubt the Gods? After all our years at the temple? After all this—?"

Inu sat in silence for so long that Kitra wondered if she was too hurt to speak. But at last she said, "I don't know what to think about the Gods, after everything that's happened to this city. We all hear the stories, growing up, and I love them, as I said. I like believing that Utu rides his chariot across the sky each day, and Inanna whispers into lovers' ears, and Énlil breathes the first breath into every newborn baby."

Kitra nodded. "I love those stories too."

"But then," Inu went on, "we have these statues of the Gods here in the temple, and the priests say the statues aren't just statues. They *are* the Gods, and we have to bow to them and make offerings. And then sometimes they say the Gods are everywhere, invisible, all around us all the time, all working together—" she trailed off, her voice trembling. "It just doesn't make sense, Kitra. None of it fits together. And that scares me, because I love the Gods. At least I think I do." Now she was actually crying, shaking as tears rolled down her face. "I want to know what's real. I feel like I'm losing my mind."

Kitra pulled her close and held her for a while as hot tears streamed down her face, and her salty breath rose between the two of them. After a while, when Inu's tears had subsided into soft sobs, Kitra asked her, "Remember playing with dolls, when you were little?"

Inu looked up, confused. "Of course."

"That's more than just play. When you set your dolls out on the bed and talked with them, you were giving them voices from inside you. There are certain conversations you can't have within yourself but that you can't share with others, either. You needed your dolls to take on those voices, to have those conversations with you. Do you understand?"

"I'm not sure." Inu sniffed and wiped her eyes. "You mean the statues are, what, dolls of Gods?"

Kitra laughed. "It sounds silly when you say it."

"But is that what you're saying?" Inu asked.

Kitra thought for a moment. "Here's what I think. We all hear so many voices in our minds," Kitra said. "Voices of fear and hope, pain and desire. It's hard to know which ones are telling the truth. But they're all real. We know that for certain. They have to be real, because we hear them. And since so many of them don't sound like us, we need somewhere else to put those voices."

"But the Gods are *truly* real," Inu protested. "I see them all around me, in the wind and the trees and the water. Not just in my mind. And the old kings walked with Gods, in the flesh, right here in Urim."

Kitra shrugged. "Maybe so. I've seen trees and water, and men who claim to be Gods. But never a God in the flesh."

Now Inu looked truly confused. "So do you believe in the Gods?" she asked. "Or don't you?"

"Of course I believe in them," Kitra said. "But it's foolish to believe every story you hear. The Gods may dwell in Heaven, but stories are dreamed up by men and women, to give reason to the things they do. Things that, in truth, may have no real reason at all."

Inu humphed, her face knotted with frustration. "You didn't answer my question," she said at last. "About what's real."

"You mean, are the old stories true?" Kitra asked. "I doubt it."

"That's not much of an answer," said Inu.

"I'm not much of a high priestess, I suppose" said Kitra. "Not after what I've done to this city. What can I say, if the Gods do nothing to stop someone like me; someone like my father, or my brothers?"

Inu stared into her eyes, as if searching for some sign there. But she found she could make no reply.

They lay back on the bed after a time. Kitra felt Inu's breathing soften, then slip into the rhythm of sleep. But she lay for a long time, eyes open, wishing she'd been able to give Inu any satisfying answers. *But to do that*, she thought, *I'd first have to find answers that satisfied me.*

She'd once been so sure of those answers, back when she'd first taken the én's crown; but the more she worked and prayed and pondered and tried to grab hold of those certainties, the more they slipped away, like water between her fingers.

203 YEARS EARLIER
2490 BC

In the city with no dogs, the fox is boss.

— Shuméru proverb

Hazi strode out onto the field outside the city of Kish, beside Lugál Susuda, the big man. The boss. Susuda's other two champions walked beside them. *Just four of us*, thought Hazi, *to meet the four from Lagash. That is, unless Lagash springs a trap…*

Lugál Susuda, boss of the fighters of Kish, asked his champions not to dress for battle. That time would come soon enough, he told them. But not this morning. So they wore only their shaggy fleece kilts, dyed in patterns of their city's colors, red and white. They wore their kilts loosely belted, in imitation of the lugál; not high and tight below the chest, as was traditional, but slung askew a handspan below the navel, so that their tasseled hems rustled in the grass, and their hands rested easily on the pommels of the long copper daggers and chisel-axes that swung at their belts.

Around their bare chests and arms curled tattoos of intricate geometric patterns: badges of the brave deeds they'd done. On their chests and bellies were inscribed their city's totem-beasts, the *lamassu*, kneeling bulls with the heads of shaggy-bearded men. The fighters wore their hair long: thick black braids bound in tight coils behind their heads, wrapped in leather headbands.

Hazi felt naked out here, without his thick armor of hard-boiled leather or his helmet of beaten copper. But this was what the lugál asked.

The fighters' sandals crunched on the dry grass. The only other sound was their slow breathing. Lugál Susuda stared straight ahead as they walked, his dark eyes scanning the horizon. Hazi glanced at the others, but none of them seemed nervous. Their hands rested easily on the pommels of their daggers. Every hair and strand of beard braided and in place. Even Girin, the lone woman in their band, had plaited her long black hair high atop her head, like a crown, which she wore with the calm of royalty.

As Susuda and his band approached the reeds of the riverbank, the men from Lagash came into view, striding toward them. Just four, like they'd promised. No shields or spears as far as Hazi could see. Just daggers in their belts. Kilts of long-curled fleece, dyed in patterns of yellow and black. Tattoos of the mythical *anzú*-bird covered their chests: symbols of the war-God Ningirsu, divine patron of Lagash, with eagle wings spread wide and lion's head roaring.

Susuda and his men stopped about ten paces away. The two groups watched each other, scanning for any detail out of place, any sign of a trap. That's what Hazi was doing, anyway. A few breaths more.

Then the boss from Lagash—the one wearing a gold headband—untied his scabbard from his belt and dropped it, jewels and all, to the ground. He and Susuda spread their arms wide, came together and embraced, arms around shoulders. Kissing each others' cheeks, laughing.

"You fat old bastard," said the boss from Lagash, still beaming. "I see they're feeding you well in Kish."

Susuda laughed. "And how're the whores up in Lagash, Temena?" he asked. "Everything still working down there, or has it finally rotted off?"

They embraced again, slapping backs, laughing, ruffling hair.

"This," said Susuda, turning to face Hazi and the others, "is Lugál Temena. The slyest old bastard I ever knew."

"And this," said Temena, turning to his men, gesturing at the other boss, "is Lugál Susuda, a son of a whore who somehow got the temple to appoint him warleader of Kish."

"Son of a fishmonger, thank you very much," said Susuda.

"Different workshop, same smell," Temena retorted.

Susuda snorted and spat.

Hazi was breathing a little easier now.

"Drop your daggers," Susuda told his men. "For one afternoon, let's at least pretend we're civilized."

Hazi and the others hesitated for a moment. Susuda widened his eyes and nodded at Hazi: *Do it now*. Hazi reached down slowly and untied his dagger and chisel-axe from his belt. Laid them slowly on the dry grass. The others followed his lead.

Temena's men were doing the same.

"Can you guess why we're here?" Susuda asked Hazi and the rest of his men. He turned to Temena and his men, too, offering them the same question.

No one answered. Hazi stepped forward.

"If you were a typical man," he said, "I would say you were planning a raid. Some caravan bringing gold and gems from the mountains, or a poorly guarded village with a fresh harvest. But you have never been a typical man, Susuda."

The lugál smiled and nodded for Hazi to go on.

"I think," Hazi said, "that you want the city of Kish for yourself."

Temena's men snorted at this. Susuda's companions were more guarded, but Hazi caught a glance from Baragi Broad-Wings: *Careful*.

"But I am already boss in Kish," said Susuda, grinning. "I already have the city to myself."

"It is true," Hazi replied, smiling back at him. "Every neighborhood pays us mutton and beer. No one sits above you." He paused, exchanging knowing looks with Susuda. "Except, of course, for the én-priestess and the temple."

Susuda nodded, spreading his arms. He was addressing the crowd now. "The én. Of course. A fat old cow, greedy as a tax collector."

"You're speaking blasphemy," one of Temena's men hissed.

Temena turned to him. "You weren't so pious last night, Merkar Short-Blade, when those girls told you they were temple virgins." A few of the others laughed.

"Our lugál speaks the truth," Baragi said calmly.

Susuda raised a finger. "As long as anyone can remember," he said, "the én and her temple have commanded, and we have obeyed. We bring them the first fruits of our fields, the fattest of our cattle, the most beautiful of our daughters and the wisest of our sons. It is they alone who decide when we will harvest barley or make beer, and which man may be married to which woman, and when we will make war, and against whom. Who can argue? Things have always been this way. They say it is," his mouth twitched in a wry smile, "the will of the Gods."

"I've heard enough!" Merkar shouted.

"But the én and her acolytes," Susuda continued, "have gotten lazy."

The lugál stared down at the dry grass. He knelt slowly, and picked a reed, running his fingers along the stem. Staring into the distance, he began picking the seedpods off the reed and tossing them to the wind, as if none of the others were here.

"Does the God Énlil speak to you?" he asked no one in particular. His dark eyes swept across his three fighters, then the men of Lagash. "Any of you?"

Hazi turned away when the lugál's eyes met his. *Those eyes are too sharp*, he thought. *As if he knows the answer in one's heart before he even asks the question.*

"No," Susuda said at last. "I thought not." He looked up, suddenly, meeting Temena's gaze. "But the God speaks to me."

Temena's brow furrowed. "What do you mean, he speaks to you—?"

"I mean exactly that," Susuda answered flatly, as if Temena had asked him what he'd eaten for breakfast. "Énlil speaks to me. The wind-God tells me that a great storm is about to sweep over this land."

"Another great flood—!" Merkar gasped.

Susuda laughed softly. "No, Merkar Short-Blade," he replied, smiling. "Not another flood. We didn't learn our lesson, you see, from the first one."

"And what lesson was that?" Temena growled.

"To listen," Susuda answered, spreading his hands as if it were the simplest thing in the world. "That is all. Simply to listen to the whispers of the Gods, rather than to the shouts of pompous men."

"I hear only one pompous man here," Merkar muttered, drawing some low laughs from the others. Temena smacked him roughly on the back of the head, and he fell silent.

Susuda nodded slowly, as if weighing Merkar's words. "Is it so, Hazi Silver-Tongue?" he asked after a moment. "Am I the pompous one here?"

Hazi hesitated a moment, then stepped forward. "In the years after the Flood," he said to Temena and his fighters, "our people, the survivors, had to cling to each other tightly. We clung tight to the Gods, too. We listened, prayed, raised great new temples atop the ruins of those destroyed by the floodwaters, performed the proper rituals and offered the right sacrifices on the right days."

"But five centuries have passed since the great Flood," Susuda said after a moment. "Our people have forgotten how terrible the Gods can be. And our priests have forgotten to fear those who hear the Gods' voices."

"I've heard enough of *your* voice, Susuda," Merkar snarled, stepping toward the lugál. Hazi's hand tensed on his belt, ready to reach for his weapons on the grass.

"Kish's temple has no walls," Susuda shouted suddenly, rising up and glowering into Merkar's eyes. The fighter backed away a step, unable to help himself. "Who will stop us?" the lugál pressed forward. "Who is left for us to fear?"

"Fear the Gods, Susuda!" Merkar cried, in a voice too high-pitched to carry much weight.

Temena gestured for calm, pulling Merkar back into line. "Is this truly your plan, Susuda?" he asked after a moment. "Tear down the temple of Kish?" He shook his head. "I wouldn't put it past you."

Susuda only sank onto his haunches again. He plucked another reed and began stripping it of its seedpods, still watching the horizon as if something would appear there.

"What is it, exactly, that you propose, you old scorpion?" Temena asked.

Susuda laughed softly. "I propose... a new kind of thing," he said. His tone was playful, as if he were flirting or making a joke.

This was the tone he'd taken when he'd convinced the temple priests to appoint him as lugál of the city of Kish, so his men could protect the city's caravans from the raiders on the mountain roads. It was the tone he'd taken when he'd proposed that "lugál" be made a permanent position, rather than a temporary one, so Kish would always be ready to respond in times of danger. It was the tone he'd taken with Hazi, privately, when he'd proposed that the men start raiding a few of the mountain caravans themselves—not enough of them to raise suspicion; just enough to make his fighters rich. It was a tone that always made Hazi smile.

"For the past five years," Susuda said, "I have watched the priests of Kish grow fat while the farmers and shepherds starve. Is it not so, Hazi?"

Hazi nodded. "It is so, lugál."

Temena stroked his beard ruefully. "It is the same in Lagash. In every city nowadays, so I hear."

"So I hear, too." Susuda said. "So I took it in my hands to help the people of Kish. I united the city's best fighters, as you, Temena, did in Lagash. You know as well as I, it was not easy, but I got all of us pulling as one, like oarsmen on a skiff. Together, we made the wild roads safe for travelers. Our workers built new dams and aqueducts. Planted new fields. Enforced the ancient laws against thieves and murderers. I've even—" he raised a finger, scowling with rage, "—commissioned new paintings and statues for the temple. And what did our temple give us in return?"

Temena's men murmured, and Hazi didn't have to hear their words to catch their tone. They knew what was coming next.

"Nothing." Susuda spread his hands. "The priests send taxmen to collect my grain, to enrich their own granaries. Sacrifice my cattle. Burn a lot of incense. Sing prayers I do not understand." The lugál looked up then, suddenly. He locked eyes with Temena and held the other boss's gaze. "So I ask you: who is it, really, who is maintaining civilization in Kish?"

A smile spread across Temena's face. "You want to kill the priests," he said.

Susuda shook his head. "No," he said, smiling. "That is not necessary. Not *all* the priests. Just the én, and those who support her."

Merkar Short-Blade gave a fresh gasp of outrage, but Hazi knew the others were ready to hear the rest. These were the moments Susuda loved most, he knew: when he could see he'd hooked his listeners like river-trout on a worm.

"And then what?" asked Temena. "You'll become én?" He laughed. "I've seen you dressed in all kinds of getup, Susuda, but can't picture you in temple robes."

"No," said Susuda, "I won't be another én. I will become," He smiled again, in his strange way. "Something new. I will talk with the God Énlil myself. Énlil and I will work out, between us, what is best for the city of Kish."

"And what about us?" Temena asked.

Susuda shrugged. "There will always be a place for you in Kish, if you like." Then he grinned, as if he'd just remembered a joke. "Or if you would prefer, I'll be in an excellent position to help you set up something similar down in Lagash."

Temena smiled, too. His men weren't smiling, though.

Merkar looked away and shook his head. "This isn't right. Even if you succeed, the Gods won't let it stand for long."

"I see two paths," said Susuda, "Or rather, I see one path well-worn, and another yet to be. I know which path I follow." He looked up sharply at Temena and his men. "What about you?"

Temena watched for a long time, eyeing Hazi and each of the others in turn.

At last he spat into the grass and turned away. Then turned back.

"You crazy bastard," he snarled at Susuda. "I hate my én as much as you hate yours. Gods damn us all, but I'm with you. Let us do this mad thing."

Susuda smiled and grasped Temena's arm.

"They may damn us," Susuda said. "But they won't stand in our way."

"Do you know when the én and her priests became weak?" Susuda asked Hazi.

"When they relaxed," Hazi replied. "Began to trust too much in the structure they'd built."

The lugál raised a finger. "Close," he said. "But not exactly."

He leaned back in his tamarisk-wood chair, gazing out across the fields surrounding his mud-brick manor-house outside the city of Kish. The two of them basked in the afternoon sun on the house's broad, flat roof, under umbrellas woven with red-and-black geometric designs that matched the colors of the stone columns adorning the estate's porches and courtyards.

Around the manor-house, fields of barley, wheat, date palms and olive trees sprawled in neat grids of clay, interrupted at intervals by neat rows of juniper and fir flanked by low bushes, to serve as windbreaks. Along the edge of the fields, a great clay channel, wide as a stream, lined by low walls of clay-covered stone, guided fresh water through the estate on a gentle downhill slope from the river, all the way out to the pastures where flocks of sheep and goats browsed verdant grass.

Hundreds of men labored in those fields, plucking dates and olives and dropping them into the woven-reed baskets on their backs, sluicing water from wood buckets into channels that ran dry, applying fresh plaster to the mud-brick walls topped with woven reed-work and dried thorn bushes, to keep the sheep and goats in their pens.

Reddish flat-topped mountains rose in the distance, stacked in layers like titanic walls and ramparts, upon which vast skrees of rocky soil lay frozen in the act of spilling downward onto the plain, step-by-giant-step. Taller snow-capped mountains towered in the distance behind the red hills, their peaks shrouded in cloud and sheets of misty rain.

Hazi was feeling slightly lazy after the mug of sweet-beer he'd just drained. Susuda, who never partook, seemed just as alert as ever.

"The én and her acolytes became weak," the lugál continued, leaning forward in his chair, "when *they themselves* began to believe in the illusion they'd conjured. When they began to think that maybe the Gods really were on their side. That they could project power without limit."

"But the rest of the people are not on their side," Hazi said, glancing to the west, toward the walls of nearby Kish.

"Exactly." Susuda grinned, snapping his fingers. "That's exactly it. When you behave like a God, and assume the privileges and rights of a God, but you fail to provide the paradise that only a God can create—well then, it is only natural that the people start to feel deceived. They ask, 'Why should I trust you, priest? Why not keep my options open?' They continue to live as they always have, but only because, for the time being, it remains the easiest path."

"But over time, that path becomes less easy," Hazi said.

Susuda nodded. "Not all at once, but bit by bit. Caravans are robbed. Villages rise in revolt. The temple must disperse its forces throughout the whole country to keep it all under control. Then one day, perhaps another city's army invades. The temple becomes exhausted. Food grows scarce. Every day, more sparks ignite."

"Until one day, the tinder catches fire." Hazi furrowed his brow.

Susuda nodded somberly. "And the flames roar up. People lash out in every direction. They've needed food, water, shelter, for so long; and suddenly they're all running riot in the streets, ripping these things from the hands of others. Robbing. Beating. Tearing down walls. And as more of them see that the law has collapsed, they begin to slake their other thirsts. Lust for that woman down the street. Long-nurtured hatred for that stingy innkeeper. The city becomes a battlefield. Men and women turn to beasts in an afternoon."

"Most of them aren't thinking beyond that stage," Hazi said. "They can't be controlled."

"Controlled, no," Susuda replied. "But they can be provided for."

Hazi stroked his beard. "You mean, if someone is already standing by, well provisioned..."

Susuda smiled. "Food. Medicine. Clothing. Shelter. Justice for the man whose daughter was murdered. Disciplined fighters who keep the streets safe for old widows and small boys. Piece by piece, some semblance of order is restored. Perhaps there's even a new school."

Now it was Hazi's turn to smile. "And what would be taught at this school?"

Susuda shrugged. "Why, whatever we wish, of course. We are the saviors, after all."

Hazi nodded slowly. "You're not trying to take down the temple."

Susuda smiled. "I don't have to." He spread his hands. "It's much easier to make the temple strike out blindly, behave in ways that infuriate the people. Then the people will do the rest on their own."

"But the people," Hazi said, "have very little idea what they really want."

"Very true," Susuda agreed. "But one thing is certain: as long as the conditions of life are tolerable, people do not want to be liberated. Freedom must be forced upon them, until it takes hold."

Hazi was pondering this when a messenger burst from the stairway below, his bare chest glistening with sweat in the hot sun as he gasped for breath.

Susuda inclined his head curiously, waiting for the message.

"There's a riot," the messenger gasped.

Hazi poured the messenger a cup of water from the pitcher on a nearby table. The boy took it with both hands and gulped it down eagerly.

"A riot, you say?" Susuda asked, a smile spreading across his lips.

The messenger nodded. "In the city, right now. The temple announced that barley rations will be cut by half this month, due to shortages. And this is the second month in a row—"

"They've been trading it." Susuda smiled. "They've had to trade the barley for copper from Umma."

Hazi's eyes widened. "To cover the costs of the lost caravans."

Susuda nodded. "And now they're short. Two seasons in a row. What a shame."

Hazi glanced around at the fields surrounding the manor-house: branches heavy with fruit, and sprawling fields of near-ripe barley.

"Soon they'll be coming for your harvest, Susuda," he said.

Susuda shook his head. "No." He smiled. "Not if we hand it out ourselves."

The lugál rose and brushed past the messenger, hurrying down the stairs into the house, tossing the words, "Take whatever you like from my table," behind him.

Hazi followed him down into the darkness of the windowless house, through the open-roofed central garden, out into the antechamber where Susuda took his dagger and helmet from their hooks on the wall.

"What are you going to do?" Hazi asked him.

"What everyone else is doing," Susuda said. "I'm going to riot. Go fetch the others. We've got work to do."

VOICES SHOUTED ALL around Hazi as he pushed through the street of tanneries, headed for the temple. The reek of the bleaching vats—water mixed with bird droppings—made Hazi and Girin gag, and the mob pushing all around them wasn't helping.

"Come on," Girin shouted over the roar of the crowd. "Let's take the back alley."

Hazi followed her down the narrow path between two mud-brick buildings, taking sharp turns among cloth-covered doorways, dodging groups of children kicking leather balls, sending cats leaping and scurrying around corners.

At last they emerged into the temple square, where a crowd of hundreds stood shoulder-by-shoulder, chanting at the towering bronze-and-wood gates of the temple.

They shouted; a cacophony: "The temple starves us!" and "We demand the barley we've reaped!" and dozens of other chants.

Hazi and Girin pushed through the crowd, searching for Susuda, or for any other fighters they recognized. But they soon gave up on trying to make a path.

The temple's vast doors were creaking open, pulled by two shaved-headed acolytes. The crowd fell silent.

A line of soldiers emerged from the temple's dim interior: stern-eyed men wearing scars and tattoos and battered copper helmets, carrying maces and long daggers in their belts. But instead of drawing these weapons, they simply descended the temple steps and took up positions before the doorway.

Behind them, the én emerged: an aged priestess clad in robes of the purest white; her silver hair neatly braided and bound atop her head, affixed with copper rings that gleamed in the sun.

"People of Kish," she said, her voice carrying clearly across the square. "My brothers and sisters, know that the Gods hear you. Know that I hear you."

Silence hung for the space of a few heartbeats.

Then someone shouted: "We need bread!"

"And beer!" another cried.

The én raised her hands for silence, but the shouts continued: "We're starving!" "What happened to the grain we harvested?"

"Listen!" bellowed the én, in a voice that astonished even Hazi with its strength. "You shall have all the grain that is owed to you, and more, with the next season. This I promise you."

"What good is next season's grain?" a farmer's wife demanded. "At this rate, my children won't see the next season!"

A legion of voices thundered in agreement.

"I understand you are hungry," the én shouted, her voice scarcely audible over the crowd's roar. "We all go hungry this season. Next season will be better, I promise you. The omens are good."

But the crowd was already pushing at the soldiers, their chants dissolving into a wordless fury. The soldiers held firm, not drawing their weapons but merely holding their ground.

Then Hazi heard Susuda's voice from across the square. He couldn't quite make out what the man was shouting, but Girin heard it too.

They fought their way through the mob, making for the sound of Susuda's voice. Even in that pushing, shouting madness, they managed to reach him. He stood at the front, nearly within spear's reach of the soldiers, crying out to the men and women gathered around him.

"See how they treat you?" he was shouting. "First they starve you. Then when you come to protest, they send their soldiers for you!"

With each proclamation, the mob shouted agreement, pumping their fists.

Susuda turned and pointed at the én, his face red with rage. "This bitch thinks she can stand up there and tell you—"

"Enough!" the én's voice echoed across the square.

The crowd's yelling dropped to a low murmur.

"So this is how you repay an old friend," she said. "I make you lugál. Give you a country estate. And now here you are, inciting a mob against me."

Susuda's expression turned incredulous. "These people are starving!" he howled. "They've come for what's rightfully theirs!"

A chorus of shouts agreed.

"We both know you're behind this, Susuda," the én replied, looking the big man square in the eye.

"And you stand behind a wall of soldiers," the lugál said. "Soldiers with orders to harm any citizen demanding his fair share of temple produce."

"These soldiers are here to protect the temple!" the én bellowed. "I have told them not to harm anyone, so long as no one attacks."

"Oh, we're far past that point now." Susuda shook his head. Hazi caught the slightest hint of a smile playing upon the lugál's face, so subtle he doubted anyone else could see it.

"We can solve this without violence!" the én cried.

"How?" Susuda demanded. "Can you produce the bread and beer these people are owed?"

"I cannot," said the én. "But that does not mean we have to fight."

"Do you even hear your own words?" Susuda asked, barking a laugh. "First you deny the people their rations. Now you send out soldiers, yet claim you want no fight. I'm tired of listening to these lies!"

The lugál turned to meet the eyes of the crowd. On those gaunt faces, contorted with anger, Hazi also saw a readiness. An eagerness to do something, anything but return home in peace. It was the look both men and women wore when a fight began.

"Those rations are ours!" Susuda cried. "And we will take them by force if we have to."

He drew his dagger, and with a roar he plunged it straight into the neck of the soldier nearest him. The man collapsed, groping frantically at the wound as bright red blood gouted down his neck.

Silence fell. For a moment, the only sound was the gasping and gurgling of the dying man.

Then the én turned and fled back into the shadows within the temple, her face contorted in despair, as the soldiers raised their spears and drew their daggers. With a roar of their own, they launched themselves at the crowd.

Hazi and Girin inspected every body sprawled on the blood-soaked sleeping mats. Some still breathed, but many more lay dead, from the spear-gashes in the throat or lung or stomach, where the blood had dried to brown. When they came to men who moaned in pain or cried out for an end, they offered gulps of joyplant milk, and let the men sink gratefully into unending sleep.

"Three weeks," Hazi muttered as he felt for a heartbeat on a young woman's neck. "How much longer do you think they can keep this up?"

"You mean our fighters?" Girin asked. "Or the temple?"

Hazi shook his head and moved on to the next body. "Either one," he said.

"These boys and grandfathers aren't fit for fighting," Girin said. "Susuda's taken the best of them, while we squat here, waiting for him."

What she said was true, Hazi knew. After the first day's massacre, the survivors had remained in the temple square, refusing to leave until the én abdicated—a demand that the mob repeated each time the temple sent a priest out to negotiate.

Meanwhile, Susuda had sent word to his estate outside the city walls, from which regular shipments of his own grain and beer arrived daily to feed the starving fighters. The lugál had won their loyalty now; Hazi could see it every time he looked in the eyes of these desperate men and women. Whatever else happened, they were Susuda's people, body and soul.

And day by day, the lugál had taken the strongest and most loyal of the young men under his wing for special training, safely out of sight of the temple guards. Boxes of strange supplies arrived by night: leopard-skins and copper ingots, leather straps and belts. At dawn each day, Susuda taught his men how to run and thrust their spears in unison; to protect their companions with shields.

Hazi could see some of the men now, sparring with their spears in a broad space Susuda had cleared for training amid the beds and bronze cookpots scattered around the square. They were getting better each day, their strokes growing more synchronized. Though Susuda's trained fighters were still outnumbered by the temple guards, Hazi was beginning to wonder if they might have a chance.

"Hazi!" the lugál called.

Hazi turned and saw Susuda approaching through the crowd. At his side strode Lugál Temena and the champion fighters of Lagash, in their black-and-yellow kilts and *anzú*-bird tattoos. Long daggers swung at their belts, and the sunlight gleamed on the polished copper tips of the spears in their hands.

"So it isn't true after all," Girin said, sauntering over. "What they say about men of Lagash."

Lugál Temena looked her over with a grin. "And what," he asked, "do they say about men of Lagash?"

"That you make a lot of promises," she replied easily, "but fail to arrive in time of need."

"Well." Temena spread his tattooed arms, smiling. "Here we are."

"How many of you?" Hazi asked.

"They brought two hundred men," Lugál Susuda answered.

"And another three hundred will be at your gates tomorrow morning," added Merkar Short-Blade, the one who'd accused Susuda of blasphemy when he'd first proposed the plan.

Girin raised her eyebrows. "Five hundred Lagash-men at our gates. It wasn't so long ago we'd be less than pleased to hear that."

"We'll be very pleased this time," Susuda said with a grin. "For these are no ordinary men."

"What are they, then?" Hazi asked. "Half-Gods? Heroes?"

"Better." A cunning smile played about Temena's lips. "A host of men who fight as one man."

"The champions of Kish already fight as one," Hazi said.

"Not like Temena's trained his Lagash-men to do." Susuda shook his head. "This is something new. Show them."

Temena clapped his hands and barked a command: "Form up!"

Fifty Lagash-men came bursting out of the crowd, arraying themselves neatly in two lines, one behind the other. They were clad in leopard-skin cloaks, and wore identical helmets of beaten copper. Each man gripped a thick-shafted spear in his right hand, and a round shield of hard boiled leather in his right. They seemed to form a wall, these two neat rows of men. A solid wall of shields, along whose top ran two lines of spear-points.

"Spears down!" Temena shouted, and the front row of men crouched as one, lowering their spear-tips to point straight at Hazi and Girin.

"Push!" barked Temena, and the men thrust their spears forward in unison, stepping forward with shields held tightly together.

Hazi glanced at Girin, whose wide eyes were locked on the lines of fighters. He glanced at Susuda, who was watching with arms folded and a tight grin on his lips.

"Push!" Temena cried again, and in one seamless motion the first line of men slid back, withdrawing their spears and raising their shields, as the rear row thrust their spears forward between the men.

"Push!" shouted Temena. "Push!" and with each shout, a line of spears shot forward as a line of shields rose to guard them. The rows of men advanced like a slow-rolling wheel, step by step, until they'd nearly reached Hazi and Girin.

A crowd of townspeople—weavers and tanners and fishwives—had gathered around the scene, watching with wide eyes and half-open mouths.

"That's enough," Susuda commanded.

The Lagash-men glanced at Temena, who gave a single nod. They raised their spear-tips, straightened their backs, and formed back into two neat lines.

"And what about yours?" Temena asked.

Hazi furrowed his brow. "Ours—?"

"They're as ready as they'll ever be," Susuda cut him off.

Hazi laughed as the pieces clicked together in his mind. "So that's what you've been up to!"

The lugál spread his hands, grinning mischievously.

"How many?" Baragi Broad-Wings demanded.

"Enough," Susuda told him.

But once they'd taken their leave of Temena and the fighters of Lagash, Hazi quietly asked Susuda how many men he truly had, ready to fight like those they'd just seen.

"In the city right now..." Susuda tilted his hand back and forth. "Only three hundred or so."

Hazi raised an eyebrow. "And outside the city?"

The lugál grinned and clapped him on the back. "Enough," he said. "More than enough to do what we have to do."

Hazi knew better than to push the lugál in moments like these. But as he and Girin lay in their bed that night, he found himself turning over that phrase in his mind: *to do what we have to do.*

It hadn't been so long ago that the lugál had told Hazi everything—all the plans in his mind, every step that would have to be climbed to secure a permanent position as lugál, to reap a profit from the caravans, to prepare and ignite the riots. But as soon as the riots had begun, Susuda had grown stranger than ever, even more distant and difficult to read than he usually was.

"What do you think that means?" Hazi asked Girin. "'To do what we have to do?'"

Girin grunted. "Only the Gods know what's in that man's mind these days." She rolled away from him, pulling the cowskin blanket over her body. "Go to sleep."

"I want to help him," he told her.

"Do you?" she asked.

They said nothing after that. Hazi lay there in the dark of the bedroom, listening to Girin's soft snores, unable to push her question from his mind. *Do I still want to help Susuda?* The question chased itself in circles. *Or have I just been saying that for too long to know whether it's true anymore?*

Hazi ducked as a clay pot smashed on the wall, just behind where his head had been a moment ago.

All around him, men and women were howling, hurling pottery and rotten fruit, smashing the wood posts beneath awnings, splashing bright red paint across the mud-brick walls of public buildings, staining the painted columns and frescoes with red and brown blotches.

Ten thousand starving farmers, herders, woodworkers, brewers, wool-spinners, cooks, cobblers, and bricklayers were laying waste to the city manors and shopfronts of the priests, who had vanished behind closed doors as soon as the people poured into the streets.

They milled and marched past porticoes and columns painted in intricate black and red; down avenues lined with palms and oaks; dashed in the shadows of bone-colored brick buildings, down narrow alleys, breaking out into the central square in other places, pushing inward, seeking the towering, columned public buildings at the center.

Hazi whirled as three old women shoved past him, bolts of expensive fabric on their backs. A crowd of young boys hurled handfuls of flour into their air like smoke clouds, while a young woman ran screaming from a gang of paint-covered teenaged boys, who chased her with hoots and whistles.

Two lines of marchers were trying to get organized in the center of the square. One group chanted "Down with the temple! The temple robs us blind!" while the other shouted "Kill the én! Spill the én's blood!" Each group's members tried to drag in nearby looters, most of whom shook off the grasping hands, while others launched into fistfights with the chanting groups.

Hazi and Girin clambered up atop a sturdy wood awning, from which they could see the crowd that filled the square; thousands of furious men and women, more than Hazi had ever seen together. Along the temple's side of the square, a thousand or more temple soldiers were forming up into three lines that partially encircled the square, barring access to the sacred precincts within.

"Where's Susuda?" Girin cried, dodging a jug of wine that shattered against the wall of a nearby building.

Suddenly a shout erupted from across the square. Ripples of movement ran through the crowd. As they parted, three columns of identically leopard-cloaked men charged across the square. Each wore an identical copper helmet, simple and round-topped, and carried a great square shield of boiled cowhide—but while some wore the red-and-white kilts of Kish, others wore the yellow-and-black of Lagash: Temena's fighters. These two armies together added up to at least a thousand men. *As many as the whole temple guard*, Hazi thought. *More, perhaps.* As the men charged, those shields came together and the spear-tips lowered in unison, pointed straight at the temple soldiers.

The combined army moved as one; a vast serpent that uncoiled and crashed into the temple guard head-on with a thunder of crashing wood and metal, splintering fragments of spears that danced in the air. They stepped back, reformed, and attacked again, holding their shields tight together to form a wall.

Hazi leaped down from the awning, drawing his dagger—but by the time he and Girin had reached the battle, the temple soldiers had drawn away from Susuda's line of warriors, who had formed up again with shields up and spear-points lowered.

Susuda stepped forth from the ranks. He wore a soft flax robe dyed bright red, embroidered with tiny gold flowers. His bronze helmet gleamed in the sun. Lugál Temena strolled behind him, resplendent in a robe of deep vermillion.

"Look at them!" Susuda roared to the lines of fighters behind him. "They're terrified of you!"

A ripple of laughter went up from the butchers, barbers and fishermen in their identical leopard-skin cloaks.

Susuda met the temple soldiers' eyes, grinning madly. "It's not your lives we want!" he cried. "This is between us and the én. Join us! Wear the leopard-skin as my fighting men do, and tonight you'll all dine on meat and beer!"

On the temple soldiers' right flank, Hazi noticed one particularly frightened-looking young soldier, scarcely more than a boy. He crept close to the young man—and at the moment the soldier caught sight of him, he reached out and wrenched the boy's spear from his hand. Grabbed him by the arm. Yanked him into Susuda's ranks.

"A wise choice!" he cried, raising the boy's arm as he struggled and cried out.

Susuda caught on immediately. "You see?" he called out to the temple soldiers. "Already you're losing men, and the fighting hasn't even begun yet."

"Gods help us all!" cried another soldier, throwing down his spear and running over to Susuda's cluster of men. Then another soldier did the same, and another. In another moment, dozens of leopard-skin cloaks were merging into the ranks on Susuda's side, even as the tattooed ranks of his fighters pressed in around the remaining few.

At last, only three temple soldiers remained. Susuda's fighters grabbed them from behind, wrenched their spears and shields away and forced them to their knees.

The crowd had fallen silent and still.

Susuda strode up to the three kneeling soldiers, who glared up at him defiantly.

"Will you not yield?" he asked calmly.

One of the soldiers, a grizzled old man, spat on the stone pavement at Susuda's feet.

Susuda locked eyes with both of the others, who only stared back impassively.

He shrugged, drew his finger across his throat, turned on his heel, and walked in the direction of the temple.

Hazi turned and followed him, with Girin and Baragi in his wake.

Behind him, Hazi heard the sound of sharp blades against flesh, the gasp of the crowd and the sounds of three bodies hitting the pavement. He didn't turn to look back. He kept his eyes on the lugál who marched ahead of him, toward the towering mud-brick temple.

𒐉
𒐉

"Shit!" Susuda slammed his fist into the wall, again and again, until his knuckles came back bloody and a dull red stain leaked down the tan brick.

Hazi came running from the adjoining room, followed by the willowy old sacrifice-priest who'd been helping him tally up the bushels of grain in the temple storehouses.

"What's going on?" Hazi asked.

Girin leaned in and whispered, "The én still squats behind her guards in the ziggurat's upper sanctuary. No word from her."

"Fat, cowardly swine!" the lugál snarled. He paced back and forth across the rug, next to a table laden with silver plates piled high with fresh plums, pears, oranges, dates and raisins—and of course, wine. There was always wine in abundance these days, though Hazi had scarcely seen the lugál indulge before. Now he held a cup formed of translucent ostrich-eggshell, its rim mosaiced with shards of red carnelian and lapis lazuli. The lugál's lips were stained red. He took a fresh gulp between each curse that flew from his lips. The food on the table sat untouched, and flies were beginning to gather.

In the five days since the coup had succeeded, Susuda had installed himself here in the city's finest manor-house, traditionally reserved for the én. Its vast, high-ceilinged rooms displayed woven wall-hangings and ornate statues carved in ivory and sandstone, claw-footed tables of tamarisk-wood surrounded by padded chairs, and high windows and skylights covered with intricately carved wood grates. Even the lugál's country manor-house seemed poor by comparison. Hazi doubted he'd ever feel truly comfortable here.

"What can the én do to us now?" Hazi approached Susuda, speaking softly, palms out in a placating gesture. "We control the city. The temple soldiers have surrendered. So have most of the priests. What does one old woman matter?"

"That fat old woman," Susuda said, whirling on Hazi, "still tethers Heaven to Earth in the eyes of this city."

"That might've been true a week ago," Girin said. "But in just five days we've gained control of the streets. Every fighter who matters has sworn loyalty to us."

"Those events, in themselves, change nothing," Susuda shot back. "The attack, the occupation of the temple—acts like these do not transfer power, any more than the act of grasping a royal sceptre makes a man a king. If that man *is* king, then the sceptre is kingship. But if that man is not king..."

"You *are* king," Girin said, slowly. "We've handed out enough of your grain to end this famine. Look out the window."

Hazi didn't have to look. The lugál himself had led his fattened bulls out of the temple stables, where the priests had locked them up when they'd confiscated them from his estate. Now ten of those bulls roasted on enormous spits in the central square, the fat on their backs crackling and steaming, while Susuda's cheering fighters tore off great chunks of meat and washed them down with sweet temple beer and date-wine. Hazi could hear the mens' songs and cheers from where he stood. He knew there'd be dancing and looting and less pleasant forms of revelry as the men got drunker. What could he do to stop it? Nothing, as far as he could see.

"The people in the streets swear loyalty to you, Susuda," Girin was saying. "Who would dare question that you and your fighters control the city of Kish?"

Hazi huffed softly. "Kish, certainly. But Kish is only one city, Susuda. Your half-brother, Lugál Anemúndu, has already sent a messenger from Kídnun, proclaiming his refusal to bend his knee."

Susuda waved his hand dismissively. "Anemúndu is no one. He has no army. No wealth. What can he do to me?"

Hazi chose his words carefully. "The noble houses of the other cities recognize our weakness, Susuda. They gather their armies in preparation. The army of Lagash—whom you invited here—now wait outside our gates. Who knows what Lugál Temena is planning?."

The lugál whirled on him, eyes afire. "Don't tell me what I already know!"

Hazi jerked away on instinct. As he regained his composure, berating himself for such a childish reaction, Hazi felt Susuda's hand on his shoulder.

"Temena and his army of Lagash were encamped to the north of our city last night," Susuda said quietly. "Do I speak truly?"

Hazi's brow furrowed. "As far as I know, they are still there—"

"Ah." The lugál raised a finger, grinning. Hazi knew that look. Susuda wrapped a muscled arm around his shoulders and guided him to the north-facing window across the room. "Tell me what you see."

Hazi gazed out through the delicately carved wood lattice covering the window. Outside, flat-topped clay towers rose amid mud-brick houses stacked block-like, among flat roofs of every height. The city's great mud-brick walls encircled this sprawl, their battlements adorned with great nests where white storks twisted their long necks and stretched their wings. Beyond it all stretched the riverplain, where innumerable fires raged, pouring thick black smoke into the morning air.

"The camp—" Hazi gasped.

But Girin was already shaking her head. "You fox," she whispered. "You truly are mad."

Though it was too far, and too dark, for Hazi to see the men who stoked those fires, he knew that the men who strode through the smoldering remains of Lagash's camp wore the red-and-white of Kish. They were Susuda's trained fighters, tossing corpses clad in black and yellow onto the pyres and setting them aflame.

"A sad fate," Susuda said quietly, "for our old friend, Lugál Temena of Lagash."

Now it was Hazi's turn to whirl on Susuda, his eyes wide with startled rage. "We could have used those men!" he howled, pointing out across the city toward the camp. "Those were five hundred loyal allies, Susuda!"

"Allies," the lugál shrugged. "Perhaps. Loyal? Most certainly not. With my men tied up keeping order in the city, Temena planned to march on my estate, then claim my crops and house for himself." He took another gulp of his wine.

"How do you know?" Hazi demanded, his voice scarcely more than a thin breath.

"Because," Susuda replied. "That's exactly what I'd have done in his place." He scratched his neck thoughtfully. "Dogs are loyal, Hazi," he said. "Foxes are not. Always remember that."

"And which are you?" Hazi asked, as the lugál strode away to pluck a plum from the table.

"Me?" the lugál asked. He shrugged and took a bit of the plum, letting the juice run down his black beard.

Hazi glanced at Girin, who watched the lugál with an unreadable expression.

"Even with Temena's help," Hazi said at last, "we'd have stood a poor chance against Umma and Girsu, and the other cities of the Riverplain. As soon as they hear of this, they'll all form a coalition against us."

"For a season, perhaps," Susuda acknowledged. "But when has any alliance lasted much longer?"

"Or any lugál," Girin added.

Susuda shot her a sharp look, but said nothing. He sipped his wine silently.

A knock sounded at the door, and a messenger boy hurried in without waiting for an answer.

"The new én awaits your pleasure, Lugál Susuda," he said, bowing low, staring at the floor.

The lugál glanced at Hazi and Girin with a look of mock surprise. "The new én, you say?" he asked the boy.

"Yes," the lad stammered, eyes still locked on the rug beneath the table. "Én-priestess Ningikuga abdicated and fled the temple this afternoon. Word has it she's gone into hiding. A priest called Shatámurrim has accepted the mantle of the Gods and taken her place as én."

He continued to stare at the floor for a long moment. Susuda chewed his plum.

"Well come on," the lugál said at last, throwing an arm around Hazi's shoulders. "Let's go meet our new én." He downed the last of his wine and tossed the ostrich-egg cup on the table behind him. It shattered to bits, dashing red wine and egg-shards across the tablecloth.

"You have my full attention," Shatámurrim, the newly appointed én of Kish, told Lugál Susuda.

The bald man eyed the lugál nervously, hands clasped atop the pressed, pleated folds of his priestly robe. With his long, sharp nose, he reminded Hazi of a river-heron, as he craned his wiry neck to try to catch Susuda's eye. He turned to whisper this thought to Girin, but her eyes, too, were fixed on Susuda.

The lugál was pacing back and forth along the table's length, like a leopard, dark eyes afire. Over his shoulder he'd thrown the fur of a leopard, the traditional cloak of a soldier, which hung about his tattooed chest. By the look in the new én's eyes, Hazi could tell the man had some choice remarks on his guests' style of dress. But he was sensible enough to hold his tongue, even as his trimmed nails plucked anxiously at imaginary dust-motes on his robe.

A dozen or so of Susuda's other fighters leaned against the room's cool mud-brick walls. They picked their nails with dagger-tips, or scratched at wounds on their tattooed arms and chests, or watched the conversation as if it were an entertainment for their benefit, wry grins on their bearded faces, thumbs notched in their low-slung belts.

"I hear you're a flexible man, Shatámurrim," Susuda said at last, in an unreadable tone.

The new én simply shrugged. "I am a practical man," he said. "My only interest is for the people of this city."

"As is ours," Girin drawled from across the table, trimming her nails with a curved bronze knife.

"What sort of arrangement did you have in mind?" Shatámurrim asked.

"Good question, priest," came a voice from the doorway.

Hazi turned to see Baragi Broad-Wings, decked out a loose-belted kilt, an oddly trimmed beard and luxuriant furs. He walked with the high-chinned regality of a priest, but none of the pious quietude. Without another word, he dropped into a chair next to the én.

Shatámurrim looked the new arrival up and down, struggling to find words. "Must we all dress this way now?" he asked after a moment.

Susuda only laughed softly, sinking into a chair and taking a fig from the plate on the table. "What word of your predecessor?" he asked the new én. "Has that fat old bitch shown her face yet?"

Shatámurrim licked his lips nervously. "She, er— remains, shall we say, recalcitrant."

"Remains what?" Susuda shook his head, irritated.

"She remains in hiding," the new én clarified, "and refuses to show herself."

"Then she will starve to death in whatever hole she's crawled into," Susuda said, munching the fig, letting its pinkish juice run down the braid of his beard. "In the meantime, I have grown tired of waiting for formal confirmation of my position. Lugál Susuda rules Kish now. I know it. All of us in this room know it. The people know it. It is time we said it out loud, in public."

Shatámurrim shrugged. "Certainly something can be arranged in the interim—"

"There will be no 'interim,'" the lugál cut him off. "The mantle of kingship has descended to me. I do not need your blessing, én. Only the blessing of the Énlil himself. And that God has already given his blessing to me, long before today."

A hush fell over the table.

Hazi took a moment to choose his words carefully. "There are precedents," he said, picking his way with care. "If a lugál is not confirmed by the temple of his own city—"

"You mean I should go to Níppúr," Susuda said flatly.

"The holy city." Shatámurrim agreed, nodding deferentially. "Make a pilgrimage to the House of the Mountain. Meet with the intercessors. Take the mantle and sceptre of kingship for yourself, directly from Énlil's high priest—"

"I need nothing from priests!" Susuda barked, so loudly that everyone in the room jumped. Shatámurrim gaped at the lugál, eyes wide in astonishment. Hazi had never seen the lugál like this, so openly hostile, like an animal in a trap.

"This," Susuda gestured around him, "is my kingship. Look out the window!" He pointed north, in the direction of his army. "*That* is my kingship." He thumped his chest with the flat of his hand. "I am kingship."

"This is blasphemy," Shatámurrim whispered.

"I'm well used to charges of blasphemy," Susuda told him. "When I asked for my position as lugál to be made permanent, the én said that was blasphemy. When I proposed to uproot the temple and rule this city, they called that blasphemy too."

The lugál gazed deep into Shatámurrim's panicked eyes. "Are you absolutely certain that you wish to make this accusation?"

"Susuda." Hazi approached the lugál, reaching out his hand.

The lugál stared at Hazi coldly, without a hint of the friendliness they'd known for so many years. Girin glanced nervously between them, her fingers playing about the hilt of the dagger at her belt.

"What's happening to you?" Hazi asked, feeling hot tears rise behind his eyes. "Susuda, it's me."

"You will address me," Susuda said, "as lugál."

"Of course you are lugál," Girin said in the most soothing voice he could muster. "You will always be our lugál."

"I warn you, too, Girin," Susuda said. "Do not speak to me like a child, like someone to be managed. Remember whom it is that you address."

"Susud—er, I mean, lugál," Hazi said. "You do not need the confirmation of any God or priest to rule here in Kish. That much is already proven. But if the other cities of the Riverplain are to acknowledge your rule, and bend the knee to you, a confirmation from the high priest will make things much easier."

Susuda stared at him for a long time, the look in his eyes frigid and unreadable.

"And you, Girin," the lugál said, without taking his eyes from Hazi. "Do you also feel this way?"

Girin swallowed. "It is an easy journey, lugál," she said. "In less than a week, you will be receiving the blessing in the House of the Mountain at Níppúr. In less than two weeks, you can be back here in Kish, confirmed as king of all Shumér."

Susuda's jaw tightened. He slowly began to nod.

"So this is the word of the council," he said quietly. "The word of *my* council, who are here to serve *me*." He huffed a dry laugh, looking from Hazi to Girin.

Hazi raised his hands. "We are only pointing out—"

"Get out of my sight," Susuda snapped.

Girin and Hazi glanced at one another, at Susuda, at Shatámurrim and Baragi, and at the other fighters around the room, who were all trying to conceal their surprise.

Susuda spread his arms, incredulous. "Stop staring at each other, and get the hell out of my city. Go!"

As he barked this last word, Hazi and Girin finally remembered themselves enough to hurry for the door.

"Perhaps tomorrow," Girin tried.

"There is no tomorrow," Susuda replied. "Not for you. I should have you slain and burned, like that traitor Temena and his men, but old friendships count for something—for more, apparently, to me than to you two."

Hazi and Girin stared at him, unable to believe the words he'd just spoken.

"Get out!" Susuda barked, pointing at the door. "If I ever see you again," he said, his voice tight with menace, "I will have you thrown on a pyre." He shook his head. "You've disappointed me, old friends. It seems loyalty does not always run both ways."

Girin grabbed Hazi's arm and dragged him from the room before he could formulate a reply.

Even as they hurried home to pack as much dried meat and cheese as they could carry, even as they walked to the city's north gate and hired a donkey-drawn wagon to carry them away from the city of Kish, then climbed into the back of the wagon and felt its bouncing wooden wheels carry them through the city gate, out into the wilderness—and even as they saw the great grassy fields of the northern Riverplain spread before them, Hazi found it impossible to believe he had been exiled from the city where he had lived all his life. Kish was all he had ever known, and now it was gone.

"*First Lugál Susuda was lord in Kish,*" the tale-teller was singing. "*Now he claims kingship over all Shumér. Yet every other city fights against him. His eyes see far but his arms are too short.*"

Hazi drained the last of his beer from his clay mug, scanning the faces around him: local manor-lords, petty nobles, and the apparently innumerable sons, daughters, uncles, cousins and wives of Lugál Anemúndu of Kídnun, who sat at the head of the central table of the manor's cramped, lamp-lit dining-room, a few seats down from Hazi and Girin.

Anemúndu was Lugál Susuda's half-brother, a tall, thickset man whose great black beard forked into twin serpentine braids. He looked as if he'd be more at home by a farm-hut's fireside than here at his dining-room in his Kídnun manor-house. He'd mimicked his half-brother's rise to power step-for-step—until Susuda had staged his coup in Kish and proclaimed himself lord of all Shumér. On that day, Anemúndu had sent a fleet-footed messenger to Susuda, proclaiming his city's independence and his refusal to bend the knee.

And since Kídnun sat only two days' wagon-ride from Kish, the small town was the most obvious place for Hazi and Girin to seek asylum in their exile. They'd ridden in the back of a lumbering donkey-drawn wagon, across the grassy fields outside Kish's mud-brick walls, past the newly erected boundary-stones carved with scenes of Lugál Susuda slaying beasts and shaking hands with Gods, the sides of the squat pillars inscribed in jagged triangular characters with the lugál's name and his deeds, and the name of this city. And for the first time in his life, Hazi had known the feeling of departing from home, out into the vast sea of the larger world.

Now he and Girin sat side-by-side in the smoke and candlelight of this dining-room, a rather shoddy imitation of Susuda's court at Kish, and watched the local nobles and lords play-act their own royal court.

"*Susuda claims to go between the Gods and men,*" the tale-teller sang as Hazi continued to scan the room, looking for a familiar face but finding none he recognized. "*But the Gods grow bored with him. All Shumér grows bored with him!*"

"Then stop singing about him!" Lugál Anemúndu hurled a steaming turnip at the tale-teller. A raucous laugh rose from all the guests as the turnip exploded against the chamber's far wall.

The tale-teller fell silent for a moment. Then he plucked a new melody on his harp, and began a different song: "*In those far-distant days, the great Flood swept over all the land...*"

Hazi leaned toward Anemúndu and gestured for his attention. "Lugál," he said, raising his voice to be heard over the harp-song and the chattering of the nobles. "I thank you for your hospitality."

Anemúndu sipped beer from a huge clay mug, foam coating his thick moustache. "Anything to irritate my pompous ass of a half-brother." He roared with laughter. "Tell me, Hazi, how is that arrogant serpent these days? Still convinced he's the cleverest man alive?"

Girin, who sat between Hazi and the lugál, reached for a pitcher and refilled the clay cup with beer. "He sees himself as a hero. Perhaps even as a God. Who knows?"

Anemúndu only huffed disdainfully.

Hazi turned Girin's words over in his mind, finding it hard to reconcile her description of Susuda with the man he'd known since they were children. Susuda had always believed he was especially clever; there was no question about that. But then, he had always been unusually cunning. He'd brought uncountable riches to the fighters of Kish, and that had always been good enough reason to trust the plans he brewed in secret—at least for Hazi.

But Hazi had always known Susuda to be, above all, a practical man. Could he truly believe he was a God? Or was this just another tool of his, another plan to bring some new idea into the world? Hazi would always have given Susuda the benefit of the doubt. Until three days ago, when the lugál had flown into a rage and exiled him and Girin on pain of death. What kind of man, Hazi wondered, turns against his oldest and truest friends? Perhaps Susuda had lost all sense of balance. Perhaps he truly did believe he was a God made flesh.

"I'll tell you a story about Susuda," Anemúndu was saying in between sips of beer. "Remember when we were all just little bastards, pickpocketing and stealing bread on the streets of Kish?"

Hazi nodded, images playing in his mind: he and Susuda and Girin and the rest of them, camped out in alleyways and basements, starving and afraid, angry at the whole world, begging outside the temple until their stomachs got the better of them and they turned to pickpocketing and theft.

Susuda had first organized them, and had taught Hazi and the others to distract passersby with questions and songs, while he sneaked up behind and lifted loaves and fruits from their purses with deft, light fingers. Strange as it seemed, Hazi remembered those days with fondness. Life hadn't been easier, but it had been simpler. Clearer. At least, that was how Hazi felt now, looking back.

"One night he woke me from a dead sleep," Anemúndu went on. "Crouched over me in the dark, in that reeking alley behind the tanneries, and told me he'd had a vision from a God. He said Énlil, the wind-God himself, had come to him in a dream. Imagine that. A boy of not ten summers, convinced he'd been given a mission from the God of breath."

"What was the mission?" Girin asked. Her face seemed calm, but Hazi had learned to read her. Something strange played behind her eyes, in the flickering lamplight.

Anemúndu's eyes narrowed. "He said the strangest thing. 'From now on,' he said, 'I will sweep over the world.'" The lugál shook his twin-bearded head. "I asked him what he meant, and he just stared at me, eyes cold as night. And he told me, 'From now on, I am apart from everyone. The temple, the priests, even the én' he said. 'I will hold myself secret from them. I'll outsmart them all, and someday they'll bow to me.'" Anemúndu's expression had turned dark, his eyes wide in the lamplight as if Susuda stood before him now. "'They'll all bow to me.' That's what he said. I remember it clear as this very morning."

Hazi and Girin watched him intently, the other nobles and the tale-teller forgotten.

Anemúndu frowned. "Didn't make much of it at the time," he said, "strange as that sounds now. We were always pretending to be heroes, fighters, rulers. He seemed very intent on it. But that was always Susuda, wasn't it? Always had to take things a bit further."

"What is to be done?" Hazi asked.

"Done?" Anemúndu grunted. "About Susuda? Well, unless you have a few thousand fighting men hidden under that kilt of yours..."

"You must have a plan," Hazi persisted. "You sent him a messenger and refused to bend your knee. You knew that would provoke his wrath." Hazi searched Anemúndu's face for some hint of the cunning that always played behind Susuda's eyes, but he saw not the slightest hint of it.

"Aye," Anemúndu replied, "and a hundred barrels of copper, along with a few woman-slaves, will calm him down again. That's how he's always been."

Girin glanced at Hazi, her eyes wide. "That's your plan?" she gasped. "Wait for him to march here, then prostrate yourself and pay him tribute?"

Anemúndu shrugged. "I've bought us enough time for one last good feast." He reached for the beer-pitcher and refilled his enormous clay mug. "You can stay here a few days, until his army shows up. After that, you'll have to go."

Girin's grip tightened around Hazi's arm. "Where will we go?"

Anemúndu spread his hands. "The world is a big place. He can't send armies everywhere."

Hazi and Girin watched the thick-shouldered man sip his beer, as the weight of his decision sank in.

"Susuda won't leave two stones standing in this city," Girin whispered at last.

But Anemúndu didn't hear her, or chose not to.

"*The great Flood's waters swept through Unúg,*" the tale-teller was singing, plucking at his lyre. "*They swept through Kish and through Lagash. The Flood's waters smashed the cities, until only ruins remained.*"

Hazi took Girin's hand, and pulled her up from the table. Together they walked out into the hallway, and found their way to their bedroom.

Later, in the dark, Hazi rolled over in bed, untangling himself from Girin's arms. He heaved himself up, climbed the ladder to the manor's roof, and looked up at the full moon and stars, casting pale light over the mud-brick labyrinth of the town of Kídnun.

A moment later, he felt her breath on the back of his neck and felt her arms wrap around him.

"Doesn't look so different from our old city, does it?" she asked quietly.

"Not so different, yet so unfamiliar," he said without turning. "All these streets I've never walked."

He turned to face her and stroked her scarred cheek.

"It's going to be war," he said after a while. "That's all there'll be, from now on."

She nodded, tears rising in her eyes. "I know," she said quietly. "We have to keep moving."

"Where?" he asked. "Where will we be safe? Where is far enough?"

She shook her head. "I don't know. But we can't stay here. Especially not now that we have a..."

Girin's words trailed off. She looked into Hazi's eyes, as if searching for something there.

"Now that we have," she said at last, "another life to protect."

He looked at her for a long moment, eyes widening as he grasped her meaning.

"Are you sure?" he gasped. "I mean—"

"My blood has not come for more than a month," she said. "On the road, I was sick in the mornings. I have craved strange foods."

He thought back to their trip here. back to the long road north from Kish, Girin's sudden disappearances in the mornings, her nauseous refusals of their common meals of dried fish and barley bread. At the time he'd only been thinking of the destination, of the town of Kídnun, the court where he'd hoped they might be safe.

"All that time," he said, "you knew, and you kept it secret."

She shook her head again. "I didn't know what to do. You are not my husband, and this is not..." she trailed off, sighing. "This is no way to raise a child."

"We must care for him," Hazi said, placing a hand gently on her belly. It was a stupid thing to say, but those were the only words he could summon.

She smiled. "How do you know it's a 'him'?"

"Her, then." He placed a hand against her belly and imagined he felt some small movement there.

She watched him for the space of several heartbeats. "I had a dream," she said at last. "On the night I first knew I'd conceived."

He looked into her eyes, brow furrowed. "What kind of dream?"

She swallowed. "A dream from the Gods, I think. I saw a woman seated atop a great mountain, holding a sceptre of gold. In her lap sat a child. A little boy. And the woman wept, though

I did not know why. She wept until her tears flooded the land, and only she and the child remained, there on the mountaintop."

Hazi was silent for a long time. "We must ask a priest the meaning—"

"No." She raised a hand, gently, to his lips. "The meaning of this dream can only be a sad one. I do not want to know it. When the time comes, I will know."

"If something so terrible is coming," Hazi said, "We must get you to safety, right away. Up to the top of that mountain, wherever it is—"

"I have a few months, still." She smiled softly. "I haven't even started to show yet. Perhaps we'll find somewhere safe."

"And then?" he asked.

"And then," she said, "we'll find someplace far from Kish. Susuda will find plenty of new acolytes to rely on."

"That," Hazi replied, "is exactly what I'm afraid of."

᭟᭟᭟
᭟᭟᭟
᭟᭟᭟

HAZI BREATHED IN the warm evening air, smelling the thick odors of reeds and mud and river-water. Simple smells, so different from the smoke and sewers and incense of the city. The evening brought a chill, but Hazi was wrapped in a hooded cloak of rough flax; as much to cover his tattoos—unchangeable marks which would reveal him instantly as a man of Kish, and thus a servant of the despot Susuda—as to keep out the cold.

He found his flat-bottomed boat anchored at the edge of the marsh, where he'd left it. Tugging on the anchor-rope, he lifted the round stone that held the boat in place, heaved it into the boat's deck and hefted the long wood pole and guided the boat out into the water.

As he poled his boat through the muddy water, back to the hut he and Girin shared, he passed small islands where cranes and herons nested amid tall stands of reeds. Beneath an orange-tinted sky, men in mud-stained wool kilts poled their own boats between the reeds and islands, calling out greetings to their friends who sat weaving baskets, spinning wool and gutting fish outside their family huts; longhouses woven of the reeds of the riverbank, daubed with clay.

Girin sat outside their reed hut, sewing a blanket of wool and sheepskin. The little one, Balih, toddled from one bank of the island to the other, picking up rocks and shellfish from among the tangled reeds, examining each discovery, then throwing it aside with excited squeals as another attraction caught his eye.

They rose to greet him as he poled the boat to the edge of the island, dropped anchor and climbed ashore. Balih ran to him and wrapped tiny plump arms around his bare muddy leg. Girin smiled softly, took his face in her hands and kissed him.

"They say in the village—" he began, but trailed off when he saw her smile fall to a frown. That furrow on her brow.

"What do they say?" she asked softly, stroking his cheek.

He bent down and lifted Balih onto his hip. "They say he claims the whole of Shumér as his own."

She snorted a laugh. "That'll be the day."

"He's taken Marad and Borsippa," Hazi said. "They say he marches with three thousand men now. They say he'll march on Umma this month."

"It rained hard yesterday," she said. "Campaigning season is nearly done."

"And then?" Hazi asked.

"And then nothing," she said. "Come inside. There's hot barley stew waiting for you."

Later, when Balih snored softly and they lay together, exhausted and panting, on a soft mattress on the hut's floor, he bit the tip of her ear and asked, "Do you ever miss it?"

She shook her head, tapping his nose with a fingertip. "Not for a moment."

"You were good at it," he whispered.

"I'm good at fishing," she said. "And caring for the little one."

"You could wield a spear or dagger like no one I've ever seen," he said. "Man or woman."

She hummed softly against his neck. "We promised," she said. "No more fighting."

He glanced across the hut. In the moonlight that pierced the reed-weaving of the roof, he could make out the outline of the tool that had once been his dagger, which he'd heated red and beaten into a sickle. Instead of blood, it now wore the stains of slain barley.

"No more fighting against kings and armies," he muttered. "But there are other fights."

"Against yourself, you mean."

"Against what I know," he said.

"No man knows the future," she whispered.

"That," he said, "is precisely why I fear it."

"Shh," she breathed softly against his ear, stroking his eyelashes. "You'll wake the baby."

"He won't be a baby much longer."

She kissed him, soft and long. "All the more reason to let him sleep."

⟨

THE FIGHTERS FROM Lagash came after the rainy season had passed, when the sun baked the mud and dried the water around the island-banks, and little Balih walked instead of toddling, and begged to accompany Hazi and Girin on boat-trips into the village.

An orange sun glared low and looming in a reddening sky, casting long shadows across the thick stands of tall reeds along the marsh-banks. Ghosts that danced among that green sea, all the way to the eastern horizon, where deep blues and purples gave way to the night's first stars. The air hung heavy, thick with moisture, humming with the drone of young mosquitoes that swarmed eagerly, scenting blood.

Ten men trudged silently through waist-high water, long-shadowed in that orange light. They wore fleece kilts dyed yellow and black, and their chests and bellies bore tattoos of the *anzû*-bird; the totem of Lagash. They breathed heavy in the humid air; swatted mosquitoes on their arms, cheeks, shoulders, pushed aside the thick-grown reeds whose stalks waved above their heads. They trod lightly on the muddy marsh-bed, giving no sign of their approach but the gentle parting of reedstalks.

Hazi stood in the trading-place, bartering a bushel of fresh-cut barley and half a basket of fish for some rope and boat-caulk, when he glanced up and saw no sign of Balih or Girin.

He glanced around frantically and saw only old men in wool kilts, who looked up, incurious and exhausted. Across the trading place, a gaggle of fishwives glanced at him suspiciously.

He approached one of them. "Have you seen my—"

Before he finished the question, three men emerged from the thick reeds on the fringe of the clearing. Tattooed, wearing black-and-yellow kilts, with *anzû*-birds on their skin. Men of Lagash. One of the fighters gripped Balih tightly by the arm. Tears streamed down the boy's face.

"This belong to you?" the fighter asked, with a sneering grin.

The fishwives and barter-men were disappearing into the nearest huts.

Hazi raised his hands. "I've got no fight with you."

The fighters chuckled. "We'll see about that." Their leader grabbed Hazi's cloak and yanked at it. "You've got the look of a fighting-man. What city do you claim? Who are you with?"

"I'm not with any city," Hazi snarled, pulling away.

But the fighter was too quick. He caught hold of Hazi's cloak and wrenched it away, revealing the tattoos beneath: the *lamassu*, man-faced bulls, herald-beasts of Kish, kneeling on his collarbones.

"Just as I thought." The Lagash-man nodded, inspecting the tattoos. "A Kish-man. Hazi Serpent-Tongue himself, unless I miss my guess."

"That's what they're calling me now?" Hazi asked. "Funny, it was 'Silver-Tongue' back in Kish."

"That was before you and the bastard Susuda betrayed your bargain with our Lugál Temena," the Lagash-man sneered. "We know it was you whispering in his ear the whole time. Everyone knows it."

"What are you talking about?" Hazi demanded.

"Don't play innocent with us," the Lagash-man snapped back. The soldier turned to his companions. "Do I really look that stupid to you? Hazi Serpent-Tongue indeed."

"I have no love for Susuda," Hazi said, "He exiled us. Me and my woman, and our child, who was unborn. He declared us his enemies and sent us into the wilderness."

"You expect me to believe that?" The Lagash-man sneered. "Oh, I've watched Kish-men kill too many of our wives and daughters, our brothers and sons. And now a Kish-man stands before me. Not just any Kish-man, but the Serpent-Tongue himself. Oh, now you'll pay, Serpent-Tongue. For all Lagash, now it's your turn to pay!"

At the last word the soldier leaped forward, drawing his dagger and slashing upward across Hazi's chest, as Hazi dodged backward. He lunged right, grabbing the arm of the soldier who held Balih, twisting it, hearing bone crack beneath his grip—the soldier squealed and let go. Hazi swept the boy into his arms and stepped back, looking for anything vaguely weapon-like.

The second soldier gasped. Thick crimson blossomed from his neck and he dropped to his knees, clutching at his throat as he fell to the dirt.

Then she was there—Girin, eyes wild and fierce as ever, stepping over the dropped soldier's body and in the same smooth motion hurling her fishing-spear into the chest of the first soldier, who stumbled backward, eyes wide with shock.

Something hard connected with the back of Hazi's head, and black clouded in at the edges of his vision. He fell, dropping Balih, twisting his body to give the boy a soft landing. He blinked, hard—the world came back, and now two more men stood over him wearing yellow-and-black kilts: Lagash-men, with long daggers in their hands.

As he scrambled to his feet, he faced another Lagash-man, stepping between him and Girin and the boy, who began to wail, his screams piercing the air as he ran for his mother's arms.

Hazi caught her eye.

"I'm sorry," she called out to him across the loose knot of encircling soldiers.

"It's not your fault," he called to her.

"No, I mean—" Eight men were closing in around her and Balih now. "—I made you make that promise. I said I was done," she called across to him. She shook her head. "But I am truly going to enjoy this."

She swept the boy up onto her hip. He clung to her tightly, wailing, tears streaming down his face. She dodged a dagger-swipe from an oncoming soldier, picked up a scythe leaning against the wall of a hut, and hooked the blade into the soldier's belly, ripping upwards, gutting him like a fish.

Hazi ducked a blow at the same time, snatched up a fishnet and flung it at the nearest soldier—flung a basket of fish into another's face—rolled away from the three men who ran at him and found a pestle-stone next to a pile of half-ground barley. He hefted the stone in his hand and felt the weight of it. A soldier rushed in at him, dagger poised for a chest strike—he faked left, leaped right, and brought the stone hard against the side of the man's skull.

More soldiers of Lagash were pouring into the trading-place now, drawn by the clamor. Across the thin-spread line of men, Hazi saw Girin ducking, whirling—little Balih still pressed tightly against her hip while her other hand thrust and hooked and parried with the sickle: slicing across a Lagash-man's hand; whipping upward to catch a Lagash-man straight through the jaw like a fish. Leopard-clad bodies dropped around her. She was a whirlwind; a one-armed storm of hooked blades that lashed out in every direction, a weeping child on her hip.

He had never loved her so much as at this moment, he thought, as he bent backward to dodge a dagger-swipe, then ducked under and caught the Lagash-man from below, shattering his jaw. Two quick stroked to the left and right dropped the Lagash-men who converged on him. They fell with hardly a grunt.

Across the trading-place, Girin was making quick work of the last three Lagash-men. As they dropped to the dirt, blood pumping from their necks and stomachs, she turned just in time to see Hazi catch a dagger-strike to the lung.

Time seemed to stop. She watched Hazi's eyes widen, watched him drop to the ground, clutching his chest, and saw blood pour from his mouth. She watched all this as if it were unfolding slowly; a moment frozen in time.

Then everything was moving again: Hazi coughing and spluttering on the ground with a pool of blood widening around him. And she was dashing to the man who'd stabbed him, faking left, dodging right, catching the killer with a blade in the neck, so fierce and deep she nearly severed his head. He went down with barely a sound, clutching stupidly at the gash.

She fell to her knees next to Hazi, kissing him, wailing, shaking him, begging. He didn't move. She knelt there with him for a long time, in a sea of broken bodies, shaking, sobbing, wanting to believe anything else but this.

⟨𐎹⟩

She did not know how long she walked after that, how many days she trudged across the wild marshes of Shumér, little Balih on her back, avoiding the areas near the rivers and places where houses were clustered, staying in the deep bush-land, where wildcats stalked amid the oaks and elms, and choruses of frogs and insects sang from sunset until morning. She speared fish from the river, or caught and cooked frogs when there were no fish.

Balih didn't like eating frogs. Balih didn't like sleeping outside in the cold, with the insects singing loudly. He cried for long stretches of every day. She could not keep him silent.

That was how the shepherd found her. One afternoon she was trudging through land she thought was empty, when a voice called out.

"Hello!" it called. It was a man's voice.

Her first instinct was to duck, to hide among the tall reeds. But Balih cried out, and the man turned and waved.

He approached them, leading a flock of sheep with his crooked staff. He wore only a simple, undyed kilt of shaggy fleece, and he bore no tattoos. His beard and hair hung unkempt about his whiskered face.

"This is no place for a woman and child," he said gently.

Girin couldn't help herself; she broke into sobs. Little Balih began to do the same.

A look of concern spread across the shepherd's face. He seemed to see them for the first time: how miserable they truly looked after days—or was it weeks?—wandering in the marshes, starving and terrified. Girin supposed they must look frightful.

"Come on," said the shepherd. "My house isn't far from here. It's not much, but we'll give you something hot to eat, and a soft bed."

"No!" Girin gasped, instinctively, pulling away.

The shepherd raised a hand gently. "It's all right," he said. "No one's going to hurt you."

She kept shaking her head, but something in her was also breaking, She shuddered, and began to cry again.

"Come on," the shepherd repeated. "We'll take care of you."

The shepherd's house was a simple hut of woven reeds, standing at a place where the marsh turned to firmer ground, and the reeds gave way to grazing-grass. The house commanded a clear view of the whole plain, from the marshes below all the way to the vast purple mountains in the distance. The whole land seemed to be empty, apart from this house.

Inside, around a crackling fire, the shepherd's wife gave Girin and Balih clay bowls of simple barley stew, which they ate ravenously, and mugs of tart-beer, which they gulped eagerly.

Balih fell asleep after that. But Girin sat up with the old couple around the fire, staring into the dancing flames, thinking of all that had happened. And before she could stop herself, the whole story came pouring out of her—Susuda and the taking of Kish, the battles against the other cities, the birth of Balih and her flight with Hazi away from the city, the attack, and Hazi's death.

The farmer and his wife listened patiently, her face contorted with the pain of sympathy. When at last Girin had run out of words, the farmer poured her a fresh mug of beer, and spoke while she sipped the foamy liquid.

"It's not just Susuda," the farmer said. "It's all of them now."

"All of who?" Girin asked.

"All the lugáls," the farmer's wife replied. "Once Susuda showed it could be done, the other lugáls drove their people to rise up against their cities' temples."

"Now armies march back and forth across the land," the farmer said. "War is everywhere. You're lucky you left when you did."

"Not just war," the farmer's wife said. "Taxes. For protection, they say."

"Protection?" Girin asked.

"Every few weeks, a band of soldiers comes marching through here," said the farmer. "Sometimes in the white and red of Kish, and sometimes in the yellow and black of Lagash. They always demand something: sheep, beer, whatever we have."

"Sometimes we have nothing," the farmer's wife said. "And then they take whatever they can find."

"It'll be the end of us," said the farmer.

"It's the end of Shumér," said his wife. "The end of civilization."

Girin thought for a long time, staring into the flames. She thought about many things: about Susuda and Hazi, about little Balih, about the farmer and his wife, about war and death and civilization.

At last she looked up and met the eyes of the farmer and his wife.

"I think I'll stay here for a while," she said.

𒌋𒐈

THE MEN FROM Kish arrived five days later: kilts of white and red, leopard-skin cloaks, bronze helmets. Girin watched them approach the reed hut from a hiding-place among the boulders of the low hill country, a little ways off across the plains.

As soon as the farmer had come running back to the hut, gasping that the soldiers were approaching, she'd handed little Balih to the farmer's wife, who doted on the boy, and hurried them away from the house, down among the reeds at the riverbank, where they wouldn't be seen.

She watched the soldiers march toward the hut, laughing and joking among themselves. Only five of them. One of her, and five of them.

As they came near to the reed hut, she crept down from her hiding-place and raced across the plains, blocked from the warriors' view by the hut. Just as they crossed the rough wood fence around the sheep-pen, she emerged from behind the reed house, sickle swinging loosely in her hand.

The soldiers' eyes widened.

She recognized one of them: Baragi Broad-Wings, who'd walked out onto the plain with her and Hazi and Susuda, to meet the men from Lagash, that morning that felt so long ago.

"It's you," Baragi said, rather stupidly.

"What are they saying of me, back in Kish?" she asked.

"That you're a traitor," Baragi said. "That you and that bastard Hazi betrayed your lugál. That you fled into the wilderness and died."

"And is that what you believe, Baragi Broad-Wings?" she asked.

He looked her up and down, carefully. "Where is Hazi?" he asked at last.

"Dead," she said. "Killed by Lagash-men."

"I'm sorry," Baragi said. "Truly, I am. I liked him."

"So did I," she said drily.

"And I liked you, too," he said. "But right now, you're standing in my way."

She nodded thoughtfully. "So this is what it comes to," she said. "A dagger-fight for some scrawny sheep. If only Susuda could see us now."

Baragi chuckled softly. "It's not too late," he told her. "Come back to Kish. Plead your case to Susuda. Maybe you'll catch him in a good mood, though those are rare these days. Anyway, old friendship's got to count for something."

"And then what?" she asked. "Fight the soldiers of Lagash over some tiny bend of river? Roam the countryside, stealing from poor farmers?"

"It's not stealing," sneered another of the soldiers, a lanky man she didn't recognize. "It's taxation."

"It's pathetic," she said. "This is why you killed the én and took over the temple?" She gestured around them at the empty grassland and at the half-ruined reed hut. "This is your glorious new Shumér?"

"All good things take time," Baragi said.

"And you've already taken too much of mine," she snarled. "Let's get this over with." She hefted her sickle. A few of the soldiers stepped back, apprehensive.

"Wait." Baragi raised a hand.

She eyed him suspiciously.

"We might not disagree as much as you think," he said.

The other men turned and furrowed their brows.

"Life's not so grand in Kish, to tell the truth," Baragi said. "Susuda's had half the old clan leaders killed. He's half-mad with drink. Spends most of his days down at the school—though it's not much of a school if you ask me. Lot of young boys swinging daggers, gulping down wine, chanting 'death to our enemies,' and all the while Susuda's marching up and down the ranks, telling them they're invincible, and that spears will break against their flesh so long as they conquer in his name."

Girin gazed at him for a long time, remembering what Hazi had told her of Susuda's promises to build new schools for the children of Kish. Half a world away, it seemed now, and half a hundred years ago.

"I'm sorry to hear it," she said at last.

"That's what Kish has become," Baragi told her. "Any day, the axe could come down on anyone's neck."

"So much for old friendship," she replied.

Baragi nodded in agreement. "What would you say to a new—eh— partnership, so to speak?"

She gaped at him, incredulous. "What me and the five of you? March back to Kish? If you want to lead me into a trap, Baragi, at least make it one that doesn't insult my intelligence." She raised the sickle again.

"Wait!" Baragi raised his hand. "It's not just us. It's a lot of fighters from Kish. And we've got backing from the Lagash fighters, too. We could use someone with your experience."

She rolled her eyes. "Wonderful. So Kish can be ruled by another despot—one from Lagash this time."

"Or," Baragi extended a hand to placate her, "we choose the new ruler together."

Girin looked into his eyes for a long time. She could see no lie there, but this was all so strange and so sudden.

"Listen," Baragi said after a moment. "Pick a place. In five days, I'll be there with three hundred fighters."

She watched him warily. Even the men by his side seemed unnerved.

"Just name the place," he said again.

She looked into his eyes one last time, searching for any hint of a lie there. She saw none.

"The big palm grove," she said at last. "The one at the crossroads, by the riverbend south of Kish. You know it?"

He nodded, smiling. "Five days," he said.

"No tricks," she told him.

〈𐎹𐎹𐎹〉

THEY CAME, AS promised. Girin could hardly believe it, but hundreds of fighters from Kish—even some of Susuda's own men—marched with the men of Lagash today. Hundreds of them assembled at the crossroads where the palm trees grew by the riverbend south of Kish.

Yesterday she'd left little Balih with the farmer and his wife, who were happy to take the boy, and had trekked to the tall cliffs overlooking this palm grove. She'd camped atop those cliffs for the night, hidden in a spot with an excellent vantage over the palm grove below, and a hidden escape route if Baragi pulled any tricks.

But she saw no tricks. She only saw what Baragi had promised: three hundred men of Kish, white-and-red kilted, tattooed with the lion-headed *anzû*-bird; and four hundred or so blue-and-gold-kilted men of Lagash, marching alongside the Kish-men as if they'd been brothers all their lives.

And so she'd gone down to greet Baragi, who walked at the head of this strange army.

"Won't Susuda notice so many of his fighters missing?" Girin asked him as they lunched on dried fish and flatbread by the riverbank.

Baragi laughed. "I forget how long it's been since you were in Kish," he said. "Susuda rarely leaves his private chambers nowadays. As long as he's well supplied with wine and women, he'll notice nothing amiss."

Girin pondered this. "And the fighters who remain loyal to him?"

"They're too afraid to fight," Baragi answered, "but they've promised to back us when the time comes."

"And when is that?" she asked.

Baragi shrugged. "We can be back in Kish in another five days."

She searched his face for some sign of a joke, but saw none.

"Why not?" he shrugged. "The sooner the better."

And so they marched the next morning, the armies of Kish and Lagash, seven hundred tattooed, kilted men with long daggers and spears and leather shields, some in leopard-skin cloaks, many others in simple homespun fabrics. Across the plains and up the river they marched, northward to the city of Kish, which loomed like a vast face of mud-brick cliffs over the crumbling canals and farmland.

No soldiers came to meet them at the gate. Only a gaggle of weary soldiers who greeted the travelers with open arms. As the Kish-men and Lagash-men marched over the crumbling flagstone streets, amid dying palm trees and cracked, untended column and porticoes, the people came out in droves to welcome them, cheering and shouting encouragement as they marched along the broad avenues, past the armory and the market-stalls, toward the palace, whose red-columned face greeted them with the only well-maintained paint left in the city: bright-painted designs of red and white.

Soldiers stood aside to let them pass. They strode through the outer courtyard, where warriors lounged on cushions by low tables, drinking wine in the shade of short-palms. They passed through the inner garden, where a long shallow pool had turned green and sludgy, dead fish floating on its surface. Drunk warriors and tavern maids glanced up without curiosity as they passed. No one seemed to be able to fathom what was happening here.

At last they reached the inner chambers of the palace, a dense maze of red columns and painted frescoes: leopards and bearded bulls, red-and-white geometric designs and awnings of intricately woven cloth.

A pack of red-kilted warriors ran out to meet them—little more than boys, really; their spears held awkwardly, their helmets fitting poorly atop their heads. They gaped out at the warriors who swarmed into the palace behind Girin and Baragi, and they gulped as they stood their ground.

Susuda burst out from the midst of them, stumbling, a hand over his eyes to shield them from the midday sun. The round wool cap of kingship sat cockeyed atop his braided black hair. A robe of bright red linen, fringed in white, hung loosely around his hairy chest, where a silver medallion gleamed. He'd grown fat as a sacrificial pig—the stretched flesh of his stomach warping his tattoos into grotesque parodies of the beard-faced *lamassu* they once were. Beneath his bulging gut hung a loosely belted kilt of deep blue, its fringed hem brushing his bare feet.

Girin could scarcely believe this was the same man who'd marched out to the field with his champion fighters, a short lifetime ago, and proposed to kick out the én and take over the city of Kish.

"What is the meaning of—" Susuda began, then paused when he recognized the attackers. "Baragi? Girin?"

"Susuda," Girin said, unable to keep the sadness from her voice. "What's happened to you? What's happened to Kish?"

"You—!" He extended a finger at her, his arm wavering drunkenly. "You're dead!"

"All too alive, I'm afraid," she replied. "Though I can't say the same for Hazi."

"Hazi..." Susuda muttered.

"Lagash-men killed him, while I watched," she said flatly. "They recognized us. Wanted vengeance for your betrayal of the pact. You invaded their lands, so now they canvass the countryside, killing every Kish man and woman they can find. All except the five hundred of them who are here with me today, to take this city back."

Susuda shook his head. "Why did you leave?"

Girin swallowed, her throat dry. "We had a son, Susuda."

A hint of a smile played at the edges of the lugál's lips. "You and Hazi. A son. I'd like to meet him."

"You never will." Girin's expression hardened.

Susuda's drunken smile warped into a snarl.

"Enough of this!" Baragi Broad-Wings barked. "You know why we're here."

Susuda laughed sadly. "To kill the lugál, eh?" He stumbled back, falling on the palace steps. "What's left of him anyway," he said, sighing.

Girin took a step closer. "Susuda," she said. "What happened to you?"

He gazed up at her, his face a mask of sadness. Whether his eyes were moist with tears or from the drink, she should not say.

"The God Énlil no longer speaks to me," Susuda said, so quietly she could scarcely hear. "He promised me I would be a great wind, sweeping over this land. I have done everything he asked. And where is he now?" He removed his wool crown and ran his hands through his hair, pulling the braids apart.

Girin and Baragi glanced at one another, unsure. There hardly seemed any satisfaction in killing such a man as this.

"For so many days and nights I prayed to my God," Susuda was saying. "But I heard no answer. I ate the sacred bread until colors and voices swirled around me, but none of those voices were Énlil's. I drank the milk of the joyplant until I slept for days and soiled my bed. But he was nowhere in my dreams."

The lugál was weeping now, tears running down his wine-stained beard. "Where is Énlil?" he cried suddenly. "Where is my God?" His eyes fixed on Girin and Baragi, as if they might hold the answer.

"Your God is everywhere in this wretched land," Girin snarled. "In every shattered city wall. In every field piled high with the dead. Do you not see him all around us?"

Susuda gazed at her for a long time. "Are those things the work of Énlil," he asked, "or of men like me?" He shook his head. "I do not know."

"Enough of this," Baragi snapped. He nodded to his fighters. "Take him."

"Take me?" Susuda barked humorlessly. "You want this?" He bent and plucked the wool crown from the tiled floor, and threw it at Baragi. "Pick it up. Take it!"

Two warriors ran forward and seized Susuda about the shoulders, pinning his arms behind his back.

"Which of you will rule in my place?" Susuda cried as they dragged him away. "Who will wear the crown and hold the sceptre? Will it be you, Baragi Broad-Wings? Is this what you hunger for—to know no guidance, and call into the empty night, to a God who will not answer?"

The fighters dragged Susuda out of the palace courtyard, still wailing and shouting in despair. When at last Girin could hear his voice no longer, she let out the breath she'd been holding.

After everything—after the battles to take the city, the flight across the countryside, so many near scrapes with death—she felt almost disappointed that it had to end this way. Was this all that was left of the great Susuda? A fat drunkard who had no wish to put up a fight?

Baragi turned to her. "In all that madness," he said, "the man did ask one good question: what do we do now?"

She pondered that for a moment, scanning the crowd of stunned court-boys and tavern women. Among the cracked tiles and wine-stains, the helmeted fighters of Lagash stood with spears at the ready, awaiting their next orders.

"Now," she told Baragi, "we work out, between us, what is truly best for the people of Kish."

WITH SUSUDA KEPT under lock and guard in a small house, the palace emptied out fairly quickly. Within a day, the drunk warriors and lounging tavern-maids were gone. Girin and Baragi agreed that the warriors of Lagash should receive some reward for their loyalty, even if they never had to lift their spears. They carried off golden chalices, tables and chairs—whatever they could strap on their backs—and began their long march back to Lagash.

A week later, Girin and Baragi sat in the council chamber with Shatámurrim, the én of Kish, trying to decide what to do now. A crowd assembled in the courtyard below, anxiously waiting to learn who their new lugál might be, and what was to become of their city.

"We can't give rulership back to the temple," Baragi said, pacing around the table. "They'll squeeze us even more mercilessly than before."

"I've already talked to them," Girin said, seated calmly in a chair. Little Balih sat in her lap, playing with his favorite toys: a wooden goat and sheep, carved for him by the farmer who'd watched over him this past week.

"While the Lagash-men were emptying out the palace yesterday," Girin said, "I went to the temple and made a deal. The én and the temple will handle collection and distribution of goods, like before—but from this day forward, the lugál will command the city's fighters and workers. And in times of crisis, his decisions will be law."

Baragi nodded thoughtfully. "Who'll be the new lugál, then?" he asked.

They turned to Shatámurrim, who fidgeted nervously in his chair. "I would recommend," the én said after a moment, "that the new lugál must be a person loyal to the temple. Someone with no personal ambitions, who values peace and stability."

A wry smile crossed Baragi's lips. "And where might we find such a lugál?"

"Let's go to the balcony," Girin said. "Ask the people what they think."

Shatámurrim opened his mouth to raise an objection, but closed it when he saw Girin shoot him a sharp look.

"Very well," Baragi said. "Why not? Let's see what the people have to say."

Girin rose and joined Baragi and Shatámurrim at the window, carrying Balih in her arms. In the courtyard below, a crowd of farmers and merchants milled about nervously, pale wool kilts mingling with colorfully woven togas; coiffed beards next to shaved bald heads and dirt-caked arms. When they saw their leaders at the window, they fill silent, pointing and nudging one another.

"People of Kish," Shatámurrim's voice boomed, surprisingly deep and strong. "Your days of tyranny are over. It is time to choose a new lugál."

The crowd murmured, glancing at one another, unsure. No one had ever offered them such a choice before.

"Who will you have as lugál?" Shatámurrim asked. "Who will command the fighters of Kish?"

Silence fell. For a long moment, Girin felt sure a fight would break out, and the whole mess might begin again. But then the people began to cheer a name. Her name.

"Girin!" They were shouting. "Girin for lugál!"

Her eyes went wide. She glanced at Shatámurrim and Baragi, who were shouting frantically over the roar of the mob. She didn't have to read their lips to know what they were saying: *Never has a woman been lugál.*

As the crowd quieted, Shatámurrim gave voice to her thoughts. "This is—most unusual," the priest declared. "Never has a woman held that position."

"Until now, perhaps," said Girin. "But now that tradition, too, is broken."

At last, she thought she might understand the meaning of the dream she'd had, on the night she'd first known that little Balih was growing inside her: a woman seated atop a mountain, with a golden sceptre in her hand and a little boy on her lap, and her tears drowning all the world. *That woman is me.* And the sceptre meant...

The crowd cheered, pumping their firsts, chanting her name: "*Gi-rin! Gi-rin! Lu-gál Gi-rin!*"

She hefted Balih on her hip, and leaned forward, shouting to be heard over the crowd. "Your days of war are ended," she told them. "I will send Susuda into exile, and send messengers to the other cities: no én or lugál in all Shumér will give him quarter. He and those like him will be banished from our land."

Baragi whirled on her, startled. "But the things he did to your family—to all of us! Surely he deserves—"

"Susuda pays for those crimes, even now," Girin said. "But the days of blood-vengeance are over in Kish. From this day forward, this city is a place of peace."

GIRIN WAS DREAMING. She knew, in some place inside herself, that she was sleeping in the royal bedchamber in Kish. But in her dream, she walked with Susuda.

Sweat ran down the lugál's plump belly. His kilt was tattered and caked in sand. He carried a leather satchel of dried fish and stale bread, stumbling west, through a wilderness of flat plains studded with thorn bushes and tall palms, and groves of juniper and elm.

Days passed before her in the dream, until she saw Susuda reach the shore of the Swift River, where he bought passage on a tiny, leaky boat. When the boat landed on the far shore, Susuda marched west again. She watched as he bartered the last of his dried fish for passage southwest across the desert, through Aram and K'nan, where a great stone city called Jericho rose above the sands, its towering walls unchanging and unfathomably ancient.

Many more days and nights passed in a whirl, as she followed Susuda across another desert even bleaker than Aram: a sprawling dead waste where only camels would go, and strange voices sang out in the starry nights above the swirling sands.

Until at last, she saw Susuda arrive at a place where the desert gave way to farms; rows upon endless rows of green barley fields, fed by far-reaching canals from a vast river that spread across the land like veins in a hand.

In the way one knows unspoken truths in dreams, Girin knew that the name of this land was Misr. Its almond-skinned people spoke a language utterly unlike anything she had ever heard. She watched as Susuda begged water from the strange people, and slept on a mat in one of their reed huts. Now it seemed as if months were passing before her eyes: she watched as he toiled in the fields and fished in the river, teaching the people the Shuméru tricks for baiting hooks and finding the right spots for fishing, and began to learn the words of Misr.

Although there were many cities in this land, the people said, there were no éns or lugáls, no battles between the temple and the local rulers, and no wars that ravaged the countryside. Instead there was one man, not a priest but a God in the flesh, who kept all the land in balance.

Girin listened as the people told Susuda that their god-king had completed a great project: a vast tomb in the desert. A shining white mountain where his body would dwell for all eternity. She followed Susuda as he made a pilgrimage to that place, where they saw that the stories were true: a gleaming white mountain rose above the sands, taller and more perfect even than the great temples of Urim and Níppúr, its majesty capped by a shining point of purest gold.

And it was there, in the strange land of Misr, in the shadow of the perfect white pyramid, that Girin's dream faded. There Susuda remained, just another poor farmer on the green banks of the Nile—gone forever from the Land Between the Rivers.

She woke among soft pillows. The first rays of dawn lanced through the thin, high-set windows of her bedchamber. Little Balih snored softly next to her. She rolled over, wrapped her arms gently around him, and smiled through the tears welling in her eyes.

567 YEARS EARLIER
3057 BC

...and then the Flood swept over.

— The King List of Shumér

Y

For as long as he could remember, Ilku had wanted to fly.

As a young boy, he climbed the tallest trees in the city gardens, watching the birds leap from the branches above, spread their wings, and take flight. He shimmied out onto the highest branches, ignoring the worried shouts of his friends below, and imagined what it would be like to have wings—to leap from the end of a branch and not fall to the ground, but to rise, into the sky, free from the pull of the ground in a sea of air.

Once, in his twelfth summer, he was napping on his family's roof, as children did during the midday heat. He dreamed of flying far above the city, watching the tiny houses passing below him as he swooped and soared in the air high above. He awoke in confusion, unable to feel the air rushing around him.

Still half-asleep, he walked to the edge of the flat roof, two stories above the ground, and leapt off, flapping his arms furiously, willing with all his might to rise into the air.

His mother heard his body hit the stones, and ran out into the street, shrieking and beating her breast amid a gathering crowd of shocked neighbors, pleading with the Gods to spare her son's life. The Gods answered her prayers, but the fall broke both Ilku's legs. He would never walk again.

But he soon learned a different way of flying. When he closed his eyes, he could fly above the great city of Unúg, and see its streets and buildings as a bird would. He could rotate any object, real or imagined, see how it fit together, and understand how to build it.

In the autumn of that long, restless year, he saw a donkey-drawn wagon roll up the road to the city gates, and had an idea. He gathered wood planks from his father's workshop and built a little wheeled cart, just high enough for his hands to reach the ground. He folded a wool blanket on top, climbed atop the blanket, and pushed. Oh, how his arms ached at first—but he was so exhilarated he barely felt the pain. Now he could travel anywhere his little wheeled chair could roll.

His father was impressed with the chair, and taught Ilku the craft of construction: the tricks of selecting the right planks for wheels and wagon-sides, of laying bricks in the right places, and of planning a canal or a barley-field. And though he stood much shorter than other men, and many still laughed at him in the streets, Ilku became a master of crafts, and earned himself a workshop in the city of Unúg, with a generous stipend of bread and beer from the temple.

But as his skills and reputation and stipend grew year by year, he held onto his dream. Someday, he told himself, he would soar above the city of Unúg, and see it for himself.

And so, amid assignments to build wagons and wheels and forges and beer-vats, he began to capture birds to keep in cages in his workshop where he could study them. He gained their trust with crumbs and morsels, and taught them to sit atop his hand while he stretched out their wings, inspecting the delicate interwoven networks of feathers and bones.

Without telling anyone, Ilku began to build a strange craft. He joined wood planks together like bones, stretched canvases and nets across them, and jointed intricate sheafs and levers beneath them, like birds' wings.

He told no one about the craft he was building. And one day, though he would not name the day, Ilku knew that he would climb into his craft and soar above the streets of Unúg, just as he dreamed of doing that summer day long ago.

TODAY WAS A festival day in Unúg. The Goddess Inanna had made the harvests of barley and dates bountiful with her heavy rains. And today the clouds had parted, as if even Inanna herself had grown tired of the ceaseless downpour. The sun shone on drying mud-brick apartments and shops and market-stalls, their walls running with half-liquified mud, now half-dried and hardening. It would be many days' work to scrape the walls clean, to apply fresh clay, and to re-paint the intricate frescoes of white and black and red.

But no one would be working during the festival. Today, the én and all the priests stood smiling atop the steps of the temple, greeting a parade of men and women who marched up Unúg's broad central avenue, past columns decorated with mosaics of tiny dots in patterns of red and black—the designs clean and perfect, not running like the paint on the shops, because every dot on every column was a tiny carved cone of colored rock, hammered into the sun-baked clay.

Up the sunlit avenue marched temple acolytes, naked, their heads and bodies shaved in keeping with ancient tradition. Around them danced women in fleece kilts, breasts bared to the sun, baskets of dates and barley in their arms. Naked children ran and squealed around the procession of people tramping joyously past the colonnades and frescoes that lined the city's central avenue, where the red-painted doorways of mud-brick houses stood in neat rows among gardens of palms and elms and cedars. *Tigi* and *zamzam* reeds whistled their harmonies to the thumping beat of *ala* and *balaj* drums.

Even the ground was cleaner in this part of the city: polished flagstone, unlike the muddy trails of the outer suburbs, where mud-brick shacks sprawled wildly amid dirt paths, bending streams and patches of grass. Here in the center, within the sacred inner walls, Unúg was a pure, orderly city. A geometrically perfect reflection of Heaven on Earth.

But Ilku could only watch from the sidelines, sitting in his wheeled chair, peering around the legs of onlookers. From down here, he could barely see what was going on up at the temple. Its broad central staircase led up a facade of pillars and carved bas-reliefs: Gods embracing priests. Trees and bowls overflowing with water. But this huge building was only the lowest platform of the temple.

Two side-staircases converged on the great square house atop the building. From that house a single staircase ran onward and upward, ascending the second layer—an imposing colonnaded facade whose roof was a great courtyard planted with palms and flowering vines. Upward from there sprang the topmost level of the ziggurat, a temple atop the mountain of temples, plated in purest white limestone, appearing tiny against the sunny sky, though Ilku knew it was the size of a palace.

To the west rose the great wall enclosing the inner temple precincts. Through its towering gates, a column of priests were leading a procession of unblemished white cattle and goats, headed for the reed house, a ritual reconstruction of an ordinary marsh-hut at the base of the ziggurat's central staircase, along whose edges bright red pennants whipped in the wind.

Someone jostled Ilku's shoulder. His chair went wheeling across the crowd. He put out his hands just in time to stop himself from slamming headlong into the legs of an old man, who whirled in surprise, dodging out of the way at the last moment.

"Sorry, Ilku. Didn't see you there." The voice was all too familiar: Namhu, tall and handsome, thick-bearded, in a long fleece kilt whose belt fit perfectly beneath his chest. Grinning, as always, in a way that made Ilku feel slightly inferior.

"Nice to see you," Ilku said, using his hands to turn his chair around to face him.

At Namhu's side stood short, wispy Erseti, his ever-present companion. And Eala. Eala was here too. Ilku's heart leapt.

"Don't look so hurt, Ilku. It was only a little joke." Namhu grinned broadly, and put out an arm for Ilku to clasp.

After a moment, Ilku accepted. His muscled hand clenched the other man's arm a bit more tightly than necessary, and he smiled inwardly at Namhu's slight flinch.

"I'm glad we ran into you," Eala said. Her breasts were bare today. Round and perfect, like ripe fruits. Her tan skin shone like polished sandstone in the sun. "It's been a while."

"Sorry I haven't been around much," Ilku told her. "I mostly sleep at the workshop these days—"

"Doesn't my wife look lovely today?" Namhu interrupted, throwing an arm around Eala's bare shoulders. Ilku had no choice but to agree, and turned away uncomfortably.

"I've been looking forward to this for weeks," Eala said. "The end of this rain."

"I'm just happy to be drinking outdoors," Erseti said, taking a swig from a skin of beer as he leered down at Ilku with his beady eyes.

"I see you're starting in early," Ilku commented.

"The only way to drink all day is to start in the morning," Erseti said with a smile, dropping into a crouch next to Ilku's chair.

Ilku couldn't hold back his laughter. "All right," he said, reaching for the beer-skin, and took a long gulp of the cool, tart liquid.

"See?" said Erseti. "I knew I'd bring you around to my point of view."

"What are you working on these days?" Eala asked.

The question startled him. For an instant he wanted to tell her everything—about his wings, and his birds, and the craft he was building. But Namhu was standing right here. Ilku felt pulled in two directions at once.

"Look!" Eala broke the silence. "They're about to kill the goats!"

Ilku broke Eala's gaze, half relieved that he hadn't had to make up his mind. He wheeled himself to the front line of the crowd, where he got a clear view of the priests at the base of the ziggurat's central staircase, raising the sacred dagger to slit the throat of the first goat.

He'd seen the ritual before. Most everyone in the city had. But it was a distraction—and it was a reason to stand near Eala, and catch her gaze every now and then. So Ilku watched, as tens of thousands like him had watched for thousands upon thousands of years, as priests at the base of the temple slit the throats of seven goats, and others at the top slaughtered ten unblemished bulls. They were almost too far away to see from down here. They looked like ants.

Ilku wondered what the scene looked like from the sky.

ᛉ

On the day the big man came to Ilku's workshop, it was raining hard again. The rain had started up a few days after the festival, and it had been pelting the city ever since. Streams of wet clay and paint ran down the sides of buildings, streaking the shops and temples, pooling in the streets.

Ilku was testing the movement of a wooden wing at a table in the back corner, when he heard footsteps in his doorway. He hurriedly threw a canvas over his secret craft in a way he hoped didn't appear suspicious.

"I hear you're the best craftsman in Unúg," boomed a voice from the entrance.

A man strolled into the workshop, enormously fat and flanked by two fierce-looking fighters. All three of them wore kilts of red and black, and were covered, neck to navel, in tattoos of hooved beasts with serpentine necks and snarling leopards' heads. The fat one wore a sash of soft leather, adorned with fine beadwork and polished carnelian.

"You have heard correctly," Ilku replied, wheeling to face them.

"Do you know who I am?" asked the one who'd spoken.

"Should I?" Ilku replied.

The man smiled. "I," he said, placing a meaty hand on his chest, "am Lugál Kalama."

"Glad to know you, lugál," Ilku replied.

"This is how you respect the big man?" grunted one of the fighters, stepping toward Ilku threateningly.

The fat man waved his hand dismissively. "You truly don't know who I am," he said. "Do you?"

Ilku shook his head helplessly, beginning to wonder if he should be afraid.

Kalama chuckled softly. "You don't get out much, do you?"

Ilku shook his head. "I don't much like it on the streets. I prefer my shop."

The lugál nodded thoughtfully, as if he approved of this. "Well, my little friend, you might say I run the streets of Unúg."

Ilku furrowed his brow. "But doesn't the temple run Unúg?"

One fighter snarled and reached for his dagger. But the lugál put out a hand to stop him.

"The temple," he said to Ilku, "might say they run this city, it's true. But I run the streets."

Ilku wasn't sure what that meant, but he nodded in agreement anyway.

"What can I do for you, lugál?" he asked.

Kalama laughed heartily, shaking the menagerie of strange beasts tattooed on his belly. The fighters laughed with him. "I like this boy," said the lugál. "I truly do. Straight to business. You two could learn something from him."

The fighters grumbled their assent.

"Well then," said Kalama. "To business. What do you know of boats, Ilku?"

"Boats?" said Ilku. "I've built them. All kinds. Fishing boats. Even a barge or two. What sort of boat do you need?"

Kalama leaned in close to Ilku. His breath reeked of beer and fish. "That's what I need you to find out," he said.

"I'm—not sure I understand," Ilku said.

"The Gods send us rain," Kalama said. "Rain every day. More rain than any of us can remember."

Ilku nodded thoughtfully. It had been raining a lot lately, now that he thought about it.

"I'm no fool," said Kalama. "Soon the great dam will burst. The rivers will overflow their banks. A flood will sweep over Unúg, and all the cities of the Riverplain. Any man with eyes can see this."

"I should hope it doesn't come to that," said Ilku. "The city dam is stronger than it looks." But even as he spoke the words, a fear crept up from his belly. The lugál was right: no one had ever seen rains like this before. Never in living memory.

"Well, maybe the dam will break, and maybe it won't," Kalama said. "But let us get one thing straight: if this flood comes, Lugál Kalama will not drown."

"Let's hope none of us will," Ilku said.

"You're going to build me a boat, Ilku," Kalama said, pointing a finger at Ilku's chest. "A boat that can survive this flood, and carry me, my men, and our families to safety."

Ilku hesitated a moment. "A boat of that size," he said at last, "has never been built before."

The lugál's belly shook with a soft laugh. "If anyone can find a way, it's you. Or so I've been told."

"There is—" Ilku cleared his throat. "—also the matter of my fee."

Suddenly the lugál was looming over Ilku. He willed himself to sit straight-backed on his chair, though his head barely reached the man's thigh, and look the lugál squarely in the eyes. The lugál gazed down at him for a few moments, his expression unreadable.

"I'd like to make you an offer," Kalama said after a moment. "One I don't make to many people."

Ilku nodded for the lugál to continue. In truth, he'd suddenly found his mouth too dry to form words.

"I could use a man like you," Kalama said. "Clever. Fearless. Good with his hands. Men like these aren't exactly—" He gestured at the two thick-muscled fighters behind him, who were poking suspiciously over neat clusters of copper pipes Ilku had arranged on a nearby table.

"Please don't touch those," said Ilku, as one of the men reached out to paw at the polished pipework. The men turned away with a sneer and a grunt.

"As you can see," Lugál Kalama continued with a dismissive gesture, "men like these are really only suited for certain tasks. Well suited, to be sure, but—limited in scope. You, on the other hand? Well. We could do some very interesting things together, you and I."

"What kinds of things?" Ilku swallowed.

A hint of a smile crossed the lugál's thick lips. "Just about anything we set our minds to, I should think."

Ilku pondered this for a moment. "I can't leave my workshop," he said at last.

Kalama looked almost hurt. "I wouldn't ask you to," he said. "I only ask one thing from you."

"Fealty, I suppose," Ilku said.

The lugál shook his head. "No. I only ask that you admit you need my help."

Ilku's brow furrowed. "And why would I need your help?"

"Because, Ilku." Now Kalama was really smiling. "The supplies for your projects don't come cheap. Oh, they're worthy projects, I've no doubt. But you owe the temple for, what, five thousand mina of wood? Two thousand of copper? Don't look so surprised, Ilku. I've seen the records. Not even the temple keeps secrets from Lugál Kalama." The lugál sank into a squat next to Ilku, meeting him on eye level. "At the rate you're going, Ilku, you'll never escape those debts. But I can wipe them all away." He waved a hand, as if brushing away a fly.

"You mean, you'll replace them with another debt," Ilku said. "A debt to you."

Kalama shrugged and rose to his feet with a grunt. "I can offer you certain things," he said. "Things the temple cannot." He glanced back at the two burly men, who were now inspecting the intricate rope nets hanging from the ceiling—the unfinished result of nearly a year's intensive work.

"Don't touch that either!" Ilku cried out, then added, "please" as the burly men rounded on him, scowling.

"I know it's not easy for you in the streets, Ilku," Kalama said, seeming not to notice the tension. "I'd have figured a smart man like you would've hired some help by now."

"What sort of help?" Ilku scanned the muscled men suspiciously, wondering what they'd paw at next.

Kalama shrugged. "I'm not as fit as I used to be, Gods know. Can't run to save my life. Can't throw a punch like I once could." He jiggled his enormous belly, smiling wistfully. "But my mind, ah—my mind is still sharp enough to get me into trouble. So these days, I let others throw the punches."

Ilku watched the fighters pick over a stack of metal plates on a table in the back of the workshop. Possibilities began to form in his mind. Thoughts he tried to push away, but couldn't.

"Maybe next time someone shoves you in the street," Kalama said, "you've got someone by your side who shoves back."

For one instant, Ilku very nearly said yes. But he managed to wrestle back control of his thoughts. No matter how much he owed the temple, he knew the temple didn't break legs or stab men in alleys. He knew what his father would've done.

"I'll just take my usual fee," he said. "Ten silver-portions per week, or the equivalent in temple credit. Plus the cost of supplies."

One of the burly men snorted. "Doesn't come cheap, does he?"

Ilku opened his mouth to reply, but Kalama spoke first: "Good work never comes cheap."

It was as if the big man had taken the words right off Ilku's tongue.

"Thank you for your offer," Ilku told the lugál. "I'm sure many others in this city would be glad to accept it."

"Ah, but I don't want another man." Kalama grinned. "I want you."

Kalama drew a deep breath, sighed, and waved away Ilku's reply. "I don't need an answer right now," the big man said. "Take a few days to think it over. In the meantime, I'll tell the temple to give you whatever supplies you need to get started. And of course, all the bread and beer you can swallow."

Ilku almost wanted to laugh at this man who talked of giving orders to the temple as if it were a common tavern. And at the same time, a strange excitement rose in his belly—the exhilaration of beginning a new project, fully supplied, for the first time in months.

"Don't worry," Kalama told him. "I'll talk with the ration-priest tomorrow morning. You'll have whatever you need. Just build my damned boat."

"I will do my very best," Ilku said.

The lugál seemed to ponder this. "I've no doubt of that," he said after a moment. "No doubt at all."

Then he called to his burly followers, who were gazing around the workshop in obvious boredom. They snapped to attention and hurried to his side, and raised a calfskin above his head as they stepped out of Ilku's workshop into the pouring rain.

Ilku watched the rain for a long while after the men left. Thoughts whirled in his mind; the same thoughts he'd been fighting back as the lugál had made him the offer, ideas he'd nurtured since childhood of having someone big and strong by his side, watching his back. They'd never been more than fantasies, but today they'd almost become real.

He turned away from the rain and the doorway. A hint of an idea was already forming in his mind, but nothing complete yet. It would have to be brought across, from the world of becoming into the world of being. Ilku rolled from table to table, extinguishing candles. When the windowless room was dark, Ilku slipped out the door, into the rain-drenched twilight, and wheeled toward the great Slow River that flowed through the city's heart.

Beneath mud-brick walls marked by tiny windows, under bridges and around market-stalls he rolled, navigating among the roots of flat-topped clay towers that rose amid clay-daubed houses of every height, heaped like children's blocks in great piles tapering toward the cloud-bruised sky. He wheeled past bundles of straw and palm leaves lain outside doors to dry, now soaked and mouldering in the rain, around open sewage ditches threatening to overflow their banks and spill their sharp-reeking contents onto the streets.

At last he emerged under open sky, onto the reed-choked banks of the Slow River, where long boats of bundled brown reeds bobbed in the waves, roped to wooden poles, canvas and hide tied tight over the cargoes as their owners drank away the evening in riverside taverns, waiting for the rain to let up. He dragged his wheeled chair through the soft green grass and tiny white flowers at the very edge of the water, pushing through the tall stands of tightly-growing reeds that swayed high above his head, swatting at mosquitoes that rose from pools of half-stagnant slime at the river's edge.

He leaned out over the slow-churning current, its muddy waves percolating with raindrops. He took seven long, slow breaths, allowing his mind to fall still and silent. Then he bowed low, bringing his face close to the water's surface, and began to pray.

How long he whispered into the murky depths, he did not know. Time always seemed to move strangely when he spoke with those in the river. But after many repetitions of his plea, he saw the gleaming backs of great brown-scaled beasts surging above the waves, diving again, then rising closer. His heart leaped with the same mixture of terror and joy he always felt at the approach of the river-sages.

The enormous fish churned and surged about the banks of the river. Dozens of them, some the length of Ilku's arms, others as fat as hogs; and a few, the most ancient of all, as vast as great boulders, their mouths yawning like caverns that could swallow Ilku whole as they thrust their faces forth from the muddy water, only a finger's length from his outstretched fingertips.

It has been a long time since we spoke, Ilku, a voice hummed in his bones, as the scaly messengers churned the river into a muddy froth. It was not the fish themselves that spoke, Ilku knew, but the God Énki, whose words passed through his appointed messengers, as it had since the world's dawn. The God's voice felt deep and wise. It sounded old but not aged; familiar yet terrifying.

Not so long ago, the voice hummed deep in Ilku's marrow, *people came to the water every day to ask my guidance. Has Unúg grown tired of its God?*

"The priests say Inanna alone is the Goddess of Unúg," Ilku whispered back after a moment. "They say the city of Eridu belongs to you, Énki, but not this city. So people here have stopped praying to you."

All except you, Ilku, the God's voice rumbled within him. *Why is it that you, alone, continue to pray to me?*

Ilku's first thought was to respond with some pious phrase about his undying faithfulness, or his love for the ancient God of the Abzu—but he knew from experience that Énki would be unimpressed with such an answer. "You are the Father of Cleverness," he whispered into the depths. "And you always tell me something clever."

And because you—and you alone—care to hear what I have to say, the God's voice hummed in his mind, *I will tell you a clever thing I have told no one else.*

Énki had once shared many secrets, Ilku knew, with people who simply came to the water and asked for them. The ideas of cities, kingship, law and marriage had all come forth from the waters of the Rivers in the world's first days. *Mhé*, these ideas were called. Special gifts from Énki. The building blocks of civilization itself.

Ilku himself had been blessed to receive a *mhé* once, when he was only a boy, in that long summer when he first learned the trick of rolling in his wheeled chair. He'd come down to the river and prayed for what felt like days, until a great river-carp rose up from the depths and whispered to him in the God's voice, telling him the trick of making a *lilis*, a goblet-shaped drum with a low, plaintive voice. When he built the first *lilis* and played it for his father, the old man had given Ilku a very strange look, as if he knew this was more than just an ordinary invention. The deep thump of the *lilis* drew many admirers, and soon Ilku was making the drum for musicians across Shumér. And all the while, Ilku's father kept looking at him strangely.

"Whatever *mhé* you choose to give me," he whispered, trembling with excitement, "I will treasure it in the very core of my heart."

Not a mhé, the God's voice hummed. *A warning.*

And as always, he felt the vast form of the God rising up from those depths to meet him, like some titan sea creature singing in a voice deeper than sound.

But this time, before the God reached him, he found himself in another place.

He was walking in a courtyard next to a temple, similar in structure to the one here in Unúg, terraced and mountainous—yet much taller and broader, its tip seeming to pierce the sky; its terraces blossoming with trees and flowering bushes. In the shadow of this vast temple he strolled across a flagstoned courtyard. A man walked next to him, young and scarcely bearded, garbed not in a typical fleece kilt, but in a strange long robe woven of blue and red.

Most strangely of all, Ilku realized, he wasn't in his wheeled chair. He was standing and walking on his own legs. The thrill of it stole the breath from his lungs.

"That's quite a costume," the young man told him.

Ilku glanced down at himself. He was clad in a fleece kilt and tattoos of red and black, as any man of Unúg might wear.

"I could say the same of you," Ilku replied. "What land do you come from?"

"From Babili," said the young man. "And you—I can see you've come all the way from ancient Shumér, before the Flood."

"The flood—?" the word rang in Ilku's ears. He stopped and placed a hand on the young man's chest. "Are you saying this flood really happens?"

The young man shook his head, confused. "Of course the Flood happened. It washed away all the cities of Shumér.

Only a few people survived. They became the founders of the new dynasties."

Even here in the dream, Ilku felt his flesh had run pale. *The flood is truly coming!* "What can we do?"

The young man furrowed his brow. "Is this some kind of a test?"

"Yes," said Ilku, nodding eagerly. "A test. How did people survive the flood?"

"I only know the story of one survivor," the young man said. "The stories say he built some kind of strange vessel that carried him over the waves."

"A strange vessel." Ilku had no idea what this meant. Perhaps Énki had yet more plans to reveal. "Perhaps that will prove to be the answer."

The young man looked more confused than ever. "What about my questions? The wisdom I asked for?"

Ilku shook his head. "What wisdom? What are you talking about?"

"What of the movement of objects on earth?" the young man demanded. "Do they obey the same laws as bodies in the heavens?"

Ilku only stared back at him, utterly baffled. "I know nothing of the heavens," he said. "But so far as I have seen, all things obey the same law: the faster one rises, the faster one falls."

The young man gazed into Ilku's eyes as if he'd just bestowed a splendid gift. "Thank you," he said, smiling.

Then the temple and the courtyard and the young man were gone, and Ilku was back on the bank of the Slow River, whispering with the great fish-sage beneath a rainy twilit sky.

This is my warning, Ilku. To you and only you, the God's voice hummed inside his very bones. *Soon the waters of my Rivers will rise, and none will be safe. Build the great boat you have been commissioned to build.*

This was what Ilku saw: a boat as tall as a house, as long as many wagons lain end to end; built of thick planks of cedar, caulked with rock-hard tar; a boat that looked too enormous to float on any water. And here it sat, in a workshop in the center of Unúg.

There in the twilight beside the Slow River, Ilku began to smile. He knew how to build it.

But build for yourself a smaller vessel, the God's voice hummed on. *Complete the craft you have been building in secret—the vessel about which no one knows save you and me. For the men on the great boat will seek to do you harm.*

And Ilku saw something else—another kind of vessel. Not quite a boat, nor a wagon, nor any kind of vehicle he recognized. But he saw, clear as a sunlit day, how it would work.

In this small vessel will I preserve you, the God's voice hummed. *For only you still listen to me.*

Then the great river-carp sank back beneath the muddy waves, returning to the vast dark kingdom below. Ilku sat for a long time in the reeds beside the river, letting the rain pelt his head.

If the God had meant this message to comfort him, it had done just the opposite. Ilku shivered in the darkening dusk, as if the River's chill currents swept about him even now.

"He asked you to build *what?*" A stunned smile spread across Eala's full red lips, revealing her lovely white teeth.

Ilku lost himself for a moment—but her giggle brought him back to himself.

"My absent-minded inventor," she teased.

He could still hardly believe his luck, bumping into her in the market alone. Namhu and the others were nowhere to be found today. Probably because of the rain, he thought. It was still pouring, as it'd been pouring for days. The onslaught of cold droplets forced Eala to walk close by his side as he rolled through mud puddles, ducking beneath awnings and wood-framed alleyways.

The last time he'd walked alone with her must've been—truth be told, he could hardly remember. Years ago, when they were scarcely more than children, and her body had just begun to flower...

"A—a boat," he answered her, suddenly, shaking his head to clear away the other thoughts. "He ordered a great boat, to carry him and his family, and all their beasts. He believes a great flood is coming."

She shook her head. "If the lugál wants it, then it must be for some evil purpose. You know what they say about that man: 'He's like a hyena. He'll eat anything that stinks.'"

Ilku shrugged. "It's a commission. He's paying for all of it, and anything I ask from the temple in the meantime."

"Oh, to have that wealth," she said. "Well, you've built boats before, haven't you?"

"Small ones," he said, turning his wheeled chair sharply to dodge around a cucumber-seller's wagon. "Fishing boats, a few barques and ferryboats for rich priests. I'm not sure anyone's ever built a boat this big. It's not like..." He paused, wondering whether it was a good idea to tell her about the boat Lugál Kalama had demanded of him.

They reached the end of a long row of awnings, and rushed together through the rain to an aisle of sheltered stalls across the street. Merchants hawked all the scents and colors of the world: sprigs of fresh green mint and coriander; striped cumin seeds and black peppercorns piled in sacks; goats and sheep in pens of reeds, rimmed with dried thorn-vines to keep the beasts from escaping. Carts piled with pale pumice stones, bright red poppyflower paste for lipstick, black kohl for eyeshadow, and vivid blue chunks of indigo-stone in woven baskets. A whole world one might fly across, if only to capture an impression of its tastes and smells.

"It's not like what?" she asked him, reminding him where he'd left off.

"Well, it's not like other boats," he told her.

"What does that mean?" she asked, pausing to sniff a tray of sweet-smelling cardamom, whose scent brought a soft smile to her lips.

He wanted to ask her if she remembered what he was remembering: those long-ago afternoons when they ran through the neighborhood, chunks of her grandmother's fresh-baked cardamom bread steaming in their hands, to the grassy riverbank where they sat among the reeds eating the sweet bread, talking of...

"I'm supposed to build it bigger than any other boat," he told her, as they moved on from the spice-seller's stall. "Big enough to carry all the lugál's men, along with his sheep and goats. Says he can tell a flood is coming. Knows it, somehow."

"It's not hard to tell that floods are coming. She furrowed her brow, raising a hand to catch the rain.

"Not any ordinary flood," Ilku said, as they crossed again, to a row of pottery stalls stacked with fired clay vessels and brightly painted vases. Nearby, Ilku could hear the grinding of bronze blades on whetstones and see sparks flashing in the clammy air. "A great flood. Powerful enough to sweep away whole cities."

She stopped, and knelt to look him in the eye. "Is such a thing really possible?"

A memory came to him, unbidden: Lugál Kalama kneeling before him in his workshop, face level with his, the big man reminding him of his debts, offering to wipe them all away, and give him much more, besides. He wondered if that offer included passage on the great boat, should the flood truly sweep through the city.

"I don't know," he told her, truthfully.

He couldn't remember the last time he'd been this close to her, looking this deeply into her dark brown eyes, and smelling the perfume in her hair. He tried to think of something to say to keep her close a while longer.

"They say this world was formed from water," he said. "Abzu and Tiamat, the sweet and salt seas, churning together where the city of Eridu stands today. If all this land was water once, perhaps it may be so again."

A worried look crossed her face, and she rose, turning away from him. Suddenly he regretted his words and wished he could make her smile instead.

"It's unlikely," he said. "Even in a great flood, the water would only reach our knees here."

But she seemed not to hear him.

"I have to go, Ilku," she said. "It was lovely to see you."

He opened his mouth to voice a protest, but she kissed the top of his head and hurried off in the direction of home, leaving him sitting beneath the awnings, rain splashing in the puddles in the street, speckling his face with muddy droplets.

After a moment, he turned his chair and wheeled in the direction of the temple.

※

"So that's—let's see—seventy planks of oakwood, twenty barrels of pitch, a barrel of nails—" The ration-priest glanced up from his clay tablet and furrowed his brow at Ilku, who sat on his wheeled chair across the desk. "By all the Gods, Ilku—what are you building this time?"

"Something big," Ilku said. "Lugál Kalama is definitely paying for all of this?"

"Shh!" The ration-priest, thick-jowled Emendurana, hissed a warning. "We don't use his name here."

Ilku rolled his eyes. "Very well. My anonymous patron is paying for all of this?"

"I could scarcely believe it myself," Emendurana muttered. "But he came by himself this morning. Told me you'd be stopping by. I told him you're in debt up to your eyebrows, and that you never pay. But the gentleman insisted."

"Your kind words are a continual inspiration," Ilku said.

"I presume you'll be wanting sweet-beer and bread, too?" the priest asked.

"And a barrel of river-trout—fresh, not salted," Ilku said. "And a rack of smoked mutton, if you've got it."

"Throwing a feast, are we?" Emendurana asked, drily, carving the symbols for sweet-beer, bread, fish and mutton into the grid inscribed on the clay tablet before him. "Or trying to impress a lady?"

Ilku almost flushed at that question, but chose to ignore it. "Perhaps I mean to make a sacrifice," he said, smiling innocently.

"That'd be the day." The priest grunted. "Why Énki favors you with such inspiration, I'll never know. It's not as if you've ever done him homage."

"Not publicly," said Ilku. "Énki and I have—a special sort of relationship."

Emendurana threw him a look of exaggerated boredom. "Will this be all?"

"Until I think of something else," Ilku said, grinning.

With deft hands, the ration-priest rolled his personal cylinder-seal across the top of the tablet, unrolling a scene of two priests chatting among stylized lions, flowers and birds into the soft clay. He tore off a smaller chunk of clay from a pile near his desk, draped in a wet rag to prevent it from drying out, pressed the chunk into a flat square, inscribed a few symbols into it, and rolled his seal across the top.

"There's your receipt," he told Ilku. "Don't lose it this time."

"And miss out on a week's ration of sweet-beer?" Ilku replied. "Unthinkable. When can I expect all this to be delivered?"

"The beer and food, by tomorrow morning," Emendurana said. "The wood and pitch—depends how soon we can get a wagon through the mud. This rain is slowing everything down."

"Even me," Ilku commented.

"One wouldn't think such a thing was possible," the priest replied. "Now if there's nothing else...?"

Ilku stuck the clay receipt into his belt and wheeled his way out through the rainy courtyard, past the temple's workshops where knife-sharpeners ran blades along sparking whetstones, coppersmiths hammered out ploughs and chisel-axes atop their anvils, pottery workers shaped wet clay on spinning wheels, brewers stirred foaming vats of sacred beer, chanting hymns to Ninkasi, Goddess of the vats; and weavers wove strong cloth of *aktum*-wool at their looms, humming songs to Uttu, the spider-Goddess in the yarn; while teams of tile-cutters, mosaic-makers, chisellers, relief sculptors, and glaziers crafted statues and paneled scenes for the temple complex's halls and sanctuaries.

He stopped in at the main public sanctuary, out of habit more than anything else,to reach up into the basin of water near the entrance—a reminder of the world's first temple at Eridu on the shores of the Abzu. He splashed a few drops on his forehead, just in case the Énki felt like blessing him with any particularly clever ideas today.

Then he wheeled out past the towering inner walls of the temple complex, where pigeons roosted, cooing softly in holes in the worn mud-brick. Raindrops began to pelt his head again as he rolled out the main gate, back onto the city's ordinary streets. He dodged among the men in fleece kilts and women in swishing *bardul*-skirts and flowing dresses of *niljam*-wool, all of them hefting reed baskets piled high with onions and shallots, or seed turnips, or bushels of hulled barley and beans; or carrying young lambs, or bleating goats, or noisily panicking ducks slung over their shoulders. Everyone was rushing on some important errand, trying to escape the downpour.

In the center of the square, a wrinkled, bald-headed priest announced, "Inanna sent this rain to punish us! We have done something to anger her. We must discover what sin we have committed, before she destroys Unúg forever!"

A soaked crowd had gathered around him: shepherds and goatherds among their flocks, yelling encouragement. Farmers' wives bearing baskets of onions and turnips, jeering and laughing at the spectacle. Young scribes from the temple, shouting disputes that were swallowed by the crowd's roar.

"This city loves Inanna," a plump goatherd shouted through the rain. "What could we possibly have done wrong?"

"I know not," the scrawny priest cried. "I pray and pray, but the Goddess does not answer me!"

"Then what are you standing here yelling for?" an aproned brickmaker shot back. "Go pray some more! Get us some answers."

"It is not Inanna we've angered," declared a long-bearded man in a linen toga. "It is the God Énlil. Our people have turned away from him!"

That remark drew more jeers. Someone threw a turnip. "You're from Níppúr, aren't you?" the brickmaker demanded of the long-bearded man. "I can tell by your dress. Énlil has your whole city to worship him! What does he want with us in Unúg?"

"Perhaps it's Énki," someone else suggested. "What if the people of Eridu have failed in their sacrifices, and now their God has turned on us?"

"It is not Énki or Énlil we have to fear!" the aged priest thundered, wiping rain from his eyes. "Each city serves its own God or Goddess, and our duty in Unúg is to serve Inanna! She will destroy us if we do not turn from our sin!"

"What sin?" the brickmaker spat through the pelting rain. "What have we done to deserve this?"

Ilku turned from the debate as more rotten fruit began to fly. Escaping, he followed the flow of the milling market-crowd along clay-plastered walls speckled with fragments of dry reeds and pebbles, lined with spiderweb cracks like crushed eggshells, worn away in spots like raw skin, revealing ragged patches of mud-brick and stone beneath—walls decorated with painted icons of wheat sheaves, birds, zigzags and other symbols that marked gangs' meeting spots and lovers' haunts.

He was wheeling under the awnings of the rain-spattered marketplace when Namhu and Erseti blocked his path, along with two other men he didn't like the look of—scowling, with beady eyes, and jagged symbols tattooed unevenly across their chests and arms.

"What luck," Namhu said, "meeting you here."

"A pleasant surprise indeed," Ilku answered, trying to keep his voice even.

"And where might you be coming from?" Namhu asked. "I mean, after passing time with my wife, of course."

A cold hand clutched in Ilku's stomach.

Namhu's mock-friendly expression turned to a snarl. "What were you thinking, filling her head with tales like that? She's spreading this story of yours about a great flood all over the neighborhood."

Ilku wiped rainwater from his eyes. "The flood wasn't my idea," he told Namhu. "In fact, I am strongly against it."

Erseti stepped forward. "One day," he sneered, "That sharp tongue will get you into something it can't get you out of." The two unknown men converged on Ilku from the sides.

"Four of you, to fight one cripple?" Ilku asked. "Am I truly so fearsome?"

"He's got it on him," snarled one of the strangers. "I saw him slip it into his belt!"

"What, this?" Ilku asked, holding up the clay receipt. "It's all yours, if you want it—though it's got my name written on it,

The Cradle and the Sword

and the priest knows me personally, so I'm not sure what good it'll do you."

The second stranger glanced at the speaker, uncertainly. "I thought you said he had gold," he snarled in a thickly accented voice.

Namhu gazed down into Ilku's furious eyes, rain dripping down his face. "Perhaps he does have gold," he said, holding his gaze. "Only one way to find out."

"Come on, then." Erseti pushed Ilku, sending his cart rolling backward. "Cough it up."

One of the strangers ran behind Ilku's cart and put out a foot to stop it.

"I don't have any gold," Ilku insisted, trying to turn to look up at Namhu and the others.

The first stranger drew a short copper dagger from his belt. "Last chance, cripple."

Erseti took hold of Ilku's hair; wrenched his head back.

"I told you," Ilku said. "I don't—"

Before he could finish, someone knocked him to the muddy ground, kicking him from behind. He coughed, spluttering rainwater and mud, trying to roll onto his stomach and push himself up. A foot slammed hard into his face, sending bright colors and pain exploding through him, knocking him onto his back.

Then hands were all over him, probing, pulling, tearing, while someone held him in the mud.

By the time they were finished, he was half naked, freezing, covered in welts already turning yellow and purple; his lip and nose split, his mouth tasting of blood.

They didn't find any gold on him, but they'd taken the clay receipt.

THE WIRY GUARD looked Ilku up and down, wearing an expression that made it clear he wasn't impressed with what he saw.

"You don't demand to see the lugál," the man said. "The lugál demands to see you, when it pleases him."

A scar ran from his mouth up the side of his face, with small symbols tattooed along its length. Leopard-headed monsters were tattooed along his arms, across his chest, and down his legs.

He reclined against the mud-brick wall of an alleyway, beneath wooden rafters that supported the rickety houses above. The whole structure looked as if it might collapse at any moment, but it kept the rain off.

"I'm not demanding to see him," Ilku said. "I'm requesting an audience."

It was difficult not to wince with every movement. The bruises on his arms and belly were throbbing, and he knew his face must be covered in angry welts and half-dried blood. The attackers had shattered the wheels of his chair, and he'd dragged himself here through the mud, like a half-formed beast from a tale of primordial earth.

"You're that builder, ain't you?" The scarred man nodded, as if confirming his own deduction. "They've been talking about you. Saying you refused the lugál's generosity."

"It was not a wise decision," Ilku said. "I see the matter with much more clarity now."

The scarred man shrugged. "Why should the lugál care what you think now?"

"He said I had a few days to think over the offer," Ilku said, looking up at him. "It's been one day, and I've made my decision."

"Have you, now." The man huffed.

"Can I see him, or not?" Ilku asked.

The scarred man grunted a laugh. "You've got fire in you, I'll give you that." He pointed a thumb at the wood door behind him. "Go on, then."

As the man kicked the door open, Ilku maneuvered into the building, half-walking on his hands, half dragging himself over stacks of boxes and piles of bags scattered across the floor. This seemed to be a storeroom. At the far end, a staircase descended into a cellar. Ilku took a deep breath, braced himself, and descended the rickety wood steps, one handhold at a time.

Before he reached the bottom, he felt himself being lifted, and carried through candlelit dimness where he was set in a chair before he could protest.

He sat across a table from Lugál Kalama, who was counting a vast pile of clay tokens into neat stacks. On either side of him, sharp-eyed men did the same, placing some tokens in bags, others in piles, others on wood shelves.

As Ilku took in the details of the scene, he realized he was sitting level with other men for the first time all day. His exhausted arms drooped at his sides. As he relaxed against the firm back of the chair, he felt the pain of his bruises and cuts welling up more fiercely than ever.

"You took quite a tumble," Lugál Kalama commented, glancing up from his counting.

"You should see how the enemy looks," Ilku replied, trying to keep the pain out of his voice.

The lugál chuckled, continuing to count and sort the clay tokens.

"I've come to tell you—" Ilku paused, searching for the right words.

Silence hung in the air, thick as the rain outside. The other men looked up, staring at Ilku.

A thin smile crossed Kalama's plump face. "All you've got to do is say the words."

Ilku licked his lips. "I need your help, lugál."

Kalama's smile grew. "You need a favor," he said.

Ilku nodded. "One might call it that."

"I do call it that," Kalama said, pausing his counting and looking Ilku in the eyes. "That is exactly what I call it. A favor."

"Thank you," Ilku said, though he wasn't entirely sure what he'd just agreed to.

Kalama turned to one of the scarred, tattooed men who always seemed to be lurking nearby. "Tizqar, fetch a mug of beer for the lad. And a healer who can put some herbs on those bruises. That one on your face looks like an angry stormcloud."

Ilku gingerly raised a hand to touch the swelling, but the pain made him jerk away, his fingertips flecked with dried blood.

The scarred man hurried up the stairs and out the door on his errand.

"You've come here asking for a special favor, and I'm glad to do it," the lugál continued, resuming counting and sorting the clay tokens. "But that means the terms of our deal have changed somewhat."

"Changed—how?" Ilku asked, nervous suspicion rising in his belly.

"Well." Kalama waved his hand dismissively, as if the answer were obvious. "You'll have protection, of course. And whoever did this to you today—oh, they'll be sorry. More than sorry. Zamug and Atab will see to that. Won't you, boys?" The lugál turned to two of the scarred, tattooed men in the corner. "Take a few of your rowdiest men and go find—" The lugál turned back to Ilku. "Who shall they go find?"

Ilku swallowed, his throat dry. "Namhu and Erseti, in the cloth-makers' street. Namhu has long braided hair—"

"Oh, I'm sure these two will have no trouble finding them." The lugál nodded to his men.

The two scarred fighters glanced at each other, grinning.

"Well, what are you waiting for?" Kalama demanded. "Get it done."

Zamug and Atab heaved themselves up from the corner, and lurched up the staircase, casting cold, unreadable looks at Ilku as they passed.

Kalama turned back to Ilku. "We'll hear from them in a day or two, I'm sure."

"The terms of the deal," Ilku interrupted, drawing sharp looks from the others. He gulped, but found the words to continue. "You said the terms of the deal had changed."

"Ah yes," said Kalama. "So I did, indeed. Well, no special favor comes for free, of course. Today I do this for you, but I won't do the other matter we discussed."

"Other matter?" Ilku asked, though he suspected he knew exactly what the lugál meant.

"You're going to make me say it out loud?" Kalama rolled his eyes. "Very well. I will not wipe away your enormous debt with the temple. Is that clear enough for you?"

A few low chuckles went up from the men around the table.

Tizqar returned with the mug of beer, climbing down the stairs and plunking the clay vessel on the table in front of Ilku without a word, spilling foam into Ilku's lap.

"Healer is coming," the man grunted.

"Thank you, Tizqar," said the lugál.

Ilku echoed the sentiment, but the scarred man ignored him.

"I'll continue to pay for all the supplies you need to build my boat," Kalama said. "And I'll keep you in bread and beer—not only for the duration of this project, but for as long as I need you. Do you understand?" The lugál looked up sharply, into Ilku's eyes. "This is no longer a temporary arrangement. You are one of the family now."

Ilku made himself hold the lugál's fierce gaze, and nod. "I understand."

"Good." Kalama smiled and returned to his counting. "We'll initiate you soon enough. Perhaps tonight, if we can find the time."

"Initiate—?" Ilku felt his stomach clench.

"How's the boat coming along?" Kalama interrupted. "Should take you weeks of planning, I'm sure, before you can get started building the damned thing. But the sooner the better. Make no mistake, Ilku—I want a boat fit to carry at least twenty men, their wives and children, and plenty of cattle and sheep besides."

Ilku opened his mouth to explain that no one had ever built such a boat, and that lugál's boat would very likely sink, as any boat of such absurd size would. But instead, he found himself saying, "Men may call you many things, lugál. But let no man ever call you unambitious."

Kalama smiled. "Don't flatter me again, Ilku," he said, smiling through the sharp words. "Just get the work done. Are we clear?"

Ilku gulped. "Clear as water, lugál."

A smile spread across the lugál's thick lips. "I'm glad," he said, "that we at last see eye to eye."

Ilku was wheeling across the market square in his newly repaired chair, dodging around the mud puddles that now covered most of the ground, when the two thieves approached him. He recognized them at once: the scarred, wiry men who'd threatened him along with Namhu and Erseti, then fled after shattering him and his chair.

"Well, well," said one of them. "Looks like our little friend has found the copper to buy himself a new chair."

"And bread and beer from the temple," said the other, "unless I miss my guess."

"Where I've been and what I've bought is none of your business," Ilku snapped, looking them sharply in the eye.

"You'd better watch your tone," the first one growled, leering over Ilku, "unless you'd like a repeat of last week."

"Perhaps he's forgetful," sneered the second. "Perhaps he needs a reminder."

Ilku caught the eyes of two men across the square—thick-muscled warriors wearing kilts of the same red and black pattern he wore. The pattern of the lugál and his family.

"What do you think you're doing to our brother?" demanded one, striding over. The drizzling rain ran over the twisting scar on his cheek; over the strange tattoos of long-necked reptilian beasts that ran around his neck and arms.

"We didn't mean no harm!" the first thief squealed.

"He has something that's ours," the second thief explained. "We just want it back."

The fighter looked down at Ilku. "Is that true, little brother? Have you taken something from these men?"

"Not unless they own the temple," Ilku said "I went to claim supplies for my project, for the lugál—"

"We know who you are, little brother," said the second fighter, a wiry old man missing an eye.

Ilku remembered these men from his meeting with the lugál, a few days ago now. What were their names, again—?.

The wiry man winked at Ilku with his one good eye, then turned and twisted the thief's arm, hard. Ilku heard a crack. The thief screamed.

"If we ever see you bothering our little brother again," the burly fighter said, twisting the first thief's arm the same way, "we'll break more than just an arm. Clear?"

"Clear," grunted the first thief, collapsing to the dirt, writhing in pain.

The wiry fighter kicked the second thief to the ground. He scrambled onto his feet and fled.

Ilku looked up at the two tattooed fighters who'd just saved his life. "I owe you my thanks," he said.

They only chuckled. "Nothing to give thanks for, little brother," said the burly one. "We're family."

"But I don't even know your names," Ilku said, immediately feeling stupid for having said it.

They laughed again. "Kuwari says you're all right," said the wiry one. "That means you're the lugál's man. That's all we need to know." He put out his hand.

In all this strangeness, it was the word "man" that leaped out at Ilku. No one had ever called him a man before. "Boy," "cripple"— even "creature," but never "man," until today. The word felt alien; and yet it filled him with warmth, even on this cool evening. Made him feel taller.

"Well, from one lugál's man to another," he said, extending his hand, "I owe you my life."

They reached down and clasped arms with him, his delicate fingers wrapping around their scarred, tattooed muscles as their calloused hands closed roughly around his skin. "I'm called Zamug," said the one who'd spoken before. "The ugly one here is Atab."

"Well, I'm glad to know you both," said Ilku. "Of that I'm certain."

"Eh, no offense," said Atab, "but I just can't help myself— can you really build this boat the lugál asked for?"

Ilku grinned. "I'll show you, if you like. Why not? Follow me."

They walked together through the tight-winding alleyways, ducking beneath awnings to avoid the worst of the rain, dodging mud puddles where children splashed, spattering the mud-brick walls with grey-brown stains. Down they went to the riverbank, where felt tents had been sewn and tied together into one sprawling structure, long as a city block, tall as a house. The frame swayed in the wind and rain, looking as if it might collapse any moment.

The fighters glanced at each other nervously as Ilku pulled aside a scrap of fabric to let them inside.

Within the great tent stood a wood boat-frame—a cage of wooden ribs so tall their upper spars scraped the tent's ceiling, and so long it stretched from one end of the great tent to the other. Dozens of workmen scrambled among these planks, spreading caulking-tar, nailing boards into place, calling out orders, their assistant-boys fetching fresh tar-pots and nails from the barrels stacked neatly along the tent's walls.

"It should be finished in a few weeks," Ilku said, scanning the latest work. "If the tent or the frame doesn't collapse first."

The two fighters gazed up at the towering wood skeleton.

"How are you going to take it to the river?" Zamug asked at last.

"Ah, that's the clever bit," Ilku replied with a grin. "I won't have to bring it to the river. The river will come to us."

Outside, rain lashed the thin felt walls of the tent.

ᚼᚼᚼ
ᚼᚼᚼ
ᚼᚼᚼ

IT WAS DARK the next morning when he woke and felt her waiting at his side.

"Where is he?" Eala demanded. He could smell the oil in her hair, a scent he'd always loved.

"Where is who?" he croaked, struggling to sit up.

"Don't lie to me!" She leaned closer. He smelled old beer on her breath.

He blinked, wiping the sleep from his eyes. "Eala, whatever you think I know, I assure you—"

"You've been telling the whole neighborhood about your contract with the lugál," she hissed.

"He paid me to build him a boat." Ilku struggled upward, looking her in the eye as best he could in the dim dawn light. "That's all."

"Then you and Namhu got into that—" she continued, "that nonsense in the marketplace. Last night he went down to the tavern for a beer and didn't come home."

Ilku's eyes widened. Rain pelted outside.

"I knew it!" she cried. "You know where he is."

"I'm not sure what I know." He raised his hands, palms out.

"You went to the lugál and asked for revenge," she said. "Didn't you? Coward that you are. And now my husband is locked in a basement somewhere."

"Your husband," Ilku snapped back, "ganged up on me with three other men, beat me bloody, and shattered my chair. They left me in the mud, to crawl home. But I didn't crawl home. I crawled to the lugál—yes, I did. I admit it. What else would you have had me do?"

"Come to me!" Her eyes were wide now, whether from fear or rage, he could not say. "You could have come to me. I'd have..."

"You'd have what?" he asked after a moment. "Cared for me? Comforted me? Asked him not to do it again?"

She only gazed back at him, her lower lip trembling.

"I'll sort this out," he said, lifting himself off the bed. "I'm going to—"

A knock sounded at the door. Her eyes widened, and she rose.

He hissed "Eala, wait—!" but a familiar pair of tattooed, scarred men were already pushing through the doorway.

"Rise and shine, brother," said Zamug. "The lugál wants a word."

Eala threw herself at him, crying. "Where is he? Where is my husband?"

Zamug dodged out of her way, chuckling. Atab threw a muscled arm around her from behind, and held her gently but firmly as she realized the futility of a trying to break his grip.

"Friend of yours?" he asked Ilku.

Ilku sighed. "You might say that."

"Lugál Kalama wants a word," said Zamug.

"I heard you the first time," Ilku said, clambering out of bed and into his wheeled chair.

"Take me with you," Eala demanded.

They all stared at her as if she'd gone mad.

"Take me with you," she repeated, glaring up at Atab, who still held her. "I need to know."

The two men laughed again. "You've got interesting taste in women, brother," Atab said.

Eala walked with them cooperatively through the winding maze of streets, beneath a gray sky that drizzled with rain, as the sky had done for weeks now. The doorman at Lugál Kalama's private warehouse eyed them warily, especially Eala. But a few quick words got them in.

As his eyes adjusted to the dark of the vast mud-brick room, lit only by a narrow skylight admitting thin rays of dawn light, Ilku saw the lugál seated behind a thick wood desk, eyebrows raised in mild surprise.

"I don't believe I invited you to bring a guest, Ilku," he said softly.

"I invited myself," Eala snarled. "What have you done with my husband?"

The lugál locked eyes with her, and they gazed into one another, like two prowling cats, for a very long moment. At last, a smile slowly began to creep across the lugál's face. Ilku did not like that smile.

"I see," said the lugál, with a note of great satisfaction. "At last, it becomes clear."

The fighters glanced at one another unsurely.

"This is about her, isn't it?" the lugál asked Ilku, sounding matter of fact. "There's always a girl." He spread his hands, as if offering an apology for his ignorance to some judge only he could see.

"What are you talking about?" Eala demanded.

"Oh, my dear, surely you're not that stupid," said the lugál, gesturing at Ilku. "He loves you. He's loved you for a long time, though he knows he could never have you. Not in his—unfortunate condition." The lugál winced, as if Ilku's condition genuinely pained him.

Eala glared at Kalama, then at Ilku, her face enraged but not surprised.

"Perhaps all this could've been avoided," said the lugál, "if—well, but there's never any point dwelling on 'what if,' is there?" He waved a hand dismissively. "Take her outside for a moment."

Atab coaxed Eala back through the door into the rain, even as she snarled and bit at him. Only Ilku, the lugál, his right-hand man Tizqar, and a few scarred warriors remained. In the quiet, Ilku heard the pattering of rain on the mud-brick walls.

"You asked for this, Ilku," Kalama said flatly.

Ilku tried to swallow, and found his throat dry. "I know," he said.

"I've got a nice surprise for you." The lugál looked up at Ilku, clearly waiting for a response.

"I think I may already know what it is," Ilku answered.

Kalama snorted a laugh. "You're going to love this one. That I promise you. We've tracked down your friends Namhu and Erseti."

"Where are they now?" Ilku asked.

The lugál laughed again. "The real question is, when would you like to pay them a visit? They're in a place where they can't do you any harm, and they're begging for the privilege of giving you an apology. Although this Namhu took a bit of convincing first." He glanced at a wiry man counting tokens beside him. "Remind me, Tizqar—how much did it take?"

"Three fingers," Tizqar rasped.

"Ah yes." The lugál grinned mirthlessly. "It was when we took the third that he begged to offer you his plea for forgiveness."

Tizqar gave a single nod. "It was as you say, lugál."

Kalama nodded, satisfied.

Ilku's blood ran cold. He sat frozen like a statue, imagining how it felt to lie chained in a dark place, hearing the same question howled in your ear with every slice of the blade…

"That was," he suppressed a shiver. "Not necessary, lugál."

"Oh, but it was." The lugál spread his hands. "When a man insults one of my brothers, it is as if that man insults me. And no insult to the lugál," he raised a finger, "can go unanswered. This is the caulk that holds our city together. Come." He heaved his great bulk up from behind the desk. "Let us pay your friends a visit."

Ilku lanced toward the door. "What about—?"

"She will be here when we return," said the lugál, in a tone that brooked no argument. "Come. We have other things to do today."

⟨

As Ilku wheeled his chair through the dark, winding passageway beneath the city, following Lugál Kalama and his ever-present escort of wiry, tattooed guards, it occurred to him that the entire city seemed to be suffused with a network of musty, lightless underground caverns whose existence most people never guessed.

While ordinary folk revered the sun, the lugál seemed to be entirely at home down here in the dark, counting his credit-tokens, holding meetings that no one would speak of above ground. Ilku wondered whether the lugál, or some man like him, would ever burst out into the light of day, to reveal that he had held the city in his grasp from beneath the ground for years. The thought made Ilku shiver.

At last, they ducked beneath a low doorway, the light of their torches casting flickering shadows across the bars of a cage deep in this burrow. In the cage cowered two men, their arms and faces spattered with dark dried blood.

"Namhu," whispered Ilku, wheeling toward the cage. Namhu jerked back, raising his hands above his head. Three fingers were missing from his right hand, whose palm wore an ugly crust of brownish scab. Erseti stared at the wall, his eyes dead.

Kalama sneered. "Namhu!" he barked, thwacking his meaty hand against the wooden bars. "You have something to say to our mutual friend."

Namhu slowly lowered his hands, trembling. His eyes wore an expression beyond fear or hate; an abject animal gaze.

"I am," he began, then trailed off, gulping and gasping for breath.

"Namhu!" the lugál barked again.

"I am sorry!" Namhu howled. He collapsed against the back wall of the cage, weeping, tears running reddish down his face. "I am sorry," he said again, not looking at Ilku; only staring blankly into the darkness. "Please. I am sorry."

The lugál nodded, satisfied. "The other one," he said, "this Erseti, broke more quickly than we expected. Now he does not speak at all; merely squats in the corner and pisses himself like a dog." The lugál kicked the cage in disgust, sending both men scurrying for the farthest corner.

Ilku reached out his hand, and both prisoners cowered away.

"Well?" Kalama demanded. "Don't you have something to say?"

Ilku tore his eyes away from the prisoners in the cage, forcing himself to look up and meet the lugál's gaze. Torchlight flickered under the man's fat face, casting his eyes in pools of shadow.

"Was this necessary?" Ilku asked.

Kalama's expression soured. "This," he said very quietly, "is what you asked for."

"No," said Ilku. "I asked for your help. I wanted protection, not—"

"You asked for my help," the lugál replied.

"Set them free," Ilku told him. "The Gods alone know what sort of life they'll have now. But there's no point in them dying down here."

"Let me make something clear." Kalama squatted eye to eye with Ilku, his vast belly bulging over his knees. "When these men attacked you, they became my enemies."

"And your enemies must be punished," Ilku said. "I know."

"You'd better watch your tone, boy," Kalama growled.

Ilku drew a deep breath, suddenly realizing just how close he was to the edge. "Please," he said. "Let them go. I'll still finish your boat."

"Oh," the lugál's eyes narrowed in the torchlight. "I've no doubt of that."

"I will," Ilku reassured him. "It's coming along nicely."

"So I'm told," Kalama replied. "Zamug and Atab say you're quite the craftsman."

From the shadows, Zamug nodded in agreement, not nearly so friendly as he'd been a few days ago, in Ilku's work-tent.

"Finish it," the lugál commanded, rising. He turned to Zamug. "And you, finish them." He nodded toward the cage.

"No—!" Ilku cried, but Zamug was prying open the cage, grasping Namhu and Erseti by the hair, dragging them kicking and wailing across the burrow's packed-dirt floor.

The lugál bent over his prisoners. He ran his thick-fingered hands over Namhu's head, over the whimpering man's eyebrows, across his cheeks, over his lips, as if feeling for something beneath the flesh.

"Do you know what happens," the lugál muttered, "to my enemies?"

He rose and turned away as Zamug and Tizqar drew their blades across the men's throats, and two bodies slumped to the dirt floor.

"I never asked for that," Ilku snarled through clenched teeth.

Kalama whirled on him. "I'll not tell you again, boy," he hissed. "Watch your tone, if you want your lady to be treated kindly."

It was only for her sake—only for the thought of Eala, still held in a scarred fighter's arms outside the warehouse, that Ilku remained quiet and lowered his gaze.

"That's what I thought," said the lugál. "Now go finish my boat."

Kalama turned away. Once he'd stalked out of the chamber, stone-faced Zamug and Tizqar led Ilku back through the dark tunnels and up into daylight, their hands stained with the blood of his departed enemies.

〈𒁹〉

THUNDER CRACKLED ACROSS the cloud-cloaked evening sky. Gusts of wind lashed the canvas of Ilku's work-tent with sheets of rain, sending workers hurrying to nail down corners that lost their moorings as the storm burst inside, extinguishing torches and soaking the great wooden hull of the boat.

The enormous craft was all but finished now, its sides looming like the walls of a fortress. Men were ascending and descending the ladders that were leaned against the heavy planks as they applied a final coat of tar, and others swept torches across the caulk to hurry its drying. Still others rushed across the great boat's sprawling deck, double-checking the hinges of the bilge-doors; the planks of the deckhouse; the ropes that tied down the rudders and oars.

In the great boat's shadow, Ilku worked in his own frenzy, dragging himself across the wood frame of a much smaller contraption. Atop a high scaffold, a lattice of light wood surrounded a small chair, behind which sat a great vat, caulked to watertightness until it gleamed like a great white river-pearl. A network of ropes and pulleys hung about a vast pile of canvas-cloth, netted and stretched across rows of pikes at the craft's rear. This project had consumed three weeks of sleepless work, along with a lot of prodding questions from the laborers, which Ilku had declined to answer.

Outside, a great crowd of farmers, shepherds, millers, bronze-smiths, bricklayers and temple acolytes pressed in against the tent, peering through every tiny rip in the fabric, weeping and ululating, raising prayers and cries for mercy to the heavens, shouting questions and accusations to the laborers within. Only Lugál Kalama's men, stationed with hands on sword pommels around the tent's perimeter, kept the panicked people from ripping through the fabric and boarding the great boat by force.

"How many of us will the boat have room for?" a scarred old shepherdess demanded.

"I'm a butcher!" called a thick-bearded man. "You've got to eat on that boat! You'll need a butcher!"

"I'm no butcher, but I know what a man likes," shouted a lady of the temple, her eyes lined in black kohl. "All the ladies of Inanna know how to please a man."

"Inanna's the reason for this whole mess!" someone else cried. "Haven't you heard?"

Ilku had promised them answers when the craft was finished. Now it very nearly was, and they were unwilling to wait much longer.

The wind tore aside a section of the tent's roof, soaking the crews with a blast of freezing rain, and blowing the torches out. The tent fell pitch dark. Workers clambered down the ladders, cursing and spluttering.

"It's no good, boss!" shouted the foreman, shielding his eyes from the rain, roaring to be heard over the thunder. "If this rain doesn't lighten up a bit, we're finished!"

Ilku's eyes adjusted to the moonlight, and he saw men climbing down from the great boat's hull, their forms silhouetted or pale against the dark sky.

"Go home," he called to the foreman; then scanned the rest of his crew, most of whom were already fleeing. "Climb onto your roofs!" he called after them. "Pray to the Gods that that's high enough," he added, more quietly.

"What about you?" the foreman called to him.

Ilku scanned his small boat; shrugged. "I'll be—"

"Where's my boat builder?" boomed a voice from behind him. He would've recognized it anywhere: Lugál Kalama, his deep voice thundering even in this storm. "Where is Ilku?"

Ilku heaved himself down from the scaffold onto his wheeled chair, turning to face the lugál. "Your boat is ready, lugál," he shouted, wiping rain from his face.

The lugál had brought only a few of his most trusted men: Tizqar, Zamug and Atab, along with a few other wiry fighters Ilku didn't recognize. Behind him, a line of slaves dragged half-panicked cows and goats toward the tent, their breath steaming as they bucked and snorted.

"You truly do love to wait until the last possible moment, don't you?" the lugál thundered.

"Perfection takes time, lugál," Ilku replied.

"We'll soon see." Kalama snorted, swaggering up to tower over Ilku, scowling at the strange craft atop the scaffold. "And what's this?"

"Just a last resort," Ilku told him. "In case of disaster."

Kalama eyed him suspiciously. "Disaster for whom?" he asked.

Ilku gazed up at him, searching for a response but finding none.

"Get on the boat," the lugál barked after a moment. He turned to his men. "Load this little craft on board. Just in case," he glowered down at Ilku, "of disaster."

The Cradle and the Sword

Ilku sat in place, eyeing the lugál and his men.

The lugál's expression softened, just a touch. "I'm going to need a clever craftsman like you," he told Ilku. "We all are, wherever this flood takes us. We'll have to rebuild. You'll be the architect of a new city—a noble, if you want. Why not? Perhaps even a lugál."

Behind him, slaves were dragging cattle and sheep up the great ship's gangplank in twos, straining against the bucking necks of the thrashing, bleating animals.

"I don't want to be a lugál," Ilku said. "And I'm not getting on that boat."

Kalama's eyes narrowed. "Why not? Perhaps because it's a trap?"

Ilku spread his hands. "No one's ever built a boat that big before. I swear before all the Gods, every bit of my craftsmanship went into it, but I simply can't predict—"

Suddenly, as if from nowhere, the lugál dragged Eala forward from among his men, placing the point of a blade against the soft flesh of her throat.

"Get on the boat, Ilku," the lugál said flatly. "I won't tell you a third time."

Ilku looked past the lugál's thick arm, into Eala's eyes. Were they filling with tears? Or was it the rain? was neither angry nor fearful but despairing in a way that drove a cold spike through Ilku's chest.

"I'm sorry," he said, though he wasn't sure whom he was speaking to. "I'm so sorry."

Kalama sneered, running the point of the dagger down Eala's neck, slipping it beneath the shoulder of her toga. She winced and tried to pull away, but his grip only tightened.

Ilku heard a great crack; the sound of a great structure shattering and thundering to the earth. For an instant he feared the din was coming from the boat—but the lugál and all his men were glancing upriver, eyes wide with fear.

"The dam!" Zamug shouted. "The dam's burst!"

"Get on the boat!" the lugál howled, dragging Eala with him as he rushed up the gangplank, pushing past panicked slaves and cows and sheep.

Something like thunder rose up from the ground. It rumbled louder, shaking the earth beneath Ilku's chair, clattering the stakes of his great tent, sending the whole structure trembling as it folded inward over their heads.

As the canvas ripped aside, the crowd poured into the tent, men and women and children all fighting to be first to the great boat's ramp, shrieking and cursing and wailing like beasts.

"Not one of them!" the lugál screamed to his men. "Not one of them gets on my boat!"

A wave of churning water crashed through the collapsing tent, sweeping men off their feet, jerking them downstream like dolls; smashing the gangplank, hurling cattle and sheep and slaves into the air to plummet headlong into the rushing current, dragged beneath the froth as they splashed and screamed for their lives.

Kalama's men backed up the great boat's gangplank, laying about them with swords and clubs, rough cudgels and weapons that had no names, shoving men and women from the ramp to plunge headlong, screaming, into the rushing torrent below. Thick-muscled bricklayers and farmers shoved back against the lugál's fighters, who struck on all sides without reason or mercy. Bones cracked, men and women howled, and the rain-drenched air grew heavy with the scent of blood.

Ilku swung himself up out of his wheeled chair; clambered up the scaffolding; fitted his shriveled body into the chair atop his light wooden craft. He yanked a knife from his belt and slashed the nets that bound the heaping pile of canvas. Then he rummaged in his bag and drew out a pair of spark-stones and clinked them frantically in the pouring rain, huddling to protect the precious sparks. At last he struck one and lit a bit of tinder, and dipped the tiny flame delicately into the great caulked vat at the craft's rear, whispering a prayer to Énki: *Please don't let this all go up in flames.*

For a long, quiet moment, nothing happened. Time seemed to stand still.

Then a great flame belched forth from the vat, blasting Ilku's back with hot air, singeing the tips of his curly black hair. He cried out in pain. But the flame grew steadier beneath the canvas, which billowed and grew, bloating outward and upward as it filled with thick waves of heat.

Ilku took a deep breath, feeling the light craft rock on the rising waves. No more time. One by one, he cut the ropes that bound the craft to the ground. And even as the hissing wind tore away the last remnants of the tent above, the craft rose steadily, smoothly, up into the windy air.

The craft rocked sickeningly, buffeted by the whirling wind. Ilku held on tight as he rose higher, watching the tent grow smaller beneath him. Soon he could see the whole city of Unúg, its mud-brick building sprawled like lamp-lit anthills amid the rising, rushing tide of the river. He gripped the handles tight, and the craft continued to rise.

All around the land below, water roared. The wind tossed the tiny craft like a seed on the wind. Ilku huddled tight against his seat, closed his eyes, and imagined himself falling backward into a deep ocean.

〈𒌋𒌋〉

How long he rode the wind on that whirling craft, he could not say. Gray clouds surrounded him, and he sailed through fog, scarcely able to tell up from down. Sometimes light filtered through the pelting rain. By night he was swallowed by blackness, tossed on winds whose churning gave no hint of their direction.

At first he tried to measure the passing of time by his sleeping and waking. But even in his dreams the craft bucked and spun, waking him for minutes or hours to soak in the frigid water pooled around him, until sleep took him again. Soon, he knew, the oil would run out, and his craft would plummet from the sky. He only hoped he would fall into deep water.

Time passed: two days; maybe three, or four. His stomach grumbled, then ached and gnawed at him as if it might devour him from within. But he'd had no time to stock the craft with bread or dried meat. Sometimes he woke thirsty, and refilled his waterskin from the pools of rainwater collecting around his feet, and gulped down the cold, fresh water until he felt he might burst. It did not help the hunger..

Sometimes when he looked down, he saw the great boat he'd built, far below, tossed on waves in the tempest, whirling like a toy. He thought of Lugál Kalama, and weeping Eala, and others he knew. And always Namhu, terrified Namhu, cowering in the corner of his cage beneath the city, cradling the blood-crusted hand from which three fingers had been sawn. Namhu reached out to him with that hand and pleaded with him. But he found no words except, "I'm sorry. I'm so sorry." He repeated those words in his dreams, and again when he woke.

One morning he woke, and the craft was still. He knew it was morning because a thin shaft of sunlight pierced the cloudy sky above him.

He strained his ears, but heard no roaring waves or rushing currents. The craft didn't even seem to be rocking.

Ilku sat up. The oil had run out during the night. But somehow, his craft had come to rest, gently, in a rocky crag, high up the side of a mountain.

Something scratched softly at the canvas pooled above his head. A raven, strutting along the edge of the door, pecking at the tar curiously.

"Hello there," he told the bird.

It eyed him warily.

"Where have you come from?" he asked.

The raven cocked its head, examining him closely, curiosity in its gleaming black eyes. Then it took wing and descended to the water far below.

The Swift River meandered across the plains, muddy pools and tangled reeds along its banks. No house or tent stood there. Only scattered piles of brick, the foundations of what had once been temples or palaces, shattered heaps of pottery and bales of straw. And in the distance, the eroded remnants of a mud-brick wall, a line of vast clay mounds along the horizon.

And on that horizon lay the wreck of the great boat he'd built, a vast hole gaping in its shattered side. Goats and sheep were picking their way down the shattered timbers, seeking the fresh green grass that had already begun to emerge from the flood-soaked mud. Ilku could make out a few human forms among those distant silhouettes. One of them might be Eala, he thought. Or the lugál. Or someone else who meant him harm. The best thing, he decided, was to wait and see.

So he waited and watched. Two herons waded through the pools along the riverside, sharp-beaked heads darting beneath the water on long necks to seek the small fish and insects below. As Ilku sat and watched, the bloated body of a cow rolled slowly past in the current, its blocky head and feet flailing. A while later, the bodies of a few men floated by; or perhaps they were women. Ilku did not go down to inspect them.

Aside from these things, all was still, the only sounds the faint rush of the breeze, the distant cries of birds, and his own ragged breath.

He gazed over the landscape below, at the foundations of the once-great houses, and the scattered bricks, and the tiny fragments of the lives those places had contained. A strange lightness came over him, as though he weighed nothing at all; as though all else might sink into the earth or under the river, except for him.

And that, he thought, *is what it feels like to fly.*

2,708 YEARS EARLIER
5765 BC

Not a reed had yet come forth,
Not a tree had been created.
All the lands were sea—
Then Eridu was made.

— The Creation of Babili

Sunlight glimmered on the rolling waves of the Slow River. The current rocked their boat gently, as a mother rocks her infant. When it drifted too close to the riverbank, Zeru's father rose with his wooden pole to push the boat back into the heart of the stream. The river was flat and placid, so there was hardly any need to row. Zeru knew, from the stories of others who'd journeyed this way, that the river's calm meant they were near the Abzu. Lying back against the scratchy bundled reeds of the stern, she tried to imagine what it was like.

When Zeru's mother and father agreed to let her come to the Abzu this year—after weeks of begging and sweet words, not to mention evenings spent cooking dinners and washing clothes so they could see how grown-up she was—they made her promise two things: first, not to go with any man this year; and second, not to stay behind at the Abzu when her people returned to the village.

"I'm not interested in men," she told them, and it was true. She only wanted to see the Abzu for herself, to learn whether the stories were real. "And why would I want to stay behind when you tell me it's time to go back home?" she added.

They seemed reassured. A few days later, they packed dried fish and bread in their sacks, and joined the aunts and uncles and cousins and grandparents on this big reed boat to push off into the great churning, splashing water. They traveled south all day, stopping only to pull the boat in for the night and rest among the thick-grown reeds of a secluded little bay; but early next morning they were off again, riding the waves that tossed the boat and sprinkled droplets of foam across their skin.

When they reached a place the aunts and uncles recognized, they dragged their boat out of the river. Then, lifting it together, they set out carrying the boat in the direction of the setting sun. They walked all the rest of that day, until nightfall, until Zeru was sure her arms would give out. At last, when the stars began to shine, they caught sight of the lazy, rolling Slow River. After setting the boat amid the reeds of the riverbank, they lay down to sleep.

In the morning, they pulled the boat into the Slow River's muddy water and pushed off again. They moved more sluggishly in this current, sometimes poling the boat over a mudflat.

As Zeru paddled, she gazed over the side of the boat, catching glimpses of great river-carp. Their dark scales glistened as they rose from the depths to break the surface. Though the muddy waters concealed their movements, Zeru could see that many were long as she was tall, and plump as her grandfather. Their thin, wiry mustaches lent them the appearance of watery sages—appropriate, Zeru thought, since everyone knew these mysterious fish consorted with the God Énki himself, somewhere in the infinite deep. They were even known to rise up and speak on occasion, whispering strange new words and ideas known as *mhé*, to certain men and women chosen to complete special projects for the Gods.

She watched the great fish closely, straining for a hint of any word they might whisper as they rose beside the boat, then slipped away into the depths. But the sages of the deep kept their silence.

Here and there Zeru and her family passed other boats like theirs, all making their way down the Slow River, which wound like a wide flat snake toward the distant southern sea. They called out to the other boats, and the people in the boats waved and answered in strange accents, sometimes using words Zeru didn't recognize. Her aunts and uncles and grandparents called back, saying strange words she'd never heard before. But one word she recognized: *Abzu*. That made her smile. Everyone else was smiling too.

"They say it has no bottom," one of her older cousins said, leaning in to whisper.

Zeru furrowed her brow. "Every lake has a bottom."

"Not the Abzu," answered her cousin, shaking her head. "It just goes down and down, forever."

All the aunts and uncles and cousins started chattering excitedly as the boat drew closer to its goal. When it wasn't their turn to row, some of Zeru's older cousins talked about the beautiful girls they'd met last year, and the girls talked about the handsome men they hoped might propose to them. The aunts and uncles talked about their friends, and about the great parties at the temple, where everyone danced until dawn. The grandparents were mostly quiet, seated in the middle, happy to be traveling with the whole big family. They didn't often spend so much time together these days, as they all had when Zeru was young.

But Zeru had her own dreams of the Abzu. Not dreams of handsome men or marriage, or of wild parties, either. No, Zeru dreamed of what happened at the climax of those parties, of tales she'd heard of people gathering around the ancient temple on the shore, and a great and terrible thing rising from the deep, and those able to master their terror at receiving new *mhé*, straight from the mouth of Énki himself.

Zeru's mother and father had told her the those tales were just stories concocted by imaginative people to explain the clever deeds of men and women whose thoughts they couldn't understand. But if there was no truth at all to those stories, she thought, then why had people built a temple on the shore of the Abzu? Why did so many of them gather here every year? Not just for fresh fish and husbands, surely.

And why did people come back from the Abzu every year with new words, new tools, clever improvements to their daily tasks?

These thoughts swirled in her mind, like the river-water around their boat, as theirs joined other boats, and still others, until the wide river was thick with boats, every one packed with excited men and women, adorned in ways Zeru had never seen.

Here came a boat whose women wore many-folded togas dyed in intricate patterns of green and red and yellow; now another filled with men in wool kilts and copper-studded belts and leather headbands sprouting with bright feathers; now one bearing men, women, and children, all shaved bald, and all wearing soft furs and what looked like fishing nets, run through with pins of polished copper and jewels.

Many of the strange people's faces and arms were painted with symbols, stripes, and swirls of white and ochre, and some also wore tattoos of animals and trees and ocean waves, inked dark-bluish across their arms and chests; sometimes even on their scalps and faces. They laughed and called out to each other, always in odd accents, or sometimes with strange words

Zeru had never heard before. She called back with friendly words of her own, but the people only laughed and shook their heads, and returned her smiles and waves.

Her family's boat had to move more slowly now, bumping against other boats. They laughed with the steersmen, their boat sending explosions of reed-flakes into the river below. This was more boats than Zeru had ever seen. She tried to count them, but she gave up when she'd counted fifty. There were at least twice that many here, all bumping and sliding against each other from one riverbank to the other.

Stretching out before them was a sea of green; an expanse of tall reeds, their leaves dancing in the wind, in waves and hillocks all the way to the distant horizon. In the midst of that lush carpet, boats fanned out across a vast lake, their wood prows bobbing along the water's dark surface as they sought places to put in on the shore.

Someone struck up a happy tune on a set of pipes, and others pulled out drums and added a tapping, rolling beat that made Zeru want to dance. Others joined in with hand-cymbals and battle-horns, and soon everyone was dancing and humming along, moving warily so their boats wouldn't tip and dump them in the muddy water, laughing and shouting when they had a close scrape.

Dancing, shouting, laughing, listening to the music, they watched the sun crawl slowly toward the horizon as they made their way to the edge of the Abzu. It was nearly night by the time they arrived. Zeru could see the first stars beyond the pinkish-blue sunset. Then at last the boats ahead of them parted, and they sailed out into the open waters of the lake.

It was the biggest lake she'd ever seen. Not as big as the sea, of course, but still so wide she could barely see the boats docked on the far side. They waved goodbye to their musical friends as they set off in their own direction. Out here on the lake, everything felt suddenly quiet. Overhead, more stars began to appear. Moonlight flickered on the dark water.

Though she could not say why, Zeru remembered an evening from a long time ago, when she was a little girl. She'd been out gathering dates in the woods all afternoon, and got lost on the way home. She wandered to the edge of a forest glade, where the date-palms gave way to thick gnarled oaks and wild undergrowth. There in the shadows, she'd caught sight of something tall and dark, rearing its long-horned head. Some kind of grazing animal—perhaps an ibex—as shocked by her as she was by it. The creature watched her for the space of a few heartbeats, and then, with a crackle of branches, bounded away into the woods.

She stared into the shadows for a long time, wondering what world that creature had run away to, what it was like to look out from its eyes, what it was like to call that world home. That was what she felt out here on the Abzu, too, under the stars, staring down at the dark water in the moonlight.

By the time they found a place on the shore to tie up the boat, she was falling asleep with her eyes open. She stumbled around with the others, getting a fire started, helping to pitch their tents in the flame-lit darkness. She was ready to lie down on the hard ground and sleep, but Mama and Papa made her drive the tent stakes while they carried their sacks of food and blankets from the boat. When the tent was ready, she shuffled inside, collapsed on her soft bed-fur, and fell into the Sea of Dreams.

𒌋𒌋

SHE DREAMED SHE was swimming in a deep ocean, immersed in endless open water on every side. Up from the depths swam a great creature, bigger than a house, swimming slowly but heading straight for her. Its body was scaled and finned, like a giant fish, but its forelegs and head were those of the beast she'd seen in the woods so long ago; a horned ibex with gracefully curving horns and stern eyes. Looking into her eyes, it opened its mouth and began to speak in a deep thundering voice. She covered her ears and thrashed and tried to swim away because she was afraid of what the beast would tell her, but she couldn't move, and the beast came closer and spoke louder, and its words became her screams. She woke just before sunrise, sweating and whimpering, afraid to fall back asleep.

She crawled out of the tent, careful not to wake Mama and Papa, who were snoring quietly. The sky was softening from black to pale blue, and the first morning-birds had started to sing. It was cold. She wrapped a fur around her and walked along the shore of the Abzu, trying to forget her dream.

He was standing a little way off, skipping pebbles across the water. As she walked closer, she could see that he was a few years older than her. Sixteen or seventeen, maybe. No older than that. Instead of a wool kilt, he wore a garment of linen, woven in a pattern of black triangles and green lines, wrapped around his waist. His hair fell to his shoulders. She'd never seen hair that long. He wasn't one of the Fishing People; that much was certain.

He turned to look at her. "Are you going to stand there staring, or are you going to throw a rock?" he asked. His accent was all rolling r's, like the waves of the Slow River, the loveliest way of speaking that Zeru had ever heard.

She took a step back. When she found her voice, she said, "I don't know how to skip it."

A hint of a smile played about his lips. "It's easy," he said.

He showed her how to toss the stone lightly along the surface of the water, so it would skip two or three times. When he skipped stones, they sailed far out into the water, like boats.

"What's your name?" he asked her.

"Zeru," she told him.

"Why are you so shy, Zeru?" he asked.

"I'm not shy," she said, raising her eyes to meet his.

He laughed. "Good," he said. "I'm glad you're not shy. Come meet my friends."

"My parents," she said, but he'd already taken her hand, and was leading her away from the lake, laughing, toward a camp where the tents were painted bright yellow and green.

"I'm Melem," he said. "Where are you from?"

"I'm from the Fishing People," she said. "Do you live here at the Abzu?"

"I suppose I do," he said, smiling. "I'm from the Farming People. But a life working in the fields—well, that was never for me. I'm a different kind of farmer."

"What kind of farmer are you?" she asked.

"You'll see," he said, smiling. "Anyway, how's life down in the marshes?"

She thought she detected a hint of mockery in his tone. "It's very nice," she said, a bit defiantly. "We have a little house on our little island, and when we're not out fishing or making nets, I make up things of my own."

"What things?" he asked.

"All sorts," she said, a note of pride in her voice. "Once I made tiny boats of all different shapes, to see which ones would float best while holding the most fish. Because of me, our village started building deeper, narrower boats; and now people come from all around to trade for them. The aunts and uncles are very proud of me."

He looked at her very strangely, in a way that made her look away. Then he smiled and said, "I think you'll fit right in here, Zeru."

When they reached his camp, he collapsed on a gazelle-skin and poured some dark liquid into a clay cup. He handed it to her, but she didn't want to take it.

"Do you always drink beer this early?" she asked him.

"It isn't beer," he said.

"What is it?" she asked.

"Joyplant."

She must have looked shocked, because he laughed and said, "It won't hurt you."

"That's only for the rituals," she said.

"Not here," he said. "Here we have different rituals."

A young man in a striped, loose-fitting robe came stumbling out of a tent, pulling a young woman by the hand. Their skin was dark and almond-colored, and their hair was long and black, braided with bright copper rings. She wore a long flax robe, and a brightly dyed scarf wrapped about her hair. On his head he wore a striped cloth, secured with a band around his forehead.

"You're up early," said the young man. He turned and squinted at her. "Who's this?"

"This is Zeru," said Melem.

"Lovely to meet you, Zeru," said the young man. "I am Ishrut, and I have a splitting headache." His accent was sharp, all hard clicks and taps of the tongue. Zeru had heard men speak like him before: the bands of wandering goat-herders who were said to dwell in the inner plains. Sometimes those tribes watered their animals at her family's ponds, as they passed through the marshes on their unspoken business.

"You're from the Herding People," Zeru said.

Ishrut and his woman looked at her like she'd just said something stupid. She didn't know what she'd said wrong.

"Yes," said Ishrut. "We are from the Herding People. And you are from the Fishing People. And I still have a splitting headache."

He sat down on a gazelle-skin, took a clay cup from Melem, and drank it all in one gulp.

The young woman rolled her eyes and smiled. "I'm Asilah," she told Zeru. "I am Ishrut's caretaker, his whore, and, when he's sober enough, his collaborator."

"You," Melem said to Asilah, "are a brilliant builder."

"You mean you all work together?" Zeru asked. "I mean, Herding People and Farming People—"

"And Fishing People, too, if we find any clever enough," Melem said in his soft-rolling accent, throwing her a wink.

Zeru blushed, not knowing what to say.

"You have never seen anything like what this woman builds," Melem told her, gesturing at Asilah. "Last spring, we wanted to plant cucumbers up on one of the hills." He pointed vaguely. "Do you know what Asilah did? She built a channel of wood and clay to carry water uphill. Water, flowing uphill. Just imagine it. And now cucumbers grow atop that hill. That's the brilliance of this woman." He filled his cup and took a deep drink.

"It was simple, really," Asilah told her, shaking her head. "I just built a tall thin vat, and when the water from the river filled it, it overflowed up and into—"

"What do you make, eh—Zeru, was it?" Ishrut, the robed one, interrupted.

They all looked at her.

She didn't know what to say. So she started telling a story.

"Back in my village, in the marsh," she said, "we caught two kinds of fish. One kind came from the salty water of the sea, and it was small, and not very good to eat. The other lived in the sweet water of the little ponds and streams, and it was delicious. Big and plump and juicy."

"Oh, I could go for some smoked fish right now," said Ishrut.

"Shut up," said Melem.

"So," she continued, "we liked to fish in the lakes and ponds, and we ignored the sea, and that made the sea angry. The sea sent a storm, and wrecked the boats we'd tied up by the rocks, and left slime on the shore that smelled horrible for months."

"I've smelled that," said Ishrut. "It's the sea plants, I think."

"Whatever it is, it smells like death," she said. "Anyway, we apologized to the sea, and paid more attention to it. This made the ponds and streams angry, and one spring they overflowed and flooded the village, washing away our whole wheat harvest and all our rare animal skins."

"I think I see where this is going," said Ishrut.

"I'm sure you do," she said. "I learned that we must pay respect to the ponds and streams, as well as to the salty sea, so neither will feel neglected. And if one becomes angry, we must pay more attention to her. And that," she smiled, "is why we sometimes have to eat the smelly fish from the salty sea, even though the juicy plump fish taste better. Everything has its place."

Melem and Asilah clapped their hands. Melem offered her the cup, and she drank without thinking. It tasted of earth and flowers—not at all how she had expected joyplant milk to taste. She tried to give the cup back to him but he gestured for her to keep it.

"Did you make that story up?" Asilah asked her.

"When I was a little girl," she said. "I told it to other girls, and now everyone in our village tells it."

Melem nodded. "That's a rare talent. A teller of tales."

"I'm no storyteller," she said. "That's a job for old men. Everyone knows that."

"Ah!" Melem raised a finger. "That idea—the idea of 'everyone knows that'—is exactly what they're trying to get away from here."

"I don't know anything," said Ishrut.

"You certainly don't," said Asilah, with a wry grin.

Then suddenly, from far away, Zeru heard voices calling her name.

Her parents' voices. Coming closer.

People stomped into the camp—aunts and uncles, Fishing People, looking worried. Before she could run away or even hide the cup holding the joyplant milk, her parents burst into the camp, howling and grabbing at her clothes, snatching the cup from her hand and hurling it away, pushing Melem and Ishrut to the ground, kicking them. Zeru thought she should be crying but the whole thing felt like a dream. She watched it all as if it were happening underwater, and she was just flowing with the stream.

Mama and Papa dragged her back to camp, slapping her about the head. She didn't really feel it. Odd.

"What is wrong with you?" Mama was shouting.

"You don't have to shout, Mama," she said.

"Can't you see?" Papa said to Mama. "She already drank it. She can't understand a word you're saying."

"I understand you fine," she said, and laughed. They were making such silly faces.

"By all the Gods!" Mama was wailing. "This is it! I told you not to bring her, and now look what's happened."

"Oh, it was *you* who told *me* not to bring her," Papa retorted. "Funny, that's not how I remember it. I remember a lot of talk about how you were going to show her off to that boy Ewi from the Longboat family, and—"

"That is not what I said!" Tears were rising in Mama's eyes. "How can you stand here and tell me that's what I said?"

"Mama! Papa!" Zeru said as loudly as she felt like. "Stop shouting. I'm fine."

"You're not fine! You're *not* fine," Mama was wailing and rubbing the sides of her face, while at the same time Papa was laughing sarcastically and saying, "Oh, she's fine! Well, we can all go home now." A lot of other people she'd never seen before were peering at her all curious and concerned, and Mama and Papa brushed them away saying they'd take care of it now.

"It's just, sweetlove, this is what we were worried about," Mama was saying.

"What were you worried about?" Zeru spread her hands.

"We don't want you getting mixed up with people like that," said Papa.

"People like what?" she asked.

Papa laughed drily. "That's a good one. People like what? Like the ones who drink joyplant and lie around and do nothing with their lives—"

"Papa, what are you talking about?" she said. "Those people are really smart. They built a river that flows uphill. They said I'm a good storyteller."

"Will you listen to her?" Papa said. "Now she's talking nonsense. How much of that stuff did she drink?"

"Baby, please, listen to your father," Mama said. "Those people are crazy."

"They're not crazy, Mama," she said. "They build things."

"What things?" Papa asked. "Did they show you any of these things?"

"Well, no, but—"

"That's what we're trying to tell you," Mama said. "The things they talk about aren't real. You're old enough to understand this now—"

"Mama, don't talk to me like a baby."

"Well this is the truth, sweetlove," said Mama. "They drink joyplant, and they eat the other plants from the rituals, but they don't use them correctly. They take them all the time, every day. Do you understand? So their thoughts are all confused, and they dream all kinds of dreams—but none of it's real. It's all just dreams. Do you see?"

Zeru shook her head. "It's not just dreams. They're really building things."

Papa was rubbing his forehead, turned away from her.

Zeru held Mama's gaze as best she could, with everything feeling so swimmy. "I'll show you. Let's go back and I'll show you."

Mama shook her head.

They made her walk with them back to the Fishing People's camp, where they lay her down on her sleeping mat. And somehow, even though she'd just woken up a little while ago, Zeru fell into a dreamless sleep. When she woke again it was midday.

She walked around some of the other camps with Mama and Papa. Mama showed her off to some of her friends from the Longboat family, who said she was growing up into a beautiful young woman. She said thank you.

In the afternoon, Papa took her down to the shore of the Abzu, and showed her how the Farming People mixed the mud with just the right amount of dried reeds, and formed the mixture into blocks that sat in the sun and turned almost as hard as rock.

"They say the Farming People have been doing this, here, for a thousand years," Papa told her. "That's how they built the temple over on the shore there." He pointed, and on the shore nearby she saw a broad low house built of these hard blocks, stacked on top of each other, to make walls like the walls of their reed houses. But these walls were taller, and they looked like they could stand up to any wind.

Back at camp, they ate dinner: juicy river-trout from the fresh water of the Abzu. Then the old men lay down to nap, and the young men drank beer and sang, and Zeru managed to slip off into the twilight.

She walked under a purplish sky, with the rush of the wind and the songs of insects in her ears. People were singing, too; songs with words she didn't understand that were still beautiful in strange ways. When she passed each camp, people looked up and smiled at her. She felt like a little girl again, wandering through her village in the evening. Except now the village was much bigger, and so was she.

Melem came running from his camp, and hugged her, and she hugged him back. Then he tried to kiss her but she slipped away and ran toward the camp, where Ishrut and Asilah lay next to a crackling fire, sipping mugs of joyplant milk, laughing and telling stories.

"You escaped!" Ishrut cried when he saw her.

"Of course I escaped," Zeru said, and immediately she wondered why she'd say such a thing. She felt as if she was turning into someone else, these past few hours—a girl she scarcely knew.

Asilah offered her a cup of joyplant milk, but she said, "My parents told me something this morning."

"Of course they did," said Ishrut, rolling his eyes.

"They told me," she said, "That none of what you talk about is real. That you haven't actually built the things you talk about."

Ishrut and Asilah looked at each other and burst out laughing. Melem was laughing too, and then so was she.

"They think we made it all up?" Ishrut asked, doubled over with laughter. This was the happiest she'd ever seen him.

"How long since your parents have been coming to the Abzu?" Melem asked her.

She shrugged. "I don't know. A few years, maybe."

Melem nodded. "Come with me."

THEY WALKED INLAND from the brightly painted camp, toward a great rounded hill where she saw a field of cucumbers, plump and green in the twilight. Asilah led her to a tall chamber made of wood, sealed with clay, like a huge, thin pitcher, set against the hillside. Water from the river flowed into the bottom of the chamber. And when the chamber filled up, water flowed out the top of it, down a network of clay channels fanning out across the hillside.

Zeru looked at Asilah. She smiled.

Then they took her to another place; a field that stretched on and on, where wheat and date palms grew; more than enough to feed ten villages. All around the palms and fields grew green grass and tall river reeds. Many narrow channels built of wood, sealed with clay, carried water far from the river, nourishing all the plants of the fields. Nearby, people were piling up baked blocks, like the ones Papa had shown her this afternoon, in a wide, complex shape, much too big to be a house.

"What is this place?" she asked Melem.

"And do you have the answer?" Zeru asked."

"Not yet," he admitted. "But I will, soon enough."

After they'd watched the brick-makers for a while, they walked back to camp and sat around the fire, sipping their cups of beer. Their eyes reflected the flames. Ishrut sat with an arm draped around Asilah, who lay her head on his shoulder. But all of them were staring intently into the flames, deep in their own thoughts.

"Something is happening here," said Ishrut after a while. "Something that has no name."

She nodded, though she wasn't sure she understood.

"This place," said Melem. "As soon as I arrived here, it felt different."

"It's not an easy place," said Asilah. She shook her head. "Not like the plains, where I grew up. The water is salty here. The river is unpredictable, and floods whenever the mood takes it. We Herding People come here when the herds come, but then we leave. Most of us, anyway."

"Is it true?" Zeru asked suddenly, "that the Abzu has no bottom?"

They all stared at her, holding their breaths as if holding back laughter.

Melem bit his lip. "Who told you that?"

She shrugged, embarrassed. "A few people. I don't know. Everyone."

"It has a bottom." Ishrut rolled his eyes. "Every lake has a bottom."

"That's what I said," Zeru told him. "But have you ever seen it? I mean, have you ever swum down there?"

Ishrut opened his mouth to say something sharp, but Melem cut him off: "Maybe it has a bottom, maybe not. But there's certainly something strange about that lake. More people keep coming here, every year. Not just Herding People, but Fishing People, and all kinds of others, to join us Farming People here on the shore. Why do we all come? What makes us stay?"

"Maybe something draws us all here," said Asilah.

"No matter the reason," said Ishrut, "We are all here, and once were are here, we no longer think like other people. So many of us, here, in one place—we think differently. You, Asilah, think of ways to build trenches and dams to direct the water."

"And this is a good place to build bigger ones," Melem said.

"Exactly," said Ishrut. "You dream of bigger trenches and dams. Asilah dreams of taking that water and growing vast fields—more dates and wheat than anyone has ever seen."

"And you?" Zeru asked Melem.

He turned to her and something in his eyes made her look down and away. But his reply was soft, as if he were talking to himself.

"I dream of great houses next to the river," he said at last. She waited for him to say more, but he sat in silence.

"Those will take a long time to build," Zeru said at last.

"Who knows?" Melem said. "No one has dreamed of building them before."

They watched the fire for a while more.

"Maybe something like this has happened a few times," said Asilah at last. "You know, in the hills far to the north of here, people live a miserable life. They wear only animal skins. They hunt and forage. They have no houses. If they cannot kill an animal or find roots or berries, they starve. If it is cold, they freeze."

"There are people like that in the forests where I come from, too," Zeru said. "Thank the Gods none of us had to grow up like that."

"Yes, but why didn't we?" Asilah asked, sitting up, clearly intent on making a point. "Why do our families live differently?"

"Because someone thought of something new," said Melem, smiling as he stared into the fire.

"Exactly," said Asilah. The fire seemed to dance in her dark eyes. "Someone dreamed new things. Mud-bricks. Houses. Robes of flax. Fields of wheat. Fruit trees and geese in the yard."

"One person dreamed all that?" Zeru asked.

"Probably not," said Ishrut. "It must've taken a lot of dreamers, who all happened to be in the right places together, at the right moments."

"And in each of those moments, something new came to be," said Asilah. "The birth of something that had no name yet."

"And now, here, there will be another," said Melem.

They stared into the fire a while longer, as if they might scry some sign of that birth in the flames that danced there.

"Melem," Zeru asked after a time. "When you look out over this plain, what do you see?"

He smiled. "I see great houses. Bigger, more glorious than anyone has ever seen—more houses than anyone can count, their tops scraping the heavens. Beautiful paintings on their pillars and walls. And inside, people dancing and eating and celebrating."

"And outside," said Asilah, "great waterworks, as vast as the Slow River itself, carrying water to distant fields that stretch as far as the eye can see."

"Fields of wheat," said Ishrut. "Date palms, fig and olive trees. Cattle and goats too numerous to count, to feed the people in this—this great village."

"No," said Melem. "Not a village. This new place that has no name yet."

Then Zeru smiled too, because—looking off into the blackness beyond the firelight, she could almost imagine the shadows of those great houses against the stars.

That night, she slipped back to her family's camp before anyone noticed she was gone.

Or so she thought. Mama and Papa caught sight of her as soon as she came within the firelight.

※

"You were with them again, weren't you," said Papa.

He and Mama were clearly not on their first beers of the night. But their eyes were sharp. Everyone else was drinking and singing, ignoring them. They'd roasted some fish, the remains speared on wooden poles stuck into the ground near the fire. Zeru tried to slip past Mama and Papa, reaching for a fish, but Papa grabbed her arm and said, "I'm talking to you, young lady."

"I just went for a walk," Zeru said.

"Don't lie to me," Mama hissed. Aunts and uncles were starting to stare now.

"Sweetlove," Papa said.

"Don't call me that," Zeru said.

"Zeru, then," he said. "We just want you to talk to us. You used to talk to us. Remember?"

"I'm talking to you now," she said.

"Will you just come and sit down?" Papa said.

She sat on the reed mat next to them, pulling her knees up to her chest. She stared into the fire.

"Want some fish?" Papa asked, offering her half a fish, still on its wood pole.

She took it wordlessly, picking off small chunks with her fingers and nibbling on them.

"Beer?" He offered her his clay cup.

Mama looked at him oddly, but said nothing. He held the cup out to Zeru, smiling slightly. After a few tense heartbeats, she reached out slowly, accepted the cup, and took a few gulps. It tasted bitter, not sweet and herbal like the joyplant milk, but she didn't let on. She smiled and handed the cup back to him.

"No, you keep it," he said. "I've had enough."

Mama began to reach for the cup. "I don't think that's a good—"

But Papa waved her off. "Let her have it," he said.

She sat drinking the beer for a while, picking at the fish. Mama and Papa rejoined the singing, leaving her to stare into the fire. Once she'd finished most of the cup, she was starting to feel a lot more relaxed.

"Did you have fun this evening?" Papa asked, dropping into the ground beside her, folding his legs beneath him.

"I did," she said. "I really did."

"What are they building now?" he asked.

Zeru opened her mouth to deny, again, that she'd been with the others. There didn't seem to be any point, though. "They want to build a new kind of place," she said. "Lots of little rivers, feeding fields and fish farms, so everyone has plenty to eat. And huge houses. Bigger than anyone has ever seen."

"Impressive," Papa said.

"What'll they do in this new place?" Mama asked, kneeling on the grass to join them.

Zeru thought about that for a moment. "I'm not sure. Dream up more new things, I guess."

"Is that what you want to do?" Papa asked. "Dream up new things?"

She shook her head. "Not exactly. But I want to help name the things. Make stories about them, and people can share the stories. Maybe other people will want to make a place like this, too."

"You were always a good storyteller," Mama said.

Zeru laughed. "Really? I thought that was just a job for old men."

Papa shook his head. "We've had all sorts of storytellers. Young men, old men. Young women, like you."

"I didn't know that," Zeru said.

"You never asked." He smiled.

Zeru set down the beer cup and lay back on the mat.

Papa turned to Mama. "You have to admit," he said, "it sounds about right."

Mama shook her head, took a sip of her beer. "Your part of it," she said to her, "sounds perfectly all right. I'd be proud for Zeru to become a great storyteller. But one sure way to ruin that talent is to lie around guzzling joyplant milk with those animals—"

"Mama." Zeru sat up. "They don't just lie around. They're strange, I know. They drink a lot of joyplant milk, it's true. But they build things. Really. They showed me."

Mama watched her for a long time. "What do they build?"

Zeru tried to think of how best to describe these things, for a moment feeling sheer panic, sure she wouldn't have the words. And then the words just—came.

"They built a tall thin vat that fills with water and overflows onto higher places, so the river can flow uphill," she said. "They built channels and tiny rivers from wood, sealed with clay, bringing the river inland, and they've planted fields of wheat and date palms all around the Abzu. I know you didn't see any of this when you were here last year, because none of this was here last year. They came together and dreamed it, and built it. And now it's here."

Mama and Papa were both staring at her now. She realized she was trembling. They watched her for the space of many breaths, their eyes wide.

"Can you take us to see these things?" Mama asked at last.

Zeru looked at her. "I don't think they'll want to see you again," she said. "Not after this morning."

Mama looked down at the fire. "I understand. But maybe if you tell them we really do want to see what they've built—"

"Maybe if you come and apologize to them," Zeru said. "That would be a good start."

She nodded. "All right. Tomorrow morning."

Then Mama came over and sat next to Zeru on the mat, and hugged her, hard. Papa wrapped his arms around them both. Some uncles and aunts and cousins came over and piled on them, and asked if she was all right, and she said yes, everything was fine.

They brought over fresh beer, and Papa insisted she drink another cup, and they sang so many songs together, and she sang louder than she'd ever sung before, and when it was over she went into the tent to fall asleep, and her sleeping mat felt like it was the softest thing in the world.

She dreamed a strange dream that night; one in which she somehow knew she was dreaming. She walked in a dark cavern lit red by flickering torches. Mist swirled about her feet, scented with strange incense. Someone had carved scenes along the walls of the cavern: warriors in combat with lions and great birds and snake-necked beasts with leopards' heads, all painted white and red and black. The carvings looked so real they frightened her, as if they might leap right off the walls.

Bones littered the cavern floor; skulls and ribs and arm-bones of men and women, and wolves and gazelle and oryx, and many other beasts besides; the newest bones gleaming white, the oldest yellowed, cracking and crumbling to dust as she trod on them.

Another woman, who a moment earlier hadn't been there, walked beside her, a soft white garment hanging off her pale, slender frame; her shiny black hair gathered up into a tight bun. She was the plainest-looking woman Zeru had ever seen: no jewelry, no tattoos, no feathers or adornments of any kind. Even her garment was strange; smooth and soft, unlike any fabric or animal-skin Zeru knew.

"Are you me?" the woman asked.

Zeru jumped, started. "What?" she asked. "Am I who?"

The other woman shook her head. "No, you can't be me. We don't look anything alike. So who are you?"

"I'm Zeru," said Zeru. "Who are you?"

The strange woman laughed. "First paintings, then riddles; now some girl who's just as confused as I am."

"Which people do you come from?" Zeru asked the woman.

"Which people?" The woman shook her head, confused. "I'm from Urim, of course. Where are you from?"

"I'm of the Fishing People," Zeru said. "What is Urim?"

"It's a city," the woman said. "You know, Urim? The great ancient city of Urim?"

Zeru furrowed her brow. "I've never heard of it. Do you have a temple there?"

The woman laughed again. "Well, yes," she said. "We have the temple, and underneath that we have the ruins of an older one, and beneath that one older still, all the way down to—to this, I suppose. Wherever this is."

"They say the temple at the Abzu is very old," said Zeru. "I wonder if yours is older."

"The Abzu?" the woman shook her head again. "But Eridu hasn't existed for—" Her eyes went wide. "That's who you are! You're the very first!"

Zeru drew back, suddenly frightened. "The first what? What's Eridu? What are you talking about?"

The woman smiled. "I don't expect you to believe me, but— on some far-distant day, people like me are going to dig up the stories left by people like you."

Zeru wrinkled her nose. "How can you dig up a story?"

The woman laughed. "That's it!" she exclaimed, waving a finger at Zeru. "That's it exactly! You don't have any way to write your stories yet. There's no writing yet. Ha! Which is why you have to tell them. But someday, someone will stamp them on clay. And we'll be able to dig them up, and find out what this was all about, at the very beginning!"

Zeru shook her head. This woman's ravings made no sense. How could one stamp a story on clay? Why would anyone want to dig it up? What did this strange woman want to find?

"You see?" the woman was shouting. "That's how we'll find out what all this was meant to be, when it all started!"

But even as she shouted these things, she was fading away into the sweet-scented mist that swirled about the bones strewn across the cavern floor. Her voice echoed from wall to carved-and-painted wall—and then Zeru felt herself flung away, and the cavern was no more.

▼▼▼
▼▼▼

Zeru woke with a thumping pain in her head. Her whole body did not want to be there. She sat up and groaned. Mama and Papa were already up.

"Good morning, sleepy girl," Papa said, poking his head into the tent.

She groaned again.

"Want some breakfast?" he asked.

The thought of food made her retch. "Maybe later," she said.

"You'll need your strength for the big night tonight," he said.

For a moment she wasn't sure what he was talking about. Then she remembered—the whole reason she'd wanted to come here. The wild ceremony on the last night at the Abzu. The strange dreams and the great beast in the water.

"I thought that was all made up," she said, rubbing her eyes.

He shrugged. "Maybe some of it is. A lot of it's not. You'll see."

Zeru managed to haul myself out of the tent into the bright sunlight, which pierced her eyes and made her head throb even more. Mama came over, chuckling, with a cup of fresh water from the Abzu.

"Drink this," she said.

She tried, but it made her feel sick. Mama sat next to her and made her finish the whole cup, then went to fetch her another. She came back with some herbs to chew, too. After the herbs, Zeru's head stopped hurting so much, and her stomach settled enough to keep down some beans and fish that Papa brought over.

"So," he said as she gulped down the last of the water. "When do we get to see these things your friends have built?"

Zeru shrugged. "We can try now."

Mama and Papa and she walked over to her friends' brightly painted camp. Ishrut and Asilah were sprawled on the reed mats outside one of the tents. Ishrut was already sipping a big mug filled with some sort of frothing brew, while Asilah rubbed his shoulders.

As soon as they saw Zeru and her parents approaching, Ishrut began to struggle to get up, but Mama and Papa said, "No, just wait a moment, please," and he sat up, eyeing them warily.

"Where's Melem?" Zeru asked.

He climbed out of the tent, an eager smile on his face—but froze when he saw Zeru's parents.

"Mama and Papa," Zeru said, spreading her arms, "meet my friends. Ishrut and Asilah, meet Mama and Papa."

Melem slowly rose to his full height, and stepped forward to greet the visitors. They all clasped arms and greeted one another, smiling nervously.

"We came," Papa said, "first of all, to apologize for yesterday morning."

"We're very sorry," said Mama. "We didn't really know anything about you."

"No," said Ishrut. "You didn't."

"We're really very sorry for acting the way we did," said Papa.

"You nearly broke one of my ribs," said Ishrut. "Look at this bruise." He lifted part of his garment, showing a big purplish blotch on his side.

Mama knelt to examine it. "I can bring you some herbs that'll keep it from swelling," she said.

Something about her tone seemed to soften him a little. "I'd appreciate that," he said.

"Well," said Asilah, "now you've apologized."

"There's something else," Zeru said.

Everyone turned to look at her, and suddenly she had the feeling she'd had yesterday, and in front of her parents last night, when she'd felt sure the words wouldn't come. But they came.

"I want to show my parents the things you've built," she said to Ishrut and Asilah.

They just looked at her. "Why?" Asilah asked.

"Because they're important. I mean, I think this is something really important, like when people first stopped roaming around, and learned to plant farms and build houses. But now something new is happening. Something different. And if my parents can see it and believe it, maybe more people will believe it."

"People here believe it," Ishrut said. "Who do you think brought the wood? Who do you think eats the food we grow? Who do you think pays for all this?" He gestured around him at the tents, and raised his mug of joyplant milk. "We're doing just fine, thank you."

Zeru nodded. "Yes, you are. But think how much more you could do if even more people believed in what you're building here. Think about what they could do if all the people—not just the people who live here, but all of them, everyone who comes to the Abzu—what if all of them helped you build the things you've been dreaming?"

Now Ishrut was nodding too. "All right," he said at last. He heaved himself up from the mat. "Let's go."

ISHRUT LED ALL of them—Zeru and Mama and Papa and Asilah and Melem—out to the hill, where Asilah had built her vat to bring water up to the top. Mama and Papa stared at it wide-eyed, and came close and examined it, touching it delicately as if it might fall apart at any moment.

"You built this yourself?" Papa asked.

"Dreamed it myself," Asilah said, proudly. "Then built it."

"Where did you get the idea?" Mama asked.

She chuckled. "I think you know." Mama and Papa smiled.

Zeru's brow furrowed. "What does she mean, she thinks you know? What's she talking about?"

"You'll see," Papa said. "Tonight."

Mama came over and hugged her, and she had no idea why.

Then Ishrut led them out to the fields, where they'd built channels of wood and clay, bringing water far inland from the river. Mama and Papa scanned the fields, astonished. This time they were like children seeing the sea for the first time. They stood and stared for a long while, saying nothing.

"What's that you're building over there?" Papa asked at last, pointing at the low walls of baked mud-brick across the fields.

"Something else new," said Ishrut. "I'm not sure yet. A big house."

As they walked closer, they heard the songs of the brick-makers who were shaping blocks from the mud and reeds of the river into little wood boxes. Taking mud from the riverbank, they tossed it into their boxes, threw in some reeds, and splashed in a little water to keep the clay soft. Then they flipped the boxes, and out came mud-bricks, ready to bake in the sun.

As she watched them, Zeru felt something exciting; the same feeling she'd had sitting around the fire with her friends last night. This was action, definitely; like grinding wheat or hustling pelts and copper to the River People on a trading-day. But this felt different, new. There were no words for it yet.

Great stacks of bricks sat all around, but she couldn't understand how these few brick-makers were going to build such a huge house. Judging by the outlines of the walls, it was going to be much bigger than the temple on the shore. Bigger than any house she'd ever seen.

"Who's going to live in this house?" Mama asked.

Ishrut chuckled. "Maybe me."

By the time they walked back to camp, it was nearly sundown. Melem and Zeru still hadn't said a word to each other since leaving the tent. Mama and Papa, on the other hand, had warmed up to Ishrut and Asilah, and the four of them were chatting excitedly now.

"At least twenty strong men," Papa was saying. "I'm sure her brothers could bring more."

Ishrut nodded. "That'd be enough to get the houses built in a year or so."

"I mix the clay with a lot of water, and keep the whole thing out of the sun," Asilah was explaining to Mama at the same time. "Once everything is in place, then I move it into the sun, and the seals harden."

"So you could put up a big shade," Mama said, "and I know a whole lot of women who could easily learn to do it, if you took a day to teach them."

Zeru listened to them all the way back to camp, trying to keep all the details in her mind, because she knew she'd want to tell this story later. The story of how the Fishing People began to work with the Farming People and the Herding People, to build something new.

"So, we'll see you tonight?" Papa asked Ishrut when they got back to their camp.

"Wouldn't miss it," said Ishrut, smiling.

They all embraced and kissed each others' cheeks, and Mama and Papa turned to go.

"You staying here?" Papa asked.

Zeru looked at her parents, then at Melem. "I think I'll stay for a while," she said.

Mama and Papa smiled, and hugged her, and headed back to their family's camp.

When they were gone, Ishrut poured a cup of joyplant milk and offered it to her. She started to refuse, but he said, "The ceremony's not long off. Better get started now."

"Yes, the ceremony," she said, taking a seat on the gazelle-skin mat. "What is it?"

Ishrut laughed. "You'll see."

Asilah poured mugs of joyplant milk for herself and Ishrut, and the two of them lay down on the mat, cuddling and speaking softly to each other.

Melem came and sat next to her.

"That took a lot of courage, what you did today," he said after a moment.

"What are you talking about?" she said.

"Talking your parents into coming here. Talking Ishrut and Asilah into showing them what they've built. I don't think I could've done it."

"I didn't do anything," she said. "All I did was tell the truth."

"You told a story," he said. "And it was a good story."

"Because it was true," she said.

He nodded. "Because it was true."

They sat for a while longer, her sipping her mug of joyplant milk, him watching her in a way that made her uncomfortable. But toward the middle of the joyplant mug, she started to feel more relaxed, and she turned to look at him for the first time all day.

"I really like you, you know," she told him, looking him square in the eye.

"I didn't know, actually," he said.

"Really?" she said.

She must've looked completely confused, because he laughed. "I thought you were afraid of me, for some reason. Of them. You kept running away."

"Because I didn't want my parents to come back here and try to kill you again."

"Fair enough. But then what about last night, before you left, around the fire?"

"What about it?"

He laughed. "I was waiting for you to come closer, so I could kiss you," he said. "All you did was stare into the fire. You looked so serious."

Zeru opened her mouth to say something, lost it, and tried to say something else. For the first time, no words were coming. "You wanted to kiss me?" she almost shouted, nearly spilling her joyplant milk.

Now he was laughing really hard. "Of course I did. You're a beautiful girl, Zeru."

"Why didn't you kiss me?"

"I just told you! You wouldn't come close to me. You looked like you were thinking about something really important."

"I was! What you're doing here is important. But you still should've tried to kiss me."

"My mistake."

They watched each other for what felt like a long time. She set her joyplant mug down and moved a little closer to him—and he moved closer to her. She felt strange all over, not just from the joyplant, but something else, a warmth down below her belly that moved lower to between her legs, and made her want to move that part of her closer to him, so she did.

He reached out and stroked her cheek, and the skin tingled there. She reached out and ran her hand through his hair, feeling the soft strands between her fingers. He leaned in and so did she, and then they were kissing. So this was what it felt like. His lips were drier than hers. A little cracked. She liked it. He smelled like earth, and something deeper, something that made her want to lift her toga over her head and take in as much of him as she could, but this felt so good too, this kissing. She thought again: so this is what kissing feels like.

Zeru glanced over at Ishrut and Asilah. They were smiling at her. They got up and slipped inside their tent, closing the flap behind them.

Now Melem and she were lying down on the mat, and he was running his hand up her leg, up inside her toga, and everywhere he touched gave her that tingling feeling, and all she wanted was for that hand to come closer, to go inside where the warm feeling was spreading, but—

"Wait," she said.

"What?" he said.

"I made a promise," she said.

"What promise?"

"Not to go with any man this year."

"No one's asking you to go anywhere," he said. "Only to stay right here."

Then he was kissing her again, and running his hand up inside to the place where it felt warm, and when he touched her there it felt even better than kissing, better in a different kind of way but it felt incredible with the kissing too at the same time, and she was saying yes and trying to catch her breath, but she didn't want to breathe. She just wanted this, more of this, and then he was on top of her slipping himself inside her, and she said yes and it hurt a lot more than she expected. Like she was going to burst. Something tore inside her, and she caught her breath.

He was moving on top of her, slowly, and the warm feeling started again. It was spreading out from between her legs all over her body, and he moved faster and the warm feeling was everywhere, and now a new feeling came from the same place, like a tingling but stronger, and as he moved the feeling built and built and then it flew outward in every direction at once, this feeling better than anything ever, shooting up through her chest and down through her arms and legs out to the tips of her fingers and toes, and her whole body was shuddering, and he was shuddering on top of her shouting yes and she was shouting yes, and it went on for what felt like forever, but then it was over, too soon.

And he collapsed beside her, and they lay there on the mat, breathing heavily, flushed and hot and panting under the setting sun.

LATER, WHEN THE sky was turning deep blue, Ishrut and Asilah came out from their tent, smiling at Zeru and Melem in a knowing way that Zeru really didn't mind. They all composed themselves as best they could, putting hair and folds of togas back into place.

Then they walked down to the shore, where all the people were leaving their camps, families and couples, groups of women and men in strangely colored togas and kilts and other garments Zeru didn't recognize, all of them heading for the shore, and the temple. In the distance, she could see a lot of people were already there, dancing by firelight to the beats of big drums.

They joined a group of women in long loincloths, who wore braided leather headbands studded with tall green feathers, and red swirls painted on their bare breasts. The women were dancing and singing, tapping small drums and playing flutes; a melody Zeru didn't recognize. She and her friends waved hello to the women, and the women nodded back. Zeru tried to exchange a few words, but could find no words the women understood. But they kept smiling anyway, as they all joined a bigger group of men and women dressed in bands of bright copper and tunics of white flax, and other men whose faces bore tattoos of jagged lines and swirls. Their group grew as they strode along the shore.

The Abzu seemed to have swelled since this morning. Water was washing up among the tall reeds, turning everything swampy. They marched through the reeds and mud, water sloshing up to their knees. It felt cool and soft against the skin of Zeru's legs.

Melem handed her something—a piece of strange-smelling bread, with dark swirls all through it. She looked at him questioningly.

He smiled. "Eat it."

"It's rotten," she said.

"Not rotten," he said. "A special thing grows on the grain. It makes the bread magical."

Zeru furrowed her brow, not understanding. She glanced over at Ishrut and Asilah, who were chewing on their own chunks of the strange, dark-swirled bread. Other people were eating it too. The dancing women were pulling small loaves out of bags, passing them around.

She put the bread in her mouth, chewed and swallowed it as best she could. It was bitter and earthy, like dirt and wood. Melem tore another piece off the loaf and handed it to her. She shook her head.

"One bite isn't enough," he said. "Take a few more."

She managed to choke a few more of them down. Her stomach rumbled, and she felt like she was about to lose control, but she stayed calm.

Their music joined with the loud music of the big drums and horns, and now they were coming near the temple she saw that it was taller than it had looked in the distance, many times taller than she was. In front of it they'd built a great fire, whose blaze roared as high as the temple's roof, sending sparks and smoke up into the twilight.

As they started dancing near the temple on the shore, something swelled inside her. Everything became more real, somehow. The colors more vivid. The music more intense. The air vibrating. She breathed it in, and now she was vibrating too. Humming inside. Everything was humming.

All around the fire they danced—more people than she'd ever seen before, all the people in the world—families and children and men and women in garments and paints and feathers and furs and flowers of every color. Long-haired men in brown leather kilts, waving their hands and stomping the ground. Bald men in white robes, tapping their feet serenely. Topless women in black skirts, with copper armbands and red-dyed hair. A knot of families in big reed masks, women and men alike painted in blue stripes from head to toe, cheering as the beat built to a crescendo—waited—thumped down again, and everyone was dancing together. Zeru and her friends were dancing too, all of them throwing their hands up and cheering and stomping their feet kicking up clouds of dust and dry grass, twisting and leaping and bouncing to the thump of the drums and flutes and horns that thudded and shook in their muscles down into their bones.

The colors of the feathers and flowers swirled. The grass and the fire were dancing with them. They were alive. Zeru knew this, suddenly, and she felt as if she'd always known it, but had somehow forgotten. It was very funny. Everyone else seemed to know it too. She started laughing. She couldn't stop laughing. It was so simple, really: everything was alive. The trees were alive. The grass was alive. The earth and the birds and even the air. And the Abzu. The Abzu was just as alive as any of them. There were Gods in all these things, Gods who wore the air and water like clothes; the fire and flowers like jewelry. How had she never noticed all these Gods before, all around them, all the time? How could anyone fail to see them? It was just hilarious, how obvious it all was. How simple. She laughed harder, and when Melem and Ishrut and Asilah saw her laughing, they started laughing too. All of them laughing together as they danced.

The drumbeats slowed; the melodies turned softer. They danced slower now, as the twilight turned to night and the stars came out, all of the lights, as if the sky itself wanted them to see everything.

People began to make their way down to the water, wading in among the reeds in the shallows. The Abzu had swelled even more in the night, and now where they had waded in the day before, the water had risen as high as their chests. Hundreds of titan river-carp had risen from their dwellings in the depths to meet the people descending into the waves. Scales gleamed as the throng of moonlit messengers churned the dark water into froth. Many of the fish were as long as Zeru's arm; some so large they could've swallowed her whole. A few, the oldest of the great scaled sages, breached the water like mountains, scanning the crowd with wise eyes.

Zeru felt she should be afraid of the fish. In a sense, she was—not afraid they'd devour her, but because they hummed with a power she did not understand. Even so, she waded through the tall reeds and deeper into the shallows. Though legends said the Abzu had no bottom, Zeru could feel soft mud squishing beneath her toes. The cool water felt wonderful. It felt alive. She liked how it caressed her.

People were swimming out into the water, slipping underneath the ripples. Some of them were watching her, singing a strange, beautiful song:

The maid, all alone, has directed her step to the Abzu,
All alone she has directed her step to the Abzu.
Let the maid enter the Abzu,
Let her enter the Abzu—

Zeru held her breath and let the water swallow her, and sank. She opened her eyes down in the dark. She could see no bottom. Nothing but rippling moonlight and the swirling shadows of titan fish; a darkness in the deep that swallowed even the moonlight far beneath her.

Now she was afraid.

⁂

From the depths, she heard a voice—or rather, felt it: deep, slow, and serene, in her bones.

I am glad you came, the voice hummed in her bones.

Who are you? she asked in her mind.

Something rose slowly out of the darkness; a great shape coming nearer. She looked around for people but there were none. Only her, alone, immersed in endless dark water; and this shape rising toward her: the most enormous fish she'd ever seen; a river-carp the size of a house, its long mustaches waving like great whips, its eyes alive with unspoken wisdom.

She tried to swim away, up toward the surface. But the fish was approaching too quickly. Its mouth yawned; a cavern of flesh and shadow. She opened her mouth to scream. A storm of bubbles escaped her lips, but she could not move. She was being sucked downward, inward, past the great fish's lips and down into its throat. Its jaws closed around her, swallowing her. She screamed again—

All was dark. So quiet she could hear her own heartbeat; and all around her, a deeper, slower beat: the heart of the great fish in whose belly she lay. She thought she ought to be afraid and expected to feel a wave of panic at any moment. But it was warm here, and the soft rhythm of the fish's heart felt like home, somehow.

A myriad of colored lights came forth from the darkness, dancing in intricate patterns, shimmering in the dark, pulsating to the deep rhythm of the great fish's heartbeat. And there, within the belly of the fish, something took shape: a beast with the fish's tail, but the head and forelegs of the ibex she'd seen in the forest, all those years ago when she was a little girl. Zeru looked into its eyes; those cold deep ibex eyes, and they became the eyes of a man; a man with long black hair and a plaited beard and a clever grin. A man with the long tail and fins of a fish.

Zeru was afraid, but not for her life. It was a deeper kind of fear, too big to contain. The fear devoured her, and became a kind of love. This was no beast, nor any man.

You're a God, she said in her mind.

I am many things, he said.

Zeru tried to get a clear view of his face, and found she could not. Sometimes he looked like the bearded man, and at the same time he looked like the great ibex. He looked like both, and like other things that were hard to make out.

Your friends have a lot of work to do here, he said. *Will you help them?*

What work? she asked, in her mind.

Sights opened up before her. Things she'd never seen and had no words for: many mud-brick houses all nestled together along the riverbank, houses of all shapes and sizes stretching to the horizon, and more people among them than blades of grass on the shore. Some houses were bigger than she'd ever seen; long, with many tall trunks like the trunks of trees, but built of stacked mud-brick, and dotted with intricate designs of red and black, with vaults that were filled with grain and figs and dates, and others filled with precious stones and gold and copper. In the houses, people were making strange new things: carts that rolled across the land atop circular pieces of wood; clay tablets bearing many tiny markings that told names and numbers and poems and songs and stories. Along the river were big boats, packed with cattle and sheep and other animals she didn't recognize, crewed by dark-skinned people in robes of black-and-white stripes.

Men in robes of shaggy fleece, wearing helmets forged of gleaming gold, paraded before towering mud-brick houses in land-boats pulled by teams of donkeys and oxen as many-colored banners snapped in the wind. Women in glistening robes of purple and emerald glided through caverns built of brick and stone, where tiny fires licked the air, casting warm glows on walls painted with scenes of forests and hunts and winged beasts. Small bricks of clay, their surfaces covered with tiny markings, lay in neat stacks along endless rows of shelves.

And in the center of this vast place, one great house that was many houses stacked atop each other, the house at the top so high it reached the clouds, and on the roofs of that house were gardens of date palms and bushes and vines, and flowers and fruit of every kind. A garden in the sky.

You will build this place, said the God.

Even in the depths of her fearful love, she knew what this meant. The God was giving her a *mhé*—a new idea, a new word to take back to the people. It was true. It was all real.

This place, said the God, *is called a city.*

City, she repeated in her mind.

And this city's name, said the God, *is Eridu.*

I will tell the story of Eridu, she promised.

I know you will, said the God.

Suddenly something cold and dark pulled at her from a deeper place. She felt herself drawn downward. All around her the colored lights scattered. She reached out for them, but they slipped away above her, hurling upward and away from the shadow that sent tendrils of icy cold up around her ankles, her legs, her belly and chest. She tasted salt, harsh and bitter in her nose and on her tongue.

Deep within that frigid salt-choked place, a voice that was a thousand voices hummed and buzzed and chittered, arguing and contradicting and berating itself, howling curses at all things. Zeru cried out to the God, but his great shape seemed distant. Unreal, somehow, as if it were fading away far above her. She reached out to him, begging, pleading, though only bubbles escaped her lips.

More sights erupted before her eyes: warriors leading long lines of men and women, shivering and in chains, away from places where many houses burned, pouring black smoke into the air. Men in wood carts drawn by donkeys thundered across the plains in clouds of dust, hurling spears at other men who fled and begged and fell in great sprays of bright red blood. Great houses burned, and crumbled, and melted in torrential rains. Rivers dried up, and starving men and women stalked a land of dead grass and bleached bones, falling on one another without mercy, like wild beasts. Long lines of men clad in crimson tunics beheaded bound prisoners, tossing the heads onto great piles, beyond which many more men and women writhed and screamed, nailed to tall wooden poles. Warriors in their tens of thousands laughed as they ripped the clothes from women's backs, and put houses and fields to the torch, and carried away fine things of gold and silver in loads that broke the backs of their beasts, to lay at the feet of men swathed in soft fabric who reclined on tall gold chairs and stroked their plaited beards and demanded more, always more.

Zeru screamed, shaking her head, but the visions whirled around her, pressing in upon her mind, choking her.

This is Tiamat, the God's voice hummed in her bones. *This is the Dragon who creates without reason, and devours without cause.*

Stop it! she pleaded. *Make it stop!*

I cannot, said the God. *And even if I could, I would not.*

I don't understand! Zeru cried, thrashing her arms and legs, trying to tread upward from these cold depths.

Yes, you do, the God's voice hummed.

And just as she thought her heart would freeze, she felt herself rising again, toward the God. His shape became clearer, ibex and fish and man all at once, and a hundred other things besides.

Tell these things, too, his voice hummed within her. *All these things, too, are part of the story.*

Then his great shape slipped away, leaving her floating alone in the belly of the fish.

Zeru felt the water churning around her, pulling her upward and outward. Before her, the fish's jaws yawned open, letting in pale rays of water-filtered moonlight. She kicked and pumped her arms, flowing with the rushing torrent, past the fish's tongue and teeth, through its lips and out into the cool, calm water of the Abzu.

Her lungs were clenching, begging for air. She kicked in the dark water, scattering river-carp the size of oxen, who turned and followed the titan back into the shadow-hidden depths.

Zeru kicked upward. Her lungs were burning. The moonlight was growing brighter.

She broke the surface and gasped.

⟨

All around her the drums were still beating. People were dancing, smiles on their faces. The fires burned under the stars. Nearby, in the water, children laughed and splashed and squealed.

She looked around. Melem appeared next to her, splashing through the shallows to wrap his arms around her. She looked into his eyes and smiled.

"It's incredible, isn't it?" he shouted over the roar of the drums and the crowd.

"Melem," she said.

His smile faded, and his face tightened with worry.

"I saw a great fish," she said, her voice trembling. "It took me into its belly. And there I... I saw the God, Melem. He told me a *mhé.*"

The Cradle and the Sword

Melem took a deep breath, his eyes wide.

Zeru's face fell. "You don't believe me."

But he nodded, eyes fixed on hers. "Of course I believe you," he said. "This is why people come to the Abzu. It's why the God called you here."

She laughed with relief and threw her arms around him. "It's true, then!" she cried. "He called me to this place."

"He called all of us," Melem said, kissing her head. "You and all the rest of us."

She looked up into his eyes. "I know the name of the place we're building," she said. "The God showed it to me."

Melem laughed, nodding with her. "All right. Yes. All right. What's it called?"

"It's going to be a *city*," she said. "The city's name will be Eridu."

"Eridu," he said. "I like it. What's it mean?"

"I didn't ask," she said.

"Maybe it doesn't matter," he said.

"Or maybe," she said, "the meaning will come later. With the story."

As she spoke, she remembered last night's dream: the woman in her long white robes, telling strange stories of cities and marks on clay. *You're the very first*, she'd said. *On some far-distant day, people like me are going to dig up the stories left by people like you.*

Suddenly she pulled free of his embrace. He followed her as she waded toward the shore. When she reached the water's edge, where the reeds were thin and the clay was soft, she knelt and pulled up a handful of it. She sculpted it into a rough ball, and pressed one side flat.

"What are you doing?" Melem asked.

Carefully, her fingers traced two sinuous lines, one atop the other. Beneath the waves she inscribed a vertical line, then a horizontal one crossing it, then two diagonals running through its center.

"The river," she said, pointing to the waves. "And the lights in the depths."

Melem's brow furrowed. "It's hard to see," he teased.

She frowned and mashed the clay ball against his chest, laughing, erasing the marks she'd made. But even as she did, she felt as if someone else was here, watching. Many people.

A shiver ran through her. "I just got the strangest feeling," she said, pulling close to Melem again.

He stroked her wet hair. "What feeling?"

"As if..." she shook her head, searching for the words. "As if someday, someone will sing of this night. This very moment. The two of us, here, on the Abzu's shore, making strange marks on clay."

"They certainly will," he said. "They'll write a hundred songs about us. We'll make sure of it."

"And when they sing of us," she went on, "they'll say, 'That was the beginning. The moment when our world was born.'"

"Rightly so," he hummed against her ear.

"But *is* this the beginning?" she asked. "You said yourself, your people have been coming here, building temples on the Abzu for as long as anyone can remember. My people have always loved the water. The Herding People have always walked the plains."

He nodded. "Those rivers have been flowing here for a long time, it's true. I suppose this is just... the moment where they all come together."

"Like the Abzu," she said. "The place all waters flow to in the end."

"And," he added, smiling, "the place where new things are born."

Zeru pressed herself closer to him, nestling against his chest. Even after the terrifying love she'd felt for the God, it was nice to have Melem here, strong arms around her, rough lips on hers. Hard in a soft way. Like the things the God had shown her: rivers that nourished nations and tore down temples; birthed cities and wore citadels to dust. Always they would flow. She could only sing of them, and pray their currents carried her words for a time.

"Let's go tell the others," Melem said, bringing her back to him.

"Not just yet," she told him. "Let's stay here a while longer."

So they stayed close, standing in the water, her head under his chin, his hand running through her soaking hair. They listened to the splashes and shouts of people all around them, the thumps of the big drums in the distance, and the roar of the fire and the sparks drifting up to the stars.

And all around them, the waters of the Abzu; so deep, and still so full of secrets.

This book was just the beginning.

Your journey continues at

TheStrangeContinent.com

CPSIA information can be obtained
at www.ICGtesting.com
Printed in the USA
LVHW11s0913071018
592717LV00001B/318/P

9 780692 922637